Josiah Cooke

Principles of Chemical Philosophy

Josiah Cooke

Principles of Chemical Philosophy

Reprint of the original, first published in 1874.

1st Edition 2024 | ISBN: 978-3-36884-625-1

Verlag (Publisher): Outlook Verlag GmbH, Zeilweg 44, 60439 Frankfurt, Deutschland
Vertretungsberechtigt (Authorized to represent): E. Roepke, Zeilweg 44, 60439 Frankfurt, Deutschland
Druck (Print): Books on Demand GmbH, In de Tarpen 42, 22848 Norderstedt, Deutschland

isting in all the three conditions of matter. Now, we find that
whenever a solid changes to a liquid, or a liquid to a gas, heat
is absorbed; and conversely, whenever a gas is liquefied, or a
liquid becomes a solid, heat is evolved; although, as a general
rule, this change of state is accompanied by no change of temperature. Thus, one kilogramme of ice, in melting, absorbs
79 units of heat, although the temperature remains at 0° during the change; and when, by boiling, a kilogramme of water
is converted into steam, under the normal pressure of the air,
no less than 537 units of heat disappear, although the temperature both of the steam and of the water is constant at 100°
during the whole period. On the other hand, when the steam
is condensed or the water frozen, absolutely the same amount
of heat is set free as was before absorbed. The heat thus absorbed or set free is generally called the *latent heat* of the liquid
or gas, and in the case of many substances the amount has
been carefully measured. Chem. Phys. (277) and (299). According to the theory we are studying, these effects are the
direct results of the molecular condition of matter. The change
of state must be accompanied by a change in the relative position
of the molecules, or in their distance from each other ; and this
change, in its turn, must be attended with a destruction or production of the moving power on which the effects of heat depend. Chem. Phys. (215 bis.).

    15. *Sources of Heat.* — The sun is the original source of
almost all the heat we enjoy on the earth, for the effect of the
earth's internal heat, at its surface, is at best very small, —
and all our artificial sources of heat have drawn their supply
either directly or indirectly from the great central luminary.
According to our theory the effect of the sun's rays is a simple
result of the transfer of molecular motion from the sun to
the earth, either by some unknown influence exerted from a
distance, or else by an actual transfer of motion through the
material particles of the ether, which is assumed to fill the in-
tervening space. The great source of all artificial heat is combustion in its many forms, and this, as we shall hereafter see, is
merely a clashing together of material molecules, and is necessarily attended with a great development of that moving power
to which we refer all thermal effects.

    16. *Specific Heat.* — The amount of heat required to raise

to the same extent the temperature of equal weights of different substances is by no means the same. The quantity is capable in any case of exact measurement, and is called the specific heat of the substance. The amount of heat required to raise the temperature of one kilogramme of water one centigrade degree has been assumed as the unit, and we express the specific heat of other substances in terms of this measure. Moreover, since with the exception of hydrogen the specific heat of water is greater than that of any substance known, the specific heat of all other bodies must be expressed by fractional numbers. In every case, unless otherwise stated, the numbers indicate what fraction of a unit of heat would be required to raise the temperature of one kilogramme of the substance from 0° to 1° centigrade. Chem. Phys. (232).

17. *Molecular Condition of Gases.* — The aeriform state is by far the simplest condition of matter, and there are two peculiarities in its properties which lead to important conclusions in regard to its molecular conditions. These characteristics are as follows : First, All true gases obey the same law of compressibility. Secondly, Equal volumes of all true gases expand equally on the same increase of temperature. Chem. Phys. (262). Now, according to the mechanical theory of heat (§ 10) these peculiar relations of the aeriform condition of matter are best explained on the assumption that *Equal volumes of all gases contain the same number of molecules;* and since, moreover, this theoretical deduction harmonizes with almost all the facts of chemistry, it has been universally adopted as a *fundamental principle* of the science. This peculiar molecular condition, however, is only found in the gas, for it is only in this state that the molecules are sufficiently separated from each other to be freed from the mutual action of those molecular forces which give rise to far more complicated relations in both liquid and solid bodies. Moreover, with our ordinary gases (in the degree of condensation in which they exist under the pressure of the atmosphere), the molecules are not yet sufficiently far apart to be wholly freed from the effects of their mutual action, and hence the theoretical condition is not absolutely fulfilled ; and in vapors, where the molecules are still closer together, the variation from the theory is quite large. In proportion as the gas ex-

2

pands, the theoretical condition is approached, and, when in a state of great expansion, equal volumes of all gases would undoubtedly contain exactly the same number of molecules. It is only then that we reach the condition of what we have called above the *true gas*, and this is our criterion of its state, — that it obeys absolutely the law of Mariotte. A very important corollary follows at once from the principle we have just deduced.

The molecular weight of all substances is directly proportioned to their specific gravities in the state of gas.

We have adopted in this book hydrogen gas as our unit of specific gravity for aeriform substances, and were we also to take the molecule of hydrogen as our unit of molecular weight, then the number which expresses the specific gravity of a gas would express also its molecular weight. But for reasons which will appear hereafter, we have selected the half hydrogen molecule as our unit, and hence *the molecular weight of any substance in terms of this unit is always twice its specific gravity in the state of gas.* In Table III. we have given, according to the most accurate experimental data, the Sp. Gr. (referred to hydrogen) of all the best known gases and vapors, and in a parallel column we have also given the Half-molecular Weights of the same substances determined by chemical analysis, in a manner which will be hereafter described. It will be seen that the numbers in the second column are almost precisely the same as those in the first, and the slight differences which will be noticed, either arise from the fact that the vapors, under the conditions in which alone their Sp. Gr. can be accurately determined, are not true gases, that is, do not exactly obey Mariotte's law; or in other cases, where the differences are more considerable, may be referred to a partial decomposition of the substance itself in the process of the experiment. In solving the problems of this book, and generally in most chemical problems, the Half-molecular weight may be taken as the true Sp. Gr. The logarithms of these values given in the last column of the table will be found useful in this connection. Although only given to four places of decimals, they exceed in accuracy the experimental data. The values in the column of 𝔖𝔭. 𝔊𝔯. referred to air, are given, as a rule, to one decimal place beyond the limit of error.

Questions and Problems.

1. Arc the qualities of a molecule of any substance, the same as those which distinguish the substance itself?

2. What is the distinction between cohesion and adhesion?

3. When the barometer stands at 76 c. m., with what weight in grammes is the air pressing against each square centimetre of surface? *Sp. Gr.* of mercury 13.596. Ans. 1033.

4. To what difference of pressure does a difference of one centimetre in the barometric column correspond?
Ans. 13.596 grammes.

5. When a mercury barometer stands at 76 c. m. how high would a water barometer stand? Also, how high would barometers stand filled with alcohol or sulphuric acid, disregarding in each case the tension of the vapor? *Sp. Gr.* of alcohol 0.81; *Sp. Gr.* of sulphuric acid 1.85. Ans. 1033; 1275 and 558.2 c. m.

6. A volume of hydrogen gas was found to be 200 $\overline{c. m.}^3$ The height of the barometer observed at the same time, was 74 c. m. What would have been the volume if observed when the barometer stood at 76 c. m. Ans. 194.7 $\overline{c. m.}^3$

7. A volume of nitrogen standing in a bell-glass over a mercury pneumatic trough measured 250 $\overline{c. m.}^3$ The barometer at the time stood at 75.4 c. m., and the level of the mercury in the bell was found by measurement to be 6.5 above the surface of the mercury in the trough. Required to reduce the volume to standard pressure.
Ans. The pressure of the air on the surface of the mercury in the trough (measured at 75.4 c. m.) was balanced first by the column of mercury in the bell, and secondly by the tension of the confined gas. Hence the pressure to which the gas was exposed was equal to 75.4 — 6.5 = 68.9 c. m. and we have 76 : 68.9 = 250 : x = 226.7 $\overline{c. m.}^3$

8. What would be the answer to the same problem, had the trough been filled with water?
Ans. The water column in the bell exerts a pressure which is as much less than the pressure of the mercury column in the previous problem, as the *Sp. Gr.* of water is less than the *Sp. Gr.* of mercury. Hence we have 13.6 : 1 = 6.5 : 0.48, also 75.4 — 0.48 = 74.92, and 76 : 74.92 = 250 : x = 246.4 $\overline{c. m.}^3$

9. A closed vessel, which displaces one litre of air, is poised on a balance with weights, whose volume is inconsiderable when compared with that of the vessel. The balance is in equilibrium when-

the barometer stands at 76 c. m.   If the barometer falls to 71 c. m.
how much weight must be added to restore the equilibrium ?

Ans. 85 milligrammes.

10. Given the weight of one litre of dry air under the normal
conditions as 14.42 criths, what will be the weight of one litre of
dry air at the normal temperature, but under a pressure of 72 c. m. ?

Ans. 13.67 criths.

11. A volume of gas measures 500 $\overline{\text{c. m.}}^3$ at 15° what will be its
volume at 288°.2 ?   In this and the next three problems the pressure
is assumed to be constant.   Ans. 1000 $\overline{\text{c. m.}}^3$

12. To what temperature must an open vessel be heated before
one quarter of the air which it contains at 0° is driven out ?

Ans. 91°.07.

13. An open vessel is heated to 819°.6.   What portion of the air
which the vessel contained at 0° remains in it at this temperature ?

Ans. ¼.

14. A closed glass vessel, which at 13° was filled with air having
a tension of 76 c. m. is heated to 559°.4.   Determine the tension of
the heated air.   Ans. 3 atmospheres.

15. Reduce the following volumes of gas measured at the temperatures and pressure annexed to 0° and 76 c. m.

1. 140 $\overline{\text{c. m.}}^3$ $H = 57$ c. m. $t = 136°.6$ Ans. 70 $\overline{\text{c. m.}}^3$

2. 320 $\overline{\text{c. m.}}^3$ $H = 95$ c. m. $t = 91°.1$ Ans. 300 $\overline{\text{c. m.}}^3$

3. 480 $\overline{\text{c. m.}}^3$ $H = 38$ c. m. $t = 68°.3$ Ans. 192 $\overline{\text{c. m.}}^3$

16. What is the weight of dry air contained in a glass globe of
640 $\overline{\text{c. m.}}^3$ capacity at the temperature 546°.4 and under a pressure
of 71.25 c. m.   Ans. 0.2583 grammes.

General Solution. — In order to make the solution general we
will represent the capacity of the globe, the temperature and the
height of the barometer by V, t and H respectively.   We can also
easily find from Table III. that one cubic centimetre of dry air at
0°, and when the barometer stands at 76 c. m., weighs 14.42 criths.
or 0.001292 grammes.   To find what one cubic centimetre would
weigh when the barometer stands at H centimetres, we make use
of proportion [6], whence we derive

$$w = 0.001292 \cdot \frac{H}{76},$$

the weight of one cubic centimetre at 0° and under a pressure of
H centimetres.   To find what one cubic centimetre would weigh

under the same pressure but at $t°$, it must be remembered that one cubic centimetre at $0°$ becomes $(1 + t\, 0.00366)$ cubic centimetres at $t°$ [7] ; therefore at $t°$ and at H centimetres of the barometer $(1 + t\, 0.00366)\ \overline{\text{c. m.}}^3$ weigh $0.00129 \cdot \dfrac{\text{H}}{76}$ grammes. By equating these two terms we obtain

$$(1 + t\, 0.00366) = 0.00129 \cdot \frac{\text{H}}{76},$$

whence .

$$1 = 0.00129 \cdot \frac{1}{1 + t\, 0.00366} \cdot \frac{\text{H}}{76}.$$

the weight of one cubic centimetre at $t°$ and under a pressure of H centimetres. The weight of V cubic centimetres (w) is evidently

$$w = 0.00129\ \text{V} \cdot \frac{1}{1 + t\, 0.00366} \cdot \frac{\text{H}}{76}. \qquad [10\ a]$$

Thus far in this solution we have neglected the change in capacity of the glass globe due to the change of temperature. This causes no sensible error when the change of temperature is small, but when the change of temperature is quite large the change of capacity of the globe must be considered. If the capacity is $\text{V}\ \overline{\text{c. m.}}^3$ at $0°$ it becomes at $t°$ $\text{V}\ (1 + t\, 0.00003)$. (See Chem. Phys. §§ 241 – 244.) Introducing this value for V into the above equations we obtain

$$w = 0.00129\ \text{V}\ (1 + t\, 0.00003) \cdot \frac{1}{1 + t\, 0.00366} \cdot \frac{H}{76}. \quad [10\ b]$$

17. Required a general method for determining the Sp. Gr. of a vapor.

Solution. — The specific gravity of a vapor has been defined as its weight compared with the weight of the same volume of hydrogen gas under the same conditions of temperature and pressure, but practically it is most convenient to determine the Sp. Gr. with reference to air, and subsequently to reduce the result to the hydrogen standard.

To find, then, the Sp. Gr. of a vapor, we must ascertain the weight of a known volume, V, at a known temperature, t, and under a known pressure, H, and divide this by the weight of the same volume of air at the same temperature, and under the same pressure. The method may best be explained by an example. Suppose, then, that we wish to ascertain the Sp. Gr. of alcohol vapor. We take a light glass globe having a capacity of from 400 to 500 $\overline{\text{c. m.}}^3$, and draw the neck out in the flame of a blast lamp, so as to leave only a fine opening, as shown in the figure at a. The first step is now to ascertain the weight of the glass globe when completely exhausted of air. As this cannot readily be done directly,

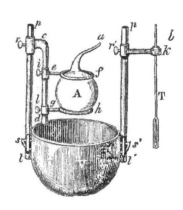

we weigh the globe full of air, and then subtract the weight of the air, ascertained by calculation from the capacity of the globe, and from the temperature and pressure of the air, by means of equation (10 a). Call the weight of the globe and air W, and the weight of the air w, then W — w is the weight of the globe exhausted of air. The second step is to ascertain the weight of the globe filled with alcohol vapor at a known temperature, and under a known pressure. For this purpose we introduce into the globe a few grammes of pure alcohol, and mount it on the support represented in the accompanying figure. By loosening the screw, r, we next sink the balloon beneath the oil contained in the iron vessel, V, and secure it in this position. We now slowly raise the temperature of the oil to between 300° and 400°, which we observe by means of the thermometer, T. The alcohol changes to vapor, and drives out the air, which, with the excess of vapor, escapes at a. When the bath has attained the requisite temperature, we close the opening a, by suddenly melting the end of the tube at a with a mouth blowpipe, and as nearly as possible at the same moment observe the temperature of the bath and the height of the barometer. We have now the globe filled with alcohol vapor at a known temperature, and under a known pressure. Since it is hermetically sealed, its weight cannot change, and we can therefore allow it to cool, clean it, and weigh it at our leisure. This will give us the weight of the globe filled with alcohol vapor at a known temperature, t', and under a known pressure, H′. Call this weight W′. The weight of the vapor is W′ — W + w. The third step is to ascertain the weight of the same volume of air at the same temperature and under the same pressure. This can easily be found by calculation from equation (10 b). The last step is to find the capacity of the globe, which, although we have supposed it known, is not actually ascertained experimentally until the end of the process. For this purpose we break off the tip of the tube (a), under mercury, which, if the experiment has been carefully conducted, rushes in and fills the globe completely. We then empty this mercury into a carefully graduated glass cylinder, and read off the volume. We find then the

Sp. Gr. by dividing the weight of the vapor by the weight of the air. The formulæ for the calculation are then

Weight of the globe and air, $\qquad$ W.

"　　" air, $\qquad w = 0.001292\ V \cdot \dfrac{1}{1 + t\ 0.00366} \cdot \dfrac{H}{76}$

"　　" globe exhausted of air, $\qquad$ W $-$ w.

"　　" " filled with vapor at a temperature t' and under a pressure H′, $\qquad$ W′.

"　　" vapor, $\qquad$ W′ $-$ W $+$ w.

"　　" air at t' and under a pressure H′, $=$

$$0.001292\ V\ (1 + t'\ 0.00003) \cdot \dfrac{1}{1 + t'\ 0.00366} \cdot \dfrac{H'}{76}.$$

$$Sp.Gr. = \dfrac{W' - W + w}{0.001292\ V\ (1 + t'\ 0.00003) \cdot \dfrac{1}{1 + t'0.00366} \cdot \dfrac{H'}{76}}$$

1. Ascertain the Sp. Gr. of alcohol vapor from the following data : —

Weight of glass globe,	W	50.804	grammes.
Height of barometer,	H	74.75	centimetres.
Temperature,	t	18°	
Weight of globe and vapor,	W′	50.824	grammes.
Height of barometer,	H′	74.76	centimetres.
Temperature,	t'	167°	
Volume,	V	351.5	cubic centimetres.

Ans. 1.575.

2. Ascertain the Sp. Gr. of camphor vapor from the following data : —

Weight of glass globe,	W	50.134	grammes.
Height of barometer,	H	74.2	centimetres.
Temperature,	t	13°.5	
Weight of globe and vapor,	W′	50.842	grammes.
Height of barometer,	H′	74.2	centimetres.
Temperature,	t'	244°	
Volume,	V	295	cubic centimetres.

Ans. 5.371.

CHAPTER IV.

18. *Definition.* — The atomic theory assumes that so long as the identity of a substance is preserved its molecules remain undivided; but when, by some chemical change, its identity is lost, and new substances are formed, the theory supposes that the molecules themselves are broken up into still smaller particles, which it calls *atoms*. Indeed it regards this division of the molecules as the very essence of a chemical change.

The word atom is derived from a, privative, and τεμνω (I cut), and recalls a famous controversy in regard to the infinite divisibility of matter, which for many centuries divided the philosophers of the world. But chemistry does not deal with this metaphysical question. It asserts nothing in regard to the possible divisibility of matter; but its modern theories claim that, practically, this division cannot be carried beyond a certain extent, and that we then reach particles which cannot be further divided by any chemical process now known. These are the chemical atoms, and the atom is simply the unit of the chemist, just as the molecule is the unit of the physicist, or the stars the units of the astronomer. The molecule is a group of atoms, and is a unit in the microcosm, of which it is a part, in the same sense that the solar system is a unit in the great stellar universe. The molecule has 'been defined as the smallest particle of any substance which can exist by itself, and the atom may be now defined as *the smallest mass of an element that exists in any molecule.*

When a molecule breaks up, it is not supposed that the atoms fall apart like grains of sand; but simply that they arrange themselves in new groups, and thus give rise to the formation of new substances. Indeed, as a rule, the atoms cannot exist in a free state, and with few exceptions every molecule consists of at least two atoms. This is thought to be true, even of the chemical elements. The difference between the molecules of an elementary substance and those of a compound, according to the theory, is merely this, that while the first are formed by the union of atoms of the same kind, the last comprise atoms of different kinds. The molecules of oxygen gas are atomic aggregates as well as those of water, only the molecules of oxygen consist of oxygen atoms alone, while the molecules of water contain both oxygen and hydrogen atoms. Such at least is the constitution of most elementary substances. Nevertheless, in the case of mercury, zinc, cadmium, and some other metallic elements, the facts compel us to believe that the molecule consists of but one atom, or, in other words, that in these cases the molecule and the atom are the same.

19. *Atomic Weights.* — There must be evidently as many kinds of atoms as there are elementary substances; and, since these substances always unite in definite proportions, it must be also true that the elementary atoms have definite weights. This once assumed, the law of multiple proportions, as well as that of definite proportions, becomes an essential part of our atomic theory; for, since the atoms are by definition indivisible, the elements can only combine atom by atom, and must therefore unite either in the proportion of the atomic weights or in some simple multiples of this proportion. We have discovered no means of measuring even approximately the absolute weight of an atom ; but, after we have determined, from considerations hereafter to be discussed, what must be the number of atoms of each kind in one molecule of any substance, we can easily calculate their relative weight from the results of analysis. A few examples will make the method plain.

1. The analysis of water, given on page 6, proves that in 100 parts it contains 11.112 parts of hydrogen and 88.888 parts of oxygen. Every molecule of water, then, must contain these two elements in just these proportions. Now we have good reason for believing that each molecule of water is a group of three atoms, — two of hydrogen and one of oxygen. Then, since $\frac{1}{2}$ (11.112) : 88.888 = 1 : 16, it follows that the oxygen atom must weigh 16 times as much as the hydrogen atom ; and, if we make the hydrogen atom the unit of our atomic weight, then the weight of the oxygen atom, estimated in these units, must be 16.

2. The analysis of hydrochloric acid gas proves that it con-

given in Table 11. These numbers are the fundamental data of chemical science, and the basis of almost all the numerical calculations which the chemist has to make. The elements of a compound body are always united either in the proportions, by weight, expressed by these numbers, or else in some simple multiples of these proportions; and whenever, by the breaking up of a complex compound, or by the mutual action of different substances on each other, the elements rearrange themselves, and new compounds are formed, the same numerical proportions are always preserved.

The atomic weights evidently rest on two distinct kinds of data ; *first*, on the results of chemical analysis, which are facts of observation, and in regard to which the only question can be as to their greater or less accuracy ; *secondly*, on our conclusions in regard to the number of atoms in each molecule of the substance analyzed. This conclusion again is based chiefly on two classes of facts, whose bearing on the subject we must briefly consider.

1. In the first place we carefully compare together all the compounds of the element we are studying, with the view of discovering the smallest weight of it which enters into the composition of any known molecule ; for this must evidently be the atomic weight of the element. An example will make the course of reasoning intelligible.

In the following table we have a list of a number of the most important compounds containing hydrogen, all of which either are gases, or can easily be changed into vapor by heat, so that their specific gravities in the state of gas can be readily determined. From these specific gravities we learn the weights of the molecules (compare § 17) which are given in the second column of the table. In the third column we have given the weight of hydrogen contained in the molecules, referred, of course, to the same unit as the weight of the molecules themselves : —

Compounds of Hydrogen.	Weight of Molecule referred to Hydrogen Atom.	Weight of Hydrogen in the Molecule.
Hydrochloric Acid	36.5	1
Hydrobromic Acid	81.0	1
Hydriodic Acid	128.0	1
Hydrocyanic Acid	27.0	1
Hydrogen Gas	2.0	2
Water	18.0	2
Sulphuretted Hydrogen	34.0	2
Seleniuretted Hydrogen	81.5	2
Formic Acid	46.0	2
Ammonia	17.0	3
Phosphuretted Hydrogen	34.0	3
Arseniuretted Hydrogen	78.0	3
Acetic Acid	60.0	4
Olefiant Gas	28.0	4
Marsh Gas	16.0	4
Alcohol	46.0	6
Ether	74.0	10

Assuming now, as has been assumed in this table, that a molecule of hydrogen gas weighs 2, it appears that the smallest mass of hydrogen which the molecule of any known substance contains, weighs just one half as much, or 1. We infer, therefore, that this mass of hydrogen cannot be divided by any chemical means, or, in other words, that it is the hydrogen atom. The molecule of hydrogen gas contains then two hydrogen atoms, and this atom is the unit to which we refer all molecular and atomic weights.

If now, in like manner, we bring into comparison all the volatile compounds of oxygen, we shall find that the smallest mass of oxygen which exists in the molecule of any known substance weighs 16, — the atom of hydrogen weighing 1, — and hence we infer that this mass of oxygen is the oxygen atom. Moreover it will appear that a molecule of oxygen gas weighs

32, and hence it follows that each molecule of oxygen gas, like the molecule of hydrogen, is formed by the union of two atoms. A similar comparison would show that, while the molecule of nitrogen gas weighs 28, the atom weighs 14, so that here again the molecule consists of two atoms. This method of investigation can be extended to a large number of the chemical elements, and the conclusions to which it leads are evidently legitimate, and cannot be set aside, until it can be shown that some substance exists whose molecule contains a smaller mass of any element than that hitherto assumed as the atomic weight, or, in other words, until the old atom has been divided.

2. The second class of facts on which we rely for determining the number of atoms in a given molecule is based on the specific heat of the elements (compare § 16). It would appear that the specific heat is the same for all atoms, and, if this is true, we might expect that equal amounts of heat would raise to the same extent the temperatures of such quantities of the various elementary substances as contain the same number of atoms, provided, of course, that these atomic aggregates are compared under the same conditions. Now we can determine accurately the number of units of heat required to raise the temperature of equal weights of the elementary substances one degree, and the results, which we call the specific heat of the elements, are given in works on physics. Chem. Phys. (232). Evidently, if our principle is true, these values must be proportional in every case to the number of atoms of each element contained in the equal weights compared. Representing then by S and S' the specific heat of two elementary substances, by m and m' the weights of the corresponding atoms, and by unity the equal weights compared, we shall have, in any case,

$$S : S' = \frac{1}{m} : \frac{1}{m'}, \text{ or } mS = m'S', \qquad [11]$$

that is, *The product of the atomic weight of an elementary substance by its specific heat is always a constant quantity.*

Taking now the atomic weights obtained by the method first given, and the specific heats of the elements as they have been determined by experimenting on these substances in the solid state, we find that, with only three exceptions, our inference is correct; and this principle not only frequently enables us to fix the atomic weight of an element, when the first method fails, but it also serves to corroborate the general accuracy of our results. It is true, owing undoubtedly to many causes which influence the thermal conditions of a solid body, that this product is not absolutely constant. It varies between 5.7 and 6.9, the most probable value being very nearly 6.34. But the variation is not important, so far as the determination of the atomic weights is concerned. This determination, as we have seen, rests chiefly on the results of analysis. The question always is only between two or three possible hypotheses, and as between these the specific heat will decide. For example, an analysis of chloride of silver proves that each molecule contains, for one atom, or 35.5 parts of chlorine, 108 parts of silver. Now, 108 parts of silver may represent one, two, three, or four atoms, or it may be that this quantity only represents a fraction of an atom. To determine, we divide 6.34 by 0.057, the specific heat of silver. The result is 111, which, though not the exact atomic weight, is near enough to show that 108 is the weight of one atom, and not of two or three. The exceptions to this rule referred to above are carbon, boron, and silicon. But the specific heat of these elements varies so very greatly with the differences of physical condition — the so-called allotropic modifications — which these elements present, — Chem. Phys. (234), — that the exceptions are not regarded as invalidating the general principle. The law simply fails in these cases, and we can see why it fails.

This important law, whose bearing on our subject we have briefly considered, was first discovered by Dulong and Petit, and was subsequently verified by the very careful experiments of Regnault. More recently it has been found, by Voestyn and others, that its application extends, in some cases at least, to chemical compounds; for it would seem that the atoms retain, even when in combination, their peculiar relations to heat, so that the product of the specific heat of a substance by its molecular weight is equal to as many times 6.3 as there are atoms in the molecule. Thus the specific heat of common salt, multiplied by its molecular weight, gives $0.214 \times 58.5 = 12.52$, which is very nearly equal to 6.3×2; while in the case of corrosive sublimate the corresponding product, $0.069 \times 271 = 18.70$, is nearly equal to 6.3×3, — results which are in accordance with our views in regard to the number of atoms in the molecules of these substances.

We have here, then, an obvious method by which we might determine the number of atoms in the molecule of any solid, and which would be of the very greatest value in investigating the atomic weights, could we rely on the general application of our law. We do not expect mathematical exactness. We know very well that the specific heat of solid bodies varies very greatly with the temperature, as well as from other physical causes, and that it is impossible to compare them under *precisely the same* conditions, as would be required in order to secure accuracy. But, unfortunately, the discrepancies are so great, and we are so ignorant of their cause, that as yet we have not been able to place much reliance on the specific heat as a means of determining the number of atoms in the molecules of a compound.

3. Lastly, assuming that both of the means we have considered fail to give satisfactory evidence in regard to the number of atoms in the molecule of a given substance (which we may have analyzed for the purpose of determining some atomic weight), we may frequently, nevertheless, reach a satisfactory, or at least a probable conclusion, by comparing the substance we are investigating with some closely allied substance whose constitution is known. Thus, if the molecule of sodic chloride (common salt) contains two atoms, it is probable that the molecules of sodic iodide, as well as those of potassic chloride and potassic iodide, contain the same number; for all these compounds not only have the same crystalline form and the same chemical relations, but also they are composed of closely allied chemical elements. Nevertheless it is true, in very many cases, that our conclusion in regard to the number of atoms which a molecule may contain is more or less hypothetical, and hence liable to error and subject to change. This uncertainty, moreover, must extend to the atomic weights of the elements, so far as they rest on such hypothetical conclusions.

If we change the hypothesis in any case, we shall obtain a different atomic weight; but then the new weight will be some simple multiple of the old, and will not alter the important relations to which we first referred. These fundamental relations are independent of all hypothesis, and rest on well-established laws.

The atomic weights are the numerical constants of chemistry, and in determining their value it is necessary to take that care which their importance demands. The essential part of the investigation is the accurate analysis of some compound of the element whose atomic weight is sought. The compound selected for the purpose must fulfil several conditions. It must be one which can be prepared in a condition of absolute purity. It must be one the proportions of whose constituents can be determined with the greatest accuracy by the known methods of analytical chemistry. It must contain a second element whose atomic weight is well established. Finally, it should be a compound whose molecular condition is known, and it is best that this should be as simple as possible. When they are once thus accurately determined, the atomic weights become essential data in all quantitative analytical investigations.

Questions and Problems.

1. Does the integrity of a substance reside in its molecules or in its atoms ?

2. We find by analysis that in 100 parts of potassic chloride there are 52.42 parts of potassium and 47.58 parts of chlorine. Moreover, we know from previous experiments that the atomic weight of chlorine is 35.5, and we have reason to believe that every molecule of the compound consists of two atoms, one of potassium and one of chlorine. What is the atomic weight of potassium ?
Ans. 39.1.

3. We find by analysis that in 100 parts of phosphoric anhydride there are 43.66 parts of phosphorus and 56.34 parts of oxygen. Moreover, we know that the atomic weight of oxygen is 16; and we have reason to believe that every molecule of the compound consists of seven atoms, 2 of phosphorus and 5 of oxygen. What is the atomic weight of phosphorus ? Ans. 31.

4. In Table III. the student will find the molecular weights of the following oxygen compounds; and we give below, following the name, the weight of oxygen (estimated like the molecular weight in hydrogen atoms) which each contains. From these data it is

required to determine the atomic weight of oxygen. Oxygen Gas, 32; Water, 16; Sulphurous Anhydride, 32, Sulphuric Anhydride, 48; Phosphoric Oxychloride, 16; Carbonic Oxide, 16; Carbonic Anhydride, 32; Osmic Anhydride, 64; Nitrous Oxide, 16; Nitric Oxide, 16; and Nitric Peroxide, 32.   Ans. 16.

5. We give below the weight of chlorine in one molecule of several of its most characteristic volatile compounds. It is required to deduce the atomic weight of chlorine on the principle of the last problem.   Chlorine gas, 71; Phosphorous Chloride, 106.5; Phosphoric Oxychloride, 106.5; Arsenious Chloride, 106.5; Phosgene Gas, 71; Stannic Chloride, 142; Stanno-triethylic Chloride, 35.5; and Hydrochloric Acid, 35.5.   Ans. 35.5.

6. Review the steps of the reasoning by which the atomic weights have been deduced in the last two problems, and show that the "*molecular weight*" and "*the weight of the element in one molecule*" are actual and independent experimental data.

7. Analysis shows that in 100 parts of mercuric chloride there are 73.80 parts of mercury and 26.20 parts of chlorine. The specific heat of mercury is 0.032. What is the probable atomic weight of mercury, that of chlorine being 35.5? Also, how many atoms of each element does one molecule of the compound contain?

Ans. Atomic weight of mercury, 200.   Each molecule consists of one atom of mercury and two of chlorine.

8. Analysis shows that in 100 parts of ferric oxide there are 70 parts of iron and 30 parts of oxygen. The specific heat of iron is 0.114. What is the probable atomic weight of iron, that of oxygen being 16? and also, how many atoms of each element does one molecule of the oxide contain?

Ans. Atomic weight of iron, 56.   One molecule of ferric oxide contains 2 atoms of iron and 3 of oxygen.

9. The molecular weight of silicic chloride is 170, and its specific heat, 0.1907. How many atoms does one molecule of the compound probably contain?   Ans. 5.

10. The molecular weight of mercuric iodide is 454, and its specific heat, 0.042. How many atoms does one molecule of the compound probably contain?   Ans. 3.

CHAPTER V.

20. *Chemical Symbols.* — The atomic theory has found expression in chemistry in a remarkable system of notation, which has been of the greatest value in the study of the science. In this system, the initial letter of the Latin name of an element is used as the symbol of that element, and represents in every case *one atom.* Thus O stands for *one atom* of Oxygen, N for *one atom* of Nitrogen, H for *one atom* of Hydrogen. When several names have the same initial, we add for the sake of distinction a second letter. Thus C stands for one atom of Carbon, Cl for one atom of Chlorine, Ca for one atom of Calcium, Cu for one atom of Cuprum (copper), Cr for one atom of Chromium, Co for one atom of Cobalt, Cd for one atom of Cadmium, Cs for one atom of Cæsium, and Ce for one atom of Cerium. The symbols of all the elements are given in Table II. Several atoms of the same element are generally indicated by adding figures, but distinguishing them from algebraic exponents by placing them below the letters. Thus Sn_2 stands for two atoms of Stannum (tin), S_3 for three atoms of Sulphur, and I_5 for five atoms of Iodine. Sometimes, however, in order to indicate certain relations, we repeat the symbol with or without a dash between them, thus $H\text{-}H$ represents a group of two atoms of Hydrogen, $Se\text{=}Se$ a group of two atoms of Selenium. We can now easily express the constitution of the molecule of any substance by simply grouping together the symbols of the atoms of which the molecule consists. This group is generally called the symbol of the substance, and stands in every case for one molecule. Thus $Na\,Cl$ is the symbol of common salt, and represents one molecule of salt. H_2O is the symbol of water, and represents, as before, one molecule. So in like manner H_3N stands for one molecule of ammonia gas, H_4C for one molecule of marsh gas, KNO_3 for one molecule of saltpetre, H_2SO_4 for one molecule of sulphuric acid,

3

$C_2H_4O_2$ for one molecule of acetic acid, H-H for one molecule of hydrogen gas. We do not, however, always write the symbols in a linear form, but group the letters in such a way as will best indicate the relations we are studying. When several molecules of the same substance take part in a chemical change, we represent the fact by writing a numerical coefficient before the molecular symbol. A figure so placed always multiplies the whole symbol. Thus $4H$-NO_3 stands for four molecules of nitric acid, $3\,C_2H_6O$ for three molecules of alcohol, $6\,O$=O for six molecules of oxygen gas. When clearness requires it, we enclose the symbol of the molecule in parentheses, thus, $4(H_3{}^{\equiv}N)$, or $(H_3{}^{\equiv}N)_4$. The precise meaning of the dashes will hereafter appear. They are used, like punctuation marks, to point off the parts of a molecular symbol, between which we wish to distinguish.

21. *Chemical Reactions.* — These chemical symbols give at once a simple means of representing all chemical changes. As these changes almost invariably result from the *reaction* of one substance on another, they are called *Chemical Reactions.* Such reactions must necessarily take place between molecules, and simply consist in the breaking up of the molecules and the rearrangement of the atoms in new groups. In every chemical reaction we must distinguish between the substances which are involved in the change and those which are produced by it. The first will be termed the factors and the last the products of the reaction. As matter is indestructible, it follows that *The sum of the weights of the products of any reaction must always be equal to the sum of the weights of the factors,* and, further, that *The number of atoms of each element in the products must be the same as the number of atoms of the same kind in the factors.* This statement seems at first sight to be contradicted by experience, since wood and many other combustibles are consumed by burning. In all such cases, however, the apparent annihilation of the substance arises from the fact that the products of the change are invisible gases; and, when these are collected, their weight is found to be equal, not only to that of the substance, but also, in addition, to the weight of the oxygen from the air consumed in the process. As the products and factors of every chemical change must be equal, it follows that *A chemical reaction may always be represented in an equation*

by writing the symbols of the factors in the first member and those of the products in the second. Thus, the following equation expresses the reaction of dilute sulphuric acid on zinc, by which hydrogen gas is commonly prepared. The products are a solution of zinc sulphate and hydrogen gas.

$$\mathbf{Zn} + (H_2SO_4 + Aq) = (ZnSO_4 + Aq) + \boxminus\!\!-\!\!\boxminus. \quad [12]$$

The initial letters of the Latin word Aqua are here used simply to indicate that the substances enclosed with it in parentheses are in solution. The symbol $\mathbf{Zn}$ is printed in "full-faced" type to indicate that the metal is used in the reaction in its well-known solid condition; while the symbol of the molecule of hydrogen is printed in skeleton type to indicate the condition of gas. This usage will be followed throughout the book; but, generally, when it is not important to indicate the condition of the materials involved in the reaction, ordinary type will be used. The molecule of hydrogen gas consists of two atoms, as our reaction indicates, and this is the smallest quantity of hydrogen which can either enter into or be formed by a chemical change. The molecule of zinc is known to consist of only one atom. When the molecular constitution of an element is not known, we simply write the atomic symbol in the reaction.

Among chemical reactions we may distinguish at least three classes. First, Analytical Reactions, in which a complex molecule is broken up into simpler ones. Thus, when sodic bisulphate is heated, it breaks up into sodic sulphate and sulphuric anhydride, —

$$Na_2S_2O_7 = Na_2SO_4 + SO_3. \quad [13]$$

So, also, by fermentation grape sugar or glucose breaks up into alcohol and carbonic anhydride, —

$$C_6H_{12}O_6 = 2C_2H_6O + 2CO_2. \quad [14]$$

Secondly, Synthetical Reactions, in which two molecules unite to form a more complex group. Thus baryta burns in an atmosphere of sulphuric anhydride, and forms baric sulphate, —

$$BaO + SO_3 = BaSO_4. \quad [15]$$

In like manner ammonia enters into direct union with hydrochloric acid to form ammonic chloride, —

$$H_3N + HCl = H_4NCl. \qquad [16]$$

Thirdly, Metathetical Reactions, in which the atoms of one molecule change place with the dissimilar atoms of another, one atom of one molecule replacing one, two, three, or more atoms of the other, as the case may be. Thus, when we add a solution of common salt to a solution of argentic nitrate, we obtain a white precipitate [1] of argentic chloride, while sodic nitrate remains in solution. The result is obtained by a simple interchange between an atom of silver and an atom of sodium, as the following reaction shows : —

$$(NaCl + AgNO_3 + Aq) = (NaNO_3 + Aq) + \mathbf{AgCl}. \quad [17]$$

In the next example, one atom of barium changes place with two atoms of hydrogen. Baric chloride and sulphuric acid yield hydrochloric acid and insoluble baric sulphate, which is precipitated from the solution in water as the reaction indicates, —

$$(BaCl_2 + H_2SO_4 + Aq) = (2HCl + Aq) + \mathbf{BaSO_4}. \quad [18]$$

Of the three classes of chemical reactions the last is by far the most common, and many chemical changes which were formerly supposed to be examples of simple analysis or synthesis are now known to be the results of metathesis. In very many cases, however, a chemical reaction cannot be explained in either of these ways alone, but seems to consist in a primary union of two or more molecules and a subsequent splitting up of this large group. Indeed, this is the best way of conceiving of all metathetical reactions, for we do not suppose that in any case there is an actual transfer of atoms from one molecule to the other. The word metathesis is merely used to indicate the result of the process, not the manner in which the change takes place, and the same is true of the words analysis and synthesis.

---

[1] The separation of a solid or sometimes of a liquid substance in a fluid menstruum, as the result of a chemical reaction, is called precipitation, and the material which separates, a precipitate; and this, too, even when the material, being lighter than the fluid, rises instead of falls.

The common method of preparing carbonic anhydride is to pour a solution of hydrochloric acid on small lumps of marble (calcic carbonate), —

$$\textbf{CaCO}_3 + (2HCl + Aq) = (CaCO_3\,H_2Cl_2 + \quad [19]$$
$$Aq) = (CaCl_2 + H_2O + Aq) + CO_2.$$

We may suppose that the molecules of the two substances are, in the first place, drawn together by the force which manifests itself in the phenomena of adhesion,[1] but that, as they approach, a mutual attraction between their respective atoms comes into play, which, the moment the molecules come into collision, causes the atoms to arrange themselves in new groups. The groups which then result are determined by many causes whose action can seldom be fully traced; but there are two conditions which, *when the substances are in solution,* have a very important influence on the result. These conditions may be thus stated : —

1. Whenever a compound can be formed, which is insoluble in the menstruum present, this compound always separates as a precipitate.

2. Whenever a gas can be formed, or any substance which is volatile at the temperature at which the experiment is made, this volatile product is set free.

The reactions 17 and 18 of this section are examples of the first, while the reactions 12 and 19 are examples of the second of these conditions. The facts just stated illustrate an important truth, which must be carefully borne in mind in the study of chemistry. A chemical equation differs essentially from an algebraic expression. Any inference which can be legitimately drawn from an algebraic equation must, in some sense, be true. It is not so, however, with chemical symbols. These are simply expressions of observed facts, and, although important inferences may sometimes be drawn from the mere form of the expression, yet they are of no value whatever unless confirmed by experiment. Moreover, the facts

[1] We find it convenient to distinguish between the force which holds together different molecules and that which unites the atoms of the molecules. To the last we give the name of chemical affinity, while we call the first cohesion or adhesion, according as it is exerted between molecules of the same kind or those of a different kind.

which are expressed in this peculiar system of notation are as purely materials for the memory as if they were described in common language.

22. *Compound Radicals.* — In many chemical reactions the elementary atoms change places, not with other elementary atoms, but with groups of atoms, which appear to sustain relations to the compounds they leave or enter similar to those of the elements themselves. Thus, if we add to a solution of argentic nitrate a solution of ammonic chloride, we get the reaction expressed by the equation

$$AgNO_3 + NH_4\text{-}Cl = NH_4\text{-}NO_3 + AgCl. \qquad [20]$$

Here the group NH_4 has taken the place of Ag. So, also, in the reaction of hydrochloric acid on common alcohol, the group C_2H_5 in the molecule of alcohol changes places with the atom of hydrogen in the molecule of hydrochloric acid, —

$$\underset{\text{Alcohol.}}{C_2H_5\text{-}O\text{-}H} + HCl = H\text{-}O\text{-}H + \underset{\text{Ethylic Chloride.}}{C_2H_5\text{-}Cl.} \qquad [21]$$

We write the symbols in this peculiar way in order to make it evident to the eye that such a substitution has taken place. Lastly, in the reaction of chloroform on ammonia, the group CH of the first changes places with the three atoms of hydrogen of ammonia gas, —

$$\underset{\text{Chloroform.}}{CH{\equiv}Cl_3} + H_3N = 3HCl + \underset{\text{Hydrocyanic Acid.}}{CH{\equiv}N.} \qquad [22]$$

Such groups as these are called compound radicals. Like the atoms themselves, they cannot, as a rule, exist in a free state; but aggregates of these radicals may exist, which sustain the same relation to the radicals that elementary substances hold to the atoms. Thus, as we have a gas chlorine consisting of molecules, represented by $Cl\text{-}Cl$, so there is a gas cyanogen consisting of molecules, represented by $CN\text{-}CN$, where CN is a compound radical called cyanogen. Again, the important radicals CO, SO_2, and PCl_3, are also the molecules of well-known gases. These *radical substances* correspond to the elementary substances previously mentioned, in which the molecule is a single atom.

But with few exceptions the radical substances have never

been isolated, and the radicals are only known as groups of atoms which pass and repass in a number of chemical reactions. Indeed, in the same compound we may frequently assume several radicals. The possible radicals of a chemical symbol correspond in fact almost precisely to the possible factors of an algebraic formula, and in writing the symbol we take out the one or the other, as the chemical change we are studying requires. A number of these radicals have received names, and among those recognized in mineral compounds a few of the most important are

Hydroxyl	HO	Sulphuryl	SO_2
Hydrosulphuryl	HS	Carbonyl	CO
Ammonium	H_4N	Phosphoryl	PO
Amidogen	H_2N	Nitrosyl	NO
Cyanogen	CN	Nitryl	NO_2.

The radicals recognized in organic compounds are very numerous, and will be tabulated hereafter.

Questions and Problems.

1. For what do the following symbols stand?

$$N; \quad Ca_2; \quad H\text{-}H; \quad H_4C; \quad 4HNO_3; \quad (C_2H_4O_2)_3.$$

2. For what do the following symbols stand?

$$Cl; \quad S_3; \quad O\text{=}O; \quad H_3N; \quad H_2SO_4; \quad 3C_2H_6O.$$

3. For what do the following symbols stand?

$$O; \quad H_5; \quad Se\text{=}Se; \quad NaCl; \quad H_2O; \quad 3KNO_3.$$

4. Analyze the following reaction. Show that the same number of atoms are represented on each side of the equation, and state the class to which it belongs.

$$\mathbf{Fe} + (\underset{\text{Hydrochloric Acid}}{2HCl + Aq}) = (\underset{\text{Ferrous Chloride.}}{FeCl_2 + Aq}) + \boxed{H}\text{-}\boxed{H}.$$

5. Analyze the following reaction. Show in what the equality consists, and state the class to which the reaction belongs.

$$\underset{\text{Ammonic Nitrate.}}{N_2H_4O_3} = \underset{\text{Water.}}{2H_2O} + \underset{\text{Nitrous Oxide.}}{N_2O}.$$

6. Analyze the following reaction. Show in what the equality consists, and state the class to which the reaction belongs.

$$\underset{\text{Carbon.}}{C} + \underset{\text{Oxygen.}}{O\text{=}O} = \underset{\text{Carbonic Anhydride.}}{CO_2}.$$

7. Analyze the following reaction. Show in what the equality consists, and state the class to which the reaction belongs.

$$2H\text{-}O\text{-}H + Na\text{-}Na = 2Na\text{-}O\text{-}H + H\text{-}H.$$
Water.   Sodium.   Sodic Hydrate.

8. The following reaction may be so written as to indicate that the products are formed by a metathesis between two similar molecules. It is required to show that this is possible.

$$2H_3N = 3H\text{-}H + N\text{-}N.$$
Ammonia gas.   Hydrogen gas.   Nitrogen gas.

9. Write the reactions [17] and [18] so as to indicate the manner in which the metathesis is supposed to take place.

10. State the conditions which determine the metathesis in the various reactions given in this chapter so far as these conditions are indicated.

11. Write the reactions [21] and [22] so as to indicate the manner in which the metathesis is supposed to take place.

12. Analyze the following reaction. Show what determines the metathesis and also what is meant by a compound radical.

$$(Pb\text{=}(NO_3)_2 + 2NH_4\text{-}Cl + Aq) =$$
Plumbic Nitrate.   Ammonic Chloride.

$$\mathbf{PbCl_2} + (2NH_4\text{-}NO_3 + Aq)$$
Plumbic Chloride.   Ammonic Nitrate.

13. Compare with [22] the following reaction and point out the two radicals, which, as we may assume, hydrocyanic acid contains.

$$(Ag\text{-}NO_3 + H\text{-}CN + Aq) = \mathbf{Ag\text{-}CN} + (H\text{-}NO_3 + Aq)$$
Argentic Nitrate.   Hydrocyanic Acid.   Argentic Cyanide.   Nitric Acid.

14. When sulphuric anhydride (SO_3) is added to water (H_2O) a violent action ensues and sulphuric acid is formed. The reaction may be written in two ways, and it is required to explain the different views of the process, which the following equations express.

$$H_2O + SO_3 = H_2SO_4$$
or $$2H\text{-}O\text{-}H + SO_2\text{=}O = H_2\text{=}O_2\text{=}SO_2 + H_2\text{=}O.$$

15. State the distinction between a chemical element and an elementary substance. Give also the distinction between a compound radical and a radical substance.

16. Give the names of the following radicals.

$$HO; \ HS; \ NH_4; \ NH_2; \ SO_2; \ CO; \ PO; \ NO_2.$$

CHAPTER VI.

STOCHIOMETRY.

23. *Stochiometry.* — The chemical symbols enable us not only to represent chemical changes, but also to calculate exactly the amounts of the substances required in any given process as well as the amounts of the products which it will yield. Each symbol stands for a definite weight of the element it represents, that is, for the weight of an atom ; but, as only the relative values of these weights are known, they are best expressed as so many parts. Thus H stands for 1 part by weight of hydrogen, the unit of our system. In like manner O stands for 16 parts by weight of oxygen, N for 14 parts by weight of nitrogen, C for 12 parts by weight of carbon, C_5 for 60 parts by weight of carbon, and so on for all the symbols in Table II. The weight of the molecule of any substance must evidently be the sum of the weights of its atoms, and is easily found, when the symbol is given, by simply adding together the weights which the atomic symbols represent. Thus H_2O stands for $2 + 16 = 18$ parts of water, H_3N for $3 + 14 = 17$ parts of ammonia gas, and $C_2H_4O_2$ for $24 + 4 + 32 = 60$ parts of acetic acid.[1]

Having then given the symbol of a substance, it is very easy to calculate its percentage composition. Thus, as in 60 parts of acetic acid there are 24 parts of carbon, in 100 parts of the acid there must be 40 parts of carbon, and so for each of the other elements. The result appears below ; and in the same way the percentage composition both of alcohol and ether has been calculated from the accompanying symbol.

[1] In this book "*the molecular weight of a substance*" will always mean the sum of the atomic weights of the atoms composing *one* molecule, and we shall use the phrase, "*the molecular weight of a symbol*," or "*the total atomic weight of a symbol*," to denote the sum of the atomic weights of all the molecules which the symbol represents.

	Acetic Acid $C_2H_4O_2$.	Alcohol C_2H_6O.	Ether $C_4H_{10}O$.
Carbon	40.00	52.18	64.86
Hydrogen	6.67	13.04	13.52
Oxygen	53.33	34.78	21.62
	100.00	100.00	100.00

The rule, easily deduced, is this : *As the weight of the molecule is to the weight of each element, so is one hundred parts to the percentage required.*

On the other hand, having given the percentage composition, it is easy to calculate the number of atoms of each element in the molecule of the substance. This problem is evidently the reverse of the last, but it does not, like that, always admit of a definite solution ; for, while there is but one percentage composition corresponding to a given symbol, there may be an infinite number of symbols corresponding to a given percentage composition. For example, the percentage composition of acetic acid corresponds not only to the formula $C_2H_4O_2$, given above, but also to any multiple of that formula, as can easily be seen by calculating the percentage composition of CH_2O, $C_3H_6O_3$, $C_4H_8O_4$, &c. They will all necessarily give the same result, and, before we can determine the absolute number of atoms of each element present, we must have given another condition, namely, the sum of the weights of the atoms, or, in other words, the molecular weight of the substance. When this is known, the problem can at once be definitely solved.

Suppose we have given the percentage composition of alcohol, as above, and also the further fact that its molecular weight is 46. We can then at once make the proportion

$100 : 52.18 = 46 : x = 24$ the weight of the atoms of carbon,
$100 : 13.04 = 46 : x = 6$ " " " " " " hydrogen,
$100 : 34.78 = 46 : x = 16$ " " " " " " oxygen.

Then it follows that

$\frac{24}{12} = 2$ the number of atoms of carbon in one molecule,
$\frac{6}{1} = 6$ " " " " " hydrogen in one molecule,
$\frac{16}{16} = 1$ " " " " " oxygen in one molecule.

It is evident from this example, that, in order to determine exactly the symbol of a compound, we must know its molecular weight. When the substance is a gas, or is capable of being changed into vapor, we can easily determine its molecular weight by the principle on page 18. The molecular weight is simply twice its specific gravity referred to hydrogen. For all the problems given in this book, which deal only with the common gases and vapors, the molecular weight can be at once taken from Table III. If we are dealing with a new substance, we must determine its specific gravity experimentally by one of the methods which will hereafter be described.

When, on account of the fixed nature of the substance, the last mode of investigation is impossible, we can still frequently determine with great probability the molecular weight, by studying the chemical reactions into which the substance enters, and connecting, by careful quantitative experiments, the molecular weight sought with that of some substance whose molecular weight is known. The methods used in such cases will be indicated hereafter; but even when all such means fail, we can nevertheless always find which of all possible symbols expresses the composition of the substance we are studying in the simplest terms, in other words, with the fewest number of atoms in the molecule. Suppose the substance to be cane sugar, which cannot be volatilized without decomposition, and of which no reaction is known which gives any definite clew to its molecular weight. Péligot's analysis, cited on page 9, shows that it contains, in 100 parts, 42.06 parts of carbon, 6.50 parts of hydrogen, and 51.44 parts of oxygen. Assume for the moment that the molecular weight is equal to 100 then

$$\frac{42.06}{12} = 3.50 \text{ the number of atoms of carbon.}$$

$$\frac{6.50}{1} = 6.50 \text{ "} \quad \text{"} \quad \text{"} \quad \text{"} \quad \text{" hydrogen.}$$

$$\frac{51.44}{16} = 3.22 \text{ "} \quad \text{"} \quad \text{"} \quad \text{"} \quad \text{" oxygen.}$$

This would be the number of atoms of each element if the sum of the atomic weight, that is, the molecular weight, of sugar, were equal to 100. As, from the very definition, fractional atoms cannot exist, these numbers are impossible, but any other possible number of atoms must be either a multiple or a submultiple of the numbers found; and we can easily discover the fewest number of whole atoms possible, by seeking for the three smallest whole numbers which stand to each other in the relation of 3.50 : 6.50 : 3.22, a proportion which is very nearly satisfied by 12 : 22 : 11. Hence, the simplest possible symbol is $C_{12}H_{22}O_{11}$, and this has been adopted by chemists as the symbol of cane sugar, although, from anything we as yet know, the symbol may be a multiple of this. If now, taking this symbol as our starting-point, we calculate the percentage composition which would exactly correspond to it, we obtain the following results, which we have arranged in a tabular form, so that the student may compare the theoretical composition with the numbers Péligot obtained by actual analysis.

Composition of Cane Sugar,
$C_{12}H_{22}O_{11}$.

	Péligot's Analysis.	Theoretical.
Carbon	42.06	42.11
Hydrogen	6.50	6.43
Oxygen	51.44	51.46
	100.00	100.00

The difference between the two is now seen to be within the probable errors of analysis, and this example illustrates the method of arranging analytical results generally adopted by chemists.

From the above discussion we can easily deduce a simple arithmetical rule for finding the symbol of a compound when its percentage composition is known. But this rule may be best expressed in an algebraic formula, which will show to the eye at once the relation of the quantities involved in the calculation, and enable us to extend our method to the solution of many classes of problems which we might not otherwise foresee. Let us then represent

By M the weight of any chemical compound in grammes.

" m the molecular weight of the compound in hydrogen atoms.

" W the weight of any constituent of that compound, whether element or compound radical, in grammes.

" w the total atomic weight of element or radical in one molecule.

Then

$$\frac{w}{m} = \text{proportion by weight of the constituent in the compound,}$$

and

$$M\frac{w}{m} = \text{weight of constituent in } M \text{ grammes of compound, or}$$

$$W = M\frac{w}{m}. \qquad [23]$$

Any three of these quantities being given, the fourth can, of course, be found. Thus we may solve four classes of problems.

1. We may find the weight of any constituent in a given weight of a compound, when we know the molecular weight of the compound and the total atomic weight of the constituent in one molecule.

Problem. It is required to find the weight of sulphuric anhydride SO_3 in 4 grammes of plumbic sulphate PbO, SO_3. Here, $w = 32 + 3 \times 16 = 80$, $m = 207 + 16 + 80 = 303$, and $M = 4$. 		Ans. 1.056 grammes.

2. We can find the weight of a compound which can be produced from, or corresponds to, a given weight of one of its constituents, when the same quantities are known as above.

Problem. How many grammes of crystallized green vitriol, $FeSO_4 . 7H_2O$, can be made from 5 grammes of iron? Here, $w = 56$, $m = 278$, $W = 5$. 		Ans. 24.821.

3. We can find the molecular weight of a compound when we have given the weight of one constituent in a given weight of the compound, and the total atomic weight of that constituent in the molecule.

Problem. In 7.5 grammes of ethylic iodide, there are 6.106 grammes of iodine; the total atomic weight of iodine in one molecule is 127. What is the molecular weight of ethylic iodide? 		Ans. 156.

4. We can find the total atomic weight of one constituent of a molecule when the molecular weight is given, and also the weight of the constituent in a known weight of the compound.

Problem. The molecular weight of acetic acid is 60, the per cent of carbon in the compound 40. What is the total atomic weight of carbon in one molecule? Ans. 24. Whence number of carbon atoms in one molecule, 2.

The last problem is essentially the same as that of finding the symbol of a compound when its percentage composition is given, while the first corresponds to the reverse problem of deducing the percentage composition from the symbol. By a slight change the formula can be much better adapted to this class of cases. For this purpose we may put $M = 100$, since we are solely dealing with per cents, and also put $w = na$, a standing for the atomic weight of any element, and n for the number of atoms of that element in one molecule of the compound we are studying. We then have

$$W = 100 \frac{na}{m} \text{ and } n = \frac{W}{100} \frac{m}{a}. \qquad [24]$$

The first of these forms is adapted for calculating the per cent of each element of a compound when the molecular weight, the number of atoms of each element in one molecule, and the several atomic weights, are known; and it is evident that all these data are given by the chemical symbol of the compound. The second of these forms enables us to calculate the number of atoms of each element present in one molecule of a compound when the percentage composition, the molecular weight, and the several atomic weights, are known, and illustrates the principle before developed, that the molecular weight is an essential element of the problem.

24. *Stochiometrical Problems.* — The principles of the previous section apply not only to single molecular formulæ, but obviously may also be extended to the equations which represent chemical changes. Since the molecular symbols which are equated in these expressions represent known relative weights, it must be true in every case that we can calculate the weight of either of the factors or products of the chemical change it represents, provided only that the weight of some one is known. If we represent by w and m the total atomic weight of any two symbols entering into the chemical equations, and by W and M the weight in grammes of the factors or products

which these symbols represent, then the simple algebraic formulæ of the last section will apply to all stochiometrical problems of this kind, as well as to those before indicated. These formulæ, however, are merely the algebraic expression of the familiar rule of three, and all stochiometrical problem are solved more easily by this simple arithmetical rule. Using the word symbol to express the sum of the atomic weights it represents, we may state the rule as applied to chemical problems in the following words, which should be committed to memory.

Express the reaction in the form of an equation ; make then the proportion, As the symbol of the substance given is to the symbol of the substance required, so is the weight of the substance given to x, the weight of the substance required ; reduce the symbols to numbers, and calculate the value of x.

This rule applies equally well to all problems, like those of the last section, in which the elements or radicals of the same molecular symbol are alone involved ; only in such cases there is of course no equation to be written. A few examples will illustrate the application of the rule.

Problem 1. We have given 10 kilogrammes of common salt, and it is required to calculate how much hydrochloric acid gas can be obtained from it by treating with sulphuric acid. The reaction is expressed by the equation

$$(2NaCl + H_2SO_4 + Aq) = (Na_2SO_4 + Aq) + 2HCl,$$

whence we deduce the following proportion,

$$\overset{117}{2NaCl} : \overset{73}{2HCl} = 10 : x = \text{Ans. 6.239 kilogrammes.}$$

Problem 2. It is required to calculate how much sulphuric acid and nitre must be used to make 250 grammes of the strongest nitric acid. The reaction is expressed by the equation

$$KNO_3 + H_2SO_4 = K, HSO_4 + HNO_3,$$

whence we get the proportions

$$\overset{63}{HNO_3} : \overset{98}{H_2SO_4} = 250 : x = \text{Ans. 1. 388.9 grammes sulphuric acid.}$$

$$\overset{63}{HNO_3} : \overset{101.1}{KNO_3} = 250 : x = \text{Ans. 2. 401.2 grammes nitre.}$$

PRINCIPLES

OF

CHEMICAL PHILOSOPHY.

BY

JOSIAH P. COOKE, JR.,

ERVING PROFESSOR OF CHEMISTRY AND MINERALOGY IN HARVARD COLLEGE.

THIRD EDITION,
REVISED AND CORRECTED.

BOSTON:
JOHN ALLYN, PUBLISHER,
LATE SEVER, FRANCIS, & CO.
1874.

CAMBRIDGE:

PRESSWORK BY JOHN WILSON AND SON.

PREFACE

TO THE SECOND EDITION.

THE object of the author in this book is to present the philosophy of chemistry in such a form that it can be made with profit the subject of college recitations, and furnish the teacher with the means of testing the student's faithfulness and ability. With this view the subject has been developed in a logical order, and the principles of the science are taught independently of the experimental evidence on which they rest. It is assumed that the student has already been made familiar with this evidence, and with the more elementary facts which the philosophy of the science attempts to interpret. At most of our American colleges this instruction is given in a course of experimental lectures ; but for less mature students a course of manipulation in the laboratory will be found a far more efficient mode of teaching, and some preliminary training of this kind ought to be made one of the requisites for admission to our higher institutions of learning.[1] The author has found by long experience that a recitation on mere facts, or descriptions of apparatus and experiments, is to the great mass of college undergraduates all but worthless, while the study of the philosophy of chemistry may be made highly profitable both for instruction and discipline. It must never be forgotten, however, that chemistry is peculiarly an experimental science, and that the chief value of its culture in a college course depends on the facilities which it affords for cultivating the power of observation, and for teaching the methods of experimental in-

[1] For such a course of practical study the student can desire no better guide than the excellent work of Professors Eliot and Storer, recently published, "A Manual of Inorganic Chemistry, arranged to facilitate the Experimental Demonstration of the Facts and Principles of the Science." By C. W. Eliot and F. H. Storer. New York, 1868.

vestigation. It is not to be expected or desired that many of
our college graduates should become professional chemists, but
it is all important that every man of culture should understand
or at least appreciate the methods and the inductive logic of
physical science. The elementary facts of chemistry can be
efficiently taught only by leading the student to observe for
himself the phenomena in which they appear, and the attempt
to learn them *memoriter* from a text-book will not only fail in
its immediate object, but miss the chief end of scientific study.
The author, therefore, would most earnestly deprecate the use
of this book except as supplementary to some course of laboratory or lecture-room instruction. It is only after the student
has become, in some limited measure at least, familiar with
chemical phenomena, that he is prepared to study the science
in a systematic way; but all who have this preparation will
acquire most rapidly *a general knowledge of the whole field*
when the subject is presented in a condensed and deductive
form. The author has had especially in view this class of students, and has endeavored to meet their wants.

Part I. of the book contains a statement of the general laws
and theories of chemistry, an explanation of its nomenclature
and mode of symbolical notation, together with so much of the
principles of molecular physics as are constantly applied in
chemical investigations. It might be figuratively called a
grammar of the science. It is intended to be studied independently in consecutive lessons, and is adapted for class-room
recitations, which should be accompanied, however, by such
experiments or further explanations as the teacher may find
necessary to render the subject intelligible.

Part II. of the book presents the scheme of the chemical
elements. It should only be studied in connection with experimental lectures or laboratory work, and will be found chiefly
useful for systematizing and reviewing the facts and phenomena
observed in the lecture-room or laboratory. It is in fact a note-
book intended to aid the student in gaining the greatest benefit
from a course of systematic lectures, enabling him to insure
the accuracy of his knowledge, and giving the teacher the
means of testing the student's acquirements.

The value of problems as means of culture and tests of attainment can hardly be overestimated, and they have therefore

been made a chief feature in this book. Since those which are here given are chiefly intended as guides to the student, the answers have always been added; and where the method was not obvious, the chief steps in the solution have been given as well. Every teacher will be able to multiply problems after these models to suit his own requirements.

The questions, which accompany the problems, form another essential feature in the plan of instruction here presented. They are intended not only to direct the student's attention to the most important points, but also to stimulate thought by suggesting inferences to which the principles stated legitimately lead.

These questions, moreover, will indicate to the teacher the manner, in which it is intended that the book should be studied. Care should be taken not to overstrain the memory, but to distribute the necessary burthen through many lessons. Thus, for the first seven chapters, the student should not be expected to reproduce the symbols and reactions, nor even to call the names of the substances represented, except those of the substances with which he is familiar. It will be sufficient for the time if he understands the principles which the symbols illustrate, and the relations of the parts of the reactions, although as yet these conventional signs may have for him no more definite meaning than the paradigms of a grammar. As he advances through chapters VIII. and IX., he should be expected to familiarize himself with the names of the compounds, and should begin to reproduce the symbols. When reciting on chapter X. he should be called upon to give not only the names of all the symbols, but also the symbols corresponding to all the names, and so on for the rest of the book. In reviewing the book a full knowledge of the names and symbols will be of course expected from the first. The questions and problems appended to each chapter will give the student a clear idea of what in any case will be required. The author has been in the habit of writing out, for his own class, similar problems on separate cards, together with the names, symbols, reactions or other data, which may in any case be given. These cards are distributed at the beginning of each recitation, and the student is not called upon to recite until he has placed his work upon the blackboard. This plan obviates many practical difficulties, and has been found to work with great success.

In arranging the chapters of Part I. the only aim has been to present the several subjects in a logical sequence, and in other respects the order adapted is not always the most philosophical; but the teacher can of course vary the order at pleasure. So also in regard to Part II., the teacher may prefer to take up the elements in his lectures in a different order from that in which they are there classified, but then the several sections may be studied in any order he would be likely to adopt with equal advantage.

The philosophy of chemistry has been developed in this book according to the " modern theories "; and the author would acknowledge his obligations to the recent works of Frankland, Kekulé, Miller, Naquet, Roscoe, Watts, Williamson, and Wurtz, all of which he has freely consulted. Careful attention has been given to the chemical notation; and a method has been devised of writing rational symbols which, while it fully exhibits the relations of the parts of the molecule, condenses the formulæ, and saves space and labor in printing. The nomenclature adopted accords with what the author regards as the best English usage. Innovations would hardly be justified in an elementary work, but every one must regret that the usage is not more uniform and consistent with the modern chemical philosophy. In the chapter on this subject, the old names are given with the new. Lastly, the metric system of weights and measures, and the centigrade scale of the thermometer, are used throughout the book.

In reviewing the work for a new edition, the chapter on the Electrical Relations of the Atoms has been rewritten, and the facts presented in the light of a new theory, which it is hoped will bring them into more intelligible relations. Important additions have also been made to the chapters on Stochiometry and Chemical Equivalency, and a new chapter has been added which treats of a number of interesting but highly complex compounds that were not included in the general plan of the book, and may be more advantageously studied in an appendix. Moreover, throughout the book the text has been altered wherever corrections have been made necessary by the recent progress of the science.

CAMBRIDGE, September 1, 1871.

CONTENTS.

PART I.

PART II.

FIRST PRINCIPLES

OF

CHEMICAL PHILOSOPHY

PART I.

CHAPTER I.

INTRODUCTION.

1. *Definitions.* — The *volume* of a body is the space it fills, expressed in terms of an assumed unit of volume. The *weight* of a body, as the word is used in chemistry and generally in common life, is the amount of material which the body contains compared with that in some other body assumed as the unit of weight. The *specific gravity* of a body is the ratio of its weight to that of an equal volume of some substance which has been selected as the standard. Solids and liquids are always compared with water at its greatest density, which is at 4° centigrade, and hence the numbers which stand for their specific gravities express how many times heavier they are than an equal volume of water at this temperature. Gases, however, are most conveniently compared with the lightest of all known forms of matter, namely, hydrogen, and in this book the number which indicates the specific gravity of a gas expresses how many times heavier it is than an equal volume of hydrogen, compared under the same conditions of temperature and pressure.

2. *Volume and Weight.* — All experimental science rests upon accurate measurements of these fundamental elements, and it is therefore very important that there should be a general agreement among scientific men in regard to them. This

1

has been secured by the almost universal adoption of the
French system of measures and weights in all scientific investigations. The details of this system are given in Table I.,
and they require no further explanation. Its great advantage over our ordinary English system is not only in its decimal subdivision, but also in the simple relation which exists
between the units of measure and of weight. Since the unit
of weight is the weight of the unit volume of water, and since
the specific gravity of solids and liquids is always referred to
water, as the standard, it is always true in this system that

$$W = V \times Sp.\ Gr. \qquad [1]$$

If the volume is given in cubic centimetres, the weight obtained is in grammes; but if the volume is given in cubic decimetres or litres, the weight is found in kilogrammes. In this
formula, $Sp.\ Gr.$ stands for the specific gravity referred to
water. If the specific gravity is referred to hydrogen, as in
the case of gases, the value must be reduced to the water-
standard before using it in the formula. The reduction is
easily made, by multiplying by 0.0000896, a fraction which
is simply the specific gravity of hydrogen itself referred to
water. Using Sp. Gr. to represent the specific gravity of a
gas referred to hydrogen, the formula becomes

$$W = V \times Sp.\ Gr. \times 0.0000896, \qquad [2]$$

and may then be used in all calculations connected with the
weight and volume of aeriform bodies. In such calculations, in
order to avoid the long decimal fractions which the use of the
gramme entails, Hofmann has proposed to introduce into
chemistry a new unit of weight which he calls the _crith._ This
unit is the weight of one cubic decimetre or litre of hydrogen
gas at the standard temperature and pressure, and is equal to
0.0896 grammes. If now we estimate the weight of all gases
in _criths_, and let W represent this weight, while W represents
the weight in grammes, and V the volume in _litres_, we shall
also have

$$W = V \times Sp.\ Gr.\ and\ W = W \times 0.0896, \qquad [3]$$

and all problems of this kind will then be reduced to their
simplest terms.

The specific gravity of gases is also frequently referred to dry air, which for many reasons is a convenient standard. The weight of one litre of air under standard conditions is 1.293187 grammes. Hence, representing specific gravity referred to air by 𝔖𝔭. 𝔊𝔯. we have

$$\text{Sp. Gr. : } \mathfrak{Sp.}\ \mathfrak{Gr.} = 1.2932 : 0.0896,$$

or

$$\text{Sp. Gr.} = \mathfrak{Sp.Gr.} \times 14.42, \cdot$$

and

$$\mathfrak{Sp.}\ \mathfrak{Gr.} = \text{Sp. Gr.} \times 0.06929.$$

3. *Chemistry and Physics.* — Among material phenomena we may distinguish two classes. First, those which are manifested without a loss of identity in the substances involved. Secondly, those which are attended by a change of one or more of the materials employed into new substances. The science of chemistry deals with the last class of phenomena, that of physics with the first, and hence the terms chemical and physical phenomena. An illustration will make this distinction plain. When a bar of iron is drawn out into wire, is rolled out into thin leaves, is reduced by mechanical means to powder, is forged into various shapes, is melted and cast into moulds, is magnetized, or is made the medium of an electric current, since the metal does not in any case lose its identity, the phenomena are all physical. When, on the other hand, the iron bar rusts in the air, is burnt at the blacksmith's forge, or is dissolved in dilute sulphuric acid, the iron is converted into a new substance, iron rust, iron cinders, or green vitriol, and the phenomena are chemical. The distinction between these two departments of human knowledge is not, however, so strongly marked as the definition would seem to imply. In fact they coalesce at many points, and a knowledge of the elements of physics is an essential preliminary to the successful study of chemistry. In the following pages it will be assumed that the student is acquainted with the most elementary principles of this science, and references will be made to the sections of the author's work on Chemical Physics. The same relation which physics bears to chemistry on the one side, chemistry bears to physiology and the natural-history sciences on the other.

Questions and Problems.

1. Reduce by Table I. at the end of the book,

30 Inches to fractions of a metre.	Ans. 0.7619 metre.
76 Centimetres to inches.	Ans. 29.92 inches.
36 Kilometres to miles.	Ans. 22.38 miles.
10 Metres to feet and inches.	Ans. 32 ft. 9.7 inches.
1 Cubic metre to quarts.	Ans. 880.66 quarts.
1 Cubic foot to litres.	Ans. 28.31 litres.
1 Pint to cubic centimetres.	Ans. 567.8 $\overline{c.\,m.}^3$
1 Litre to cubic inches.	Ans. 61.027 cubic inches.
1 Pound Avoirdupois to grammes.	Ans. 453.6 grammes.
1 Kilogramme to ounces avoirdupois.	Ans. 35.27 ounces.
1 Ounce to grammes.	Ans. 28.35 grammes.

2. If the globe were a perfect sphere what would be the circumference and what the diameter in kilometres?

Ans. Circumference 40,000 kilometres,
Diameter   12,732.4   "

3. The length of the metre was determined by measuring the distance between Dunkirk (in France), Latitude 51° 2′ 9″, and Formentera (one of the Balearic Islands), Latitude 38° 39′ 56″, both on the same meridian. This distance was found by triangulation to be equal to 730,430 toises. What is the length of a metre in terms of this old French unit of measure? What, also, was the length measured in English miles? No account is to be taken of the ellipticity of the earth.   Ans. The metre, 0.5314 toise.

The length was 854 miles.

4. The *Sp. Gr.* of iron is 7.84. What is the weight of 10 c. m.³ of the metal in grammes? What is also the weight in kilogrammes of a sphere of iron whose diameter equals one decimetre?

Ans. 78.4 grammes and 4.105 kilogrammes.

5. What is the weight in grammes of 50 $\overline{c.\,m.}^3$ of oil of vitriol, when the *Sp. Gr.* of the liquid is 1.8?   Ans. 90 grammes.

6. The *Sp. Gr.* of alcohol being 0.8, what volume in litres would weigh 7.2 kilogrammes?   Ans. 9 litres.

7. Assuming that the earth is spherical, and its mean *Sp. Gr.* 5.67, what would be its weight, using as the unit of weight a kilometre cube of water at its greatest density?   Ans. 6,130,000,000,000.

8. Determine the *Sp. Gr.* of absolute alcohol from the following data: — weight of empty bottle 4.326; weight of same filled with water 19.654; weight of same filled with alcohol 16.741.

Ans. 0.8095.

9. Determine the *Sp. Gr.* of lead from the following data : — weight of bottle filled with water 19.654; weight of lead shot 15.456; weight of bottle filled in part with the shot and the rest with water 33.766. Ans. 11.5.

10. Determine the *Sp. Gr.* of iron from : — weight of iron in air 3.92, weight under water 3.42. Ans. 7.84.

11. Determine *Sp. Gr.* of wood from : — weight of wood in air 25.35; weight of sinker under water 9.77; weight of wood with sinker under water 5.10 grammes. Ans. 0.8445.

12. How much volume must a hollow sphere of copper have, weighing one kilogramme, which will just float in water? What must be the volume of the copper? Sp. Gr. of copper 8.8.
Ans. One cubic dicemetre and 113.6 $\overline{c. m.}^3$

13. How much volume must a hollow cylinder of iron have, which weighs 10 kilogrammes and sinks one half in water, and what must be the volume of the metal? Ans. 20 and 1.276 cubic decimetres.

14. What is the weight in grammes (under standard conditions) of 128 $\overline{c. m.}^3$ of oxygen gas (Sp. Gr. = 16)?
Ans. 0.1834 grammes.

15. How many litres of carbonic anhydride gas (Sp. Gr. = 22) would weigh (under normal conditions) 4.480 kilogrammes?
Ans. 2274 litres.

16. Solve the last two problems by [3], and show in what respect the method differs from that indicated by [2].

17. What is the weight in criths (under standard conditions) of one litre of nitrogen gas (Sp. Gr. = 14), of one litre of chlorine gas (Sp. Gr. = 35.5), of one litre of marsh gas (Sp. Gr. = 8), and of one litre of ammonia gas (Sp. Gr. = 8.5)?
Ans. 14, 35.5, 8, and 8.5 criths respectively.

18. What is the weight in grammes of one litre of each of the same gases under the same conditions?
Ans. 1.254, 3.180, 0.7165, and 0.7617 respectively.

19. The weight of one litre of hydrochloric acid gas is 1.642 grammes; of carbonic oxide gas 1.2500 grammes; of cyanogen gas 2.335 grammes, and of hydrogen gas 0.0896 grammes. What is the specific gravity of each of these gases referred to air?
Ans. 1.270, 0.9665, 1.806, and 0.0693 respectively.

20. What is the volume (under standard conditions) of 12.54 grammes of nitrogen gas, when specific gravity referred to air is 0.9703? Ans. 10 litres.

21. What is the weight of one litre of air in criths?

Ans. 14.42.

22. What would be the ascensional force of one thousand litres if hydrogen, under normal conditions?

Ans. The ascensional force is the difference between the weight of the hydrogen and that of the air displaced. Hence in the present example, the ascensional force would be 14,420 — 1000 = 13420 criths, or 1,201 grammes.

23. What is the value of a crith in grains, English weight.

Ans. 1.382 grains.

CHAPTER II.

4. *Compounds and Elements.* — With sixty-three exceptions,
all known substances, by various chemical processes, may
be decomposed, and hence are called *chemical compounds;*
while the sixty-three substances which have as yet never
been resolved into simpler parts are called *chemical elements.*
There is some reason for believing that many, if not all, of
these elementary substances may hereafter be decomposed, and
hence they can only be considered chemical elements provis-
ionally; but, however this may be, all known materials may still
be regarded as formed by the union of the particles of one or
more of these sixty-three substances. A list of the chemical
elements is given in Table II. The names of the more abundant or otherwise more important elements are printed in Roman letters. The others are very rare substances, and are
practically unimportant. Of these elementary substances more
than three fourths possess metallic properties, and among them
are all the useful metals, including the liquid metal mercury.
The rest present every variety of physical character. Oxygen,
hydrogen, and nitrogen are permanent gases. Chlorine, and
probably fluorine, though gases under ordinary conditions, may
by pressure and cold be condensed to liquids. Bromine is a
very volatile liquid; and among the solids we have every gradation between the highly volatile iodine, or the easily fusible
phosphorus, on the one hand, and carbon, which has never
even been melted, on the other. We find, also, among the elements every difference as regards density. Hydrogen gas is
the lightest, and the metal platinum the heaviest substance
known. Several of the elementary substances occur in a free
state in nature, for example, oxygen and nitrogen in the atmosphere, carbon in the coal beds, sulphur in the neighborhood
of active volcanoes, iron in meteoric stones, while arsenic, an-

timony, bismuth, copper, gold, silver, mercury, and platinum,
with a few other rare associates, are sometimes found in a
more or less pure state in metallic veins. Gold and platinum
are usually found in a free condition, though as a rule slightly
alloyed with their associated metals; but all the other elements
are generally found in combination, and the greater number
appear in nature only in this condition. From such compounds
the elements may be extracted by various chemical processes,
which will appear as we proceed. Among these elements the
useful metals are the tools of civilization, carbon is our universal fuel, while sulphur, phosphorus, arsenic, chlorine, bromine, and iodine have found important applications in the arts,
and are therefore articles of commerce; but the greater number
of the elements are only to be seen in the chemist's laboratory,
and are solely objects of chemical investigation. The elements
are distributed in nature in very unequal proportions. At
least one half of the solid crust of the globe, eight ninths of
the water on its surface, and one fifth of the atmosphere which
surrounds it, consist of the one element, oxygen. Moreover,
the other elements are usually found in combination with
oxygen, so that oxygen may be regarded as the cement by
which these elementary parts of the world are held together.
Next in abundance is silicon, which, after oxygen, is the chief
constituent of the rocks, and makes up about one fourth of the
earth's crust. Silicon is always found combined with oxygen,
and more than one half of the oxygen of the globe is in combination with this element. Hence, the compound of the two,
which we call silica or quartz, must make up more than one
half of our solid globe, at least as far as its composition is
known. After silicon in the order of abundance would follow
the elements aluminum, calcium, magnesium, potassium, sodium, iron, carbon, sulphur, hydrogen, chlorine, nitrogen,
which, without attempting to discriminate between them, make
up altogether very nearly the other fourth of the earth's mass;
for the remaining fifty elements — including all the useful
metals except iron — do not constitute altogether more than
one one-hundredth. Of the sixty-three known elements, then,
thirteen alone make up at least $\frac{99}{100}$ of the whole known mass
of the earth.

 5. *Analysis and Synthesis.* — The composition of a chemical

compound may be made evident in two ways. First, by breaking up the compound into its constituent parts; secondly, by reuniting these parts and reproducing the original substance. The first of these methods of proof is called *analysis*, the second, *synthesis*. The study of the processes by which the composition of a body may be discovered, and the relative amounts of its various constituents determined, forms an important branch of practical chemistry, which is known as *Chemical Analysis*, and this is subdivided into Qualitative and Quantitative Analysis, according to the object we have in view. Synthesis is chiefly used to prove the results of analysis.

6. *Law of Definite Proportions.* — Numberless analyses have proved that *any given chemical compound always contains the same elements combined in the same proportions.* Thus, when we analyze water, sugar, and salt, we always obtain the result given below; and this result is invariable, saving small errors of observation, from whatever source these materials may be drawn. The composition is given in per cents, as is usual in such cases.

Water (Dumas).		Salt.		Sugar (Péligot).	
Hydrogen,	11.112	Sodium,	39.32	Carbon,	42.06
Oxygen,	88.888	Chlorine,	60.68	Hydrogen,	6.50
				Oxygen,	51.44
	100.		100.		100.

Chemists have not yet succeeded in making sugar by combining its elements, but the synthesis both of water and salt is easily effected, and illustrates still more forcibly the same law. Thus we may *mix* together hydrogen and oxygen gas in *any* proportion, but when, by passing an electric spark through the mixture, we cause the elements to combine, then the gases unite in the exact proportion indicated above, and any excess of one or the other which may be present is left over. The law of definite proportions gives to chemistry a mathematical basis; for, since the analyses of all compounds have been made and tabulated in a way that will be soon explained, it is always possible, when the weight of a compound is given, to calculate the weights of its constituents, and, when the weight of one of its elements is known, to calculate the weights of all the other elements present.

7. *Mixture and Chemical Compound.* — The law of definite proportions gives a simple criterion for distinguishing between a mixture and a true chemical compound. In the first the elements may be mixed in any proportion, but in the true compound they are always combined in definite proportions. Thus we may mix together copper-filings and sulphur in any proportion, but as soon as we apply heat, and cause the elements to combine, then the copper combines with one half of its own weight of sulphur, and the excess of either element above these proportions is discarded. Again, in a mixture however homogeneous, we can generally, by mechanical means alone, distinguish the ingredients. Thus, in the mixture just referred to, a microscope would show the grains of sulphur and metallic copper, with all their characteristic appearances; and by means of carbonic sulphide we can easily dissolve out all the sulphur from the mixture; but after the chemical union has taken place, the characteristic properties of the elements are *merged* in those of the compound, and no such simple mechanical separation is possible. But although these distinctions are generally sufficient, nevertheless we find in some alloys, in solutions, and in a few other classes of compounds, less intimate conditions of chemical union where these criterions fail.

8. *Law of Multiple Proportions.* — It is generally the case that the same elements unite in more than one proportion, forming two or more different compounds. Now we always find that the proportions of the elements in such compounds are simple multiples of each other. This law is best illustrated by the compounds of nitrogen and oxygen, which are five in number, and have the names indicated in the table below. In order to make evident the law, we give, not the percentage composition as above, but the amount of oxygen, which is in each case combined with one and three fourths parts of nitrogen.

COMPOUNDS OF NITROGEN WITH OXYGEN.

	Nitrogen. By weight.	Oxygen. By weight.	Nitrogen. By volume.	Oxygen. By volume.
Nitrous Oxide,	1.75	1	2	1
Nitric Oxide,	1.75	2	2	2
Nitrous Anhydride,	1.75	3	2	3
Nitric Peroxide,	1.75	4	2	4
Nitric Anhydride,	1.75	5	2	5

CHAPTER III.

MOLECULES.

9. *Molecules.* — In order to bring the facts of chemistry into relation with each other, and unite them in an harmonious system, the following theory, first proposed by the English chemist, Dalton, and known as the Atomic Theory, is generally accepted by chemists. This theory assumes, in the first place, that every body, whatever its substance may be, is formed by the aggregation of minute particles of the same kind, which cannot be further subdivided without destroying the *identity* of the substance. Thus a lump of sugar is an aggregate of minute particles of sugar. If the sugar is burnt, these particles will be further subdivided; but the sugar will be thus changed into new substances. In like manner, a drop of water is an aggregate of minute particles of water. By passing a current of electricity through the drop, these particles will be subdivided, but then we shall have no longer water, but the two elementary gases, oxygen and hydrogen. *The smallest particles of any substance which can exist by themselves, we call molecules.*

10. *Physical Properties of Matter.* — The physical qualities of a body depend solely on the relations of its molecules. The physicist has therefore no occasion to continue the subdivision beyond the molecule, which is his unit.

Solid. — In a solid the molecules firmly cohere, and the force which binds them together has been called cohesion. On the form and size of the molecules, and also on the mode of aggregation, is supposed to depend the crystalline form of each substance, which is one of the most important and characteristic properties of matter, and one to which we shall have occasion hereafter to refer. On certain relations of the molecules, which we do not fully understand, depend undoubtedly elasticity, tenacity, ductility or malleability, hardness, transparency, diathermancy, and the allied qualities of solid bodies.

Liquid. — In the liquid condition of matter the molecules have more freedom of motion than in the solid, but still the motion is circumscribed within the liquid mass. Moreover, a certain cohesion still exists between the molecules, and on this depends the form of the rain-drop. The various phenomena of capillary action also are effects of the *cohesion* of the liquid molecules modified by their *adhesion* to the surfaces of solids, and the solvent power of liquids is a still further effect of the same mutual action. Connected also with this freedom of molecular motion is the property of liquids of transmitting pressure in all directions, and the well-known principles of hydrostatics to which it leads; but this property belongs to the third condition of matter as well.

Gas. — In the aeriform condition of matter, the motion of the molecules is only circumscribed by the walls of the containing vessel, or by some force acting on the mass from without. The molecules of a gas are constantly beating against the walls which confine them, and were they not thus restrained would fly off into space. The molecules of the atmosphere are restrained by the force of gravitation, and, as they fly upwards like a ball thrown into the air, they are at last brought to rest, and fall back again to the earth. Hence gases always exert pressure against any surface with which they are in contact, and we measure the pressure, or, as we frequently call it, the tension of the gas, by the height to which it will raise a column of mercury. Chem. Phys. (158). The instrument used for this purpose is called a barometer.

The height of the mercury column which represents the pressure or tension of a gas is always represented by *H*.

In our latitude, at the surface of the sea, the atmosphere in its normal conditions will raise a column of mercury 76 c. m. high. Hence $H = 76$, and to this standard we always refer in comparing together the volumes of different gases.

11. *Mariotte's Law.* — The most characteristic feature of the aeriform condition is the great change of volume which gases undergo, under varying pressure, and the special law of compressibility which they obey. If we represent by *H* and *H'* two conditions of pressure to which the *same body* of gas is at different times exposed, then the law is expressed by the formula

$$V : V' = H' : H. \qquad [4]$$

Moreover, since the specific gravity of a *given mass* of gas must be the greater the less its volume, it is also true that

$$Sp.\ Gr. : Sp.\ Gr'. = H : H', \qquad [5]$$

and lastly, since the weight of a *given volume* of gas is obviously proportional to its specific gravity, we also have

$$W : W' = H : H', \qquad [6]$$

in which W and W' represent the weight of an equal volume of the same gas under the two pressures H and H'.

12. *Heat a Manifestation of Molecular Motion.* — The effects of what we call heat are supposed to be merely manifestations of the motion of the molecules of bodies. The greater the moving power of the molecule, the more forcibly it strikes against our nerves of feeling, and hence the more intense is the sensation of heat produced; and to the condition of matter which produces this sensation we give the name of *temperature*. The greater the moving power of the molecules, the higher the temperature; the less the moving power, the lower the temperature. Moreover, since by the very definition all molecules at the *same temperature* are in the condition to produce the *same sensation* of heat, we must assume further, that, whatever their size or weight, they must all have, at the same temperature, the same moving power. The light molecule of hydrogen must move much faster than the heavy molecule of carbonic anhydride in order to produce the same effect. If now we represent the mass of any molecule by m, and by V its velocity at any given temperature, then the moving power will be represented by $\frac{1}{2}m\ V^2$, Chem. Phys. (42), and this will have the same value for every molecule at the same temperature. With a few exceptions, all bodies expand with an increasing temperature, and in the case of mercury the change of volume is so nearly proportional to the change of temperature that we may use the varying volume of a confined mass of this liquid as a measure of temperature. This is the simple theory of the common mercurial thermometer, and in this book we shall refer all temperatures to the degrees of the centigrade scale. These degrees are purely arbitrary; but to each one corresponds a definite value of $\frac{1}{2}m\ V^2$, although we have not as yet been able to connect our arbitrary with our theoretical measure.

When we increase the temperature of a body, we must of course increase the moving power of all the molecules, each by the same amount, and the sum of the moving powers which they thus acquire is the legitimate measure of the amount of heat which the body receives. Hence, while $\frac{1}{2}m\ V^2$ represents the temperature of a body, $\Sigma\ \frac{1}{2}m\ V^2$ represents the whole amount of heat which it contains. Practically, however, we measure quantity of heat by an arbitrary standard, and we shall use in this book as our unit the amount of heat required to raise the temperature of a kilogramme of pure water from 0° to 1° centigrade. This we call the *Unit of Heat*, and it has been found, by careful experiments, that this unit of heat represents an amount of moving power which is adequate to raise a weight of 423 kilogrammes one metre, or to do any other equivalent amount of work.

13. *Expansion by Heat.* — The amount of expansion which bodies undergo when heated has been carefully measured for many different substances, and the results are tabulated in all works on physics. Chem. Phys. Table XV. In each case is given the coefficient of expansion, which is the small fraction of its volume which a body increases when heated one centigrade degree. If, now, K represents this fraction, V the initial volume, V' the new volume, t the initial temperature, and t' the new temperature, then, if we assume that the expansion is proportional to the temperature, we easily deduce the formula, Chem. Phys. (239),

$$V' = V\left(1 + K\left(t' - t\right)\right). \qquad [7]$$

This formula serves to calculate the change of volume both of solids and gases, which expand, nearly at least, proportionally to the temperature. The same, however, is not true of liquids, whose rate of expansion frequently increases, with the temperature, very rapidly ; and for such bodies we are obliged to use the following formula, which is of the general form in which every algebraic function may be developed, and is much less simple : —

$$V' = V\left(1 + A\,t + B\,t^2 + C\,t^3 + \&c.\right). \qquad [8]$$

In this formula, V' represents the required volume at some temperature, t, and V, the volume at 0°, which is assumed to be known ; while A, B, C, &c., are numerical constants, which have been determined by experiment in the case of most liquids. Chem. Phys. (255).

Both solids and liquids expand with irresistible force, and we have, therefore, only this one effect to consider in regard to the action of heat upon them. It is different, however, with gases. By enclosing a gas in a tight vessel, we can raise its temperature without changing its volume, except so far as the vessel itself becomes enlarged by the heat. The effect of the heat is, then, to increase the tension or pressure of. the gas. Hence, in the case of a gas, we may have two distinct effects; first, an increase of volume, when the pressure is constant; secondly, an increase of tension, when the volume is constant. The increased volume may always be calculated from the initial volume and difference of temperature, by means of the formula,

$$V' = V\left(1 + 0.00366\ (t' - t)\right), \qquad [9]$$

which differs from that just given only in that the numerical value has been substituted for K, — this being the same for all gases. On the other hand, the increased tension may always be calculated from the initial tension, by means of the corresponding formula,

$$H' = H\left(1 + 0.00366\ (t' - t)\right), \qquad [10]$$

in which H and H' stand for the heights of the mercury columns which measure the initial and final tension respectively. The last formula is easily deduced from the first, on the principles of Mariotte's law, stated above. Chem. Phys. (261) and [201].

Variations of temperature produce such important changes in the volume and specific gravity of all bodies, and especially of gases, that it becomes frequently essential, before comparing together different observations, to reduce them all to some standard temperature. Most scientific men use, as this standard temperature, 0° centigrade, and scientific measures are generally adjusted to this standard; but 60° Fahrenheit, corresponding to 15°.5 centigrade, is often a more convenient standard, because it is nearer the mean temperature of the air, and is, therefore, not unfrequently employed.

14. *Change of State.* — Many substances are capable of ex-

The student should also solve by the same rule the problems given in the last section.

25. *Gay-Lussac's Law.* — This eminent French chemist was the first to state clearly the important truth, that, when gases or vapors react on each other, the volumes both of the factors and of the products of the reaction always bear to each other some very simple numerical ratio. This truth is generally known as the law of Gay-Lussac, but, since the principle is a direct consequence of the atomic theory, it is best studied in that relation. It is, as we have seen, a fundamental postulate of the theory that equal volumes of all substances, when in the aeriform condition, contain the same number of molecules. Hence it follows, that the volumes of all single molecules are the same, and, if we take this common volume as our unit of measure, it follows, further, that the total molecular volume represented by any symbol is always equal to the number of molecules. We are thus led to a most important fact, which gives an additional meaning to our chemical symbols, for it appears that *Every chemical equation, when properly written, represents not only the relative weights, but also the relative volumes of its factors and products, when in the state of gas.*

This principle is illustrated by the following equations:

$$\boxed{CH_4} \;+\; 2\boxed{O\!=\!O} \;=\; \boxed{CO_2} \;+\; 2\boxed{H_2O}$$

Marsh Gas. Oxygen Gas. Carbonic Anhydride. Aqueous Vapor.

$$2\boxed{NO} \;+\; 5\boxed{H\text{-}H} \;=\; 2\boxed{NH_3} \;+\; 2\boxed{H_2O}$$

Nitric Oxide Gas. Hydrogen Gas. Ammonia Gas. Aqueous Vapor.

The squares which here serve to indicate equal volumes, and to impress on the mind the meaning of the symbols, are evidently unnecessary and will not be used hereafter.

The important rule of the last section may be expressed by the following proportion

$$n\,m : n'\,m' = W : W' = \mathrm{W} : \mathrm{W}'$$

Here m and m' represent the molecular weights of any two substances, n and n' the number of molecules of these substances, which take part in a chemical reaction whether as factors or products, while n m and n' m' represent what in the statement of our rule we have called *the symbols of the substances*, and the equation expresses the fact that the sum of the atomic weights indicated by the symbols is proportional to the weights of the substances involved in the chemical reaction, whether these weights are estimated in grammes or in criths (2).

Now by (17) m' $=$ 2 Sp. Gr. and by [3] W' $=$ V $\times$ Sp. Gr.

Making these substitutions we may reduce the above proportion to the following form

$$\tfrac{1}{2}n \ m : n' = W : V$$

and this gives us another stochiometrical rule, by which we can calculate the *volume* of a gas or vapor involved in a chemical reaction, when the *weight* of some other factor or product is known, or inversely, when the volume is given calculate the weight.

Express the reaction in an equation ; make then the proportion, As one half of the symbol of the first substance is to the number of molecules of the second, so is the weight in criths of the first to the volume in litres of the second ; reduce the symbol to numbers, and calculate the value of the unknown quantity.

This rule has the same general application as the first, and a few examples will illustrate the use of it.

Problem 1. How much chlorate of potash must be used to obtain one litre of oxygen gas? The reaction is expressed by the equation

$$2KClO_3 = 2KCl + 3\,O\text{=}O,$$

whence we get the proportion

$$\tfrac{1}{2}(2\overset{122.6}{K\,ClO_3}) : 3 = x : 1. \quad x = 40.9 \text{ criths,}$$

$$40.9 \times 0.0896 = \text{Ans. } 3.664 \text{ grammes.}$$

Problem 2. How many litres of oxygen gas can be obtained from 500 grammes of chlorate of potash ? The reaction is the same as before, but in this case the grammes must first be reduced to criths. The proportion will then be written

$$\overset{122.6}{KClO_3}:3 = \frac{500}{0.0896} : x = \text{Ans. } 136.6 \text{ litres.}$$

In applying the rules of this chapter to the solving of stochiometrical problems, the student should carefully bear in mind, *first*, that the rule of (24) applies to all those cases in which the *weight* of one substance is to be calculated from the *weight* of another; *secondly*, that when *volume* is to be deduced from *volume* the answer can be found by mere inspection of the equation according to the principles stated in (25), and *thirdly*, that the rule of page 49 applies only to those problems in which volume is to be calculated from weight, or the reverse. In using this last rule it must be remembered that the "first substance" is always the one whose *weight* is given or sought, while the "second substance" is always the one whose *volume* is given or sought.

Moreover, the student will notice that the volume of any aeriform factor or product may also be found by dividing its weight in grammes, — calculated by the rule of (24), — by the known weight of one litre of the gas or vapor, found from Table III. by [3].

Questions and Problems.

1. What is the molecular weight of plumbic sulphate, $Pb{=}O_2{=}SO_2$? Of calcic phosphate, $Ca_3{\equiv}O_6{\equiv}(PO)_2$? Of ammonia alum, $(NH_4)_2, [Al_2]{\equiv}O_8{\equiv}(SO_2)_4 \cdot 24H_2O$? Ans. 303, 310, and 906.8.

2. What are the molecular weights of the symbols

$$3\,C_2H_4O_2;\ 5(FeSO_4 \cdot 7H_2O)\ \text{and}\ 7K_2{=}O_2{=}CO?$$

Ans. 180, 1390, and 967.4.

3. Are the total atomic weights of the two members of the following reaction equal?

$$Fe + (H_2SO_4 + Aq) = (FeSO_4 + Aq) + H\text{-}H.$$

Ans. The total weight of each member of the equation is 154.

4. Calculate the percentage composition of ammonic chloride, NH_4Cl. Ans. Nitrogen, 26.17; Hydrogen, 7.48; Chlorine, 66.35.

5. Calculate the percentage composition of nitrobenzole, $C_6H_5NO_2$. Ans. Carbon, 58.53; Hydrogen, 4.07; Nitrogen, 11.39; Oxygen, 26.01.

6. Given the percentage composition of chloroform as follows: Carbon, 10.04; Hydrogen, 0.83; Chlorine, 89.13. Required the symbol, knowing that the Sp. Gr. of chloroform vapor equals 59.75.

Ans. $CHCl_3$.

7. Given the percentage composition of stanno-diethylic bromide as follows: Tin, 35.13; Carbon, 14.29; Hydrogen, 2.97; Bromine, 47.61. Required the symbols, knowing that the Sp. Gr. of the vapor equals 168. Ans. $SnC_4H_{10}Br_2$.

8. Given the percentage composition of ethylene chloride as follows: Carbon, 24.24; Hydrogen, 4.04; Chlorine, 71.72. Required the symbol, knowing that the Sp. Gr. of the vapor equals 49.5.

Ans. $C_2H_4Cl_2$.

9. Given the percentage composition of cream of tartar as follows: Potassium, 20.79; Hydrogen, 2.66; Carbon, 25.52; Oxygen, 51.03. Required the simplest symbol possible. Ans. $KH_5C_4O_6$.

10. Given the percentage composition of crystallized ferrous sulphate as follows: Iron, 20.15; Sulphur, 11.51; Oxygen, 23.02; Water, 45.32. Required the simplest symbol possible.

Ans. Estimating the number of molecules of water (H_2O), as if water were a fourth element with an atomic weight of 18, we get $FeSO_4. 7H_2O$.

11. The percentage composition of morphia according to Liebig's analysis is Carbon, 71.35; Hydrogen, 6.69; Nitrogen, 4.99; Oxygen (by loss), 16.97. What is the symbol of this alkaloid, and how closely does this symbol agree with the results of analysis?

Ans. The symbol $C_{17}H_{19}NO_3$ would require 71.58 Carbon, 6.66 Hydrogen, 4.91 Nitrogen, and 16.85 Oxygen.

12. It is required to find the weight of phosphorus in 155 kilos. of calcic phosphate ($Ca_3P_2O_8$). Ans. 31 kilos.

13. It is required to find the weight of sulphuric anhydride (SO_3) in 284 kilos. of sodic sulphate, Na_2SO_4. Ans. 160 kilos.

14. How many grammes of plumbic sulphate, ($PbSO_4$) can be made from 2.667 grammes of sulphuric anhydride (SO_3)

Ans. 10.1 grammes.

15. How many grammes crystallized cupric sulphate ($CuSO_4. 6H_2O$) will yield 317 grammes of copper? Ans. 1337 grammes.

16. Required the total molecular weight of crystallized sodic phosphate, knowing that 71.6 parts of the salt contain 9.2 parts of sodium, and that the total atomic weight of sodium in one molecule of the compound is 46. Ans. 358.

17. The molecular weight of potassic nitrate is 101.1, and 2.359 grammes of the salt contain 1.120 grammes of oxygen. What is the total atomic weight of oxygen, and also the number of oxygen atoms in one molecule?

Ans. Total atomic weight 48. No. of oxygen atoms 3.

18. How much nitric acid (HNO_3) is required to dissolve 3.804 grammes of copper (Cu) and how much cupric nitrate (CuN_2O_6) and how much nitric oxide (NO) will be formed in the process? The reaction is expressed by the equation

$$3\,Cu + (8HNO_3 + Aq) = (3\,CuN_2O_6 + 4H_2O + Aq) + 2NO.$$

Ans. 10.08 grammes of nitric acid; 11.244 grammes of cupric nitrate and 1.20 grammes of nitric oxide.

19. How much common salt ($NaCl$) must be added to a solution containing 30 grammes of argentic nitrate ($AgNO_3$) in order to throw down the whole of the silver, and how much argentic chloride ($AgCl$) will be thus precipitated?

$$(AgNO_3 + NaCl + Aq) = \mathbf{AgCl} + (NaNO_3 + Aq).$$

Ans. 10.32 grammes of salt and 25.32 grammes argentic chloride.

20. How many litres of ammonia gas (NH_3) and how many of chlorine gas $Cl\text{-}Cl$ are required to make one litre of nitrogen gas $N\text{=}N$? How many litres of hydrochloric acid gas (HCl) are also formed?

$$2NH_3 + 3\,Cl\text{-}Cl = 6HCl + N\text{=}N.$$

Ans. 2 litres of ammonia gas; 3 litres of chlorine gas, and 6 litres of hydrochloric acid gas.

21. How many litres of hydrochloric acid gas (HCl) and how many of oxygen gas ($O\text{=}O$) can be obtained from one litre of aqueous vapor (H_2O), and how many litres of chlorine gas ($Cl\text{-}Cl$) must be used in the process?

$$2H_2O + 2\,Cl\text{-}Cl = 4HCl + O\text{=}O.$$

Ans. 2 litres of hydrochloric acid gas, ½ litre of oxygen gas, and 1 litre of chlorine gas.

22. How many litres of oxygen gas ($O\text{=}O$) are required to burn completely (i. e. to combine with) one litre of alcohol vapor (C_2H_6O), and how many litres of carbonic anhydride (CO_2) and how many of aqueous vapor (H_2O) are formed by the process? The chemical reaction which takes place when alcohol burns is expressed by the equation

$$C_2H_6O + 3 O=O = 2 CO_2 + 3 H_2O.$$

Ans. 3 litres of oxygen gas; 2 litres of carbonic anhydride, and 3 litres of aqueous vapor.

23. How many litres of oxygen gas are required to burn one litre of arseniuretted hydrogen (H_3As), and how many litres of arsenious acid vapor (AsO_3) and how many of aqueous vapor are formed in the process?

$$4 H_3As + 9 O=O = 4 AsO_3 + 6 H_2O.$$

Ans. $2\frac{1}{4}$ litres of oxygen gas; 1 litre arsenious acid vapor and $1\frac{1}{2}$ litres of aqueous vapor.

24. How many litres of chlorine gas can be made with 19.49 grammes of manganic oxide (MnO_2)?

$$\mathbf{MnO_2} + (4HCl + Aq) = (MnCl_2 + 2H_2O + Aq) + Cl\text{-}Cl.$$

Ans. 5 litres.

25. How many grammes of chalk ($CaCO_3$) are required to yield one litre of carbonic anhydride?

$$\mathbf{CaCO_3} + (2HCl + Aq) = (CaCl_2 + H_2O + Aq) + CO_2.$$

Ans. 4.48 grammes.

26. How many litres of hydrochloric acid gas (HCl) can be made with 8.177 kilogrammes of common salt ($NaCl$)?

$$(2NaCl + H_2SO_4 + Aq) = (Na_2SO_4 + Aq) + 2 HCl.$$

Ans. 3120.

27. How many grammes of ferrous sulphide (FeS) are required to yield 568 $\overline{c.\,m.}^3$ of sulphuretted hydrogen (H_2S)?

$$\mathbf{FeS} + (H_2SO_4 + Aq) = (FeSO_4 + Aq) + H_2S.$$

Ans. 2.24 grammes.

CHAPTER VII.

CHEMICAL EQUIVALENCY.

26. *Chemical Equivalents.* — If in a solution of argentic sulphate we place a strip of metallic copper, we find after a short time that all the silver has separated from the solution, and that a certain quantity of copper has dissolved in its place.

$$(Ag_2SO_4 + Aq) + \mathbf{Cu} = (CuSO_4 + Aq) + \mathbf{Ag_2}. \quad [25]$$

If now we pour off the solution of cupric sulphate, and place in this solution a strip of metallic zinc, the metallic copper in its turn will all separate, and to replace it a certain amount of zinc will dissolve.

$$(CuSO_4 + Aq) + \mathbf{Zn} = (ZnSO_4 + Aq) + \mathbf{Cu}. \quad [26]$$

Lastly, if we pour off the solution of zincic sulphate, and place in this a strip of metallic magnesium, the zinc will in like manner be replaced by magnesium.

$$(ZnSO_4 + Aq) + \mathbf{Mg} = (MgSO_4 + Aq) + \mathbf{Zn}. \quad [27]$$

In experiments like these, we can by proper analytical methods determine the relative quantities by weight of the several metals which thus replace each other, and we find that they are always the same. Thus, if our first solution contained 108 milligrammes of silver, the amount of each metal successively dissolved and precipitated would be, of copper, 31.7 *m. g.*, of zinc, 32.6 *m. g.*, of magnesium, 12 *m. g.* Moreover, if, instead of using in our experiments a metallic sulphate, we take a metallic chloride, nitrate, acetate, or any other compound of the metals, we find that the same definite ratios are preserved, at least in every case where the substitution is possible. It would appear then that these relative quantities of the several metals exactly replace each other in all such cases. They are, therefore, regarded as the chemical equivalents of each other, in the sense that they are capable of filling each other's place.

In a strict sense, two quantities of different elements can be said to be equivalent to each other only when they are actually capable of replacing each other in some known chemical reaction, but formerly the word was used with a much wider significance, and quantities of two different elements were said to be equivalent to each other if they had been proved to be equivalent to the same quantity of some third element which served as a link of connection. In this way an equivalency may be established between all the chemical elements, and the system of chemistry still used in many textbooks is based on a system of equivalency so determined. If the table of chemical equivalents on this old system is compared with a table of atomic weights on the new, it will be found that the numbers of the one are either the same as those of the other, or else some very simple multiples of them. The one set of numbers can be used in all stochiometrical calculations in the same way as the other, and on the old system the symbols stand for equivalents, as in the new they stand for atomic weights. The equivalents have this advantage, that they are the result of direct experiments, and are based on no hypothesis in regard to the molecular constitution of matter. But this hypothesis is necessary, in order to correlate a large number of facts which modern chemical investigation has brought to light, and when once made, the rest of the system follows as a necessary consequence.

27. *Quantivalence and Atomicity of the Elements.* — If now, starting with the atomic weights as they have been determined or assumed in Table II., we compare together the different elements from the point of view taken in the last section, it will be found, that, while in some cases one atom of one element is the equivalent of one atom of another, in other cases, it may be the equivalent of two, three, or four atoms. Since in the system of this book the symbols always stand for atomic weights, the relation here referred to is made evident whenever any metathetical reaction is expressed in the form of an equation. A few examples will illustrate the point, and make clear what is meant. The reaction of aqueous hydrochloric acid on a solution of argentic nitrate is expressed by the equation,

$$(\overset{\text{I}}{Ag}NO_3 + HCl + Aq) = (HNO_3 + Aq) + \mathbf{AgCl}, \quad [28]$$

and here evidently Ag changes places with H, and hence one atom of silver is equivalent to one atom of hydrogen. Take now the reaction of dilute sulphuric acid on zinc, which is expressed by the equation,

$$\overset{\text{II}}{Zn} + (H_2SO_4 + Aq) = (ZnSO_4 + Aq) + \boxed{H}\text{-}\boxed{H}, \quad [29]$$

and it will be seen that Zn has changed places with H_2, and hence that one atom of zinc is the equivalent of two atoms of hydrogen. Lastly, in the reaction of water on phosphorous trichloride, expressed by the equation,

$$H_3H_3O_3 + \overset{\text{III}}{P}Cl_3 = 3HCl + \underset{\text{Phosphorous Acid.}}{H_3PO_3}, \quad [30]$$

it is equally evident that P has changed places with H_3, and hence in this reaction one atom of phosphorus is equivalent to three atoms of hydrogen.

This relation of the elements to each other is called by Hofmann *quantivalence*; and selecting here, as in the system of atomic weights, the hydrogen atom as our standard of reference, the atoms of different elements are called *uni*valent, *bi*valent, *tri*valent, or *quadri*valent, according as they are in the sense already indicated *equi*valent to one, two, three, or four atoms of hydrogen. These terms are very appropriate, since they are all derived from the same root as our common English word equivalent, which best expresses the fundamental idea that underlies the whole subject. We shall therefore adopt them in this book, and, as Hofmann recommends, designate the quantivalence, whenever important, by a Roman numeral placed over the atomic symbol thus,

$$\overset{\text{I}}{Cl}, \quad \overset{\text{II}}{O}, \quad \overset{\text{III}}{N}, \quad \overset{\text{IV}}{C}.$$

In most cases, however, the quantivalence is indicated with sufficient clearness by the dashes, which are also used in this book to separate the parts of a molecular symbol. The number of these dashes is always the same as the quantivalence of the atoms, or groups of atoms, on either side.

With these additions to our notation we are able to express by our symbols all that was valuable in the old system of equivalents, and at the same time all that is peculiar to our modern theories.

Precisely the same relations of quantivalence are manifested even more fully by the compound radicals, whenever in a chemical reaction they change places with elementary atoms, and their replacing value is indicated in the same way. Thus, in the following reaction,

$$C_2H_3\overset{\text{I}}{O}\text{-}Cl + H\text{-}O\text{-}H = H\text{-}Cl + H\text{-}O\text{-}C_2H_3\overset{\text{I}}{O}, \quad [31]$$

Acetyl chloride.   Water.   Acetic Acid.

the radical C_2H_3O, named acetyl, changes places with one atom of hydrogen, and is therefore univalent, while in the next,

$$\overset{\text{III}}{C}H \equiv Cl_3 + H_3N = 3HCl + \overset{\text{III}}{C}H \equiv N, \quad [32]$$

Chloroform.   Hydrocyanic Acid.

the radical CH is as evidently trivalent.

The quantivalence of an element or radical is shown, not only by its power of replacing hydrogen atoms, but also by its power of replacing any other atoms whose quantivalence is known. Moreover, what is still more important, the quantivalence of an element or radical is shown, not only by its replacing power, but also by what we may term its *atom-fixing power*, that is, by its power of holding together other elements or radicals in a molecule. We may take as examples the molecules of four very characteristic compounds, namely, hydrochloric acid, water, ammonia, and marsh gas, whose symbols may be written thus,

$$\overset{\text{I}}{H}\text{-}Cl \qquad H, \overset{\text{II}}{H}\text{=}O \qquad H, H, \overset{\text{III}}{H}\text{=}N \qquad H, H, H, \overset{\text{IV}}{H}\equiv C.$$

Hydrochloric Acid.   Water.   Ammonia.   Marsh Gas.

By these symbols it appears, that, while the univalent atom of chlorine can hold but one atom of hydrogen, the bivalent atom of oxygen holds two, the trivalent atom of nitrogen three, and the quadrivalent atom of carbon four atoms of the same element. It appears, then, that the Roman numerals or dashes, which represent the replacing power of the atoms or radicals, represent also the *atom-fixing power* of the same, measured in each case by the number of atoms of hydrogen, or their equivalents, with which these atoms or radicals can combine to form a single molecule. On account of the importance of this principle we will extend our illustrations to a number of other compounds, and the student should carefully compare in each case the quantivalence on the two sides of the dash or dashes, which mark the atom-fixing power of the dominant atom in the molecule.

$$\overset{I}{Na}\text{-}\overset{I}{Cl} \qquad \overset{I}{K}\text{-}\overset{I}{I} \qquad \overset{I}{C_2H_5}\text{-}\overset{I}{Br} \qquad \overset{I}{K}\text{-}\overset{I}{CN};$$
Sodic Chloride.   Potassic Iodide.   Ethylic Bromide.   Potassic Cyanide.

$$\overset{I}{K}\text{-}\overset{II}{O}\text{-}\overset{I}{H} \qquad \overset{II}{Pb}\text{=}\overset{II}{O} \qquad \overset{I}{H}\text{-}\overset{II}{O}\text{-}\overset{I}{NO_2} \qquad \overset{I}{H}\text{-}\overset{II}{O}\text{-}\overset{I}{C_2H_3O};$$
Potassic Hydrate.   Plumbic Oxide.   Nitric Acid.   Acetic Acid.

$$\overset{I}{H.}\ \overset{I}{H.}\ \overset{I}{C_2H_5}\text{=}\overset{III}{N} \qquad (\overset{I}{C_2H_5})_3\text{=}\overset{III}{P} \qquad \overset{I}{CH_3},\ \overset{I}{C_2H_5},\ \overset{I}{C_5H_{11}}\text{=}\overset{III}{N}.$$
Ethylamine.   Triethyl phosphine.   Methyl-ethyl-amyl-amine.

The quantivalence of the chemical elements, especially as indicated by their atom-fixing power, is by no means always the same. They constantly exhibit under different conditions an unequal atom-fixing power. Thus we have

$$\overset{II}{Sn}Cl_2 \text{ and } \overset{IV}{Sn}Cl_4, \qquad \overset{III}{P}Cl_3 \text{ and } \overset{V}{P}Cl_5, \qquad \overset{III}{N}H_3 \text{ and } \overset{V}{N}H_4Cl.$$

Each element, however, has a maximum power, which it never exceeds. This we shall call its *atomicity*, and we shall distinguish the elements as monads, dyads, triads, &c., according to the number of univalent atoms or radicals they are able at most to bind together. Thus nitrogen is a pentad, although it is more commonly trivalent, and lead is a tetrad, although it is usually bivalent. Again, sulphur is a hexad, although in most of its relations it is, like lead, bivalent. In like manner with other elements, one of the few possible conditions is generally much more common and stable than the rest, and this prevailing quantivalence of an element is a more characteristic property than its maximum quantivalence or atomicity. A classification of the elements based on their atomicity alone would contravene their most striking analogies, while one based on the prevailing quantivalence very nearly satisfies all natural affinities. Moreover, it should be added, that, while the prevailing quantivalence of the elements is generally well established, their atomicity is frequently

still in doubt ; for the first can generally be discovered by studying the simple compounds of the elements with chlorine or hydrogen, while the last is often only manifested in those more
complex combinations, in regard to which a difference of opinion is possible.

The possible degrees of quantivalence of an elementary
atom are related to each other by a very simple law. They
are either all even or all odd. Thus the atom of sulphur may
be sextivalent, quadrivalent and bivalent, but is never trivalent or univalent; and on the other hand the atom of nitrogen
may be quinquivalent, trivalent and univalent, but not quadrivalent or bivalent. Atoms like those of sulphur, whose quantivalence is always even, are called *artiads*, while those like
nitrogen, whose quantivalence is always odd, are called
perissads.

A change in the quantivalence of an atom implies a change
in all its chemical relations, and the differences between the
reactions of the same atom in its several states of quantivalence
are frequently as great as those between the atoms of different
elements. Indeed, the first distinction appears to be only less
fundamental than the last, to which chemists have attached so
great and perhaps undue importance. The ferrous and ferric
compounds of iron, for example, would be referred to different
elements, were it not for the single circumstance that they may
be derived from the same substance and are so readily convertible into each other. The classes of compounds to which they
are most closely related belong indeed to wholly different elements ; for the ferrous compounds resemble those of zinc, and
the ferric compounds those of aluminum. A multitude of similar facts will be brought to notice in Part II. of this work.

28. *Atomicity or Quantivalence of Radicals.* — When in the
molecule of any compound the dominant or central atom is
united to as many other atoms as it can hold of that kind, the
molecule is said to be saturated ; thus

$$HCl, \qquad H_2O, \qquad H_3N, \qquad H_4C$$

are all saturated molecules ; for, although nitrogen is a pentad,
it cannot without the intervention of some other atom or radical
hold more than three atoms of hydrogen. While on the other
hand the molecules

$$\overset{II}{C}O, \qquad \overset{II}{P}Cl_3 \text{ and } \overset{II}{Sn}Cl_2$$

are not saturated, for they can combine directly with more oxygen or chlorine, forming thus the saturated molecules

$$CO_2, \qquad PCl_5 \text{ and } SnCl_4.$$

If now from a saturated molecule we withdraw one or more atoms of hydrogen, or their equivalents, *the residue may be regarded as a compound radical with an atomicity equal to the number of hydrogen atoms, or their equivalents, withdrawn.* Thus, if from the saturated molecule of marsh gas H_4C we withdraw one atom of hydrogen, we get the radical methyl H_3C, which is a monad; if we withdraw two atoms, we have the radical, H_2C, which is a dyad; if we withdraw three, there results HC, which is a triad; and lastly, if we withdraw all four, we fall back on the tetrad atom of carbon. Again, if from the saturated molecule of nitric anhydride N_2O_5 we withdraw one atom of the dyad oxygen O, it falls into two atoms of NO_2 each of which is a monad. If now we withdraw from NO_2 one of its remaining atoms of oxygen, we have left NO, which is a triad. Lastly, a molecule of sulphuric anhydride SO_3, which is saturated, gives, by withdrawing one atom of oxygen, SO_2, which acts as a bivalent radical. These considerations lead us to a simple rule, first stated by Wurtz, which in almost every case will enable us to infer the atomicity of any given radical. *The atomicity*[1] *of a compound radical is always equal to the number of hydrogen atoms, or their equivalents, which the radical may be regarded as having lost.*

It must not be supposed, however, that all such radicals are possible compounds. In a few cases only these residues, of which we have been speaking, form non-saturated molecules, which are capable of existing in a free state, like those of carbonic oxide, nitric oxide and sulphurous acid. At other times they are compound radicals, which, *by doubling*, form molecules that can exist in a free state, as those of cyanogen gas, and perhaps also of some hydrocarbons. Again, they appear as compound radicals, which pass and repass in so many chemical reactions as to almost force upon us the belief that they have a real existence, and represent the actual grouping of the atoms in the compounds of which they seem to be an integral part. Still again, and even more frequently, they can only be regarded as convenient factors in a chemical equation.

[1] The quantivalence of a compound radical is always the same as its atomicity.

Questions and Problems.

1. Analyze the following metathetical reactions, showing in each case how many parts of the several elements are equivalent to one part by weight of hydrogen, and also to how many atoms of hydrogen one atom of each of the interchanging elements corresponds. For the atomic weights refer to Table II.

$$2H\text{-}O\text{-}C_2H_5 + K\text{-}K = 2K\text{-}O\text{-}C_2H_5 + H\text{-}H.$$
Alcohol.   Potassium.   Potassic Ethylate.

$$2H\text{-}O\text{-}H + Mg = Mg\text{=}O_2\text{=}H_2 + H\text{-}H.$$
Water.   Magnesic Hydrate.

$$Sb\text{=}O_3\text{=}H_3 + 3HCl = SbCl_3 + 3H\text{-}O\text{-}H.$$
Antimonious Hydrate.   Antimonious Chloride.

$$4H\text{-}O\text{-}H + SiCl_4 = H_4\text{=}O_4\text{=}Si + 4HCl.$$
Silicic Chloride.   Silicic Acid.

2 Make out a table of chemical equivalents so far as the reactions of this chapter will enable you to deduce them from the atomic weights given in Table II.

3. Analyze the following metathetical reactions, showing in each case how the quantivalence of the several compound radicals involved in the metathesis, is indicated.

$$H\text{-}O\text{-}H + (C_2H_3O)\text{-}O\text{-}(C_2H_5) = (C_2H_3O)\text{-}O\text{-}H + H\text{-}O\text{-}(C_2H_5).$$
Water.   Acetic Ether.   Acetic Acid.   Alcohol.

$$2K\text{-}(CN) + (C_2H_4)\text{=}Br_2 = (C_2H_4)\text{=}(CN)_2 + 2KBr.$$
Potassic Cyanide.   Ethylene Bromide.   Ethylene Cyanide.   Potassic Bromide.

$$3H\text{-}O\text{-}H + (C_3H_5)\text{=}Cl_3 = (C_3H_5)\text{=}O_3\text{=}H_3 + 3HCl.$$
Water.   Glyceryl Chloride.   Glycerine.   Hydrochloric Acid.

The names of the radicals are as follows: C_2H_3O, Acetyl; C_2H_5, Ethyl; C_2H_4, Ethylene; C_3H_5, Glyceryl; CN, Cyanogen.

4. What is the atom-fixing power or quantivalence of the different atoms and radicals in the following symbols?

$$K_3\text{=}S_3\text{=}SbS$$
Potassic Sulphantimoniate.

$$H_2Na\text{=}O_2\text{=}CO$$
Acid Sodic Carbonate.

$$(NH_4)\text{-}O\text{-}NO$$
Ammonic Nitrite.

$$H_4\text{=}N_2\text{=}C_2O_2$$
Oxamide.

$$(HO).(H_2N)\text{=}(C_4H_4O_2)$$
Succinamic Acid.

$$K,Sb\text{=}O_4\text{=}C_4H_2O_2.$$
Tartar Emetic (dried).

5. If H_2O; C_2H_6; C_2H_6O (alcohol); $COCl_2$ (phosgene gas); $C_2H_4O_2$ (acetic acid) and $C_2H_2O_4$ (oxalic acid) are saturated molecules, what is the atomicity of the radicals HO (hydroxyl); C_2H_5 (ethyl); C_2H_4 (ethylene); C_2H_5O (aldehyde); CO (carbonyl); C_2H_3O (acetyl) and C_2O_2 (oxalyl).

CHAPTER VIII.

CHEMICAL TYPES.

29. *Types of Chemical Compounds.* — There are three modes or forms of atomic grouping, to which so large a number of substances may be referred, that they are regarded as molecular types, or patterns, according to which the atoms of a molecule are grouped together. These types may be represented by the general formulæ : —

$$\overset{\text{\tiny I}}{R}\text{-}\overset{\text{\tiny I}}{R} \qquad \overset{\text{\tiny I}}{R},\overset{\text{\tiny I}}{R}\text{=}\overset{\text{\tiny II}}{R} \quad \text{or} \quad \overset{\text{\tiny I}}{R}\text{-}\overset{\text{\tiny II}}{R}\text{-}\overset{\text{\tiny I}}{R} \qquad\qquad [33]$$

$$\overset{\text{\tiny I}}{R},\overset{\text{\tiny I}}{R},\overset{\text{\tiny I}}{R}\text{=}\overset{\text{\tiny III}}{R} \quad \text{or} \quad \overset{\text{\tiny I}}{R},\overset{\text{\tiny I}}{R}\text{=}\overset{\text{\tiny III}}{R}\text{-}\overset{\text{\tiny I}}{R}.$$

It will be noticed, that in the first of these types a single univalent atom or radical [1] is united to another single univalent atom, that in the second a bivalent atom binds together two univalent atoms or their equivalents, and that in the third a trivalent atom binds together three univalent atoms, or their equivalents. The dashes are used to separate what has been callèd the *central*, the *dominant*, or the *typical* atom from those which it thus unites into one molecular whole, and serve at the same time to point out the parts of the symbol to which its affinities are directed. Commas are used to separate the subordinate atoms so united. It will be further noticed, that in each case the quantivalence of the dominant atom is equal to the sum of the quantivalences of the subordinate atoms, or radicals, on either side; and the peculiarity in each case consists solely in the relations of the parts of the molecule which we thus attempt to indicate by the symbol. The three compounds, hydrochloric acid, water, and ammonia,

$$\overset{\text{\tiny I}}{H}\text{-}\overset{\text{\tiny I}}{Cl}, \qquad \overset{\text{\tiny I}}{H},\overset{\text{\tiny I}}{H}\text{=}\overset{\text{\tiny II}}{O}, \qquad \overset{\text{\tiny I}}{H},\overset{\text{\tiny I}}{H},\overset{\text{\tiny I}}{H}\text{≡}\overset{\text{\tiny III}}{N},$$

---

[1] Here, as elsewhere through the book, we use the symbol R for any univalent, $\overset{\text{\tiny II}}{R}$ for any bivalent, and $\overset{\text{\tiny III}}{R}$ for any trivalent atom or radical. Moreover, to avoid unnecessary repetition, we shall for the future conform to the general usage, and speak of the atoms of a radical as well as of those of an element, and use the word "atom" as applying to both, although the usage frequently involves an obvious solecism.

are generally taken as representatives of these types, and substances are described as belonging to the type of hydrochloric acid, to the type of water, or to the type of ammonia, as
the case may be.   These substances, however, are regarded as
types in no other sense than that their molecules present the
same mode of grouping which is indicated above by the more
general symbols.   Substances belonging to the same type may
have widely different properties.   To the type of water belong the strongest alkalies and the most corrosive acids known.
In what, then, it may be asked, does the type outwardly consist, or in what is it manifested? for the grouping of the atoms
can only be a matter of inference.   The answer is, that the
type of the molecules of a substance is manifested solely by
its chemical reactions.   Substances belonging to the same type
are simply those whose reactions may be classed together according to some one general plan.   Thus water, alcohol, and
acetic acid are classed in the same type, because, when submitted to the action of the same or similar reagents, they undergo
a like transformation, which seems to point to a similarity of
atomic grouping.

$$H, H{=}O + PCl_5 = PCl_3O + H\text{-}Cl + H\text{-}Cl$$
Water.   Phosphoric Chloride.   Hydrochloric Acid.

$$H, C_2H_5{=}O + PCl_5 = PCl_3O + H\text{-}Cl + C_2H_5\text{-}Cl \quad [34]$$
Alcohol.   Phosphoric Oxy-chloride.   Ethylic Chloride.

$$H, C_2H_3O{=}O + PCl_5 = PCl_3O + H\text{-}Cl + C_2H_3O\text{-}Cl.$$
Acetic Acid.   Acetylic Chloride.

On studying these reactions, it will be seen that both the manner in which the three compounds break up, and the probable
constitution of the products formed, point to the conclusion, that,
in each, one bivalent atom holds together two univalent atoms
or radicals.   It will be found, in the first place, that in all three
cases the reaction consists primarily in the substitution of two
atoms of chlorine for one of oxygen in the original molecule.
It will appear, in the next place, that as soon as this dominant
atom, which holds together the parts of the molecule, is taken
away, each of the three molecules splits up into two others of a
similar type; and lastly, it is evident from the third example
that one of the oxygen atoms of acetic acid stands in a very
different relation to the molecule from the other.   All this

points to the inference just made. At least, these and a vast number of similar reactions are best explained on this hypothesis, and herein its only value lies and its probability rests. In section 27 we have already given the symbols of a number of chemical compounds so printed that they can be at once referred to one or the other of the three types here alluded to, and it will not, therefore, be necessary to multiply examples in this place.

30. *Condensed Types.* — In the same way that a bivalent atom may bind together two univalent atoms or their equivalents, so, also, it may serve to bind together two *molecules*, and, in like manner, a trivalent atom may bind together three *molecules* into a more complex molecular group; and thus are formed what are called condensed types. We may represent a double molecule of the type of water thus, $\overset{\text{I}}{R_2} = \overset{\text{II}}{R_2} = \overset{\text{I}}{R_2}$, but it must be borne in mind that such a symbol stands for two molecules, since, by the very definition, two molecules of the same kind cannot chemically combine. We can, however, solder them, as it were, into one molecular whole by substituting for the two univalent atoms $\overset{\text{I}}{R_2}$ a single bivalent atom $\overset{\text{II}}{R}$, when we obtain a mode of molecular grouping represented by

$$\overset{\text{I}}{R_2} = \overset{\text{II}}{R_2} = \overset{\text{II}}{R}, \qquad\qquad [35]$$

which may be called the type of water doubly condensed. The constitution of common sulphuric acid is best represented after this type by the symbol, —

$$H_2 = O_2 = \overset{\text{II}}{S}O_2. \qquad\qquad [36]$$

The soldering atom is here the bivalent radical $\overset{\text{II}}{S}O_2$. In like manner, by using a trivalent atom, we can solder together three molecules of the same water-type, as in the general symbol, —

$$\overset{\text{I}}{R_3} = \overset{\text{II}}{R_3} = \overset{\text{III}}{R}, \qquad\qquad [37]$$

which represents the type of water trebly condensed. In the same way we may derive the symbol, —

$$\overset{\text{I}}{R_2}, \overset{\text{I}}{R_2} = \overset{\text{III}}{R_2} = \overset{\text{II}}{R}, \qquad\qquad [38]$$

which represents the type of ammonia doubly condensed. The substance urea, one of the most important of the animal secretions, is best represented by a symbol after this last type,—

$$H_2, \ H_2 \overset{\text{III}}{\equiv} \overset{\text{II}}{N_2} = \overset{}{C}O \qquad [39]$$

where the soldering atom is the bivalent radical carbonyl.

Chemists have also been led to admit the existence of what are called *mixed types*, which are formed by the union of molecules of different types soldered together by a single multivalent atom or radical as before. Thus, the molecules of sulphurous acid may be regarded as formed of a molecule of water soldered to a molecule of hydrogen by an atom of sulphuryl, $\overset{\text{II}}{S}O_2$; thus, H-O-H and H-H, united by $\overset{\text{II}}{S}O_2$ give

$$H\text{-}\overset{\text{II}}{O}\text{-}\overset{\text{II}}{S}O_2\text{-}H. \qquad [40]$$

So, also, the composition of a complex organic compound called sulphamide, or sulphamic acid, is most simply expressed when regarded as formed by the union of water and ammonia soldered together by the same radical sulphuryl; thus, from

$$H, \ H \overset{\text{III}}{=} \overset{}{N}\text{-}H, \text{ and } H\text{-}\overset{\text{II}}{O}\text{-}H \text{ we have } H, \ H \overset{\text{III}}{=} \overset{\text{II}}{N}\text{-}\overset{\text{II}}{S}O_2\text{-}O\text{-}H. \qquad [41]$$

Lastly, if we bind together on the same principle molecules of the type of hydrochloric acid, we shall simply reproduce the types of water and of ammonia, thus showing that all the types are only condensed forms of the simplest. We must not, therefore, attach to the idea of a chemical type any deeper significance than that indicated above. It is simply a convenient mode of classifying certain groups of chemical reactions, and a help in representing them to the mind; and we may regard the same substance as formed on one type or on the other, as will best help us to explain the reactions we are studying. Moreover, it is frequently convenient to assume other types besides those here specially mentioned.

31. *Substitution.* — When cotton-wool is dipped in strong nitric acid (rendered still more active by being mixed with twice its volume of concentrated sulphuric acid), and afterwards washed and dried, it is rendered highly explosive, and,

5

although no important change has taken place in its outward aspect, it is found on analysis to have lost a certain amount of hydrogen and to have gained from the nitric acid an equivalent amount of nitric peroxide NO_2 in its place.

$$C_6 \, (H_{10}) \, O_5 \quad \text{becomes} \quad C_6\!\left(H_7(NO_2)_3\right)O_5.$$
Cotton.   Gun-Cotton.

Under the same conditions glycerine undergoes a like change, and is converted into the explosive nitro-glycerine, —

$$C_3 \, (H_8) \, O_3 \quad \text{becomes} \quad C_3\!\left(H_5(NO_2)_3\right)O_3.$$
Glycerine.   Nitro-glycerine.

So, also, the hydrocarbon naphtha, called benzole, is changed into nitro-benzole, —

$$C_6 \, H_6 \quad \text{becomes} \quad C_6\!\left(H_5, NO_2\right).$$
Benzole.   Nitro-benzole.

The last compound is not explosive, and the explosive nature of the first two is in a measure an accidental quality, and is evidently owing to the fact that into an already complex structure there have been introduced, in place of the indivisible atoms of hydrogen, the atoms of a highly unstable radical rich in oxygen. The point of chief interest for our chemical theory is that this substitution does not alter, at least essentially, the outward aspect of the original compound. Every one knows how closely gun-cotton resembles cotton-wool. In like manner nitro-glycerine is an oily liquid like glycerine, and nitro-benzole, although darker in color, is a highly aromatic volatile fluid like benzole itself. Products like these are called *substitution products*, and they certainly suggest the idea that each chemical compound has a certain definite structure, which may be preserved even when the materials of which it is built are in part at least changed. If in the place of firm iron girders we insert weak wooden beams, a building, while retaining all its outward aspects, may be rendered wholly insecure, and so the explosive nature of the products we have been considering is not at all incompatible with a close resemblance, in outward aspects and internal structure, to the compounds from which they were derived.

The idea that each body has a definite atomic structure is

even more forcibly suggested by another class of substitution products first studied by Dumas, in which atoms of chlorine, bromine, or iodine have taken the place of the hydrogen atoms of the original compound. Thus, if we act upon acetic acid with chlorine gas, we may obtain three successive products, as shown in the following table, although only the first and the last have been fully investigated.

Acetic acid	$C_2H_4O_2$	or	$(\overset{\text{I}}{C_2H_3}\overset{\text{II}}{O})\text{-}\overset{\text{I}}{O}\text{-}H$
Chloracetic acid	$C_2(H_3Cl)O_2$	"	$(\overset{\text{I}}{C_2H_2}Cl\overset{\text{II}}{O})\text{-}\overset{\text{I}}{O}\text{-}H$
Dichloracetic acid	$C_2(H_2Cl_2)O_2$	"	$(\overset{\text{I}}{C_2}HCl_2\overset{\text{II}}{O})\text{-}\overset{\text{I}}{O}\text{-}H$
Trichloracetic acid	$C_2(HCl_3)O_2$	"	$(\overset{\text{I}}{C_2}Cl_3\overset{\text{II}}{O})\text{-}\overset{\text{I}}{O}\text{-}H$

We cannot, however, replace the fourth atom of hydrogen by chlorine; and this fact seems to prove that there is a real difference between this atom of hydrogen and the other three, and gives an additional ground for the distinction we make when we write the symbol of acetic acid after the type of water, as in the second column. The three atoms of hydrogen in the radical placed on the left-hand side of the dominant atom may all be replaced by chlorine, but the single atom of hydrogen placed on the right cannot. These products all resemble acetic acid in that they form with the alkalies crystalline salts, when the fourth atom of hydrogen is replaced by an atom of sodium or potassium, as the case may be.

It was the study of these and similar substitution products which first led to the conception of *chemical types*, and the word as first used was intended to convey the idea of a definite structure, although perhaps as yet unknown; but as the theory was extended more and more, and to widely different chemical compounds, it was found that the first definite conception could not be maintained, and the idea gradually assumed the shape we have given it in the last section. Still, the facts from which the original conception was drawn remain, and they point no less clearly now than they did before to the existence of a definite structure in all chemical compounds as the legitimate object of chemical investigation.

32. *Isomorphism.* — Closely associated with the facts of the last section, which find their chief manifestation in substances of organic origin, are the phenomena of isomorphism, which are equally conspicuous among artificial salts and native min-

Fig. 1.

erals. There seems to be an intimate connection between chemical composition and crystalline form, and two substances which under a like form have an analogous composition are said to be *isomorphous.* Thus the following minerals all crystallize in rhombohedrons (Fig. 1,) which have very nearly the same interfacial angles, and, as the symbols show, they have an analogous composition. They are therefore isomorphous.

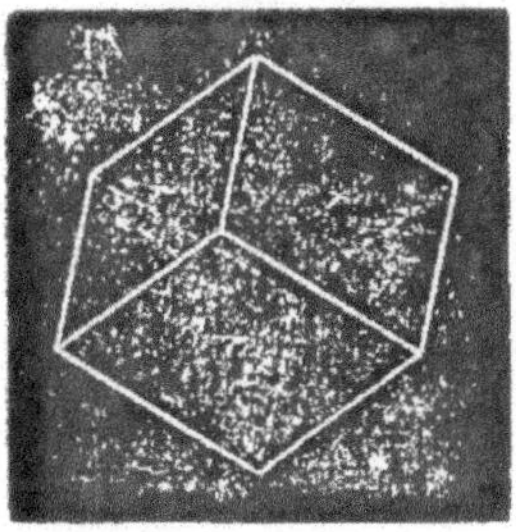

Calcite or calcic carbonate	$\overset{II}{C}a\overset{II}{=}O_2\overset{II}{=}CO$
Magnesite or magnesic carbonate	$\overset{II}{M}g\overset{II}{=}O_2\overset{II}{=}CO$
Chalybdite or ferrous "	$\overset{II}{F}e\overset{II}{=}O_2\overset{II}{=}CO$
Diallogite or manganous "	$\overset{II}{M}n\overset{II}{=}O_2\overset{II}{=}CO$
Smithsonite or zincic "	$\overset{II}{Z}n\overset{II}{=}O_2\overset{II}{=}CO$

The most cursory examination of these symbols will show that they differ from each other only in the fact that one metallic atom has been replaced by another. It is not, however, every metallic atom which can thus be put in without altering the form. This is a peculiarity that is confined to certain groups of elements, which for this reason are called groups of isomorphous elements. Moreover, as a rule, there is a close resemblance between the members of any one of these groups in all their other chemical relations. These facts, like those of the last section, tend to show that the molecules of every substance have a determinate structure, which admits of a limited substitution of parts without undergoing essential change, but which is either destroyed or takes a new shape when in place of one of its constituents we force in an unconformable element. A well-known class of artificial salts, called the alums, affords even a more striking illustration of the principles of isomorphism than the simpler example we have chosen; but all the bearings of the subject cannot be understood without a knowledge of crystallography, and we must therefore refer for further details to works on mineralogy.

33. *Rational Symbols.* — Chemical formulæ, like those of the last few sections, which endeavor, by grouping together the elementary symbols, to illustrate certain classes of reactions, and to illustrate the manner in which a complex molecule may break up, are called *rational symbols*, and are to be distinguished from the simpler symbols used earlier in the book, which express only the relative proportions in which the elements are combined, and which, since they are simply expressions of the results of analysis on a concerted plan, are called *empirical symbols.* Whether these rational symbols can be regarded in any sense as indicating the actual grouping of the material atoms is very doubtful, although facts like those stated above would seem to indicate that such may be the case, at least to a limited extent. It is difficult, for example, to resist the conclusion that in alcohol and its congeners the atoms C_2H_5 are grouped together in sóme sense apart from the rest of the molecule; but then we have no evidence of this grouping apart from the reactions of these compounds, and, until greater certainty is reached, it is not best to attach a significance to our symbols beyond the truths they are known to illustrate.

It is objected to the use of rational symbols that they bias the judgment on the side of some theory, of which they are more or less the exponents. But when they are used in the sense stated above, this objection has no force, for the reactions they prefigure are no less facts than the definite proportions they conventionally represent, and we employ one mode of grouping the symbols or another, as will best indicate the reactions we are studying. Moreover, as science advances, we have every reason to believe that we shall gain more and more knowledge of the actual relations between the parts of a material molecule, and as has already been intimated, there can hardly be a doubt that in some cases our rational symbols do express even now actual knowledge of this sort, however crude and partial it may be. Our present typical symbols are indeed the expressions of partial generalizations, which, however imperfect, have an element of truth. Hence it is that they have pointed out new lines of investigation, have led to new discoveries, and have been of the greatest value to science. They will doubt-less soon be superseded by other rational symbols, expressing other partial generalizations, to serve the same purpose in their turn and be likewise forgotten. We must not, however, de-spise these temporary expedients of science. They are not only useful, but necessary, and cannot mislead the student if he re-members that all such aids are merely the scaffoldings around the science, on which the builders work. It is from this point of view alone that we are to look at the whole idea of chemi-cal atoms, which lies at the basis of our modern chemical philosophy. That this idea is actually realized in the concrete form which it takes in some minds, can hardly be believed. The true chemical idea of the *atom* is more nearly represented by the corresponding Latin word *individuum*. The atom is the chemical individual, the unit, in which the mind seeks to repose for the time the individuality of that as yet undivided substance we call an element.

34. *Graphic Symbols.* — A more graphic method of repre-senting the relations between the atoms of a molecule than that of our ordinary rational symbols has been contrived by Kékulé, and has a similar value in aiding the conceptions, and thus facilitating the study of chemistry. In describing this system we shall speak of the possibilities of combination of any polyad atom with monad atoms as so many centres of at-traction or points of attachment, and, also, as so many affinities. Kékulé represents a monad atom, with its single centre, thus, $\odot$, while the symbols $(\cdot\ \cdot)$, $(\cdot\ \cdot\ \cdot)$, $(\cdot\ \cdot\ \cdot\ \cdot)$, &c., represent polyad atoms of different atomicities. When the several affini-ties are satisfied, the points are exchanged for lines pointing in the direction of the attached atoms. Thus, the symbol represents a dyad atom with its two affinities satisfied by two monad atoms, as, for example, in a molecule of water $H\text{-}\overset{\text{II}}{O}\text{-}H$.

In like manner the symbol repre-sents a molecule of nitric anhydride $\overset{\text{V}}{N_2}\overset{\text{II}}{O_5}$, and the symbol a molecule of sulphuric anhydride $\overset{\text{VI}}{S}O_3$. Mole-cules like these, in which all the affinities are satisfied, are said to be *saturated* or *closed*, while the atomic group $\overset{v}{N}O_2$, represented

by ⬭⬭ has one point of attraction still open, and,

therefore, acts as a monad radical. So, also, the molecular

group SO_2 represented by ⬭⬭, acts as a dyad radical.

These graphic symbols enable us to illustrate several important principles which could not readily be understood without their aid.

First. In the examples given in this section thus far, the quantivalence of a group of atoms of the same element is equal to the sum of the quantivalences of all the atoms of the group. Thus, in the molecule $\overset{v}{N_2}\overset{\scriptstyle{ii}}{O_5}$, the group of two pentad atoms presents ten affinities, and is saturated by the group of five dyad atoms, which presents the same number of affinities in return. So, also, in the molecule SO_3, a group of three dyad atoms just saturates the single hexad atom S. Such, however, is not necessarily the case, for it frequently happens that the similar atoms of such groups are united among themselves, and that a portion of the affinities (necessarily always an even number) are thus satisfied. For example, although C is a tetrad atom, the hydrocarbons, C_2H_6, C_2H_4, and C_2H_2, are all saturated molecules, as is shown by the following graphic symbols,

C_2H_6 C_2H_4 C_2H_2

and it is evident that in the first the two carbon atoms have been united by two, in the second by four, and in the third by six, of their eight affinities, while a corresponding number of points to which hydrogen atoms might otherwise have been attached are thus closed.

In like manner we have a well-known series of hydrocarbons, whose symbols are

$$CH_4, \quad C_2H_6, \quad C_3H_8, \quad C_4H_{10}, \quad C_5H_{12}, \quad C_6H_{14}, \quad \&c.,$$

the molecule of each one differing from that of the last by the group CH_2. In all these compounds the carbon atoms are united among themselves at the smallest possible number of points, as is shown, in a single case, by the following graphic symbol,

$$C_5H_{12}$$

and by constructing the graphic symbols of the other members of the series, it will be easily seen that the number of affinities thus closed is in every case equal to $2n - 2$, while the number remaining open is $4n - (2n - 2) = 2n + 2$, where n stands for the number of carbon atoms in the molecule. Hence, while the groups just mentioned form saturated molecules, the atomic groups

$$\underset{\text{Methyl.}}{CH_3} \qquad \underset{\text{Ethyl.}}{C_2H_5} \qquad \underset{\text{Propyl.}}{C_3H_7} \qquad \underset{\text{Butyl.}}{C_4H_9} \qquad \underset{\text{Amyl.}}{C_5H_{11}} \ \&c.,$$

act as univalent radicals. The graphic symbol of ethyl is , and in a similar way the graphic symbols of the other radicals may be easily constructed. In like manner may be also constructed the graphic symbols of the following important compound radicals, which form a series parallel to the first, and are all evidently dyads: —

$$\underset{\text{Ethylene.}}{C_2H_4} \qquad \underset{\text{Propylene.}}{C_3H_6} \qquad \underset{\text{Butylene.}}{C_4H_8} \qquad \underset{\text{Amylene.}}{C_5H_{10}} \ \&c.$$

Here again the graphic symbols enable us to explain a remarkable fact. These last atomic groups act not only as compound radicals, but also form the molecules of definite hydrocarbons (the first in the series being the well-known olefiant gas), and the difference in these two conditions may be represented to the eye, in the case of amylene, for example, as below: —

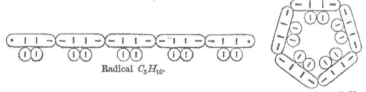

Radical C_5H_{10}.

Hydrocarbon C_5H_{10}.

The molecule in the first case is open, and presents two points of attraction, while in the second case it is closed.

The members of the two classes of hydrocarbon radicals mentioned above are the characteristic constituents of an important class of compounds called alcohols, and hence they are usually called alcohol radicals. If, in these atomic groups, we substitute oxygen for a portion of the hydrogen, one atom of oxygen always taking the place of two atoms of hydrogen, we obtain still other series of radicals, which are the characteristic constituents of several important organic acids, and belong to the class of acid radicals, which will be defined in the next chapter. Among the most important of the radicals thus derived are those of the following series : —

$$CHO \qquad C_2H_3O \qquad \cdot C_3H_5O \qquad C_4H_7O \qquad C_5H_8O$$

Formyl. Acetyl. Propionyl. Butyryl. Valeryl.

and the student should construct the graphic symbol of each.

The compounds of carbon have been selected to illustrate the apparent change of atomicity which frequently accompanies the grouping together of similar atoms, because this element is peculiarly susceptible of such a mode of combination, and in fact the almost infinite variety of its compounds may be traced to this circumstance. The same phenomenon, however, is presented, although to a less marked degree, by other elements. Thus arises the remarkable fact that a group of two atoms of a bivalent element has not unfrequently only the same quantivalence as a single atom. For example, there are two compounds of mercury and chlorine $Hg = Cl_2$ represented graphically by (⌣) and $[Hg_2] = Cl_2$ represented by (⌣). So also we have $Cu = O$ and $[Cu_2] = O$. We also frequently meet with another illustration of the same principle in an important class of tetrad elements whose atoms readily pair together, forming an atomic group which is sexivalent. Thus are formed the well-known compounds

$$[Al_2] \equiv Cl_6 \qquad [Fe_2] \equiv O_3 \qquad [Cr_2] \equiv O_3, \text{ \&c.}$$

When these same elements enter into combination by single atoms, they are almost invariably bivalent, and thus we have, in several cases, two very distinct classes of compounds, the one formed with the single and the other with the double atom of the element; for example,

$Fe = Cl_2$ and $[Fe_2] \overset{\equiv}{\equiv} Cl_6$ $Fe = O$ and $[Fe_2] \overset{\equiv}{\equiv} O_3$.

It will be noticed that although in the compounds of the second class the quantivalence of the single atoms is twice as great as it is in the first, yet their atom-fixing power is only increased by one half, and hence the name of *sesqui*-oxides or *sesqui*-chlorides, &c., which is frequently applied to them.

In order to distinguish the groups of similar atoms whose affinities are all open, from those groups where the affinities are in part closed by the union of the atoms among themselves, we may, as above, enclose the symbols of the last in brackets; and this rule will generally be followed. In most cases, however, the relations of the parts of the symbol are sufficiently evident without this aid.

Secondly. The graphic symbols illustrate another important theoretical principle, which, although almost self-evident, might be overlooked if not dwelt upon specially; namely, that on the multivalence of one or more of its atoms depends the integrity of every complex molecule. According to our present theories, no molecule can exist as an integral unit unless its parts are all bound together by such atomic clamps. Moreover, the whole virtue of a compound radical consists in the circumstance that it is an incomplete structure of the same sort, and its quantivalence is in every case equal to the number of univalent atoms (or their equivalents) which are required to complete it, or which it may be regarded as having lost. Hence the law of Wurtz finds a perfect expression in this system of graphic notation.

Thirdly. The graphic symbols illustrate most forcibly the relations of the parts of a complex molecule. Thus, for example, the symbols of alcohol and acetic acid given below show

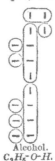

Alcohol.
$C_2H_5 \cdot O \cdot H$.

that in these compounds the dominant atom of oxygen acts as a bond uniting a complex radical to a single monad atom. They also show how it is possible that three of the atoms of hydrogen in acetic acid may stand in a very different relation to the molecule from the fourth (31). Again they show that the molecule of acetic acid differs from that of alcohol in the

Acetic Acid.
$C_2H_3 O \cdot O \cdot H$.

fact that one dyad atom has taken the place of two monad atoms; and, lastly, they give form to the idea of chemical types, so far as it has any real significance. When the composition of a compound is represented in this way, all the accidental or arbitrary divisions of our ordinary notation disappear, and only those are preserved which are fundamental. We gain thus more accurate conceptions of molecular structure. We understand better the relations of the various compound radicals (compare § 28), and, above all, we thus realize the full meaning of the fundamental tenet of our new philosophy, which holds that each chemical molecule is a completed structure bound together in all its parts by a system of mutual attractions.

There is another system of graphic symbols, frequently used in works on modern chemistry, which has some advantages over the one just described. In this system the atoms are represented by small circles circumscribing the ordinary symbol, and the atomicity is indicated by dashes radiating from these circles. A few examples will sufficiently illustrate the application of this method.

Water
H-O-H

Alcohol.
C_2H_5-O-H.

Acetic Acid.
C_2H_3O-O-H.

It is obvious, however, that the circles here used are not essential, and if we omit them, and only use dashes between the dominant atoms, and also, for convenience in printing, bring the whole expression into a linear form, using commas to separate disconnected atoms, and such other signs as may be necessary to avoid ambiguity, we have at once the ordinary system of notation adopted in this book. The graphic symbols last described are merely an expansion of this system. Nevertheless, the practice of developing the ordinary symbols into either of the more graphic forms will tend to impress the full meaning of the symbols on the mind of the student, and will thus greatly aid him in acquiring a clear conception of the theory of modern chemistry.

We may, however, extend the use of dashes so as to indicate the relations of all the parts of a complex molecule by our ordinary notation. Thus we may write the symbol of alcohol

$$([C\text{-}C]^{\underline{\underline{\underline{=}}}}H_5)\text{-}O\text{-}H,$$

or that of acetic acid

$$([C\text{-}C]^{\underline{=}}H_3, O)\text{-}O\text{-}H,$$

and these expanded symbols may frequently be used to advantage in place of the graphic forms. When thus developed, the symbol indicates the quantivalence of each of the atoms of the molecule, and in every case, if the symbol is correctly written, the number of dashes will be one half of the total quantivalence of all the atoms which are thus grouped together, for each dash evidently represents two affinities.

The remarks at the close of the last section apply, of course, still more forcibly to such bold and material conceptions as these graphic symbols appear to represent, and when we recall the hooked atoms of an elder philosophy, we cannot but smile to think how closely our modern science has reproduced what we once considered as strange and grotesque fancies. But, absurd as such conceptions certainly would be, if we supposed them realized in the concrete forms which our diagrams embody, yet, when regarded as aids to the attainment of general truths, which in their essence are still incomprehensible, even these crude and mechanical ideals have the very greatest value, and cannot well be dispensed with in the study of science.

Questions and Problems.

1. To what types may the following symbols be referred, and what is the quantivalence of the different compound radicals here distinguished? Study with the same view the symbols already given in the previous chapter.

$$H\text{-}(C_6H_5)$$
Benzole.

$$H\text{-}(C_7H_5O)$$
Oil of Bitter Almonds.

$$C_2H_4$$
Ethylene.

$$H_2\text{=}O_2\text{=}(C_2H_2O)$$
Glycollic Acid.

$$H\text{-}O\text{-}(C_6H_5)$$
Phenic Acid.

$$H\text{-}O\text{-}(C_7H_5O)$$
Benzoic Acid.

$$H_2\text{=}O_2\text{=}(C_2H_4)$$
Glycol.

$$H_2\text{=}O_2\text{=}(C_2O_2)$$
Oxalic Acid.

$$H, H, (C_6H_5)\text{≡}N$$
Aniline.

$$H, H, (C_7H_5O)\text{≡}N$$
Benzamide.

$$H_2, H_2, (C_2H_4)^{\underline{\underline{=}}}N_2$$
Ethylene diamine.

$$H_2, H_2, (C_2O_2)^{\underline{\underline{=}}}N_2$$
Oxamide.

$$H, H\text{=}N\text{-}(C_2H_2O)\text{-}O\text{-}H$$
Glycocol.

$$H, H\text{=}N\text{-}(C_2O_2)\text{-}O\text{-}H$$
Oxamic Acid.

$$H, (C_7H_5O)\text{=}N\text{-}(C_2H_2O)\text{-}O\text{-}H$$
Hippuric Acid.

$$H, H\text{=}N\text{-}(C_2O_2)\text{-}O\text{-}(C_2H_5)$$
Oxamethane.

2. Analyze the following reactions, and show that by comparing the reactions in each group, the typical structure of the various compounds may be inferred.

$$Cl\text{-}Cl \quad + \quad H\text{-}H \quad = \quad HCl \quad + \quad HCl$$
Chlorine gas.   Hydrogen gas.   Hydrochloric Acid.   Hydrochloric Acid.

$$Cl\text{-}Cl \cdot + (C_7H_5O)\text{-}H = (C_7H_5O)\text{-}Cl + HCl$$
Oil of Bitter Almonds.   Benzoyl Chloride.

$$H\text{-}Cl \quad + \quad K\text{-}O\text{-}H \quad = \quad KCl \quad + \quad H\text{-}O\text{-}H$$
Potassic Hydrate.   Potassic Chloride.   Water.

$$H\text{-}Cl \quad + \quad (C_2H_5)\text{-}O\text{-}H \quad = \quad (C_2H_5)\text{-}Cl \quad + \quad H\text{-}O\text{-}H$$
Alcohol.   Ethylic Chloride.

$$H, H\text{=}S \quad + \quad P\text{≡}Cl_5 \quad = \quad P\text{≡}Cl_3, S \quad + \quad HCl \quad + \quad HCl$$
Sulphohydric Acid.   Phosphoric Chloride.

$$H, (C_2H_3O)\text{=}S + P\text{≡}Cl_5 = P\text{≡}Cl_3, S + (C_2H_3O)\text{-}Cl + HCl$$
Thiacetic Acid.   Acetyl Chloride.

$$K_2\text{=}O_2\text{=}H_2 + (CO), H\text{≡}N = K_2\text{=}O_2\text{=}(CO) + H, H, H\text{≡}N$$
Potassic Hydrate.   Cyanic Acid.   Potassic Carbonate.   Ammonia.

$$K_2\text{=}O_2\text{=}H_2 + (CO), (C_2H_5)\text{≡}N = K_2\text{=}O_2\text{=}(CO) + H, H, (C_2H_5)\text{≡}N$$
Cyanic Ether.   Ethylamine.

3. What would be the symbols of cyanic acid and cyanic ether (see last problem), on the supposition that they contain the radical cyanogen, and are formed after the water type? Is the following reaction compatible with that last given?

$$K\text{-}O\text{-}H + (C_2H_5)\text{-}O\text{-}(CN) = (C_2H_5)\text{-}O\text{-}H + K\text{-}O\text{-}(CN).[1]$$
Cyanetholine.   Alcohol.   Potassic Cyanate.

and if not, what conclusion must you draw in regard to the two compounds cyanic ether and cyanetholine?

4. What bearing have the phenomena of substitution on the doctrine of chemical types? Does the circumstance that the proper-

---

[1] This product in the actual process is decomposed by the excess of potash into potassic carbonate and ammonia.

ties of the substitution products are frequently quite different from those of the original substance invalidate the doctrine ?

5. How does the action of chlorine on acetic acid indicate that this compound is fashioned after a determinate type ? On what particular fact does this evidence chiefly rest ?

6. What bearing have the phenomena of isomorphism on the doctrine of types ? Enforce the argument by some familiar illustration.

7. The radical allyl C_3H_5 is univalent in oil of garlic $(C_3H_5)_2\text{-}S$, and in allylic alcohol $(C_3H_5)\text{-}O\text{-}H$, but trivalent in glycerine $(C_3H_5)\equiv O_3\equiv H_3$. Moreover, this radical when set free doubles, forming a volatile hydrocarbon oil, which has the composition $(C_3H_5)\equiv(C_3H_5)$, and which combines directly with bromine, the resulting product having the symbol $(C_3H_5)\text{-}(C_3H_5)\equiv Br_4$. Represent these symbols by the graphic method, and thus explain the different relations of the radical.

8. Represent the symbols of phenic acid and benzoic acid by the second graphic method, and explain why the radical phenyl (C_6H_5) and benzoyl (C_7H_5O) are only univalent.

9. Why is it that the addition of the atoms CH_2 does not change the atomicity of a radical ?

10. What is the quantivalence of Al in the symbol $[Al\text{-}Al]\equiv Cl_6$? Is there any difference in the quantivalence of Fe in the two compounds $Fe\equiv O_2\equiv CO$ and $[Fe\text{-}Fe]\equiv O\equiv(SO_2)_3$? Answer the questions by the aid of graphic symbols.

11. Is there any difference in the quantivalence of nitrogen in potassic nitrite $K\text{-}O\text{-}NO$ and potassic nitrate $K\text{-}O\text{-}NO_2$?

12. Represent by graphic symbols the difference between cyanic ether and cyanetholine (see problems 2 and 3 above).

13. The symbol $[Hg_2]Cl_2$ represents a single molecule, while Na_2Cl_2 represents two molecules, and would be more properly written $2NaCl$. What is the difference in the two cases ?

14. Represent by the graphic method the symbols of potassic carbonate $K_2\equiv O_2\equiv(CO)$ and potassic oxalate $K_2\equiv O_2\equiv(C_2O_2)$, and show that both form a perfect molecular unit.

15. Represent by the graphic method the following symbols ;

$$H_2\equiv O_2\equiv(C_3H_6) \qquad \text{(Propyl Glycol.) ;}$$

$$H_2\equiv O_2\equiv(C_3H_4O) \qquad \text{(Lactic Acid.) ;}$$

$$H_2{=}O_2{=}(C_3H_2O_2) \quad \text{(Malonic Acid)};$$

$$H_2{=}O_2{=}(C_3O_3) \qquad \text{(Unknown)},$$

and thus show that they are formed after the same type.

16. What is the atom-fixing power or quantivalence of the elements and radicals, which appear in the various symbols given in this chapter? Develop these symbols, and show that they represent in each case a single perfect molecule.

N. B. The student should practice developing the ordinary molecular symbols into the graphic forms described above, until he is perfectly familiar with the method, and has acquired a clear conception of the different types of molecular structure.

CHAPTER IX.[1]

BASES, ACIDS, AND SALTS.

35. *Hydrates, Alkalies, Bases.* — It is not unfrequently the case that the technical terms of a science remain in use long after they have lost their original meaning. This is peculiarly true of those which we have placed at the head of this section. They have, with the exception of the first, come down to us from the period of alchemy, and are still retained in the language of trade and in many works on practical science, with a peculiar meaning which they have acquired during the last hundred years under the teaching of the dualistic theory. Since they, in many cases at least, suggest erroneous conceptions in regard to the constitution of chemical compounds, it would be well if they could be discarded altogether; but, as this is impracticable, we must endeavor to give to them as definite a meaning as possible.

The term "hydrate" is applied to a class of compounds which were formerly supposed to contain water as such, but which are now believed to have no closer relation to water than is indicated by the circumstance that they have the same type, and may be formed from water by replacing one of its hydrogen atoms with some metal. Thus, by acting on water with potassium, we obtain potassic hydrate; or, if we use sodium, we obtain sodic hydrate.

$$2H\text{-}O\text{-}H + K\text{-}K = 2K\text{-}O\text{-}H + H\text{-}H$$

Water. Potassium. Potassic Hydrate. Hydrogen Gas.

[42]

$$2H\text{-}O\text{-}H + Na\text{-}Na = 2\,Na\text{-}O\text{-}H + H\,H$$

Water. Sodium. Sodic Hydrate. Hydrogen Gas.

Both of these hydrates, and also those of the very rare but closely allied metals, lithium, cæsium, and rubidium, are very

---

[1] In studying this chapter the student should endeavor to remember the names and symbols of the different compounds mentioned. Hitherto we have been chiefly employed with the forms of the symbols, and this exercise of the memory has not been expected.

soluble in water, and yield solutions which corrode the skin, and convert the fats into soaps. To all the substances known to them which possessed these caustic qualities the alchemists gave the name of *alkalies,* and this term is now applied to the five hydrates just enumerated. The first two of these are commercial products, and have important applications in the arts. They all differ from the hydrates of other metals in that they cannot be decomposed by heat alone.

Again, if we act on water with calcium or magnesium, we obtain calcic or magnesic hydrate; but the double atom of water is then decomposed by these bivalent metals.

$$H_2\text{-}O_2\text{=}H_2 + \overset{II}{Ca} = Ca\text{=}O_2\text{=}H_2 + H\text{-}H$$
<small>Water.   Calcium.   Calcic Hydrate.   Hydrogen Gas.</small>

$$[43]$$

$$H_2\text{-}O_2\text{=}H_2 + \overset{II}{Mg} = Mg\text{=}O_2\text{=}H_2 + H\text{-}H$$
<small>Water.   Magnesium.   Magnesic Hydrate.   Hydrogen Gas.</small>

These two hydrates, as well as those of the allied metals, barium and strontium, although much less soluble in water than the alkalies, still dissolve in this common solvent to a limited extent, and manifest decided caustic qualities. When dry they have an earthy appearance, and hence are frequently known as the alkaline earths. They also differ from the true alkalies in the fact that they are readily decomposed by heat; and since they are then resolved into water and a metallic oxide, as the following reaction shows, the opinion formerly entertained in regard to their composition was not unnatural.

$$Mg\text{=}O_2\text{=}H_2 = MgO + H_2O \qquad [44]$$
<small>When heated.</small>

Moreover, when the anhydrous oxides are mixed with water, they enter into direct union with a portion of the liquid. This combination is usually attended with the evolution of great heat, and the process is known as slaking.

$$CaO + H_2O = Ca\text{=}O_2\text{=}H_2. \qquad [45]$$

There are many other metallic hydrates which are still more readily decomposed by heat. These, as a rule, cannot be formed by the direct union of the corresponding metallic oxide and water, but may be obtained by adding to a solution of

6

a salt of the metal one of the soluble hydrates mentioned above. Thus, —

$$(CuCl_2 + 2Na\text{-}O\text{-}H + Aq) = (Cu{=}O_2{=}H_2 + 2NaCl + Aq)$$
Cupric Chloride.   Cupric Hydrate.   Sodic Chloride.

[46]

$$(ZnCl_2 + 2K\text{-}O\text{-}H + Aq) = (Zn{=}O_2{=}H_2 + 2KCl + Aq)$$
Zincic Chloride.   Zincic Hydrate.   Potassic Chloride.

$$([Fe_2]Cl_6 + 3Ba{=}O_2{=}H_2 + Aq) = ([Fe_2]^{\underline{\underline{\text{iii}}}}O_6^{\underline{\underline{\text{iii}}}}H_6 + 3BaCl_2 + Aq)$$
Ferric Chloride.   Ferric Hydrate.   Baric Chloride.

The hydrates are regarded by some chemists as compounds of the metal with the compound radical hydroxyl, and their symbols are then written after a simpler type, thus,—

$$Ca{=}(\overset{\text{I}}{HO})_2 \qquad Fe{=}(\overset{\text{I}}{HO})_2 \qquad [\overset{\text{VI}}{Cr_2}]^{\underline{\underline{\text{iii}}}}(\overset{\text{I}}{HO})_6$$
Calcic Hydrate.   Ferrous Hydrate.   Chromic Hydrate.

Ammonia. — Closely allied to these metallic hydrates is a very remarkable compound, formed by dissolving ammonia gas, NH_3, in water. Although the product resembles, in many of its physical relations, a simple solution of gas in water, yet the compound in all its chemical relations acts like a metallic hydrate,

$$NH_3 + H_2O = \overset{\text{I}}{NH_4}\text{-}O\text{-}H$$
Ammonia Gas.   Water.   Ammonic Hydrate.

which has led chemists to write its symbol after the type of water, and to assume the existence of a univalent compound radical $\overset{\text{I}}{NH_4}$, to which has been given the name of ammonium.

Metallic Oxides or Basic Anhydrides. — Closely allied to the metallic hydrates, in the relation we are now considering, are many of the simple compounds of the metals with oxygen which are called in general metallic oxides. Such compounds as

$$Ca{=}O \qquad Ba{=}O \qquad Pb{=}O \qquad Fe{=}O \qquad Cu{=}O \qquad Ag_2{=}O$$
Calcic Oxide.   Baric Oxide.   Plumbic Oxide.   Ferrous Oxide.   Cupric Oxide.   Argentic Oxide.

may be regarded as formed from one or more molecules of water, by replacing all the atoms of hydrogen with those of some metal; and these oxides as well as the hydrates before mentioned are frequently classed together under the common title of *bases,* although it would be best to confine this term to the metallic hydrates alone, and to distinguish the *basic oxides* as *basic anhydrides*. (37)

Salts. — The atoms of hydrogen still remaining in a metallic hydrate may be replaced with the atoms of a well-defined class of non-metallic elements and compound radicals; and, for a reason which will soon appear, the replacing atoms are called acid or negative radicals.[1]

From this replacement results a new class of compounds we call *salts*. Thus, —

$$K\text{-}O\text{-}H \text{ gives } K\text{-}O\text{-}Cl, \text{ also } K\text{-}O\text{-}NO_2 \text{ and } K\text{-}O\text{-}(C_2H_3O)$$
Potassic Hydrate.   Potassic Hypochlorite.   Potassic Nitrate.   Potassic Acetate.

$$Ca\text{=}O_2\text{=}H_2 \text{ gives } Ca\text{=}O_2\text{=}SO_2, \text{ } Ca\text{=}O_2\text{=}CO \text{ } Ca\text{=}O_2\text{=}(C_2H_3O)_2$$
Calcic Hydrate.   Calcic Sulphate.   Calcic Carbonate.   Calcic Acetate.

36. *Acids.* — Opposed in chemical properties to the so-called bases is another very important class of compounds called *acids*. They derive their name from the fact that they are generally soluble in water and have a sharp or sour taste, although there are many exceptions to the rule. Like the bases, they all contain hydrogen; but this hydrogen can no longer be replaced by non-metallic elements or negative radicals, but only by metallic elements and positive radicals, and it is herein that the chief distinction lies. Moreover, the opposition of these two classes of compounds also appears in the fact that, while in bases the replaceable hydrogen atoms are united to a metallic atom or positive radical, which for this reason we frequently call a basic radical, in the acids, on the other hand,

---

[1] The word radical, as used in chemistry, stands for any atom or group of atoms, which is, for the moment, regarded as the principal constituent of the molecules of a given compound, and which does not lose its integrity in the ordinary chemical reactions to which the substance is liable. The distinction between basic and acid radicals (or positive and negative radicals as they are more frequently called) will become clear as we advance. It is sufficient for the present to state that, although these terms imply an *opposition of relations* rather than a difference of qualities, yet, as a general rule, the metallic atoms are basic radicals, while the non-metallic atoms are acid radicals. Moreover it may be added, that among compound radicals those consisting of carbon and hydrogen alone are usually basic, and those containing also oxygen usually acid; and, further, that of the two most important radicals containing nitrogen, ammonium (NH_4) is strongly basic, and cyanogen (CN) as decidedly acid. In this book, with few exceptions, the basic radicals are always placed on the left-hand, and the acid radicals on the right-hand side, of the molecular symbols.

these same hydrogen atoms are united as a rule to a non-metallic atom or negative radical, frequently, also, called as above an acid radical.   In most cases there is a vinculum which unites the two parts of the molecule ; and both in acids and in bases this vinculum consists usually of one or more oxygen atoms, although in a large class of acids the hydrogen atoms are united directly to the radical without any such connection.   The acids of this class have by far the simplest constitution ; and we will give examples of these first, adding in each case a reaction to illustrate the acid relations of the compound.   In studying these reactions, it must be borne in mind that the evidence of acidity is in each case to be found in the fact that one or more of the hydrogen atoms of the compound may be replaced by positive radicals or metallic atoms. This replacement may be obtained in one of four ways, — by acting on the acid, either with the metal itself, or with a metallic oxide, or with a metallic base, or with a metallic salt.

$$(2\,HCl + Aq) + NaNa = (2\ NaCl + Aq) + \boxed{H}\text{-}\boxed{H}$$
Hydrochloric Acid.   Sodium.   Sodic Chloride.

$$(2\,HCl + Aq) + ZnO = (ZnCl_2 + H_2O + Aq)$$
Zincic Oxide.   Zincic Chloride.

[47]

$$(HBr + K\text{-}O\text{-}H + Aq) = (KBr + H_2O + Aq)$$
Hydrobromic Acid. Potassic Hydrate.   Potassic Bromide.

$$(HI + Ag\text{-}O\text{-}NO_2 + Aq) = AgI + (H\text{-}O\text{-}NO_2 + Aq)$$
Hydriodic Acid. Argentic Nitrate.   Argentic Iodide.   Nitric Acid.

We will next give examples of more complex acids, in which the two parts of the molecule are united by a vinculum of oxygen atoms.

$$(H\text{-}O\text{-}(C_2H_3O) + Na\text{-}O\text{-}H + Aq) = (Na\text{-}O\text{-}(C_2H_3O) + H_2O + Aq)$$
Acetic Acid.   Sodic Hydrate.   Sodic Acetate.

$$(H_2\text{=}O_2\text{=}SO_2 + Aq) + CuO = (Cu\text{=}O_2\text{=}SO_2 + H_2O + Aq)$$
Sulphuric Acid.   Cupric Oxide.   Cupric Sulphate.

$$(H_3\text{=}O_3\text{=}PO + 3K\text{-}O\text{-}H + Aq) = (K_3\text{=}O_3\text{=}PO + 3H_2O + Aq)$$
Phosphoric Acid. Potassic Hydrate.   Potassic Phosphate.

Such acids as these are called oxygen acids.   Like the hydrates, they may be regarded as compounds of hydroxyl, but with negative instead of positive radicals, thus : —

$$HO\text{-}NO_2 \qquad (HO)_2\text{=}SO_2 \qquad (HO)_3\text{=}PO.$$

Nitric Acid.   Sulphuric Acid.   Phosphoric Acid.

This mode of writing the symbols is not only frequently convenient, but has been of real value by bringing out unexpected and important relations. It does not, however, indicate any fundamental difference of opinion in regard to the constitution of these hydrates, and this at once appears when the symbols are put into the graphic form.

When an acid, like acetic acid, contains but one atom of hydrogen, which is replaceable by a metallic atom or a positive radical, it is called monobasic; when, like sulphuric acid, it contains two such hydrogen atoms, it is called dibasic; when, like phosphoric acid, it contains three, it is tribasic, &c. Moreover, one evidence of this difference of basicity is found in the fact that whereas a monobasic acid can only form one salt with a univalent radical, a dibasic acid can form two, and a tribasic three. Thus, while we have only one sodic nitrate, there are two sodic sulphates and three sodic phosphates.

$$Na\text{-}O\text{-}NO_2 \qquad\qquad H_2Na\text{=}O_3\text{=}PO$$

Sodic Nitrate.   Acid Sodic Phosphate.

$$H,Na\text{=}O_2\text{=}SO_2 \qquad\qquad HNa_2\text{=}O_3\text{=}PO$$

Acid Sodic Sulphate.   Neutral Sodic Phosphate. [48]

$$Na_2\text{=}O_2\text{=}SO_2 \qquad\qquad Na_3\text{=}O_3\text{=}PO$$

Neutral Sodic Sulphate.   Basic Sodic Phosphate.

There is, however, but one calcic sulphate, for, since the calcium atoms are bivalent, a single one is sufficient to replace both of the hydrogen atoms in the acid.

37. *Acid Anhydrides.* — Besides the acids properly so called, all of which contain hydrogen, there is another class of compounds which bear the same relation to the true acids which the metallic oxides bear to the true bases. To avoid confusion, compounds of this class have been distinguished as *anhydrides*,[1] and they may be regarded as one or more molecules of water in which all the hydrogen has been replaced by negative or acid radicals. As among the most important of these we may enumerate Sulphuric Anhydride $SO_2\text{=}O$ or SO_3, Nitric Anhy-

---

[1] More precisely *acid anhydrides*, but as the basic anhydrides are usually called simply metallic oxides, the qualifying term is seldom added.

dride $(NO_2)_2$=O or N_2O_5, Carbonic Anhydride CO=O or CO_2, Phosphoric Anhydride $(\overset{\text{I}}{P}O_2)_2$=$O$ or P_2O_5, and Silicic Anhydride $\overset{\text{IV}}{Si}$≡O_2. Most of the anhydrides unite directly with water to form acids, and several of the acids, when heated, give off water and are resolved into anhydrides. [Compare 44 and 45.]

$$H_2O \;+\; SO_3 = H_2\text{=}O_2\text{=}SO_2$$

$$3H_2O \;+\; P_2O_5 = 2H_3\text{=}O_3\text{=}PO$$

$$\underset{\text{Silicic Acid.}}{H_4\text{=}O_4\text{≡}Si} = \underset{\text{Silicic Anhydride.}}{SiO_2} + 2H_2O$$

$$\underset{\text{Boric Acid.}}{2H_3\text{=}O_3\text{=}B} = \underset{\text{Boric Anhydride.}}{B_2O_3} + 3H_2O$$

[49]

Moreover in many cases these anhydrides will combine directly with the metallic oxides to form salts; and the reactions are best indicated by a rational formula, which represents the oxide and anhydride as radicals in the resulting compound. Thus, baric oxide burns in the vapor of sulphuric anhydride, yielding baric sulphate; and lime also unites directly with the same anhydride, although with less energy, forming calcic sulphate.

$$BaO + SO_3 = BaO,\ SO_3 \text{ and } CaO + SO_3 = CaO,\ SO_3$$

We are thus led to the old formulæ of the dualistic system, according to which the metallic oxides were the only true bases, the anhydrides were the only true acids, and the two were regarded as paired in all true salts. But, although in its modern theories our science has fortunately left the ruts to which the dualistic ideas for so long limited its progress, yet it must be remembered, that, according to our present definitions, these dualistic formulæ are perfectly legitimate, and still give the simplest exposition of a large number of important facts.

38. *Salts.* — The definition of the term "salt" has been clearly implied in the definitions of "base" and "acid" already given. It is any acid in which one or more atoms of hydrogen have been replaced with metallic atoms or basic radicals; it is any base in which the hydrogen atoms have been more or less replaced by non-metallic atoms or acid radicals; or it may be the

product of the direct union of a metallic oxide and an anhydride. A neutral salt is, properly speaking, one in which all the hydrogen atoms, whether of base or acid, have been replaced as just stated. A basic salt is one in which one or more of the hydrogen atoms of the base remain undisturbed, and therefore still capable of replacement by acid radicals. An acid salt is one in which one or more of the hydrogen atoms of the acid remain undisturbed, and therefore capable of replacement by basic radicals.

But, besides the basic and acid salts, which come under these definitions, there are also others which can be most simply defined as consisting of several atoms of the metallic oxide to one of anhydride, or of several atoms of anhydride to one of the metallic oxide.

As an example of acid salts of the second class we have, besides the two sodic sulphates mentioned on page 85, also a third, which may be written $Na_2O, 2SO_3$. This is easily obtained by simply heating the acid sulphate.

$$2(H, Na=O_2=SO_2) = Na_2O, 2SO_3 + H_2O \qquad [50]$$
$$\text{Acid Sodic Sulphate.} \qquad \text{Sodic Bisulphate.} \qquad \text{Water.}$$

If heated to a still higher temperature, one atom of the anhydride is set free, and the salt falls back into the neutral sulphate.

$$Na_2O, 2SO_3 = Na_2O, SO_3 + SO_3$$
$$\text{Bisulphate.} \qquad \text{Neutral Sulphate.} \qquad \text{Anhydride.}$$

This reaction justifies the dualistic form given to the symbol; but other relations of the bisulphate may be better expressed by the following typical formula, —

$$Na_2=O_2=(SO_2-O-\overset{\text{II}}{S}O_2) = Na_2=O_2=SO_2 + SO_3$$
$$\text{Sodic Bisulphate.} \qquad \text{Neutral Sulphate.} \qquad \text{Anhydride.}$$

in which a group of two atoms of SO_2, soldered together by one atom of oxygen, acts as a bivalent radical.

As an example of a basic salt of the second class we have, in addition to the two plumbic acetates of the normal type,

$$Pb=O_2=(C_2H_3O)_2 \qquad \text{and} \qquad Pb=O_2=(C_2H_3O), H$$
$$\text{Neutral Plumbic Acetate.} \qquad \qquad \text{Basic Plumbic Acetate.}$$

a third salt containing three times as much lead, —

$$(Pb\text{-}O\text{-}Pb\text{-}O\text{-}\overset{\text{II}}{Pb}) = O_2 = (C_2H_3O)_2, \qquad [51]$$

Triplumbic Acetate.

in which a group of three atoms of lead, soldered together by two atoms of oxygen, acts as a bivalent radical. It is evident that, theoretically, any number of multivalent radicals might be united in this way, and also that the complex radical thus formed will have a quantivalence easily determined by estimating the number of bonds which remain unsatisfied; but, practically, the grouping cannot be carried to a very great extent, for the stability of the radical diminishes with its complexity, and a condition is soon reached when it can no longer sustain, if we may so express it, its own weight. Moreover, while some radicals, like the atoms of lead, copper, mercury, and iron, are prone to group themselves in this way, the larger number show but little tendency to this mode of union.

The symbols of these acetates may also be written on the dualistic type, which represents them as compounds of plumbic oxide, PbO, and acetic anhydride, $C_4H_6O_3$. We have, then, —

$$PbO, \ C_4H_6O_3 \qquad \text{and} \qquad 3PbO, \ C_4H_6O_3 \qquad [52]$$

Neutral Plumbic Acetate.   Triplumbic Acetate.

and we may thus best illustrate the important fact that the second compound is prepared by combining with the first an additional quantity of plumbic oxide.

It will appear on reviewing the symbols of the acids, bases, and salts given in this section, that, in by far the greater number, the two parts of the molecule are held together by one or more atoms of oxygen, which act as a vinculum. Such compounds are called oxygen salts, using the word salt, as is frequently done, to stand for acids and bases, as well as for the true metallic salts; and in fact they all belong to the same type of chemical compounds. Since oxygen plays so important a part in terrestrial nature, we might well expect that these oxygen compounds would hold a very conspicuous place in our chemical science, — and such is indeed the fact. During the dualistic period the study of chemistry was almost wholly confined to the oxygen compounds, and, even now, they occupy by far the largest share of a chemist's attention.

There is, however, another element, namely, sulphur, which is capable of filling the place occupied by oxygen in many of its compounds, and thus may be formed a distinct class of bodies which are called sulphur salts. These compounds are not nearly so numerous as the oxygen salts, and have not been so well studied, so that a few examples will be sufficient to illustrate their general composition, and the relations which they bear to the corresponding oxygen compounds.

Oxygen Salts.	Sulphur Salts.
$H\text{-}O\text{-}H$	$H\text{-}S\text{-}H$
Water or Hydric Acid.	Sulphohydric Acid.
$K\text{-}O\text{-}H$	$K\text{-}S\text{-}H$
Potassic Hydrate.	Potassic Sulphohydrate.
$K_2\text{=}O_2\text{=}CO$	$K_2\text{=}S_2\text{=}CS$
Potassic Carbonate.	Potassic Sulphocarbonate.

39. *Test-Papers.* — The soluble bases and acids, when dissolved in water, cause a striking change of color in certain vegetable dyes, and these characteristic reactions give to the chemist a ready means of distinguishing between these two important classes of compounds. The two dyes chiefly used for this purpose are turmeric and litmus, and strips of paper colored with the dyes are employed in testing. Turmeric paper, which is naturally yellow, is turned brownish red by bases, while litmus paper, which is naturally blue, is turned red by acids, and in both cases the natural color is restored by a compound of the opposite class.

If to a solution of a strong base, like sodic hydrate, we add slowly and carefully a solution of a strong acid, like sulphuric, we shall at last reach a condition in which the solution affects neither test-paper, and it is then said to be *neutral.* On evaporating this solution we obtain a neutral salt, like sodic sulphate, and the presence in the solution of the slightest excess of acid or base beyond the amount required to form this salt would have been made evident by the test-papers. In such cases, we may therefore use these test-papers to distinguish between acid, basic, and neutral salts, but only with great caution; for we find that when, as in acid-carbonate of soda, a strong base is associated with a weak acid, the reaction is still basic, although the acid may be greatly in excess, and, on the other hand, when, as in cupric sulphate, a weak base has been associated with a strong acid, the reaction may be strongly acid even in the basic salts. The explanation of these apparent anomalies is to be found in the fact that these colored reagents are all salts themselves, and the reactions examples of metathesis. The coloring matter of these dyes is an acid which varies its tint according as the hydrogen atoms have or have not been replaced; and when, for any reason, the acid or base of the salt examined is not in a condition to determine the necessary metathesis, the characteristic change of color does not take place.

Unfortunately, the facts just stated have led to great confusion in the use of the words "acid" and "basic" as applied to salts, since these terms sometimes have reference solely to the number of atoms of hydrogen, in the acid or base, which have not been replaced in the formation of the salt, and at other times refer to the reactions of the salt on the colored reagents just described. A confusion of this sort must have been noticed in the names of the three phosphates of soda on page 85. The so called neutral phosphate is theoretically an acid salt, and the basic phosphate a neutral salt, but the salts give with test-papers the reactions which their names indicate. The theoretical is the only legitimate use, and the one we shall adhere to in this book, except in regard to names of compounds which cannot be arbitrarily changed.

40. *Alcohols, Fat Acids, Ethers.* — The hydrocarbon radicals mentioned in § 34 yield a very large number of compounds after the type of water, which are closely allied to the hydrates and anhydrides, both acid and basic, just described. If one of the hydrogen atoms in the molecule of water is replaced by either of the univalent basic radicals, methyl, ethyl, propyl, &c., we obtain a class of compounds, called alcohols, of which our common alcohol is the most important. On the other hand, if the atom of hydrogen is replaced by one of the univalent acid radicals, formyl, acetyl, propionyl, &c., we obtain an important class of acid compounds, of which acetic acid (vinegar) is the best known, but which also includes a large number of fatty substances closely related to our ordinary fats. Hence the name Fat Acids, by which this class of compounds is generally designated.

Basic Hydrates or Alcohols.

Methylic Alcohol (wood spirits)	$CH_3\text{-}O\text{-}H.$
Ethylic Alcohol (common alcohol)	$C_2H_5\text{-}O\text{-}H.$
Propylic Alcohol	$C_3H_7\text{-}O\text{-}H.$
Butylic Alcohol	$C_4H_9\text{-}O\text{-}H.$
Amylic Alcohol (fusel oil)	$C_5H_{11}\text{-}O\text{-}H.$

(With six others already known.)

Acid Hydrates, Fat Acids.

Formic Acid	$H\text{-}O\text{-}CHO.$
Acetic Acid	$H\text{-}O\text{-}C_2H_3O.$
Propionic Acid	$H\text{-}O\text{-}C_3H_5O.$
Butyric Acid	$H\text{-}O\text{-}C_4H_7O.$
Valerianic Acid	$H\text{-}O\text{-}C_5H_9O.$

(With fifteen others already known.)

If now we replace both of the hydrogen atoms of water by the same basic radicals mentioned above, we obtain a class of compounds called ethers, which correspond to the metallic oxides or basic anhydrides; and if we replace the two hydrogen atoms by the corresponding acid radicals, we obtain a similar series of acid anhydrides. Lastly, if we replace one of the hydrogen atoms by a basic radical, and the other by an acid radical, we get a class of compounds also called ethers (but distinguished as compound ethers), which correspond to the salts.

Examples of Anhydrides.

1. Simple Ethers.

Methylic Ether	$CH_3\text{-}O\text{-}CH_3$ or $(CH_3)_2\text{=}O.$
Ethylic Ether (common ether)	$C_2H_5\text{-}O\text{-}C_2H_5$ or $(C_2H_5)_2\text{=}O.$

2. Mixed Ethers.

Methyl-ethyl Ether	$CH_3\text{-}O\text{-}C_2H_5.$
Ethyl-amyl Ether	$C_2H_5\text{-}O\text{-}C_5H_{11}.$

3. Compound Ethers.

Acetic Ether	$C_2H_5\text{-}O\text{-}C_2H_3O.$
Butyric-methyl Ether	$CH_3\text{-}O\text{-}C_4H_7O.$

4. Acid Anhydrides.

Acetic Anhydride	$C_2H_3O\text{-}O\text{-}C_2H_3O$ or $(C_2H_3O)_2\text{=}O.$
Valerianic Anhydride	$C_5H_9O\text{-}O\text{-}C_5H_9O$ or $(C_5H_9O)_2\text{=}O.$

The positive radicals, of which the alcohols consist, hold an intermediate position between the strong basic radicals on the one hand, and the strong acid radicals on the other, and the same is true of the alcohols themselves, which hold a middle place between the strong basic and the strong acid hydrates. This is indicated by the following reactions; in what way it is left to the student to inquire.

$$2H\text{-}O\text{-}C_2H_5 + K\text{-}K = 2K\text{-}O\text{-}C_2H_5 + H\text{-}H$$

$$2\ CH_3\text{-}O\text{-}H + H_2\text{:}O_2\text{:}SO_2 = (CH_3)_2\text{:}O_2\text{:}SO_2 + 2\ H_2O$$

41. *Glycols.* — The class of hydrates described in the last section belong to the simple type of water. But we have also a class of analogous compounds belonging to the type of water doubly condensed. If in the double molecule of water $(H_2\text{:}O_2\text{:}H_2)$ we replace one of the pairs of hydrogen atoms by either of the bivalent positive radicals, ethylene, propylene, butylene, &c., we obtain a series of compounds closely resembling the alcohols, called glycols, and by substituting the related negative radicals we obtain two series of acid hydrates, which stand in the same relation to the glycols that the fat acids bear to the alcohols. These relations are shown in the following scheme, which, however, includes only the five first members of each of these three series of compounds. It should be noticed in this connection that each of the *bivalent positive* radicals yields *two* related *negative* radicals, while the *univalent positive* radicals of the last section yield only one such negative radical; and moreover that the acids in the first series, although diatomic, are only monobasic, while those in the second series are both diatomic and dibasic (43).

$C_2H_4\text{:}O_2\text{:}H_2$ Ethylic Glycol.	$H_2\text{:}O_2\text{:}C_2H_2O$ Glycolic Acid.	$H_2\text{:}O_2\text{:}C_2O_2$ Oxalic Acid.
$C_3H_6\text{:}O_2\text{:}H_2$ Propylic Glycol.	$H_2\text{:}O_2\text{:}C_3H_4O$ Lactic Acid.	$H_2\text{:}O_2\text{:}C_3H_2O_2$ Malonic Acid.
$C_4H_8\text{:}O_2\text{:}H_2$ Butylic Glycol.	$H_2\text{:}O_2\text{:}C_4H_6O$ Oxybutyric Acid.	$H_2\text{:}O_2\text{:}C_4H_4O_2$ Succinic Acid.
$C_5H_{10}\text{:}O_2\text{:}H_2$ Amylic Glycol.	$H_2\text{:}O_2\text{:}C_5H_8O$ Valerolactic Acid.	$H_2\text{:}O_2\text{:}C_5H_6O_2$ Pyrotartaric Acid.
$C_6H_{12}\text{:}O_2\text{:}H_2$ Hexyl Glycol.	$H_2\text{:}O_2\text{:}C_6H_{10}O$ Leucic Acid.	$H_2\text{:}O_2\text{:}C_6H_8O_2$ Adipic Acid.

Corresponding to these basic and acid hydrates we have also been able to obtain in several cases the basic and acid anhydrides, besides a very large number of compound ethers.

42. *Glycerines and Sugars.* — In the alcohols one hydrogen atom from the original typical molecule (*typical hydrogen*) remains undisturbed. In the glycols there are two such hydrogen atoms, and hence these compounds are frequently called diatomic alcohols. Our common glycerine is a triatomic alcohol, and may be regarded as formed from a molecule of water trebly condensed ($H_3^= O_3^= H_3$), by replacing one of the groups of hydrogen atoms with the trivalent radical glyceryl ($C_3 H_5$). It is probable that a large number of triatomic alcohols or glycerines may hereafter be obtained, but only two are now known.

Propylic Glycerine (common glycerine) $H_3^= O_3^= C_3 H_5$.
Amylic Glycerine $\qquad\qquad\qquad\qquad H_3^= O_3^= C_5 H_9$.

From the glycerines we may derive acids, anhydrides, and compound ethers, bearing to each other the same relations as those derived from the alcohols of a lower order, but only a few of the possible compounds which our theory would foresee are yet known. The natural fats are compounds of glycerine with the fat acids, and it is probable that our common sugars are likewise derived from alcohols of a still higher order of atomicity.

43. *Atomicity and Basicity of an Acid.* — By the *atomicity of a compound* is meant the number of hydrogen atoms which it retains from the original typical molecule still unreplaced, and the use of this term with reference to the *basic hydrates* has been already abundantly illustrated in this chapter. In the case of the acids a distinction must be made between atomicity and basicity, which is frequently important.

The formula of every acid may be written on the type of one or more atoms of hydrochloric acid, as $H_n R^n$, in which H_n stands for the replaceable atoms of hydrogen, and R^n for all the rest of the atoms of the molecule, which may be regarded as forming a radical with an atomicity equal to the number of replaceable hydrogen atoms. The symbols $H\text{-}\overset{\text{I}}{N}O_3$ $H_2^=\overset{\text{II}}{S}O_4$ $H_3^=\overset{\text{III}}{P}O_4$ are written on this principle. In each case the acid is said to have the atomicity of the radical. The basicity of the acid, on the other hand, depends, not on the *total* number of replaceable hydrogen atoms, but on the number which may be replaced by *metallic* atoms or *basic* radicals. As a general rule, it is true that the basicity is the same as the atomicity, but this is not always the case. Thus lactic acid is diatomic but monobasic, and the same is true of the other acids homologous with it (page 92).

$$\overset{+}{H}, \; \overset{-}{H}{=}(C_3H_4\overset{II}{O_3}) \quad Na, \; H{=}(C_3H_4\overset{II}{O_3}) \quad Na, \; (C_7H_5\overset{I}{O}){=}(C_3H_4\overset{II}{O_3})$$
Lactic Acid.   Sodic Lactate.   Sodic Benzolactate.

$$K, \; C_2H_5{=}(C_3H_4O_3) \qquad C_2H_5, \; C_2H_5{=}(C_3H_4O_3)$$
Potassic Ethyl-lactate.   Diethylic-lactate.

Only one atom of hydrogen can be replaced by a metallic radical, but a second may be replaced by either a negative or an alcoholic radical, as in the last three symbols, and in designating the atoms, thus differently related to the molecular structure, it is usual to call the first basic and the other alcoholic hydrogen.

We might, in like manner, distinguish between the atomicity and the *acidity* of a base, but this distinction has not been found as yet to be of practical importance.

44. *Water of Crystallization.* — Among the most striking characteristics of the class of compounds we call salts is their solubility in water and their tendency on separating from it, in consequence of either the evaporation or the cooling of the fluid, to assume definite crystalline forms. These crystals, as a general rule, are complex crystalline aggregates of molecules of the salt and molecules of water. The water is held in combination by a comparatively feeble force, and may be generally driven off by exposing the salt to the temperature of 100° C., when the crystals fall to powder. Sometimes it escapes at the ordinary temperature of the air, when the crystals, as before, fall to powder and are said to effloresce. It thus evidently appears that the water, although an essential part of the crystalline structure, is not inherent in the chemical molecule, and hence the name Water of Crystallization. The presence of

water of crystallization in a salt is expressed by writing after the symbol of the salt, and separated from it by a period, the number of molecules of water with which each salt molecule is associated. Thus we have

$$FeSO_4.7H_2O \qquad\qquad Na_2CO_3.10H_2O$$

Crystallized Ferrous Sulphate or Green Vitriol.   Crystallized Sodic Carbonate or Sal Soda.

The same salt, when crystallized, at different temperatures not unfrequently combines with different amounts of water of crystallization, the less amounts corresponding to the higher temperatures. Thus manganous sulphate may be crystallized with three different amounts of water of crystallization. We have

$MnSO_4.7H_2O$ when crystallized below 6° C.
$MnSO_4.5H_2O$ "   "   between 7° and 20°.
$MnSO_4.4H_2O$ "   "   between 20° and 30°.

The crystalline forms of these three compounds are entirely different from each other ; and this fact again corroborates the view that the molecules of water, while a part of the crystalline structure, are not a part of the chemical type of the salt. It will be well to distinguish the molecular aggregate, which the symbols of this section represent, from the simpler chemical molecules by a special term, and we propose to call them crystalline molecules. While, however, there is little room for difference of opinion in regard to the relations in which the molecules of water stand to the structure of most crystals, there are cases where the condition is apparently far less simple, and where we find the water so firmly bound to the salt itself that it seems to form a part of its atomic structure.

Questions and Problems.

1. Analyze reactions [42]. Show what is meant by a metallic hydrate, and define the term alkali. Write the similar reactions which may be obtained with lithium, caesium, and rubidium. Name in each case the class of compounds to which the factors and products belong. Also represent these reactions by graphic symbols.

2. Analyze reactions [43]. State the distinction between an alkaline earth and an alkali, and write the similar reactions which may be obtained with barium and strontium. Name in each case

the class of compounds to which the factors and products belong. Also represent the reactions by graphic symbols.

3. Analyze reactions [44] and [45], and write the similar reactions which may be obtained with either of the metals, calcium, strontium, barium, and magnesium. What theory of the constitution of the metallic hydrates do these reactions suggest?

4. In what respects do the hydrates $Ca = O_2 = H_2$ and $Mg = O_2 = H_2$ differ from $K\text{-}O\text{-}H$ and $Na\text{-}O\text{-}H$?

5. Analyze reactions [46], and show that the principal products must be regarded as hydrates. Name the class of compounds to which the other products and factors belong.

6. State the third theory which is held in regard to the constitution of the hydrates, and write the symbols of the different hydrates according to this view. Also bring these symbols into comparison with those of the same compounds written after the other two plans, and show by means of graphic symbols how far these forms are arbitrary, and how far they represent fundamental differences.

7. In what sense may the solution of ammonia gas in water be regarded as an hydrate? Write reactions [46], using ammonic hydrate instead of the hydrates of sodium, potassium, and barium.

8. In what relation do the metallic oxides stand to the hydrates? Define the term *base*.

9. Define the term *salt*, and illustrate your definition by examples.

10. Define the term *acid*. How does an acid differ from a metallic hydrate? Is an acid necessarily an hydrate? What two classes of acids may be distinguished?

11. What is the distinction between an acid and a basic radical. How are they related to the two hydrogen atoms of water? Assuming that there is no difference between these two atoms in the original molecule of water, does not the replacement of one of the atoms by a radical of either class alter the relations of the second? Is there not an analogy between these phenomena and those of magnetism?

12. Analyze reactions [47 et seq.], and point out the evidence of acidity in each case.

13. Analyze the following reactions.

$$K\text{-}O\text{-}H + HF = KF + H_2O$$

$$Ca = O_2 = H_2 + H_2 = O_2 = CO = Ca = O_2 = CO + 2H_2O$$

$$Cu = O_2 = H_2 + 2H\text{-}O\text{-}NO_2 = Cu = O_2 = (NO_2)_2 + 2H_2O$$

$$NaCl \ + \ H_2\text{=}O_2\text{=}SO_2 \ =. \ H, Na\text{=}O_2\text{=}SO_2 + HCl$$

$$2NaCl \ + \ H_2\text{=}O_2\text{=}SO_2 \ = \ Na_2\text{=}O_2\text{=}SO_2 \ + 2HCl.$$

Point out the different acids and bases. In what does the evidence of their acidity or basicity appear either in these or in reactions previously given ? Show in each case how the replacement of the hydrogen atoms is obtained, and illustrate the difference between the hydrogen atoms of an acid and those of a base. What two classes of acids may be distinguished ?

14. Regarding the hydrates as compounds of hydroxyl, how can you define the acids and bases of this class ?

15. Represent the composition of nitric, sulphuric, and phosphoric acid by graphic symbols, and show that the two modes of writing their symbols embody essentially the same idea.

16. Hydrochloric acid, acetic acid, nitric acid, hydriodic acid, hydrobromic acid, sulphuric acid, carbonic acid, and phosphoric acid have what basicity ? Point out, in the various reactions given in this chapter, the evidence in each case, and write the symbols of the possible sodic salts of the different acids.

17. What class of compounds do the symbols SO_3, N_2O_5, P_2O_5, CO_2, and SiO_2 represent ? By a comparison of symbols show how these compounds may be regarded as formed from water, and how they are related to the corresponding acids. To what class of compounds do they stand in direct antithesis ?

18. Define the terms basic and acid hydrate ; basic and acid anhydride, and compare reactions [49] with [44 and 45].

19. Analyze the reaction, $BaO \ + \ SO_3 \ = \ BaO, SO_3.$

What reason may be urged for writing the symbol of baric sulphate in this way ? What was the theory of the dualistic system in regard to such compounds ? Represent the symbol by the graphic method, and seek to determine whether the dualistic form is compatible with the theory of molecular unity.

20. The following symbols represent compounds of what class ?

$$H\text{-}O\text{-}H; \ H_3\text{=}O_3\text{≡}PO; \ Fe\text{=}O_2\text{=}H_2; \ 2H\text{-}(HO); \ (PO_2)_2\text{=}O;$$

$$K\text{-}O\text{-}H; \ Ca\text{=}O_2\text{=}H_2; \ C_2H_5\text{-}O\text{-}H; 2Na\text{-}O\text{-}H; \ (C_5H_9O)_2\text{=}O;$$

$$H_4\text{≡}O_4\text{≡}Si; \ H\text{-}O\text{-}NO_2; H_2\text{=}O_2\text{=}SO_2; (Fe\text{-}Fe)\text{≡}O_3; H\text{-}O\text{-}C_2H_3O;$$

$$Ca_2\text{≡}O_4\text{≡}Si; K\text{-}O\text{-}NO_2; (C_4H_9)_2\text{=}O; Na_2\text{=}O_2\text{=}SO_2; C_2H_5\text{-}O\text{-}C_2H_3O.$$

7

Give in each case the name of the compound so far as you are able to infer it from examples previously given, and show how the symbol is related to that of water.

21. Point out the acid basic and neutral salts among the compounds represented by the following symbols : —

$$H, Na = O_2 = CO \qquad H, K = O_2^= (C_2O_2) \qquad (Hg\text{-}O\text{-}Hg\text{-}O\text{-}Hg) = O_2^= SO_2$$

$$Na_2^= O_2 = CO \qquad K_2^= O_2^= (C_2O_2) \qquad [Hg\text{-}Hg] = O_2^= (NO_2)_2$$

$$H_2, Cu \equiv O_4 \equiv Si \qquad Cu = O_2^= (NO_2), H \qquad [Fe\text{-}Fe] \equiv O_6^\equiv (SO_2)_3$$

$$Bi \equiv O_3^= (NO_2), H_2 \qquad H_2, K = O_3^= As \qquad K_2^= O_2^= (SO_2\text{-}O\text{-}SO_2).$$

What two classes of basic salts may be distinguished ? Convert the symbols into the dualistic form.

22. Analyze reactions [49 and 50], and show how far they justify the dualistic form given to the symbols. Represent the same reactions in the graphic form.

23. What class of compounds do the following symbols represent ?

$$Ag_3 = S_3 \equiv As \qquad Ag\text{-}S\text{-}SbS \qquad Ca = S_2 = H_2.$$

Write the symbols of the corresponding oxygen compounds.

24. Explain the theory of the colored test papers, and the use of the terms acid and basic in connection with them. To what confusion does the double meaning of these terms sometimes lead ?

25. The members of the series of alcohols stand in what relation to each other ? Does the same relation exist between the members of the series of fat acids, glycols, &c. ? Find a general symbol, which will represent the composition of each of these classes of compounds.

26. In what relations do the alcohols stand to the fat acids, and the glycols to the acids derived from them ?

27. Select examples from each of the classes of compounds described in sections 40, 41, and 42, and bring the symbols into comparison with those of some simple hydrate or anhydride with which they exactly correspond.

28. We are acquainted with a class of compounds known as condensed glycols, one of which has the following symbol : —

$$(C_2H_4\text{-}O\text{-}C_2H_4\text{-}O\text{-}C_2H_4) = O_2 = H_2.$$

To what class of salts does this correspond ?

29. Judging from the following symbols of a few of the salts of tartaric acid, what conclusion should you reach in regard to the atomicity and basicity of this acid ?

$$H_4^{\equiv}O_4^{\equiv}(C_4H_2O_2) ; \quad K, H_3^{\equiv}O_4^{\equiv}(C_4H_2O_2) ; \quad K_2, H_2^{\equiv}O_4^{\equiv}(C_4H_2O_2) ;$$

$$(C_2H_5)_2, H_2^{\equiv}O_4^{\equiv}(C_4H_2O_2) ; \quad (C_2H_5)_2, (C_2H_3O)_2^{\equiv}O_4^{\equiv}(C_4H_2O_2)$$

30. What is the atomicity and basicity of the different acids whose symbols have been given in this chapter ? Does the basicity of the different hydrocarbon acids (§ 40 to § 43) appear to have any connection with the number of oxygen atoms in the radical ?

31. How do you explain the state of combination of the water which enters into the composition of most crystalline salts ? Show by an example how this mode of combination is represented symbolically. What facts may be adduced in support of the opinion that the molecules of water are not a part of the chemical type of the salt.

NOTE. — Should the teacher think it best to introduce in this connection definitions of the several compounds formed after the type of ammonia gas, he will find them given in sections 166 to 171 of Part II.; and, if he finds it necessary, he should dwell more at length on the acids and salts of the type of hydrochloric acid than has been thought necessary in this chapter.

CHAPTER X.[1]

45. *Origin of Nomenclature.* — Previous to the year 1787 the names given to chemical compounds were not conformed to any general rules ; and many of these old names, such as *oil of vitriol, calomel, corrosive sublimate, red precipitate, saltpetre, sal-soda, borax, cream of tartar, Glauber's* and *Epsom salts*, are still retained in common use. As chemical science advanced, and the number of known substances increased, it became important to adopt a scientific nomenclature, and the system which came into use was due almost entirely to Lavoisier, who reported to the French Academy on the subject, in behalf of a committee, in the year named above. In the Lavoisierian nomenclature the name of a substance was made to indicate its composition ; and at the time of its adoption, and for fifty years after, it was probably the most perfect nomenclature which any science ever enjoyed. It was based, however, on the dualistic theory, of which Lavoisier was the father ; and, when at last the science outgrew this theory, the old names lost much of their significance and appropriateness. Within the last few years the English chemists have attempted to modify the old nomenclature so as to better adapt the names to our modern ideas. Unfortunately the result, like most attempts to mend a worn-out garment, is far from satisfactory, although it is probably the best which under the circumstances could be attained. The new nomenclature has not the simplicity or unity of the old, and its rules cannot be made intelligible until the student is more or less acquainted with the modern chemical theories. Fortunately, however, the admirable system of chemical symbols supplies the defects of the nomenclature, and for many

---

[1] In studying this chapter, the student is expected to remember the names corresponding to the different symbols, and also the symbols corresponding to the names.

purposes may be used in its place. We have, therefore, developed this system first, but have also used, meanwhile, the corresponding scientific names, so that the student might become familiar with the nomenclature, and gather its rules as he advanced. A brief summary of these rules is all that will be necessary here.

46. *Names of Elements.* — The names of the elements are not conformed to any fixed rules. Those which were known before 1787, such as sulphur, phosphorus, arsenic, antimony, iron, gold, and the other useful metals, retain their old names. Several of the more recently discovered elements have been named in allusion to some prominent property or some circumstance connected with their history: as *oxygen*, from ὀξὺς γεννάω (acid-generator) ; *hydrogen*, from ὕδωρ γεννάω (water-generator) ; *chlorine*, from χλωρός (green) ; *iodine*, from ἰωδής (violet) ; *bromine*, from βρῶμος (fetid odor). The names of the newly discovered metals have a common termination, *um*, as *potassium, sodium, platinum ;* and the names of several of the newly discovered metalloids end in *ine*, as *chlorine, bromine, iodine, fluorine.* Equally arbitrary names have been given to the compound radicals ; but, with a few exceptions, they all terminate in *yl* or *ene*, as *ethyl, acetyl, hydroxyl,* and *ethylene, acetylene,* &c.

47. *Names of Binary Compounds.*[1] The simple compounds of the elements with oxygen are called oxides, and the specific names of the different oxides are formed by placing before the word "oxide" the name of the element, but changing the termination into *ic* or *ous*, to indicate different degrees of oxidation, and using the Latin name of the element in preference to the English, both for the sake of euphony and in order to secure more general agreement among different languages. When the same element unites with oxygen in more than two proportions, the Greek numeral prefixes, di, tri, tetra, penta, &c., are added to the word "oxide," in order to indicate the additional degrees. Formerly these compounds were called oxides of the different elements, the degrees of oxidation being indicated solely by the prefixes ; and, as the old names are still in very general use, they are also given in the following examples : —

---

[1] Compounds of two elements.

		New Names.		Old Names.
AgO	is	Argentic Oxide	or	Oxide of Silver
N_2O	"	Nitrous Oxide	"	Protoxide of Nitrogen
NO	"	Nitric Oxide	"	Deutoxide of Nitrogen
NO_2	"	Nitric Dioxide	"	Peroxide of Nitrogen
FeO	"	Ferrous Oxide	"	Protoxide of Iron
Fe_2O_3	"	Ferric Oxide	"	Sesquioxide of Iron.

An exception to the above rules is sometimes made in the case of those oxides which, when combined with the elements of water, form acids. As has been already stated, page 85, such compounds are called anhydrides, but the degrees of oxidation are distinguished as before, thus : —

		New Names.		Old Names.
SO_2	is	Sulphurous Anhydride	or	Sulphurous Acid
SO_3	"	Sulphuric Anhydride	"	Sulphuric Acid
N_2O_3	"	Nitrous Anhydride	"	Nitrous Acid
N_2O_5	"	Nitric Anhydride	"	Nitric Acid
P_2O_3	"	Phosphorous Anhydride	"	Phosphorous Acid
P_2O_5	"	Phosphoric Anhydride	"	Phosphoric Acid
CO_2	"	Carbonic Anhydride	"	Carbonic Acid
SiO_2	"	Silicic Anhydride	"	Silicic Acid.

The names in common use, even among chemists, of the earths, the alkaline earths, and the alkaline oxides, make another important exception to the general rules given above, thus : —

Al_2O_3	Aluminic Oxide	is commonly called			Alumina
BaO	Baric Oxide	"	"	"	Baryta
SrO	Strontic Oxide	"	"	"	Strontia
CaO	Calcic Oxide	"	"	"	Lime
MgO	Magnesic Oxide	"	"	"	Magnesia
K_2O	Potassic Oxide	"	"	"	Potassa
Na_2O	Sodic Oxide	"	"	"	Soda.

As this last class of oxides stands in the same relation to the bases in which the previous class stands to the acids, they have also been called by some chemists anhydrides.

The names of the binary compounds of the other elements are formed like those of the oxides.

Compounds	of Chlorine	are called	Chlorides
"	" Bromine	" "	Bromides
"	" Iodine	" "	Iodides
"	" Fluorine	" "	Fluorides
"	" Sulphur	" "	Sulphides
"	" Nitrogen	" "	Nitrides
"	" Phosphorus	" "	Phosphides
"	" Arsenic	" "	Arsenides
"	" Antimony	" "	Antimonides
"	" Carbon	" "	Carbonides.

Moreover, the specific names of the several compounds also follow the analogy of the oxides, thus : —

		New Names.		*Old Names.*
$SnCl_2$	is	Stannous Chloride	or	Protochloride of Tin
$SnCl_4$	"	Stannic Chloride	"	Perchloride of Tin
Fe_2S	"	Diferrous Sulphide	"	Subsulphide of Iron
FeS	"	Ferrous Sulphide	"	Protosulphide of Iron
Fe_2S_3	"	Ferric Sulphide	"	Sesquisulphide of Iron
FeS_2	"	Ferric Disulphide	"	Bisulphide of Iron
$CaFl_2$	"	Calcic Fluoride	"	Fluoride of Calcium.

Here, again, must be noticed several exceptions to the general rule. Several simple compounds of the elements with hydrogen, of which the hydrogen is easily replaced with a metal or positive radical, are called acids, and retain the specific names of the old nomenclature, thus : —

HCl	or	Hydric Chloride	is called	Hydrochloric Acid
HBr	"	Hydric Bromide	" "	Hydrobromic Acid
HI	"	Hydric Iodide	" "	Hydriodic Acid
HFl	"	Hydric Fluoride	" "	Hydrofluoric Acid
H_2S	"	Hydric Sulphide	" "	Hydrosulphuric Acid.

The last compound is frequently called also sulphuretted hydrogen, and several other hydrogen compounds are named after the same analogy, while others again are always called by their well-known trivial names, thus : —

H_3Sb	is	Antimoniuretted Hydrogen
H_3As	"	Arseniuretted Hydrogen
H_3P	"	Phosphuretted Hydrogen
H_3N	"	Ammonia Gas
H_4C	"	Marsh Gas or Light Carburetted Hydrogen
H_4C_2	"	Olefiant Gas or, as a radical, Ethylene.

48. *Ternary Compounds.* — Of the old class of ternary compounds, it is only those which are formed after the type of water for which the rules of the nomenclature need at present be explained.

49. *Bases.* — These we call simply hydrates, and for the specific name we take the name of the positive radical, changing the termination into *ic* or *ous*, and using such prefixes as circumstances may require, thus : —

	New Names.	Old Names.
K-O-H	is Potassic Hydrate or Hydrate of Potassa	
$Ca=O_2=H_2$	" Calcic Hydrate "	Hydrate of Lime
$Fe=O_2=H_2$	" Ferrous Hydrate "	{ Hydrate of Protoxide of Iron.
$Fe_2O_6H_4$	" Ferric Hydrate "	{ Hydrate of Sesquioxide of Iron.

ZoO_4H_4 Zirconic Hydrate or Hydrate of Zirconia.

50. *Acids.* — The inorganic acids all take their specific names from the name of the most characteristic element of the negative radical, which is modified by terminations and prefixes as before, only the last are usually taken from the Greek rather than the Latin. Here the old and the new names coincide.

H-O-NO_2	is called Nitric Acid
$H_2O_2=SO_2$	" " Sulphuric Acid
$H_2O_2=SO$	" " Sulphurous Acid
$H_2O_2=(S$-O-$\overset{\pi}{S})$	" " Hyposulphurous Acid

The specific names of the **organic** acids are, as a rule, arbitrary, like tartaric acid, citric acid, malic acid, gallic acid, uric acid, and the like.

51. *Salts.* — The name of a salt is formed from the name of the acid from which the salt is derived, preceded by the names of the basic radicals. When the name of the acid ends in *ic* the termination is changed into *ate*, when in *ous* into *ite*. Moreover, the terminations *ous* and *ic* are retained in connection with the name of the basic radical, and such prefixes are used as may be necessary for distinction, thus : —

	New Names.		Old Names.
$Ca=O_2=CO$	is Calcic Carbonate	or	{ Carbonate of Lime
$Ca=O_2=(S-O-\overset{\pi}{S})$	" Calcic Hyposulphite	"	{ Hyposulphite of Lime
$Ba=O_2=SO$	" Baric Sulphite	"	{ Sulphite of Baryta
$Fe=O_2=SO_2$	" Ferrous Sulphate	"	{ Protosulphate of Iron
$Fe_2\equiv O_6\equiv (SO_2)_3$	" Ferric Sulphate	"	{ Persulphate of Iron
$(NH_4), Mg=O_2=PO$	" Ammonio-magnesic Phosphate		
$H, (NH_4), Na\equiv O_3\equiv PO$	" Hydro-ammonio-sodic Phosphate.		
$H, Na_2=O_3=PO$	" Hydro-disodic Phosphate.		
$H_4, Ca^{vi}O_6{}^{vi}(PO)_2$	" Tetrahydro-calcic Diphosphate.		
$Na_2=O_2=B_4O_5$	" Disodic Tetraborate (Borax).		

NOTE. — The rules of the nomenclature given above conform to what the author regards as the best present use among chemists. There is, however, an important departure from the more general use, which must not be overlooked. Several English authors, who think that the adjectives derived from the Latin names of the elements, with terminations in *ic* and *ous*, are not in harmony with English idioms, use such terms as Gold Chloride, Silver Nitrate, and Iron Sulphate, instead of Auric Chloride, Argentic Nitrate, and Ferrous Sulphate. This usage, however, appears to the writer open to equally just criticism, besides abridging greatly the capabilities of the nomenclature, which is full of similar incongruities. Nor does he sympathize with the same class of writers in rejecting the word "anhydride" as a part of the name of a substance, on the ground that it does not express its constitution, but only a mode of its derivation; for a similar objection might be urged with equal force against the terms "acid" and "hydrate." Moreover, he has thought it best, in a work designed chiefly for instruction, not only to introduce no novelties, but also to represent the actual usage, so far as possible, in all its phases. He would, however, offer the following suggestions as guides to the student in selecting for his own use a more uniform and consistent system, hoping that before long some agreement will be reached among chemists, by which greater uniformity may be secured. He would recommend, —

First, that the terminations *ic, ous, ate,* and *ite,* with the modifying Greek and Latin prefixes, should be used so far as possible to distinguish the quantivalence of the chief multivalent radical of the compound. Secondly, that the Greek numeral prefixes should be used when necessary to indicate the number of atoms of any radical which each molecule of such compound contains. Thirdly, that in forming the name of a compound it should be the great object to indicate its composition, and that the use of such terms as acid, basic, or anhydride as parts of the name should be avoided, except when it is desired to make conspicuous the peculiar chemical relations which they express.

By referring to the list of sulphates on page 319, and to the list of sulphites on page 315, the student will find good examples of the application of these principles. He will notice that salts in which the quantivalence of sulphur is six are called sulphates, while those in which it is four are called sulphites, and those in which it is two hyposulphites. Again, on page 230 he will find the proper application of the term anhydride explained, the term acid and basic having been already defined on page 82.

Questions and Problems.

1. Give the names of the compounds represented by the following symbols: —

a. KCl; K_2O; K_2S; $K_2^=O_2^=SO$; $K_2^=O_2^=SO_2$; $K_2^=O_2^=(S\text{-}O\text{-}S)$;

b. FeO; $Fe^=O_2^=H_2$; $Fe^=O_2^=CO$; $Fe^=O_2^=C_2O_2$; $[Fe_2]^{\underline{\underline{\underline{\equiv}}}}O_3$; $Fe_2^{\underline{\underline{\underline{\equiv}}}}O_6^{\underline{\underline{\underline{\equiv}}}}H_6$; $[Fe_2]^{\underline{\underline{\underline{\equiv}}}}O_6^{\underline{\underline{\underline{\equiv}}}}(NO_2)_6$

c. $H\text{-}Cl$; $H\text{-}F$; $H\text{-}O\text{-}NO_2$; $H\text{-}O\text{-}NO$; $H_2^=O_2^=SO_2$; $H_2^=O_2^=SO$; $H_3^{\underline{\underline{\underline{\equiv}}}}O_3^{\underline{\underline{\underline{\equiv}}}}PO$.

2. Write the symbols of the following compounds:

a. Calcic Sulphide; Calcic Sulphite; Calcic Hyposulphite; Calcic Sulphate; Calcic Hydrate; Calcic Sulphohydrate; Calcic Carbonate; Calcic Sulphocarbonate; Calcic Silicate.

b. Water; Potassic Hydrate; Nitric Acid; Potassic Nitrate; Nitric Anhydride; Potassic Oxide.

c. Magnesic Oxide; Magnesic Hydrate; Magnesic Nitrate; Magnesic Carbonate; Magnesic Phosphate; Ammonio-magnesic Phosphate.

N. B. Examples like the above should be greatly multiplied by the teacher, pains being taken to group together the names and symbols in the way best calculated to exhibit their relations and to assist the memory.

CHAPTER XI.

52. *Solution.* — The solvent power of water is one of the most familiar facts of common experience, and all liquids possess the same power to a greater or less degree, but they differ very widely from each other in the manifestation of their solvent power, which for each liquid is usually limited to a certain class of solids. Thus mercury is the appropriate solvent of metals, alcohol of resins, ether of fats, and water of salts and of similar compounds of its own type. Water is by far the most universal solvent known, and for this reason, as well as on account of its very wide diffusion in nature, it becomes the medium of most chemical changes. The phenomena of aqueous solution form therefore a very important subject of chemical inquiry, and these alone will be considered in this connection.

The solvent power of water, even on bodies of its own type, differs very greatly. Some solids, like potassic carbonate, or calcic chloride, liquefy in the atmosphere by absorbing the moisture it contains. Such salts are said to *deliquesce*, and are rendered liquid by a very small proportion of water. Other salts, like calcic sulphate, require for solution several hundred times their weight of water, and others again, like baric sulphate, are practically insoluble.

As a general rule the solvent power of water increases with the temperature; but here, again, we observe the greatest differences between different substances. While the solubility of some salts increases very rapidly with the temperature, that of others increases not at all, or only very slightly; and there are a few which are actually more soluble in cold water than in hot. The solubility of each substance is absolutely definite for a given temperature, and we can determine by experiment the exact amount which 100 parts of water will in any case dissolve. The results of such experiments are best represented to the eye by means of a curve drawn as in the accompanying figure on the principles of analytical geometry.

Fig. 2.

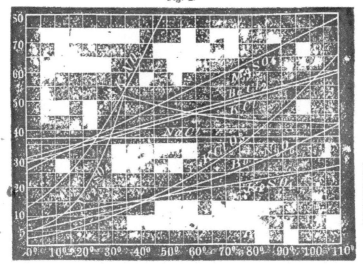

The figures on the horizontal line indicate degrees of temperature, and those on the vertical line parts of salt soluble in 100 parts of water. To find the solubility of any salt, for a stated temperature, the curve being given, we have only to follow up the vertical line corresponding to the temperature until it reaches the curve, and then, at the end of the horizontal line which intersects the curve at the same point, we find the number of parts required. These curves also show in each case the law which the change of solubility obeys.

When a liquid has dissolved all of a solid that it is capable of holding at the temperature, it is said to be saturated; but when saturated with one solid the liquid will still exert a solvent power over others; indeed, in some cases the solvent power is thereby increased. When several salts are dissolved together in water, a definite amount of metathesis seems always to take place, and the different positive radicals are divided between the several acids in proportions which depend on the relative strength of their affinities, and on the quantities of each present. If in this way either an insoluble or a volatile product is formed, the solid or the gas at once falls out of the solution, and, the equilibrium being thus destroyed, a new metathesis takes place, and this goes on so long as any of these products can be formed. Here, then, we find a simple explanation of the two important laws already stated on page 37.

53. *Solution of Gases.* — Most liquids, but especially water and alcohol, exert on gases a greater or less solvent power, which is marked by differences of manifestation similar to those we have already studied in the case of solids, although the peculiar physical conditions of the gas somewhat modify the result. Under the same conditions, the volume of gas dissolved is always the same ; but it varies with the pressure of the gas on the surface of the liquid, with the temperature, and with the peculiar nature of the gas and the absorbing liquid. The quantity[1] of gas dissolved by one cubic centimetre of a liquid on which it exerts a pressure of 76 c. m. is called the coefficient of absorption. This coefficient, in almost every instance, diminishes with the temperature ; but, as in the case of solids, each substance obeys a law of its own, which must be determined by experiment. The observed values for several of the best known gases, when absorbed by water and alcohol, are given in the Chemical Physics. Table VII. With these data we can easily calculate the quantity of any of these gases which a given volume of water or alcohol will absorb, assuming that the gas exerts on the liquid a pressure of 76 c. m. Moreover, since *the quantity of a gas absorbed by a liquid varies directly as the pressure which the gas exerts upon it*, we can easily calculate from the first result the quantity absorbed at any given pressure. Again, it is a direct consequence of the last principle that at a fixed temperature a given mass of liquid will dissolve the *same volume* of gas, whatever may be the pressure. Lastly, if a mass of liquid is exposed to an atmosphere of mixed gases, it will absorb of each the same quantity as if this gas was alone present and exerting on the liquid the same partial pressure which falls to its share in the atmosphere. The amount dissolved of each gas is easily calculated when the partial pressure and the coefficient of absorption are known. It is thus that water absorbs the oxygen and nitrogen gases of our terrestrial atmosphere ; and the fact that these two gases are found dissolved in the ocean in very different proportions from those present in the atmosphere is a conclusive proof that the air is a mixture, and not, as was formerly supposed, a chemical compound.

[1] By quantity of gas is here meant the volume in cubic centimetres measured under the standard conditions of temperature and pressure.

54. *Solution and Chemical Change.* — There seems at first sight to be a wide difference between solution and chemical change; for, while in the first the solid body becomes diffused through the liquid menstruum without losing its chemical identity or destroying that of the liquid, there is in the second a complete identification of the combining substances in the resulting compound.

The same wide difference appears also between mechanical and chemical solution, which are sometimes confounded by students, because, unfortunately, the same term has been applied to both. When salt or sugar is dissolved in water, the differences between salt and solvent are preserved; but when chalk is dissolved in hydrochloric acid, or copper in nitric acid, there is a complete *identification of the differences* in the resulting compound; and the only ground for calling such chemical changes solution is the fact that the solution of the resulting salt in the water, used as the medium of the chemical change, is frequently an essential condition of the process.

But if, instead of comparing extreme cases, we study the whole range of chemical phenomena, we shall find that the distinction is by no means so clearly marked. In many cases what seems to be a simple solution can be shown to be a mixed effect at least of solution and chemical combination; and between this condition of things, where the evidence of chemical combination is unmistakable, and a simple solution, like that of sugar in water, we have every degree of gradation. To such an extent is this true, that the facts seem to justify the opinion that solution is in every case a chemical combination of the substances dissolved with the solvent, and that it differs from other examples of chemical change only in the weakness of the combining force.

The metallic alloys afford another striking illustration of the same principle. They are originally solutions of one metal in another; but in many cases the result is greatly modified by the chemical affinities of the metals and their tendency to form definite chemical compounds.

55. *Liquid Diffusion.* — Closely connected with the phenomena of solution are those of liquid diffusion. These phenomena may be studied in their simplest form, by placing an open vial filled with a solution of some salt in a much larger jar of pure water, as shown in Fig. 3, and so carefully arranging the details of the experiment that the surfaces of the two liquids may be brought in contact without mixing them mechanically. It will then be found that the salt molecules will slowly escape from the vial and spread throughout the whole volume of the water. The rate of the diffusion increases with the temperature equally for all substances, and the whole phenomenon is probably caused by that same molecular motion to which we refer the effects of heat. At best, however, the diffusion is very slow, as we should expect, considering the limited freedom of motion which the liquid molecules possess. It is found, also, that the rate of diffusion differs very greatly for the different soluble salts; but these may be divided into groups of equidiffusive substances, and the rates of diffusion of the several groups bear to each other simple numerical ratios. If a mixture of salts be placed in the vial, it is found that the presence of one salt affects to some degree the diffusion of the other; but if the difference of rate is considerable, a partial separation may be effected, and even weak chemical compounds may be thus decomposed.

Fig. 3.

56. *Crystalloids and Colloids.* — There is a very great difference of diffusive power between the ordinary crystalline salts (including most of the common acids and bases) and such substances as gum, caramel, gelatine, and albumen, which are incapable of crystallizing, and which give insipid viscid solutions, readily forming into jelly; hence the name colloids, from κόλλη, glue. The last class is distinguished by a remarkable sluggishness and indisposition to diffusion; as is illustrated by the fact that sugar, one of the least diffusible of the crystalloids, diffuses seven times more rapidly than albumen, and fourteen times more rapidly than caramel. Our theories would lead us to believe that this great difference of diffusive power is caused by the fact that the molecules of colloids are far more complex atomic aggregates than those of crystalloids, and therefore are heavier and move more slowly. Moreover, the diffusive power

is only one of many characters which point to a great molecular difference between these two classes of substances.

57. *Dialysis.* — The difference of diffusive power between the two classes of compounds distinguished in the last section is still further increased when the aqueous solution is separated from the pure water by some colloidal membrane, and upon this fact Professor Graham of London, to whom we owe our whole knowledge of this subject, has based a simple method of separating crystalloids from colloids, which he calls dialysis.

A shallow tray is prepared by stretching parchment paper (which is itself an insoluble colloid) over one side of a gutta-percha hoop, and holding it in place by a somewhat larger hoop of the same material. The solution to be *dialysed* is poured into this tray, which is then floated on pure water whose volume should be eight or ten times greater than that of the solution. Under these conditions the crystalloids will diffuse through the porous septum into the water, leaving the colloids on the tray, and in the course of two or three days a more or less complete separation of these two classes of substances will have taken place.

In this way arsenious acids and similar crystalloids may be separated from the colloidal materials, with which, in cases of poisoning, they are frequently found mixed in the stomach ; and by an application of the same method alumina, ferric oxide, chromic oxide, stannic, metastannic, titanic, molybdic, tungstic, and silicic acids have all been obtained dissolved in water in a colloidal condition. All these substances usually exist in a crystalline condition. The colloidal condition appears to be an abnormal state, and in almost all such substances there is a tendency towards the crystalloid form.

58. *Diffusion of Gases.* — Gases diffuse much more rapidly than liquids, as we should naturally expect from the greater freedom of motion which their molecules possess. Moreover, if the theory of the molecular condition of gases is correct, we ought to be able to calculate the relative rates of diffusion of different gases from their respective molecular weights. If it is true, as stated on page 13, that at any given temperature

$$\tfrac{1}{2} m V^2 = \tfrac{1}{2} m' V'^2$$

then it follows that

$$V : V' = \sqrt{\tfrac{1}{2} m'} : \sqrt{\tfrac{1}{2} m} = \sqrt{\text{Sp. Gr}'.} : \sqrt{\text{Sp. Gr.}}$$

Hence, if two masses of gas are in contact, the molecules of either gas must move into the space filled by the other with velocities which are inversely proportional to the square roots of the respective specific gravities. If one gas is hydrogen (Sp. Gr. $=$ 1), and the other oxygen (Sp. Gr. $=$ 16), the molecules of hydrogen must move past the section separating the two masses four times as rapidly as those of oxygen; and, since all gas molecules occupy the same volume, it follows further that four volumes of hydrogen must enter the space filled by the oxygen, while one volume of oxygen is passing in the opposite direction. Numerous experiments have fully confirmed this theoretical deduction, and the close agreement between theory and experiment furnishes important evidence in favor of the theory itself. Such experiments can be made, moreover, with great accuracy, since the molecular motion is not arrested by various porous septa, which may be used to separate the two masses of gas, and which entirely prevent the passage of gas currents that might otherwise vitiate the results.

8

CHAPTER XII.

59. *The Atmosphere.* — The earth is surrounded by an ocean of aeriform matter called the atmosphere, and many of the most important chemical changes which we witness in nature are caused by the reaction of this atmosphere on the substances which it surrounds and bathes. The great mass of the atmosphere consists of the two elementary gases, oxygen and nitrogen, mixed together in the proportions indicated in the following table : —

Air contains.	Composition By Volume.	Composition By Weight.
Oxygen,	20.96	23.185
Nitrogen,	79.04	76.815
	100.	100.

That the air is a mixture, and not a chemical compound, is proved by the action of solvents upon it (§ 53) ; but, nevertheless, the analyses of air collected in different countries, and at different heights in the atmosphere, show a remarkable constancy in its composition. Besides these two gases, which make up over 93 per cent of its whole mass, the air always contains variable quantities of aqueous vapor, carbonic anhydride, and ammonia, and sometimes also traces of various other gases and vapors.

60. *Burning.* — Of the two chief constituents of the atmosphere, nitrogen gas is a very inert substance, and serves chiefly to restrain its more energetic associate. Oxygen gas, on the other hand, is endowed with highly active affinities, and tends to enter into combination with other elementary substances, and with many compounds which are not already saturated with this all-pervading element. Many of these substances, such as phosphorus, sulphur, petroleum, coal, and wood, have such a strong affinity for oxygen, that, under certain conditions, they will absorb it from the atmosphere, and combine with it

under the evolution of heat and light. These substances are said to be combustible, and the process of combination is called combustion. Moreover, all burning with which we are familiar in common life consists in the union of the burning body with the oxygen of the air. The chemical process in these cases may be expressed, like any other chemical reaction, in the form of an equation.

Burning of Hydrogen Gas.

$$2\,H\text{-}H + O\text{=}O = 2\,H_2O. \qquad [53]$$

Burning of Carbon (Charcoal).

$$C + O\text{=}O = CO_2. \qquad [54]$$

Burning of Benzole.

$$2\,C_6H_6 + 15\,O\text{=}O = 12\,CO_2 + 6\,H_2O. \qquad [55]$$

Burning of Alcohol.

$$C_2H_6O + 3\,O\text{=}O = 2\,CO_2 + 3\,H_2O. \qquad [56]$$

Burning of Sulphur.

$$S\text{-}S + 2\,O\text{=}O = 2\,SO_2. \qquad [57]$$

Burning of Phosphorus.

$$P_2\text{≡}P_2 + 5\,O\text{=}O = 2\,P_2O_5. \qquad [58]$$

Burning of Magnesium.

$$2\,Mg + O\text{=}O = 2\,MgO. \qquad [59]$$

The four substances, hydrogen gas, charcoal, benzole, and alcohol, may be regarded as types of our ordinary combustibles; and, as the first four reactions show, the products of their combustion are aeriform. Moreover, these products are wholly devoid of any sensible qualities, and hence the apparent annihilation of the burning substance, and the reason that for so long a period the nature of the process remained undiscovered. That these qualities of the products of ordinary combustion are not necessary conditions of the process, but remarkable adaptations in the properties of those combustibles which are our artificial sources of light and heat, is shown by the fact, that, in the last two reactions, the products of the combustion are solids, while in [57] the product is a noxious suffocating gas.

A careful inspection of the reactions will also teach the student several other important facts in regard to the processes here represented. It will be seen that, in the burning of hydrogen gas, two volumes of hydrogen gas and one volume of oxygen gas combine to form two volumes of aqueous vapor. It will further be noticed, that, in the burning of carbon and of sulphur, a given volume of oxygen gas yields in each case its own volume of the aeriform product. The carbon in the one case, and the sulphur in the other, are absorbed, as it were, by the gas, without any increase of volume. Further, if the experiments are made, which these reactions represent, it will appear that, in all those cases where the combustible is represented as a gas, the combustion is accompanied by flame, while in the case of carbon, which is a fixed solid, there is no proper flame. Hence we learn that flame is burning gas, and that only those substances burn with flame which are either gases themselves, or which, at a high temperature, become volatilized, or generate combustible vapors. Still other important facts connected with the process of combustion will be learned by solving the following problems according to the rules already given (§§ 24 and 25).

Problem. How many cubic centimetres of hydrogen gas, and how many of oxygen gas, are required to form one cubic centimetre of liquid water?[1] Ans. 1,240 $\overline{cm}^3$ of hydrogen gas, and 620 $\overline{cm}^3$ of oxygen gas.

Problem. How many cubic metres of air are required to burn 448 kilogrammes of coal, assuming that the coal is pure carbon? Ans. 833.333 $\overline{m}^3$ of oxygen gas, or 3,975.83 $\overline{m}^3$ of atmospheric air.

[1] Here, as in all other problems throughout the book, it is understood, unless otherwise expressly stated, that the measurements and weights are all taken at the standard temperature and pressure. (Compare §§ 10 and 13.)

Problem. How many cubic metres of carbonic anhydride are formed by the burning of 1,000 kilogrammes of coal, assuming, as before, that the coal is pure carbon? Ans. 1,860.

Problem. How many litres of carbonic anhydride, and how many of aqueous vapor, would be formed by burning one litre of benzole vapor? Ans. Simple inspection of the equation shows that 6 litres of the first and 3 litres of the second would be formed.

Problem. How many litres of carbonic anhydride, and how many of aqueous vapor, would be formed by burning one litre of liquid alcohol (C_2H_6O)? Sp. Gr. of liquid at $0°=0.815$. Ans. One litre of alcohol weighs 815 grammes or 9,097 criths, and, since the Sp. Gr. of alcohol vapor is 23, this quantity of liquid would yield 395.6 litres of vapor. Hence there would be formed $2 \times 395.6 = 791.2$ litres of carbonic anhydride, and $3 \times 395.6 = 1,186.8$ litres of aqueous vapor.

61. *Heat of Combustion.* — The reactions of the last section represent only the chemical changes in the processes of burning. The physical effects which accompany the chemical changes our equations do not indicate, but it is these remarkable manifestations of power which chiefly arrest the student's attention, and on this power the importance of the processes of combustion as sources of heat and light wholly depends.

The immediate cause of the power developed in the process of combustion is to be found in the clashing of material atoms. Urged by that immensely powerful attractive force we call chemical affinity, the molecules of oxygen in the surrounding atmosphere rush, from all directions, and with an incalculable velocity, upon the burning body. The molecules of oxygen thus acquire an enormous moving power; and when, at the moment of chemical union, the onward motion is arrested, this moving power is distributed among the surrounding molecules, and is manifested in the phenomena of heat and light.[1] (Compare § 12.)

---

[1] According to our best knowledge, the phenomena of light are merely another manifestation of the same molecular motion which causes the phenomena of heat. When we speak of the amount of heat produced, we refer always to the total amount of molecular motion; although, even in the most brilliant illumination, the amount of mechanical power manifested as light appears to be inconsiderable as compared with that which takes the form of heat.

The quantity of heat evolved during combustion varies very greatly with the nature of the combustible employed, but it is always constant for the same combustible if burnt under the same conditions, and is exactly proportional to the weight of combustible consumed. We give in the following table the amount of heat evolved by one kilogramme of several of the most common combustibles when they are burnt in oxygen gas in their ordinary physical state. The numbers represent what is called the calorific power of the combustible. With the exception of the two last, which are only approximate values, they are the results of very accurate experiments made by Favre and Silbermann.

Calorific Power of Combustibles.

	Units.		Units.
Hydrogen,	34,462	Sulphur,	2,221
Marsh Gas,	13,063	Wood Charcoal,	8,080
Olefiant Gas,	11,858	Carbonic Oxide,	2,400
Ether,	9,027	Dry Wood (about),	3,654
Alcohol,	7,184	Bituminous Coal, "	7,500

The calorific power of our ordinary hydrocarbon fuels may be calculated approximately when their composition is known. Most of these combustibles contain more or less oxygen, and it is found, as might be expected, that the amount of heat developed by the perfect combustion of the fuel is equal to that which would be produced by the perfect combustion of all the carbon, and of so much of the hydrogen as is in excess of that required to form water with the oxygen present. The rest of the hydrogen may be regarded, so far as relates to the present problem, as in combination with oxygen in the state of water; and in estimating the available heat produced, we must deduct the amount of heat required to convert, not only this water into steam, but also any hygroscopic water which may be present. Moreover, if we use in our calculation the value of the calorific power of hydrogen given in the table above, we must also deduct the amount of heat required to convert into vapor all the water formed in the process of burning, because, in the experiments by which this value was obtained, the aqueous vapor formed was subsequently condensed to water and gave out its latent heat.

Problem. Given the average composition of air-dried wood as in the table, to find the calorific power.

		From the results of analysis we easily	
Carbon,	400	deduce	
Hydrogen,	48	Quantity of H in combination with O	41
Oxygen,	328	" " available as fuel	7
Nitrogen and Ash,	24	Quantity of water formed by burn-⎱	432
Hygroscopic Water,	200	ing 48 parts hydrogen ⎰	
	1000	Hygroscopic Water	200
		Total quantity of water evaporated	632

Units of Heat.

400 grammes of carbon yield 3,232

7 "   " hydrogen " 241

3,473

Deduct amount of heat required to convert 632 grammes of water into vapor. (See § 14.) 339

Calorific power of air-dried wood 3,134

From the mechanical equivalent of heat given on page 14, and from the data of the above table, we can easily calculate the mechanical power developed in ordinary combustion, and the student will be surprised to find how great this power is. The burning of one kilogramme of charcoal produces an amount of heat which is equivalent to $8,080 \times 423 = 3,417,840$ kilogramme metres; that is, the moving power which is developed by the clashing of the atoms during the combustion of this small amount of coal is equal to that which would be produced by the fall of a mass of rock weighing 8,080 kilogrammes over a precipice 423 metres high, and, could this power be all utilized, it would be adequate to raise the same weight to the same height, or to do any other equivalent amount of work. The steam-engine is a machine for applying this very power to produce mechanical results; but, unfortunately, in the best engines we do not utilize much more than $\frac{1}{20}$ of the power of the fuel; and to find a more economical means of converting heat into mechanical effect is one of the great problems of the present age.

62. *Calorific Intensity.* — The calorific intensity of fuel is to be carefully distinguished from its calorific power. By *calorific power* is meant, as we have seen, the total quantity of heat developed by the combustion of a given amount of fuel. By *calorific intensity*, we mean the maximum temperature developed in the process of combustion. Provided the products are the same, the total amount of heat produced in any case is

not materially influenced by the rapidity of the process; but it is evident that the temperature of the burning fuel will depend, other things being equal, on the rapidity with which the heat is developed as compared with the rapidity with which it is dissipated through surrounding objects; and, when the combination with oxygen is very slow, the heat may be dissipated as fast as it is generated, and then the temperature of the burning body will not rise above that of the surrounding atmosphere, as is the case in many of the processes of slow combustion.

Assuming, however, that all the heat is retained by the products of combustion, we can calculate the maximum temperature which can in any case be produced, provided the calorific power of the fuel and the specific heat of the products of combustion are known. The calorific intensity is simply the temperature to which the heat generated by the burning of each portion of the fuel can raise the products of its own combustion. Assume that the quantity burnt is one kilogramme, that the calorific power or number of units of heat produced is C, that the weights of the various products of combustion are W, W', W'', &c., and that the specific heats of these products are S, S', S'', &c. Then $WS + W'S' + W''S''$ + &c., represents the amount of heat required to raise the temperature of the whole mass of the products one centigrade degree (§ 16), — and the maximum temperature, to which these products can be raised in the process of combustion, must be

$$T = \frac{C}{WS + W'S' + W''S''} \qquad [60]$$

Problem. Find the calorific intensity of charcoal burnt in pure oxygen, and also in air under constant atmospheric pressure.

Solution. By [54] we easily find that each kilogramme of carbon yields, by burning, 3.67 kilogrammes of carbonic anhydride, which is the sole product of its combustion when burnt in pure oxygen. The specific heat of carbonic anhydride (Chem. Phys. 235) is 0.2164. The calorific power of charcoal is 8,080. By substituting these values in [60] we get $T =$ 10,174°.

When the charcoal burns in air, the 3.67 kilogrammes of carbonic anhydride formed by the combustion are mixed with a large mass of inert nitrogen, which must be regarded as one of the products of the combustion. The weight of this nitrogen is easily calculated from the known composition of air by weight (§ 59) and from the amount of oxygen consumed in the process.

$$23.2 : 76.8 = 2.67 : x; \text{ or } x = 2.67 \times 3.31 = 8.84.$$

We have now, besides the values given above, $W' = 8.84$ and S' the specific heat of nitrogen, equal to 0.244. Whence $T' = 2,738°$.

Problem. Find the calorific intensity of hydrogen gas burnt in oxygen and burnt in air.

Solution. One kilogramme of hydrogen yields 9 kilogrammes of aqueous vapor. The specific heat of aqueous vapor is 0.4805. The calorific power of hydrogen is not so great when the gas is burnt under ordinary conditions as that given in the table on page 118; for in the experiments of Favre and Silbermann the vapor formed by the combustion was subsequently condensed to water, and gave out its latent heat, while in a burning flame of hydrogen no such condensation takes place. Hence $C = 34,462 - (537 \times 9) = 29,629$. We also have $W = 9$ and $S = O. 480$. Whence $T = 6,853°$.

When hydrogen is burnt in air, the nitrogen, mixed with the aqueous vapor, weighs 26.49 kilogrammes and S' is the same as in the previous problem. Whence $T' = 2,746°$.

It appears then from these problems, that, although the calorific power of hydrogen is much greater than that of carbon, its calorific intensity is less. But it must be remembered that the conditions assumed in these problems are never realized in practice, for the heat generated by the combustion is never wholly retained in the products. The process of combustion requires a certain time, and during this time a portion of the heat escapes. Moreover, more air passes through the combustible than is required for perfect combustion, and many of the data which enter into the calculation are uncertain. The results, therefore, can only be regarded as approximate. The theoretical conditions are most nearly realized in a gas flame, and especially in that form of burner known as the Bunsen lamp. The temperature of the flame of this lamp, when carefully regulated, is very nearly that which the theory would assign.

63. *Point of Ignition.* — In order that a combustible body should take fire, and continue burning in the atmosphere, it must be heated to a certain temperature, and maintained at this temperature. This temperature is called the point of ignition; and although it cannot always be accurately measured, and is undoubtedly more or less variable under different conditions, yet, nevertheless, it is tolerably constant for each substance. For different substances it differs very greatly. Thus phosphorus takes fire below the boiling point of water, sulphur at 260°, wood at a low red heat, anthracite coal only at a full red heat, while iron requires the highest temperature of a forge. If a burning body is cooled below its point of ignition, it goes out; and our ordinary combustibles continue burning in the air only because the heat evolved by the burning maintains the temperature above the required point. If the temperature of the combustible is not maintained sufficiently high, either because the chemical union is too slow, or because the calorific power is too small, then the combustible will not continue to burn in the air of itself, although it may burn most readily if its temperature is sustained by artificial means. Hence many of the metals which will not burn in the air burn readily in the flame of a blowpipe, and an iron watch-spring burns like a match in an atmosphere of pure oxygen. The calorific intensity of all combustibles, when burnt in the atmosphere, is, as we have seen, greatly reduced by the presence of nitrogen; and hence it is that, although the burning watch-spring is maintained above the point of ignition in pure oxygen, it soon falls below this temperature, and goes out when ignited in the air. Thus it is that the nitrogen of our atmosphere exerts a most important influence on the action of the fire element; and it can easily be seen that, were it not for these provisions in the constitution of nature, by which the active energies of oxygen are kept within certain limits, no combustible material could exist on the surface of the earth.

64. *Calorific Power derived from the Sun.* — The great mass of the crust of our globe consists of saturated oxygen compounds, or, in other words, of burnt materials; and the total amount of combustible materials which exists on its surface is, comparatively, very small. That which exists naturally consists almost entirely of carbon and its compounds, — such as coal,

naphtha, and wood ; and all these substances are the results of vegetable growth, either of the present age or of earlier geological epochs. Moreover, whatever subsequent changes the material may have undergone, it was all originally prepared by the plant from the carbonic acid and water of our atmosphere ; for, in the economy of nature, these products of combustion have been made the food of the vegetable world. The sun's rays, acting on the green leaves of the plant, exert a mysterious power, which decomposes carbonic anhydride, and perhaps also water ; and, as the result of this process, oxygen is returned to the atmosphere, while carbon and hydrogen are stored up in the growing tissues of the plant. The sun thus undoes the work of combustion, and parts the atoms which the chemical affinities had drawn together. In doing this, the sun exerts an enormous power ; and the work which it thus accomplishes is the precise measure of the calorific power of the combustible material, which it then prepares. When we wind up the weight of a clock, we exert a certain power which reappears in its subsequent motions ; and so, when the sun's rays part these atoms, the great power it exerts is again called into action, when in the process of combustion the atoms reunite. Moreover, what is true of calorific power is true of all manifestations of power on the surface of the earth. Every form of motion is sustained by the running down of some weight which the sun has wound up ; and, according to the best theory we can form, the sun's power itself is sustained by the gradual falling of the whole mass of the solar system towards its common centre. However varying in its manifestation, all power in its essence is the same, and the total amount of power in the universe is constant.

65. *Heat of Chemical Combinations.* — The heat of combustion is only a striking manifestation of a very general principle, which holds true in all chemical changes. It would appear that whenever, in a chemical reaction, atoms or molecules are drawn together by their mutual affinities, a certain amount of moving power is developed, which takes the form of heat ; and whenever, on the other hand, these same atoms or molecules are drawn apart by the action of some superior force, the same amount of moving power is expended, and heat disappears. Every chemical reaction is a mixed effect of such combina-

tions and decompositions, and it is simply a complex problem in the mechanical theory of heat to determine what must be in any case the ' thermal effect. The numerous facts with which we are acquainted in regard to the heat of chemical combination generally agree with the mechanical theory ; and, where the facts do not appear to conform to it, the discrepancy probably arises from our ignorance of the nature of the chemical change in question. It would be incompatible with our design to discuss these facts in this book. It must be sufficient to state a few general results, which may be summed up in the following propositions : —

First. The heat absorbed in the decomposition of a compound is equal to the heat evolved in its formation, provided the initial and the final states are the same.

Second. The heat evolved in a series of successive chemical changes is equal to the sum of the quantities which would be evolved in each separately, provided the bodies are finally brought into identical conditions.

Third. The difference between the quantities of heat evolved in two series of changes starting from two different states, but ending in the same final state, is equal to that which is evolved or absorbed in passing from one initial condition to the other.

For example, if a body m evolves a certain amount of heat in uniting with n to form $m\,n$, and if the body $m\,n$ is decomposed by a third body p, so that $m\,p$ is formed, the quantity of heat evolved in this last reaction is less than that which would be evolved in the direct union of m and p by the amount evolved in the formation of $m\,n$.

All these propositions, however, are but special cases under a more general principle which is at the basis of the whole mechanical theory of heat, and which may be enunciated as follows : Whenever a system of bodies undergoes chemical or physical changes, and passes into another condition, whatever may have been the nature or succession of the changes, the quantity of heat evolved or absorbed depends solely on the initial and final conditions of the system, provided no mechanical effect has been produced on bodies outside.

Questions and Problems.

1. How many times more space does the carbonic anhydride formed by burning charcoal (*Sp. Gr.* = 2) occupy than the charcoal burnt ?

Ans. One cubic centimetre or two grammes of charcoal yields 3.720 litres. Hence the gas occupies 3,720 times the volume of the charcoal.

2. How many litres of oxygen gas are required to burn one litre of alcohol vapor, and how many litres of aqueous vapor, and how many of carbonic anhydride, will be formed in the process ?

Ans. 3 litres of oxygen, 3 litres of aqueous vapor, 2 litres of carbonic anhydride.

3. Given the symbol of alcohol C_2H_6O to find its calorific power.

Ans. 6,572 units, or 7,200 units, assuming that the steam formed was condensed.

4. The composition of dried peat is as follows : Carbon, 625.4 ; Hydrogen, 68.1 ; Oxygen, 292.4 ; Nitrogen, 14.1. Find the calorific power. Ans. 5,521 units.

5. Find the calorific intensity of marsh gas burnt in oxygen.

$$CH_4 + 2 O = O = CO_2 + 2H_2O$$

Calorific power of marsh gas, 13,063. Specific heat of steam, 0.4805 ; of CO_2, 0.2164. Ans. 7,793.

6. Find the calorific intensity of olefiant gas burnt in oxygen.

$$C_2H_4 + 3 O = O = 2 CO_2 + 2H_2O$$

Calorific power of C_2H_4 11,858. Specific heat of steam and carbonic anhydride as in last problem. Ans. 9,136°.

7. Find the calorific intensity of marsh gas and olefiant gas burnt in air. Besides the data already given, we have also specific heat of nitrogen 0.244. Ans. 2,662°, and 2,916°.

CHAPTER XIII.

MOLECULAR WEIGHT AND CONSTITUTION.

66. *Determination of Molecular Weights.* — It has already been stated that the molecular weight of a substance is an essential element in fixing its symbol and in judging of its chemical relations, but until now the student has not possessed the knowledge necessary in order to understand the methods by which this important constant is determined.

Whenever the substance is a gas, or is capable of being volatilized without decomposition at a manageable temperature, we always ascertain the molecular weight from the specific gravity on the principle already several times enforced (§ 17). The problem then resolves itself into finding the specific gravity of the substance in the state of gas. The methods used in such cases are described on page 21, and more in detail in the author's work on Chemical Physics (330 *et seq.*), and in the same book tables are given which very greatly facilitate the calculation of the results. The specific gravity of the gas or vapor having been found by either of these methods, and referred to hydrogen gas as the unit, the molecular weight of the substance is simply twice the number thus determined. But in applying this important principle, on which our modern chemical philosophy so greatly rests, two precautions are essential.

It is only true that equal volumes of all substances contain the same number of molecules when they are in the condition of true gases. Now, while some substances, like alcohol, assume this condition at temperatures only a few degrees above their boiling point, at least nearly enough for all practical purposes, others, like acetic acid, only attain it at temperatures one or two hundred degrees above their boiling point, and others still, like sulphur, only at the very highest temperatures at which we have been able to experiment. For this reason, the specific gravity of sulphur vapor was for a long time an anomalous fact in the science, and it was not until St. Clair Deville, by

using a porcelain globe, succeeded in determining its specific
gravity at a very high temperature, that its value was found to
correspond with the probable molecular weight, and it is possible that a similar anomaly which still exists in the case of
phosphorus and arsenic may be due to the same cause.

The chemist, however, can always have a sure criterion of
the condition of any vapor whose specific gravity he is determining by repeating his experiment at a somewhat higher temperature. If the second result does not agree with the first, it
is a proof that the vapor is not yet in a proper condition, and
that the temperature employed in the experiment was too low.
A series of determinations of the specific gravity of the vapor
of acetic acid made by Cahours furnish an excellent illustration of the importance of the precaution we are discussing, and
will also point out another important relation of this whole subject. This acid when in the most concentrated state boils at
120°, and the specific gravity of its vapor referred to hydrogen
at the same temperature and pressure was found to have the
following values at the temperatures annexed : —

At 125°	45.90	At 170°	35.30	At 240°	30.16
" 130	44.82	" 180	35.19	" 270	30.14
" 140	41.96	" 190	34.33	" 310	30.10
" 150	39.37	" 200	32.44	" 320	30.07
" 160	37.59	" 220	30.77	" 336	30.07

It will be noticed that, as the temperature increases, the
specific gravity diminishes, at first very rapidly, afterwards
more slowly, and does not become constant until the temperature has risen 200° above the boiling point, when we have the
true specific gravity of acetic acid in the state of gas. This
gives for the molecular weight of acetic acid 60 very nearly,
which corresponds to the received formula, $C_2H_4O_2$. The slight
difference between the theoretical and the observed results
may be in part due to errors of observation, but is most probably to be referred to the same cause which determines even
in the permanent gases, when under the atmospheric pressure,
a variation from Mariotte's law. We do not expect, moreover,
to find from the specific gravity the exact molecular weight.
*The precise value is determined by the results of analysis, which
are, as a rule, far more accurate, and the specific gravity is*

only used to decide which of several possible multiples must be the true value. (Compare carefully § 23.)

67. *Disassociation.* — But, besides taking care that the temperature is sufficiently high to bring the substance we are studying into the condition of a true gas, we must look out that the compound is not decomposed in the process. It is now well known that at very high temperatures the disassociation of the elements of a compound body is a constant result, and it is probable that in some cases the same effect is produced at the much lower temperatures which are employed in the determination of vapor densities. The specific gravity of the vapor of ammonic chloride, instead of being 26.75, as we should expect from the undoubted weight of its molecule, NH_4Cl, is only about one half of this amount; and the reason probably is, that, when heated, the molecule breaks into two, and in consequence the volume of the vapor doubles.

$$\boxed{NH_4Cl} = \boxed{NH_3} + \boxed{HCl}$$

It is very difficult, however, to obtain any further evidence that such a change has taken place; for, as soon as the temperature falls, the molecules recombine in assuming the solid condition, and all the phenomena attending the change of state are precisely the same as those observed in any other volatile body. Indeed, although many very ingenious experiments have been made with a view of settling the question, it is still uncertain, not only in this, but also in several other cases, whether disassociation has taken place or not. The question is of great importance to the theory of chemistry. If disassociation does not take place, the cases referred to are exceptions to the law of equal molecular volumes, and specific gravity can no longer be regarded, as now, the sole measure of molecular weight. If, however, it can be proved that such a change does take place, then the unity of our present theory is preserved, and the chemist has only to guard against this cause of error in his experiments.

68. *Indirect Determination of Molecular Weight.* — Although our modern chemical theories rest in great measure on the molecular weight of a few typical compounds determined,

at least approximately, by their specific gravities, yet it is only in a comparatively few cases that we are able to refer the molecular weight of a substance directly to this fundamental measure. Most substances are so fixed, or so easily decomposed by heat, that it is impossible to determine the specific gravity of their vapor, even when such a condition is possible. In these cases, however, we endeavor to refer the molecular weight indirectly to the fundamental measure, by establishing a relation of chemical equivalency between the substance whose molecular weight is sought and some *closely allied* volatile substance whose molecular weight has been previously determined in the manner described above. A few examples will make the application of this principle intelligible.

It is required to determine the molecular weight of nitric acid. A careful study of the numerous nitrates leads to the conclusion that this acid, like hydrochloric acid, HCl, contains but one atom of replaceable hydrogen. For example, we find but one potassic nitrate and one sodic nitrate, whereas we should expect to find several, if the acid were polybasic. Hence we conclude that one molecule of argentic nitrate, like one molecule of argentic chloride, $AgCl$, contains but one atom of silver. Next, we analyze argentic nitrate, and find that 100 parts of the salt contain 63.53 parts of silver. We know the atomic weight of silver, 108, and evidently this must bear the same relation to the molecular weight of argentic nitrate that 63.53 bears to 100. But $63.53 : 100 = 108 : x = 170$, which is the molecular weight of argentic nitrate, and, since the molecule of nitric acid differs from that of argentic nitrate only in containing an atom of hydrogen in place of the atom of silver, its own weight must be $170 - 108 + 1 = 63$.

It is required to determine the molecular weight of sulphuric acid. A comparison of the different sulphates shows that sulphuric acid is dibasic. We find two sulphates of potassium and sodium, an acid sulphate and a neutral sulphate, and hence we conclude that this acid contains two replaceable atoms of hydrogen, and hence that one molecule of neutral potassic sulphate contains two atoms of potassium. In analyzing potassic sulphate it appears that 100 parts of the salt contain 44.83 parts of potassium, and evidently this weight

9

bears the same relation to 100 that the weight of two atoms of potassium bears to the weight of the molecule of potassic sulphate. Thus we have, —

44.83 : 100 = 78 : x = 174 ; the *M. W.* of Potassic Sulphate,
and 174 — 78 + 2 = 98 ; the *M. W.* of Sulphuric Acid.

By a similar course of reasoning we may deduce from the results of analysis, and from the general chemical relations, the molecular weight of any other acid or base. If there is any question in regard to the basicity of the acid or the acidity of the base, there will be the same question as to the molecular weight; but we cannot be led far into error, for the true weight will be some simple multiple or submultiple of the one assumed, and the progress of science will sooner or later correct our mistake. From the molecular weight of any acid we easily deduce the molecular weights of all its salts.

When the substance is not distinctively an acid or a base, but is capable of entering into combination with other bodies, we can frequently discover its molecular weight by determining experimentally how much of this substance is equivalent to a known weight of some allied but volatile substance whose molecular weight is known. Thus ammonia gas, whose molecular weight is one of the best-established data of chemistry, enters into direct union with a compound of platinic chloride and hydrochloric acid ($PtCl_6H_2$) to form a definite crystalline salt whose composition is exactly known.

$$PtCl_6H_2 + 2NH_3 = PtCl_6(NH_4)_2. \qquad [61]$$

Now a very large number of substances allied to ammonia form with this same platinum salt equally definite products, so that by simply determining the weight of platinum in these compounds, which is very easily done, their molecular weights may at once be referred to the molecular weight of ammonia.

Lastly, if other means fail, we may sometimes discover the molecular weight of a compound by carefully studying the reactions by which it is formed or decomposed, and inferring the weight of the compound from that of its factors or products. We seek to express the reaction in the simplest possible way, and give that value to the molecular weight which best satisfies the chemical equation. Evidently, however, such results are less trustworthy than those obtained by either of the other methods.

69. *Constitution of Molecules.* — It is a favorite theory with some chemists that no molecule can exist in a free condition with any of its affinities unsatisfied, but those who hold this view are compelled to admit that two points of attraction in the same atom may, in certain cases, neutralize each other. Hence, they would distinguish between a dyad atom like that of oxygen ⊙, with its affinities open, and a dyad atom like that of mercury ⊖, with its affinities closed through their own mutual attraction. The first could not exist in a free condition, while the last could. In like manner any atom, having an even number of points of attraction, can exist in a free state because all its affinities may be satisfied within itself; but an atom having an uneven number of points cannot, for at least one of its affinities must be open as is shown by the symbol ⊖. As thus interpreted it must be admitted that the theory explains many facts.

For example, among the univalent elements, chlorine, bromine and iodine are all known to have molecules consisting of two atoms. So, also, the molecule of cyanogen gas consists of two atoms of the radical CN, and the same is true of ethyl, propyl, &c., at least if the hydrocarbons so named have really the constitution first assigned to them.

Passing next to the dyads, we find that, while oxygen, sulphur, selenium and tellurium have molecules consisting of two atoms, the metals mercury and cadmium, and the radicals ethylene, propylene, &c. (C_2H_4 and C_3H_6), have molecules which coincide with their atoms.

Of the well-defined triad elements none are volatile, but the two triad radicals which have been obtained in a free state — allyl[1] (C_3H_5) and kakodyl ($(CH_3)_2As$) — both have double atomic molecules.

In like manner none of the tetrad elements are volatile, and the only tetrad radicals known in a free state have single atomic molecules.

Of the pentad elements nitrogen has a molecule of two atoms, while phosphorus and arsenic have molecules of four

---

[1] See page 78, Problem 7.

atoms. No compound radicals of this order are known in a free state.

Lastly, the only hexad radical known in a free state, benzine, C_6H_6, has a molecule which coincides with its atom.

Thus it appears that in general the theory is sustained by the facts. Nevertheless, there are several well-marked exceptions to it. Thus the well-known compounds $\overset{III}{N}O$ and $\overset{I}{N}O_2$ have molecules which act as radicals of uneven atomicities and yet contain but one complex atom. We must be careful, therefore, not to give too much weight to this hypothesis, but still it may be useful in co-ordinating facts. It leads at once to three general principles which will be found to be almost universally true.

The first is that the sum of the atomicities of the atoms of every molecule is an even number.

The second is that the atomicity of any radical is an odd or even number according as the sum of the atomicities of its elementary atoms is odd or even.

The third is that the quantivalence of elementary atoms must be, as stated on page 59, either even or odd. They are *artiads* or *perissads*, and the two characters can never be manifested by the same elements.

It has also been a question among chemists whether molecular combination was possible; in other words, whether it is possible for molecules of different kinds to combine chemically, each preserving its integrity in the compound. Some of the advocates of the unitary theory, in the reaction against the dualistic system, have been inclined to doubt the possibility of such compounds, and have attempted to represent the symbols of *all* compounds in a single molecular group; but any antecedent improbability, on theoretical grounds, is far more than outweighed by the evidence of a large number of compounds whose constitution is most simply explained on the hypothesis of molecular combination. For example, in the crystalline salts it is impossible to doubt that the water exists as such, not as a part of the salt molecule, but combined with it as a whole. So, also, there are a number of double salts whose constitution is most simply explained on a similar hypothesis, and, in the present state of the science, it seems unnecessary to complicate their symbols by forcing them into the unitary mould. It is a characteristic of such molecular compounds as are here assumed, that the force which holds together the molecules is much feebler than that which binds together the atoms in the molecule. When the molecular attraction is very strong, it is probable that in almost all cases the different molecules coalesce into one; and between the extreme limits we find compounds in which it is difficult to determine whether true molecular combination exists or not. Such coalescing of distinct molecules seems always, however, to be attended with a greater development of heat, and, in general, with a more marked manifestation of physical energies, than usually attends either molecular aggregation or atomic metathesis.

In the notation of this book molecular combination is indicated by writing together the symbols of the different molecules thus united, but separating these symbols by periods. Thus the symbols $4KCl.PtCl_4$, and $3NaF.SbF_3$ represent compounds of this class.

70. *Isomerism, Allotropism, Polymorphism.* — We should infer from the doctrine of chemical types that the same atoms might be grouped together in different ways, so as to form different molecules which in their aggregation would present essentially distinct qualities. Hence, we should expect to find distinct substances having the same composition; and in fact our science, organic chemistry especially, is rich in examples of this kind. Such substances are said to be isomeric, and the phenomenon is called isomerism. There are different phases of isomerism, which it will be well to distinguish, not so much on account of any essential differences in the phenomena as in order to make ourselves better acquainted with its manifestations.

In the first place, we have examples of isomeric bodies having the same centesimal composition, but showing no relation to each other in their properties or in their chemical reactions. Sometimes we have assigned to them the same formula, but in other cases the symbol of one is a simple multiple of that of the other. Thus aldehyde and oxide of ethylene have both the symbol C_2H_4O; cane sugar and gum arabic, the common formula $C_{12}H_{22}O_{11}$; lactic acid, the formula $C_3H_6O_3$; and glucose, $C_6H_{12}O_6$. These compounds bear no resemblance to each other, and have no relations in common save the single fact that their centesimal composition is the same.

In the second place, we have numerous examples of isomeric compounds, which, with the same centesimal composition, have also the same molecular weight, and whose molecules, therefore, consist of the same number of ·atoms, but where a fundamental difference in the grouping of the atoms may be inferred from the nature and products of the chemical reactions, by which such isomeric compounds are formed or decomposed. Thus, for example, ethylic formiate (C_2H_5)-O-(CHO) has exactly the same composition and molecular weight as methylic acetate (CH_3)-O-(C_2H_3O). The same is true of cyanic ether and cyanetholine, whose symbols have already been given (page 77) in connection with the reactions, which indicate their molecular constitution, and another still more remarkable case will be found in Part II. of this work [164] and [165].

In the third place, we have several groups of isomeric compounds, especially among the hydrocarbons, which have the same general properties and the same percentage composition, but which differ from each other in their molecular weights; so that the symbol of one is a multiple of that of the rest. The hydrocarbons ethylene C_2H_4, propylene C_3H_6, butylene C_4H_8, form a group of this kind. Compounds of this class are frequently called *polymeric*, and sometimes the heavier compounds may be regarded as condensed forms of the lighter.

Lastly, we may distinguish still a fourth class of isomeric compounds which have the same general properties, the same symbol, and the same general system of reactions, but which differ in a few marked qualities, physical or chemical, and which preserve these characteristics to a greater or less extent in their compounds. The two forms of toluic acid, $C_8H_8O_2$, belong to this class, and such compounds are isomeric in the fullest sense of the word.

In all the above examples the differences between the isomeric compounds are sufficiently great to lead chemists to assign to each a distinct name. When, however, the differences are not sufficiently great to justify a distinct name, the two bodies are said to be different *allotropic* states of the same substance. Thus there are two varieties of tartaric acid; the first of which deviates the plane of polarization of a ray of light to the left, while the second deviates it to the right; but since in almost every other respect these two bodies are identical, we do not speak of them as different substances, but merely as different allotropic states of tartaric acid. There are also three other varieties of tartaric acid, but these differ so greatly from the normal acid in crystalline form, in solubility, and also in other relations, that they may fairly be regarded as distinct substances.

Again, there are many substances where the difference of state or *allotropism* is associated with difference of crystalline form; and when this difference of form is fundamental, the substance is said to be dimorphous or trimorphous, as the case may be, and the phenomenon is called polymorphism. Thus common calcic carbonate crystallizes in two fundamentally distinct forms, corresponding to the two mineralogical species, calcite and aragonite. Such difference of form, however, is invariably accompanied by a marked difference of properties, so that polymorphism is merely one of the indications of allotropism.

Differences of condition similar to those we have described manifest themselves even more markedly among elementary substances; and indeed the word allotropism was first applied to phenomena of this last class. Thus there are two allotropic states of phosphorus, which differ so much from each other that no one would suspect from their external characters that there was any identity between them, and to these two states correspond two fundamentally different crystalline forms. In some cases the differences between the allotropic states of the same element are far greater than any which are seen between the most unlike isomeric compounds. No substances could be better defined by well-marked and utterly distinct qualities than diamond, plumbago, and charcoal, and yet they are all three allotropic modifications of the one elemental substance we call carbon; and such phenomena as these give us strong grounds for believing that our present elements may have a composite structure.

Questions and Problems.

1. What are the molecular weights of alcohol and camphor as deduced from the results of the 𝕾𝖕. 𝕮𝖗. determinations given on page 23 ?

    Ans. 45.5 and 155, which, although not closely agreeing with the theoretical numbers, enables us to decide that the symbols of these compounds are C_2H_6O and $C_{10}H_{16}O$ as the simplest interpretation of the analyses would indicate.

2. At the temperature of 470° the 𝕾𝖕. 𝕮𝖗. of the vapor of sulphuric acid is approximately 1.697. How does this result agree with the generally received symbol of this compound, and how do you explain the discrepancy ?

3. A study of the different tartrates has led to the conclusion already expressed that tartaric acid, although tetratomic, is dibasic. It also appears that one hundred parts of neutral argentic tartrate yield when ignited 55.39 parts of metallic silver. Required the molecular weight of tartaric acid.   Ans. 176.

4. An hundred parts of baric oxide, BaO, (whose composition is assumed to be known) yield when treated with sulphuric acid 152.3 parts of baric sulphate. Further it is assumed, as the result of careful study, that sulphuric acid is dibasic, and the metal barium a bivalent radical. Required the molecular weight of sulphuric acid.

    Ans. 98.

5. The well-known base aniline gives with platinic chloride a definite crystalline product, one hundred parts of which yield on ignition 32.99 parts of platinum. Required the molecular weight of aniline. How does this result agree with the 𝕾𝖕. 𝕮𝖗. of aniline vapor, which has been found by observation to be 3.210. ?

    Ans. 93; which corresponds to 𝕾𝖕. 𝕮𝖗. of 3.223.

6. The base triethylamine gives in like manner a platinum salt, one hundred parts of which yield on ignition 32.13 parts of platinum. Required the molecular weight.   Ans. 101.

7. Compare together the symbols of the compounds of the various alcohol radicals on pages 90 to 93 and point out the examples of isomerism.

CHAPTER XIV.

CRYSTALLINE FORMS.

71. *Relations to Chemistry.* — Almost every substance affects a definite polyhedral form, although it may manifest this tendency only under favorable conditions. Such forms are called crystals, and the process of crystalline growth, or development, is called crystallization. The one essential condition of crystallization is a certain freedom of motion, and crystals, more or less perfect, are usually formed whenever a molten liquid " sets," or a solid is deposited from a condition of solution or of vapor ; and in each case the slower the process the larger and the more perfect are the crystals. The crystalline condition is, in fact, the normal state of solid matter. It is true that there are a few substances which, like glue, are only known in the colloid state; but in most of the so-called colloid substances this state is abnormal, and there is a constant tendency to crystallization. Moreover, its peculiar crystalline form is one of the most characteristic, and apparently one of the most essential, properties of a substance, and is therefore of great value in determining its chemical affinities. The study of the geometrical relations of these forms is, however, in itself a separate science, and in this connection we can only dwell on the few elementary principles of the subject on which our system of chemical classification in part rests.

72. *Definitions.* — In the forms of crystals the idea of symmetry is the great controlling principle. Each substance follows a certain law of symmetry, which seems to be inherent, and a part of its very nature ; and. when, from any cause, the character of the symmetry changes, the substance loses its identity, and, even if its chemical composition remains the same, it becomes, to all intents and purposes, a different substance. In every crystal the symmetry points to a few *directions*, to which not only the position of the planes, but also the physical properties of the body, are closely related. Certain of these *directions*, more or less arbitrarily chosen, are called the *axes* of the crystals, and a *crystalline form* may be defined as a group of *similar* planes symmetrically disposed around these

Fig. 4.

axes. As is evident from this definition a crystalline form, like a geometrical form, is a pure abstraction, and this conception is carefully to be kept distinct from the idea of a crystal, which implies not only a certain form, but also a certain structure. Moreover, in by far the larger number of cases the same crystal is bounded by several forms. Thus, in Fig. 4, which represents a crystal of common quartz, the planes of the prism and the planes of the pyramid are distinct crystalline forms.

73. *Systems of Crystals.* — A careful study of the forms of crystals has shown that these forms may be classified under six crystalline systems, each of which is distinguished by a peculiar plan of symmetry. These divisions, it is true, are in a measure arbitrary ; for here, as elsewhere in nature, no sharp dividing lines are found ; but nevertheless the distinctions on which the classification rests are clearly marked. We can only give in this book a very imperfect idea of these several plans of symmetry by representing with figures a few of the more characteristic forms of each.

74. *First or Isometric System.*[1] — The three most frequently occurring forms of this system are the regular octahedron, the

Fig. 5.   Fig. 6.

Fig. 7.

rhombic dodecahedron and the cube, Figs. 5, 6, and 7. These and all the other forms of the system may be regarded as

[1] Called also monometric.

grouped around three equal and similar axes at right angles to each other, and hence the name isometric (equal dimensions). They present the same symmetry on all sides, and the appearance of the form is identical, whichever axis is placed in a vertical position.' In this system no variation in the relative positions or lengths of the axes is possible, for this would change the plan of symmetry on which the system is based.

75. *Second or Tetragonal System.*[1] — The plan of symmetry in this system is best illustrated by the square octahedron, Fig. 8. Of this form the basal section, Fig. 9, is a square, and to

Fig. 9.

Fig. 8.

Fig. 10.

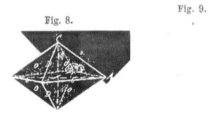

this fact the name of the system refers. The vertical section, on the other hand, is a rhomb, Fig 10. Here, as in the first system, the forms may all be referred to three rectangular axes, but only two have the same length; the third may be either longer or shorter than the others. The last is the dominant axis of the form, and hence we always place it in a vertical position and call it the vertical axis. The length of the vertical axis bears a constant ratio to that of the lateral axes in all crystals of the same substance, but this ratio differs very greatly for different substances, and is therefore an important crystallographic character. The familiar square prism is another very characteristic form of this system.

Fig. 11.

Fig. 12.

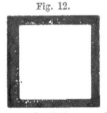

Moreover, the planes both of the prism and of the octahedron may have different positions with reference to the lateral axes, as is shown by the two basal sections, Figs. 11 and 12;

---

[1] Called also dimetric.

and this leads us to distinguish two square prisms and two square octahedrons, one of which is said to be the inverse of the other.

76. *Third or Hexagonal System.* — In the last system the planes were arranged by fours around one dominant axis, while in this system they are arranged by sixes. The most characteristic forms of this system are the hexagonal pyramid, Fig. 13, and the hexagonal prism, Fig. 14. The basal section through either of these forms is a regular hexagon, Fig. 15, and, besides

Fig. 13.

Fig. 14.

Fig. 15.

the dominant or vertical axis, we also distinguish as lateral axes the three diagonals of this hexagonal section. These lateral axes stand at right angles to the vertical axis, but between themselves they subtend angles of 60°. Here, as before, the ratio of the length of the vertical axis to the common length of the lateral axes has a constant value on crystals of the same substance, but differs very greatly with different substances, the vertical axis being sometimes longer and sometimes shorter

Fig. 16.

Fig. 17.

than the other three. The rhombohedron, Fig. 16, and the scalenohedron, Fig. 17, are also forms of this system, and occur even more frequently than the more typical forms first mentioned. Lastly, a difference of position in the planes of the prism or pyramid with reference to the lateral axes gives rise in this system to the same distinction between the direct and the inverse forms as in the last.

77. *Fourth or Orthorhombic System.*[1] — The most characteristic forms of this system are the rhombic octahedron, Fig. 18, and the right rhombic prism, from which the system takes its name. The three principal sections of the octahedron, represented by Figs. 19, 20, and 21, and also the basal section of the

Fig. 18.   Fig. 19.   Fig. 20.

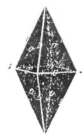

Fig. 21.

prism, are all rhombs, whose relations to the form are indicated by the lettering of the figures. We easily distinguish here three axes at right angles to each other, but of unequal lengths, and in regard to the ratios of these lengths, the remarks of the last two sections are strictly applicable.

78. *Fifth or Monoclinic System.* — The forms classed together under this system may be referred to three unequal axes, one of which stands at right angles to the *plane* of the other two, while they are inclined to each other at an angle, which, though constant on crystals of the same substance, varies very greatly with different substances, as vary also the relative dimensions of the axes themselves. Fig. 22 represents an octahedron of this system, and Figs. 23 and 24 represent two sections made through the edges FF and DD' of this form. A section through the edges CC would be similar to Fig. 23, and these three sections give a clear idea of the relative positions of the axes. The section, Fig. 24, containing the two oblique axes,

[1] Called also trimetric.

is called the plane of symmetry, and the faces on all monoclinic crystals are disposed symmetrically solely with reference to this plane.   In a word, the symmetry is bilateral, and corresponds

Fig. 22.   Fig. 23.   Fig. 24.

to the type with which we are so familiar in the structure of the human body.   This plan of symmetry is well illustrated by Figs. 25, 26, and 27, which represent the commonly occurring forms of gypsum, augite, and felspar, three of the most common minerals.   These figures, however, do not, like those of the previous sections, represent simple crystalline forms.   The crystals here represented are in each case bounded by several forms, and indeed in this system such compound forms are alone possible, for no simple monoclinic form can of itself enclose space.

Fig. 25.   Fig. 26.   Fig. 27.

79. *Sixth or Triclinic System.* — This system is distinguished by an almost complete want of symmetry.   Only opposite planes

Fig. 28.

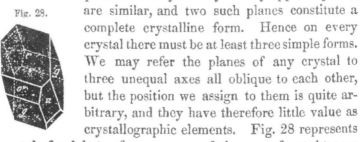

are similar, and two such planes constitute a complete crystalline form.   Hence on every crystal there must be at least three simple forms. We may refer the planes of any crystal to three unequal axes all oblique to each other, but the position we assign to them is quite arbitrary, and they have therefore little value as crystallographic elements.   Fig. 28 represents a crystal of sulphate of copper, one of the very few subtances which crystallize in this system.

80. *Modifications on Crystals.* — When several crystalline forms appear on the same crystal, some one is usually more prominent or *dominant* than the rest, and gives to the crystal its general aspect, the planes of the secondary forms only appearing on its edges or solid angles, which are then said to be modified or replaced. Thus, in Figs. 29, 30, and 31, the solid angles of a cube are replaced (or truncated) by the faces of an octahedron; in Fig. 32 the edges of the cube are replaced by the faces of the dodecahedron; in Fig. 33 the edges of the octahedron are modified in the same way; and in Fig. 34 the solid angles of a dodecahedron are replaced by the faces of an

Fig. 29.   Fig. 30.   Fig. 31.

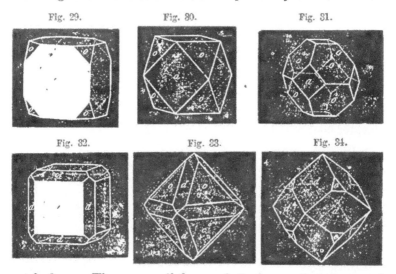

Fig. 32.   Fig. 33.   Fig. 34.

octahedron. These are all forms of the isometric system, and the relations of the simple forms to each other, which determine in every case the position of the secondary planes, will be readily seen on comparing together the figures already given on page 138. These figures, like all crystallographic drawings, are geometrical projections, and represent the planes in the same relative position towards the crystalline axes which they have on the crystal itself. Moreover, since in all figures of crystals of this system the axes are drawn in absolutely the same position on the plane of the paper, the same face has also the same position throughout.

As a general rule, *all the similar parts of a crystal are simultaneously and similarly modified.* This important law, which is a simple inference from the principles already stated, is illustrated by the figures just given, and also by Figs.

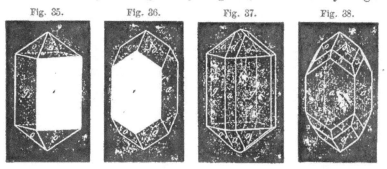

Fig. 35.   Fig. 36.   Fig. 37.   Fig. 38.

35 to 50. By carefully studying these figures, as well as Figs. 25 to 28 on page 142, the student will be able to refer each of

Fig. 39.   Fig. 40.   Fig. 41.

the compound crystals here represented to one or the other of the systems of symmetry already described, and from this and

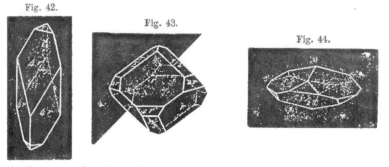

Fig. 42.   Fig. 43.   Fig. 44.

similar practice he will learn, better than from any descriptions, how clearly the modifications on a crystal point out its crystallographic relations.

81. *Hemihedral Forms.* — To the law governing the modifications of crystals just stated, there is one important excep-

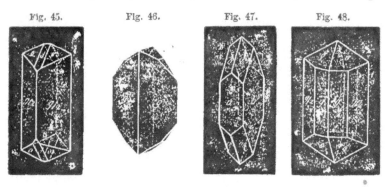

Fig. 45.   Fig. 46.   Fig. 47.   Fig. 48.

tion.   It not unfrequently happens that *half the similar parts of a crystal are modified independently of the other half.*   Thus

Fig. 49.

Fig. 50.

in Fig. 51 only one half of the solid angles of the cube are truncated.   The modifying form in this case is the tetrahedron,

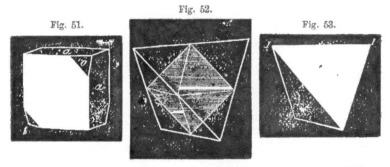

Fig. 52.

Fig. 51.   Fig. 53.

Fig. 53, also a simple form of the isometric system.   When all the solid angles of the cube are truncated, the modifying form, as has been shown, is the octahedron, and the relation which the tetrahedron bears to the octahedron is shown by Fig. 52.   The rhombohedron, Fig. 54, stands in a similar relation to the hexagonal pyramid, Fig. 55.   From these figures it is evident that while the octahedron and the hexagonal pyramid have all the planes which perfect symmetry requires, the

Fig. 54.

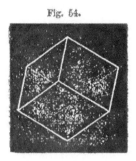

Fig. 55.

tetrahedron and the rhombohedron have only half the number, and in crystallography all forms which bear a similar relation to the forms of perfect symmetry are said to be *hemi*hedral, while the forms of perfect symmetry are distinguished as *holo*hedral. The hemihedral forms are quite numerous in all the systems, but with the exception of the tetrahedron, rhombohedron, and scalenohedron (Fig. 17), they seldom appear except as modifying planes on the edges or solid angles of the more perfect forms. As a general rule, they are easily recognized, but not unfrequently they give to a crystal the aspect of a different system from that to which it really belongs, and may lead to false inferences; but these can, in most cases, be corrected by a careful study of the interfacial angles.

82. *Identity of Crystalline Form.* — As has already been stated, every substance is marked by certain peculiarities of outward form, which are among its most essential qualities, and we must next learn in what these peculiarities consist. As a general rule, the same substance crystallizes in the same form, but under unusual circumstances it frequently appears in other forms of the same system. Thus fluorspar is usually found crystallized in cubes, but in large collections crystals of this mineral may be seen in almost all the holohedral forms of the isometric system, including their numerous combinations. In like manner common salt usually crystallizes in cubes, but out of a solution containing urea it frequently crystallizes in octahedrons. Moreover, the same principle holds true in regard to substances crystallizing in other systems, most of whose forms never appear except in combination. Thus the mineral

quartz generally shows the simple combination represented in Fig. 4 ; but more than one hundred other forms, all, however, belonging to the same system, have been observed on crystals of this well-known substance.   So also the crystals of gypsum, augite, and felspar, in most cases present the forms already figured on page 142, although other forms are common, which, however, in each case all belong to the same crystalline system. We never find the same substance in the forms of different systems except in those cases of polymorphism already described, page 135, where the differences in other properties are so great that the bodies can no longer be regarded as the same substance.

Among substances crystallizing in the isometric system the crystalline form is not so distinctive a character as it is in other cases.   In this system the relative dimensions are invariable, and the octahedron, the dodecahedron, and the cube, more or less modified by different replacements, are the constantly recurring forms.   Even here, however, specific differences may at times be found in the fact that some substances affect hemihedral forms on modification, while others do not.   In all the other systems the dimensions of the crystal (the relative lengths of its axes and the values of the interaxial angles) distinguish each substance from every other.   But here, also, the general statement must be somewhat modified.

We frequently find on the crystals of the same substance several forms having different axial dimensions.   Thus, on the crystal represented by Fig. 56, belonging to the tetragonal system, there are three different octahedrons, and three corresponding values of the vertical axis.   But if, beginning with the planes of the octahedron O, we determine the ratio which its vertical axis bears to the common length of the two lateral axes, and call this value a, we shall find that the corresponding values for the two other octahedrons are $2a$ and $\frac{1}{2}a$ respectively.   Moreover, if we extend our study we shall also find that this example illustrates a general principle, and that *the crystalline forms of a given substance include not only those of identical axial dimensions, but also those whose dimensions bear to each other some simple ratio.*

Fig. 56.

This most important law gives to the science of crystallography a mathematical basis, and enables us to apply the exhaustive methods of analytical geometry in discussing the various relations of the subject. Among the actual forms of a given substance we fix on some one as the fundamental form, and, taking
the values of its axial dimensions as our standards, we are able
to express the position of the planes of all the possible forms by
means of very simple symbols, and also to express by mathe-
mátical formulæ the relations of the interfacial angles to the
same fundamental elements of the crystal; so that the one
may readily be calculated from the other.

It may seem at first sight that the crystallographic distinction
between different substances, insisted on above, is greatly obscured by the important limitations just made. But it is not
so, at least to any great extent. The selection of the fundamental form of a given substance is not arbitrary, although it is
based on considerations which it lies beyond the scope of this
book to discuss. Moreover, an error in this choice is not fundamental, since the true conception of the form of a substance
includes not only the fundamental form, but all those which are
related to it. This conception, though not readily embodied in
ordinary language, is easily expressed by a general mathematical formula, and is as tangible to one familiar with the subject
as the general statement first made.

But however obscure, to those who are not familiar with
mathematical conceptions, may be the distinction between the
forms of different substances in the same system, the difference
between the different systems is clear and definite, and it is
with this broad distinction that we have chiefly to deal in our
chemical classification.

83. *Irregularities of Crystals.* — It must not be supposed
that natural crystals have the same perfection of form and
regularity of outline which our figures might seem to indicate.
In addition to being more or less bruised or broken from accidental causes, crystals are rarely terminated on all sides, — one
or more of the faces being obliterated where the crystal is im-
planted on the rock, or where it is merged in other crystals.
But by far the most remarkable phase which the irregularities
of crystals present is that shown by Figs. 57 to 67. By comparing together the figures which have been here grouped to-

gether on the page, and which represent in each case different phases of the same crystalline form, it will be seen that the variations from the normal type are caused by the undue de-

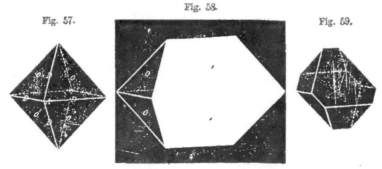

Fig. 57.　　　　　Fig. 58.　　　　　Fig. 59.

velopment of certain planes at the expense of their neighbors, or by an abnormal growth of the crystal in some one direction.

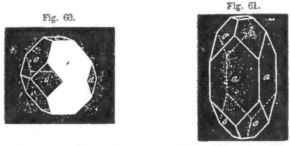

Fig. 60.　　　　　Fig. 61.

Such forms as these, however, although great departures from the ideal geometrical types, are in perfect harmony with

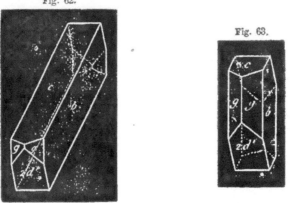

Fig. 62.　　　　　Fig. 63.

the principles of crystallography. The axis of a crystal is not a definite line, but a definite direction; and the face of a crystal is not a plane of definite size, but simply an extension in two definite directions. These directions are the only fundamental elements of a crystalline form, and they are preserved under

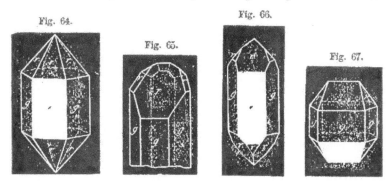

Fig. 64.

Fig. 65.

Fig. 66.

Fig. 67.

all conditions, as is proved by the constancy of the interfacial angles, and of the modifications, on crystals of the same substance, however irregular may have been the development.

84. *Twin Crystals.* — Every crystal appears to grow by the slow accretion of material around some nucleus, which is usually a molecule or a group of molecules of the same substance, and which we may call the crystalline molecule or germ. Now we must suppose that these molecules have the same differences on different sides which we see in the fully developed crystal, and which, for the want of a better term, we may call polarity. As a general rule, in the aggregation of the molecules a perfect parallelism of all the similar parts is preserved. But, if molecular polarity at all resembles magnetic polarity, it may well be that two crystalline molecules might become attached to each other in a reversed position, or in some other definite position determined by the action of the polar forces. Assume now that each of these crystalline molecules "germinates," and the result would be such twin crystals as we actually find in nature. The result is usually the same as if a crystal of the normal form were cut in two by a plane having a definite position towards the crystalline axes, and one part turned half round on the other; and twins of this kind are therefore called hemitropes. Figs. 68 to 71. At other times the germinal molecules seem to have become attached with their dominant axes at right angles to each other, and then there result twins such as are represented in Figs. 72 and 73; and many other modes of twin-

ning are possible. Some substances are much more prone to the formation of twin crystals than others, and the same substance generally affects the same mode of twinning, which may

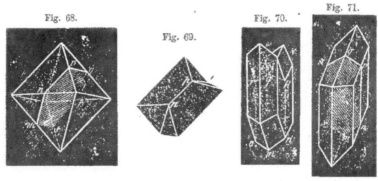

Fig. 68.

Fig. 69.

Fig. 70.

Fig. 71.

thus become an important specific character. The plane which separates the two members of a twin crystal, called the plane

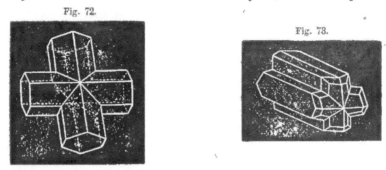

Fig. 72.

Fig. 73.

of twinning, has always a definite position, and is in every case parallel either to an actual or to a possible face on both of the two forms.

Twin crystals always preserve the same symmetry of grouping, and the values of the interfacial angles between the two forms are constant on crystals of the same substance, so that they might sometimes be mistaken for simple crystals by unpractised observers. There is, however, a simple criterion by which they can be generally distinguished. Simple crystals never have re-entering angles, and, whenever these occur, the faces which subtend them must belong to two individuals.

The same principle which leads to the formation of twin crystals may determine the grouping of several germinal molecules, and lead to the formation of far more complex combinations. Frequently, as it would seem, a large number of molecules arrange themselves in a line with their principal axes parallel and their dissimilar ends together, and hence result linear groups of crystals alternating in position, but so fused into each other as to leave no evidence of the composite character except the re-entering angles, and frequently these are marked only by the striations on the surface of the resulting faces. Such a structure is peculiar to certain minerals, and the resulting striation frequently serves as an important means of distinction. The orthoclase and the klinoclase felspars are distinguished in this way.

85. *Crystalline Structure.* — The crystalline form of a body is only one of the manifestations of its crystalline structure. This also appears in various physical properties, which are frequently of great value in fixing the crystallographic relations of a substance, and such is especially the case when, on account of the imperfection of the crystals, the crystalline form is obscure. Of these physical qualities one of the most important is *cleavage.*

As a general rule, crystallized bodies may be split more or less readily in certain definite directions, called planes of cleavage, which are always parallel either to an actual or to a possible face on the crystals of the substance, and are thus intimately associated with its crystalline structure. At times the cleavage is very easily obtained, when it is said to be *eminent,* as in the case of mica or gypsum, which can readily be split into exceedingly thin leaves, while in other cases it can only be effected by using some sharp tool and applying considerable mechanical force. With a few unimportant exceptions the cleavage planes have the same position on all specimens of the same substance. Thus specimens of fluor-spar may be readily cleaved parallel to the faces of an octahedron, Fig. 5, those of galena parallel to the faces of a cube, Fig. 7, those of blende parallel to the faces of a dodecahedron, Fig. 6, and those of calc-spar parallel to the faces of a rhombohedron, Fig. 16. In these cases, and in many others, the cleavage is a more distinctive character than the external form, and can be more frequently observed, and we generally regard the form produced by the union of the several planes of cleavage as the fundamental form of the substance.

Again, we always find that cleavage is obtained with equal

ease or difficulty parallel to similar faces, and with unequal ease or difficulty parallel to dissimilar faces. Moreover, the dissimilar cleavage faces thus obtained may generally be distinguished from each other by differences of lustre, striation, and other physical character; and such distinctions are frequently a great help in studying the crystallographic relations of a substance. Similar differences on the natural faces of crystals are also equally valuable guides.

But, of all the modes of investigating the crystalline structure of a body, none can compare in efficiency with the use of polarized light. It is impossible to explain the theory of this beautiful application of the principles of optics without extending this chapter to a length wholly incompatible with the design of this book. It must suffice to say, that if we examine with a polarizing microscope a thin slice of any transparent crystal of the second or third system, cut perpendicular to the dominant axis, we see a series of colored rings, intersected by a black cross, and it is evident that the circular form of the rings answers to the perfect symmetry which exists in these systems around the vertical axis. If, however, we examine in a similar way a slice from a crystal of one of the last three systems, cut in a definite direction, which depends on the molecular structure, and must be found by trial, we see a series of oval rings with two distinct centres, indicating that the symmetry is of a different type. Moreover, the distribution of the colors around the two centres corresponds in each case to the peculiarities of the molecular structure, and enables us to decide to which of the three systems the crystal belongs.

The use of polarized light has revealed remarkable differences of structure in different crystals of the same substance, connected with the hemihedral modifications described above. The Figures 74 and 76 represent crystals of two varieties of tartaric acid, which only differ from each other in the position of two hemihedral planes, and are so related that when placed before a mirror the image of one will be the exact representation of the other. The intermediate Figure, 75, represents the same crystal without these modifications. Since the solid angles are all similar, we should expect to find them all modified simultaneously; but, while on crystals of common tartaric acid only the two front angles (as the figure is drawn) are replaced, a variety of this acid has been discovered having similar crystals, whose back angles only are modified. Now, it is found that a solution of the common acid rotates the plane of polarization of a beam of light to the right, while a similar so-

Fig. 74.   Fig. 75.   Fig. 76.

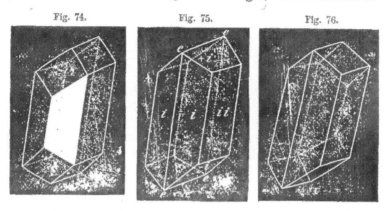

lution of this remarkable variety rotates the plane of polarization to the left. This difference of crystalline structure, moreover, is associated with certain small differences in the chemical qualities of the two bodies ; but the difference is so slight that we cannot but regard them as essentially the same substance, and the polarized light thus reveals to us the beginnings of a difference of structure, which, when more developed, manifests itself in the phenomena of isomerism. It is a remarkable fact, worthy of notice in this connection, that these two varieties of tartaric acid chemically combine with each other, forming a new substance called racemic acid.

Questions.

1. By what peculiar mode of symmetry may each of the six crystalline systems be distinguished ? How may crystals belonging to the 1st system be recognized ? How may crystals of the 2d, 3d, and 4th systems be distinguished by studying the distribution of the similar planes around their terminations or dominant axes ? By what peculiar distribution of similar planes may the crystals of the 5th and 6th systems be distinguished from all others ? State the system to which each of the crystals, represented by the various figures of this chapter, belongs, and give the reason of your answer in every case.

2. We find in the mineral kingdom two different octahedral forms of titanic acid belonging to the tetragonal system. In one of these forms the ratio of the unequal axes is 1 : 0.6442, in the other it is 1 : 1.7723. Can these forms belong to the same mineral substance ?

CHAPTER XV.

86. *General Principles.* — If in a vessel of dilute sulphuric acid (one part of acid to twenty of water) we suspend a plate of zinc and a plate of platinum, opposite to each other, and not in contact, we find that no chemical action whatever takes place, provided the zinc and the acid are perfectly pure. As soon, however, as the two plates are united by a copper wire, as represented in Fig. 77, chemical action immediately ensues, and the following phenomena may be observed. First: Bubbles of hydrogen gas are evolved from the surface of the platinum plate. Secondly: The zinc plate slowly dissolves, the zinc combining with the radical of the acid to form zincic sulphate, which is soluble in water. Lastly: A peculiar mode of atomic motion called electricity is transmitted through the copper wire, as may be made evident by appropriate means. If the connection between the plates is broken by dividing the conducting wire, the chemical action instantly stops, and the current of electricity ceases to flow; but, as soon as the connection is renewed, these phenomena again appear.

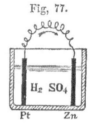

Fig, 77.

Similar effects may be produced by other combinations than the one just mentioned, provided only certain conditions are realized. In the first place, the two plates must consist of materials which are unequally affected by the liquid contained in the vessel, or cell; and the greater the difference in this respect, within manageable limits, the better. In the second place, the materials, both of plates and connector, must be conductors of electricity; and, lastly, the liquid must contain some substance for one of whose radicals the material of one of the plates has sufficient affinity to determine its decomposition under the conditions present. Such a combination is called a

Voltaic Cell. The mode of action of this instrument, which since its first discovery has been a subject of controversy, is very obscure, but the following theory gives an intelligible explanation of the general phenomena, and may serve a useful purpose until greater certainty can be attained.

Polarity. The phenomena of magnetism have made us familiar with a condition of matter we call *polarity*, in which bodies manifest a mode of energy known as *polar force.* The characteristics of polar force are as follows : —

1. *The energy is chiefly concentrated at opposite points of the polarized body called its poles.* 2. *The poles differ in kind in so far that, while unlike poles attract, like poles repel each other, and while unlike poles neutralize, like poles enhance each the other's effect.* 3. *With every pole is always associated its opposite, either on the same or a neighboring body, and in every polar system the sum* [1] *of the polar energies of one kind is exactly equal to that of those of the opposite kind.* 4. *A polarized body induces a similar state in all neighboring bodies susceptible of this condition, a pole of a given kind determining nearest to itself a pole of the opposite kind.* 5. *Induction is attended with no loss of energy in the inducing body, whose condition is frequently exalted by the reaction of the induced polarity.* 6. *Polarity appears of different kinds as well as in different degrees; the phenomena of magnetic, electrical, and chemical polarity, though similar in their general features, differing widely in their modes of manifestation.* 7. *Substances differ from each other, not only in their susceptibility to polarity of any given kind, but also in their power of retaining it.* [2]

The study of this class of phenomena has shown that the energy manifested by polarized bodies is always the effect of an attraction or repulsion between poles, and that whenever they appear to act on a neutral body the last is always first polarized by induction. Thus the nails attracted by a magnet or the straws attracted by an electrified stick of sealing-wax are all in a polar condition. A horseshoe magnet, with its keeper attached, affords a familiar illustration of these principles, which will aid us in explaining the more obscure phenomena of the Voltaic cell. The horseshoe magnet was originally polarized by induction, and since it is made of hardened steel retains its magnetism. The soft-iron keeper while in contact with the magnet is as truly polarized as the steel. It has a north pole in contact with the south pole, and a south pole in contact with the north pole of the magnet. But the moment it is withdrawn, all its polarity disappears. Again, while the magnetic circuit, as we call it, is closed, the keeper, by reacting on the source of power, greatly enhances the energy of the magnet, which will lift a much greater weight suspended from the keeper than it can when the two poles act separately.

Fig. 77 *a.*

Lastly, if we break a steel magnet, each of the parts will be found to be magnetized with poles relatively situated as is shown in Fig. 77 *a*, and since this relation of parts is pre-

---

[1] There may be several poles on the same mass of matter, and the polarity may be very irregularly distributed. Such is frequently the condition of the lode-stone or of a steel bar irregularly magnetized.

[2] For example, the metals iron, nickel, and cobalt, with a few of their compounds, are the only substances susceptible of magnetic polarity to a high degree. Again, a hardened steel bar retains the polar condition more or less permanently as in the common magnet, but soft iron loses its magnetic virtue the moment the inducing cause ceases to act.

served, however far we may carry the subdivision, we are led to the conclusion that the polarity is a quality inherent, not in the bar as a whole, but in the molecules of which it consists, and picture to ourselves as the condition of a magnetized bar that which is rudely represented in Fig. 77 b.

Fig. 77 b.

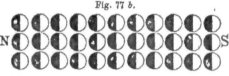

Theory of Chemical Polarity. As the molecules of iron may be magnetically polarized, we infer that the molecules of all substances are susceptible of different polar states, and we conceive that chemism[1] is a manifestation of a molecular condition, which we may distinguish as chemical polarity. It must be remembered, however, that we do not understand the cause of the differences in the various modes of polar energy; and in saying that the molecules of matter may be chemically polarized, we mean merely that they are susceptible of a condition whose general features have been indicated above. Our theory further assumes that with some molecules the polarity is inherent and therefore permanent, while with others it can only be induced by extraneous causes. These last, however, may become polarized by induction to as high or even a higher degree than the first, but the condition, like that of an electromagnet, is transient, varying with the inducing cause. Again, as every analogy would lead us to believe, our theory further assumes that different substances are susceptible of chemical polarity (whether it be inherent or assumed) to very different degrees, and that the susceptibility varies under different conditions. Lastly, our theory supposes that the chemical activity of a substance depends on the degree of polarity inherent in its molecules, and it refers the well-known active qualities of acids and alkalies to the fact that their peculiar constitution renders their molecules strongly polarized, while the inert qualities of most of the elementary substances is explained by the neutral condition which their homogeneous structures would naturally produce in their molecules. Thus, for example, we suppose that every molecule of sulphuric acid, $H_2 SO_4$, or of hydrochloric acid, H-Cl, or of sodic hydrate, H-NaO, is naturally polarized, while on the other hand the molecules of zinc, Zn, of magnesium, Mg, of hydrogen, H-H, and of oxygen, O=O, are all normally neutral. As soon, however, as we place zinc in contact with dilute sulphuric acid, the metallic molecules become polarized by induction to the degree of which they are susceptible under the influence of this acid. A powerful attraction is thus developed and a familiar chemical change is the result. If magnesium is treated in a similar way, the action is more energetic, because, as we suppose, the molecules of this metal are susceptible of a higher degree of polarity, and the force developed is therefore proportionally stronger. On the other hand, with metallic copper there is no action under the same conditions, because the molecules of the metal do not acquire a sufficient degree of polarity to determine chemical change.

While, however, the molecular structure appears to be the most important, it is evidently by no means the only cause which determines chemical polarity. The highly active qualities of the alkaline metals and of the chlorine group of elementary substances indicate that their molecules, although apparently homogeneous in structure, must be permanently polarized. Moreover, the fact that a high degree of energy is developed in many of the elementary substances, as in oxygen gas, by a simple elevation of temperature, and the general principle that heat hastens chem-

---

[1] This term is synonymous with the old term *chemical affinity*, to which it is on many accounts to be preferred.

ical changes, seem to indicate that the polar condition may be frequently produced by this agent alone. So also the process of photography is most simply explained by the theory that the sun's rays excite a similar condition in the silver compounds on the surface of the sensitive plate, and the effect of continuous electrical discharges in converting oxygen gas into that peculiar active modification of this substance called ozone, may be regarded as a direct result of their polarizing power.

Theory of Electricity. The study of the phenomena of optics has led physicists to the conclusion that there exists throughout space, filling not only the interplanetary but also the intermolecular spaces, a highly attenuated but at the same time wonderfully elastic medium which is called the ether. (92). Again, the phenomena of heat indicate that the molecular forces have an energy which is adequate to cope with this very great elasticity; and we can conceive that they condense around these molecules greater or less quantities of this ether, thus giving to each a distinct atmosphere, but one which merges into that universally diffused medium in which molecule and planet alike float. Now our theory supposes that electrical phenomena are caused by disturbances in the composition of these ethereal atmospheres. The electrical ether,[1] as we assume, consists of two separable materials, which, adopting names long used in science, we will call positive and negative or vitreous and resinous electricities. In all the terrestrial region of the solar system at least these electricities are blended in certain definite proportions, like the constituents of the earth's atmosphere, but by various causes they may become separated and more or less isolated either on the same or on different molecules. Whenever this takes place, the two electricities tend to flow together until the normal condition is restored in accordance with the law of diffusion; but the force of diffusion in these molecular atmospheres is vastly greater and the process vastly more rapid than it is in the terrestrial atmosphere, because the elasticity of the ether so greatly exceeds that of the air. This being granted, our theory further supposes that every process of electrical excitement causes a separation of the constituents of the ether, and that an electrified body is one on whose molecules one or the other of the two electricities is to a greater or less degree isolated; and again, that the familiar phenomena of attraction and repulsion between electrified bodies are the effects of pressure caused by the diffusive force; and lastly, that an electrical current consists in an actual transfer of the ethereal material between the molecules of the conductor. We have not space, however, to follow out the theory into its mechanical details, and we must content ourselves with applying it to the explanation of the phenomena of the Voltaic cell.

Theory of Voltaic Cell. In studying chemical reactions we have thus far overlooked the molecular atmospheres; but it is evident that, if the above theory is correct, they must enter as important factors into every chemical change. This theory assumes that the condition of the atmosphere is intimately connected with that of the molecule, although in what way it does not attempt to explain. When the molecule is polarized, the two electricities are more or less fully separated and isolated around the molecular poles; and if the polarity is inherent this condition is permanent. If, however, the polar state is induced, the neutral condition is restored as soon as the inducing force ceases to act. Let us study now from this new point of view the familiar reaction of sulphuric acid on zinc referred to above.

$$\mathbf{Zn} + (H_2SO_4 + Aq) = (ZnSO_4 + Aq) + \boxed{H}\cdot\boxed{H}.$$

[1] As it is not important for our present purpose to inquire whether the electrical ether is identical or only is mingled with the luminiferous ether, this question is here left in abeyance.

The molecule H_2SO_4 is inherently polarized and induces at once a similar condition in the normally neutral molecule Zn. At the poles of each of these molecules we have therefore free electricity. When now Zn replaces H_2 in H_2SO_4 it takes with it into its new combination only free positive electricity, leaving behind the corresponding negative electricity on the adjacent molecule of zinc. Meanwhile the hydrogen atoms thus liberated bring with them to form the molecule H-H only positive electricity. We have thus set free on opposite molecules at the same time equivalent quantities of the two electricities, and the equilibrium being thus disturbed, an interchange at once takes place between them, by which the normal condition of their atmospheres is restored. In order to make this point clearer, we have endeavored to illustrate the reaction in the following diagram : —

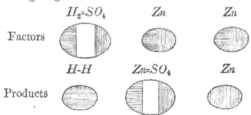

Factors H_2-SO_4 Zn Zn

Products H-H Zn-SO_4 Zn

This diagram, however, indicates very imperfectly the conception we have formed of the process, and there are certain quantitative relations between the parts which must not be overlooked, although they can be as yet but very imperfectly understood. We should naturally infer that the quantity of ethereal atmosphere would be determined in every case by the mass of the molecule, but the quantities of free electricities separated from this atmosphere under different conditions seem to depend on the atomicities of the radicals of which the molecule consists. At least, the facts indicate that the amount of free electricity which any group of atoms takes out of the molecule from which it is parted is exactly measured by the number of atomic bonds thus broken. Hence in our diagram the amount of positive electricity which H_2 takes from H_2SO_4 is a definite quantity and exactly equal to that which Zn carries in to take its place. Moreover, this last quantity came originally, not from one, but from two zinc molecules, and the chemical metathesis between H_2 and Zn was accompanied by an interchange of electricities between the zinc molecules, by which all the free positive electricity passed to the one which entered into combination, and all the free negative electricity to the one left behind ; and further, as already stated, this free negative electricity is equivalent to the free positive electricity on the hydrogen molecule formed at the same time.

If, as in the usual form of the reaction we have been studying, the acid sufficiently diluted is poured upon clippings of sheet zinc, it is found that, although the mass of the metal is polarized throughout, the polarity is very irregularly distributed. A multitude of negative polar points are formed upon the surface, from which bubbles of hydrogen gas are evolved, and around these are spaces positively polarized where the metal enters into solution. According to our theory, when the molecules of metal replace the atoms of hydrogen they take with them positive electrical charges, leaving behind equivalent negative charges, and these are transmitted from molecule to molecule of the metal, until they reach one of the negative polar points above mentioned. It is there that the interchange takes place with the positive charges on the molecules of hydrogen gas as rapidly as these are formed. The polar points just referred to appear to be determined by variations of texture or bits of impurity in the metal, and this is the reason that the general polarity of the mass is so irregularly distributed. If the metal is absolutely pure and uniform in texture, or if the surface of the common sheet zinc is previously amalgamated, there is no local action, and the zinc will not dissolve unless we fasten to the metal a piece of some material less readily acted on by the acid, which must be also a conductor of electricity. But when this is done, the whole mass becomes polarized uniformly throughout, after the pattern represented in Fig. 77 b. Of this system the surface of the zinc forms the positive pole, and the surface of the second material the negative pole. Chemical action ensues as before, and while zinc dissolves at the positive pole, hydrogen gas is evolved from the negative pole.

We are now prepared to understand the conditions in the Voltaic cell represented in Fig. 77. Here we have a plate of zinc and a plate of platinum, united by a metallic wire and dipping together into the acid liquid, with their surfaces opposed to each other and not touching. Here, also, the two plates with the conductor form one uniformly polarized system, of which the surface of the zinc is the positive and the surface of the platinum the negative pole. The polarity of this arrangement is induced by the action of the acid, whose molecules are inherently polarized.

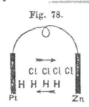

Fig. 78.

Moreover, under these conditions the mass of acid between the plates forms also a uniformly polarized system, the molecules arranging themselves in polar lines as represented in Fig. 78. We may compare the combination thus formed to a magnetic circuit, consisting of a horseshoe magnet and its armature, or rather of a bar magnet with a horseshoe armature. The inherently polarized liquid corresponds to the permanent magnet, the system of metallic plates to the armature with its induced polarity. Now just as in the magnetic circuit we have a strong attractive force at the surfaces where the armature touches the magnet, so in the Voltaic circuit we have a powerful force exerted at each of the corresponding surfaces. A mutual attraction is exerted between the hydrogen end of the acid molecule and the platinum surface on one side, and the sulphion end[1] of the same molecules and the zinc surface on the other side. These forces are adequate to decompose the acid. The sulphion atoms enter into union with the zinc to form zincic sulphate, which dissolves in the acid liquid, while the hydrogen atoms combine with each other to form molecules of hydrogen gas, which collects in bubbles that rise along the surface of the platinum plate. Meanwhile, every molecule of zinc which enters into solution leaves behind a charge of negative electricity, and every molecule of hydrogen gas carries to the surface of the platinum plate a charge of positive electricity, and these opposite charges flow together through the conductor, forming what we call an electrical current, which tends to restore the electrical equilibrium that the chemical action destroys.

Electrical Current. According to our theory an electrical current consists in the last analysis in the transfer of the ethereal medium between neighboring molecules, the one giving up a quantity of positive electricity and receiving an equivalent portion of negative electricity in its stead. This transfer is supposed to take place at the surface of contact between the molecular atmospheres by a process similar to diffusion (58), and implies an oscillation of the molecules by which each is brought alternately in near proximity to its neighbors on either side. The oscillatory motion is maintained by the alternate attractions and repulsions, which the varying phases of the molecules necessarily determine, and is a most important

---

[1] For the sake of simplicity we have represented in the figures molecules of H-Cl instead of H_2-SO_4, but the theory applies equally to both.

element of the electrical current. It can easily be imitated by suspending with silk threads small metallic balls between two brass knobs connected with the conductors of an electrical machine, so that they hang near but at equally small distances from each other on the same line. The continuous oscillation of these balls, while the machine is in action, illustrates what we conceive to be the mode of motion in the molecules of a conductor.

If the above explanation is correct, it is obvious that an electrical current in a solid conductor has two distinct elements: first, an oscillatory motion of the molecules; secondly, a mutual transfer of the two modifications of the electrical ether from molecule to molecule, along the lines uniting the opposite poles of the polar system, which every current implies. But in the acid liquid, which not only originates the current but also forms a part of the circuit, the relations are somewhat different. There the transfer of the two electricities is attended with a decomposition of the acid molecules, and the opposed atoms, each bearing its charge of electricity, actually travel from one plate to the other. Thus we have the singular phenomenon produced of two coexisting atomic currents throughout the mass of the liquid, a stream of sulphion atoms constantly setting towards the zinc plate, and a stream of hydrogen atoms flowing in the opposite direction in the same space towards the platinum plate. The result is produced by a constant metathesis along the whole line of molecules between the two plates, so that for every atom of sulphion which enters into union with the zinc a double atom or molecule of hydrogen is set free at the face of the platinum plate.

As our theory shows, the opposite currents of atoms in the liquid and the opposite currents of electricity in the solid conductor are mutually dependent. Hence, if the connection is broken so that the motion can no longer be transmitted through the conductor, the motion in the liquid itself ceases; and if by any means the motion through the conductor is checked the motion of the atoms in the liquid is reduced to the same extent. The two currents, which, as we have seen, are continuous throughout the whole circuit, take the names of the two kinds of electricity which they respectively carry; that flowing into the conducting wire from the platinum, or inactive plate, being called the positive current, and that from the zinc, or active plate, the negative current. Reasoning from certain mechanical phenomena, the physicists originally concluded that the electrical current flowed in but one direction, that is, through the conducting wire from the platinum plate to the zinc, and from the zinc plate through the liquid back again to the platinum; and now, when the direction of the current is spoken of, it is this direction, that of the positive current, which is always meant.

87. *Electrical Conducting Power or Resistance.*— Different materials transmit the electric current with very different degrees of facility; for while in some this peculiar form of molecular motion is easily maintained, in others the molecules yield to it only with difficulty, and many substances seem not to be susceptible of it. The conducting powers of different metallic wires have been very carefully studied, and some of the most trustworthy results are collected in the following table. Silver is the best conductor known, and, assuming that a silver wire of definite size and 100 centimetres long is taken as the standard, the number opposite the name of each metal is the length in centimetres of a wire made of this metal, and of the same size

as the first, which will oppose the same resistance to the transmission of the current. The second column gives the relative resistances of wires of the same materials when of equal size and of equal lengths. The relative or *specific resistances* of two such wires must evidently be inversely proportional to their conducting powers, and thus the numbers of the second column are easily calculated from those of the first. For the results collated in this table we are indebted to the careful investigations of Professor Matthiessen.

Pure Metals.		Conducting Power.		Specific Resistance.	
		At 0°.	At 100°.	At 0°.	At 100°.
Silver	(*hard drawn*)	100.00	71.56	1.000	1.397
Copper	(*hard drawn*)	99.95	70.27	1.0005	1.423
Gold	(*hard drawn*)	77.96	55.90	1.283	1.788
Zinc		29.02	20.67	3.445	4.838
Cadmium		23.72	16.77	4.216	5.964
Cobalt		17.22		5.808	
Iron	(*hard drawn*)	16.81		5.948	
Nickel		13.11		7.628	
Tin		12.36	8.67	8.091	11.53
Thallium		9.16		10.92	
Lead		8.32	5.86	12.02	17.06
Arsenic		4.76	3.33	21.01	30.03
Antimony		4.62	3.26	21.65	30.68
Bismuth		1.245	0.878	80.34	113.9

Commercial Metals.	C. P.	Sp. R.	C°.	Commercial Metals.	C. P.	Sp. R.	C°.
Copper	77.43	1.291	18.8	Iron	14.44	6.924	20.4
Sodium	37.43	2.672	21.7	Palladium	12.64	7.911	17.2
Aluminum	33.76	2.962	19.5	Platinum	10.53	9.497	20.7
Magnesium	25.47	3.926	17.0	Strontium	6.71	14.90	20.5
Calcium	22.14	4.516	16.8	Mercury	1.63	61.35	22.8
Potassium	20.85	4.795	20.4	Tellurium	0.00077	129,800	19.6
Lithium	19.00	5.262	20.0	Red Phosphorus	0.00000123	81,300,000	24.0

If, next, we compare wires of the same material, but of different sizes, we find that the resistance increases as the length, and diminishes as the area, of the section. Moreover, if we adopt some absolute standard of resistance, like that selected by the English physicists, we can easily express the resistance of any given conductor in terms of this unit. It must be remembered, however, in making such comparisons, that the resistance varies with the temperature, and also that the conducting power of the same metal is materially influenced both by its physical condition and by the presence of impurities.

88. *Ohm's Law.* — The first effect of the chemical forces in the cell of an electrical combination is to marshal the dissimilar atoms of the active liquid between the plates into lines, which at once begin to move in parallel columns, but in opposite directions (Fig. 78). Moreover, each one of these lines of *moving* atoms is continued by a corresponding line of *oscillating* atoms in the conducting wire, and thus is formed a continuous circuit returning upon itself. The union of all the *lines of force* in the two opposite coexisting streams constitutes in any case the electrical current, and the different parts of this continuous chain are so related that *the total amount of motion is always the same at every point on the circuit,* and *no more lines of moving atoms form in the liquid between the plates than can be continued through the oscillating atoms of the solid conductors.*

If we adopt this theory, it is obvious that the strength of any electrical current must depend, — first, on the number of continuous lines of force, and secondly, on the strength of the polarity transmitted through each of these channels. Of these two elements, the first is determined solely by the total resistance which the various parts of the circuit oppose to the electrical motion, and the greater this resistance the less will be the number of the lines of force. The second element is determined by the value of the resultants of all the polar forces acting in any combination, which draw the dissimilar atoms towards the opposite plates, — a value which depends solely on *the chemical relations of the materials of the plates to that of the active liquid,* and is what is called the *electromotive force* of the combination, a quantity we will represent by E.

It appears, then, from the above analysis, that an electrical current is a continuous chain, which is sustained in a regulated and equable motion in all its parts by the chemical activity in the cell, and that the strength of this current at any point of the chain must be directly proportional to the electromotive force, and inversely proportional to the sum of the resistances throughout the circuit. If, then, we represent the resistance in the conducting wire by r, the resistance of the liquid between the plates of the cell by R,[1] and also the strength of the current by C, we shall have, in every case,

$$C = \frac{E}{R + r} \qquad [62]$$

1 The resistance of any circuit may be conveniently divided into two parts,

The quantities C, R, r, and E may all be accurately measured, and stand in each case for a certain number of arbitrary units, whose relations will hereafter be stated.

89. *Electromotive Force and Strength of Current.* — It would seem at first sight as if the strength of an electric current might be increased by simply enlarging the size of the plates in the combination employed, and obviously the number of *possible* lines of moving atoms which could be marshalled in the liquid between the plates would thus be increased; but, as has been stated, the parts of the circuit are so intimately connected that no greater number of lines of atoms can form between the plates than can be continued through the whole circuit, and practically there may be formed between the smallest plates a vastly greater number of atomic lines than can be continued through any conductor, however good its quality or however ample its size. Hence it is, that by increasing the size of the plates we multiply the lines of force only in so far as we thereby lessen the resistance in the liquid part of the circuit. We thus simply lessen the value of R in Ohm's formula [62]; but if this value is already small as compared with r, that is, if the resistance in the cell is small compared with that in the conductor, no material gain in the power of the current, or in the value of C, will result. On the other hand, if the exterior resistance, r, is small, or nearly nothing, as when the plates are connected by a thick metallic conductor, then the value of C will increase in very nearly the same proportion as the size of the plates is enlarged, and the value of R, in consequence, diminished. Under these conditions, the number of lines of moving atoms is greatly multiplied, and we obtain a current of very great volume, but only flowing with the limited force which the single cell is capable of maintaining. Such a current has but little power of overcoming obstacles; and if we attempt to condense it by using a smaller conductor, we reduce, as has been said, the chemical action which keeps the whole in motion, and thus lessen the volume of the flow. This is generally expressed by saying

first, the resistance of the conducting wire, and secondly, the resistance of the liquid portion of the circuit between the two plates of the cell. The resistance of the solid conductor may be readily estimated on the principles stated in the last section, and the resistance of liquid may be measured in a similar way. The last depends, — 1. On the conducting power of the liquid; 2. On the length of the liquid circuit, which is determined by the distance apart of the plates; 3. On the area of the section of the liquid conductor, which is determined by the size of the plates; and, 4. On the temperature.

that the current has large *quantity*, but small *intensity*, or more properly, *electromotive power*.

It must now be obvious from the theory, that we cannot increase effectively the intensity of a current (its power of overcoming obstacles) without in some way increasing the chemical activity, or, in other words, the electro-motive force of the combination employed, and Ohm's formula leads to the same result. If the value of r in our formula is very large as compared with R, we cannot increase it still farther without lessening the total value, C, unless at the same time we increase the value of E. Now, this electro-motive force may be, to a certain extent, increased by using a more active combination; but the limit in this direction is soon reached, and the construction of the cell which has been found practically to be the most efficient will be described below.

We can, however, increase the effective electro-motive force to almost any extent by using a number of cells, and coupling them together in the manner represented by Fig. 79, the platinum plate of the first cell being united by a large metallic connector to the zinc plate of the second, and so on through the line, until finally the external conductor establishes a connection between the platinum plate of the last cell and the zinc plate of the first. Such a combination as this is called a Galvanic or Voltaic[1] battery, and the current which flows through such a combination has a vastly greater power of overcoming resistance than that of any single cell, however large.

The increased effect obtained with such a combination will be easily understood, when it is remembered that each of the innumerable closed chains of moving molecules now extends through the whole combination, and that all its parts move in the same close mutual dependence as be-

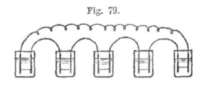

Fig. 79.

fore. But whereas with a single cell the motion throughout any single chain of molecules is sustained by the chemical energy at only one point, it is here reinforced at several points;

[1] From the names of Galvani and Volta, two Italian physicists, who first investigated this class of phenomena.

and the polar energy at any point of the circuit is the effect of the induction of the acid molecules between each pair of plates concurring with that produced by the similar molecules between every other pair. The electro-motive power is then increased in proportion to the number of cells; and the effect on the current would be increased in the same proportion, were it not for the fact that the current must keep in motion a greater mass of liquid, and hence the resistance is increased at the same time. The value of this resistance, however, is easily estimated, since it is directly proportional to the distance through which the current has to flow in the liquid; and hence, if the liquid is the same in all the cells, and the plates are at the same distance apart in each, the liquid resistance will be n times as great in a combination of n cells as it is in one. Moreover, since the effective electro-motive force is n times as great also, while the external resistance remains unchanged, the strength of the current from such a combination will still be expressed by formula [62] slightly modified.

$$C = \frac{nE}{nR + r} \qquad [63]$$

This formula shows at once, that, when the exterior resistance is very small, or nothing, very little or no gain will result from increasing the number of cells, for the ratio of nE to nR is the same as that of E to R; and, under such conditions, in order to increase the strength of the current, we must increase the surface of the plates. If, on the contrary, the exterior resistance is very large, the formula shows that great gain will result from increasing the number of the cells, and that little or no advantage will accrue from enlarging the surface of the plates. Moreover, the formula enables us in any case to determine what proportion the number of cells should bear to the size of the plates in order to obtain the full effect of any battery in doing a given work; and in the numerous applications of electricity in the arts we find abundant illustrations of the principles it involves. The methods used in finding the values of the quantities represented in the formula lie beyond the scope of this work, and for such information the student is referred to works on Physics.

90. *Constructions of Cells.* — It is found practically that the

simple combination of plates and acid first described must be slightly modified in order to obtain the best results.

In the first place, both the zinc and sulphuric acid of commerce contain impurities, which give rise to what is called local action, and cause the zinc to dissolve in the acid when the battery is not in action. Fortunately, however, it has been found that such local action can be wholly prevented by carefully amalgamating the surface of the zinc and filtering the acidulated water.

The mercury on the surface of the zinc plates acts as a solvent, and gives a certain freedom of motion to the particles of the metal. These, by the action of the polar forces, are brought to the surface of the plate, while the impurities are forced back towards the interior, so that the plate constantly exposes a surface of pure zinc to the action of the acid.

By filtering we remove the particles of plumbic sulphate which remain floating in the sulphuric acid for a long time after it has been diluted with water, and which, when deposited on the surface of the zinc, become points of local action, even when the plates have been carefully amalgamated.

In the second place, the continued action of the simple combination first described develops conditions which soon greatly impair, and at last wholly destroy, its efficiency.

The hydrogen gas, which by the action of the current is evolved at the platinum plate, adheres strongly to its surface, and with its powerful affinities draws back the lines of atoms moving towards the zinc plate, and thus diminishes the effective electro-motive force. Moreover, after the battery has been working for some time, the water becomes charged with zincic sulphate ; and then the zinc, following the course of the hydrogen, is also deposited on the surface of the platinum, which after a while becomes, to all intents and purposes, a second zinc plate, and then, of course, the electric current ceases.

Both of these difficulties, however, have also been surmounted by a very simple means discovered by Mr. Grove, of London. The Grove cell, Fig. 80, consists of a circular plate of zinc well amalgamated on its surface, and immersed in a glass jar containing dilute sulphuric acid. Within the zinc cylinder is placed a cylindrical vessel of much smaller diameter, made of porous earthenware, and filled with the strongest nitric acid, and in this hangs the plate of platinum, Fig. 81. The walls of

Fig. 80.

Fig. 81.

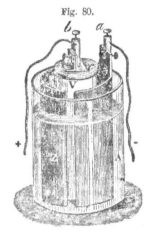

the porous cell allow both the hydrogen and the zinc atoms to
pass freely on their way to the platinum plate; but the moment
they reach the nitric acid they are at once oxidized, and thus
the surface of the platinum is kept clean, and the cell in condition to exert its maximum electro-motive power.   In this combination we may substitute for the plate of platinum a plate
of dense coke, such as forms in the interior of the gas retorts,
which is very much cheaper, and enables us to construct large
cells at a moderate cost.   The use of gas coke was first suggested by Professor Bunsen of Heidelberg, and the cell so
constructed generally bears his name.   The Bunsen cell, such
as is represented in Fig. 82, is exceedingly well adapted for use

Fig. 82.

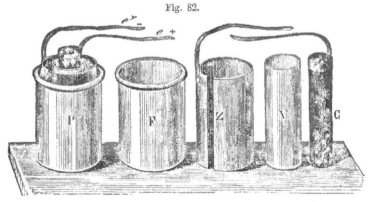

in the laboratory.   These cells are usually made of nearly a uniform size, the zinc cylinders being about 8 c. m. in diameter by 22 c. m. high, and they are frequently referred to as a rough standard of electrical power. They may be united so as to produce effects either of intensity or of quantity. The intensity effects are obtained in the manner already described (see Fig. 79), and the quantity effects are obtained with equal readiness; since by attaching the zinc of several cells to the same metallic conductor, and the corresponding coke plates to a similar conductor, we have the equivalent of one cell with large plates. Many other forms of battery, differing in more or less important details from those here described, and adapted to special applications of electricity, are used in the arts, and are fully described in the larger works on physics.

91. *Electrolysis.* — As our theory indicates, the electrical current has the remarkable power of imparting to the unlike atoms of almost all compound bodies motion in opposite directions, like that in the battery cell itself, and this, too, at whatever point in the circuit they may be introduced. The galvanic battery thus becomes a most potent agent in producing chemical decompositions, and it is in consequence of this fact that the theory of the instrument fills such an important place in the philosophy of chemistry.

If we break the metallic conductor at any point of a closed circuit, the two ends, which in chemical experiments we usually arm with platinum plates,[1] are called poles. The end connected with the platinum or coke plate, from which the positive current is assumed to flow, is called the *positive pole*, and the end connected with the zinc plate, from which the negative current flows, is called the *negative pole*. Let us assume that Fig. 83 represents the two platinum poles dipping in a solution of hydrochloric acid in water, which thus becomes a part of the circuit. The moment the circuit is thus closed, the *H* and *Cl* atoms begin to travel in opposite directions, just as in the battery cell below. The hydrogen atoms move *with the positive current* towards the negative pole, and hydrogen gas is disengaged from the surface of

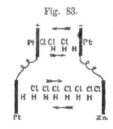

Fig. 83.

---

[1] We use platinum plates because this metal does not readily enter into combination with the ordinary chemical agents.

the negative plate, while the chlorine atoms move *with the negative current* towards the positive pole, and chlorine gas is evolved from the surface of the positive plate. Moreover, it will be noticed that each kind of atoms moves in the same direction on the closed circuit, that is, follows the course of the same current, both in the battery cell below and in the decomposing cell above; and wherever we break the circuit, and at as many places as we may break it, the same phenomena may be produced, provided only that our battery has sufficient power to overcome the resistance.thus introduced.

If next we dip the poles in water, the atoms of the water will be set moving, as shown in Fig. 84; hydrogen gas escaping as before from the negative pole, and oxygen gas from the positive. We find, however, that pure water opposes a very great resistance to the motion of the current; and, unless the current has great intensity, the effects obtained are inconsider

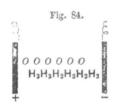

Fig. 84.

able. But if we mix with the water a little sulphuric acid, the decomposition at once becomes very rapid; but then it is the atoms of the sulphuric acid, and not those of the water, which are set in motion. The molecule H_2SO_4 divides into H_2 and SO_4; the hydrogen atoms moving in the usual direction, and the atoms of SO_4 in the opposite direction. As soon, however, as the last are set free at the positive pole, they come in contact with water, which they immediately decompose, $2H_2O + 2SO_4 = 2H_2SO_4 + O = O$, and the oxygen gas thus generated escapes from the face of the platinum plate. Thus the result is the same as if water were directly decomposed, but the actual process is quite different.

So also in many other cases of electrolysis, — as these decompositions by the electrical current are called, — the process is complicated by the reaction of the water, which is the usual medium employed in the experiments. Thus, if we interpose between the poles a solution of common salt, *Na Cl*, the chlorine atoms move towards the positive pole, and chlorine gas is there evolved as in the first example. The sodium atoms move also, but in the opposite direction. As soon, however, as they are set free at the negative pole, they decompose the water present; hydrogen gas is formed, which escapes in bubbles from the platinum plate, while sodic hydrate (caustic soda) remains in solution,

$$2H_2O + 2Na = 2H, Na\text{-}O + H\text{-}H.$$

We add but one other example, which illustrates a very important application of these principles in the arts. We assume, in Fig. 85, that the positive pole is armed with a plate of copper, and that to the negative pole has been fastened a mould of some medallion we wish to copy, the surface of which, at least, is a good conductor. We

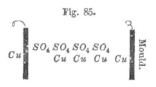

Fig. 85.

assume further that both copper plate and mould are suspended in a solution of sulphate of copper, $Cu\text{=}SO_4$. In this case the atoms of the compound are set in motion as before. Those of copper accumulate on the surface of the mould ; and at last the coating will attain such thickness that it can be removed, furnishing an exact copy of the original medallion. Meanwhile the atoms of SO_4 have found at the positive pole a mass of copper, with whose atoms they have combined ; and thus fresh sulphate of copper has been formed, and the solution replenished. The process has in effect consisted in a transfer of metal from the copper plate to the medallion ; and, by using appropriate solvents, silver and gold can be transferred and deposited in the same way.

In all these processes of electrolysis, one remarkable fact has been observed, which has a very important bearing on the theory of the battery. If in any given circuit we introduce a number of decomposing cells, containing acidulated water, we find that in a given time exactly the same amount of gas is evolved in each ; thus proving, what we have thus far assumed, that the moving power is absolutely the same at all points on the circuit. Moreover, the amount of gas which is evolved from such a decomposing cell in the unit of time is an accurate measure of the strength of the current actually flowing in any circuit, and this mode of measuring the quantity of an electrical current is constantly used.

We should infer from the facts already stated, and the principle has been confirmed by the most careful experiments, that the chemical changes which may take place at different points of the same closed circuit are always the exact equivalents of each other. If, for example, we have a series of Grove's cells, arranged as in Fig. 79, and interpose in the external circuit two decomposing cells, as in Figs. 84 and 85, we shall find (provided there is no local action) that the weight of zinc dissolved in each of the five Grove's cells is the exact *chemical equivalent*, (26) not only of the weight of hydrogen gas evolved from the first decomposing cell, but also of the weight of metallic copper deposited on the mould in the second. For every 63.4 grammes of copper deposited, 2 grammes of hydrogen are evolved, and 65.2 grammes of zinc are dissolved in *each* cell of the battery. If there is also local action in the cells, the chemical change thus induced is added to the normal effect of the battery-current.

This important principle (discovered by Faraday) is in entire harmony with the theory of electricity developed in this chapter. In the single Voltaic cell, Fig. 77, there is but one source of free electricity, which all flows through the same conductor, In a Voltaic battery, Fig. 79, there are as many sources of free electricity as there are separate cells; but only the free electricity received on the end plates flows through the longer conductor,[1] for that received on the intermediate plates becomes neutralized in the shorter conductors[1] uniting the cells. In either case, if a liquid forms a part of the principal conductor, as in Fig. 83, then the molecules of the liquid decomposed by the current become an additional source of electricity, and the currents flowing from the two ends of the battery are neutralized by the charges of electricity, which the atoms liberated from the electrolyte[2] bring with them to either electrode.[2] Thus, in Fig. 83, the positive electricity flowing from the inactive plate of the battery is neutralized by the negative electricity, which the chlorine atoms yield, and the negative electricity from the active plate of the battery by the positive electricity, which the hydrogen atoms yield. Now, since, according to our theory, the strength of a current is necessarily the same at all points of a

---

[1] It will be noticed that each of the five conductors in Fig. 79 sustains the same relations to the battery as a whole.

[2] The liquid submitted to electrolysis is frequently called an *electrolyte*, and the inactive poles dipping into the liquid are also called *electrodes*.

continuous circuit, however extended, and since the amount of
electricity set free in the decomposing cell, as in the battery
cells, must be proportional to the number of atomic bonds
broken (86), it is evident that it would require, for example,
twice as many hydrogen as copper atoms, liberated on the face
of an electrode in a given time, to supply the same current, and
this is equivalent to the principle stated above.

The examples which have been given are sufficient to illustrate the remarkable power which the electric current possesses
of setting in motion the atoms of compound bodies.   Innumerable experiments have shown that, in reference to their relations to the current, the atoms, both simple and compound, may
be divided into two great classes : first, those which travel on
the line of the circuit in the direction of the positive current
and follow in the lead of the hydrogen atoms ; and, secondly,
those which follow the lead of the chlorine atoms, and move in
the opposite direction with the negative current.   The first
class of atoms, or radicals, we call *positive ;* and the second class,
negative.

The opposition in qualities of the chemical atoms, which the
study of these electrical phenomena has revealed, is, in many
cases at least, relative, and not absolute.   For, while there are
some atoms which always manifest the same character, there
are others which appear in some associations positive, and in
other associations negative.   To such an extent is this true,
that the electrical relations of the atoms are best shown by
grouping the elements in series, which may be so arranged that
each member of the series shall be electro-positive when in
combination with those elements which follow it, and electro-
negative when combined with those which precede it.

NOTE. — Questions and problems bearing on this chapter will
be found in the Appendix, page 567.

CHAPTER XVI.

RELATIONS OF THE ATOMS TO LIGHT.

92. *Light a Mode of Atomic Motion.* — It has already been intimated (§ 61, note), that the phenomena of vision are the effects of an atomic motion transmitted from some luminous body to the eye through continuous lines of material particles, and such lines we call rays of light. This motion may originate with the atoms of *various* substances; but in order to explain its transmission, we are obliged to assume the existence of a medium filling all space, of extreme tenuity, and yet having an elasticity sufficiently great to transmit the luminous pulsations with the incredible velocity of 186,000 miles in a second of time. This medium we call the ether, but of its existence we have no definite knowledge except that obtained through the phenomena of light themselves, and these require assumptions in regard to the constitution of the ethereal medium which are not realized even approximately in the ordinary forms of matter; for while the assumed medium must be vastly less dense than hydrogen, its elasticity must surpass that of steel.

According to the undulatory theory, motion is transmitted from particle to particle along the line of each luminous wave very much in the same way that it passes along the line of ivory balls in the well-known experiment of mechanics. The ethereal atoms are thus thrown into waves, and the order of the phenomena is similar to that with which all are familiar in the grosser forms of wave motion. But in this connection we have no occasion to dwell on the mechanical conditions attending the transmission of the motion. The motion itself may be best conceived as an oscillation of each ether particle in a plane perpendicular to the direction of the ray, not necessarily, however, in a straight line; for the orbit of the oscillating molecule may be either a straight line, an ellipse, or a circle, as the case may be.   Such oscillations may evidently differ both as regards their amplitude and their duration, and on these fundamental elements depend two important differences in the effect of the motion on the organs of vision, viz. intensity and quality, or brilliancy and color.

If our theory is correct, it is obvious that the intensity of the luminous impression must depend upon the force of the atomic blows which are transmitted to the optic nerves, and it is also evident that this force must be proportional to the square of the velocity of the oscillating atoms, or what amounts to the same thing, to the square of the amplitude of the oscillation; assuming, of course, that the oscillations are isochronous.

The connection of color with the time of oscillation is not so obvious, and why it is that the waves of ether beating with greater or less rapidity on the retina should produce such sensations as those of violet, blue, yellow, or red, the physiologist is wholly unable to explain.   We have, however, an analogous phenomenon in sound, for musical notes are simply the effects of waves of air beating in a similar way on the auditory nerves; and, as is well known, the greater the frequency of the beats, or, in other words, the more rapid the oscillations of the aerial molecules, the higher is the pitch of the note.   Red color corresponds to low, and violet to high notes of music, and, the gradations of color between these extremes, passing through various shades of orange, yellow, green, blue, and indigo, correspond to the well-known gradations of musical pitch.

From well-established data we are able to calculate the rapidity of the oscillations which produce the different sensations of color, and also to estimate the corresponding lengths of the ether waves, and the following table contains the results.   It must be understood, however, that these numbers merely correspond to a few shades of color definitely marked on the solar spectrum by certain dark lines hereafter to be mentioned; and that equally definite values may be assigned to the infinite number of intermediate shades which intervene between these arbitrary subdivisions of the chromatic scale.

Color.	Number of waves or oscillations in one second.		Length of waves in fractions of a millimetre.	
Red	477	million million.	650	millionths.
Orange	506	" "	609	"
Yellow	535	" "	576	"
Green	577	" "	536	"
Blue	622	" "	498	"
Indigo	658	" "	470	"
Violet	699	" "	442	"

93. *Natural Colors.* — It follows, as a necessary consequence of the fundamental laws of mechanics, that an oscillating molecule can only transmit to its neighbor motion which is isochronous with its own. Hence a single ray of light can only produce a definite effect of color, and this quality of the ray will be preserved however far the motion may travel. A beam of light is simply a bundle of rays, and if the motion is isochronous in all its parts, that is, if the beam consists only of rays of one shade of color, such a beam will produce the simplest chromatic sensation possible, — that of a pure color. If, however, the beam contains rays of different colors, we shall have a more complex effect, and the infinite variety of natural tints are thus produced. When, lastly, the beam contains rays of all the colors mingled in due proportion, we receive an impression in which no single color predominates, and this we call white light.

The colors of natural objects, whether inherent or imparted by various dyes, are simply effects upon the retina produced by the beam after it has been reflected from the surface or transmitted through the mass of the body, and the peculiar chromatic effects are due to the unequal proportions in which the different colored rays are thus absorbed. The color reflected, and that absorbed or transmitted, are always complementary to each other, and if mingled they would reproduce white. It is obvious, moreover, that no beam of light, however modified by reflection or transmission, could produce the sensation of a given color, if it did not contain from the first the corresponding colored rays. Hence it is that the colors of objects only appear naturally by daylight, and when illuminated by a monochromatic light, all colors blend in that of this one pure tint.

94. *Chromatic Spectra and Spectroscopes.* — When a beam of light is passed through a glass prism placed as shown in Fig.

Fig. 86.

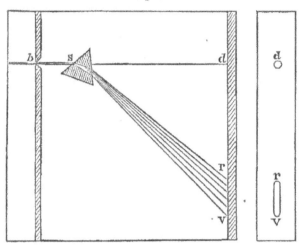

86, it is not only *refracted,* that is, bent from its original rectilinear course, but the colored rays of which the beam consists, being bent unequally, are separated to a greater or less extent, and falling on a screen produce an elongated image colored with a succession of blending tints, which we call the spectrum. The red rays, which are bent the least, are said to be the *least refrangible*, while the violet rays are the *most refrangible*, and intermediate between these we have, in the order of refrangibility, the various tints of orange, yellow, green, blue, and indigo. Thus a prism gives an easy means of analyzing a beam of light, and of discovering the character of the rays by which a given chromatic effect is produced. Such observations are very greatly facilitated by a class of instruments called spectroscopes, and Figs. 87 and 90 will illustrate the principles of their construction.

In the very powerful instrument first represented, the beam of light is passed in succession through nine prisms (each having an angle of 45°), and the extreme rays are thus widely separated, while the beam itself is bent around nearly a whole circumference. The only other essential parts of the instrument are the collimator A and the telescope B. The light first enters the collimator through a narrow slit, and having passed through the prisms is received by the telescope. The telescope is adjusted as it would be for viewing distant objects,

and a lens at the end of the collimator serves to render the
rays diverging from the slit parallel, so that when the two

Fig. 87.

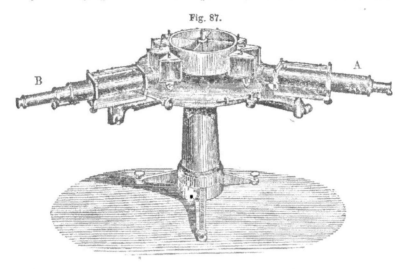

tubes are in line, one sees through the telescope a mag-
nified image of the slit, just as if the slit were at a great

Fig. 88.

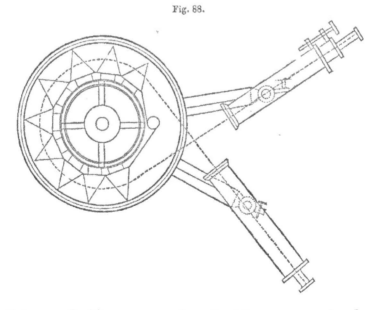

distance.   In like manner when the telescopes are placed as
in Fig. 88, and when the light before reaching the telescope

Fig. 89.

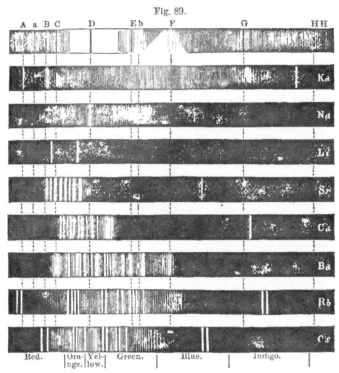

passes through the whole series of prisms, we still see a single
definite image whenever the slit is illuminated by a pure
monochromatic light. Moreover, this image has a definite
position in the field of view, which, when the instrument is
similarly adjusted, depends solely on the refrangibility of the
light.

Thus, if we place in front of the slit a sodium flame, which
emits a pure yellow light, we see a single yellow image of this
longitudinal opening, as in Fig. 89, Na. If we use a lithium
flame, we see a similar image,[1] but colored red, and at some
distance from the first, to the left, if the parts of our instrument are disposed as in Fig. 88. If we use a thalium
flame, we in like manner see a single image, but colored
green, and falling considerably to the right of both of the
other two. If now we illuminate the slit by the three
flames simultaneously, we see all three images at once in the
same relative position as before. So also if we examine the

---

[1] The second image shown in Fig. 89, Li is not ordinarily seen.

flame of a metal, which emits rays of several definite degrees of refrangibility, we see an equal number of definite images of the slit. If, next, we illuminate the slit with sunlight, which contains rays of all degrees of refrangibility, we see an infinite number of images of the slit spread out along the field of view, and these, overlapping each other, form that continuous band of blending colors which we call the solar spectrum. If, lastly, we examine with our instrument the light reflected from a colored surface, or transmitted through a colored medium, we also see a band of blending colors, but at the same time we observe that certain portions of the normal solar spectrum are either wholly wanting or greatly obscured.

With a spectroscope of many prisms like the one represented by Fig. 87, we can only see a small portion of the spectrum at once. By moving the telescope, which, fastened to a metallic arm, revolves around the axis of the instrument, different portions of the spectrum may be brought into the field of view; while a vernier, attached to the same arm and moving over a graduated arc, enables us to fix the position of the spectrum lines, as the images of the slit are usually called. The other mechanical details shown in the figure are required in order to adjust the various parts of the instrument, and especially in order to bring the prisms to what is termed the angle of minimum deviation. But an instrument of this magnitude and power is not required for the ordinary applications of the spectroscope in chemistry. For this purpose a small instrument consisting of a collimator, a single prism, and a telescope, all in a fixed position, are amply sufficient. In the field of such a spectroscope the whole spectrum may be seen at once; and the position of the spectrum lines is very easily determined by means of a photographic scale placed at one side, and seen by light reflected into the telescope from the face of the prism.

The various parts of the instrument, as arranged for observation, are shown in Fig. 90. A is the collimator, P the prism, and B the telescope. The tube C carries the photographic scale, and has at the end nearest to the prism a lens of such focal length that the image both of the slit and the scale may be seen through the telescope at the same time, the one appearing projected upon the other. The screw e serves to adjust the width of the slit. Moreover, one half of the

Fig. 90.

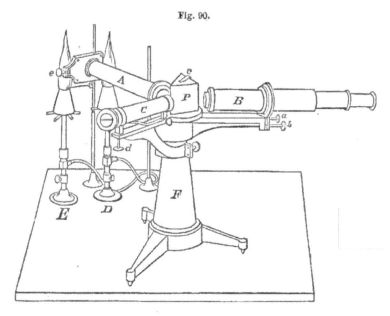

length of the slit is covered by a small glass prism so arranged
that it reflects into the collimator tube the rays from a lamp
placed on one side.   Thus the two halves of the slit may be
illuminated independently by light from different sources, and
the two spectra, which are then seen superimposed upon each
other (see Fig. 91), exactly compared.   The various screws,
which appear in Fig. 90, are used for adjusting the different
parts of the instrument.

95. *Spectrum Analysis.* — The atoms of the different chemical elements, when rendered luminous under certain definite
conditions, always ' emit light whose color is more or less
characteristic, and which, when analyzed with the spectroscope,
exhibit spectra similar to those which are represented in Fig.
89, so far as is possible without the aid of color.   Sometimes
we see only a single line in a definite position, as in the case
of Na, Li, and Th, already referred to.   At other times
there are several such lines ; and, still more frequently, to
these lines (or definite images of the slit) there are super-
added more or less extended portions of a continuous spectrum.
Moreover, not only is the general aspect of each spectrum
exceedingly characteristic, but also the occurrence of its
peculiar lines is, so far as we know, an absolute proof of the

presence of a given element, and these lines may be readily recognized by their position, even when the character of the spectrum is otherwise obscure. It is evident then that we have here a principle which admits of most important applications in chemical analysis, and it only remains to consider under what conditions the elementary atoms emit their characteristic light.

First. All bodies when intensely heated are rendered luminous, and, other things being equal, the higher the temperature the more intense is the light. The brilliancy of the light emitted at the same temperature by different bodies varies very greatly, the densest bodies being, as a general rule, the most intensely luminous.

Secondly. — Solid and liquid bodies, if opaque, emit when ignited white light, or at least light which shows with the spectroscope a continuous spectrum more or less extended. At a red heat the light from such bodies consists chiefly of red rays, but as the temperature rises first to a white and then to a blue heat, the more refrangible rays become more abundant and finally predominate.

Thirdly. — The elementary substances give out their peculiar and characteristic light only in the state of gas or vapor. Hence, when we examine with a spectroscope a source of light, we may infer that a continuous spectrum indicates the presence of solid or liquid bodies, while a discontinuous spectrum, with definite lines or images of the slit, indicates the presence of gases and vapors; and in the last case we can, as has been seen, infer from the position of the lines the nature of the luminous atoms. It would seem, however, from recent investigations, that under certain conditions even a gas may show a continuous spectrum, and there are other seeming exceptions which admonish us that the general principles just stated should be applied with caution.

Fourthly. — At the very high temperatures at which alone gases or vapors become luminous, compound bodies, as a rule, appear to be decomposed, and the elementary atoms disassociated. Hence the observations with the spectroscope have been almost entirely confined to the spectra of the elementary substances, and our knowledge of the spectra of compound substances is exceedingly limited. In some few cases where the spectrum of a compound has been obtained, it has been noticed that, as the temperature rises, this spectrum is suddenly resolved into the separate spectra of the elements of which the compound consists.

Fifthly. — At a high temperature the metallic atoms of a compound body are far more luminous than those of the other elementary atoms with which they are associated. Hence, when the vapor of a metallic compound is rendered luminous, the light emitted is so exclusively that of the metallic atoms, disassociated by the heat, that when examined with the spectroscope the spectrum of the metal is alone seen; and this is the probable explanation of the fact that the salts of the same metal, when treated as will be described in the next paragraph, all show, as a general rule, the same spectrum as the metal itself.

Lastly. — The substance, on which we wish to experiment, may be rendered luminous in several ways. If the substance is a volatile metallic salt, the simplest method is to expose a bead of the substance (supported on a loop of platinum wire) to the flame of a Bunsen's burner (Fig. 90), which by itself burns with a nearly non-luminous flame. The flame soon becomes filled with the disassociated atoms of the metal and shines with their peculiar light.

In order to study the spectra of the less volatile metals like aluminum, iron, or nickel, we use two needles of the metal, and pass between the points, when about one fourth of an inch apart, the electric discharges of a powerful Ruhmkorff coil, condensed by a large Leyden jar. The metal is volatilized by the heat of the electric current, and the space between the points becomes filled with the intensely ignited vapor, which then shines with its characteristic light."[1]

In a similar way we can experiment on the permanent gases and lighter vapors, enclosing them in a glass tube with platinum electrodes, and before sealing the tube reducing the tension with an air pump, when the discharge will pass through a length of several inches of the attenuated gas. The light then emitted comes from the atoms or molecules of the gas, and where the electric current is condensed as in the capillary por-

[1] An electric spark is in every case merely a line of material particles rendered luminous by the current.

tion of the tubes constructed for this purpose, the light is sufficiently intense to be analyzed with the spectroscope.

The three different modes of experimenting just described do
not by any means always give the same spectrum when applied to the same chemical element. It constantly happens
that as the temperature rises new lines appear, which are usually those corresponding to the more refrangible rays, and at
the very high temperatures generated by the electric discharge
many of the spectra change their whole aspect. The ill-defined
broad bands or luminous spaces which are so conspicuous at a
low temperature (see Fig. 89), disappear, and are replaced by
a greater or less number of definite spectrum lines. Generally, however, the characteristic lines which mark the element at the lower temperature are seen also at the higher; but
sometimes there is a sudden and complete change of the whole
spectrum. The cause of these differences is not understood,
but it has been thought by some investigators that the normal
spectra of the elementary atoms consist of bright bands alone,
and that the more or less continuous spectra, which are also
seen at the lower temperatures, are to be referred to the imperfect disassociation of the atoms, whose mutual attractions
or partial combinations produce a state of aggregation ap-
proaching the condition which determines the continuous spectra of liquid or solid bodies.

96. *Delicacy of the Method.* — Having now stated the
general principles of spectrum analysis, and the conditions
under which these principles may be applied, it need only be
added that the method is one of extreme delicacy. It enables
us to detect wonderfully minute quantities of many of the
metallic elements, and has already led to the discovery of four
elements of this class which had eluded all methods of investigation previously employed. The names of these elements,
Rubidium, Caesium, Thallium and Indium, all refer to the
color of their most characteristic spectrum bands.[1]

97. *Solar and Stellar Chemistry.* — When a beam of sunlight is examined with a powerful spectroscope, the solar
spectrum is seen to be crossed by an almost countless number
of *dark lines* distributed with no apparent regularity, and dif-

[1] The different bands of the same element are usually distinguished by
Greek letters, following the order of relative brilliancy.

fering very greatly in relative strength or intensity. These
lines were first accurately described by the German optician
Fraunhofer, and have since been known as the Fraunhofer
lines. A few of the most prominent of these lines are shown
in Fig. 89, with the letters of the alphabet by which they are
designated. These lines, like the bright lines of the elements,
correspond in every case to a definite degree of refrangibility,
and therefore have a fixed position on the scale of the spectroscope. Moreover, what is very remarkable, the bright and
the dark lines have in several cases absolutely the same
position.

It is easy to construct the spectroscope so that the two halves
of the slit may be illuminated from different sources. If then
we admit a beam of sunlight through one half, and the light
of a sodium flame through the other half, we shall have the
two spectra super-imposed in the same field, as in Fig. 91,

Fig. 91.

Red ←——   ——→ Green

and it will be seen that the two parts of the sodium band,
which appears as a double line under a high power, coincide
absolutely in position with the double dark line D in the
solar spectrum. But a still more striking coincidence has
been observed in the case of iron, for the eighty well-marked
bright lines in the spectrum of this metal correspond absolutely
both in position and in strength with eighty of the dark lines
of the solar spectrum. Now, the chances that such coinci-
dences are the result of accident, are not one in one billion
billion; and we are therefore compelled to believe that the
two phenomena must be connected. A simple experiment
shows what the relation probably is.

If we place before the spectroscope a sodium flame, we see,
of course, the familiar double line. If now we place behind

the sodium flame a candle flame, so that the candle also shines into the slit, but only through the sodium flame, we shall see the same bright lines projected upon the continuous spectrum of the candle. If, however, we put in place of the candle an electric light, we shall find that while the continuous spectrum is now far more brilliant than before, the sodium lines appear black. The explanation of this singular phenomenon is to be found in a principle, now well established both theoretically and experimentally, that a mass of luminous vapor, while otherwise transparent, powerfully absorbs rays of the same refrangibility which it emits itself. Hence, in our experiment, the very small portion of the spectrum covered by the sodium line is illuminated by the sodium flame alone, while all the rest of the spectrum is illuminated from the source behind, and the effect is merely one of contrast, the sodium lines appearing light or dark according as they are brighter or darker than the contiguous portions of the spectrum.

In a similar way the bright lines of a few other elements have been inverted, and these experiments would lead us to infer that the Fraunhofer lines themselves are formed by a brilliant photosphere shining through a mass of less luminous gas. In other words, it would appear that the sun's luminous orb is surrounded by an immense atmosphere which intercepts a portion of his rays, and that we see as dark lines what would probably appear as bright bands, could we examine the light from the atmosphere alone.

If then our generalization is safe, the dark and the bright lines are the same phenomena seen under a different aspect, and the one as well as the other may be used to identify the different chemical elements. Hence, then, there must be both iron and sodium in the sun's atmosphere, and for the same reason we conclude that our luminary must contain Hydrogen, Calcium, Magnesium, Nickel, Chromium, Barium, Copper, and Zinc, while there is equally good evidence that Gold, Silver, Mercury, Cadmium, Tin, Lead, Antimony, Arsenic, Strontium, and Lithium are not present, at least in large quantities. It is, moreover, worthy of notice that the lines neither of oxygen, nitrogen, nor indeed of any of that class of bodies formerly called metalloids, have been recognized in the solar spectrum ; but then the spectra of these elements, so abundant on the earth's surface, are so much feebler than those of the metals, that it is doubtful whether the negative evidence of the spectroscope is trustworthy in these cases.

The elements thus recognized in the sun only account for a small portion of the dark lines, and the scheme of the chemical elements is apparently so incomplete on the earth, at least so far as we know it (103), that we should not be surprised to find a multitude of new forms of elementary matter at the centre of the solar system. But, on the other hand, the meteorites have brought to us no new elements, and their evidence, therefore, as far as it goes, is adverse to the assumption that there exists in the sun's atmosphere such a great number of unknown elements as the dark lines would indicate, and this obvious explanation of their vast number cannot be regarded as probable.

If next we turn the spectroscope on some of the brighter fixed stars, we shall see continuous spectra like the solar spectrum, of greater or less extent, and covered by dark lines. A careful comparison of these lines would seem to indicate that the stars differ very greatly from each other, although in general they are bodies similar to our sun ; and if our theory is correct, we have been able to detect the presence of sodium, magnesium, hydrogen, calcium, iron, bismuth, tellurium, antimony, and mercury in Aldebaran, and other elements in other stars.

The most remarkable result of stellar chemistry remains yet to be noticed. On examining the nebulæ with the spectroscope, it has been found that while some of them show a continuous spectrum, there are a number of these remarkable bodies which exhibit the phenomena of bright lines. This would lead us to the conclusion that the last are really, as the nebular theory assumes, masses of incandescent gas, while the first are not true nebulæ, but simply clusters of very distant stars. An examination of the comets has confirmed the previous conclusion that they also are mere masses of gas, but, singularly enough, the light from the coma of one of those bodies gave a continuous spectrum, due probably to reflected sunlight.

98. *Absorption Spectra.* — When a luminous flame is viewed with a spectroscope through a solution of any salt of the metal *Erbium*, the otherwise continuous spectrum of the flame

is seen to be interrupted by several broad bands, which have a definite position, and are a valuable means of recognizing the presence of this very rare element. This absorption spectrum, as it is called, is simply the reverse, the "negative" of the luminous spectrum of the same element.

In like manner the salts of *Didymium* give an equally characteristic, although very different, absorption spectrum, which is in fact the only sure test we possess for this remarkable elementary substance ; and as the bands may under some conditions be seen with reflected, as well as with transmitted light, we may apply the test even to opaque solids. Also, the same absorption bands are obtained either when the light is transmitted through a *liquid* solution, or through a *solid* crystal of *any* salt of the metal ; and, moreover, the incandescent vapor of the metal shows bright bands corresponding to the dark bands in position. These facts would seem to show that the characteristic spectrum bands of an element may be, at least to some extent, independent both of the state of aggregation, and of the condition of combination of the elementary atoms.

Many substances besides the compounds of the elements just noticed, give characteristic absorption spectra which have been found to be useful chemical tests, especially in the case of blood, and certain other bodies of organic origin. The most remarkable phenomena of this class are the absorption spectra which are seen when a luminous flame is viewed with a spectroscope through various colored vapors, such as those of nitric per-oxide, bromine, and iodine. The dark bands are then very numerous, and in some cases may be resolved into well-defined lines. Indeed, the absorption bands are a class of phenomena closely allied to the Fraunhofer lines, many of which are known to result from the absorption by the earth's atmosphere of solar rays of certain degrees of refrangibility : and all these facts, with many others, prove that gases and vapors may exert their peculiar power of elective absorption at the ordinary temperature, as well as when incandescent. As a general rule, however, the absorption bands are not, like the bright lines of the metallic spectra or their representatives among the dark lines of the solar spectrum, definite images of the slit, but they are darker portions of the spectrum more or less regularly shaded, and correspond to the broad bands or

luminous spaces in the spectra of the metallic vapors when
not intensely heated. In each case the effect results from the
blending of a greater or less number of images of the slit,
differing in relative position and intensity.

99. *Theory of Exchanges.* — The facts of the two last
sections are all illustrations of a general principle already
referred to in connection with the reversal of the sodium
spectrum. This principle is known as the " Theory of Exchanges," and has been stated as follows: " The relation
between the power of emission, and power of absorption
for each kind of rays (light or heat) is the same for all
bodies at the same temperature." . . . . " Let R denote the
intensity of radiation of a particle for a given description of
light at a given temperature, and let A denote the proportion
of rays of this description incident on the particle which it
absorbs; then $R \div A$ has the same value for all bodies at the
same temperature, — that is to say, this quotient is a function
of the temperature only."

The law of exchanges finds its widest application in the
phenomena of radiant heat, and so far as experiments have
been made, it appears to be true in its greatest generality. In
applying it to explain the reversal of the spectra of colored
flames, we have only to deal with a single body in its relations
to rays of different qualities. If the principle is true, the
absorbing power of such a body at a given temperature must
bear a fixed ratio to its power of emission for each kind of
ray. If, for example, it has a great power of emitting certain
rays of red light, it has a proportionally great power of
absorbing the same rays. If, again, it has a feeble power of
emitting violet rays of definite quality, its power of absorbing
such rays is proportionally feeble, and bears the same ratio to
the power of emission as before ; and, lastly, it has no power
of absorption over such rays as it does not itself emit. Moreover, it would follow that, although the relation of the absorbing to the radiating power might vary very greatly, so that,
as the temperature falls, the last may become inconsiderable
as compared with the first, or even vanish, no essential change
in the character of the elective absorption would be thus induced. Hence, we should expect that bodies would absorb
when cold rays of the same quality which they emit when hot,

and also that opaque solids when heated would emit white light. We have seen that the general order of the phenomena is that which the law of exchanges would predict, and here, for the present, our knowledge stops. We have as yet been able to form no satisfactory theory in regard to the relations of the molecular structure of bodies to the medium through which the waves of light or heat are transmitted. It is, however, worthy of notice that Euler, one of the earliest and ablest investigators of undulatory motion, predicted the discovery of the law of exchanges, in assuming as a fundamental principle of the undulatory theory that a body can only absorb oscillations isochronous with those of which it is itself susceptible.

100. *General Conclusions.* — The facts that have been stated in this chapter are sufficient to show, that, although yet in its infancy, spectrum analysis promises to be one of the most powerful instruments of investigation ever applied in physical science. It seems to be the key which will in time open to our view the molecular structure of matter ; and even now the results actually obtained suggest speculations in regard to the ultimate constitution of matter, of the most interesting character. The several monochromatic rays which the atoms of the elements emit, must receive their peculiar character from some motion in the atoms themselves which is isochronous with the motion they impart. Is it not then in this motion that the *individuality* of the element resides, and may not all matter be alike in its ultimate essence? Such speculations, however wild, are not wholly unprofitable, if only they stimulate investigation and thus lead to further discoveries.

CHAPTER XVII.

CHEMICAL CLASSIFICATION.

101. *General Principles.* — The glimpses that we have been able to gain of the order in the constitution of matter give us grounds for believing that there is a unity of plan pervading the whole scheme, and encourage a confident expectation that hereafter, when our knowledge becomes more complete, chemists may attain to at least such a partial conception of this plan as will enable them to classify their compounds under some natural system; and in imagination we may even look forward to the time when science will be able to express all the possibilities of this scheme with a few general formulæ, which will enable the chemist to predict with absolute certainty the qualities and relations of any given combination of materials or conditions. But although to a very slight extent the idea has been realized for a small class of the compounds of carbon, yet as a whole this grand conception is as yet but a dream. The more advanced student will find that in limited portions of some few fields of investigation a fragmentary classification is possible, as in mineralogy; but, when he attempts to comprehend the whole domain, he becomes painfully aware of the immense deficiencies of his knowledge; he is confused by the numerous chains of relationship, which he follows, with no result, to sudden breaks, and soon becomes convinced that all such efforts must be fruitless until more of the missing links are supplied.

The best that can now be done in an elementary treatise on chemistry is to group together the elements, or, rather, the elementary atoms, in such families as will best show their natural affinities; and then to study, under the head of each element, the more important and characteristic of its compounds. However little value such a classification may have in its scientific aspect, it will bring together, to a greater or less extent, the allied facts of the science, and thus will help the mind to retain them in the memory.

In classifying the elementary atoms, the three most important characters to be observed are the *Prevailing Quantivalence*,
the *Electrical Affinities*, and the *Crystalline Relations*. The
first of these characters serves more particularly to classify the
elements in groups, the second to determine their position in
the groups, and the last to control the indications of the other
two.

The crystalline relations of the atoms can only be determined by comparing the crystalline forms of allied compounds,
and involve the principles of isomorphism already discussed.
Moreover, in order to reach the most satisfactory scheme of
classification, we must take into consideration other properties
of these compounds besides the crystalline form; which, although they may not be so precisely formulated, are frequently
important aids in forming correct opinions as to the relations of
the atoms. It will also be evident, from what has previously
been stated, that more trustworthy inferences as to these relations may frequently be drawn from the crystalline form and
properties of allied compounds than from those of the elementary substances themselves; for, in addition to the fact that so
many of these substances crystallize in the isometric system,
whose dimensions admit of no variation, it is also true that, in
our ignorance of the molecular constitution of most of them, we
often have more certainty, in the case of compounds, that our
comparisons are made under identical molecular conditions.

102. *Metallic and Non-Metallic Elements.* — In all works on
chemistry since the time of Lavoisier, the elementary substances have been divided into two great classes, — the *metals*
and the *non-metals;* and the distinction is undoubtedly fundamental, although too much importance has been frequently
attached to the accident of a brilliant lustre. The characteristic qualities of a metal, with which every one is more or less
familiar, are the so-called *metallic lustre*, that peculiar adapt-
ability of molecular structure known as *malleability* or *ductility*,
and the *power of conducting electricity or heat*. These qualities
are found united and in their perfection only in the true metals,
although one or even two of them are well developed in several
elementary substances which, on account of their chemical
qualities, are now almost invariably classed with the non-
metals, — as, for example, in selenium, tellurium, arsenic,

antimony, boron, and silicon. Besides the properties above named, many persons also associate with the idea of a metal a high specific gravity; but this property, though common to most of the useful metals, is by no means universal; and, among the metals with which the chemist is familiar, we find the lightest, as well as the heaviest, of solids. The non-metallic elements, as the name denotes, are distinguished by the absence of metallic qualities; but the one class merges into the other.

The presence or absence of metallic qualities in the elementary substances is for some unknown reason intimately associated with the electrical relations of their atoms, — those of the metals being electro-positive, while those of the non-metals are electro-negative, with reference, in each case, to the atoms of the opposite class. In the classification given in Table II. we have associated together in the same family both the metals and the non-metals having the same quantivalence, believing that such an arrangement not only best exhibits the relations of the atoms, but also that in a course of elementary instruction it presents the facts of chemistry in the most logical order.

103. *Scheme of Classification.* — The classification of the elementary atoms which has been adopted in this book is shown in Table II.

In the first place the atoms are divided into two large families, the Perissads and the Artiads (27).

Secondly, these families are subdivided into groups (separated by bars in the table) of closely allied elements. The atoms of any one of these groups are isomorphous; and they are arranged in the order of their weights, which is found to correspond also, in almost every case, to their electrical relations. Each group forms a very limited chemical series; and not only the weights and the electrical relations of the atoms, but also many of the physical qualities of the elementary substances, vary regularly as we pass from one end of the series to the other. The order of the variation, however, is not always the same; for while in some cases the lightest atoms of a series are the most electro-negative, in other cases they are the most electro-positive.

Thirdly, in arranging the groups of allied atoms we have followed the prevailing quantivalence of the group, and those groups whose elementary atoms exhibit in general the lowest quantivalence are, as a rule, placed first in order; but with our present limited knowledge there must be some uncertainty in regard to the details of such an arrangement, and the principle has sometimes been violated so as to bring together those groups of atoms which are most allied in their chemical relations.

The remarks already made in regard to the general scheme of chemical classification apply with almost equal force to the partial system here attempted. The very attempt makes evident the fragmentary character of our knowledge, even in regard to the exceedingly limited portion of the subject with which we are dealing. The idea of classification by series was first developed in the study of organic chemistry, where the principle is much more conspicuous than among inorganic compounds. Thus, as has been shown (40), we are acquainted with twenty acids resembling acetic acid, which form a series beginning with formic acid and ending with melissic acid. Each member of this series differs in composition from the preceding member by CH_2, or by some multiple of this symbol; and the properties of the compounds vary regularly between the extreme limits, according to well-established laws. Moreover, many other similar, although more limited, series of compounds are known, and the principle realized in these organic series seems to be the true idea of all chemical classification. But, in attempting to apply it to the chemical elements, we find only two or three groups of atoms where the series is of sufficient extent to make the relations of the members evident. In most cases it would seem as if we only knew one or two members of a series, and this apparent ignorance not only throws doubt on the general application of our principle, but also renders uncertain the details of our scheme, even assuming that the principle of the classification is correct. Hence, also, great differences of opinion may be reasonably entertained in regard to the position which the different atoms ought to occupy in such a scheme.

Another very important cause of uncertainty in any scheme of classifying the elements arises from the double relationships which many of them manifest. Thus iron, which we have associated with manganese and aluminum, is in some of its relations closely allied to magnesium and zinc. Many other elements resemble iron in having a similar two-fold character, and different authors may reasonably assign to such elements different places in their systems of classification, according as they chiefly view them from one or the other aspect. Hence arises a degree of uncertainty which affects our whole system, and cannot be avoided in the present state of the science.

Indeed, no classification in independent groups can satisfy the complex relations of the elements. These relations cannot be represented by a simple system of parallel series, but only by a web of crossing lines, in which the same element may be represented as a member of two or more series at once, and as affiliating in different directions with very different classes of elements. In the present fragmentary state of our knowledge, such a classification as we have just indicated is not attainable. The scheme adopted in this book only indicates in each case a single line of relationship; but we have always endeavored to place each element in that relation which is the most characteristic; and, however imperfect such a scheme may be, it will nevertheless assist study by bringing before the student's mind the facts of the science in a systematic and natural order.

104. *Relations of the Atomic Weights.* — If the principle of classification which we have adopted is correct, and the elements actually belong to series like those of the compounds of organic chemistry, we should naturally expect that the atomic weights would conform to the same serial law; and it is a remarkable fact that the differences between the atomic weights of the elements of the same group are in most cases very nearly multiples of 16. The value of this common difference varies between 15 and 17, and we must admit in some cases the simplest fractional multiples; but the mean value is very nearly 16, and the frequent occurrence of this difference is very striking. This numerical relation is not absolutely exact, but here, as in the periods of the planets, in the distribution of leaves on the stem of a plant, and in other similar natural phenomena, there is a marked tendency towards a certain numerical result, which is fully realized, however, only in comparatively few cases.

Other numerical relations which have been noticed between the atomic weights are probably only phases of the same law of distribution in series. Thus the atomic weight of sodium is very nearly the mean between that of lithium and potassium ; and the atomic weights of chlorine, bromine, and iodine, of glucinum, yttrium and erbium, of calcium, strontium, and barium, of oxygen, sulphur, and selenium, are similarly related. Again, there are several pairs of allied elements, between whose atomic weights there is very nearly the same difference. Thus the difference between the atomic weights of indium and cadmium is very nearly the same as that between the atomic weights of magnesium and zinc, and the difference between the atomic weights of niobium and tantalum the same as that between the atomic weights of molybdenum and tungsten. A careful study of the atomic weights will also reveal many other approximate relations of the same sort ; but although the study of these relations is highly interesting, and may lead hereafter to valuable results, yet no great importance can be attached to them in the present state of the science.

PART II.

INTRODUCTION.

HAVING developed in Part I. the fundamental principles of chemical science, we shall next give, in Part II., a brief summary of the more important elements and compounds, exhibiting their constitution and relations by means of formulæ and reactions, and adding a number of questions and problems, which will serve to direct the attention of the student to the more important facts and principles, or to those which, being only implied in the context, might be otherwise overlooked, and which will also give him the means of testing the thoroughness and accuracy of his knowledge. The answers to the problems have been calculated with the four-place logarithms, which will be found at the end of the volume. Used in connection with the table of antilogarithms which accompanies them, the logarithms give results which are accurate to the fourth significant figure, and this degree of accuracy exceeds in almost every case that of the experimental data given in the problems. With certain exceptions referred to below, the answers to the questions are either stated or implied in the immediate context, or in the sections and formulæ to which reference is made. The references to sections are enclosed in parentheses, and those to formulæ in brackets. Direct questions on the facts stated in the summary are seldom given, and obviously would be superfluous; but the student should make himself thoroughly acquainted with the subject-matter of each section before he attempts to answer the questions or solve the problems which follow. In studying the book, however, he should aim to acquire a knowledge of the general principles and mutual relations which are exhibited, rather than to commit to memory the isolated facts. He must never forget that he is dealing, not with abstractions, but with real things and actual phenomena, and that chemical formulæ are merely expressions of definite facts ascertained by experiment. Moreover, he must discriminate with the greatest care between the facts directly stated or expressed by the reactions, and the inferences drawn from them, and he should be required to state clearly the successive steps in every process of inductive reasoning. As was stated in the preface, this portion of the book is only intended as an auxiliary to lecture-room or laboratory instruction, and the closer the lessons can be connected with the experimental illustrations the better.

The elements are studied in the following chapters in the order in which they are arranged in Table II., and in connection with each element we describe, or at least mention, the more important compounds which it forms with the elements preceding it in our classification. At least this is the general rule, but, so far as regards the compounds, we do not follow this order invariably, departing from it whenever it may be necessary to illustrate the relations of the element we may be studying. Thus we describe with each element its chief oxygen and sulphur compounds from the first. No attempt has been made to embrace the whole field, but the aim has been to illustrate fully the principles of chemical philosophy, and to give a clear idea of that phase of the scheme of nature which has been revealed by the study of chemistry. As stated in the Preface, the "Questions and Problems" are an essential feature in the plan of the work, and serve to supplement as well as to illustrate the text. The student will find that the knowledge which he gains inferentially, while seeking the answers to the questions or solving the problems, is peculiarly valuable, and the acquisition has something of the zest of new discovery. As he advances, he will meet with questions which he cannot fully answer without consulting more extended works, and which are intended to direct his study beyond the limits of this book. He may consult in such cases Watts's Dictionary of Chemistry, Miller's Elements of Chemistry, Percy's Metallurgy, and Dana's System of Mineralogy.

CHAPTER XVIII.

THE PERISSAD ELEMENTS.

Division I.

105. HYDROGEN. $H = 1$. — Monad. The lightest atom, and the standard of quantivalence. Very widely diffused in nature. Forms one ninth of water, and is a constituent of almost all vegetable and animal substances as well as of many minerals. The essential constituent of all acids and bases, from which it is readily displaced by other atoms.

106. *Hydrogen Gas. H-H.* — The lightest substance known in nature. Sp. Gr. $= 1$, the standard of comparison. Seldom found in a free state in nature. Best prepared by the action of zinc or iron on dilute sulphuric acid.

$$\mathbf{Zn} + (H_2SO_4 + Aq) = (ZnSO_4 + Aq) + \text{H-H}. \quad [64]$$

Very combustible. Has the greatest calorific power of any substance known. Aqueous vapor sole product of its combustion.

$$2\,\text{H-H} + \text{O-O} = 2\,H_2O. \quad\quad [65]$$

107. *Hydric Oxide (Water).* H_2O. — The universally diffused liquid of the globe. The life-blood of nature, and the chief constituent of organized beings. Below 0° a crystalline solid (hexagonal system, Figs. 14 and 16). *Sp. Gr.* $= 0.918$. Under the ordinary pressure of the air it boils at 100°, but exists in the atmosphere in the state of vapor, at all temperatures. For maximum tension of vapor at different temperatures see Chem. Phys. (284 and 312). Water is an almost universal solvent and the medium of most chemical changes. Its molecular structure is regarded as the type of a very large class of chemical compounds. Its composition may be determined, — First, by electrolysis (91 and [65] reversed).

9 *

Secondly, by passing a mixture of steam and chlorine gas through a red-hot tube.

$$2H_2O + 2Cl\text{-}Cl = 4HCl + O\text{-}O. \qquad [66]$$

Thirdly, by exploding in an eudiometer-tube a mixture of oxygen and hydrogen gas [65]. Fourthly, by passing hydrogen gas over heated cupric oxide.

$$\mathbf{CuO} + H\text{-}H = \mathbf{Cu} + H_2O. \qquad [67]$$

Water combines with anhydrides to form acids, as

$$SO_3 + H_2O = H_2{=}O_2{=}SO_2,$$
or $$P_2O_5 + 3H_2O = 2H_3{=}O_3{=}PO. \qquad [68]$$

It combines with metallic oxides to form hydrates, bases, or alkalies, as

$$Na_2O + H_2O = 2Na\text{-}O\text{-}H \text{ or } CaO + H_2O = Ca{=}O_2{=}H_2. \quad [69]$$

It combines with many salts as water of crystallization, as

$$Fe{=}SO_4 \cdot 7H_2O \text{ Cryst. Ferrous Sulphate.}$$

108. *Hydroxyl. HO.* — An important compound radical, which may be regarded as a factor (28) in the molecules of many chemical compounds, and for this reason it is sometimes convenient to write its symbol *Ho* (22). The oxygen bases may be considered as compounds of hydroxyl with electro-positive atoms or radicals, and the oxygen acids as compounds of the same with electro-negative atoms or radicals. Thus we may write the symbols of the following compounds as shown below : —

Sodic Hydrate	$Na\text{-}O\text{-}H$	or	$Na\text{-}Ho,$
Baric Hydrate	$Ba{=}O_2{=}H_2$	"	$Ba{=}Ho_2,$
Ferric Hydrate	$[Fe_2]{\equiv}O_6{\equiv}H_6$	"	$[Fe_2]{\equiv}Ho_6,$
Nitric Acid	$H\text{-}O\text{-}NO_2$	"	$Ho\text{-}NO_2,$
Sulphuric Acid	$H_2{=}O_2{=}SO_2$	"	$Ho_2{=}SO_2,$
Phosphoric Acid	$H_3{\equiv}O_3{\equiv}PO$	"	$Ho_3{\equiv}PO.$

[70]

109. *Hydric Peroxide (Oxygenated Water).* H_2O_2 or $Ho\text{-}Ho.$

—Best regarded as the "radical substance" (22 and 69) corresponding to hydroxyl. In its most concentrated form it is a colorless liquid of the consistency of syrup, and having a decided odor resembling chlorine. Soluble in water in all proportions. Prepared by action of carbonic acid on baric peroxide.

$$\mathbf{BaO_2} + (H_2CO_3 + Aq) = \mathbf{BaCO_3} + (H_2O_2 + Aq). \quad [71]$$

Carbonic anhydride is passed through water in which BaO_2 is suspended and the solution of H_2O_2 subsequently evaporated in vacuo. Decomposed by fine metallic powders, and also spontaneously at temperatures higher than 22°, into water and oxygen gas.

$$(2H_2O_2 + Aq) = (2H_2O + Aq) + \odot \cdot \odot. \quad [72]$$

It liberates iodine from its compounds.

$$2KI + (Ho\text{-}Ho + Aq) = \mathbf{I\text{-}I} + (2K\text{-}Ho + Aq). \quad [73]$$

It generally acts as an oxidizing agent.

$$\mathbf{PbS} + (4H_2O_2 + Aq) = \mathbf{PbSO_4} + (4H_2O + Aq). \quad [74]$$

It sometimes, however, acts as a reducing agent.

$$\mathbf{Ag_2O} + (H_2O_2 + Aq) = \mathbf{Ag_2} + (H_2O + Aq) + \odot \cdot \odot. \quad [75]$$

Questions and Problems.[1]

1. What distinction can be drawn between a chemical element and an elementary substance, it being understood that the word element is used in a restricted sense, as applying only to the ultimate atoms into which matter may be resolved? Illustrate the distinction by the case of hydrogen. (69; 18 and 22.)

2. What is the essential characteristic of an acid and of a base? (35 and 36.)

3. What is the ground for the belief that each molecule of hydrogen gas consists of two atoms? (19.)

---

[1] It is assumed in all the problems of this book that the temperature is 0° C., and the pressure 76 c. m., unless otherwise stated. The following abbreviations will be used: c. m., centimetre; $\overline{c.\,m.}^3$, cubic centimetre; $\overline{d.\,m.}^3$, cubic decimetre; kilo., kilogrammes, &c. (See Table I.)

4. The litre and the crith, the molecular weight of hydrogen and its molecular volume, sustain what relation to each other? State the reason for the rule on page 49. (2 and 25.)

5. How many grammes of zinc and how many of sulphuric acid will yield one litre of hydrogen gas?
Ans. 2.92 grammes of zinc, and 4.39 grammes of sulphuric acid.

6. If 45 grammes of zinc are used in reaction [64], how many cubic centimetres of sulphuric acid must be used also, and how many grammes of zincic sulphate, and how many litres of hydrogen gas, will be formed in the process (Sp. Gr. of H_2SO_4 = 1.843)?
Ans. 36.7 $\overline{c.\,m.}^3$ of sulphuric acid, 111.3 grammes of zincic sulphate, and 15.4 litres of hydrogen.

7. What volume of water should be mixed with the sulphuric acid in the last problem, assuming that the reaction takes place at 20°, and that 100 parts of water at that temperature will dissolve 53 parts of zincic sulphate?
Ans. 209.9 $\overline{c.\,m.}^3$, or enough to dissolve all the zinc salt formed.

8. What weight of iron must be used to generate sufficient hydrogen to raise in the atmosphere by its buoyancy a total weight of 121 grammes (Sp. Gr. of air 14.5 nearly)?
Ans. 100 litres of hydrogen gas will be required, and this can be made from 250.9 grammes of iron.

9. Assuming that the principle of (17) is correct, why does it follow from reaction [65] that the molecule of oxygen gas must contain at least two atoms?

10. What is the volume of 4.480 grammes of hydrogen at 273°.2 [9]?   Ans. 100 litres.

11. What is the volume of 4.480 grammes of hydrogen at 0° and under a pressure of 38 c. m. [4]?   Ans. 100 litres.

12. A block of ice weighs 36.72 kilos. What is its volume [1]?
Ans. 40 $\overline{d.\,m.}^3$

13. An iceberg is floating in sea water (Sp. Gr. = 1.028). What proportion of its bulk is submerged?   Ans. 0.8932.

14. One kilogramme of steam at 100° will melt how many kilos. of ice?
Ans. The steam by condensing and cooling would give out 637 units of heat, which is adequate to melt 637 ÷ 79 = 8 + kilogrammes of ice. (14 and 16.)

15. What is the weight of one litre of confined steam at the temperature of 144°? Tension of steam at 144° equals 4 atmospheres.
Ans. Weight of litre of steam at 0° and 76 c. m. would be theoretically 9 criths. Hence weight at 144° and 4 × 76 c. m. is, by [6] and [10], 23.58 criths or 2.113 grammes.

16. What is the weight of one litre of superheated steam under normal pressure, and at 546°.4 ? Ans. 0.2688 grammes.

17. Water is forced into a glass globe containing dry air, at the temperature of 100° C. and under the normal pressure, as long as it continues to evaporate. What will be the tension of the moist air ?

Ans. Water or any other liquid evaporates into a confined space until the vapor attains its maximum tension for the existing temperature, even when the space is filled with another gas; and the tension of the mixture of gas and vapor is equal to the sum of the tension which each would exert separately. Chem. Phys. (312). The maximum tension of aqueous vapor at 100° is 76 c. m., and hence the tension of the moist air in the globe must be 152 c. m.

18. A volume of hydrogen gas standing in a bell-glass over a pneumatic trough, and consequently saturated with moisture, measures 100 c. m.³ The temperature is 22°.3 and pressure on the gas 76 c. m. What would be the volume under the same conditions if the air were perfectly dry ?

Ans. The maximum tension of aqueous vapor at given temperature is 2 c. m. Hence if vapor were removed, the tension of the gas would become 74 c. m., provided the volume remained constant. But the exterior pressure being 76 c. m., the volume must accommodate itself to this condition, and hence by [4] would be reduced to 97.36 c. m.

19. What is the Sp. Gr. of aqueous vapor? What is meant by the term Sp. Gr. as applied to a vapor, and under what conditions is it assumed to be taken ? (1 and 17.) Ans. 9.

20. In Table III. the weight of one litre of aqueous vapor under the standard conditions of temperature and pressure is given as 9 criths. Why is this value a fiction ? and why is an impossible value given in the table? Chem. Phys. (329).

21. In the experiment indicated by reaction [66] the oxygen gas was collected in a bell-glass over water. It measured 1,101 c. m.³ at the temperature 22°.3 and under a pressure of 76 c. m. What was the volume of chlorine gas used, measured under the normal conditions? The tension of aqueous vapor at 22°.3 is 2 c. m.

Ans. 2 litres.

22. How much copper will be *reduced* in the formation of nine grammes of water, and what volume of hydrogen gas will be used in the reaction ?

Ans. 31.7 grammes of copper and 11.16 litres of hydrogen.

23. It has been found by exact experiments that for every nine

grammes of water formed by reaction [67] the cupric oxide lost in weight eight grammes. What is the percentage composition of water? Ans. 11.112 of hydrogen and 88.888 of oxygen.

24. Given percentage composition of water and the Sp. Gr. of aqueous vapor, and assuming that the molecule of water contains only one oxygen atom, how can you deduce the atomic weight of oxygen? (23.)

25. Assuming that all the heat of combustion is utilized, how many litres of hydrogen must be burnt to convert into free steam one kilogramme of boiling water, and how does the volume of steam generated compare with the volume of gas burnt?

Ans. 176.8 litres of hydrogen gas and 1,240 litres of steam, when reduced to standard conditions. (14 and 17.) (61.)

26. Assuming that all the heat of combustion is retained in the aqueous vapor formed from the burnt hydrogen, how will the volume of the expanded vapor compare with that of the gas consumed?

Ans. By problem on page 121 it appears that the temperature of the vapor would be, under the conditions assumed, 6,853°. Hence the volume would be 26.08 times as great as that of the gas [9].

27. Assuming that the whole volume of gas resulting from the electrolysis of water is retained in the space previously occupied by the water, what would be its tension? Ans. 1,860 atmospheres.

28. What is the relation of an anhydride to an acid, or of a metallic oxide to a hydrate? (37 and 47.)

29. What objections may be raised to the method of writing the symbols of acids and bases used in [70]?

30. What is the distinction between a compound radical and a radical substance?

31. Why does reaction [73] sustain the view that hydric peroxide contains the radical hydroxyl? Do not reactions [72], [74], and [75] point to another view of its constitution?

32. Analyze reaction [75], and show that it is in harmony with the modern theory of the constitution of the oxygen molecule.

Division II.

110. FLUORINE. $F = 19.$ — Quantivalence usually one, but its atomicity is probably of higher order. A chief constituent of fluor-spar, CaF_2, and of cryolite, $Na_6Al_2F_{12}$. Found also, but in small quantities, in Apatite, Tourmaline, Mica, and a few other minerals. Also in the bones of animals, especially in the teeth. The elementary substance $F\text{-}F$ is undoubtedly a gas, but it has not with certainty been isolated.

111. *Hydrofluoric Acid. HF.* — The anhydrous acid is at 15° a colorless mobile liquid, extremely volatile, boiling at 19.5°, densely fuming in the air, and attracting greedily water from the atmosphere. It is exceedingly corrosive, and a highly dangerous substance. The dilute acid is obtained by distilling a mixture of powdered fluor-spar and sulphuric acid in a platinum or lead retort.

$$\mathbf{CaF_2} + (H_2SO_4 + Aq) = \mathbf{CaSO_4} + 2HF + Aq. \quad [76]$$

Cryolite may be used advantageously instead of fluor-spar. This acid is distinguished for its power of dissolving silica, with which it forms volatile products. Hence it is much used in chemical analysis for decomposing siliceous minerals, and in the arts for etching glass.

112. CHLORINE. $Cl = 35.5.$ — Quantivalence usually one, but atomicity probably of a higher order. Very widely distributed in nature, chiefly in combination with sodium, forming common salt.

113. *Chlorine Gas. Cl-Cl.* — Yellowish-green gas, which may be liquefied by pressure, but has never been frozen. Soluble in water, with which it forms at 0° a crystalline hydrate. Highly corrosive, and enters into direct union with most of the elementary substances. Discharges vegetable colors and destroys noxious effluvias, and hence much used in the arts as a bleaching and disinfecting agent. Best prepared by gently heating in a glass flask a mixture of hydrochloric acid and manganic dioxide.

$$\mathbf{MnO_2} + (4HCl + Aq) =$$
$$(MnCl_2 + 2H_2O + Aq) + Cl\text{-}Cl. \quad [77]$$

Chlorine gas is a very important chemical reagent. It not

only converts many simple chlorides into perchlorides, but, with
the intervention of water or of some other oxygen compound,
it also acts as an oxidizing agent, and to this effect its bleaching
power is probably in great measure owing.

$$(Sn\,Cl_2 + Cl_2 + Aq) = (Sn\,Cl_4 + Aq). \qquad [78]$$

$$3\,Co\text{=}(HO)_2 + (Cl\text{-}Cl + Aq) =$$
$$[Co_2]\overset{=}{\equiv}(HO)_6 + (Co\,Cl_2 + Aq). \quad [79]$$

Chlorine has also a remarkable power of replacing hydrogen in
many of its compounds. (31)

114. *Hydrochloric Acid. H-Cl.* — A colorless gas which
may be liquefied by cold and pressure, but has not been frozen.
Exceedingly soluble in water, which at 4° absorbs its own
weight or about 480 times its volume of the gas. This solution is very much used in the laboratory as a reagent, and an
impure solution called muriatic acid is manufactured on a large
scale for the uses of the arts. From the *Sp. Gr.* of the liquid
acid we can determine very closely the quantity of gas held in
solution, by means of tables in which the results of careful experimental determinations have been tabulated. The following
extracts from a table of Dr. Ure's give all the data required for
calculating the problems in this book.

Sp. Gr. 15° C.	Per Cent. HCl.	Sp. Gr. 15° C.	Per Cent. HCl.	Sp. Gr. 15° C.	Per Cent. HCl.	Sp. Gr. 15° C.	Per Cent. HCl.
1.2000	40.777	1.1410	28.544	1.0899	18.349	1.0397	8.155
1.1893	38.330	1.1308	26.505	1.0798	16.310	1.0298	6.116
1.1802	36.292	1.1206	24.466	1.0697	14.271	1.0200	4.078
1.1701	34.252	1.1102	22.426	1.0597	12.233	1.0100	2.039
1.1599	32.213	1.1000	20.388	1.0497	10.194	1.0060	1.124

Muriatic acid is prepared by heating common salt with sulphuric acid in large iron retorts, and conducting the gas formed
into large glass vessels containing water.

$$2Na\,Cl + H_2SO_4 = Na_2SO_4 + 2\,HCl. \qquad [80]$$

When we make pure hydrochloric acid in the laboratory, we
only use half as much salt. The gas is then given off at a
much lower temperature, and glass retorts may be employed.

$$Na\,Cl + (H_2\text{=}SO_4 + Aq) = (H,Na\text{=}SO_4 + Aq) + HCl. \quad [81]$$

Hydrochloric acid may also be obtained by directly uniting hydrogen and chlorine gas.

$$H\text{-}H + Cl\text{-}Cl = 2HCl. \qquad [82]$$

By electrolyzing the aqueous solution, the last reaction is reversed and the acid is decomposed. It may also be readily decomposed by metallic sodium.

$$2HCl + \mathbf{Na\text{-}Na} = 2NaCl + H\text{-}H. \qquad [83]$$

Liquid hydrochloric acid dissolves most of the metals and the metallic oxides, and its uses in practical chemistry are illustrated by the following reactions. See also [77].

$$\mathbf{Sn} + (2HCl + Aq) = (Sn\,Cl_2 + Aq) + H\text{-}H. \quad [84]$$

$$\mathbf{ZnO} + (2HCl + Aq) = (Zn\,Cl_2 + H_2O + Aq). \quad [85]$$

$$[\mathbf{Al_2}]\mathbf{O_3} + (6HCl + Aq) = ([Al_2]\,Cl_6 + 3H_2O + Aq). \quad [86]$$

115. *Compounds of Chlorine and Oxygen.* — All of them unstable and most of them explosive. In regard to their molecular constitution different views are entertained.

Hypochlorous Anhydride	Cl_2O	$Cl\text{-}O\text{-}Cl,$
Hypochlorous Acid	$HClO$	$H\text{-}O\text{-}Cl,$
Chlorous Acid	$HClO_2$	$H\text{-}O\text{-}O\text{-}Cl,$
Chlorous Anhydride	Cl_2O_3	$Cl\text{-}O\text{-}O\text{-}O\text{-}Cl,$
Chloric Acid	$HClO_3$	$H\text{-}O\text{-}O\text{-}O\text{-}Cl,$
Chloric Peroxide	Cl_2O_4	$Cl\text{-}O\text{-}O\text{-}O\text{-}O\text{-}Cl,$
Perchloric Acid	$HClO_4$	$H\text{-}O\text{-}O\text{-}O\text{-}O\text{-}Cl.$

116. *Potassic Chlorate.* — The most important salt of any of the chlorine oxygen acids. Obtained by passing a stream of chlorine gas through a warm solution of caustic potash.

$$(6K\text{-}O\text{-}H + Aq) + 3\,Cl\text{-}Cl = (KClO_3 + 5KCl + 3H_2O + Aq). \quad [87]$$

Potassic chlorate, being much the less soluble, is readily freed from the potassic chloride by two or three crystallizations. It is decomposed by heat alone into potassic chloride and oxygen gas.

$$2KClO_3 = 2KCl + 3\,O\text{-}O. \qquad [88]$$

N

Much used for making oxygen gas, and also in fireworks and the preparation of detonating powder.

117. BROMINE. $Br = 80.$ — Quantivalence usually one, but atomicity probably of a higher perissad order. Associated with chlorine in minute quantities in saline waters and certain silver ores. The elementary substance (Br-Br) is a very volatile deep-red liquid. $Sp.\ Gr. = 3.187.$ Boils at 63°. Freezes. at 7°.3. Prepared from the bittern of certain salt springs, by treating with chlorine and dissolving out the liberated bromine with ether.

118. IODINE. $I = 127.$ — Quantivalence and atomicity same as with bromine. Associated with chlorine in still smaller quantities than bromine. The elementary substance is obtained from the ashes of certain seaweeds. Crystalline solid; $Sp.\ Gr.$ $= 4.95.$ Melts at 107°. Boils at 175°, forming a dense violet vapor. Very slightly soluble in water, but is readily dissolved by alcohol, ether, and carbonic sulphide. Imparts to starch paste a deep blue color.

The three elements, chlorine, bromine, and iodine, form a well-defined natural group, and a careful comparison will show that the properties both of the elementary substances and of their compounds conform closely to the law of progression which marks a chemical series. These elements are all highly electro-negative bodies, but as we descend in the series we find that this character becomes less marked, and hence their chemical energy, as manifested by the strength of their affinity for elements of the opposite class, such as hydrogen and the electro-positive metals, diminishes as the atomic weight increases; and this law, as will appear, obtains with few exceptions in all the chemical series. Moreover, it will also be found, as might indeed be anticipated, that elements so closely related as these are almost invariably found associated in nature.

119. *Characteristic Reactions.* — The soluble chlorides, bromides, and iodides all give, with a solution of argentic nitrate, precipitates insoluble in water and acids. The iodide of silver may be distinguished from both the chloride and the bromide of the same metal by its yellow color and insolubility in aqua ammonia, in which the last two readily dissolve. Bromine and iodine may both be expelled from their salts by chlorine gas, when the first may be recognized by the red color which it im-

parts to ether or chloroform, and the last by the exceedingly characteristic blue color which it gives to starch paste. Fluorine is easily discovered because its compounds, when heated in a glass tube with potassic bisulphate, yield hydrofluoric acid which etches the glass. This element, although closely allied to the other three, differs so greatly in some of its chemical relations that it is doubtful whether it belongs to the same chemical series.

Questions and Problems.

1. It appears that 10 grammes of pure fluor-spar yields 17.436 grammes of calcic sulphate [76]. Assuming that the atomic weight of calcium is 40, that of SO_4 96, and also that the symbol of fluor-spar is CaF_2, what is the atomic weight of fluorine?   Ans. 19.

2. How much fluor-spar and how much sulphuric acid must be used to generate sufficient hydrofluoric acid to neutralize 53 grammes of sodic carbonate?
       Ans. 39 grammes of fluor-spar and 49 of sulphuric acid.

3. How much liquid hydrochloric acid, *Sp. Gr.* 1.1893, and how much MnO_2, will yield one litre of chlorine gas?
Ans. 3.897 grammes of MnO_2 and 17.06 grammes of hydrochloric acid.

4. Fifty-nine grammes of metallic tin were dissolved in hydrochloric acid [84], and into this solution chlorine gas was passed until all the tin was converted into perchloride. How many litres of hydrogen gas were evolved in the first process, and how many of chlorine gas absorbed in the second?   Ans. 11.16 litres of each.

5. Analyze reactions [66 and 79], and show in what way the chlorine gas acts as an oxidizing agent.

6. Five grammes of liquid hydrochloric acid are mixed with a solution of argentic nitrate, the last being in excess. The precipitated argentic chloride was collected, washed, dried, and weighed. The weight was 3.206 grammes. Required the per cent of *HCl* in the solution.   Ans. 16.31.

7. One volume of common muriatic acid, *Sp. Gr.* 1.2, contains how many volumes of *HCl* gas?
Ans. 1 $\overline{\text{c. m.}}^3$, or 1.200 grammes, contains 0.489 grammes of *HCl*, or 315.8 $\overline{\text{c. m.}}^3$ measured at 15° [9].

8. In order to make one litre of common muriatic acid of *Sp. Gr.*

1.16, how much salt and how much sulphuric acid must be used, and how much water must be placed in the condenser? [81]

    Ans. 598.9 grammes of salt, 1003. grammes of sulphuric acid, and 786.3 grammes of water.

9. On what does the economy of the process [80] over [81] depend?

10. The reaction [82] is said to prove that both hydrogen and chlorine gas have molecules consisting of two atoms. On what postulates does the proof rest? (17) (19.)

11. One litre of hydrochloric acid gas will yield by [83] how many litres of hydrogen gas?   Ans. $\frac{1}{2}$ of a litre.

12. Point out the differences between the reactions [84, 85, 86, and 87], and the relations on which the differences depend.

13. Show that the compounds of chlorine and oxygen may be regarded as compounds of chlorine and hydroxyl, less a certain number of molecules of water. What atomicity would it then be necessary to assign to chlorine?

    Ans. For one case, $(HO)_7 \overset{\text{vii}}{Cl} - 3H_2O = (HO) \text{-} \overset{\text{vii}}{Cl} \frac{7}{2} O,O,O.$

14. It has been found by very careful experiments that 100 parts of potassic chlorate yield by [88] 60.85 parts of potassic chloride; and further, that 100 parts of potassic chloride give by precipitation 192.4 parts of argentic chloride. Assuming that the symbols of these compounds are those given above, what must be the atomic weights of chlorine, potassium, and silver? It is also assumed, as found by previous experiments, that the atomic weight of oxygen is 16, and that 100 parts of silver combine with 32.87 of chlorine.

    Ans. $Cl = 35.5$, $K = 39.1$, $Ag = 108$.

15. The chlorine gas evolved from 1.740 grammes of MnO_2 is passed into a solution of potassic iodide. How much iodine will be thus set free?   Ans. 5.081 grammes.

16. Bromine and iodine form both with hydrogen and oxygen compounds similar to those of chlorine. Compare together the several compounds and point out the resemblances and differences in their properties. (See Miller's Chemistry.)

Division III.

120. SODIUM. $Na = 23$. — Monad. Combined with chlorine it forms common salt, a substance which is very widely distributed throughout nature. It also enters into the composition of a few other minerals as an essential constituent, and several of its salts find important applications both in the arts and in common life.

121. *Metallic Sodium. Na-Na.* — Soft, white metal with brilliant lustre, but rapidly tarnishing in the air. *Sp. Gr.* = 0.97. Fuses at 90°, and boils at a red heat. When heated in the air, it burns with intensely yellow flame. Decomposes water at the lowest temperatures. Prepared by distilling in an iron retort a mixture of sodic carbonate and charcoal.

$$Na_2CO_3 + 2C = Na\text{-}Na + 3CO. \qquad [89]$$

Used in the extraction of aluminum, and in the chemist's laboratory as a powerful reducing agent.

122. *Sodic Chloride (Common Salt). Na Cl.* — White crystalline salt (Isometric, Fig. 7). *Sp. Gr.* = 2.078. Melts at red heat. Volatilizes at white heat. Soluble in about three times its weight of water. Obtained from salt-beds and by the evaporation of saline waters. An essential article of food. The source of almost all the sodium salts. Used for preserving meat.

123. *Sodic Carbonate (Sal Soda). Na_2CO_3.* — The crystallized salt contains in addition $10 H_2O$, but effloresces in dry air. White soluble salt, having an alkaline reaction. Formerly prepared by the lixiviation of the ashes of certain marine plants called barilla. Now almost universally made from common salt by Leblanc's process. This consists, — First, in treating common salt with sulphuric acid, which converts sodic chloride into sodic sulphate.

$$2NaCl + H_2SO_4 = Na_2SO_4 + 2HCl. \qquad [90]$$

Secondly, in melting on the hearth of a reverberatory furnace the sodic sulphate with chalk and fine coal.

$$5Na_2SO_4 + 20C = 5Na_2S + 20CO. \qquad [91]$$

$$5Na_2S + 7CaCO_3 =$$
$$5Na_2CO_3 + 5CaS, 2CaO + 2CO. \qquad [92]$$

Thirdly, by lixiviating the non-volatile product of the last reaction (called black-ball) with water, which dissolves only the sodic carbonate. Used in washing, in the manufacture of glass and soap, and in the preparation of other sodium salts. Also an important reagent in the laboratory. Precipitates from solution of their salts most of the metals, generally as carbonates.

$$(Ca\,Cl_2 + Na_2\,CO_3 + Aq) = \mathbf{CaCO_3} + (2Na\,Cl + Aq). \quad [93]$$

When fused in large excess with insoluble silicates or sulphates, it decomposes them. Sodic silicate or sulphate is formed, which is soluble in water, and metallic carbonates, soluble in acids.

$$BaSO_4 + xNa_2\,CO_3 =$$
$$Ba\,CO_3 + Na_2SO_4 + (x-1)\,Na_2\,CO_3. \quad [94]$$

124. *Acid Sodic Carbonate* (*Bicarbonate of Soda*). $H,Na\text{=}CO_3$. — The crystallized neutral carbonate, when exposed to an atmosphere of carbonic anhydride, absorbs the gas and is converted into this product (a white powder).

$$Na_2\,CO_3 \cdot 10H_2O + CO_2 = 2H,Na\text{=}CO_3 + 9H_2O. \quad [95]$$

Used, under the name of saleratus, for raising bread, and in the preparation of various effervescing powders.

$$(H,Na\text{=}CO_3 + H,K\text{=}C_4H_4O_6 + Aq) =$$
$$\underset{\text{Cream of Tartar.}}{}$$
$$(Na,K\text{=}C_4H_4O_6 + H_2O + Aq) + CO_2. \quad [96]$$
$$\underset{\text{Rochelle Salts.}}{}$$

125. *Sodic Hydrate* (*Caustic Soda*). $Na\text{-}O\text{-}H$. — Amorphous white solid, having very strong attraction for water, in which it dissolves in all proportions, evolving considerable heat. Solution powerfully alkaline and strongly caustic. Prepared by adding milk of lime to a solution of sodic carbonate.

$$(Na_2\text{=}CO_3 + Ca\text{=}(HO)_2 + Aq) =$$
$$\mathbf{Ca\text{=}CO_3} + (2Na\text{-}HO + Aq). \quad [97]$$

To obtain the solid, the solution must be decanted from the insoluble chalk ($Ca\,CO_3$) and evaporated to dryness. The solution itself is a very valuable reagent in the laboratory, and a crude solution (lye) is used in the arts for making soap.

Caustic soda will completely neutralize the strongest acids. On evaporating the neutral solution, we obtain the sodic salt of the acid used.

$$(NaO\text{-}H + HO\text{-}NO_2 + Aq) = $$
$$NaO\text{-}NO_2 + H_2O + Aq). \quad [98]$$

$$(2NaO\text{-}H + \underset{\text{Oxalic Acid.}}{(HO)_2\text{=}C_2O_2} + Aq) = $$
$$((NaO)_2\text{=}C_2O_2 + 2H_2O + Aq). \quad [99]$$

Sodic salts of weak acids have an alkaline reaction.

126. *Oxides of Sodium.* — Sodic Oxide, Na_2O. Sodic Peroxide, $Na_2(O\text{-}O)$.

127. *Sodic Nitrate (Chili Saltpetre or Cubic Nitre).* $Na\text{-}NO_3$. — A natural product found incrusting the soil in the desert of Atacama. Crystallizes in rhombohedrons resembling cubes. Much used for making nitric acid.

128. POTASSIUM. $K = 39.1$. — Monad. An important constituent of felspar and mica, two very widely distributed siliceous minerals. A constituent also of all fertile soils which are formed in part by the disintegration of rocks containing these minerals. By the action of atmospheric agents on the soil, soluble potassium salts are formed which are absorbed by the growing plants, whose ashes are the chief source of the potassium salts of commerce. But these salts are now also obtained from the salt-beds of Stassfurt in Germany.

129. *Metallic Potassium. K-K.* — Resembles sodium, but has a bluish tinge of color; *Sp. Gr.* $= 0.865$. Brittle at $0°$. Soft at $15°$. Melts at $55°$. Sublimes in green vapors at a low red heat. Burns when heated in the air, and takes fire spontaneously on water. Prepared by distilling in an iron retort the intimate mixture of potassic carbonate and charcoal obtained by charring crude tartar. Reaction same as [89], substituting K for Na. More powerful reducing agent than sodium; hence obtained with greater difficulty. More expensive, and less used on that account.

130. *Potassic Carbonate.* K_2CO_3. — White deliquescent salt, with strong alkaline reaction. The crude salt (*Pot-ashes* of commerce) is obtained by lixiviating wood-ashes and evaporating the lixivium. Purified by dissolving in a small quantity of boiling water, and crystallizing out the impurities. Largely

consumed in the arts for manufacturing glass and soap, and for preparing other compounds of potassium.

131. *Acid Potassic Carbonate* (*Bicarbonate of Potash*). H,K=CO_3. — White crystalline salt, prepared by passing CO_2 through a strong solution of the neutral carbonate. Reaction like [95], substituting K for Na.

132. *Potassic Hydrate* (*Caustic Potash*). H,K=O. — White amorphous solid, prepared like caustic soda [97], which it closely resembles, but is more deliquescent and more strongly alkaline. Forms with fats "soft soaps," while soda forms "hard soaps." Like caustic soda, an important reagent in the laboratory. Precipitates from solutions of their salts most of the metals, generally as hydrates, but sometimes as oxides. In some cases the precipitate is soluble in an excess of the reagent.

$$(Ca\text{=}SO_4 + 2K\text{-}(HO) + Aq) =$$
$$Ca\text{=}(HO)_2 + (K_2\text{=}SO_4 + Aq). \quad [100]$$

$$(2Ag\text{-}NO_3 + 2K\text{-}(HO) + Aq) =$$
$$Ag_2O + (H_2O + 2K\text{-}NO_3 + Aq). \quad [101]$$

$$([Al_2]Cl_6 + 6K\text{-}(HO) + Aq) =$$
$$[Al_2]\text{=}(HO)_6 + (6KCl + Aq). \quad [102]$$

$$[Al_2]\text{=}(HO)_6 + (6K\text{-}HO + Aq) =$$
$$(K_6\text{=}O_6\text{=}[Al_2] + 6H_2O + Aq). \quad [103]$$
Potassic Aluminate.

133. *Oxides of Potassium.* — Potassic Oxide, K_2=O. Potassic Dioxide, K_2=$(O\text{-}O)$. Potassic Tetroxide, K_2=$(O\text{-}O\text{-}O\text{-}O)$.

134. *Potassic Chloride* (*Sylvine*). KCl. — Isomorphous with $NaCl$. Found associated with Carnallite (KCl . $MgCl_2$. $6H_2O$) in the mines of Stassfurt.

135. *Potassic Nitrate* (*Nitre*). KNO_3. — White crystalline salt. Dimorphous. Usual form of crystals orthorhombic prisms, but under certain conditions crystallizes in rhombohedra like $NaNO_3$ (Hexagonal). Melts at 339° without decomposition. Is decomposed at a red heat, giving off a mixture of oxygen and nitrogen gas. Deflagrates on glowing coals. Nitre is a natural product, and is chiefly used in the manufacture of gunpowder. It is also employed in curing meat, and the fused salt (sal prunelle) is a useful medicine

136. *Characteristic Reactions.* — Salts of potassium are distinguished from those of sodium by giving a precipitate with an excess of tartaric acid and with acid platinic chloride.

$$(KCl + \underset{\text{Tartaric Acid.}}{H,H\text{=}C_4H_4O_6} + Aq) =$$
$$\underset{\text{Acid Potassic Tartrate.}}{\mathbf{H,K\text{=}C_4H_4O_8}} + (HCl + Aq). \quad [104]$$

$$(2KCl + PtCl_6H_2 + Aq) =$$
$$\mathbf{PtCl_6K_2} + (2HCl + Aq). \quad [105]$$

137. *Lithium, Rubidium, and Cæsium* are found in very minute quantities in certain mineral waters, in lepidolite mica, and in a few other rare minerals. They are always associated with potassium and sodium, to which they are closely allied in all their chemical relations. They form with sodium and potassium a series of electro-positive elements quite as well marked as the series of electro-negative elements of the previous group; and, following the same law, the most electro-positive elements are the lowest in the series and have the highest atomic weights. Hence, therefore, the chemical energy of the elements of this group, as manifested by the strength of their affinities for elements of the opposite class, like those of the chlorine group, increases as we descend in the series.

138. *Characteristic Reactions.* — The compounds of each of the five "alkaline metals" impart a peculiar color to the flame of the Bunsen lamp. These colored flames, when examined with the spectroscope, exhibit characteristic bands, by which the elements may be distinguished, and both rubidium and cæsium were discovered by this means. (Chapter XVI.)

Questions and Problems.

1. What is the Sp. Gr. of sodium vapor ? Ans. 23.

2. What is the weight of one litre of sodium vapor at 1,093°, but under the normal pressure ? [9] and (1).

Ans. Weight of hydrogen gas under the conditions named is $\frac{1}{5}$ of a crith. Hence, weight of sodium vapor is 4.6 criths or 0.4121 of a gramme.

3. In the preparation of sodium [89] what weight of metal ought to be obtained from 20 kilos. of sodic carbonate, and how many litres

of carbonic oxide gas should be formed for every gramme of sodium obtained ?

Ans. 8.680 kilos. of sodium and 1.456 litres of carbonic oxide.

4. One cubic decimetre of rock-salt contains how many cubic decimetres of metallic sodium, and how many litres of chlorine gas?

Ans. 0.8422 $\overline{\text{d. m.}}^3$ of sodium and 896.5 litres of chlorine.

5. To what extent is the solubility of common salt influenced by the temperature ? (Fig. 2, page 108.)

6. Given the specific heat of common salt (0.214), and the atomic weights of its elements (sodium and chlorine), to find its symbol.

7. How much carbonate of soda can be made from 500 kilogrammes of common salt ? How much sulphuric acid ? How much coal and how much chalk are required in the process, according to the theory ?

Ans. 453 kilos. of $NaCO_3$, 418.8 kilos. of H_2SO_4, 205 kilos. of C, and 598.2 of $CaCO_3$.

8. What relation ought the price of crystallized carbonate of soda to bear to that of the dry salt, if the intrinsic value is alone considered ?   Ans. Price of dry salt 2.7 of crystallized.

9. In order to convert ten kilogrammes of crystallized sodic carbonate into acid carbonate, what volume of CO_2 will be absorbed ?

Ans. 780.3 litres.

10. What is the difference between the two sodic carbonates, and what is the reason for the name *acid* carbonate ? (36).

11. What volume of CO_2 can be obtained from 3.72 grammes of acid sodic carbonate ? [96].   Ans. 1 litre.

12. The symbol of sodic hydrate may be written $Na\text{-}O\text{-}H$, or $Na\text{-}Ho$, or $(NaO)\text{-}H$, and to what three possible views of its constitution do these symbols correspond? [70] (235). Why should the radicals HO or NaO be monads, and what advantage would be gained by writing the symbol in one way or the other ? (22) and (28).

13. Why does calcic hydrate, a comparatively weak base, decompose sodic carbonate ? (21) (52).

14. A solution of caustic soda was exactly neutralized by 0.630 of a gramme of crystallized oxalic acid ($Ho_2\text{=}C_2O_2 \cdot 2H_2O$). What weight of sodium does it contain ?   Ans. 0.230 of a gramme.

15. In what different ways may you write the symbol of potassic nitrate ? Illustrate by diagrams like those of (34). State what rules must be followed in grouping the atoms. (22, 28, 34, and 69.)

Ans. $K\text{-}NO_3$, $KO\text{-}NO_2$, or $K\text{-}O\text{-}NO_2$.

16. What conclusions may be drawn in regard to the distribution of the soluble salts of sodium and potassium based on the nature of the plants from which they are obtained?

17. On what relations of solubility does the process of purifying potassic carbonate depend?

18. If in a chemical process potassic or sodic carbonates may be used indifferently, what relation ought their prices to bear to each other in order that they may be used with equal profit?

Ans. 138 : 106.

19. Analyze equations [100, 101, 102, 103], and show that the various symbols are written in conformity to the rules referred to above, No. 15.

20. If a saturated solution of nitre is made at 38°, and subsequently cooled to 10°, what proportion of the salt will crystallize out? (Fig. 2.) Ans. Two thirds.

21. The difference between the two kinds of soap corresponds to what difference of properties between sodic and potassic carbonate? Ans. The one effloresces and the other deliquesces in the air.

22. Draw diagrams illustrating the constitution of the different potassic oxides. (34.)

23. Why would not the salts of sodium be precipitated by the same reagents used in [104 and 105]? Apply the same principle to the interpretation of the other reactions of this section.

Division IV.

139. SILVER. $Ag = 108$. — Monad. Found in small quantities in nature, chiefly in the metallic state, or in combination with chlorine, sulphur, arsenic, or antimony.

140. *Metallic Silver.* $Ag\text{-}Ag?$ — *Sp. Gr.* 10.474. Fuses at about 1,000°. The principal ores are

Native Silver	$Ag\text{-}Ag,$
Horn Silver	$Ag\,Cl,$
Silver Glance	$Ag_2S,$
Light-red Silver Ore (Proustite)	$(AgS)_3{=}As,$
Dark-red Silver Ore (Pyrargyrite)	$(AgS)_3{=}Sb.$

These ores are found chiefly in mineral veins either by themselves or associated with ores of lead and copper, with which they are frequently smelted, and the silver subsequently separated from the regulus thus obtained. Silver does not oxidize when heated in contact with the air, and for this reason is readily separated from lead in the process of cupellation.

$$xAg_2 \cdot yPb + \tfrac{1}{2}yO{=}O = xAg\text{-}Ag + yPbO. \quad [106]$$

The cupel furnace is so arranged that the melted litharge (PbO) runs off as fast as formed, and leaves the silver pure. Melted silver can dissolve about twenty-two times its volume of oxygen gas; but the gas is given off, in great measure, when the metal solidifies.

141. *Argentic Nitrate.* $AgNO_3$. — The most important soluble salt of silver. Obtained by dissolving silver in dilute nitric acid.

$$3Ag\text{-}Ag + (8HNO_3 + Aq) =$$
$$(6AgNO_3 + 4H_2O + Aq) + 2NO. \quad [107]$$

White crystalline solid which melts at 219°. Fused salt is called lunar caustic, and is much used in surgery as a cautery. Argentic nitrate, although not changed by the light when pure, is readily decomposed when in contact with organic matter, and the black stain of metallic silver thus formed cannot be removed by washing. Hence its application for making hair dyes and indelible ink.   It is also used in large quantities in the art of photography.

142. *Argentic Chloride. Ag Cl.* — White crystalline solid (Fig. 7).   Melts at about 260°, and on cooling forms a horny sectile mass, whence the mineralogical name, horn silver.   Prepared by adding to a solution of argentic nitrate any soluble chloride.

$$(AgNO_3 + NaCl + Aq) = \mathbf{AgCl} + (NaNO_3 + Aq). \quad [108]$$

We thus obtain a white curdy precipitate, which is insoluble in water and acids, but soluble in ammonia, in potassic cyanide, and in sodic hyposulphite.   Owing to a partial reduction, the white powder blackens in the light, especially in the presence of organic matter and an excess of argentic nitrate.   On this property is based the ordinary process of photographic printing. In contact with dilute acids, argentic chloride is very readily reduced by metallic zinc.

$$2AgCl + Zn = ZnCl_2 + Ag_2. \qquad [109]$$

It may also be reduced by hydrogen or hydrocarbon gas passed over the chloride in a heated tube.

$$2\mathbf{AgCl} + \mathbf{H\text{-}H} = \mathbf{Ag\text{-}Ag} + 2\mathbf{HCl}. \qquad [110]$$

In the process of electro-plating, argentic chloride, dissolved in an aqueous solution of potassic cyanide, is decomposed by the electric current.   (91).

143. *Argentic Bromide, AgBr,* and *Argentic Iodide, AgI,* resemble argentic chloride, and are formed in a similar way. The last, however, has a yellow color, and is insoluble in ammonia.   In presence of an excess of argentic nitrate, and after exposure to light, they are at once reduced to the metallic state by solution of ferrous sulphate.   Before exposure the reduction takes place very slowly, and on this reaction is based the art of photography.   The steps of the process are: 1. Spreading over a glass plate a film of collodion, holding in solution a mixture of metallic bromides and iodides; 2. Immersing the coated plate in a solution of argentic nitrate until a mixture of argentic bromide and iodide is formed in the film; 3. Exposing the plate to light in the camera, where the image formed by a lens falls upon it; 4. Developing the latent image by a solution of

ferrous sulphate; 5. Dissolving out the undecomposed silver salt by a solution of sodic hyposulphite.

144. *Argentic Oxide.* Ag_2O.   *Argentic Peroxide.* Ag_2O_2. — The first is very slightly soluble in water, and the solution has an alkaline reaction.

145. *Characteristic Tests.* — Most silver compounds may be reduced to pure silver before the blow-pipe; and whenever they are brought into solution the silver can be recognized and the amount very accurately determined by the reaction just given. [108]. Silver is remarkable for forming anhydrous salts; and whenever we wish to determine the molecular weight of an acid, it is generally best to analyze its silver salt. (68).

Division V.

146. THALLIUM. $Tl = 204$. — Usual quantivalence one, but atomicity probably three. A very rare element, found in some varieties of pyrites. Its oxide, Tl_2O, is soluble in water, and absorbs carbonic anhydride from the air. Its vapor imparts a green color to the flame of a Bunsen lamp, and shows a single green band in the spectroscope.

Division VI.

147. GOLD. $Au = 197$. — Triad. Probable molecular symbol of metal, $Au=Au$. Almost always found in the native state, or only slightly alloyed with other metals. The only well-defined native compounds are those with Tellurium. Very sparingly but very widely disseminated through many of the crystalline rocks and in the alluvium resulting from their disintegration. In the gold-bearing rocks the metal is frequently found accumulated to a greater or less extent in veins of quartz (auriferous quartz). It is also constantly associated in minute quantities with other metallic ores, especially with those of silver, and in some localities the veins of iron and copper pyrites yield large amounts of the precious metal. It is extracted either by simple washing or by bringing the finely pulverized ore in contact with metallic mercury, which has a great affinity for gold and picks out the minute particles from the mass of

refuse. The process is very simple, and the cost of the product depends, to a great extent, on the very large amount of material which must be handled; for gold ores do not on the average contain but a few ounces of metal to the ton. From the resulting amalgam the mercury is recovered by distillation, and the residual metal may then be melted and cast into bars. The gold thus obtained, however, is more or less alloyed, chiefly with silver, and is refined before being used for coinage. This is best accomplished by dissolving the metal in aqua-regia, evaporating to dryness to remove the excess of nitric acid, dissolving in a large volume of water, and precipitating the gold with ferrous sulphate. Lastly, the precipitate is collected and melted under borax. If the proportion of alloy is very large, it is best removed by boiling the metal with nitric or sulphuric acid. When nitric acid is used for parting gold from silver, the separation is not complete when the amount of gold is more than one fourth of the weight of the alloy; and since in most cases the alloy must be first reduced to this proportion, the process is called quartation. When sulphuric acid is used, the amount of gold must not exceed one fifth.

Gold has been called the king of metals; for it not only possesses the qualities distinguishing a metal in their highest perfection, but also, under all ordinary conditions, preserves its brilliant lustre unimpaired. With the exception of platinum, iridium, and osmium, gold is the densest solid known; *Sp. Gr.* 19.34. It may be drawn into wire of such fineness that three kilometres only weigh a single gramme, and may be beaten into leaves not more than one ten-thousandth of a millimetre thick. Gold has a familiar yellow color, but thin leaves transmit a green light. It has been found that an exceedingly thin film of gold attached to the surface of a glass plate, and heated to a temperature not exceeding 315°, loses its metallic lustre and appears ruby-red by transmitted light; and finely divided gold, when suspended in water or melted into glass, imparts to the medium the same beautiful color. Gold is nearly as soft as lead, and pieces of pure gold may be welded together without heat by pressure or concussion, as in dentistry. In order to increase its hardness it is alloyed with copper. The standard gold of both the United States and the French coinage contains one tenth copper, that of the English one twelfth of the same alloy. Gold melts at about 1,100°. It is only slightly volatile at the highest furnace heat; but before the compound blow-pipe it is dispersed in purple vapor. It is an excellent conductor of heat and electricity, but is inferior in this respect both to silver and copper.

Gold is not dissolved by any of the common acids, and is not attacked by the fused caustic alkalies. It enters, however, into direct union both with chlorine and bromine, and is readily dissolved by any liquid mixture which liberates chlorine. The usual solvent is a mixture of four parts of hydrochloric acid with one of nitric acid, called, on account of its power of dissolving gold, aqua-regia.

$$Au \underline{=} Au + (2HNO_3 + 6HCl + Aq) =$$
$$(2AuCl_3 + 4H_2O + Aq) + 2NO. \quad [111]$$

When gold is dissolved in aqua-regia, if hydrochloric acid is used in excess, the solution, evaporated at a gentle heat, yields *yellow* needle-shaped crystals, which appear to be a molecular compound of $AuCl_3$ with HCl. If, however, the evaporation is pushed still further, but at a temperature not exceeding 120°, a *red* crystalline mass is obtained, which is essentially *Auric Chloride*, $AuCl_3$, although it is difficult to expel the last traces of HCl without still further decomposing the salt. If this product is heated above 160° it loses two atoms of chlorine, and there is left a pale-yellow, sparingly soluble powder, which is *Aurous Chloride*, $AuCl$, and at 200° this last is also decomposed and reduced to metallic gold. Auric chloride is deliquescent, and yields an orange-colored solution easily distinguished from the solution of $AuCl_3 . HCl$, which is yellow. It also forms yellow crystalline salts with the alkaline chlorides, similar in constitution to the compounds with HCl. Their formulas are $AuCl_3 . KCl . 5H_2O$, and $AuCl_3 . NaCl . 4H_2O$. In like manner it unites with ammonic chloride and with the chlorides of most of the organic bases, forming crystallizable salts, which are often employed to determine the molecular weight of these alkaloids. Auric chloride is a very unstable compound, and is readily reduced to the metallic state. Solutions of ferrous sulphate, of antimonious chloride, of oxalic acid, and of sulphurous acid, all precipitate the gold in a finely-divided state. Phosphorous and hypophosphorous acid and solutions of their salts produce the same effect, as do also phosphorus itself and many of the metals. The brown gold powder thus obtained is much used for gilding porcelain. A solution of stannous chloride mixed with stannic chloride produces in neutral solution of auric chloride a beautiful purple precipitate called Purple of Cassius, which is much used for coloring glass and porcelain. The compound contains both gold and tin combined with oxygen, but its chemical constitution is still in question. Metallic tin gives a similar precipitate. There appear to be two iodides of gold, AuI and AuI_3, but only one bromide, $AuBr_3$, has been described. There are also two oxides, Au_2O_3 and Au_2O. The first acts as an acid, the second as a very feeble basic anhydride. The following reactions illustrate the formation and relations of these compounds.

$$(AuCl_3 + 6K\text{-}O\text{-}H + Aq) =$$
$$(K_3^{\equiv}O_3^{\equiv}Au + 3KCl + 3H_2O + Aq). \quad [112]$$

$$K_3^{\equiv}O_3^{\equiv}Au + 3H\text{-}O\text{-}C_2H_3O + Aq) =$$
$$H_3^{\equiv}O_3^{\equiv}Au + (3K\text{-}O\text{-}C_2H_3O + Aq). \quad [113]$$

$$2H_3^{\equiv}O_3^{\equiv}Au = Au_2O_3 + 3H_2O. \quad [114]$$

To obtain these reactions, the solution of $AuCl_3$ should be boiled after the addition of $K\text{-}O\text{-}H$ and then acidified with acetic acid. The precipitate thus obtained has, when dried, the composition of Au_2O_3. The compound Au_2O is obtained as an insoluble violet powder by digesting $AuCl$ with a solution of caustic alkali.

$$(2AuCl + 2Na\text{-}O\text{-}H + Aq) =$$
$$Au_2O + (2NaCl + H_2O + Aq). \quad [115]$$

It does not enter into direct combination with acids, but there is an hyposulphite of gold and sodium which plays an important part in photography, and appears to have the formula $Au,Na\text{-}O_2\text{-}(S\text{-}O\text{-}S)$. Singularly, however, gold is not precipitated from the solution of this salt by the ordinary reagents. There are two sulphides of gold, Au_2S_3 and Au_2S. The first is precipitated by H_2S from a cold solution and the last from a boiling solution of $AuCl_3$ by the same reagent. They both dissolve in alkaline sulphides and form sulphur salts. Thus

$$Au_2S_3 + (6K\text{-}S\text{-}H + Aq) =$$
$$(2K_3^{\equiv}S_3^{\equiv}Au + Aq) + 3H_2S. \quad [116]$$

148. *Characteristic Reactions.* — With the exception just noticed, gold, when in solution, can be distinguished by the fact that it is precipitated by ferrous sulphate, provided the solution, though acid, does not contain an excess of nitric acid.

$$(2AuCl_3 + 6Fe\text{-}O_2\text{-}SO_2 + Aq) =$$
$$\mathbf{Au\text{-}Au} + ([Fe_2]\tfrac{3}{2}Cl_6 + 2[Fe_2]\tfrac{3}{2}O_6\tfrac{3}{2}(SO_2)_3 + Aq). \quad [117]$$

The formation of purple of Cassius, and the easy reduction of all the compounds to the metallic state by simple ignition, are other indications by which the presence of gold may be readily recognized. The reduced gold, even when in fine powder, acquires its peculiar lustre if rubbed against a hard surface, as in the process of burnishing. Besides the important uses of gold for coinage and for articles of ornament or luxury, the metal is peculiarly well adapted, both by its softness and its power of resisting corrosive agents, for its applications in dentistry. It is also largely employed in the various methods of gilding, which consists either in directly applying thin gold-leaf to the surface to be covered, or, when the surface is metallic, by depositing upon it a thin film of gold with the aid of galvanism or by the simple action of chemical affinity.

Questions and Problems.

1. Given the percentage composition of Proustite. Silver, 65.45; Sulphur, 19.39; Arsenic, 15.16. Required the symbol.

Ans. Ag_3S_3As.

2 How much greater is the per cent of silver in Proustite than in Pyrargyrite? Ans. 5.68 per cent.

3. Draw diagrams illustrating the molecular constitution of the different silver ores.

4. Analyze reaction [107], and point out the difference between it and the class of reactions of which [64] is the type.

5. If a given mass of argentiferous lead contains three fourths of one per cent of silver, how many kilogrammes of litharge will be made in the process of cupellation to each kilogramme of silver extracted, and how many cubic metres of oxygen gas will be absorbed by the process?

Ans. 142.5 kilos. of litharge, and 7.134 $\overline{m.}^3$ of oxygen.

6. One gramme of silver treated as indicated by [107] and [108] yielded 1.328 grammes of argentic chloride. What is the atomic weight of silver? The atomic weight of chlorine is assumed to be known, 35.5, and also the specific heat of argentic chloride, 0.091.

Ans. 108.

7. One gramme of argentic chloride reduced by hydrogen [110] yielded 0.7526 of a gramme of silver. What is the atomic weight of silver? The same values are assumed as in the last problem.

Ans. 108.

8. One gramme of argentic oxalate yields when heated 0.7105 of a gramme of silver. We have reason to believe that oxalic acid is bibasic. What is its molecular weight? (68). Ans. 90.

9. Write the reactions of sulphurous acid and of oxalic acid on solution of auric chloride, assuming that sulphuric acid in one case, and CO_2 in the other, are a part of the products.

10. What evidence do you find of the quantivalence of gold in the above sections?

11. Does gold act as an acid or a basic radical?

12. What is the chief chemical characteristic of gold?

13. There has been a question about the cause of the color which purple of Cassius imparts to glass and porcelain glaze. Do the facts stated above explain this phenomenon?

Division VII.

149. BORON. $B = 11.$ — Triad. Very sparingly distributed. Always found in combination with oxygen. In boric acid
and in various borates, including the minerals Datholite and
Danburite, boron is the electro-negative element, while in Axi-
nite and Tourmaline, and in many artificial salts, it acts the part
of a basic radical. The elementary substance $(B{=}B?)$ may be
obtained both in an amorphous and a crystalline form. The
first is obtained by decomposing boric anhydride with sodium.

$$B_2O_3 + 3Na\text{-}Na = 3Na_2O + B{=}B. \qquad [118]$$

It is an infusible dark-brown powder, which soils the fingers
and dissolves slightly in water. At about 300° it takes fire in
the air and burns into B_2O_3, and it is also oxidized when heated
with sulphuric acid or with the alkaline nitrates, sulphates, carbonates, or hydrates. It decomposes nitric acid even when
slightly concentrated and cold.

$$B{=}B + 3H_2{=}O_2{=}SO_2 = B_2O_3 + 3H_2O + 3SO_2. \quad [119]$$

$$B{=}B + 6KNO_3 = 2K_3{=}O_3{=}B + 6NO_2. \qquad [120]$$

Boron is one of the very few elements which unite directly with
nitrogen.

$$B{=}B + N{=}N = 2B{=}N. \qquad [121]$$

If amorphous boron is heated intensely in a closed crucible, it
becomes much denser, and is then less easily oxidized. It dissolves in melted aluminum, and when the molten metal sets, the
boron crystallizes in quadratic octohedrons (75) more or less
highly modified. These crystals are nearly as hard as the diamond, have an adamantine lustre, and *Sp. Gr.* $= 2.68$. They
may also be obtained directly from boric anhydride, which is
decomposed by aluminum.

$$[Al_2] + B_2O_3 = [Al_2]O_3 + B{=}B. \qquad [122]$$

The crystals thus prepared are sometimes nearly colorless,
but more frequently they have a yellow or red color, and sometimes the color is so deep that they appear black. They are

probably never wholly pure, and it is worthy of remark that they sometimes, if not always, contain a considerable quantity of carbon. They resist the action of all acids, and even of fused nitre, but are oxidized when fused with acid potassic sulphate. It appears, from recent investigations, that the so-called graphitoidal boron, which is formed with the crystals just mentioned, is a compound of aluminum and boron.

150. *Boric Acid.* $H_3^= O_3^= B$. — A product of volcanic action. Found in some natural waters, and has been detected in the waters of the ocean. It is collected in large quantities, but in an impure condition, from the hot vapors of the "*fumerolles*" in the Maremma of Tuscany. The pure acid is best prepared from borax by the reaction

$$(Na_2^= O_2^= B_4 O_5 + 2HCl + 5H_2O + Aq) =$$
$$4H_3^= O_3^= B + (2NaCl + Aq). \quad [123]$$

The hydrochloric acid should be mixed with a hot saturated solution of borax, which as it cools deposits boric acid in white nacreous crystalline scales. Boric acid is sparingly soluble in cold water, but dissolves in three times its weight of boiling water. It is also soluble in alcohol, and imparts to the flame of burning alcohol a peculiar green tint, which exhibits in the spectroscope five well-marked green bands. The solution both in water and in alcohol cannot be evaporated without loss, as the vapor always takes with it an appreciable amount of the acid. The solution evaporated on turmeric paper changes the color to brown, like an alkali, but it affects litmus paper like other weak acids. At the temperature of 100° it loses one atom of water.

$$H_3^= O_3^= B = H\text{-}O\text{-}BO + H_2O. \quad [124]$$

The compound $H_3^= O_3^= B$ is called orthoboric acid. The product $H\text{-}O\text{-}BO$ is frequently described as the first anhydride of this acid, and is called metaboric acid. If this is heated to a still higher temperature two molecules unite, while at the same time they lose another atom of water, forming the second and last anhydride, boric anhydride.

$$2H\text{-}O\text{-}BO = B_2O_3 + H_2O. \quad [125]$$

At a red heat B_2O_3 fuses to a viscid glass, which remains clear

as it cools, but soon becomes opaque and crumbles if exposed
to the air. It also forms fusible compounds with the metallic
oxides. Hence the use of boric acid and the borates as fluxes.

151. *Borates.* — It is evident from the principles of (38)
that, besides orthoboric acid, many others are theoretically possible. Thus : —

Boric Acid	$H_3 \equiv O_3 \equiv \overset{\text{III}}{B},$
Diboric Acid	$H_4 \equiv O_4 \equiv (B\text{-}O\text{-}\overset{\text{IV}}{B}),$
Triboric Acid	$H_5 \equiv O_5 \equiv (B\text{-}O\text{-}B\text{-}O\text{-}\overset{\text{V}}{B}),$
Tetraboric Acid	$H_6 \equiv O_6 \equiv (B\text{-}O\text{-}B\text{-}O\text{-}B\text{-}O\text{-}\overset{\text{VI}}{B}),$
Polyboric Acid	$H_{n+2} O_{n+2} (B_n O_{n-1})^{n+2}.$

These may be regarded as formed by the coalescing of several molecules of orthoboric acid, and the elimination from this
condensed molecule of a sufficient number of molecules of water
to set free the number of oxygen atoms required to cement together the atoms of boron in the resulting radical. By eliminating additional molecules of water, we may obtain from either
of the above acids a series of anhydrides (distinguished as the
first, second, &c., anhydrides), and the number of possible anhydrides in any case is equal to the number of pairs of hydrogen atoms which the acid contains. It must be understood that
all these possible forms are not real compounds. Indeed, only
the three already mentioned have been actually prepared ; but
there are several borates whose constitution is best explained
when we regard them as salts of acids derived from orthoboric
acid in the way just indicated. The most important of these
is common borax, which may be regarded as the sodium salt of
the second anhydride of tetraboric acid.

152. *Borax,* $Na_2 \equiv O_2 \equiv (B \equiv O_2 \equiv B\text{-}O\text{-}B \equiv O_2 \equiv \overset{\text{II}}{B}) . 10H_2O$, was originally brought from a salt lake in Thibet, and was called Tincal.
It also occurs in large crystals in the mud of Borax Lake, in
California, and it has been found in solution in many mineral
springs, and even in minute quantities in the ocean. Is manufactured in large quantities from the crude boric acid of the
Tuscan lagoons. White crystalline salt, which when heated
gives up its water of crystallization. At a red heat melts to a
transparent glass, which has the property of dissolving almost

all the metallic oxides. Many of them impart to the glass characteristic colors; and these reactions, which are readily obtained with a small bead of borax supported by a loop of platinum wire, are useful blow-pipe tests. It is also used for soldering metals, for making enamels, for fixing colors on porcelain, and as a flux in various metallurgical processes. The ordinary crystals contain as above $10 H_2 O$, and belong to the monoclinic system; but the salt can be crystallized with only $5 H_2 O$ in octahedrons belonging to the isometric system.

153. *Boric Chloride*, BCl_3, can be obtained by passing chlorine gas over an intimate mixture of $B_2 O_3$ and carbon, heated to a red heat in a porcelain retort.

$$B_2 O_3 + 3 C + 3 Cl\text{-}Cl = 3 CO + 2 BCl_3. \quad [126]$$

It is a very volatile liquid (*Sp. Gr.* 1.35 at 7°), boiling at 17°, and yielding a dense vapor whose Sp. Gr., as found by experiment, is 56.85; chiefly interesting as establishing the quantivalence of boron. It is at once decomposed by water.

$$BCl_3 + 3 H_2 O = H_3 \equiv O_3 \equiv B + 3 HCl. \quad [127]$$

154. *Boric Bromide*, BBr_3, prepared like the chloride, is a volatile liquid (*Sp. Gr.* 2.69), boiling at 90°, and giving a vapor whose Sp. Gr. has been found by experiment equal to 126.8. Decomposed by water like the chloride.

155. *Boric Fluoride*, BF_3, is best prepared by intensely heating a mixture of $B_2 O_3$ and fluor-spar.

$$2 B_2 O_3 + 3 CaF_2 = Ca_3 \equiv O_6 \equiv B_2 + 2 BF_3. \quad [128]$$

A colorless gas, whose Sp. Gr. has been found by experiment equal to 34.2. This gas is eagerly absorbed by water, which dissolves seven hundred times its volume and forms a corrosive acid liquid called *borofluoric acid*, whose constitution is not well understood. If its composition is that usually assigned to it, its formation will be expressed by the reaction

$$2 BF_3 + 3 H_2 O = B_2 O_3 . 6 HF. \quad [129]$$

The same compound may be also prepared by dissolving $B_2 O_3$ in $HF + Aq$, and then concentrating the solution.

If borofluoric acid is largely diluted with water, one fourth of the boron separates in the form of boric acid, and there is left in solution what has been called hydrofluoboric acid.

$$(4(B_2O_3 . 6HF) + Aq) =$$
$$2H_3^{=}O_3^{=}B + (6(HF . BF_3) + 6H_2O + Aq). \quad [130]$$

Hydrofluoboric acid forms salts with basic radicals, and the compound with potassium may be formed by the action of boric acid on a dilute solution of potassic fluoride.

$$(8KF + 2H_3^{=}O_3^{=}B + Aq) =$$
$$2(KF . BF_3) + (6K\text{-}O\text{-}H + Aq). \quad [131]$$

156. *Characteristic Reactions.* — The peculiar green color which boric acid imparts to an alcohol or blow-pipe flame is the best indication of its presence, and this test is made still more decisive by analyzing the colored light with the spectroscope. The acid, however, must first be set free before the reaction can be obtained. In many of its relations boron resembles carbon.

Questions and Problems.

1. Write the reaction of sulphuric acid on solution of borax.

2. What test can be applied to determine when an excess of sulphuric acid has been added?

3. Define an ortho acid, regarding orthoboric acid as a type of the class.

4. Make a table showing the relations of the various possible derivatives of boric acid.

5. The empirical symbol of boracite is $Mg_3O_{15}B_8$. What is its rational symbol, and what is its relation to the ortho-borates?

6. Boric sulphide, B_2S_8, may be prepared by passing over a mixture of carbon and boric anhydride the vapor of carbonic sulphide, CS_2. The products are $2B_2S_8$ and $6CO$. Write the reaction.

7. Boric sulphide is readily decomposed by water, giving boric acid and sulphuretted hydrogen. Write the reaction.

8. In reaction [126] what double affinities are called into play?

9. In what respect do you find reaction [131] remarkable?

10. What evidence do you find of the prevailing quantivalence of boron? Are there any facts which would indicate that boron is a pentad?

Division VIII.

157. NITROGEN. $N = 14.$ — Pentad, but as frequently trivalent or univalent. Chief constituent of the atmosphere; but to this and the materials of organized beings it is almost exclusively confined. It is the characteristic ingredient of animal tissues, which are composed mainly of the four elements carbon, hydrogen, oxygen, and nitrogen. Vegetable tissues, on the other hand, consist chiefly of only the first three of these elements; but nitrogen is never entirely absent from plants, and is an essential ingredient of many important vegetable products, as, for example, of the albuminoid compounds and of the vegetable alkaloids. Nitrogen is marked by weak affinities, and hence its compounds are usually unstable, as is illustrated by the well-known tendency of animal substance to decay.

158. *Nitrogen Gas,* $N\equiv N$, constitutes four fifths of the volume of the atmosphere, and can be obtained in a pure condition, — First, by slowly or rapidly burning phosphorus in a confined volume of air. Secondly, by passing air over ignited copper-turnings, which combine with the oxygen. Thirdly, by passing chlorine gas through a solution of ammonia, —

$$(8H_3N + Aq) + 3\,Cl\text{-}Cl = (6H_4NCl + Aq) + N\equiv N. \quad [132]$$

Fourthly, by heating ammonic nitrite or a mixture of potassic nitrite and ammonic chloride, —

$$(H_4N)\text{-}O\text{-}NO = 2H_2O + N\equiv N. \quad [133]$$

$$K\text{-}O\text{-}NO + (H_4N)Cl = KCl + 2H_2O + N\equiv N. \quad [134]$$

Nitrogen gas has never been condensed to a liquid condition. According to Regnault, one litre of nitrogen gas, under standard conditions, weighs 1.256167 grammes. It is remarkable for its inertness, and one of its chief offices in the atmosphere is to moderate the action of its violent associate. The only elementary substances with which it directly combines are boron and titanium. Nevertheless, nitrogen has a great capacity for combination, and is distinguished by the large number and varied

nature of its compounds; but these can only be formed by indirect methods.

Oxides of Nitrogen.

Nitrous Oxide	N_2O,		
Nitric Oxide	NO,		
Nitrous Anhydride	N_2O_3,	Nitrous Acid	$H\text{-}O\text{-}\overset{\text{III}}{N}O$,
Nitric Peroxide	NO_2,		
Nitric Anhydride	N_2O_5,	Nitric Acid	$H\text{-}O\text{-}\overset{\text{V}}{N}O_2$.

159. *Nitric Acid. HNO_3.* — When electrical discharges are
passed through air which is in contact with caustic or carbo-
nated alkalies, or when organic matter decays in the atmosphere
under the same conditions, a partial union of the elements of the
atmosphere takes place, and nitrates of potassium, sodium, or
calcium are the usual result. From either of these native nitrates, or *nitres*, the acid may be obtained. It is usually prepared by distillation from a mixture of sodic nitrate (127) and
sulphuric acid.

$$Na\text{-}O\text{-}NO_2 + H_2\text{=}O_2\text{=}SO_2 = H,Na\text{=}O_2\text{=}SO_2 + H\text{-}O\text{-}NO_2. \quad [135]$$

One molecule of sulphuric acid is adequate to decompose two
molecules of nitre; but the temperature required is then much
higher, and the nitric acid is in part decomposed. The strongest acid thus prepared is a colorless, fuming liquid, boiling at $86°$
and freezing at $-49°$. Its *Sp. Gr.* $= 1.552$ at $20°$. It is unstable, and is partially decomposed when exposed to the light.

$$4H\text{-}O\text{-}NO_2 = 2H_2O + 4NO_2 + O\text{=}O. \quad [136]$$

The remaining acid is thus diluted, while the nitric peroxide
colors it yellow. A similar decomposition takes place during
the distillation of the acid. This decomposition continues until
the hydrate $2HNO_3 . 3H_2O$ is formed, which is far more stable
and distils unchanged at $123°$. This is the common strong
nitric acid of commerce, but it is not a definite compound, the
composition varying with the pressure under which the acid
distils. A still weaker acid is much used in the arts under the
name of aqua-fortis. The strength of the acid may be determined from its specific gravity by means of tables prepared for
the purpose.

Sp. Gr.	Per Cent. HNO_3	Sp. Gr.	Per Cent. HNO_3	Sp. Gr.	Per Cent. HNO_3
1.500	92.98	1.395	64.17	1.228	36.28
1.470	82.71	1.343	51.50	1.165	26.95
1.435	73.10	1.289	45.62	1.105	17.62

Nitric acid is one of the most corrosive agents known. With a very few exceptions, it oxidizes all the elementary substances, converting them into oxides, acids, or nitrates, as the case may be. In these reactions, as a general rule, nitric oxide is evolved; but the products vary to a certain extent with the conditions of the experiments, and examples will be found under the different elements, and also in [107], [142], [151], and [156], illustrating the different phases which the reaction may assume. Nitric acid corrodes all organic tissues, oxidizing them, and forming various products, among which the most common are water, carbonic acid, and oxalic acid. When more dilute, it stains the skin, wool, silk, and other albuminoid bodies of a bright yellow color. Very strong nitric acid, when mixed with strong sulphuric acid, acts on some organic compounds in a very remarkable way. It removes one or more atoms of hydrogen, and substitutes an equal number of atoms of the radical NO_2 in their place. (31).

$$C_6H_6 + H\text{-}O\text{-}NO_2 = C_6H_5(NO_2) + H_2O. \qquad [137]$$
$$\text{Benzol.} \hspace{4.5cm} \text{Nitro-Benzol.}$$

With the various bases it forms a large class of important salts. When the radical is univalent, these salts have the general symbol $\overset{\mathrm{I}}{R}\text{-}O\text{-}NO_2$. When the radical is bivalent, the general formula becomes $\overset{\mathrm{II}}{R}\text{=}O_2\text{=}(NO_2)_2$, or $\overset{\mathrm{II}}{R}\text{=}O_2\text{=}N_2O_4$. Salts of these types are, in the ordinary use of the term, the normal or ortho-nitrates; but, theoretically, nitrogen is capable of fixing five univalent radicals, and hence some chemists regard the assumed compound $H_5\text{≡}O_5\text{≡}N$ as orthonitric acid, and salts of that type as orthonitrates. By eliminating from this orthoacid first one and then two molecules of water, we obtain the following anhydrides, the last of which is the ordinary acid.

Orthonitric Acid	$H_5\text{≡}O_5\text{≡}N$,	or	$H\text{-}O\text{-}NO_2 . 2H_2O$,
Metanitric "	$H_3\text{=}O_3\text{=}NO$,	or	$H\text{-}O\text{-}NO_2 . H_2O$,
Dimetanitric "	$H\text{-}O\text{-}NO_2.$		

Salts are known whose symbols may be written on all these types, but they may also be written on the ordinary type as well. Thus

$$H_2Bi^{\equiv}O_5{}^{\equiv}N \qquad \text{or} \qquad Bi^{\equiv}O_3{}^{=}NO_2,H_2,$$
Dihydro-bismuthic Orthonitrate.   Basic bismuthic Nitrate.

[138]

$$Mg_3^{\equiv}O_4^{\equiv}(NO)_2 \quad \text{or} \quad (Mg\text{-}O\text{-}Mg\text{-}O\text{-}Mg)^{=}O_2^{=}(NO_2)_2.$$
Magnesic Metanitrate.   Trimagnesic Nitrate.

Such distinctions are of no practical importance, but they are of value in pointing out the many-sided relations of our subject. Under no condition does potassic hydrate form more than one salt with nitric acid, and the important theoretical bearing of this fact is evident.

160. *Nitric Anhydride*, N_2O_5, may be obtained by passing dry chlorine gas over dried argentic nitrate heated to 95°.

$$4AgNO_3 + 2\,Cl\text{-}Cl = 4Ag\,Cl + 2N_2O_5 + O\text{=}O. \quad [139]$$

It is a white solid, crystallizing in prisms of the fourth system, melting at 29°.5, and boiling at 45°. Very unstable, undergoing spontaneous decomposition in a sealed glass tube. By the action of water it forms nitric acid.

$$N_2O_5 + H_2O = 2HNO_3. \qquad\qquad [140]$$

161. *Nitrous Anhydride*. N_2O_3. — Best prepared by the action of dilute nitric acid (*Sp. Gr.* 1.25) on starch. Is also formed in the following reactions : —

$$As_2O_3 + 2HNO_3 = As_2O_5 + N_2O_3 + H_2O. \quad [141]$$

$$2Ag\text{-}Ag + 6HNO_3 = 4AgNO_3 + N_2O_3 + 3H_2O. \quad [142]$$

$$4N\!O + O\text{=}O = 2N_2O_3. \qquad\qquad [143]$$

In each case brownish-red fumes are formed, which, at a low temperature, become condensed into a very volatile blue liquid, boiling at about 0°. With a small quantity of water it yields nitrous acid, $H\text{-}O\text{-}NO$, but a large quantity at once decomposes it.

$$3N_2O_3 + H_2O = 4NO + 2HNO_3. \qquad [144]$$

If the red vapor is passed into a solution of potassic hydrate, we obtain potassic nitrite, and in a similar way other nitrites may be made.

$$(2KOH + Aq) + N_2O_3 = (2K\text{-}O\text{-}NO + H_2O + Aq). \quad [145]$$

According to the theory of the last section, ordinary nitrous acid is the first anhydride of an assumed acid, $H_3^{\equiv}O_3^{\equiv}N$. This would be called orthonitrous acid, and the ordinary acid would then be metanitrous acid. The compound $Pb_3^{\equiv}O_6^{\equiv}N_2$, according to this view, is plumbic orthonitrite, but it may be also regarded as a triplumbic nitrite of the ordinary type ($Pb\text{-}O\text{-}Pb\text{-}O\text{-}Pb$)$\text{=}O_2\text{=}(NO)_2$.

162. *Nitric Peroxide*, NO_2, is best prepared by mixing two volumes of nitric oxide with one of oxygen gas, both *absolutely dry*.

$$2\dot{N}O + O\text{=}O = 2NO_2. \quad [146]$$

The two gases when mixed immediately combine, yielding a deep brownish-red vapor, which, if passed into perfectly dry tubes cooled by a freezing mixture, is condensed to a crystalline solid. This solid melts at —9° to an orange-colored liquid, which boils at 22°, but when once melted it does not freeze even at —20°. The substance is decomposed by water with the greatest readiness. A mere trace of water is sufficient to prevent the formation of the crystals, occasioning instead the production of a green liquid, which appears to be a solution of nitrous anhydride in nitric acid.

$$4NO_2 + H_2O = 2HNO_3 + N_2O_3. \quad [147]$$

If a larger amount of water is present, we obtain nitric oxide in place of nitrous anhydride, and the equation becomes

$$3NO_2 + H_2O = 2HNO_3 + NO. \quad [148]$$

In a similar way, when acted on by metallic hydrates and basic anhydrides, it yields a mixture of nitrate and nitrite. Thus

$$2K\text{-}O\text{-}H + 2NO_2 = K\text{-}O\text{-}NO + K\text{-}O\text{-}NO_2 + H_2O. \quad [149]$$

Nitric peroxide may also be obtained by distilling plumbic nitrate, —

$$2Pb\text{=}O_2\text{=}(NO_2)_2 = 2PbO + 4NO_2 + O\text{=}O. \quad [150]$$

Owing to the presence of a little moisture, we first obtain the green liquid mentioned above, but towards the end of the process the anhydrous peroxide comes over and may be crystallized. Nitric peroxide appears also to be formed in the reaction of nitric acid on tin, — ·

$$Sn_5 + 20HNO_3 = H_{10}O_{10}Sn_5O_5 + 5H_2O + 20NO_2; \quad [151]$$

but in this, as in other reactions of nitric acid on the metals, the main product is more or less mixed with other oxides of nitrogen.

163. *Nitric Oxide, NO*, is best prepared by the action of dilute nitric acid (*Sp. Gr.* about 1.2) on copper-turnings.

$$3Cu + (8HNO_3 + Aq) =$$
$$(3Cu(NO_3)_2 + 4H_2O + Aq) + 2NO. \quad [152]$$

The reaction appears to consist, first, in a metathesis of the metal with the hydrogen of the acid, and secondly, in the reduction of a further portion of the acid by the hydrogen thus liberated. In order to obtain a pure product it is important that the acid should be in excess. Nitric oxide may also be obtained perfectly pure by heating together a mixture of ferrous chloride, nitre, and hydrochloric acid.

$$(6FeCl_2 + 2KNO_3 + 8HCl + Aq) =$$
$$(3[Fe_2]Cl_6 + 2KCl + 4H_2O) + 2NO. \quad [153]$$

A mixture of ferrous sulphate, nitre, and dilute sulphuric acid (*Sp. Gr.* 1.18) may also be used.

Nitric oxide is a colorless permanent gas (Sp. Gr. $= 15$), but slightly soluble in water (one volume of water dissolves one twentieth of a volume of NO). It extinguishes a burning candle, but both phosphorus and charcoal, if burning vigorously, continue to burn, and with great intensity, when plunged into the gas. It is the most stable of the oxides of nitrogen, and is not decomposed by a red heat. It is neither an acid nor a basic anhydride, but it is marked by its avidity for oxygen, with which it forms the brownish-red fumes either of NO_2 or of N_2O_3, according to the proportions present. [143] and [146]. It dissolves freely in a solution of ferrous sulphate, forming a deep reddish-brown liquid, from which the gas may be expelled by heat. A similar product may be obtained with other ferrous salts, and this reaction may be used as a test for nitric acid.

164. *Nitrous Oxide*, N_2O, is best prepared by gently heating ammonic nitrate in a glass flask or retort.

$$NH_4\text{-}O\text{-}NO_2 = 2H_2O + N_2O. \qquad [154]$$

It may also be obtained by exposing nitric oxide gas to the action of moistened iron-filings, which absorb one half of the oxygen.

$$4NO - O\text{=}O = 2N_2O. \qquad [155]$$

It is also evolved when zinc dissolves in dilute nitric acid, or, more surely, when a mixture of equal parts of nitric and sulphuric acids, diluted with eight or ten parts of water, is used for dissolving the metal.

$$4Zn + (10HNO_3 + Aq) =$$
$$(4Zn(NO_3)_2 + 5H_2O + Aq) + N_2O. \quad [156]$$

Nitrous oxide is a colorless gas (Sp. Gr. 22), which, by pressure and cold, may be condensed to a colorless liquid, boiling at —88° and freezing by its own evaporation at about —101°. It is less stable than nitric oxide. It is decomposed by heat, and all combustibles burn in it with nearly the same readiness and brilliancy as in pure oxygen gas. When pure, it can be inhaled without danger, and is much used as an anæsthetic agent. With some patients it produces at first a transient intoxication, attended at times with uncontrollable laughter. Hence the popular name of laughing-gas. It manifests no tendency to unite with more oxygen. It is soluble in water to a limited extent, and to a much greater degree in alcohol. At 0° one volume of water dissolves 1.3 volumes, and one volume of alcohol 4.18 volumes, of this gas.

165. *Oxychlorides of Nitrogen.* — If in reaction [111] no gold or other metal is present to unite with the chlorine evolved by the aqua-regia, this element combines with the nitric oxide set free at the same time, and besides chlorine gas we obtain, as products of the reaction, two compounds which we may call nitrous oxychloride and nitric oxydichloride respectively.

$$(HNO_3 + 3HCl + Aq) =$$
$$(2H_2O + Aq) + NOCl + Cl\text{-}Cl. \quad [157]$$

or $(2HNO_3 + 6HCl + Aq) =$
$$(4H_2O + Aq) + 2NOCl_2 + Cl\text{-}Cl. \quad [158]$$

During the early stages of the decomposition of aqua-regia the second of the two reactions prevails, and the product is nearly pure $NOCl_2$; but as the process advances this becomes more and more mixed with $NOCl$. At the ordinary temperature both substances are gases, $NOCl$ having an orange, and $NOCl_2$ a deep lemon-yellow color; but by cold they may be readily condensed to liquids, which have a red color and resemble each other in odor and aspect. They have neither acid nor basic relations, but are readily decomposed by chemical agents into nitric oxide and chlorine; and by mixing together these two gases the same or similar compounds may be reproduced. By the action of dry hydrochloric acid on anhydrous nitric peroxide, still a third compound is formed, which has the symbol NO_2Cl, and resembles the other two. The last compound may also be obtained by mixing phosphoric oxytrichloride with plumbic nitrate.

$$3Pb^=O_2^=(NO_2)_2 + 2POCl_3 = Pb_3^{\equiv}O_6^{\equiv}(PO)_2 + 6NO_2Cl. \quad [159]$$

166. *Compounds with Hydrogen.* — *Ammonia Gas.* NH_3. — Nitrogen and hydrogen gases will not directly combine; but through various indirect methods, not well understood, this union is constantly taking place in nature, and ammonia gas is the chief product. This gas, or some one of its numerous compounds, is constantly formed whenever an organic substance decays or is charred, as in the process of dry distillation. It is also formed in many chemical reactions when nitrogen and hydrogen atoms are brought together at the moment of chemical change. Thus when a mixture of nitric oxide and hydrogen gas is passed over heated platinum sponge, we have the reaction

$$2NO + 5H\text{-}H = 2H_2O + 2NH_3. \quad [160]$$

So also when nitric acid is added in very small quantities at a time to a mixture of zinc and dilute hydrochloric acid, from which hydrogen gas is being slowly evolved, we have the reaction

$$HNO_3 + 4H\text{-}H = NH_3 + 3H_2O. \quad [161]$$

But the ammonia thus produced unites at once with the hydrochloric acid present to form ammonic chloride, and in a similar way ammonia salts are frequently formed to a limited extent when zinc and similar metals are dissolved in nitric acid. Practically, we always prepare ammonia gas from the commercial ammonic chloride by the reaction

$$2NH_4Cl + Ca\text{=}O_2\text{=}H_2 = CaCl_2 + 2H_2O + 2NH_3. \quad [162]$$

It is a colorless gas, so light (𝔖𝔭. 𝔊𝔯. 0.591) that it can be collected in an inverted bottle by displacement. By pressure and cold it may be readily condensed to a liquid, which boils at —38°.5 and freezes at —75°. The evaporation of the liquefied gas is attended with great reduction of temperature, and this principle is applied in the apparatus of Carré to the artificial production of cold. Ammonia has a familiar pungent odor, and is useful in medicine as an irritant, but when pure it is wholly irrespirable. It is incombustible in air, but burns in an atmosphere of oxygen, yielding aqueous vapor and nitrogen gas.

The composition of ammonia gas may be thus ascertained: First, by passing a series of electrical discharges through a confined volume of the gas in a eudiometer the volume doubles.

$$2NH_3 = N\text{=}N + 3H\text{-}H. \quad [163]$$

If next we add to this product one half of its volume of oxygen gas, then explode the mixture, and subsequently remove with pyrogallic acid the residual oxygen, we shall find that the volume of nitrogen gas remaining in the tube is exactly one half of the volume of the ammonia gas with which we started. Secondly, if we shake up in an eudiometer-tube a measured volume of chlorine gas with a weak solution of aqua ammonia, taking care after the reaction is finished to expel by heat all the nitrogen from the liquid, it will be found that the volume of chlorine has been replaced by one third of its volume of nitrogen gas.

With colored test-paper ammonia gas, even when dry, gives a strong alkaline reaction, and it directly combines with several of the acid anhydrides. These unimportant compounds, however, must not be confounded with the important class of ammonia salts. In part they correspond to the amides mentioned below, but the constitution of others is not well understood. The last are frequently called ammonides, and of these sulphuric ammonide $(NH_3)_2 . SO_3$, will serve as an example. Ammonia gas forms also equally anomalous compounds with many anhydrous metallic salts. Thus, argentic and calcic chlorides absorb large volumes of ammonia gas, forming what appear to be molecular compounds, $Ag\,Cl . 2H_3N$ and $Ca\,Cl_2 . 8H_3N$, in which the ammonia seems to play somewhat the same part as water of crystallization in ordinary salts. But by far the most important quality of ammonia is its power of combining directly with water and with the acids, as such, to form the large class of ammonia salts. In forming these compounds, however, nitrogen changes its quantivalence, and it will therefore be convenient to class them under a different head. When ammonia gas comes in contact with the fumes of a volatile acid, the formation of the ammonia salt gives rise to a dense white smoke, which is one of the most characteristic tests for this substance.

167. *Amines or Compound Ammonia.* — Ammonia gas is the type of a large class of compounds, most of them volatile, in all of which nitrogen is trivalent. These compounds may be regarded as derived from one or more molecules of ammonia by replacing the hydrogen atoms either wholly or in part with various positive radicals. According as they are fashioned after the type of one, two, three, or more molecules of ammonia they are called monamines, diamines, &c., and they are distinguished as primary, secondary, or tertiary, according as one, two, or three hydrogen atoms in the monamines, or the corresponding groups of atoms in the polyamines, have been replaced. We may represent the type of ammonia either as in (29), or more graphically in the vertical form as in table below, which contains the symbols of a few of the compound ammonias.

Monamines.

Primary.			Secondary.		Tertiary.
$\left.\begin{array}{l}H\\H\\H\end{array}\right\}N$	$\left.\begin{array}{l}CH_3\\H\\H\end{array}\right\}N$	$\left.\begin{array}{l}C_6H_5\\H\\H\end{array}\right\}N$	$\left.\begin{array}{l}C_2H_5\\C_2H_5\\H\end{array}\right\}N$	$\left.\begin{array}{l}C_6H_5\\C_2H_5\\H\end{array}\right\}N$	$\left.\begin{array}{l}CH_3\\C_2H_5\\C_6H_5\end{array}\right\}N$
Ammonia.	Methylamine.	Phenylamine. (Aniline.)	Diethylamine.	Phenylethylamine.	Methyl ethylphenylamine.

Diamines.

Primary.

$$\left.\begin{array}{c} H_2 \\ H_2 \\ H_2 \end{array}\right\} N_2$$

Ammonia.
Doubly condensed.

$$\left.\begin{array}{c} C_2H_4 \\ H_2 \\ H_2 \end{array}\right\} N_2$$

Ethylene diamine.

Tertiary.

$$\left.\begin{array}{c} C_2H_4 \\ C_2H_4 \\ (C_2H_5)_2 \end{array}\right\} N_2$$

Diethylene-diethyl-diamine.

Many of the ammoniated compounds of the metals may be arranged under this same type. Thus, when potassium is heated in dry ammonia gas, an olive-green compound is formed, which has the composition $K,H,H \ddot= N$; and other examples will be given hereafter.

The amines are all basic, and like ammonia gas combine directly with acids to form salts; but this character is the less strongly marked in proportion as the hydrogen atoms have been replaced. The volatile organic bases belong to the same class of compounds.

168. *Amides.* — The atoms of hydrogen in ammonia gas may be replaced by negative as well as by positive radicals; but then the product, instead of being basic, is either neutral or acid. They are classified and named like the amines, but with few exceptions only one or one set of the hydrogen atoms can be thus replaced. The following are a few examples:—

Monamides.

$$\left.\begin{array}{c} C_2H_3O \\ H \\ H \end{array}\right\} N$$

Acetamide.

$$\left.\begin{array}{c} C_7H_5O \\ H \\ H \end{array}\right\} N$$

Benzamide.

Diamides.

$$\left.\begin{array}{c} C_2O_2 \\ H_2 \\ H_2 \end{array}\right\} N_2$$

Oxamide.

$$\left.\begin{array}{c} C_4H_4O_2 \\ H_2 \\ H_2 \end{array}\right\} N_2$$

Succinamide.

These compounds may also be regarded as formed by the union of the compound radical amidogen (H_2N) with the acid radical, and hence the name amides. They differ, then, from the corresponding acids only in containing amidogen in place of hydroxyl. Thus,

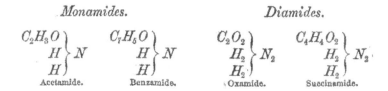

$Ho-C_2H_3O$,
Acetic Acid.

$Ho_2=CO$,
Carbonic Acid.

$Ho_2=C_2O_2$,
Oxalic Acid.

$Ho_2=C_4H_4O_2$.
Succinic Acid.

$H_2N-C_2H_3O$,
Acetamide.

$(H_2N)_2=CO$,
Carbamide (Urea ?).

$(H_2N)_2=C_2O_2$,
Oxamide.

$(H_2N)_2=C_4H_4O_2$.
Succinamide.

These amides are all neutral; but if in the dibasic acids we re-place only one of the atoms of hydroxyl, it is evident that we shall obtain a class of amides still containing an atom of basic hydrogen, and which are, therefore, acids. Thus are formed

$$HO,H_2N{=}CO. \qquad HO,H_2N{=}C_2O_2, \qquad HO,H_2N{=}C_4H_4O_2.$$
Carbamic Acid.[1]   Oxamic Acid.   Succinamic Acid.

Lastly, if we take an acid like lactic acid, $\overset{+}{H}O,\overset{-}{H}O{=}C_3H_4O$, or glycollic acid, $\overset{+}{H}O,\overset{-}{H}O{=}C_2H_2O$, which, although diatomic, is only monobasic (43), we can obtain from each acid, at least theoretically, two distinct amides, according as we replace the basic hydrogen $(\overset{+}{H})$ or the alcoholic hydrogen $(\overset{-}{H})$, see (43). The first will be neutral, the second acid; but although several of the acid amides are known, the only neutral amide of this class which has been investigated is that derived from lactic acid.

$$NH_2,\overset{-}{H}O{=}C_3H_4O, \qquad \overset{+}{H}O,NH_2{=}C_3H_4O, \qquad \overset{+}{H}O,NH_2{=}C_2H_2O.$$
Lactamide (Neutral).   Lactamide (Acid).   Glycolamide (Acid) or Glycocoll.

From these various amides a large number of compounds may be derived by replacing the hydrogen atoms either of the amidogen or of the acid with different compound radicals. The following are a few examples :—

$$\left.\begin{array}{l}C_7H_5O\\C_6H_5\\H\end{array}\right\}N \qquad \left.\begin{array}{l}C_2O_2\\(C_2H_5)_2\\H_2\end{array}\right\}N_2 \qquad \left.\begin{array}{l}((C_2H_5)O{-}C_2O_2)\\H\\H\end{array}\right\}N$$
Phenyl-benzamide.   Diethyl-oxamide.   Oxamethane.

$$\left.\begin{array}{l}HO{-}C_2H_2O\\C_7H_5O\\H\end{array}\right\}N \qquad \left.\begin{array}{l}HO{-}C_3H_4O\\C_2H_5\\H\end{array}\right\}N \qquad \left.\begin{array}{l}(C_2H_5)O{-}C_3H_4O\\H\\H\end{array}\right\}N$$
Hippuric Acid.   Lactethylamide.   Lactmethane.

The last two compounds are isomeric, the only difference being that in the first the radical ethyl replaces an atom of hydrogen of the amidogen, while in the second it replaces the alcoholic hydrogen of the lactic acid. That there is a real difference between the two is proved by the following reactions :—

$$\left.\begin{array}{l}(C_2H_5)O,{-}C_2H_4O\\H\\H\end{array}\right\}N+K{-}O{-}H=K,(C_2H_5){=}O_2{=}C_3H_4O+\left.\begin{array}{l}H\\H\\H\end{array}\right\}N\ [164]$$
Potassic Ethyl-lactate.

---

1 The acid has not been isolated, but the ammonic salt is well known.

$$\left.\begin{array}{l} HO\text{-}C_3H_4O \\ C_2H_5 \\ H \end{array}\right\} N + K\text{-}O\text{-}H = \underset{\text{Potassic Lactate.}}{K,H\text{=}O_2\text{=}C_3H_4O} + \left.\begin{array}{l} C_2H_6 \\ H \\ H \end{array}\right\} N. \quad [165]$$
Ethylamine.

These complex amide compounds may also be referred to a system of mixed types. (Compare 30, Part I.)

169. *Imides.* — If from an *acid* monamide we eliminate a molecule of water, or if from a neutral diamide we eliminate a molecule of ammonia gas, we obtain as the product a compound which may be regarded as formed by the union of the acid radical with the compound radical HN. Thus,

$$\overset{+}{H}O,H_2N\text{=}C_3H_4\underset{\text{Lact-amide.}}{\underline{O}} = H\text{-}O\text{-}H + \underset{\text{Lact-imide.}}{HN\text{=}C_3H_4O}. \quad [166]$$

$$\underset{\text{Succin-amide.}}{(H_2N)_2\text{=}C_4H_4O_2} = H_3N + \underset{\text{Succin-imide.}}{HN\text{=}C_4H_4O_2}. \quad [167]$$

Such compounds are called *Imides*, and they always act as monobasic acids.

170. *Nitriles.* — If from a *neutral* monamide we eliminate a molecule of water, the residue, which may be regarded as a compound of nitrogen with a trivalent radical, has been called a *Nitrile.* Thus,

$$\underset{\text{Acetamide.}}{H_2N\text{-}C_2H_3O} = H_2O + \underset{\text{Acetonitrile.}}{C_2H_3\text{≡}N}. \quad [168]$$

$$\underset{\text{Valeramide.}}{H_2N\text{-}C_5H_9O} = H_2O + \underset{\text{Valeronitrile.}}{C_5H_9\text{≡}N}. \quad [169]$$

These compounds are weak bases, like ammonia, combining directly with acids to form salts, and they may be regarded as a part of the class of amines.

171. *Ammonium Compounds.* — In all the above compounds nitrogen is trivalent, and a single atom of this element, unassisted, does not appear to be able to hold together more than three atoms of hydrogen or of other univalent positive radicals; but when the different ammonias are brought in contact with acids, the nitrogen atoms suddenly manifest two additional affinities, and a most important class of compounds is formed, in which nitrogen is quinquivalent. The cause of this sudden accession of power is not well understood, but it evidently de-

pends on the reflex influence which the negative atoms or radicals of the acids exert. In all these cases the ammonias combine with the acids as a whole, and the reaction is an example
of synthesis and not of metathesis. The following are a few
examples: —

$$N^{\equiv}H_3 + HCl = N^{\equiv}H_4, Cl = NH_4\text{-}Cl \quad \text{like} \quad KCl. \quad [170]$$
Ammonic Chloride.

$$N^{\equiv}H_3 + H_2O = N^{\equiv}H_4,(HO) = NH_4\text{-}O\text{-}H \text{ like } K\text{-}O\text{-}H. \quad [171]$$
Ammonic Hydrate.

$$N^{\equiv}H_3 + H\text{-}NO_3 = N^{\equiv}H_4,(NO_3) =$$
$$NH_4\text{-}O\text{-}NO_2 \text{ like } K\text{-}O\text{-}NO_2. \quad [172]$$
Ammonic Nitrate.

$$(N^{\equiv}H_3)_2 + H_2^{=}SO_4 = N_2\text{x}H_8,(SO_4) =$$
$$(NH_4)_2^{=}O_2^{=}SO_2 \text{ like } K_2^{=}O_2^{=}SO_2. \quad [173]$$
Ammonic Sulphate.

The products thus obtained resemble very closely the salts of
the alkaline metals. With certain limitations they are susceptible of the same reactions, and in these reactions the atomic
group NH_4 plays the same part as the metallic atoms in the
other salts. Thus we have

$$(Ag\text{-}NO_3 + NH_4\text{-}Cl + Aq) =$$
$$Ag\,Cl + (NH_4\text{-}NO_3 + Aq). \quad [174]$$

$$(CaCl_2 + (NH_4)_2^{=}O_2^{=}CO + Aq) =$$
$$Ca^{=}O_2^{=}CO + (2NH_4Cl + Aq). \quad [175]$$

Hence we conclude that the ammonia salts are compounds of
this univalent radical which we call ammonium, and therefore
we write their symbols as above. But although many attempts
have been made to obtain the radical substance corresponding
to NH_4, these attempts have been hitherto unsuccessful. It is
true that when we electrolyze a solution of ammonic chloride,
using as the negative pole of the battery a quantity of mercury,
we obtain a material resembling a metallic amalgam, which,
when kept, slowly changes back to metallic mercury, evolving
a mixture of hydrogen and nitrogen gases; but it would now
appear that in this pasty mass the gases are merely mixed, and
not chemically combined, and, moreover, the total amount of

material which the mercury thus singularly encloses is exceedingly small.

172. *Ammonic Chloride* (*Sal Ammoniac*), NH_4Cl, is the most important of the ammonia salts, and the material from which the other ammonia compounds are prepared. It is manufactured in large quantities from the ammoniacal liquid of the gas-works, one of the products of the dry distillation of coal. It is a white crystalline salt, very soluble in water, but only slightly soluble in alcohol. It sublimes below redness without first melting. It is isomorphous with sodic and potassic chloride, and resembles these salts, especially the last, very closely. Like potassic chloride, it is precipitated from aqueous solutions by platinic chloride, with which it forms a double salt insoluble in water.

$$(2NH_4Cl + PtCl_4 + Aq) = (NH_4Cl)_2 . PtCl_4 + (Aq). \quad [176]$$

173. *Ammonic Hydrate* (*Aqua Ammonia*). ($NH_4\text{-}O\text{-}H +$ Aq.) — At $0°$ water absorbs 1,050 times its own volume of ammonia gas, but the quantity absorbed rapidly diminishes as the temperature rises, so that at $15°$ it can only hold 727 times its volume, and at $24°$ 600 times its volume. Water saturated at $15°$ contains about one third of its weight of ammonia, but in consequence of the great expansion which attends the absorption, the solution is lighter than water. This solution has the pungent odor of ammonia, because the gas slowly escapes even at the ordinary temperature of the air, and by prolonged boiling the whole may be driven off. In this and in other physical relations the compound of ammonia with water acts like the solution of a gas, but in all its chemical relations it behaves like an alkaline hydrate. It is strongly caustic; it precipitates metallic hydrates from solutions of their salts, and is very much used in the laboratory as an alkaline reagent. It has been called the *volatile alkali*. It differs, however, from *the fixed alkalies, soda, and potassa*, in two important particulars. First, it is decomposed by heat into ammonia gas and water, and is not, therefore, properly speaking, volatile. Secondly, it forms with many metallic radicals soluble double salts, and other compounds of peculiar constitution, which can have no counterparts among the compounds of the alkaline metals. Hence it is that in many important particulars the reactions of the ammonia salts are wholly

different from those of the corresponding salts of sodium and potassium. They either do not give precipitates under the same conditions, or the precipitates obtained have a wholly different character. Compare [174], [175], with (265), (276), and (316).

174. *Ammonic Carbonate.* — The commercial salt is a *translucent* white solid, obtained by subliming a mixture of sal-ammoniac with chalk. It is very soluble in water, has the odor of ammonia, and a strong alkaline reaction. Its composition is not unvarying, but the usual product appears to be a mixture of hydro-ammonic carbonate and ammonic carbamate (168) in equivalent proportions. Exposed to the air it loses about 44 per cent of its weight, owing to the dissipation of the ammonic carbamate, which is resolved into CO_2 and NH_3, and the *opaque spongy* residue consists of hydro-ammonic carbonate. From the commercial salt there may be prepared well-defined crystals of the three following compounds : —

Acid or Hydro-ammonic Carbonate $H, NH_4 = O_2 = CO$.

Neutral or Diammonic Carbonate $(NH_4)_2 = O_2 = CO \cdot H_2 O$.

Dihydro-tetra ammonic Tricarbonate $H_2 \cdot (NH_4)_4{}^{vi} O_6{}^{vi} (CO)_3 \cdot H_2 O$.

A solution of the neutral salt prepared by mixing a solution of the commercial substance with the requisite amount of aqua ammonia is very much used in the laboratory as a reagent.

175. *Characteristic Reactions of the Ammonia Salts.* — These compounds, when heated with caustic alkalies or alkaline earths, give off ammonia gas, which may be recognized by its odor, or by the cloud it forms with HCl. The ammonia salts are all volatile at a moderate temperature (except in the few cases in which the acid is fixed), and are thus readily distinguished from those of the non-volatile bases. This quality is of great importance in chemical analysis, and leads us to select the ammonia salts, whenever it is possible, as reagents, because the excess of the reagent and all the ammoniacal products can so readily be eliminated by heat.

176. *Ammonium Bases.* — The salts formed by the union of the compound ammonias, or amines, with acids, closely resemble those of ammonia, and may be regarded as consisting of radicals derived from ammonium by replacing one or more of its hydrogen atoms with other positive radicals. Of these com-

pounds the most interesting are those corresponding to ammonic hydrates, but in which all four of the hydrogen atoms have been thus replaced. They may be prepared from the ternary amines in a manner which is illustrated by the following reactions : —

$$\left.\begin{array}{c} C_2H_5 \\ C_2H_5 \\ C_2H_5 \end{array}\right\} N + (C_2H_5)I = \left.\begin{array}{c} C_2H_5 \\ C_2H_5 \\ C_2H_5 \\ C_2H_5 \end{array}\right\} N\text{-}I. \qquad [177]$$

Triethylamine. Iodide of Tetrathyl-ammonium.

$$Ag_2O + 2\left[(C_2H_5)_4 N\text{-}I\right] + H_2O =$$
$$2AgI + 2([(C_2H_5)_4 N]\text{-}O\text{-}H). \ [178]$$

The solutions of the amines in water, although, like aqua ammonia, they may be regarded as compounds of an ammonium radical, are decomposed when evaporated into the volatile amine and water, and it might have been anticipated that the hydrate of tetrathyl-ammonium would break up in a similar way, but such is not the case. This compound is stable, and on evaporating the solution resulting from the last reaction the hydrate is obtained as a white solid resembling caustic potash. It absorbs water and carbonic acid from the air; it precipitates the metallic oxides from their salts; it saponifies fats, and it neutralizes the stróngest acids, just as potash does. Several similar compounds have been prepared; and since it appears that the four hydrogen atoms of ammonium may be replaced by the same or by different atoms at will, it is evident that an infinite number of such compounds are, theoretically at least, possible. These hydrates have a bitter taste, and cannot be volatilized without decomposition. In both of these particulars they very closely resemble the non-volatile organic alkaloids, which are evidently formed after the same type. There are, therefore, two classes of bases derived from ammonia; the one volatile. after the type of H_3N; the other non-volatile, after the type of $NH_4\text{-}O\text{-}H$; and corresponding to these there are two classes of organic alkaloids, the first volatile like nicotine and conine, the second non-volatile like quinine.and morphine. In all these bases the parts are grouped around one or more atoms of nitrogen, and the difference between the two classes of compounds depends primarily on the fact that these atoms are tri-

11 *

valent in the first class and quinquivalent in the second. The two classes of compounds are, however, intimately related, and may be regarded from different points of view. Thus the amides, imides, and nitriles, which we have considered as formed after the type of ammonia gas, may also be regarded as anhydrides of the salts of the ammonium radicals, and in many cases may be prepared from these salts by a simple process of dehydration. Moreover, careful study will open up many other relations of these bodies, all of which must be considered before we can command a comprehensive view of the subject.

177. *Chloride of Nitrogen*, NCl_3, is a very volatile, yellow, oily liquid, obtained by the action of chlorine gas on a strong solution of sal-ammoniac.

178. *Bromide of Nitrogen*, NBr_3, is obtained by digesting bromide of potassium with chloride of nitrogen, and is similar to the last in appearance, but has a much darker color.

179. *Iodide of Nitrogen*, NI_3, is a black powder, formed when aqua ammonia is added in large excess to an alcoholic solution of iodine. They are all three highly explosive, and illustrate in a most marked manner the instability of all the compounds of nitrogen.

180. PHOSPHORUS. $P = 31.$ — Found in nature, chiefly in combination with calcium, in calcic phosphate, a mineral substance very widely but sparingly disseminated, and an essential but subordinate constituent of many plants, and of all the higher animal structures. In order to obtain the elementary substance, the calcic phosphate (generally bone ashes) is first partially decomposed with sulphuric acid. The *soluble* acid calcic phosphate thus obtained is easily separated from the nearly *insoluble* calcic sulphate, by filtration. The solution is then evaporated, the acid phosphate mixed with pulverized charcoal, and the thoroughly dried mass distilled in earthen retorts. The distillation proceeds slowly, and requires a very high temperature.

$$Ca_3O_6(PO)_2 + 2H_2O_2SO_2 =$$
$$2Ca\text{-}O_2SO_2 + H_4,Ca O_6(PO)_2.$$

When dried, $H_4,Ca O_6(PO)_2 = Ca\text{-}O_2(PO_2)_2 + 2H_2O,$ [179]

$$3Ca\text{-}O_2(PO_2)_2 + C_{10} = Ca_3O_6(PO)_2 + 10CO + P_4.$$

181. *Common Phosphorus*, P_4, when perfectly pure, is a

colorless, transparent solid, but ordinarily it has a yellowish tint, and is only translucent. At low temperatures it is brittle, but at 20° it is soft like wax. It melts at 45°, and boils at 290°. *Sp. Gr.* of solid 1.83. Insoluble in water, slightly soluble in alcohol and ether, still more soluble in both the fixed and volatile oils, and very soluble in sulphide of carbon or chloride of sulphur. Phosphorus is by far the most combustible of the chemical elements. It takes fire below the boiling point of water, and slowly combines with the oxygen of the air at the ordinary temperature. If in not too small quantity, the heat evolved by its slow combustion soon raises the temperature to the point of ignition, and it is therefore always preserved under water or alcohol. The product of the rapid combustion is phosphoric anhydride; that of the slow combustion in moist air chiefly phosphorous acid. Exposed to the air in the dark, phosphorus emits a greenish light, and hence its name, from φῶς φορός; but this phosphorescence, though always accompanying the slow combustion, does not appear to be necessarily connected with it. Sticks of phosphorus, when kept under water, become covered after some time with a white crust, which consists of a mass of microscopic crystals; and in the course of many years these crystals may acquire considerable size. The form of the crystals is the regular dodecahedron of the first system (Fig. 6), and crystals of the same form are obtained by slowly evaporating the solution of phosphorus in sulphide of carbon.

182. *Red Phosphorus.* — Exposed to the direct sunlight under water, phosphorus becomes covered with a red coating, and the same red modification is formed in great abundance when ordinary phosphorus is heated for several hours to a temperature below 235° and 250° in an atmosphere of carbonic anhydride, or some other inert gas. Red phosphorus is insoluble in carbonic sulphide, and is thus easily separated from the portion which has not been changed. Iodine facilitates the conversion, and if a solution of phosphorus in sulphide of carbon, containing a little iodine, is sealed up in a glass flask and heated for some time to only 100°, red phosphorus is slowly precipitated. As usually obtained, red phosphorus is an amorphous powder; but it has been crystallized, and it appears that the crystals are rhombohedrons belonging to the third system.

Hence phosphorus is dimorphous, and in this respect resembles arsenic and antimony. The *Sp. Gr.* of red phosphorus is about 2.1. It undergoes no change in dry air, and may even be heated to 250° without taking fire; but at a slightly higher temperature it changes back to common phosphorus and inflames. The specific heat of red phosphorus is 0.1700, while that of the ordinary variety is 0.1387; and hence, as we should anticipate, this reverse change is attended with the evolution of heat. Moreover, the calorific power of common phosphorus is to that of red phosphorus in the proportion of 1.15 to 1. In general, red phosphorus is less active, chemically, than common phosphorus, and is not, like the latter, poisonous. Both varieties are largely used in the manufacture of friction-matches. The red variety is not used in making the match itself, but only in the preparation of the surface on which it is rubbed.

183. *Phosphorus and Oxygen.* — The following compounds of phosphorus with oxygen, or with both oxygen and hydrogen, have been observed : —

Phosphorous Anhydride	P_2O_3,
Phosphoric Anhydride	P_2O_5,
Hypophosphorous Acid	$H\text{-}O\text{-}(P^{\equiv}O,H_2)$,
Phosphorous Acid	$H_2^{=}O_2^{=}(P^{\equiv}O,H)$,
Orthophosphoric Acid	$H_3^{\equiv}O_3^{\equiv}(P^{=}O)$,
Metaphosphoric Acid	$H\text{-}O\text{-}(P^{\equiv}O_2)$,
Pyrophosphoric Acid	$H_4^{\equiv}O_4^{\equiv}(P^{=}O_3^{\equiv}P)$,
Sodium salt of Hexabasic Acid	$Na_6^{\equiv}O_6^{\equiv}(P^{=}O_2^{=}P^{\equiv}O_3^{\equiv}P^{=}O_2^{=}P)$,
Sodium salt of Dodecabasic Acid	$Na_{12}\text{xii}\,O_{12}\text{xii}(P_{10}O_{19})$.

The relations of these compounds will be best understood by taking as our first starting-point an assumed compound, $H_5^{\equiv}O_5^{\equiv}P$, in which the atoms of phosphorus are united to hydroxyl by all their five affinities. Ortho[1] and metaphosphoric acids are now simply the successive anhydrides of this pentatomic acid. Starting next from the double molecule of our assumed compound, the following anhydrides are possible : —

	$H_{10}\text{x}\,O_{10}\text{x}\,P_2$,	3d.	$H_4^{\equiv}O_4^{\equiv}(P^{\equiv}O_3^{\equiv}P)$,
1st.	$H_8\text{viii}\,O_8\text{viii}(P\text{-}O\text{-}P)$,	4th.	$H_2^{=}O_2^{=}(P^{\equiv}O_4^{\equiv}P)$,
2d.	$H_6^{\equiv}O_6^{\equiv}(P^{=}O_2^{=}P)$,	5th.	$(P^{\equiv}O_5^{\equiv}P)$.

----

[1] The assumed pentatomic acid is by some called orthophosphoric.

Of these possible compounds the second and fourth are identical with ortho and meta-phosphoric acids, of which the symbols represent two molecules, while the third and the fifth are the pyrophosphoric acid and phosphoric anhydride of the above list. The first anhydride of this series has not yet been observed. In like manner we may take three, four, or more molecules of the first compound, and deduce from each of these condensed molecules another series of anhydrides; but of the infinite number of compounds thus possible, only the salts of the hexabasic and dodecabasic acid mentioned above are known. This scheme, however, does not include hypophosphorous and phosphorous acids, which have an anomalous constitution. They may be regarded as orthophosphoric acids in which atoms of hydroxyl (two in the first case and one in the second) have been replaced with atoms of hydrogen. The molecules of both acids contain three atoms of hydrogen, but the first is only monobasic and the second dibasic; and this fact illustrates an important principle. In all the so-called oxygen salts, only those atoms of hydrogen are replaceable by metallic atoms, which are united to the negative radical by a vinculum consisting of an equal number of *oxygen* atoms. The hydrogen and oxygen atoms thus paired are equivalent to so many atoms of the radical hydroxyl [70]. Phosphorous anhydride is the only one of this class of compounds in which the phosphorus atoms are not quinquivalent.

184. *Phosphoric Anhydride* is readily prepared by burning phosphorus in dry air. It is an amorphous white powder, having an intense affinity for water, and is sometimes used as an hygroscopic agent. It hisses when dropped into water, and gives a solution of

185. *Metaphosphoric Acid.* — This compound is obtained as a vitreous solid (glacial phosphoric acid) by heating orthophosphoric acid to redness. Its solution coagulates albumen, and one molecule of the acid saturates only one molecule of sodic hydrate. By boiling the solution the acid loses its power of coagulating albumen, and acquires greater capacity of saturation, having changed into

186. *Orthophosphoric Acid.* — This is much the most important of these compounds. It is readily prepared by boiling phosphorus in not too strong nitric acid, and evaporating the liquid product to the consistency of syrup. The ordinary phos-

phates are all salts of this acid, and one molecule of acid is capable of saturating three molecules of base. Many of the phosphates are thus constituted, and these are, theoretically (38), the neutral salts; but evidently we may also have for each base two acid salts. Thus in the case of soda we have

$$Na_3{}^{=}O_3{}^{=}PO, \qquad H,Na_2{}^{=}O_3{}^{=}PO, \qquad H_2,Na{}^{=}O_3{}^{=}PO;$$

so in the case of lime we have

$$Ca_3{}^{\equiv}O_6{}^{\equiv}(PO)_2, \qquad H_2,Ca_2{}^{\equiv}O_6{}^{\equiv}(PO)_2, \qquad H_4,Ca{}^{\equiv}O_6{}^{\equiv}(PO)_2.$$

Here, as in many other cases, a diatomic metal serves to solder together two molecules of the acid.

187. *Common Sodic Phosphate*, $H,Na_2{}^{=}O_3{}^{=}PO . 12H_2O$, is by far the most important of the salts which phosphoric acid forms with the bases previously studied. It is, moreover, the chief soluble salt of the acid, and is much used in the laboratory as a reagent. It is also highly interesting, theoretically, because it illustrates by its reactions the relations we have just been considering. A solution of the salt is neutral to test-paper, but when mixed with a solution of argentic nitrate, also perfectly neutral, we obtain a yellow precipitate of argentic phosphate, $Ag_3{}^{=}O_3{}^{=}PO$, and at the same time the solution becomes acid. Heat now the salt to 120°, and it will be found that it loses twelve molecules of water; but when the dried mass is dissolved in water, and the solution evaporated, we obtain crystals of the same form (rhombic prisms, Fig. 45) and composition as before, and which give again the same reaction. But heat the same salt to a red heat, and we have a wholly different result. The salt has lost thirteen molecules of water; the residue is less soluble than before. On evaporation we obtain crystals of a different form and composition ($Na_4P_2O_7 . 10H_2O$), and the solution, after precipitation with argentic nitrate, although previously alkaline, becomes neutral. Moreover, the precipitate, instead of being yellow, is white, and has the composition $Ag_4P_2O_7$.

188. *Microcosmic Salt*. $H,NH_4,Na{}^{=}O_3{}^{=}PO . 4H_2O.$ — If we mix together hot saturated solutions of common sodic phosphate and sal ammoniac, we obtain the following reaction: —

$$(H,Na_2{}^{=}O_3{}^{=}PO + NH_4Cl . 4H_2O + Aq) =$$
$$H,NH_4,Na{}^{=}O_3{}^{=}PO . 4H_2O + (NaCl + Aq). \quad [180]$$

As the solution cools, the microcosmic salt crystallizes out, leaving sodic chloride in solution. This salt, when ignited, loses both its water and its ammonia, and the sodic metaphosphate, which remains, fuses into a colorless glass at a red heat. This glass acts very much like borax, and is used in the same way as a blow-pipe flux.

189. *Phosphorus and Hydrogen.* — When phosphorus is boiled with strong potash or soda lye, or with milk of lime, a gas is evolved, called phosphuretted hydrogen, which on coming in contact with the air inflames spontaneously. This gas consists almost entirely of the compound H_3P; and when soda is used, the reaction by which it is formed is as follows: —

$$P_4 + (3Na\text{-}O\text{-}H + 3H_2O + Aq) =$$
$$(3Na\text{-}O\text{-}POH_2 + Aq) + H_3P. \quad [181]$$

This crude product, however, is not pure H_3P; for when it is passed through a tube cooled by a freezing mixture it deposits a small amount of a very volatile yellow liquid, which has been found to be a second compound of phosphorus and hydrogen, H_4P_2, and has the property of inflaming spontaneously to a high degree. Moreover, the *gas* thus treated loses its power of self-lighting, and this quality in the crude product is evidently due to a small admixture of the liquid substance. When exposed to the direct sunlight, the liquid compound gives off H_3P, and deposits a yellow solid, which is a third compound of phosphorus and hydrogen, H_2P_4.

$$5H_4P_2 = H_2P_4 + 6H_3P. \quad [182]$$

This same solid compound is deposited on the sides of the vessel when the crude product first mentioned is exposed to the sunlight, and in this case, also, the gas loses its self-lighting power.

There are, then, three distinct compounds of hydrogen and phosphorus. But of these the first is by far the most important, and the other two are chiefly interesting as explaining the singular phenomena just noticed. The compound H_3P is the analogue of ammonia gas, and differs from it in composition only in containing in the place of nitrogen the next lower element of the same chemical series. But the differences in properties

are so great that to superficial observation it would seem as if
there were no similarity between the two compounds. Thus
phosphuretted hydrogen is insoluble in water, except to a very
slight degree, and does not unite with any of the common acids.
A more careful study, however, discovers very marked resemblances, for it appears that H_3P does unite with HBr and HI
to form the compounds $(H_4P)Br$ and $(H_4P)I$, which resemble
$(H_4N)Br$ and $(H_4N)I$. Moreover, the atoms of hydrogen in
H_3P may be replaced by methyl, CH_3, ethyl, C_2H_5, and other
radicals yielding compounds similar to the tertiary amines, which
we call the phosphines; and it further appears that the phosphines have a strong basic character, combining with all the
ordinary acids to form a class of salts corresponding to those of
the compound ammonias, and yielding also, by reactions similar
to [177] and [178], compounds analogous to the hydrates of
the ammonium radicals. There are, however, even here, differences to be noted, — quite important, because they point to a
tendency in the series which develops into a marked character
in the next element, arsenic. The compounds trimethylphos-
phine, $(CH_3)_3P$, and triethylphosphine, $(C_2H_5)_3P$, not only
combine with acids, but they also unite as diatomic radicals
either with two atoms of chlorine, bromine, or iodine, or with
one atom of sulphur or of oxygen. Thus are formed the crystalline compounds

$$(C_2H_5)_3P = Cl_2, \qquad (C_2H_5)_3P = O, \qquad (C_2H_5)_3P = S.$$

Lastly, a compound has been described corresponding to liquid
phosphuretted hydrogen, and having the symbol $(CH_3)_2P$-
$(CH_3)_2P$, which, like the former, is both liquid and spontaneously inflammable. It has, moreover, the properties of a feeble
basic radical, and in the chemical series finds its analogue on
one side in the radical amidogen, and on the other in the remarkable compound kakodyl (198).

190. *Phosphorus and Chlorine.* — Phosphorus combines
with chlorine in two proportions. When the phosphorus is in
excess, phosphorous chloride, PCl_3, is formed, which is a fuming,
colorless liquid. When, on the other hand, the chlorine is in
excess, we obtain phosphoric chloride, PCl_5, a white crystalline
solid. Both compounds are decomposed by water, and when
the water is in large excess the reactions are as follows: —

$$PCl_3 + (3H_2O + Aq) = (H_2^=O_2^=PHO + 3HCl + Aq). \quad [183]$$

$$PCl_5 + (4H_2O + Aq) = (H_3^=O_3^=PO + 5HCl + Aq). \quad [184]$$

If in the last reaction water is not present in sufficient quantity, we obtain quite a different result.

$$PCl_5 + H_2O = PCl_3O + 2HCl. \qquad [185]$$

The first of the three reactions is important, because it gives an easy method of preparing phosphorous acid, and the last has a special interest because it illustrates a valuable application of phosphoric chloride. This reagent gives us the means of replacing an atom of oxygen with two atoms of chlorine, and (as is illustrated not only by [185], but also by [34]) this simple change frequently gives a clew to the molecular constitution of a chemical compound. The compound PCl_3O is called phosphoric oxychloride, and there is also a phosphoric sulphochloride, PCl_3S. Both are fuming, colorless liquids. The last, when heated with a solution of caustic soda, gives the following remarkable reaction : —

$$(PCl_3S + 6Na\text{-}O\text{-}H + Aq) =$$
$$(Na_3^=O_3^=PS + 3NaCl + 3H_2O + Aq). \quad [186]$$

191. ARSENIC. $As = 75.$ — Trivalent or quinquivalent. One of the less abundant elements, but in minute quantities quite widely distributed. Found native, and in combination both with sulphur and with many of the metals. The most abundant of the native compounds is *Mispickel*, $FeS_2 . FeAs_2$, and by simply heating this mineral in a closed vessel the elementary substance is easily obtained.

$$2Fe_2As_2S_2 = 4FeS + As_4. \qquad [187]$$

It is also prepared by subliming a mixture of arsenious anhydride and charcoal.

$$2As_2O_3 + 3C = As_4 + 3CO_2. \qquad [188]$$

192. "*Metallic Arsenic*," As_4, has a bright, steel-gray lustre, and conducts electricity with readiness. It is, therefore, frequently classed among the metals, and hence the trivial name.

On the other hand, it is very brittle, and closely allied in all its chemical relations to the class of elements with which it is here grouped. Arsenic, like phosphorus, is dimorphous, and may readily be crystallized both in octahedrons of the first system, and in rhombohedrons of the third. Corresponding to these two forms are two allotropic modifications, distinguished also by differences of density and of other physical qualities, although these differences are not so marked as those between the two states of phosphorus. In its ordinary condition, arsenic, when heated out of contact with the air, begins to volatilize at about 130° without previously melting, and it cannot be brought into the liquid condition except under pressure. The *Sp. Gr.* of the solid is 5.75, and that of the vapor referred to air 10.6. Heated in contact with the air, it burns with a pale blue flame, and the product of the combustion is arsenious anhydride, As_2O_3. It cannot, however, maintain its own combustion, and goes out unless the temperature is kept above the point of ignition by external means. At the ordinary temperature it rapidly tarnishes in the air, and, when in large bulk, the oxidation is sometimes sufficiently rapid to ignite the mass. Serious accidents have originated from this cause. The burning of arsenic is attended with a peculiar odor resembling garlic, which is very characteristic. It is insoluble in water or any of the ordinary solvents.

193. *Arsenic and Oxygen.* — *Arsenious Anhydride.* As_2O_3. — The white powder which is formed by the burning of arsenic is the most important and the best known of the compounds of this element. It is obtained in very large quantities as a secondary product in the roasting of many metallic ores. Like arsenic itself, this compound is dimorphous, and may be obtained crystallized both in octahedrons of the first system and in rhombic prisms of the fourth. Moreover, when freshly sublimed, it appears as a vitreous solid, and in this third state it is three times more soluble in water than in the crystalline condition. Common white arsenic is only sparingly soluble in water, but by continuous boiling with water this crystalline condition is changed into the vitreous (or colloidal) modification, and a much larger amount enters into solution. This change, however, is not permanent, and after long standing the excess before dissolved is all deposited in octahedral crystals. When digested

with the mineral acids, or with aqua ammonia, white arsenic dissolves still more readily than in water, but on standing, the larger part of the As_2O_3 is deposited from these solutions in octahedral crystals as before, and by evaporation the whole may be thus recovered, indicating that no stable compound had been formed.

194. *Arsenites.* — Arsenious acid, $H_3{=}O_3{=}As$, is only known in solution; and indeed there is no evidence that As_2O_3 forms with water a definite hydrate. There are, however, several well-defined arsenites.

Potassic Arsenite (Fowler's Solution)	$H_2,K{=}O_3{=}As,$
Cupric Arsenite (Scheele's Green)	$H,Cu{=}O_3{=}As,$
Argentic Arsenite (Brilliant Yellow)	$Ag_3{=}O_{=}As.$

The first is obtained by adding to a solution of caustic potash an excess of As_2O_3, and the last two are precipitated when a solution of the first is added to the solution of a silver or copper salt. Arsenious anhydride is a most violent mineral poison. It is also a powerful antiseptic, and is much used in packing hides and for preserving anatomical preparations.

195. *Arsenic Acid,* $H_3{=}O_3{=}As\,O$, is readily obtained by treating As_2O_3 with nitric acid.

$$As_2O_3 + 2H\text{-}O\text{-}NO_2 + 2H_2O = 2H_3{=}O_3{=}As\,O + N_2O_3. \quad [189]$$

On evaporating the resulting solution under regulated conditions of temperature, definite hydrates, all white solids, may be obtained corresponding to the three conditions of phosphoric acid. But they differ from the latter in that when dissolved in water they all yield solutions having the same properties and containing the same tribasic acid. From this acid a large number of arseniates may be prepared. The following, all of which may be obtained in well-defined crystals, are isomorphous with the corresponding phosphates : —

$$Na_3{=}O_3{=}As\,O\,.\,12H_2O, \quad H,Na_2{=}O_3{=}As\,O\,.\,12H_2O, \quad [190]$$
$$H_2Na{=}O_3{=}As\,O\,.\,H_2O, \quad H_2,K{=}O_3{=}As\,O.$$

These salts may be all rendered anhydrous by heat, and from the acid salts products may be thus obtained corresponding in composition to the meta and pyro-phosphates; but when dissolved they reunite with water and become tribasic. Hence aqueous solutions of all these arseniates give, with argentic nitrate, the same precipitate, $Ag_3{=}O_3{=}As\,O$. This precipitate has a brick-red color, and enables us to distinguish an arseniate from an arsenite. It is not formed, however, if an excess of ammonia or a free acid is present. On adding a solution of magnesic sulphate containing an excess of ammonia to a solution of an arseniate, a precipitate is obtained, $(H_4N),Mg{=}O_3{=}As\,O\,.\,6H_2O$, which very closely resembles the corresponding precipitate obtained with a phosphate under the same conditions.

196. *Arsenic Anhydride*, As_2O_5, is obtained as a white amorphous solid when arsenic acid is heated nearly to redness. At a higher temperature it fuses and is decomposed into As_2O_3 and $O{=}O$.

197. *Arsenic and Hydrogen.* — There are two compounds, a solid, H_4As_2, and a gas, H_3As. The gas is formed whenever hydrogen, in its nascent condition, comes in contact with a compound of arsenic, and its formation gives us one of the most delicate means of detecting the presence of arsenic in cases of poisoning. Thus, when arsenious acid is introduced into an apparatus evolving hydrogen, we have the reaction

$$H_3{=}O_3{=}As + 3H{-}H = 3H_2O + H_3As. \qquad [191]$$

As thus obtained, however, the gas is more or less mixed with hydrogen. It may be obtained pure by the following reaction : —

$$Sn_3As_2 + (6HCl + Aq) = (3Sn\,Cl_2 + Aq) + 2H_3As. \ [192]$$

It is a colorless gas (Sp. Gr. 33.9), which may be condensed to a liquid boiling at 30°. It has a repulsive odor, and is exceedingly poisonous. It burns in the air, forming As_2O_3 and H_2O. In the interior of the flame the combustion is imperfect, and hence the flame deposits on a cold surface, which is pressed upon it, a brilliant mirror of metallic arsenic. The gas is decomposed when passed through a red-hot glass tube, and a similar mirror is formed on the inner surface in front of the heated portion. By careful experimenting these mirrors may be obtained with hydrogen gas, which contains only a mere trace of arsenic. When arseniuretted hydrogen is passed into a solution of argentic nitrate, we obtain the following remarkable reaction : —

$$H_3As + 8Ag\text{-}O\text{-}NO_2 + 4H_2O =$$
$$4Ag_2 + 8H\text{-}O\text{-}NO_2 + H_3{=}O_3{=}AsO. \quad [193]$$

198. *Compounds with the Alcohol Radicals.* — Arsenic forms compounds analogous to the amines, phosphines, and their derivatives. The compounds trimethyl-arsine, $(CH_3)_3As$, and triethyl-arsine, $(C_2H_5)_3As$, do not, however, like the corresponding phosphines, combine directly with HCl and the similar acids, but they do unite very readily with two atoms of chlorine, bromine, or iodine, or with one atom of oxygen or sulphur, forming such compounds as

$$(CH_3)_3As\text{=}Cl_2, \quad (C_2H_5)_3As\text{=}Br_2, \quad (CH_3)_3As\text{=}O, \quad (C_2H_5)_3As\text{=}S.$$

They also unite with the iodides and bromides of the alcohol radicals, forming such compounds as

$$(CH_3)_4As\text{-}I \quad \text{or} \quad (C_2H_5)_4As\text{-}Br,$$

and from these may be derived basic compounds analogous to ammonic hydrate, like

$$(CH_3)_4As\text{-}O\text{-}H \quad \text{or} \quad (C_2H_5)_4As\text{-}O\text{-}H.$$

But by far the most important of this class of compounds are those which may be regarded as derived from a remarkable radical substance, $(CH_3)_2As\text{-}(CH_3)_2As$, called kakodyl, which is formed when a mixture of arsenious anhydride and potassic acetate is submitted to distillation in a closed retort. A crude complex product is thus obtained, from which the radical substance may be subsequently separated. Pure kakodyl is a spontaneously inflammable, exceedingly fetid, fuming liquid, resembling in many respects the corresponding compound of phosphorus. It enters into direct combination with several of the elements, and is one of the best defined of the radical substances. Representing the group of atoms $(CH_3)_2As$ by Kd, the symbols of a few of the more characteristic compounds will be as follows : —

Kakodyl	$Kd\text{-}Kd,$
Kakodylous Oxide	$Kd_2O,$
Kakodylic Oxide	$Kd_2O_2,$
Kakodylic Acid	$H\text{-}O\text{-}KdO,$
Kakodylic Anhydride?	$Kd_2O_3,$
Kakodylous Sulphide	$Kd_2S,$
Kakodylic Sulphide	$Kd_2S_2,$
Sulpho-kakodylic Acid	$H\text{-}S\text{-}KdS,$
Sulpho-kakodylic Anhydride	$Kd_2S_3,$
Kakodylous Chloride, Bromide, or Iodide	$KdCl, KdBr,$ or $KdI,$
Kakodylic Chloride, Bromide, or Iodide	$KdCl_3, KdBr_3,$ or $KdI_3.$

The mutual relations of the different compounds studied in this section are illustrated by the following scheme, which includes all the known compounds of arsenic with methyl ($Me = CH_3$) and chlorine : —

Type $H_3N.$	Type $ClH_4N.$
$Me,Me,Me \equiv As,$	$Cl,Me,Me,Me,Me \equiv As,$
$Cl,Me,Me \equiv As,$	$Cl,Cl,Me,Me,Me \equiv As,$
$Cl,Cl,Me \equiv As,$	$Cl,Cl,Cl,Me,Me \equiv As,$
$Cl,Cl,Cl \equiv As,$	$Cl,Cl,Cl,Cl,Me \equiv As.$

By direct union with Cl_2, the compounds of the first column may be changed into the compounds of the second column on the next lower line, and the compounds of the second column, when heated, break up into $MeCl$, and the corresponding compound of the first column on the same line. Moreover, the first compound of the first column unites directly with $MeCl$ to form the first compound of the second column. Besides the compounds mentioned above, this scheme includes another class of compounds, which may be regarded as formed from the radical (CH_3)As (corresponding to HN), not yet isolated. Such are

$(CH_3)As \cdot I_2,$	$(CH_3)As \cdot O,$
$(CH_3)As \equiv Cl_4,$	$H_2 \cdot O_2 \cdot ((CH_3)As \cdot O).$

They are called arsenmonomethyl iodide, oxide, &c., and the last, arsenmonomethylic acid. It is evident that the atomicity of the radical is not the same in all the compounds.

199. *Compounds with Chlorine, Bromine, and Iodine.* —
These elements unite directly with arsenic, but only in one
proportion forming $AsCl_3$, $AsBr_3$, and AsI_3. The first is a
liquid, the last two are volatile solids at the ordinary temperature of the air. They are all decomposed by water.

$$2AsBr_3 + 3H_2O = As_2O_3 + 6HBr. \qquad [194]$$

200. *Compounds with Sulphur.* — Arsenic and sulphur may
be melted together in all proportions. They also form several
distinct compounds. The most important are

201. *Realgar, As_2S_2,* a brilliant *red* solid, much used as a
pigment, and found in nature well crystallized.

202. *Orpiment, As_2S_3,* a brilliant *yellow* solid, also used as a
paint. Formed whenever arsenic is precipitated from its solutions by H_2S. Also found crystallized in nature. Soluble in
ammonia and caustic alkalies, and precipitated from such solutions by acids.

203. *Arsenic Sulphide. As_2S_5.* — Only known in combination.

The last two compounds are "sulphur anhydrides," and form
with the sulphur bases a very large and important class of sulphur salts, many of which are native compounds and important
metallic ores. The following reactions will illustrate the formation of compounds of this class : —

$$As_2S_3 + (4K\text{-}O\text{-}H + Aq) =$$
$$(H,K_2\equiv O_3\equiv As + H,K_2\equiv S_3\equiv As + H_2O + Aq), \quad [195]$$

$$(H,Na_2\equiv O_3\equiv As + 3H_2S + Aq) =$$
$$(H,Na_2\equiv S_3\equiv As + 3H_2O + Aq). \quad [196]$$

Sulpho-arsenites.

Proustite,	Hexagonal	$Ag_3\equiv S_3\equiv As,$
Tennantite,	Isometric	$[Cu_2]_3\equiv S_6\equiv As_2 . FeS,$
Sartorite,	Orthorhombic	$Pb\equiv S_2\equiv As_2S_2,$
Dufrénoysite,	Orthorhombic	$Pb_2\equiv S_4\equiv As_2S.$

Sulpho-arseniates.

| Enargite, | Orthorhombic | $[Cu_2]_3\equiv S_6\equiv(AsS)_2.$ |

These symbols should be compared with those of the corresponding compounds of antimony, in connection with which their mutual relations will be explained.

204. *Characteristic Reactions.* — The importance of proving the presence or absence of arsenic in cases of suspected poisoning has led to a most careful study of the characteristic reactions of this element, and hence our knowledge on these points is unusually accurate and full. The most striking of these reactions have already been given. Further details or descriptions of methods by which arsenic, even when in minute quantities, may be detected and distinguished from antimony lie beyond the scope of the present work.

205. ANTIMONY. $Sb = 122.$ — Trivalent or quinquivalent. This element is less abundantly distributed than arsenic, although found in similar associations. The most abundant native compound is the gray sulphide (Antimony Glance), Sb_2S_3, which occurs not only in a pure state, but also in combination with other metallic sulphides. Antimony is sometimes, although rarely, found in the metallic state, and likewise in combination with oxygen.

206. *Metallic Antimony, Sb?*, is most readily extracted from the native sulphide by smelting the ore with metallic iron.

$$Sb_2S_3 + 3Fe = 3FeS + Sb_2. \qquad [197]$$

It is also extracted by first roasting the ore,

$$2Sb_2S_3 + 9O\text{-}O = 2Sb_2O_3 + 6SO_2, \qquad [198]$$

and then melting with charcoal and sodic carbonate. The last converts into oxide the small portion of the sulphide which escaped oxidation in the roasting process,

$$Sb_2S_3 + 3Na_2\text{-}O_2\text{-}CO = Sb_2O_3 + 3Na_2S + 3CO_2, \ [199]$$

and the charcoal reduces the oxide to metallic antimony,

$$Sb_2O_3 + 3C = Sb_2 + 3CO. \qquad [200]$$

By oxidizing the crude metal with nitric acid, and again reducing with charcoal, the antimony may be obtained in a pure condition.

Antimony is closely allied to arsenic, but possesses the properties of a metal to a still higher degree. It has a bright metallic lustre, which it preserves in the air. It has a high *Sp. Gr.* (6.7), and conducts heat and electricity with facility. Its conducting power, however, is inferior to that of the perfect metals, and, moreover, it is very brittle and may be readily reduced to powder. It has also a highly crystalline structure, and like arsenic it may be obtained crystallized both in rhombohedrons of the third system, and in octahedrons of the first. The first is the common form, and lumps of the metal may sometimes be cleaved parallel to the rhombohedral planes, which are always more or less evident on the fractured surface. Antimony melts at 430°, and it volatilizes, but only very slowly, at a full red heat. The melted metal, when heated in the air, slowly oxidizes, and before the blow-pipe it burns, the product of the oxidation being in either case Sb_2O_3. Antimony is only very slightly acted on by pure hydrochloric acid, even when concentrated and boiling; but on the addition of a *very small* amount of nitric acid the metal dissolves easily, forming a solution of $SbCl_3$.

$$Sb_2 + (6HCl + 6HNO_3 + Aq) =$$
$$(2SbCl_3 + 6H_2O + Aq) + 6NO_2. \ [201]$$

With the aid of heat it dissolves in strong sulphuric acid.

$$Sb_2 + 6H_2SO_4 = Sb_2O_6(SO_2)_3 + 3SO_2 + 6H_2O. \ [202]$$

Nitric acid, when in excess, converts the metal into a white powder insoluble in the acid (chiefly Sb_2O_4). If, however, the nitric acid contains a little hydrochloric acid, the product is metantimonic acid.

$$Sb_2 + 4H\text{-}O\text{-}NO_2 =$$
$$2H\text{-}O\text{-}SbO_2 + H_2O + N_2O_3 + 2NO. \ [203]$$

Lastly, antimony dissolves readily in a mixture of tartaric and nitric acids, which is one of the best solvents of the metal. Metallic antimony is chiefly used in the arts to alloy with other metals, to which it imparts a greater hardness and durability. Type-metal is an alloy of four parts of lead and one of antimony. This alloy expands in "setting," and therefore takes a sharp impression of the mould in which it is cast; and this property, as well as the hardness, renders type-metal peculiarly suitable to the important use to which it is applied. Britannia metal, an alloy of brass, antimony, tin, and lead, much used as the base of plated silver-ware, also owes its hardness and durability to the antimony it contains.

207. *Antimony and Chlorine.* — *Antimonious Chloride.* $SbCl_3$. — A solution of this compound is readily obtained either by [201] or by dissolving the native sulphide in hydrochloric acid. On evaporating the excess of acid, and distilling the residue, the chloride is obtained as a white crystalline solid. It is deliquescent, very volatile, and melts so readily (72°) that it was formerly known as butter of antimony. The Sp. Gr. of its vapor, as found by experiment, is 112.7. Antimonious chloride may also be obtained by distilling antimony or antimonious sulphide with mercuric chloride, and also by distilling a mixture of antimonious sulphate with common salt.

$$Sb_4 + 4HgCl_2 = Sb_2Hg_2 + [Hg_2]Cl_2 + 2SbCl_3. \quad [204]$$

$$Sb_2S_3 + 3HgCl_2 = 3HgS + 2SbCl_3. \quad [205]$$

$$Sb_2O_6(SO_2)_3 + 6NaCl = 3Na_2O_2SO_2 + 2SbCl_3. \quad [206]$$

Antimonious chloride is decomposed by water, forming an insoluble oxychloride and hydrochloric acid. Hence the solution obtained by [201] becomes turbid when diluted with water. The presence of tartaric acid in sufficient quantity prevents the decomposition, and a solution of this acid dissolves the oxychloride when formed. By long-continued washing the oxychloride may be converted into antimonious oxide.

$$(SbCl_3 + H_2O + Aq) = \mathbf{SbOCl} + (2HCl + Aq). \quad [207]$$

$$\mathbf{2SbOCl} + (H_2O + Aq) = \mathbf{Sb_2O_3} + (2HCl + Aq). \quad [208]$$

Antimonious chloride combines with the chlorides of the metals of the alkalies and of the alkaline earths, and forms soluble crystalline salts. Hence it may be mixed with concentrated solutions of these chlorides, as also with strong hydrochloric acid, without undergoing decomposition. The following are the symbols of a few of these double chlorides, which are best regarded as molecular compounds: —

$$3(H_4N)\,Cl\,.\,SbCl_3\,.\,1\tfrac{1}{2}H_2O,^1 \qquad 2(H_4N)\,Cl\,.\,SbCl_3\,.\,H_2O,$$
$$3KCl\,.\,SbCl_3, \qquad\qquad 2KCl\,.\,SbCl_3,$$
$$3NaCl\,.\,SbCl_3, \qquad\qquad BaCl_2\,.\,SbCl_3\,.\,2\tfrac{1}{2}H_2O.^{\iota}$$

208. *Antimonic Chloride*, $SbCl_5$, may be formed by passing chlorine gas over $SbCl_3$, or by acting on the metal with an excess of the same reagent. It is a volatile, fuming liquid, which readily parts with two fifths of its chlorine, and is therefore sometimes used, like PCl_5, as a chloridizing agent. It is at once decomposed by water. With only a small quantity it forms an oxychloride (compare [185]).

$$H_2O + SbCl_5 = 2HCl + SbCl_3O. \qquad [209]$$

With an excess of water, either ortho-antimonic acid or pyro-antimonic acid results.

$$SbCl_5 + 4H_2O = H_3{\equiv}O_3{\equiv}SbO + 5HCl, \qquad [210]$$

or $$2SbCl_5 + 7H_2O = H_4{\equiv}O_4{\equiv}Sb_2O_3 + 10HCl. \qquad [211]$$

The presence of tartaric acid prevents these reactions. By the action of H_2S on $SbCl_5$ a sulpho-chloride may be formed.

$$SbCl_5 + H_2S = SbCl_3S + 2HCl. \qquad [212]$$

A bromide of antimony, $SbBr_3$, and an iodide, SbI_3, are readily formed by the direct action of these elements on the metal, but no penta-bromide or iodide has yet been obtained. They are both fusible and volatile solids, and when acted on by water are converted into $SbBrO$ and $SbIO$. The corresponding fluoride dissolves in water without decomposition, and forms with the alkaline fluorides a number of double salts.

$$3NaF\,.\,SbF_3, \qquad 2(H_4N)F\,.\,SbF_3, \qquad KF\,.\,SbF_3.$$

209. *Antimony and Oxygen.* — *Antimonious Oxide.* Sb_2O_3. — This compound, already mentioned as a product of the direct oxidation of antimony, may, like As_2O_3, be obtained crystallized both in octahedrons of the first system or in rhombic prisms of the fourth, and on this difference of form depends the distinc-

---

[1] These symbols are thus written to show the relations of the compounds. To be strictly accurate they should be doubled.

tion between the two minerals Senarmontite and Valentinite, both of which consist of this same substance. The oxide is most readily prepared artificially by pouring a solution of $Sb\,Cl_3$ [201] into a boiling solution of sodic carbonate.

$$(3Na_2{=}O_2{=}CO + 2\,Sb\,Cl_3 + Aq) =$$
$$\mathbf{Sb_2O_3} + (6Na\,Cl + Aq) + 3\,\textcircled{C}\textcircled{O}_2. \quad [213]$$

Antimonious oxide acts both as a basic and as an acid anhydride, although the first is by far its most marked character. It is but very slightly soluble in water. When the solution of $Sb\,Cl_3$ is poured into a cold solution of sodic carbonate, we have the reaction,

$$(3Na_2{=}O_2{=}CO + 2\,Sb\,Cl_3 + H_2O + Aq) =$$
$$2\mathbf{H\text{-}O\text{-}SbO} + (6Na\,Cl + Aq) + 3\,\textcircled{C}\textcircled{O}_2, \quad [214]$$

and the product may be regarded as metantimonious acid, for it dissolves in caustic alkalies and forms definite, although very unstable, salts. On the other hand, the oxide dissolves in fuming sulphuric and fuming nitric, as well as in hydrochloric acids, forming crystalline salts, in which the antimony plays the part of a basic radical.

The most important salt of this class is that formed by dissolving Sb_2O_3 in a solution of acid potassic tartrate (cream of tartar). This compound is very much used in medicine as an emetic, and hence the trivial name *tartar emetic*. Tartaric acid is tetratomic, but only bibasic (43), and we have the following series of compounds : —

Tartaric Acid	$\overset{+}{H}_2 , \overline{H}_2{\equiv}O_4{\equiv}(C_4H_2O_2),$
Neutral Potassic Tartrate	$K_2 , \overline{H}_2{\equiv}O_4{\equiv}(C_4H_2O_2),$
Acid Potassic Tartrate	$K,H, \overline{H}_2{\equiv}O_4{\equiv}(C_4H_2O_2),$
Tartar Emetic (crystallized)	$K,SbO , \overline{H}_2{\equiv}O_4{\equiv}(C_4H_2O_2) . H_2O,$
" after heating to 200°	$K,Sb{\equiv}O_4{\equiv}(C_4H_2O_2).$

It will be noticed that in forming tartar emetic the radical SbO of the compound $H\text{-}O\text{-}SbO$ takes the place of one atom of basic hydrogen, which still remains unreplaced in cream of tartar. On heating the crystallized salt to 100° it gives up its water of crystallization. At 200° it gives off an additional atom of water, formed at the expense of the oxygen in the radical just named and of the two atoms of hydrogen distinguished as negative in the acid; and it will be seen that, in the anhydrous salt thus obtained, one atom of antimony takes the place of three typical atoms of hydrogen in tartaric acid. Compounds similar to tartar emetic may be made in a similar way with the oxides of arsenic, bismuth, and uranium. Their symbols differ from that of tartar emetic only in having the radicals $As\,O$, $As\,O_2$, $Bi\,O$, or $U\,O$, in place of $Sb\,O$, and they undergo a similar decomposition when heated. Compounds of the same class may also be obtained with other anhydrides than those of the group of elements we are now studying (as Fe_2O_3 Cr_2O_3, B_2O_3, &c.), and when it is further added that the potassium in these compounds may be replaced by other univalent radicals, or even by bivalent radicals soldering together two molecules of the ordinary type, it will be seen that a very large number of such salts are possible. Lastly, the fact that a compound has been prepared in which two of the typical atoms of hydrogen are replaced by the positive radical ethyl, while the other two are replaced by the negative radical acetyl, and the additional fact that no salt can be obtained in which all the four atoms are replaced by a well-defined positive radical, give a strong presumption in favor of the formulæ of the tartrates adopted above.

Antimonious oxide, when heated out of contact with the air, volatilizes unchanged, but under the same conditions in the air it burns like tinder, forming a higher oxide, Sb_2O_4, which is fixed, even at a high red heat. By ignition with charcoal or hydrogen, all the oxides are readily reduced to the metallic state.

210. *Antimonic Acid.* — The reactions have already been given [203], [210], [211] by which the three conditions of this acid may be prepared. They are

Metantimonic Acid	$H\text{-}O\text{-}Sb\,O_2$,
Orthoantimonic Acid	$H_3\equiv O_3\equiv Sb\,O$,
Pyroantimonic Acid	$H_4\equiv O_4\equiv Sb_2O_3$.

Pyroantimonic acid may also be prepared by acidifying the solution of acid potassic pyroantimoniate mentioned below,

$$(H_2K_2\equiv O_4\equiv Sb_2O_3 + 2HCl + Aq) =$$
$$H_4\equiv O_4\equiv Sb_2O_3 + (2KCl + Aq), \quad [215]$$

but when this precipitate is dried, it loses water and changes into metantimonic acid,

$$H_4\!\equiv\!O_4\!\equiv\!Sb_2O_3 = 2H\text{-}O\text{-}SbO_2 + H_2O.\qquad [216]$$

The existence of orthoantimonic acid has not been as yet well established, but the other two are well known, and many of their salts have been investigated. The most interesting of these salts is obtained by fusing antimonic anhydride with an excess of potassic hydrate, and extracting the fused mass with water. An alkaline solution is obtained, containing a salt whose composition is expressed by the symbol $H_2K_2\!\equiv\!O_4\!\equiv\!Sb_2O_3$. This solution produces a precipitate in solutions of salts of sodium, and is sometimes used as a reagent in testing for this element. The sodic salt thus precipitated has the composition $H_2Na_2\!\equiv\!O_4\!\equiv\!Sb_2O_3 \cdot 6H_2O$. Antimonic acid, in either of its conditions, is insoluble in water, as well as the antimoniates, with a few exceptions. In this respect they frequently differ from the corresponding compounds of phosphorus and arsenic, which they closely resemble in molecular constitution.

211. *Antimonic Anhydride*, Sb_2O_5, is readily prepared by gently heating metantimonic acid, the product of reaction [203]. It is a pale yellow powder, insoluble in water. Fused with alkaline hydrates or carbonates it yields various antimoniates. When ignited alone it gives off one fifth of its oxygen, and the product is the same white powder, Sb_2O_4, which is formed by the oxidation of antimonious oxide. This intermediate oxide is the most stable of the oxides of antimony. It is sometimes called antimonious acid, and when fused with the alkalies it enters into combination with them, but the products thus obtained may be regarded as mixtures of an antimonite and an antimoniate, and the oxide itself appears to be an antimoniate of antimony, $SbO\text{-}O\text{-}SbO_2$. A rare mineral called Cervantite has the same composition.

212. *Antimony and Hydrogen.* — *Antimoniuretted Hydrogen.* H_3Sb. — When any soluble compound of antimony is added to an apparatus evolving hydrogen [64], we obtain a product closely resembling arseniuretted hydrogen, but containing antimony instead of arsenic.

$$SbCl_3 + 3H\text{-}H = H_3Sb + 3HCl.\qquad [217]$$

The antimony compound thus formed is always mixed with much hydrogen gas, and has not yet been obtained in a pure condition. When burnt in air it yields water and antimonious oxide.

$$2H_3Sb + 3\,O{=}O = Sb_2O_3 + 3H_2O. \qquad [218]$$

If burnt against a cold surface, so that the combustion is incomplete, the antimony is deposited and a metallic mirror is formed.

$$4H_3Sb + 3\,O{=}O = Sb_4 + 6H_2O. \qquad [219]$$

The compound is decomposed and a similar mirror formed when the gas is passed through a red-hot tube.

When the gas is transmitted through a solution of argentic nitrate we get the reaction

$$(3Ag\text{-}O\text{-}NO_2 + Aq) + H_3Sb =$$
$$Ag_3Sb + (3H\text{-}O\text{-}NO_2 + Aq). \; [220]$$

This reaction, and the well-established trivalent character of antimony, fix the composition of antimoniuretted hydrogen beyond all reasonable doubt.

Compounds of antimony with the alcohol radicals have been prepared, both after the type of ammonia and that of the ammonium salts. Thus we have

Trimethyl-stibine	$(CH_3)_3Sb,$
Trimethyl-stibine Chloride	$(CH_3)_3SbCl_2,$
Trimethyl-stibine Oxide	$(CH_3)_3SbO,$
Tetramethyl-stibonium Iodide	$(CH_3)_4SbI,$
Tetramethyl-stibonium Hydrate	$(CH_3)_4Sb\text{-}O\text{-}H,$

and the corresponding compounds of ethyl and amyl. The reaction of triethyl-stibine on hydrochloric acid is interesting, as it illustrates the serial relations among the group of elements we are studying. $(C_2H_5)_3Sb$ not only does not combine with HCl, but actually decomposes the acid, yielding $(C_2H_5)_3SbCl_2$ and $H\text{-}H$. Compounds of antimony corresponding to those of the kakodyl group are not known.

213. *Antimony and Zinc.* — There are two very well marked crystalline compounds of antimony and zinc, Zn_3Sb_2 and Zn_2Sb_2, which give still further evidence of the usual trivalent charac-

ter of antimony. The compound Zn_3Sb_2, moreover, decomposes water with the evolution of hydrogen gas.

214. *Antimony and Sulphur (Crude Antimony).* — *Antimonious Sulphide.* Sb_2S_3.— The gray sulphide of antimony has already been noticed as a native product. It is known to mineralogists as Antimony Glance, and is distinguished by its great fusibility. Large splinters of the mineral readily melt in a candle flame. Hence it is easily separated by fusion from the gangue with which it is found associated, and the process is termed "liquation." Its crystals have a bright metallic lustre, and the form of rhombic prisms of the fourth system; but a strong tendency to longitudinal cleavage gives to them a bladed appearance.

When antimony and sulphur, or antimonious oxide and sulphur, are melted together in proper proportions, a compound is obtained similar to the native sulphide. Moreover, a precipitate of the same composition falls when H_2S is passed through the solution of any antimonious compound. This precipitate, however, has a brick *red color*, and is probably an isomeric modification of the native gray compound. It is insoluble in dilute hydrochloric acid when cold, but readily dissolves in the hot acid if moderately concentrated. It is also soluble in solutions of alkaline hydrates.

$$Sb_2S_3 + (6K\text{-}O\text{-}H + Aq) =$$
$$(K_3{\equiv}S_3{\equiv}Sb + K_3{\equiv}O_3{\equiv}Sb + 3H_2O + Aq). \quad [221]$$

From this solution it is again precipitated on the addition of an acid.

$$(K_3{\equiv}S_3{\equiv}Sb + K_3{\equiv}O_3{\equiv}Sb + 6HCl + Aq) =$$
$$Sb_2S_3 + (6KCl + 3H_2O + Aq). \quad [222]$$

In like manner it dissolves in solutions of alkaline sulphohydrates.

$$Sb_2S_3 + (6K\text{-}S\text{-}H + Aq) =$$
$$(2K_3{\equiv}S_3{\equiv}Sb + Aq) + 3H_2S. \quad [223]$$

Antimonious sulphide is a strong sulpho-anhydride, and many of its salts are important minerals. The following are a few examples. We give the symbols in their simplest form, but in the minerals themselves the antimony is frequently more or less replaced by arsenic, and the principal metallic radical by others isomorphous with it. These compounds are best classified by referring them to a series of assumed sulphur acids, related to each other like the successive anhydrides of the oxygen acids (181), but derived from the normal compound of the series by eliminating successive molecules of H_2S. They may be distinguished as ortho, meta, and pyro-sulphantimonites, but these terms have no special appropriateness except so far as they imply a distinction analogous to that which obtains between similar oxygen compounds.

Ortho-sulphantimonites.

Pyrargyrite	Hexagonal	$Ag_3{=}S_3{\equiv}Sb,$
Stephanite	Orthorhombic	$Ag_3{=}S_3{\equiv}Sb . Ag_2S,$
Polybasite	Orthorhombic	$Ag_3{=}S_3{=}Sb . 3Ag_2S,$
Bournonite	Orthorhombic	$[Cu_2], Pb_2 {\equiv}S_6{\equiv}Sb_2,$
Meneghinite	Monoclinic ?	$Pb_3{\equiv}S_6{\equiv}Sb_2 . PbS,$
Tetrahedrite	Isometric	$[Cu_2]_3{\equiv}S_6{\equiv}Sb_2 . ZnS.$

Meta-sulphantimonites.

Miargyrite	Monoclinic	$Ag{-}S{-}SbS,$
Zinkenite	Orthorhombic	$Pb{=}S_2{=}Sb_2S_2,$
Chalcostibite	Orthorhombic	$Cu{=}S_2{=}Sb_2S_2,$
Berthierite		$Fe{=}S_2{=}Sb_2S_2.$

Pyro-sulphantimonites.

Jamesonite (feather ore)	Orthorhombic	$Pb_2{\equiv}S_4{\equiv}Sb_2S,$
Freieslebenite	Monoclinic	$3Ag_{10}{\times}S_{10}{\times}Sb_4S . 4Pb_5{\times}S_{10}{\times}Sb_4S.$

A few points in connection with the above formulæ require further explanation. Of the three dyad atoms which compose the basic radical of the mineral Bournonite, two are atoms of lead, and one a double atom (34) of copper. Now we may either suppose that each molecule of the mineral is constituted as our symbol would indicate, or we may regard it as a molecular aggregate of two distinct compounds, namely, $[Cu_2]_3{\equiv}S_6{\equiv}Sb_2$ and $Pb_3{\equiv}S_6{\equiv}Sb_2$, and as containing for every two molecules

12 *   R

of the last one molecule of the first. In Freieslebenite, however, the proportions of silver and lead are such that the composition of the mineral can only be accurately expressed in the second of the two ways just indicated, and this is the general rule in the mineral kingdom. Again, the minerals Stephanite, Polybasite, Meneghinite, and Tetrahedrite may be best regarded as molecular aggregates of an ortho-sulphantimonite and a simple metallic sulphide, in which the last plays very much the same part as the water of crystallization in our ordinary salts.

In all the above cases the results of analysis would indicate a great constancy in the relative number of heterogeneous molecules which enter into the composition of the mineral; but in other cases no such constancy is observed, and one element is found replacing another in almost any proportion. In tetrahedrite, for example, we frequently find the copper more or less replaced by silver or mercury, the antimony in like manner replaced by arsenic or bismuth, and the zinc by iron. This we express by writing the symbols of the replacing elements together within the same brackets. Thus $[[Cu_2], Ag_2, Hg]$ stands for only one atom, but indicates that in the mineral the copper is more or less replaced by silver and mercury. So also the symbol $[Zn, Fe]$ represents only one atom, but indicates that the zinc is to a certain extent replaced by iron. In its most general form the symbol of tetrahedrite would be written, —

$$[[Cu_2], Ag_2, Hg]_3 S [Sb, As, Bi]_2 . [Zn, Fe] S.$$

This symbol indicates nothing in regard to the relative proportions of the elements enclosed in the same brackets, and in fact this proportion is variable in different specimens of the same mineral, but it does show that, so far as the number of atoms is concerned, $[[Cu_2], Ag_2, Hg] : [Sb, As, Bi] : [Zn, Fe] = 3 : 2 : 1$.

It is, of course, impossible, according to our present theories, that each molecule should have this complex constitution; but we may suppose that in the mineral there are certain molecules containing one set of elements, and other molecules a different set, the actual specimen being an aggregate of all; and further, we must suppose that there are two kinds of molecular aggregation, one in which the molecules are united in more or less definite proportions, and a second where they are merely mixed in any proportions which accident may have determined.

215. *Antimonic Sulphide.* Sb_2S_5. — When H_2S is passed through a solution of $SbCl_5$, an orange-colored precipitate is formed, having the composition which our symbol indicates. It may be questioned, however, whether the precipitate is not an intimate mixture of Sb_2S_3 and $S=S$, for when treated with sulphide of carbon two fifths of the sulphur is dissolved, Sb_2S_3 being left; and, moreover, it is decomposed by boiling hydrochloric acid into $SbCl_3$, H_2S, and $S=S$. On the other hand, it is dissolved in alkaline hydrates and sulphides, forming sulphantimoniates, and from these solutions the same substance is again precipitated on the addition of an acid.

$$4Sb_2S_5 + (24K\text{-}O\text{-}H + Aq) =$$
$$(3K_3\text{=}O_3\text{=}SbO + 5K_3\text{=}S_3\text{=}SbS + 12H_2O + Aq). \quad [224]$$

$$Sb_2S_5 + (3K_2S + Aq) = (2K_3\text{=}S_3\text{=}SbS + Aq). \quad [225]$$

$$(2K_3\text{=}S_3\text{=}SbS + 6HCl + Aq) =$$
$$Sb_2S_5 + (6KCl + Aq) + 3H_2S. \quad [226]$$

216. *Characteristic Reactions.* — The formation of the red sulphide by the action of H_2S is one of the most characteristic indications of the presence of antimony; but, before this test can be applied, the antimony must be separated from all those elements which would obscure the reaction, by the well-known methods of qualitative analysis. The blow-pipe reactions of antimony are also very characteristic. They consist in the formation of a brittle metallic bead or a coating of volatile oxide on charcoal, and in the peculiar bluish-green color which this oxide imparts to the blow-pipe flame.

217. BISMUTH. $Bi = 210$. — Trivalent and quinquivalent. One of the rarer elements. Usually found native, sometimes combined with sulphur, in bismuth glance, Bi_2S_3, and rarely with both sulphur and tellurium, in tetradymite, Bi_2Te_2S. Metallic bismuth is readily extracted from the native mineral by fusion (liquation). After the analogy of phosphorus and arsenic, we assign to the elementary substance the molecular formula Bi_4; but since the metal does not volatilize except at a very high temperature, we have not been able to determine its molecular weight experimentally. Bismuth melts at 265°, and forms alloys which are remarkable for their great fusibility.

An alloy containing two parts of bismuth, one of lead, and one of tin, melts at about 94°, and the addition of cadmium reduces the melting-point still lower. These alloys expand on hardening, and are, therefore, useful for making casts.

As we descend in the series from antimony to bismuth, the metallic qualities become still more marked. The *Sp. Gr.* of bismuth equals 9.83. Its lustre is brilliant, with a reddish tinge. It is less brittle than antimony, and even is slightly malleable. Bismuth may readily be crystallized in rhombohedrons isomorphous with those of antimony; but it has not yet been crystallized in forms of the isometric system. Bismuth is not dissolved by strong hydrochloric acid, nor even by sulphuric acid, except when concentrated and boiling. Nitric acid readily dissolves it with evolution of NO_2, forming a well-crystallized nitrate (distinction from antimony). The metal also dissolves in aqua-regia, and combines directly with chlorine, bromine, and iodine.

218. *Bismuth and the Alcohol Radicals.* — No compound of bismuth and hydrogen is known, but bismuth combines with ethyl, forming a very unstable liquid, which inflames spontaneously in the air and explodes at 150°. It has the composition $(C_2H_5)_3Bi$, and from it may be obtained the compound $(C_2H_5)_3 BiI_2$ in yellow six-sided crystalline plates. This is the iodide of a bivalent radical, which forms also definite but very unstable compounds with chlorine and oxygen, and is capable of replacing the hydrogen of nitric or sulphuric acids.

219. *Bismuth and Chlorine.* — Only one compound of bismuth and chlorine is known, $BiCl_3$, and this may be obtained either by passing chlorine over the metal, by distilling the metal with corrosive sublimate, or by distilling the residue obtained when a solution of the metal in aqua-regia is evaporated to dryness. The product in either case is a very fusible and volatile solid resembling the corresponding compound of antimony. It dissolves in hydrochloric acid, but is decomposed by water into hydrochloric acid and insoluble oxychloride of bismuth, $BiOCl$. The same oxychloride is precipitated when a solution of bismuthous nitrate is poured into a solution of common salt. It is a brilliant white powder, known under the name of pearl white, and much used as a cosmetic. It is insoluble in tartaric acid, ammonic sulphide, or solution of potash, and is thus distinguished

from oxychloride of antimony precipitated under similar conditions. Bismuthous chloride combines with hydrochloric acid and the alkaline chlorides to form double salts, and, like $SbCl_3$, may be mixed with concentrated solutions of these compounds without undergoing decomposition.

The compounds of bismuth with bromine, iodine, and fluorine are $BiBr_3$, BiI_3, and $BiFl_3$.

220. *Bismuth and Oxygen.* — Metallic bismuth does not tarnish in the air, but at a red heat the melted metal slowly oxidizes, and before the compound blow-pipe it burns brilliantly. The product of the oxidation is Bismuthous Oxide, Bi_2O_3. The same compound is obtained by heating the nitrate to a *low* red heat. It is a pale yellow powder, which melts at a full red heat to a dark yellow liquid. It is insoluble in water, and will not directly combine with it; but by pouring a solution of bismuthous nitrate in dilute nitric acid into dilute aqua ammonia, or into a solution of potassic hydrate, a white hydrate of the metal is precipitated. This hydrate, when dried, has the composition $BiO\text{-}O\text{-}H$; but there are reasons for believing that the precipitate falls of the composition $Bi^\equiv O_3^\equiv H_3$. By a gentle heat, or by boiling with caustic alkalies, all the water is expelled and Bi_2O_3 is left. Bismuthous oxide is a decided basic anhydride. It is dissolved by hydrochloric, nitric, and sulphuric acids, forming definite salts. Nevertheless, by fusing the oxide with sodic carbonate, an unstable compound is obtained, in which the metal is the basic radical ($Na\text{-}O\text{-}BiO$).

By passing chlorine through a solution of $K\text{-}O\text{-}H$, holding Bi_2O_3 in suspension, a red deposit is obtained, which is a mixture of bismuthic acid, $H\text{-}O\text{-}BiO_2$, and bismuthic anhydride, Bi_2O_5.

$$Bi_2O_3 + (4K\text{-}O\text{-}H + 2Cl\text{-}Cl + Aq) =$$
$$2H\text{-}O\text{-}BiO_2 + (4KCl + H_2O + Aq). \quad [227]$$

The two products may be separated by means of cold nitric acid, which dissolves only the anhydride. Bismuthic acid dissolves in a solution of potassic hydrate, giving a blood-red solution; but the salt thus formed is very unstable and is decomposed by mere washing. The other compounds of the acid are little known. At a temperature of 130° the red-colored acid is resolved into water and the brown anhydride.

Bismuthic anhydride, when gently heated, changes into an intermediate oxide, Bi_2O_4, or rather into a mixture of this oxide and Bi_2O_3. If heated in a current of hydrogen, it is at once completely reduced to the lower degree of oxidation. When heated with sulphuric or nitric acids it evolves oxygen, producing bismuthous sulphate or nitrate; and when heated with hydrochloric acid it evolves chlorine, yielding bismuthous chloride.

221. *Bismuthous Nitrate,* $Bi^{=}O_3^{=}(NO_2)_3 . 5H_2O$, is the most important of the salts of bismuth. It forms large deliquescent crystals. It readily dissolves in water strongly acidified with nitric acid, but when mixed with a large volume of water it is decomposed, and a white basic salt of somewhat variable composition, formerly called the magistery of bismuth, is precipitated. The first precipitate appears to consist mainly of the compound $Bi^{=}O_3^{=}(NO_2),H_2$; but this is more or less decomposed by the subsequent washings. The product is now generally known as the basic nitrate of bismuth, and is used medicinally.

222. *Bismuthous Sulphate.* — When bismuthous oxide dissolves in sulphuric acid, the normal sulphate $Bi_2^{\,}O_6^{=}(SO_2)_3$ is undoubtedly formed; but when the solution is evaporated this salt loses the larger part of its acid, and the yellow product obtained, when the residue is gently heated, has, approximately at least, the composition $(BiO)_2^{=}O_2^{=}SO_2$; although, being easily decomposed by heat, it is difficult to obtain the compound in a pure condition. The formula of the basic nitrate may also be written $BiO\text{-}O\text{-}NO_2 . H_2O$, and the formation of salts of this type is characteristic of the class of elements we are studying.

223. *Bismuth and Sulphur.* — The native compound of bismuth and sulphur already mentioned, Bi_2S_3, is isomorphous with antimony glance, Sb_2S_3, which it closely resembles. The same compound may be obtained by fusing bismuth with sulphur in proper proportions, and also by passing H_2S through the solution of a bismuth salt. The precipitated sulphide is black, and is not dissolved by alkaline hydrates or sulpho-hydrates. It is also insoluble in all the dilute mineral acids, but it dissolves in hot nitric acid. When, however, the solution is mixed with water, most of the bismuth is again precipitated as basic nitrate. When heated in the air, Bi_2S_3 is oxidized and yields SO_2 and Bi_2O_3, which melts to dark yellow globules. Bismuthous sulphide is a sulpho-anhydride, and the following minerals may be regarded as sulpho-bismuthites: —

Kobellite	Orthorhombic?	$Pb_3 \vline S_6 \vline Bi, Sb,$
Needle Ore	"	$([Cu_2], Pb_2) \vline S_6 \vline Bi_2,$
Wittichenite	"	$[Cu_2]_3 \vline S_6 \vline Bi_2,$
Emplectite	"	$[Cu_2] = S_2 = Bi_2 S_2.$

224. Characteristic Reactions. — The decomposition of the soluble salts of bismuth by water, with the formation of an insoluble basic salt, is the most characteristic reaction of this metal. The salts of bismuth are easily reduced on charcoal before the blow-pipe, and yield a metallic bead, surrounded by a yellow coating of oxide.

Questions and Problems.

Nitrogen.

1. In order to determine the composition of the air, 863.7 $\overline{c.\,m.}^3$ of air measured under a pressure of 55.76 c. m., and at 5°.5, were mixed in an eudiometer-tube with a quantity of pure hydrogen. After addition of hydrogen the volume measured 1006.7 $\overline{c.\,m.}^3$, under pressure of 69.11 c. m. The mixture was next exploded by an electric spark, and after the explosion the residual gas measured 800.7 $\overline{c.\,m.}^3$, under a pressure of 49.14 c. m., and at 5°.6. Required composition of air by volume in 100 parts.

Solution. By [4] and [9] it will be found that the three volumes given above would have measured, under the normal conditions, respectively 621.20, 897.38, and 507.38. The absorption due to the combustion of the hydrogen is then 897.3 — 507.3 = 390 $\overline{c.\,m.}^3$ Of this $\frac{1}{3}$ or 130 was oxygen. Hence 621.20 $\overline{c.\,m.}^3$ of air contained 130 $\overline{c.\,m.}^3$ of oxygen and 491.2 $\overline{c.\,m.}^3$ of nitrogen, or 100 parts contained 20.92 oxygen and 79.08 nitrogen.

2. In another experiment 885.4 $\overline{c.\,m.}^3$ of air at 53.88 c. m., and 0°.5 were taken. After addition of hydrogen, volume measured 1052.7 $\overline{c.\,m.}^3$, at 70.31 c. m. and 0°.5. After explosion the volume was reduced to 858.3 $\overline{c.\,m.}^3$, at 51.36 c. m. and 0°.5. Required composition of air by volume in 100 parts.

Ans. Oxygen 20.93, nitrogen 79.07.

3. One cubic metre of dry air, measured under normal conditions, was passed over ignited copper-turnings. How much must the copper have increased in weight? Ans. 299.9 grammes.

4. In preparing nitrogen gas by [132], what volume of nitrogen is obtained for every litre of chlorine used? Ans. $\frac{1}{3}$ of a litre.

5. What weight of nitric acid, *Sp. Gr.* = 1.47, can be made from 170 kilos. of soda nitre, and what weight of sulphuric acid must be used in the process ? [135.]

　　　　　　Ans. 196 kilos. of sulphuric acid, 152.4 nitric acid.

6. When, in the preparation of nitric acid, two molecules of nitre are used to each molecule of sulphuric acid, one half of the nitric acid is given off with great readiness; but to obtain the second half we must heat the materials to a much higher temperature. In the first stage of the reaction sodic bisulphate is formed, and in the second, neutral sodic sulphate. Write the two successive reactions.

7. How much sulphuric acid is required for the decomposition of 303.3 grammes of potassic nitrate ?　　　　Ans. 294 grammes.

8. Write the reaction of nitric acid on sulphur, assuming that the products are sulphuric acid and nitric oxide.

9. Write the reaction of nitric acid on copper, assuming that the products are cupric nitrate and nitric oxide.

10. How much nitric acid (*Sp. Gr.* 1.228) is required to dissolve 14.7 grammes of copper ?　　　　Ans. 107.6 grammes.

11. How much to dissolve 16.7 grammes cupric oxide ?

　　　　　　　　Ans. 73.21 grammes.

12. A quantity of plumbic nitrate, weighing 0.993 grammes, yields on ignition 0.669 gramme of plumbic oxide. By another determination it appears that 1.324 grammes of the same salt, ignited in a glass tube with copper-turnings, yield 89.34 $\overline{\text{c. m.}}^3$ of nitrogen. Deduce the percentage composition and symbol of nitric acid, assuming that the composition of plumbic oxide and the atomic weight of lead, oxygen, and nitrogen are known. What reason have you for assuming that the acid molecule contains only one atom of hydrogen ?

13. Write the reaction of nitric acid on phosphorus, assuming that phosphoric acid and one or more of the oxides of nitrogen are the products of the reaction.

14. Write the reaction of nitric acid on cotton. (31.)

15. Illustrate by means of a table the relations of the various acids and anhydrides which may be theoretically derived from orthonitric acid.

16. In nitric acid and the nitrates, what is the quantivalence of nitrogen ?

17. In nitrous acid and the nitrites, what is the quantivalence of nitrogen ?

18. Illustrate by means of a table the relations of the various acids and anhydrides which may be theoretically derived from orthonitrous acids.

19. Can nitrite ever be isomeric with a nitrate ? What is the essential difference between the two classes of compounds ?

20. The Sp. Gr. of nitric peroxide vapor referred to air has been found to be 1.72. How does this value agree with the number deduced from theory ?

21. With what volumes of oxygen gas must one litre of nitric oxide be mixed, to prepare respectively nitrous anhydride and nitric peroxide ?

22. The Sp. Gr. of nitric peroxide would seem to compel us to assign to the compound the symbol we have adopted, and the same group of atoms also constantly acts as a univalent radical. Can you harmonize these facts with the theory of (69) ?

23. What volume of oxygen is required to convert 3 grammes of nitric oxide (in presence of water) into nitric acid ?

Ans. $1674.6 \overline{c.m.}^3$

24. Write the reaction of nitric peroxide on calcic hydrate.

25. In the preparation of nitric oxide by [152], why should you anticipate that nitrous oxide, or even nitrogen gas might be evolved, when the nitric acid was nearly exhausted ?

26. Analyze the reaction [152], and represent the two stages by separate equations.

27. Analyze the reaction [153], and determine the amounts of the different factors which should be used in order to make 10 litres of nitric oxide gas.

28. Write the reaction when ferrous sulphate, sulphuric acid, and nitre are heated together.

29. The Sp. Gr. of nitric oxide referred to air is 1.038. How does this compare with the theoretical number ?

30. When sodium is heated in a confined quantity of NO, the volume of the gas is reduced to one half, and the residue is found to be pure nitrogen. Assuming that the Sp. Gr. is known, show that this fact proves that the symbol we have assigned to the compound must be correct.

31. Analyze reaction [154], and show in what it differs from [133].

32. What weight and what volume of nitrous oxide can be obtained from 240 grammes of ammonic nitrate ?

Ans. 132 grammes, or 66.9 litres.

33. One litre of nitric oxide gas will yield by [155] what volume of nitrous oxide ?   Ans. ½ litre.

34. Analyze reaction [156], and represent the two stages by separate equations.

35. What evidence is given that nitrous oxide is less stable than nitric oxide ?

36. When sodium is heated in nitrous oxide no change of volume results, and the residue is pure nitrogen. The Sp. Gr. of nitrous oxide is 22. Deduce from these facts the symbol of the compound.

37. What volume of gas would a litre of nitrous oxide yield when decomposed by heat ?   Ans. 1½ litres.

38. What is the quantivalence of nitrogen in nitrous oxide, and what in nitric oxide ?

39. What are the relations of the oxychlorides of nitrogen to the oxides ?

40. What strong reason may be adduced for doubling the formula of nitric oxydichloride ? Would not the same principle require us to double the symbols of two of the oxides ? and what argument can you urge in favor of the symbols adopted in this book ?

41. What is the specific gravity of ammonia gas referred to air, and referred to hydrogen ?   Ans. 0.591, and 8.5.

42. What would be the volume of 3.0464 grammes of ammonia gas at 273°.2 and 38 c. m. ?   Ans. 16 litres.

43. What weight of ammonia would be obtained from one litre of NO by reaction [160] ?   Ans. 0.7614 grammes.

44. Ammonia gas may also be formed by the action of metallic zinc (when in contact with platinum or iron) on a mixture of a nitrate with a solution of potash. Write the reaction [161].

45. In order to determine the amount of nitric acid present in a specimen of crude soda nitre, 1.000 gramme was treated as in the last reaction. The ammonia evolved was conducted into a solution of hydrochloric acid, and subsequently precipitated with platinic chloride. This precipitate weighed 2.1017 grammes. What was the per cent of pure soda nitre ?   Ans. 80%.

46. In order to obtain 10 litres of ammonia gas, how many grammes of sal ammoniac must be taken ?   Ans. 23.96.

47. What volume of nitrogen would be formed by burning one litre of ammonia ? Write the reaction.   Ans. ½ litre.

48. When an organic substance is heated with soda lime (a mix-

ture of caustic soda and lime), all the nitrogen present is evolved as ammonia, which may be collected in hydrochloric acid and combined with platinic chloride as above. In a given determination the weight of the precipitate thus obtained was 2.232 grammes. What was the weight of nitrogen in the compound?

Ans. 0.140 grammes.

49. Deduce from the results of the eudiometric experiments described on page 241 the symbol of ammonia gas. Must we know the specific gravity in order to fix the formula definitely?

50. Show that the result of the experiment with chlorine gas confirms the formula just deduced.

51. Write the symbols of the different amines according to the plan of (29).

52. The amides may be derived from the corresponding acids through what replacement?

53. After what two types may the symbols of the amides be written?

54. Write the symbols of oxamic and succinamic acids after the water type.

55. Explain the meaning of the terms basic and alcoholic, as applied to the atoms of hydrogen.

56. Write the symbols of the two lactamides after the ammonia type.

57. How may the imide and nitrile compounds be regarded as constituted on the type of ammonia?

58. The nitriles (170) may be regarded as cyanides of what radicals?

59. Why should you anticipate that the imide compounds would have an acid, and the nitrile compounds a basic character?

60. Write the reactions which take place when acetic, benzoic, lactic, and oxalic acids combine with ammonia.

61. Write the reactions corresponding to [174 and 175], using the sodium instead of the ammonium salts.

62. What proof do you have that ammonium is a univalent radical?

63. What per cent of NH_3 does the platinum salt contain?

64. When aqua ammonia is added to a solution of ferric chloride, $(Fe_2)Cl_6$, ferric hydrate, $(Fe_2)Ho_6$, is precipitated. Write the reaction.

65. Write two reactions in which aqua ammonia acts like a solution of caustic soda, and two others in which it does not.

66. Write the reaction which takes place when a mixture of ammonic chloride with calcic carbonate is sublimed.

67. Write the reaction by which the sublimed carbonate when exposed to the air changes to the acid carbonate.

68. When a solution of ammonic chloride is boiled with a solution of caustic soda, ammonia gas is evolved. Write the reaction.

69. Write the symbols of the compounds formed by the union of the amines described in (167), both with hydrochloric acid and with water.

70. Write the symbol of the ammonium base which contains the radicals phenyl, C_6H_5, amyl, C_5H_{11}, ethyl, C_2H_5, and methyl, CH_3.

71. Show what different compounds may be formed by the dehydration of the acetate, lactate, and oxalate of ammonia.

Phosphorus.

72. The Sp. Gr. of phosphorus vapor has been observed to be 63.8, and according to Deville no material change is effected by a temperature of 1,040°. Moreover, the specific gravities of the vapors of the following compounds have been determined, and also the per cent of phosphorus which they contain.

	Sp. Gr.	Per cent of Phosphorus.
Phosphuretted Hydrogen,	17.1	91.18
Phosphorous Chloride,	68.4	22.55
Phosphoric Oxychloride,	76.6	20.19

Given these results of observation, show how the atomic weight of phosphorus and the molecular constitution of the elementary substance may be determined.

73. The atomic weight of phosphorus, now received, was found by burning a known weight of red phosphorus in perfectly dry air, and weighing the phosphoric anhydride thus formed. Assuming that one gramme of phosphorus yields 2.2903 grammes of phosphoric anhydride, what must be the atomic weight of phosphorus? How far does this experiment modify the conclusion reached in the last problem?

74. How much phosphorus can be obtained from 9.3 kilos. of pure calcic phosphate by [179]?   Ans. 1.24 kilos.

75. Can you discover any connection between the difference of specific heat of the two varieties of phosphorus, and the difference

of calorific power ? Does the first difference wholly explain the last ?

76. Show that ortho- and meta-phosphoric acid may be derived from the assumed pentatomic acid by successive dehydration, and make a table which shall exhibit the different possible derivatives of this compound.

77. Taking orthophosphoric acid as the starting-point, in place of the assumed pentatomic acid, show how the different varieties of phosphoric acid may be deduced.

78. What is the basicity of phosphorous and hypophosphorous acids ? and what is the quantivalence of phosphorus in these compounds ?

79. When either phosphorous or hypophosphorous acids are heated, they break up into orthophosphoric acid and PH_3. Write the reaction in each case.

80. Compare together the nitrates and phosphates of the univalent and bivalent metallic radicals.

81. Write the reaction of a solution of argentic nitrate on a solution of common sodic phosphate, and show why, after precipitation, the solution must be acid.

82. Write the reaction which takes place when common sodic phosphate is heated to redness.

83. Write the reaction of a solution of argentic nitrate on a solution of sodic pyrophosphate. If the first salt is used in excess, why must the solution after the precipitation be neutral ?

84. Pyrophosphoric acid may be prepared by first adding plumbic acetate to a solution of sodic pyrophosphate, when plumbic pyrophosphate is precipitated, and then decomposing this precipitate suspended in water with H_2S. The solution thus obtained evaporated *in vacuo* gives crystals of the compound. Write the reactions. Why may not the solution be evaporated by heat in the usual way ?

85. Write the reaction which takes place when PH_3 burns.

86. Write the symbols of Trimethyl-phosphine ; Tetramethyl-phosphonium Hydrate ; Trimethyl-amyl-phosphonium Iodide.

87. Write the symbols of the platinum and gold salts of tetraethyl-phosphonium. (136) (147).

88. Write the symbols of Triethyl-phosphine Oxide and Triethyl-phosphine Iodide. How does the last differ from Triethyl-phosphonium Iodide ?

89. Explain the use of PCl_5 as a reagent, and give illustrations of its peculiar action.

90. Can you devise a method by which the reaction [183] may be applied in the preparation of phosphorous acid ?

91. Does the reaction [186] throw any light on the constitution of phosphoric acid ?

92. What different degrees of quantivalence does phosphorus manifest in the compounds described above ?   Point out the examples of each condition.

93. Make a summary of the resemblances and differences between the compounds of nitrogen and those of phosphorus.

Arsenic.

94. Represent by graphic symbols the constitution of Mispickel, and show how it is possible that the double atom of sulphur should replace the double atom of arsenic.

95. What should be theoretically the specific gravity of arsenic vapor referred to air ?   Ans. 10.4.

96. Compare together the formulæ of nitrous and arsenious acids, and point out their relations to each other. Is phosphorous acid allied to the other two ?

97. Write the reactions by which cupric and argentic arsenites are formed.

98. Write the symbols of the three hydrates of arsenic acid, and give their names, following the analogy of phosphoric acid.

99. If the arseniates [190] are heated until all the water is expelled, what will be the symbols of the compounds left ?

100. Write the reaction of argentic nitrate on a solution of either of the compounds. [190.]

101. Write the reaction of a solution of magnesic sulphate and ammonia on a solution of either of the compounds. [190.]

102. State the differences between phosphoric and arsenic acids.

103. Write the reaction which takes place when H_3As burns, both with a sufficient and with a limited supply of oxygen.

104. How may the reactions described in (197) be used to detect the presence of arsenic in a suspected liquid ?

105. How could you discover the presence of the arsenic acid formed by reaction [193] ?

106. State the resemblances and differences between the amines, the phosphines, and the arsines.

107. Is the quantivalence of arsenic the same in all the compounds of kakodyl?

108. In what respects does kakodyl resemble, and in what does it differ from, the corresponding compound of phosphorus?

109. Does the relation of arsenic to chlorine differ materially from the relation of phosphorus to the same element?

110. Write the reaction of H_2S on a solution of As_2O_3 in dilute hydrochloric acid.

111. Analyze the reactions [195] and [196], and give the names of the products which are formed.

112. What would be the chemical names of the minerals Proustite and Enargite, and what are the corresponding oxygen compounds? Define the class of compounds to which these minerals belong.

Antimony.

113. Why is the molecular weight of antimony doubtful?

114. Theoretically, what weight of metallic antimony should be obtained from 1,020 kilos. of antimony glance? Ans. 732 kilos.

115. The most common impurities of commercial antimony are arsenic, iron, copper, and lead. Why should the process described (206) tend to remove these substances?

116. Write the reaction when antimony burns.

117. Write the reaction of nitric acid on antimony, assuming that the products are Sb_2O_4 and NO.

118. Write the reaction of hydrochloric acid on Sb_2S_3. What will prevent the resulting solution from becoming turbid when mixed with water?

119. What should be theoretically the Sp. Gr. of $SbCl_3$?

120. Why is it probable that the double chlorides (207) are molecular compounds?

121. When $SbCl_3$ is mixed with strong $HCl + Aq$, what compound would analogy lead us to suppose is formed in the solution?

122. Write the reaction of chlorine gas (in excess) on antimony and on $SbCl_3$.

123. Write the reaction of water on $SbBr_3$ and SbI_3.

124. Write the reactions when Sb_2O_3 dissolves in $HCl + Aq$ and H_2SO_4. [202.]

125. Write the reaction when Sb_2O_3 dissolves in cream of tartar.

126. Write the reaction when tartar emetic is heated to 200°.

127. Write the symbols of the compounds formed by dissolving As_2O_3, As_2O_5, or Bi_2O_3 in cream of tartar.

128. Write the symbols of the compounds of the same class derived from Fe_2O_3, Cr_2O_3, and B_2O_3, assuming that the radicals Fe_2O_2, Cr_2O_2, and BO replace the SbO of tartar emetic.

129. Write the reaction when to a solution of tartar emetic is added a solution of calcic chloride, knowing that the corresponding lime compound, being insoluble, is precipitated. Calcium, it must be remembered, takes the place of two atoms of potassium.

130. Write the symbol of diaceto-diethylic tartrate.

131. State the grounds for the distinction between the three sets of hydrogen atoms which tartaric acid contains. By what names do you distinguish the different sets of atoms, and what other examples have been studied in which a similar distinction has been made?

132. What is the name of the compound $H_2.K_2 \equiv O_4 \equiv Sb_2O_3$? Write the reaction of a solution of this reagent upon a solution of $NaCl$.

133. On boiling its solution, the acid potassic pyroantimoniate changes into a metantimoniate which does not precipitate soda. Write the reaction.

134. Write the reaction of $(HCl + Aq)$ on Zn_3Sb_2, assuming that the product is H_3Sb.

135. Write the symbols of the ethyl and amyl compounds of antimony, following the analogy of the methyl compounds whose symbols are given.

136. Write the reaction of triethyl-stibine on hydrochloric acid.

137. Represent by graphic symbols the constitution of Zn_3Sb_2 and Zn_2Sb_2, and give the symbols of other compounds formed after the same type.

138. Write the reaction when antimonious oxide and sulphur are melted together.

139. Write the reaction when H_2S is passed through a solution of tartar emetic.

140. Analyze reactions [221], [222], and [223], and name the classes of compounds to which the several products belong.

141. Show by symbols the relations of the assumed sulphur acids to which the several sulphantimonites are referred.

142. Explain the distinction between a chemical compound and a molecular aggregate. What different orders of combination do the facts and the atomic theory require of us to assume in such a mineral as Tetrahedrite?

143. How are the phenomena of isomorphous substitution in the mineral kingdom to be explained in harmony with the atomic theory?

144. Write the reaction of H_2S on a solution of $SbCl_5$.

145. Write the reaction of hydrochloric acid on the precipitate obtained by the last reaction.

Bismuth.

146. Represent by graphic symbols the constitution of Bismuth Glance, and Tetradymite.

147. Compare the qualities of metallic bismuth with those of the other elementary substances belonging to the same series, considering especially the crystalline form and the specific gravity.

148. Write the reaction of nitric acid on bismuth, and compare this reaction with that of nitric acid on antimony.

149. Write the reaction of aqua-regia on bismuth.

150. Compare the compounds of the alcohol radicals with the different members of the nitrogen series of elements, and present the subject in a written form.

151. Write the different reactions by which $BiCl_3$ may be formed.

152. Write the reaction of water on $BiCl_3$, and the reaction when a solution of bismuthous nitrate is poured into a solution of common salt.

153. Why does the presence of a large amount of H_4NCl prevent a solution of $BiCl_3$ from becoming turbid when mixed with water?

154. Compare $BiCl_3$ with the corresponding chlorides of the same series. What inference do you draw from the fact that the compound $BiCl_5$ has not been obtained? Have any other facts been mentioned pointing to the same conclusion? What is the evidence that bismuth is ever quinquivalent?

155. Write the reaction when bismuth burns, or is more slowly oxidized.

156. Write the reaction when bismuthous nitrate is heated to a

13   S.

low red heat. Why in this process is it important to avoid a higher temperature ?

157. Write the reaction when a solution of bismuthous nitrate (in dilute nitric acid) is poured into a solution of potassic hydrate.

158. Write the reactions when bismuthous oxide dissolves in hydrochloric, nitric, or sulphuric acid.

159. Compare the oxides and hydrates of the elements of the nitrogen series, and, by tabulating their symbols, show that their molecular constitution is analogous. Trace also the variation in their properties as you descend in the series.

160. Write the reaction of water on bismuthous nitrate, assuming that the basic salt whose symbol is given above, together with free nitric acid, are the resulting products.

161. If Bi_2S_3 and Sb_2S_3 are precipitated together, how may the two be separated ?

162. Write the reaction when Bi_2S_3 is roasted in a current of air.

163. To which of the three classes of salts, distinguished on page 273, must the several sulpho-bismuthites be referred ?

164. Compare the sulpho-salts of bismuth, antimony, and arsenic, and point out their mutual relations.

Division IX.

225. VANADIUM. $V = 51.21$. — Trivalent and quinquivalent. A very rare element, discovered in 1830 in the iron ores of Taberg in Sweden. It has since been found associated with the iron and uranium ores of other localities, and more recently it has been found in considerable quantities in certain remarkable metalliferous sandstone beds occurring in the county of Cheshire in England. Vanadium is also the essential constituent of a few very rare minerals. Of these the most important is Vanadinite, which is a vanadate of lead, and so closely resembles the native phosphate and arseniate of the same metal as to leave no doubt that all three have a similar molecular constitution, and hence that vanadium is a perissad element like phosphorus and arsenic. Thus we have the following minerals, which are all isomorphous with each other : —

| Apatite | (Ca_5F) ix O_9 ix $(PO)_3$, |
| Pyromorphite | (Pb_5Cl) ix O_9 ix $(PO)_3$, |

Mimetine $(Pb_5 Cl)$ ix O_9 ix $(As O)_3$,
Vanadinite $(Pb_5 Cl)$ ix O_9 ix $(VO)_3$.

The study of the other compounds of vanadium leads to the same conclusion, and shows that the same character already noticed in Bismuth and Antimony is developed in this element to a still higher degree. The lowest oxide of vanadium, VO, is a powerful univalent or trivalent radical, and combines with chlorine or replaces hydrogen like an elementary substance, and almost all of the compounds of the element, formerly known, and which can be directly prepared from the native vanadates, are compounds of this radical, now called *vanadyl*, but which was for a long time mistaken for the element itself. We have, for example, $(VO) Cl_3$, a yellow fuming volatile liquid boiling at 126° 7 with *Sp. Gr.* = 1.84 and Sp. Gr. = 88.2, also $(VO) Cl_2$ in brilliant green tubular crystals, next $(VO) Cl$, a light brown powder, and lastly, $(VO)_2 Cl$, a brownish yellow powder resembling mosaic gold. The true chlorides of vanadium can only be prepared from the metal or its nitride, and the air must be carefully excluded during the process. The following have been recently described by Roscoe: VCl_2, a bright apple green, solid in hexagonal plates, with a micacious lustre; VCl_3, in brilliant tubular crystals with color of peach blossoms; and VCl_4, a dark reddish-brown volatile liquid, boiling at 154°, with *Sp. Gr.* at 0° = 1.858 and Sp. Gr. = 93.3. Roscoe was unable to obtain the pentad compound.

The oxides of vanadium are, — first, $V_2 O_2$ or $VO\text{-}VO$, obtained as a gray metallic powder when the vapor of $VO Cl_3$ mixed with hydrogen is passed over red-hot carbon. It dissolves in dilute acids with the evolution of hydrogen, and cannot be deprived of its oxygen except with the greatest difficulty. Secondly, $V_2 O_3$, obtained as a black powder when $V_2 O_5$ is reduced by hydrogen at a red heat. It is insoluble in acids. Thirdly, $V_2 O_4$, obtained in the form of blue shining crystals by allowing $V_2 O_3$ to absorb oxygen from the air. Fourthly, $V_2 O_5$, vanadic anhydride, a brownish-red crystalline solid, fusible at a red heat, and sparingly soluble in water. The solution has a yellow color, and is strongly acid; but no definite hydrate has been described. Vanadic anhydride dissolves in concentrated sulphuric acid when boiling, giving a dark red solution. If this is diluted with fifty times its volume of water, and heated with metallic zinc, it rapidly changes color, passing through all shades of blue and green until it attains a permanent lavender tint. To each of these shades corresponds a certain degree of oxidation of the dissolved vanadium, thus bright blue to V_2O_4, green to V_2O_3, and lavender to V_2O_2; and by using less active reducing agents the change may be arrested at any desired point. The lavender solution absorbs oxygen with such avidity as " to bleach indigo and other vegetable coloring matters as quickly as chlorine, and far more powerfully than any other known agent."

From vanadic anhydride we derive the vanadates, of which there appear to be three classes corresponding to the phosphates.

1. Metavanadates as in $NH_4\text{-}O\text{-}VO_2$　　　　or $Pb\text{=}O_2\text{=}(VO_2)_2$.
　　　　　　　　　　　　　　　　　　　　　　　　Dechenite.

2. Pyrovanadates as in $Na_4\text{≡}O_4\text{≡}V_2O_3$　　or $Pb_2\text{≡}O_4\text{≡}(V_2O_3)_2$.
　　　　　　　　　　　　　　　　　　　　　　　　Descloizite.

3. Orthovanadates as in $Na_3\text{=}O_3\text{=}VO$. $16H_2O$ or $Ca_3{}^{vi}O_6{}^{vi}(VO)_2$.

Of these salts the metavanadates are the most and the ortho-vanadates the least stable, the reverse of what is true in the case of the phosphates.

There are two nitrides of vanadium, VN and VN_2. The first is a black powder obtained by acting on $(VO)Cl_3$ with dry NH_3. Its composition has been determined by analysis, and it is interesting not only as fixing the atomic weight of the metal, but also as the starting-point from which the true chlorides of vanadium, and the metal itself, have been reached.

Metallic vanadium has been obtained by reducing VCl_2 with hydrogen. It is a light whitish-gray powder, which under the microscope appears as a brilliant crystalline metallic mass with a silver-white lustre. This metallic powder has a *Sp. Gr.* = 5.5, and is not magnetic. It does not volatilize or fuse when heated to redness in an atmosphere of hydrogen. It does not tarnish in the air or decompose water at the ordinary tempera-tures, but when thrown into a flame it burns with brilliant scin-tillations. It does not dissolve in hydrochloric acid hot or cold, and only slowly in hot sulphuric acid, but nitric acid of all strengths attacks it with violence. It is not acted upon by solutions of the caustic alkalies, but when fused with sodic hydrate hydrogen gas is evolved and a vanadate formed. It unites directly with chlorine gas to form VCl_4, and with nitro-gen gas to form VN, and it is capable of absorbing as much as

1.3 per cent of hydrogen gas. It attacks all glass and porcelain in which it is heated, a compound of silicon and the metal
being formed. It yields also an alloy with platinum, and for
these reasons, as well as on account of its very great avidity
(when heated) for both oxygen and nitrogen, it has been one of
the most difficult of all the elements to isolate.

Division X.

226. URANIUM. $U = 120.$ — One of the rarer elements.
Always found in nature combined with oxygen, chiefly in
Pitchblende, which is essentially the compound U_3O_4, and in
a rare mineral called Uranite. Of the last there are two varieties: the first is a phosphate of uranium and calcium, and
the second a phosphate of uranium and copper.

$$Ca_4(UO)_4O_6(PO)_2 . 8H_2O \quad \text{or} \quad Cu_4(UO)_4O_6(PO)_2 . 8H_2O.$$

In many of its chemical characteristics, uranium very closely
resembles vanadium. Like the last element, it forms an oxide,
UO, which acts as a univalent radical, replacing hydrogen and
combining directly with chlorine; and all the most important
stable and characteristic compounds of uranium may be regarded as compounds of this radical. Moreover, U_2O_2, like
V_2O_2, cannot be decomposed by the ordinary reducing agents,
and was formerly mistaken for the metal itself. Uranyl acts
both as a basic and as an acid radical. Of the uranyl compounds, the most important, besides the native phosphates already mentioned, are Uranyl Chloride, $(UO)Cl$, Uranyl Fluoride, $(UO)F$, Uranyl Hydrate, $(UO)\text{-}O\text{-}H$ (a yellow powder),
Uranyl Nitrate, $(UO)\text{-}O\text{-}NO_2 . 3H_2O$ (a beautiful yellow salt,
crystallizing in long striated prisms), and Uranyl-potassic Sulphate, $K_4(UO)=O_2=SO_2 . H_2O$; and to these may be added a
number of remarkable double salts, which may be formed by
the union both of the chloride and the fluoride of uranyl with
the chlorides or fluorides of the metals, of the alkalies, or earths.
Indeed, these double salts are a characteristic feature of uranium, and one which becomes still more marked in the next
element, Columbium.

If to a solution of a uranyl salt we add ammonia, or the solution of any other alkali or earth, we obtain a yellow precipitate. This is not, however, as might have been expected, the hydrate of uranyl, but a compound of the radical with the alkali, in which uranyl acts as an acid radical. The constitution of these compounds is not well understood, but they are probably mixtures of uranyl hydrate with a compound of the form R-O-(UO). The so-called yellow uranium oxide of commerce is a hydrate thus prepared, retaining about two per cent of ammonia. All these uranyl compounds have a yellow color, and the yellow oxide is used to communicate a beautiful and peculiar yellow to glass. Glass thus colored, and the transparent uranyl salts, are to a high degree fluorescent.

Judging from the uranyl compounds alone, we should conclude that uranium was a perissad closely allied to vanadium and the nitrogen group of elements; but there are other compounds of uranium which do not readily conform to this theory. Thus we have a chloride, UCl_2, and a series of *uranous* salts (all having a green color), in which one atom of the metal appears to combine with two atoms of chlorine, or to replace two atoms of hydrogen. These would seem, on the other hand, to indicate that uranium was an artiad element allied to iron; and the important fact that the native oxide, U_3O_4, is isomorphous with the magnetic oxide of iron sustains this view. Uranium thus appears to stand between the nitrogen group of elements of the perissad family and the iron group of the artiad family. It belongs in a measure to both, and its compounds may be interpreted according to the one or the other plan of molecular grouping. In classing it with the perissads we merely follow what appear to be its normal relations; but others may reasonably entertain a different view, and further investigation is required to determine its quantivalence. Uranium thus illustrates very forcibly the remarks already made on chemical classification. (103.)

Of metallic uranium but little is known. It has been obtained by decomposing the chloride UCl_2 with potassium, and appears to be a steel-white metal (*Sp. Gr.* = 18.4), which is slightly malleable, and not readily oxidized by atmospheric agents. If heated, however, it burns in the air, and dissolves in dilute acids with the evolution of hydrogen. The compounds of uranium have found but few applications in the arts. The "yellow oxide" is used, as already stated, for coloring glass, and the so-called black oxide (U_4O_5), obtained by igniting the nitrate, is employed as a black pigment in painting on porcelain. The nitrate, which is the most common soluble salt, has been thought to have some valuable qualities in photography.

Questions and Problems.

1. State the grounds on which the conclusion in regard to the atomicity of vanadium is based, and represent by . graphic symbol the constitution of Vanadinite.

2. How does the Sp. Gr. of the vapor of vanadic oxytrichloride compare with the theoretical value?

3. It has been shown by careful analysis that the above chloride contains 61.276 per cent of chlorine. What is the atomic weight of vanadyl, and what that of vanadium? Ans. 67.29, and 51.29.

4. In order to determine the atomic weight of vanadium from vanadic anhydride, Roscoe reduced V_2O_5 by hydrogen to vanadic oxide, V_2O_3. Four experiments gave the following results: —

	Weight of V_2O_5 used.	Weight of V_2O_3 obtained.
1st,	7.7397 grammes,	6.3827 grammes.
2d,	6 5819 "	5.4296 "
3d,	5.1895 "	4.2819 "
4th,	5.0450 "	4.1614 "

Deduce the atomic weight of vanadium.

5. Berzelius assigned to Vanadic Anhydride the symbol VO_3, and to Vanadyl Chloride the symbol VCl_3. On this hypothesis he found for the atomic weight of vanadium, by the method of the last problem, the value 137 (when $O = 16$), which would be reduced to 134.74 by the more accurate determinations of Roscoe. State the reasons for believing that the true atomic weight of the element is 51.21, and that the compounds have the symbols assigned to them above. Show how far these conclusions have been proved, and point out the cause of the former error.

6. State the grounds for classing uranium with vanadium, as well as the reasons which might be urged for associating it with iron, and write the rational symbols of the uranium compounds on the assumption that this element is an artiad.

Division XI.

227. COLUMBIUM (*Niobium*). $Cb = 94.$ — Pentad. This element forms the acid radical of Pyrochlore, Columbite, Samarskite, Euxenite, Aeschynite, Fergusonite, and a few other rare minerals. They are all compounds of columbic anhydride, Cb_2O_5, with various metallic oxides, — among which those of cerium, yttrium, and their associated elements are especially to be distinguished. The columbium, however, is almost invariably replaced to a greater or less extent by tantalum. Columbite, the most abundant of these minerals, has the symbol $[Fe,Mn]\text{=}O_2\text{=}([Cb,Ta]O_2)_2$. It has a black color, a submetallic lustre, and a specific gravity from 5.4 to 6.5, increasing as the proportion of tantalum increases. When finely powdered it is easily decomposed by fusion with potassic bisulphate, and on subsequently boiling the fused mass with water a white insoluble residue is obtained, which consists chiefly of Cb_2O_5, and from this the different compounds of columbium may be prepared. Of these the most characteristic are the following : —

228. *Columbic Anhydride.* Cb_2O_5. — A white powder, which becomes crystalline when heated, and is afterwards insoluble in all acids. It has a *Sp. Gr.* between 4.37 and 4.53. Before ignition, and when in condition of hydrate (Columbic Acid?), it dissolves in strong sulphuric and in hydrofluoric acids. After boiling with strong hydrochloric acid, in which it is nearly insoluble, the product dissolves in water, and the solution treated with zinc turns blue and finally deposits a blue-colored oxide. When a large excess of hydrochloric acid is present, the solution deposits a brown oxide under the same conditions; but the constitution of neither of these compounds is as yet known. It has been stated that oxides having the composition Cb_2O_2 and Cb_2O_4 have also been obtained. Columbic acid forms salts called columbates, and, besides the native compounds mentioned above, we are acquainted with several potassic columbates, three of which have been obtained in well-defined crystals, but they have a very complex constitution.

229. *Columbic Chloride.* $CbCl_5$. — A yellow crystalline solid, melting at 194°, and boiling at 241°. It has been found

by analysis to contain 65.28 per cent of chlorine, and the $\mathfrak{Sp.}$ $\mathfrak{Gr.}$ of its vapor, by experiment, is 9.6.

230. *Columbic Oxychloride.* $CbOCl_3$. — A white solid, crystallizing in silky tufts, which volatilizes in the air, without previously melting, at 400°. It contains, according to analysis, 48.9 per cent of chlorine, and the $\mathfrak{Sp.}$ $\mathfrak{Gr.}$ of its vapor has been found to be 7.9. Moreover, it has been recently *proved* that it contains oxygen. Both chlorides, when treated with water, yield columbic acid.

231. *Columbic Oxyfluoride.* $CbOF_3$. — This compound is probably formed when columbic acid is dissolved in hydrofluoric acid, but it has not yet been isolated in a pure condition. The solution, however, forms definite crystalline salts with several metallic fluorides, and these are among the most important compounds of columbium. The salt $2KF . CbOF_3 . H_2O$ is very readily obtained in nacreous scales, and being far more soluble than the compound of tantalum formed under the same conditions, $2KF . TaF_5$, it gives us the only useful means yet discovered of separating this element from columbium. A salt has also been formed, having the composition $2KF . CbF_5$, and isomorphous with the compound of tantalum just mentioned. It is interesting as pointing to a fluoride of columbium, CbF_5, which is not otherwise known.

The metal columbium has not with certainty been obtained. The black powder described as such by Rose is said to be the oxide Cb_2O_2.

An infusion of gall-nuts gives with *acid* solutions containing columbium a deep orange-red precipitate; and by this reaction columbium may be distinguished from tantalum, which, under the same conditions, gives a bright brown precipitate.

232. TANTALUM. $Ta = 182$. — This element, associated with columbium in the native columbates named above, is the chief constituent of Tantalite, Yttrotantalite, and of a few other minerals equally rare. Tantalite is isomorphous with columbite, has the same composition, save only that the acid radical is wholly tantalum, and differs chiefly in having a higher *Sp. Gr.*, which varies from 7 to 8. Although tantalum is so closely allied to columbium, yet its compounds differ from those of this last element in several important respects. There appears to be no tendency to form oxychlorides or oxyfluorides, — at least

no such compounds are known. . The chloride is $TaCl_5$, a pale yellow solid, melting at 211°, boiling at 242°, and having a vapor density $= 12.8$. It contains by analysis 48.75 of chlorine, and is decomposed by water, yielding tantalic acid. The fluoride, is in like manner, TaF_5. It forms double salts with the metallic fluoride, the most important of which is the potassic fluotantalate, $2KF . TaF_5$, mentioned above. Tantalic anhydride, Ta_2O_3, is a white powder, insoluble in acids. It closely resembles columbic anhydride, and is prepared in a similar way from the native tantalates, but it has a higher density (*Sp. Gr.* $= 7.6$ to 8), and forms with the alkalies a larger number of crystallized salts. There is a hydrate (Tantalic Acid?), and also probably several lower oxides of the element. A solution of $TaCl_5$ in strong sulphuric acid, when diluted with water and reduced with zinc becomes colored blue, but yields no brown oxide as in the case of columbium. By reducing sodio-tantalic fluoride with sodium, a black powder is obtained which has been supposed to be metallic tantalum.

Questions and Problems.

1. Calculate the percentage composition of columbite, on the assumption that the basic radical is wholly iron and the acid radical wholly columbium.   Ans. 21.17 FeO and 78.83 Cb_2O_5.

2. Explain the meaning of the symbol of columbite in (227).

3. How far do the theoretical Sp. Gr. of columbic chloride and oxychloride compare with the experimental results?

4. The mean of twenty analyses of the potassio-columbic oxyfluoride, $2KF . CbOF_3 . H_2O$, gave the following results: From 100 parts of the salt there were obtained by the process of analysis adopted 5.87 parts of water, 44.36 of columbic anhydride, 57.82 of potassic sulphate, and 31.72 of fluorine. Assuming that the symbol of columbic anhydride is Cb_2O_5, and estimating the per cent of oxygen by the loss, deduce the percentage composition of the compound and its symbol.

Ans. Columbium, 31.12; Potassium, 25.92; Oxygen, 5.37; Fluorine, 31.72; Water, 5.87.

5. What would be the atomic weight of columbium if deduced from the result of the above analyses?   Ans. 93.9.

6. Previous to the recent investigations of Marignac, the symbol

of columbic acid was usually written CbO_3 when $O = 8$, or Cb_2O_5 when $O = 16$. What proofs have been given of the correctness of the symbol adopted in this book? What was the probable cause of the error made by the earlier investigators?

7. By what general method may tantalum be separated from columbium? How can you tell when the separation is complete?

8. What compounds of tantalum and columbium are isomorphous? What bearing does this fact have on the symbol of tantalic anhydride? Does the vapor density of tantalic chloride agree with the symbol which has been adopted? Why is there a necessary connection between the symbol of the chloride and that of the anhydride?

9. How may tantalite be distinguished from columbite?

10. State the resemblances and the differences between the two members of this group of elements.

CHAPTER XIX.

THE ARTIAD ELEMENTS.

Division I.

233. OXYGEN. $O = 16.$ — Dyad. The most abundant, and the most widely diffused of the elements. Forms one fifth of the atmosphere, eight ninths of water, more than three fourths of organized beings, and one half of the solid crust of the globe.

234. *Oxygen Gas.* $O{=}O.$ — Exists in a free state in the atmosphere, but mixed with nitrogen gas. May be extracted from the air by either of the following double reactions. Metallic mercury or baric oxide is first heated in the air, and then the products of the first reaction raised to a much higher temperature.

$$1.\ 2Hg + O{=}O = 2HgO. \qquad 1.\ 2BaO + O{=}O = 2BaO_2.$$
$$2.\ 2HgO = 2Hg + O{=}O. \qquad 2.\ 2BaO_2 = 2BaO + O{=}O. \qquad [228]$$

Generally obtained from commercial or natural products, rich in oxygen, by one of the reactions given below. The materials must in each case be heated to a definite temperature, and the last two reactions require a full red heat.

$$2KClO_3 = 2KCl + 3\,O{=}O.^{[1]} \qquad\qquad [229]$$

$$2K_2Cr_2O_7 + 10H_2SO_4 =$$
$$4(HKSO_4) + 2([Cr_2]3SO_4) + 8H_2O + 3\,O{=}O. \quad [230]$$

$$2MnO_2 + 2H_2SO_4 = 2MnSO_4 + 2H_2O + O{=}O. \quad [231]$$

$$3MnO_2 = Mn_3O_4 + O{=}O. \qquad\qquad [232]$$

$$2H_2SO_4 = 2H_2O + 2SO_2 + O{=}O. \qquad\quad [233]$$

Also by electrolysis of water and by [66]. Oxygen gas is a chief product of vegetable life. Under the influence of the

---

[1] This reaction is greatly facilitated by mixing the potassic chlorate with cupric oxide or manganic dioxide, which, however, undergo in the process no apparent change.

sun's rays the plants decompose the carbonic acid of their food, fixing the carbon and liberating the oxygen. Oxygen gas manifests intense affinities, but these are only called into play under regulated conditions. (Review Chapter XII. on Combustion.) When an elementary substance unites with oxygen it is said to be *oxidized*, and when the compound is decomposed the oxide is said to be *reduced*.

235. *Oxygen Compounds.* — The most important classes of oxides are illustrated by the following symbols and examples:—

1.	$\overset{I}{R_2}O$	or	$\overset{I}{R},\overset{I}{R}\ O$	as in	H_2O	K_2O	Ag_2O,
2.	$\overset{I}{R_2}O_2$	"	$\overset{I}{R},(\overset{I}{R}\text{-}O)=O$	"	H_2O_2	K_2O_2	Ag_2O_2,
3.	$\overset{II}{R}O$	"	$\overset{II}{R}=O$	"	FeO	CaO	PbO,
4.	$\overset{II}{R_2}O$	"	$(\overset{II}{R}\text{-}\overset{II}{R})=O$	"	Cu_2O	Hg_2O	Pb_2O,
5.	$\overset{II}{R}O_2$	"	$(\overset{II}{R}\text{-}O)=O$	"	MnO_2	BaO_2	PbO_2,
6.	$\overset{III}{R_2}O_3$	"	$(\overset{III}{R}\text{-}O\text{-}\overset{III}{R})\equiv O_3$	"	B_2O_3	Au_2O_3	Bi_2O_3,
7.	$\overset{IV}{R}O_2$	"	$\overset{IV}{R}\equiv O_2$	"	SnO_2	SiO_2	CO_2,
8.	$\overset{IV}{R_2}O_3$	"	$(\overset{IV}{R}\text{-}\overset{IV}{R})\equiv O_3$	"	Fe_2O_3	Al_2O_3	Sn_2O_3,
9.	$\overset{II\,\&\,IV}{R_3}O_4$	"	$\overset{V}{R}=O_2=[\overset{V}{R_2}]\equiv O_2$	"	Fe_3O_4	Cr_3O_4	Co_3O_4,
10.	$\overset{V}{R_2}O_5$	"	$(\overset{V}{R}\text{-}O\text{-}\overset{V}{R})\equiv O_4$	"	N_2O_5	P_2O_5	As_2O_5,
11.	$\overset{V}{R_2}O_4$	"	$(\overset{V}{R}\text{-}\overset{V}{R})\equiv O_4$	"	V_2O_4	Sb_2O_4	Bi_2O_4,
12.	$\overset{VI}{R}O_3$	"	$\overset{VI}{R}\equiv O_3$	"	SO_3	SeO_3	MoO_3.

As a rule, the oxides of the forms 1 and 3 act as anhydride bases (47), and are called protoxides. On the other hand, the oxides of the forms 6, 7, 10, and 12 generally act as anhydride acids. The oxides of the form 8 are called sesquioxide. They usually act as basic, but sometimes as acid anhydrides, and at other times like the hyperoxides mentioned below. The oxides of the forms 9 and 11 are very indifferent bodies, and those of the first class are sometimes called saline oxides. The oxides of the forms 2 and 5 are called di or hyper-oxides. They act as powerful oxidizing agents, readily giving up one half of the oxygen they contain [74] [77]. The oxides of the form 4 are called suboxides. They sometimes act as anhydride bases, but in most cases when acted on by acids they change into protox-

ides, either giving up one half of the metal or taking up as much
again oxygen as they contain. The relation of the oxides to
the acids, bases, and salts has been already explained. (Review
Chapters IX. and X.)

Besides the above classes of oxides, all of which comprise
actual compounds, there are others, most of which are only
known as compound radicals. With many of these radicals the
student is already familiar, such as SO_2, SO, NO_2, NO, PO, in
all of which the oxygen atoms only satisfy a part of the affinities of the multivalent atoms, with which they are grouped, and
the quantivalence of the radical is easily found by Wurz's rule.
(28.) The chemists have also been led to assume a very different type of oxygen radicals, in which the affinities of the oxygen
atoms predominate, and, moreover, it is frequently convenient,
in expressing the composition of complex compounds, to indicate
these radicals by a single symbol. The following examples
illustrate the most important classes of these radicals: —

Radicals.		Symbols.	Examples.		
$\overset{\text{I}}{R}O$	$(R\text{-}O)$	$\overset{\text{I}}{Ro}$	Ho	Ko	$(NH_4)o.$
$\overset{\text{II}}{R}O_2$	$(O\text{-}R\text{-}O)$	$\overset{\text{II}}{Ro}$	Cao	Zno	$Feo.$
$[\overset{\text{VI}}{R_2}]O_6$	$(O_3\overset{=}{=}R\text{-}R\overset{=}{=}O_3)$	$\overset{\text{VI}}{R_2}o$	Al_2o	Fe_2o	$Cr_2o.$

It will be noticed that the number of oxygen atoms in all
these cases corresponds to the quantivalence of the metallic element with which they are united, and that the quantivalence of
the radical is the same as that of its characteristic element.
Hydroxyl, Ho, is the type of this class of radicals, and names
may be given to them all formed after the same analogy as
Potassoxyl, Zincoxyl, — but such names are rarely used. The
relations of this type of radicals to the three great classes of
chemical compounds has been already in part illustrated (108),
and will be still further developed in the present chapter.

236. *Ozone.* $(O\text{-}O)\text{-}\overline{O}.$ — The best opinion that can at present be formed in regard to the constitution of this remarkable
substance is expressed by the rational symbol here given.
Ozone is formed under a great variety of conditions, as, — 1.
During the passage of electric sparks through air or oxygen.
2. During the electrolysis of water. 3. During the slow com-

bustion of phosphorus in *moist* air. 4. During the slow combustion of alcohol, ether, and volatile oils. 5. By decomposing potassic permanganate with sulphuric acid, and by several other similar reactions. Ozone as thus obtained, however, is very largely diluted with air or oxygen gas, and we have not yet succeeded in preparing it in a pure condition. It differs from ordinary oxygen gas, — 1. In having a peculiar odor, with which we are familiar, as a concomitant of electrical action. 2. In acting as a powerful oxidizing agent at the ordinary temperature of the air. It corrodes cork, india-rubber, and other organic materials. It bleaches indigo. It even oxidizes silver, and displaces iodine from its metallic compounds. If a slip of paper moistened with starch and potassic iodide is inserted in a jar containing the smallest trace of ozone, it is immediately colored blue, owing to the liberation of the iodine (119). In like manner, paper wet with a solution of manganous sulphate is turned brown by ozone, owing to the oxidation of the manganese, and paper stained with plumbic sulphide is bleached by the same agent, because the black sulphide is changed to the white sulphate. 3. In the fact that its Sp. Gr. is 24 instead of 16. The formation of ozone in a confined mass of oxygen gas is attended with a reduction of volume ; and since the ozone thus formed may be absorbed by oil of turpentine, we have thus the means of determining its specific gravity, and the results, if correct, prove that the molecule of ozone consists of three oxygen atoms. Again, during most cases of oxidation by ozone, the volume of the ozonized oxygen does not change, and this fact is consistent with the theory of its constitution which our molecular formula expresses, as is illustrated by the following reaction : —

$$Ag\text{-}Ag + 2(O\text{-}O)\text{=}\bar{O} = Ag_2\bar{O}_2 + 2O\text{=}O. \quad [234]$$

It has been shown, however, that oil of turpentine absorbs the molecule of ozone as a whole, and is, therefore, an exception to the general rule. The metal in the above reaction is raised to the condition of peroxide, and it is probable that several of the oxides and oxygen acids contain one or more atoms of oxygen in the same condition as in ozone. Such compounds have been called ozonides, and among them are classed the peroxides of silver, lead, and manganese, the sesquioxides of nickel and

cobalt, as also chromic, manganic, and permanganic acids, with
their various salts.　Ozone appears to be constantly present in
the atmosphere, and important effects have been attributed to
its influence.　It has been thought to be the active agent in all
processes of slow combustion and decay, and to play an important part in the economy of nature.　At a temperature of 300°
ozone is instantly changed into common oxygen gas, and at a
temperature no higher than boiling water, it slowly returns to
the same condition.

237. *Antozone.* $(O\text{-}O)\text{=}\overset{+}{O}.$ — Whenever ozone is prepared,
there appears to be formed at the same time a second modifica-
tion of oxygen gas, which presents such a singular antithesis to
ozone as to lead us to believe that it is in fact the same substance, only oppositely polarized.　Hence we have called it antozone, and assigned to it the symbol at the head of this section,
although our theory is not based on any conclusive experiments,
and our knowledge of the substance is still very imperfect.　It
may be obtained in several ways, — 1.　When *dry* electrified air
is passed through a solution of pyrogallic acid or potassic iodide,
the ozone is absorbed and the air is left charged with antozone.
2.　When baric peroxide is dropped into sulphuric acid, the oxygen evolved is more or less charged with the same agent.　3.
When phosphorus is burnt in *dry* air, a small amount of oxygen
is always left unconsumed, and this appears to be in the condition of antozone.　Indeed, it has been supposed that, in all similar processes of oxidation, both ozone and antozone are formed;
but that, while the oxygen atoms of the first enter into combination with the burning body, those of the last do not, owing to
their polar condition.

Antozone has an odor like ozone, but much more repulsive.
It does not displace iodine or color the iodized paper.　It does
not oxidize silver or the solution of manganous sulphate, but, on
the contrary, removes from the paper prepared with the manganous salt the brown stain which ozone had made.　On all
ozonides it acts as a reducing agent.　[236.]　There is, however, another class of substances which it oxidizes, and among
these the most important is water, with which it forms hydric
peroxide.

$$H_2O + (O\text{-}O)\text{=}\overset{+}{O} = H,Ho\text{=}\overset{+}{O} + O\text{=}O. \qquad [235]$$

' In many processes of ozonizing air, the antozone unites with and thus condenses the vapor present, although, in most cases at least, the union appears to be rather mechanical than chemical. The reaction is consequently attended with the formation of mists or clouds, which is one of the most striking properties of antozone. The smoke of gunpowder, tobacco, and smouldering wood has been thought to be an antozone cloud, and the clouding of gas jars in many chemical experiments has been referred to the same cause. Opposed to the ozonides we have a class of antozonides, among which have been classed, besides the peroxide of hydrogen, the peroxides of barium, strontium, sodium, and potassium, and reactions may be obtained between these two classes of compounds which are very interesting. They mutually decompose each other, with the evolution of oxygen gas, thus:—

$$(Pb\text{-}O)\text{=}\overset{-}{O} + H,Ho\text{=}\overset{+}{O} = PbO + H_2O + O\text{=}O. \ [236]$$

Compare also [75]. Antozone is more unstable than ozone, and changes back to oxygen gas at a still less elevation of temperature.

Questions and Problems.

1. What is the reason for writing the symbol of oxygen gas $O\text{=}O$? (17) and (19.)

2. What is the difference between the condition of oxygen gas in the atmosphere, and that of the same gas in a pure condition contained in a bell-glass standing over a pneumatic trough?

3. Were the nitrogen gas of the atmosphere removed, would the physical condition of the oxygen gas be changed?

4. If by either of the methods [228] oxygen gas is obtained directly from the atmosphere, how many litres of air would be required to yield one litre of oxygen gas at same temperature and pressure? (59.)   Ans. 4.77 litres of air.

5. How much potassic chlorate must be used to yield 100 litres of oxygen gas at 30° and 38 c. m. pressure?   Ans. 165 grs.

6. What weight of potassic dichromate [230] must be used to yield a litre of oxygen gas, Sp. Gr. = 96?   Ans. 52.77 grs.

7. If 32.05 grammes of potassic chlorate are decomposed in a

T

closed vacuous vessel of 1,010 $\overline{c.\,m.}^3$ capacity, what will be the tension of the gas in the vessel at 273° ?   Ans. 131.6 c. m.

8. What weight of oxygen gas is required to fill a globe of 10 litres' capacity at 27°.3′ and 38 c. m. pressure ?   Ans. 6.515 gram.

9. From a given weight of MnO_2 how much more oxygen gas can be obtained by reaction [231] than by [232] ?   Ans. ½ more.

10. A volume of air measuring 100 $\overline{c.\,m.}^3$ is mixed with 50 $\overline{c.\,m.}^3$ of hydrogen gas and exploded. What volume of gas is left, assuming that the volumes are all measured under standard conditions, and that all the water formed is condensed? (59.)

Ans. 87.12 $\overline{c.\,m.}^3$.

11. In an experiment like the last, with the same initial volume of air and hydrogen, the volume of the residual gas measured 89.41 $\overline{c.\,m.}^3$ What is the composition of the air? It is assumed that the volumes are measured under a constant pressure of 76 c. m., and at a temperature at which the tension of aqueous vapor equals 2 c. m.

Ans. 20.96 oxygen, 79.04 nitrogen.

12. Analyze reaction [230], and show from which of the factors the oxygen is derived.

13. Represent reaction [232] by graphic symbols.

14. What volume of chlorine gas is required to decompose one litre of aqueous vapor ?   Ans. 1 litre.

15. If one gramme of water is decomposed by galvanism in a closed glass globe containing 1.86 litres of air under normal conditions, what will be the tension of the resulting gas mixture, leaving out of the account the tension of the aqueous vapor which may be present ?   Ans. 152 c. m.

16. Represent by graphic symbols the constitution of the various classes of oxides and oxygen radicals.

17. In the symbols of acids, hydrates, and salts (35) written on the water type, to what do the oxygen radicals correspond ?

18. Explain the change of color which takes place when paper moistened with a solution of starch and potassic iodide is exposed to the action of ozone.

19. Explain the method of finding the Sp. Gr. of ozone.

20. Can you devise a method of finding the Sp. Gr. of ozone based on the principle of (58) ?

21. Explain the reasons for writing the symbol of ozone $(O\text{-}O)\text{=}\overline{O}$.

22. How would you write the symbols of argentic peroxide and plumbic peroxide, on the same principle?

23. Why is it essential in preparing antozone that the electrified air should be dry?

24. In what different ways may the symbol of hydric peroxide be written, and what theories of its composition do the symbols suggest? By what reactions are these theories sustained?

Division II.

238. SULPHUR. $S = 32.$ — Usually bivalent when in combination with metals or positive radicals, but in other associations frequently quadrivalent and sexivalent. Widely and abundantly distributed in nature, chiefly in combination, forming various metallic sulphides and sulphates. The most abundant of these are iron pyrites, FeS_2, and gypsum, $CaSO_4 . 2H_2O.$ Found also native in volcanic districts. It is, moreover, an essential, although a very subordinate, ingredient of the animal tissues. Sulphur is very closely allied to oxygen, and, corresponding to each metallic oxide, there is usually a sulphide of the same form ; and, substituting the symbol of sulphur for that of oxygen, the table of oxides on page 301 will serve equally well as a classification of the sulphides. Moreover, we have found it convenient to assume a number of sulphur radicals corresponding in all respects to the oxygen radicals, and we represent them by separate symbols formed in a similar way. Thus, $\overset{\text{I}}{Hs}$, $\overset{\text{II}}{Pbs}$, $\overset{\text{II}}{Cu_2s}$, $\overset{\text{VI}}{Sb_2s}$ stand for the radicals HS, PbS_2, Cu_2S_2, Sb_2S_6 respectively.

The greater part of the sulphur of commerce comes from the mines of Sicily, where it is either melted or distilled from the volcanic earth. A small quantity is obtained by roasting or distilling iron pyrites. Common sulphur is a very brittle, yellow solid, melting at $114°$, and boiling at $440°$, when it forms a dense red vapor. It is insoluble in water, and nearly so in alcohol, ether, and chloroform, but readily soluble in carbonic bisulphide, benzole, and oil of turpentine, the solvent power of the last two liquids being greatly increased by heat. Sulphur assumes a great variety of allotropic modifications, which are manifested by differences of crystalline form, specific gravity, solubility, and color. At the ordinary temperature it crystallizes in octahedrons of the orthorhombic system, $Sp. Gr.$ 2.05, and above $105°$ in oblique prisms of the monoclinic systems, $Sp. Gr.$ 1.98. Moreover, the one crystalline condition passes into the other at the temperature at which it is normally formed. If heated to $230°$, melted sulphur becomes darker colored, thick, and pasty, and if suddenly cooled the mass remains plastic for

some time. At 100° this plastic material suddenly changes back
to brittle sulphur, with evolution of heat, and the same change
soon follows, although more slowly, at the ordinary temperature.
If sulphur is heated to 230°, and suddenly cooled several times
in succession, it is in part converted into a peculiar dark-colored
variety, wholly insoluble in all solvents, and easily separated
by carbonic sulphide from the unchanged portion.　Moreover,
ordinary flowers of sulphur (formed by condensing the vapor
of sulphur in *cold* brick chambers) consist in part of a yellow
powder, insoluble in carbonic sulphide, which appears to be still
another condition of sulphur, and several other modifications,
including a black and a red variety, have been described as
distinct allotropic states.　Some chemists have thought to find
among these various modifications a difference of polar condition
similar to that observed in the modifications of oxygen.　Sulphur appears, even in the state of vapor, to present differences
of condition.　Just above its boiling point the Sp. Gr. of sulphur vapor is 96, which corresponds to the molecular formula
$S\substack{=\\=}S_3$; and not until the temperature reaches 1,000° does the
Sp. Gr. become 32, corresponding to the formula $S\text{=}S$, like that
of oxygen gas.　Sulphur has strong affinities for the metals,
many of which burn in its vapor with great brilliancy.　It has
also a strong affinity for oxygen.　It is very combustible, taking
fire at a low temperature, and forming by burning SO_2.　It is
chiefly used for making sulphuric acid, and vulcanizing india-
rubber; but it has many subordinate applications both in the
arts and in medicine.　The so-called milk of sulphur, used in
pharmacy, is obtained by dissolving flowers of sulphur in alkaline liquids, and subsequently precipitating with acid.

239. *Hydric Sulphide, Sulphohydric Acid, Sulphuretted
Hydrogen,* H_2S. — A colorless gas, which by pressure and cold
may be condensed to a limpid, colorless liquid (*Sp. Gr.* $= 0.9$),
boiling at —62°, and freezing at —86°.　Is soluble in water
and alcohol, one measure of water at 0° dissolving 4.37 measures, and one volume of alcohol dissolving 17.9 measures, of the
gas at the same temperature.　Has a repulsive odor, and is a
constant product of decaying animal tissues.　Generally obtained
by the reaction

$$FeS + (H_2SO_4 + Aq) = (FeSO_4 + Aq) + H_2S; \quad [237]$$

but as the ferrous sulphide commonly used contains more or less metallic iron, the gas thus prepared is mixed with hydrogen. It is obtained in a purer condition from

$$Sb_2S_3 + (6HCl + Aq) = (2SbCl_3 + Aq) + 3H_2S. \quad [238]$$

Hydric sulphide is very combustible, and burns with a pale blue flame.

$$2H_2S + 3O{=}O = 2H_2O + 2SO_2. \quad [239]$$

The solution of the gas exposed to the air soon becomes turbid, owing to the oxidation of the hydrogen and consequent separation of sulphur.

$$(2H_2S + Aq) + O{=}O = (2H_2O + Aq) + S{=}S. \quad [240]$$

If the action is assisted by porous solids, the oxidation is more complete.

$$(H_2S + Aq) + 2O{=}O = (H_2{=}O_2{=}SO_2 + Aq). \quad [241]$$

The substance is also decomposed by chlorine, bromine, or iodine.

$$(2H_2S + 2I{-}I + Aq) = (4HI + Aq) + S{=}S. \quad [242]$$

On this last reaction is based a simple process of determining volumetrically the amount of H_2S in a given solution. The compound may be analyzed by heating metallic tin in a confined volume of the gas.

$$H_2S + Sn = SnS + H{-}H. \quad [243]$$

Although the sulphur is removed by the tin, the volume of the gas does not change. Hydric sulphide is not unfrequently formed in nature from calcic sulphate, which in contact with decaying animal or vegetable matter loses its oxygen, when the carbonic acid of the atmosphere, acting on the resulting calcic sulphide, sets free the compound in question. It is thus that the soluble sulphides in many mineral springs probably originate.

Hydric sulphide is one of the most important chemical reagents, and is used to convert into sulphides various metallic hydrates and other salts.

1. Action on alkaline hydrates.

$$(K\text{-}O\text{-}H + H_2S + Aq) = (K\text{-}S\text{-}H + H_2O + Aq). \quad [244]$$

$$(K\text{-}S\text{-}H + K\text{-}O\text{-}H + Aq) = (K_2S + H_2O + Aq). \quad [245]$$

Thus may also be formed $Na\text{-}Hs$, Na_2S, $NH_4\text{-}Hs$, $(NH_4)_2S$. (38.)

2. Action on salts of the more electro-negative metals.

$$(CdSO_4 + H_2S + Aq) = CdS + (H_2SO_4 + Aq). \quad [246]$$

So also may be precipitated from *acid* solutions of their salts

As_2S_3,	Sb_2S_3,	Sb_2S_5,	SnS,	SnS_2,	PtS_2,	Au_4S_4,
Yellow.	Red.	Orange.	Brown.	Yellow.	Brown.	Black.

all of which are soluble in alkaline sulphides, and

CdS,	CuS,	Bi_2S_3,	Ag_2S,	HgS,	$[Hg_2]S$,	PbS,
Yellow.	Black.	Black.	Black.	Black.	Black.	Black.

all of which are insoluble in alkaline sulphides.

3. Action on salts of the more electro-positive metals. The following sulphides, although not precipitated from *acid* solutions, are precipitated when sufficient ammonia is added to neutralize all the acids present, or when an alkaline sulphide is used in place of H_2S.

ZnS,	MnS,	FeS,	NiS,	CoS.
White.	Pink.	Black.	Black.	Black.

At the same time aluminum and chromium are also precipitated as hydrates. The remaining common metals, viz.: *Ba*, *Sr*, *Ca*, *Mg*, *K*, and *Na*, forming sulphides soluble in water, are not precipitated by H_2S under any conditions. Thus H_2S serves to divide the metallic radicals into groups, and on these relations the ordinary methods of qualitative analysis are based.

4. Action as reducing agent.

$$([Fe_2]Cl_6 + H_2S + Aq) =$$
$$(2FeCl_2 + 2HCl + Aq) + S. \quad [247]$$

$$(K_2[Cr_2]O_7 + 8HCl + 3H_2S + Aq) =$$
$$([Cr_2]Cl_6 + 2KCl + 7H_2O + Aq) + S_3, \quad [248]$$

(Red.) (Green.)

$$10H_2S + 10SO_2 = 5S_2 + 8H_2O + 2H_2S_5O_6. \quad [249]$$

Pentathionic Acid.

240. *Hydric Persulphide*, H_2S_2, analogous to H_2O_2, can be obtained by gradually adding to hydrochloric acid sodic bisulphide. It is a yellow, oily liquid, and very unstable.

241. *Alkaline Sulphides* and *Sulphohydrates*. — Solutions of the simple sulphides and sulphohydrates are best formed as above. These solutions readily dissolve sulphur, and various persulphides are thus formed. The following six sulphides of potassium are known : K_2S, K_2S_2, K_2S_3, K_2S_4, K_2S_5, and K_2S_7. Other modes of preparing similar compounds are illustrated by the following reactions : —

$$K_2{=}O_2{=}SO_2 + 4H{-}H = K_2S + 4H_2O. \qquad [250]$$
Ignited in gas current.

$$12S + (6K{-}O{-}H + Aq) =$$
Boiled in solution.
$$(2K_2S_5 + K_2S_2O_3 + 3H_2O + Aq). \quad [251]$$
Pentasulphide.   Hyposulphite.

$$16S + 8K{-}O{-}H = 3K_2S_5 + K_2SO_4 + 4H_2O. \quad [252]$$
Melted together at a high temperature.

$$8S + 3K_2{=}O_2{=}CO = 2K_2S_3 + K_2S_2O_3 + 3CO_2, \text{ or}$$
$$12S + 3K_2{=}O_2{=}CO = 2K_2S_5 + K_2S_2O_3 + 3CO_2. \qquad [253]$$
Melted together at a lower temperature.

The products of the last two reactions are not constant, but various persulphides are formed, depending on the temperature and the conditions of the process. The resulting mixture is a yellow solid called liver of sulphur. When treated with acids, the various sulphides react as follows : —

$$(K{-}Hs + HCl + Aq) = (KCl + Aq) + H_2S. \quad [254]$$

$$(K_2S + 2HCl + Aq) = (2KCl + Aq) + H_2S. \quad [255]$$

$$(K_2S_3 + 2HCl + Aq) = (2KCl + Aq) + S_2 + H_2S. \quad [256]$$

$$(2K_2S_5 + K_2S_2O_3 + 6HCl + Aq) =$$
$$(6KCl + SO_2 + H_2O + Aq) + 9S + 2H_2S. \quad [257]$$

Solutions of the alkaline sulphides or sulphohydrates absorb oxygen from the air, and are thus changed into persulphides and hyposulphites.

$$(8NH_4{-}S{-}H + Aq) + 5O{=}O =$$
Colorless solution.
$$(2(NH_4)_2S_2 + 2(NH_4)_2S_2O_3 + 4H_2O + Aq). \quad [258]$$
Yellow solution.

Sulphur and hydric sulphide react on the alkaline earths in nearly the same ways as on the alkalies.

$$Ca\,O + H_2S = CaS + H_2O. \qquad [259]$$
Ignited in gas current.

$$CaSO_4 + 4H\text{-}H = CaS + 4H_2O. \qquad [260]$$
Ignited in gas current.

$$CaSO_4 + 4C = CaS + 4CO. \qquad [261]$$
Ignited together.

$$2\,CaS + H_2^{=}O_2^{=}H_2 = Ca^{=}S_2^{=}H_2 + Ca^{=}O_2^{=}H_2. \qquad [262]$$
Mixed with water.

$$(Ca^{=}O_2^{=}H_2 + 2H_2S + Aq) =$$
Passing H_2S through milk of lime.
$$(Ca^{=}S_2^{=}H_2 + 2H_2O + Aq). \qquad [263]$$

By boiling sulphur with milk of lime, a mixture of calcic hyposulphite with various calcic persulphides is obtained, among which may be distinguished CaS_2 and CaS_5. By melting together sulphur and calcic hydrate or carbonate, there results a mixture of calcic sulphide and calcic sulphate. If pulverized charcoal is also added, the product is chiefly calcic sulphide.

242. *Compounds of Sulphur and Oxygen.* — The following are known : —

Sulphurous Anhydride	SO_2,
Sulphurous Acid	$H_2^{=}O_2^{=}SO$,
Hyposulphurous Acid	$H_2^{=}O_2^{=}(S\text{-}O\text{-}S)$,
Sulphuric Anhydride	SO_3,
Sulphuric Acid	$H_2^{=}O_2^{=}SO_2$,
Nordhausen Acid	$H_2^{=}O_2^{=}(SO_2\text{-}O\text{-}SO_2)$,
Dithionic Acid	$H_2^{=}O_2^{=}(SO_2\text{-}SO_2)$,
Trithionic Acid	$H_2^{=}O_2^{=}(SO_2\text{-}S\text{-}SO_2)$,
Tetrathionic Acid	$H_2^{=}O_2^{=}(SO_2\text{-}S\text{-}S\text{-}SO_2)$,
Pentathionic Acid	$H_2^{=}O_2^{=}(SO_2\text{-}S\text{-}S\text{-}S\text{-}SO_2)$.

243. *Sulphurous Anhydride.* SO_2. — Colorless gas, having a familiar suffocating odor. It is easily condensed to a colorless liquid. boiling at —10° and freezing at —76° ; $\mathfrak{Sp. Gr.} = 1.49$. Natural product of volcanic action, and abundantly evolved during the roasting of copper pyrites and other sulphurous ores. May be prepared by either of the following reactions : —

14.

$$S\text{=}S + 2\,⊙\text{=}⊙ = 2\,S⊙_2. \qquad [264]$$
Burning.

$$2H_2SO_4 + Hg = HgSO_4 + 2H_2O + S⊙_2. \qquad [265]$$

$$2H_2SO_4 + C = 2S⊙_2 + C⊙_2 + 2H_2⊙. \qquad [266]$$

$$S\text{=}S + MnO_2 = MnS + S⊙_2. \qquad [267]$$

May be decomposed by the reactions

$$2SO_2 + 4H\text{-}H = 4H_2O + S\text{=}S. \qquad [268]$$

$$SO_2 + 3H\text{-}H = 2H_2O + H_2S. \qquad [269]$$

The first reaction is obtained by passing a mixture of the two gases through a red-hot tube; the second, by adding to the solution containing SO_2 a small amount of hydrochloric acid with a few pieces of zinc. The H_2S may be detected by a strip of paper moistened with a solution of acetate of lead, and the reaction gives us the means of discovering small quantities of SO_2.

Sulphurous anhydride is a powerful reducing agent. Thus

$$(2HIO_3 + 5SO_2 + 4H_2O + Aq) =$$
Iodic Acid.
$$(I\text{-}I + 5H_2SO_4 + Aq). \quad [270]$$

$$(As_2O_5 + 2SO_2 + 2H_2O + Aq) =$$
$$(As_2O_3 + 2H_2SO_4 + Aq). \quad [271]$$

$$(SO_2 + I\text{-}I + 2H_2O + Aq) = (H_2SO_4 + 2HI + Aq.) \quad [272]$$

$$(2SO_2 + 2H_2O + Aq) + ⊙\text{=}⊙ = (2H_2SO_4 + Aq). \quad [273]$$

$$\mathbf{PbO_2 + S⊙_2 = PbSO_4.} \qquad [274]$$

It is also a powerful disinfecting and antiseptic agent, and is much used for retarding fermentation and putrefaction. It also bleaches some of the more fugitive colors, but the effect is frequently transient, and the reaction not well understood.

244. *Sulphites.* — At 0° water absorbs 68.8 times its bulk of SO_2, and three crystalline hydrates have been described, one of which has the composition $SO_2 . H_2O$, and has been regarded as sulphurous acid, but this opinion may be questioned. The aqueous solution acts in all its mechanical relations like the simple

solution of a gas. Nevertheless, in its chemical relations it acts like an acid, and yields, with many of the metallic oxides, hydrates, or carbonates, a numerous class of salts called the sulphites. The following examples will illustrate their general composition : —

Hydro-sodic Sulphite	$H,Na=O_2=SO . 4H_2O,$
Disodic Sulphite	$Na_2=O_2=SO . 7H_2O,$
Calcic Sulphite	$Ca=O_2=SO.$

The sulphites are generally best prepared by transmitting a stream of SO_2 through water in which the metallic oxide, hydrate, or carbonate is suspended. The alkaline salts are the only sulphites which are freely soluble in water. The sulphites of barium, strontium, and calcium dissolve to some extent in water charged with SO_2, and in this respect the sulphites resemble the carbonates. Argentic sulphite, which may be readily obtained by precipitation, undergoes a remarkable reaction when boiled with water.

$$Ag_2=O_2=SO + (H_2O + Aq) =$$
$$Ag-Ag + (H_2=O_2=SO_2 + Aq). \quad [275]$$

245. *Hyposulphites.* — Hyposulphurous acid has never been isolated; but several hyposulphites may be obtained by passing a stream of SO_2 through solutions of the corresponding sulphides, or digesting a solution of the sulphite on powdered sulphur.

$$S + (Na_2=O_2=SO + Aq) = (Na_2=O_2=(S-O-S) + Aq. \quad [276]$$

Calcic hyposulphite is formed spontaneously in large quantities, both in the refuse lime taken from the purifiers of the gasworks, and in the refuse after the lixiviation of the black-ball at the alkali works, and from this source sodic hyposulphite is now obtained. It is the only hyposulphite of practical value, and is not only used in photography, but also for removing the last traces of chlorine from the bleached pulp used in papermaking, and in the treatment of silver ores.

246. *Sulphuric Anhydride.* SO_3. — Soft, white, silky-looking crystalline solid, melting at 25°, and volatilizing at 35°. May be obtained either by distillation from the Nordhausen acid or

from sodic disulphate, or else by passing a mixture of SO_2 and $O=O$ through a heated tube filled with platinum sponge.

$$H_2^{=}O_2^{=}(SO_2^{-}O\text{-}SO_2) = H_2^{=}O_2^{=}SO_2 + SO_3. \quad [277]$$

$$Na_2^{=}O_2^{=}(SO_2^{-}O\text{-}SO_2) = Na_2^{=}O_2^{=}SO_2 + SO_3. \quad [278]$$

$$2SO_2 + O\text{-}O = 2SO_3. \quad [279]$$

It unites with many metallic oxides to form sulphates, and baryta burns in its vapor.

$$\mathbf{BaO + SO_3 = BaO,SO_3.} \quad [280]$$

It has an intense affinity for water, and the heat developed by the union is so great that the solid hisses like red-hot iron when dropped into the liquid. The product is common sulphuric acid.

247. *Sulphurylic Chloride.* SO_2Cl_2. — May be formed by the direct union of SO_2 and $Cl\text{-}Cl$ under the influence of the sunlight, also by the reaction

$$H_2SO_4 + 2PCl_5 = SO_2Cl_2 + 2PCl_3O + 2HCl. \quad [281]$$

The product is a liquid boiling at 80°; *Sp. Gr.* 1.68. Slowly decomposed by water.

$$SO_2Cl_2 + 2H_2O = H_2SO_4 + 2HCl. \quad [282]$$

There have also been described the allied compounds $H\text{-}O\text{-}SO_2\text{-}Cl$ and SO_2I_2. The relations of these compounds to sulphuric acid will be made more evident by writing the symbols thus : —

$$Ho_2^{=}SO_2, \qquad Ho,Cl^{=}SO_2, \qquad Cl_2^{=}SO_2, \qquad I_2^{=}SO_2.$$

248. *Sulphuric Acid.* $H_2^{=}O_2^{=}SO_2$ or $Ho_2^{=}SO_2$. — The following reactions are interesting as illustrating the constitution of this important acid, although of no practical value as methods of making it :—

$$Ho\text{-}Ho + SO_2 = Ho_2^{=}SO_2. \quad [283]$$

$$H_2O + SO_3 = H_2O,SO_3. \quad [284]$$

$$2H_2^{=}O_2^{=}SO + O=O = 2H_2^{=}O_2^{=}SO_2. \quad [285]$$

$$S^{=}S + 4H\text{-}O\text{-}NO_2 = 2H_2^{=}O_2^{=}SO_2 + 4NO. \quad [286]$$

For the uses of the arts the acid is made in enormous quantities by burning sulphur in large brick ovens, and conveying the SO_2 thus formed, together with steam and nitric acid fumes, generated simultaneously [135], into large chambers lined with sheet lead.

1. $$SO_2 + 2HNO_3 = H_2SO_4 + 2NO_2.$$ [287]

2. $$3NO_2 + H_2O = 2HNO_3 + NO.$$ [288]

3. $$2NO + O{=}O = 2\,NO_2.$$ [289]

These reactions may be repeated indefinitely, and it is evident that the same quantity of nitric acid would serve to convert an infinite amount of SO_2 into H_2SO_4, were it not for the loss occasioned by the constant draft of air through the chambers. The reaction consists essentially in a transfer of oxygen from the air to the SO_2, the nitrogen compounds acting as the mediator, and the draft yields the requisite supply of oxygen gas. When the amount of aqueous vapor is insufficient, there forms in the chambers a white crystalline compound of somewhat uncertain composition, but to which has been assigned the symbol $(NO_2)_2{=}(SO_2{-}O{-}SO_2)$. When mixed with water, this compound breaks up into sulphuric acid and nitrous anhydride, so that the formation of the acid may also be represented by the following equations, which are thought by some chemists to represent the process more accurately than those given above:—

1. $$SO_2 + 2HoNO_2 = Ho_2SO_2 + 2NO_2.$$ [290]

2. $$4NO_2 + 4SO_2 + O{=}O = 2(NO_2)_2{=}(SO_2{-}O{-}SO_2).$$ [291]

3. $$(NO_2)_2{=}(SO_2{-}O{-}SO_2) + 2H_2O = 2Ho_2SO_2 + N_2O_3.$$ [292]

4. $$3N_2O_3 + H_2O = 2HoNO_2 + 4NO.$$ [293]

5. $$2NO + O{=}O = 2NO_2.$$ [294]

In manufacturing sulphuric acid iron pyrites is now frequently used instead of sulphur. This ore, burnt in kilns adapted to the purpose, yields a plentiful supply of SO_2, which is converted into sulphuric acid in lead chambers as before. The acid drawn from the chambers is very dilute, and for most uses must be concentrated by evaporation, which is begun in leaden pans, but completed in retorts of glass or platinum. The strongest acid thus obtained corresponds to the symbol H_2SO_4. It is an oily liquid (oil of vitriol), *Sp. Gr.* = 1.842, boiling at 327°, and crystallizing at a low temperature. If during the evaporation the temperature is limited to 205° C., an acid is obtained of the composition $H_2SO_4 \cdot H_2O$, and *Sp. Gr.* 1.78, which crystallizes at 9°, and by limiting the temperature to 100°, still a second definite hydrate may be obtained, $H_2SO_4 \cdot 2H_2O$, which has *Sp. Gr.* = 1.62. Oil of vitriol may be mixed with water in any proportion, and the hydration of the acid is accompanied by a condensation of volume and a great evolution of heat, the maximum of condensation and the maximum of heat being attained when the proportions are such as to form the second hydrate. A definite *Sp. Gr.* corresponds to each degree of dilution, and tables have been prepared by which, when the specific gravity is known, the strength of the acid may be determined. The short table which follows gives all the data required for the problems in this book: —

Per Cent of H_2SO_4.	Sp. Gr. at 15°.	Per Cent of SO_3.	Per Cent of H_2SO_4.	Sp. Gr. at 15°.	Per Cent of SO_3.
100	1.8426	81.63	50	1.3980	40.81
95	1.8376	77.55	45	1.3510	36.73
90	1.8220	73.47	40	1.3060	32.65
85	1.7860	69.38	35	1.2640	28.57
80	1.7340	65.30	30	1.2230	24.49
75	1.6750	61.22	25	1.1820	20.40
70	1.6150	57.14	20	1.1440	16.32
65	1.5570	53.05	15	1.1060	12.24
60	1.5010	48.98	10	1.0680	8.16
55	1.4480	44.89	5	1.0320	4.08

In consequence chiefly of its strong attraction for water, sulphuric acid disorganizes and blackens both animal and vegetable tissues. It is also used as a hygroscopic agent, and, under limited conditions, for the dehydration of various chemical compounds. Its action on different chemical agents has been already repeatedly illustrated. (See [64], [231], [265].) It forms several classes of salts, as is illustrated by the following examples: —

Hydro-sodic Sulphate	$Ho,Nao\text{-}SO_2,$
Disodic Sulphate	$Nao_2^=SO_2$ and with $10H_2O,$
Sodic Disulphate	$Nao_2^=(SO_2\text{-}O\text{-}SO_2),$
Cupric Sulphate	$Cuo\text{-}SO_2 . 5H_2O,$
Ferrous Sulphate	$Feo\text{-}SO_2 . 7H_2O,$
Potassio-ferrous Disulphate	$Feo\text{-}(SO\text{-}O_2\text{-}SO)\text{-}Ko_2 . 6H_2O,$
Aluminic Sulphate	$Al_2o^{\equiv}(SO_2)_3 . 18H_2O,$
Common Alum	$Ko_2^=(SO_2)_4^{\equiv}Al_2o . 24H_2O,$
Zincic Sulphate	$Zno\text{-}SO_2,$
Dizincic Sulphate	$Zno_2^{\equiv}SO,$
Trizincic Sulphate	$Zno_3^{\equiv}S.$

The last may be regarded as an orthosulphate, but salts of this class are wholly exceptional.

249. *Nordhausen Sulphuric Acid, $Ho_2^=(SO_2\text{-}O\text{-}SO_2)$,* corresponding to the disulphates in constitution, may be prepared by dissolving SO_3 in H_2SO_4, and has been manufactured for many years at the German town whence it takes its name, by the distillation of ferrous sulphate. The manufacture of sulphuric acid is one of the most important branches of industry in a civilized community, as there is hardly an art or a trade into which, in some form or other, it does not enter.

250. *Sulphurous Chloride. S_2Cl_2.* — Yellow, volatile, fuming liquid, formed by distilling sulphur in an atmosphere of chlorine gas. It is a powerful sulphur solvent, and has been used for vulcanizing india-rubber. It is decomposed by water, but mixes with benzole and carbonic sulphide. Sulphuric chloride, SCl_2, and several oxychlorides of sulphur are also known.

251. SELENIUM. *$Se = 79.4.$* TELLURIUM. *$Te =$* 128. — Two very rare elements, closely allied to sulphur, but presenting such differences as might be anticipated in elements of the same chemical series. They form compounds with hydrogen, H_2Se and H_2Te, analogous to H_2S, and compounds with oxygen and hydrogen resembling sulphurous and sulphuric acids.

Selenium, which follows in the series next to sulphur, manifests its relationship in many ways. The elementary substance, which in its ordinary condition is a brittle solid having a glassy fracture and a dark brown color, *Sp. Gr.* 4.3, may be obtained in several allotropic states, and in one of these, when its *Sp. Gr.*

$= 4.8$, it has the same monoclinic form and molecular volume[1] as the corresponding condition of sulphur. It readily melts at a varying temperature above 100°, depending on its condition, and at 700° is converted into a deep yellow vapor which has been observed to have, at a high temperature, Sp. Gr. $= 82$. It burns in the air with a blue flame, forming chiefly SeO_2, and emits an offensive odor resembling putrid horseradish. Hydric selenide, also, is a gas with a disgusting smell, which, like H_2S, precipitates many of the metals from solutions of their salts as selenides. Selenic acid is a thick oily liquid like sulphuric acid, and many of the selenates cannot be distinguished by merely external characters from the corresponding sulphates. Selenium, moreover, is almost invariably found in nature associated with sulphur, and is extracted from the residues resulting from the treatment of sulphur ores. There are, however, a few rare minerals which consist mainly of metallic selenides. Among the most important of these may be named Clausthalite, $PbSe$, Berzelianite, $CuSe$, Naumannite, Ag_2Se, and Onofrite, $HgSe$.

When we descend in the series to Tellurium, we find more marked differences. The elementary substance has a silver-white color, a bright metallic lustre, and outwardly resembles a metal. It is closely allied in many of its physical properties to bismuth. It crystallizes in rhombohedrons, and the mineral Tetradymite has been regarded as an isomorphous mixture of native tellurium with native bismuth. Its $Sp. Gr. = 6.2$, and its atomic volume is very much nearer that of bismuth and antimony, than that of selenium and sulphur. Nevertheless, in other relations it is closely allied to selenium. It is hard and brittle, a poor conductor of heat and electricity. It fuses between 425° and 475°, and at a high temperature yields a yellow vapor which has a specific gravity corresponding to the molecular formula $Te=Te$. When heated in the air, it burns with a greenish blue flame, and is converted into tellurous anhydride, TeO_2. Lastly, hydric telluride resembles closely hydric selenide, and the salts of tellurous and telluric acids are similar to the corresponding selenites and selenates; but telluric acid does not, like selenic acid, form salts corresponding to the alums, and its

---

[1] The quotients obtained by dividing the molecular weights of different solid substances by their respective specific gravities may be regarded as proportional to their molecular volumes in the solid state.

salts are less stable. Tellurium is the chief constituent of a few native compounds which are highly prized as minerals. Besides Tetradymite, Bi_2Te_3, we have Hessite, Ag_2Te, Sylvanite, $AgAuTe_4$, Altaite, $PbTe$, and Nagyagite, which is a sulphotelluride of lead and gold of somewhat uncertain composition. The elements of this group form then, evidently, a very well-marked series, in which, as in the chlorine series, the chemical energy diminishes as the atomic weight increases.

Division III.

252. MOLYBDENUM. $Mo = 96$. One of the rarer elements, but not unfrequently met with in the mineral kingdom, usually in combination with sulphur forming the mineral Molybdenite, MoS_2, which so closely resembles foliated graphite that the two might easily be mistaken for each other. From this mineral we readily obtain by roasting, at a low red heat in a current of air, molybdic anhydride, MoO_3, which is the most characteristic compound of the element. When pure, the anhydride is a pale buff-colored powder, fusing to a straw-colored glass at a red heat, and volatilizing at a higher temperature. It is only sparingly soluble in water, but readily dissolves in ordinary acids, in aqua ammonia, and in solutions of the alkaline hydrates or carbonates, and forms with metallic oxides a numerous class of salts called molybdates. Plumbic molybdate (Wulfenite), $Pb\text{=}O_2\text{=}MoO_2$, is sometimes found in beautiful yellow or red crystals associated with other lead ores, and molybdate of ammonia, $(NH_4)_2\text{=}O_2\text{=}MoO_2$, is much used in the laboratory as a test for phosphoric acid. Besides MoO_3, the element also forms compounds with one and with two atoms of oxygen, MoO and MoO_2, which act as basic anhydrides, and there is also an intermediate oxide having a beautiful blue color, and another having a dull green color, which are formed by the action of $SnCl_2$ and other reducing agents on acid solutions of the molybdates, and the accompanying change of color serves as a very striking test for molybdenum. In solutions of molybdic acid or of molybdates, when acidified with hydrochloric acid, H_2S, gives a brownish-black precipitate of MoS_3, and there is still a third sulphide, MoS_4, which, as well

14* U

as the last, acts as a sulphur acid. There are also two chlorides, $MoCl_2$ and $MoCl_4$. The elementary substance is a brittle silver-white metal ($Sp. Gr. = 8.6$), which is unalterable in the air and very infusible. It can be obtained without difficulty by reducing the oxides with charcoal or hydrogen, but unless the temperature is very high the metal is left as a gray powder. The name is from the Greek, and signifies "a mass of lead."

253. TUNGSTEN. $W = 184$. — This element occurs in tolerably large quantities combined with calcium in the mineral Scheelite, $CaWO_4$, and with both iron and manganese in Wolfram, of which there are two varieties, $2FeWO_4 + 3MnWO_4$ and $4FeWO_4 + MnWO_4$. Both minerals are decomposed by acids, and by this means we readily obtain tungstic anhydride, WO_3, a yellow powder insoluble in water and acids, but readily dissolving in ammonia and solutions of alkaline hydrates, and even decomposing with effervescence the alkaline carbonates, when heated in solutions of their salts. From a boiling alkaline solution of tungstic anhydride the common acids throw down a yellow precipitate of tungstic acid, H_2WO_4. This acid forms with bases a numerous class of salts called tungstates, which, although of little practical importance, are theoretically very interesting, and have been the object of careful investigation. There are several (at least two) distinct types of these salts, and there are also two modifications of tungstic acid; for, besides the ordinary insoluble condition, both molybdic and tungstic acids have been obtained in a colloidal condition, in which they are very soluble in water (57). The tungstates have the same crystalline form as the corresponding molybdates, and a tungstate of lead, isomorphous with Wulfenite, is a well-known mineral called Scheeltine. Besides WO_3 there is an oxide, WO_2, which also acts as an acid anhydride, and there is also an intermediate oxide of a splendid blue color, which may be produced by the action of reducing agents on the anhydride or the soluble tungstates. Tungsten is not, like molybdenum, precipitated by H_2S, but the sulphide, WS_2, has been prepared artificially, and resembles very closely the native molybdenite. There is also a sulphide, WS_3, and there are two volatile chlorides, WCl_4 and WCl_6. The metal itself ($Sp. Gr.$ 17.6) is easily reduced, but, in consequence of its great infusibility, cannot be obtained in a compact state except at a very high temperature. It has an

iron-gray color, and, when alloyed with steel to the extent of 8 or 10 per cent, renders the metal exceedingly hard. The compounds neither of tungsten nor of molybdenum have found any important applications in the arts, although sodic tungstate has been used, mixed with starch, in finishing cambrics, because it has been found to render these light fabrics less inflammable. The name tungsten had a Swedish origin, and signified in the original "heavy stone."

Questions and Problems.

1. What is the per cent of sulphur in gypsum and iron pyrites?
Ans. 18.6 per cent and 53.33 per cent.

2. Write the symbols of the different classes of sulphides.

3. Express by graphic symbols the constitution of the various sulphur radicals.

4. What are the atomic volumes of the two crystalline varieties of sulphur? Ans. 15.60 and 16.16.

5. By heating 10.000 grammes of silver in the vapor of sulphur, Dumas obtained 11.4815 grammes of argentic sulphide. What is the atomic weight of sulphur? What assumption is made in your calculation, and what ground have you for this assumption?
Ans. 32.000.

6. What is the specific gravity of H_2S gas referred to hydrogen and to air? Ans. 17 and 1.1764.

7. What weight of sulphur is contained in one litre of H_2S?
Ans. 1.434 grammes.

8. How much antimonious sulphide is required for the preparation of one litre of hydric sulphide? How much to prepare 340 grammes?
Ans. 5.076 grammes, 1133.33 grammes.

9. What volume of oxygen gas is required to burn one litre of H_2S, and what are the volumes of the aëriform products?
Ans. $1\frac{1}{2}$ litres of oxygen gas, one litre of aqueous vapor, and one of sulphurous anhydride.

10. One litre of $(H_2S + Aq)$ saturated at $0°$ will absorb what volume of oxygen gas, and will yield what weight of sulphur?
Ans. 2.185 litres, 6.263 grammes.

11. Assuming that a solution of iodine in a solution of potassic iodide has been prepared of known strength, how may this be used to measure the quantity of H_2S in a mineral water?

12. The specific gravity of hydric sulphide has been found by experiment to be 17.2, and by reaction [243] it is shown that one volume of the gas contains an equal volume of hydrogen. Show that these results agree quite closely with the molecular symbol assigned to the compound. How do you explain the slight discrepancy?

13. Write the reactions by which hydric sulphide is formed from calcic sulphate.

14. Write the reaction by which NH_4-Hs may be formed from aqua ammonia.

15. Write the reaction of H_2S gas on solution of plumbic acetate, and calculate what volume of $(H_2S + Aq)$ saturated at 0° would be required to precipitate 0.207 grammes of lead.

$$\text{Ans. } 5.109 \; \overline{\text{c. m.}}^3 \text{ of } H_2S + Aq.$$

16. Write the reaction of H_2S on solution of acetate of zinc. What inference would you draw from the fact that Zn is precipitated by this reagent from an acetic acid solution, while Fe and Mn are not?

17. Into what groups may the metallic radicals be divided by means of the two reagents hydric sulphide and ammonic sulphide, and how must the reagents be used in order to separate these groups from a given solution?

18. In reducing 28 grammes of iron from the condition of ferric to that of ferrous chloride, how much sulphur is precipitated?

$$\text{Ans. } 8 \text{ grammes.}$$

19. Analyze the reactions [248] and [249], and show how the H_2S gas acts as a reducing agent in each case.

20. Write the reaction of hydrochloric acid on sodic bisulphide.

21. Represent by graphic symbols the constitution of the various potassic sulphides.

22. Analyze reactions [250] to [263].

23. Write reaction when sulphur and milk of lime are boiled together, assuming, first, that CaS_2, and second, that CaS_5, is produced.

24. Write reaction when sulphur and calcic hydrate are melted together, assuming that CaS_5 and $CaSO_4$ are produced.

25. Represent by graphic symbols the composition of the compounds of sulphur and oxygen.

26. Is the quantivalence of sulphur in the sulphites and hyposulphites the same as in the sulphates, &c.?

27. What volume of sulphurous anhydride would be formed by burning 2.8672 grammes of sulphur?   Ans. 2 litres.

28. It has been observed that when sulphur burns in oxygen the volume of the product is the same as the initial volume of oxygen gas. It has been found by experiment that the Sp. Gr. of sulphurous anhydride equals 32.25. How do these facts correspond with the molecular symbol usually assigned to the compound? What is the Sp. Gr. of SO_2 referred to air?   Ans. 2.234.

29. How much mercury is required to make one litre of SO_2?
          Ans. 8.96 grammes.

30. Leaving out of view the value of the mercury used, as it may be easily recovered, by which of the two reactions [265] or [266] may SO_2 be most profitably prepared?

31. How much MnO_2 would be required to yield by reaction [267] sufficient SO_2 to neutralize 1.29 grammes of sodic carbonate?
          Ans. 1.059 grammes.

32. Point out the volumetric relations in reaction [268].

33. Are the conditions under which the reaction [269] is obtained in any way peculiar?

34. Compare reactions [271] and [272], and inquire whether a method of volumetric analysis based upon them might not be devised.

35. Represent by graphic symbols the sulphites whose symbols are given in (244).

36. The refuse lime of the gas and alkali works contains calcic disulphide, CaS_2. In what way would this be changed by exposure to the air into calcic hyposulphite, and how from this product could sodic hyposulphite be prepared?

37. Write the reaction of hydrochloric acid on sodic hyposulphite, knowing that hyposulphurous acid, when liberated, breaks up into sulphurous anhydride and sulphur.

38. The specific gravity of the vapor of sulphuric anhydride has been found by experiment to be 39.9. How does this agree with the theoretical value? Compare the densities of $O=O$, SO_2, and SO_3 as regards the relative degree of condensation in each.

39. What are the relations of the compounds SO_2Cl_2, SO_2ClHO, SO_3, and H_2SO_4 to each other?

40. Analyze the two sets of reactions [287 *et seq.*] and [290 *et seq.*], and show from whence the oxygen required to oxidize the sulphurous acid is derived, and what part the oxides of nitrogen play in the process.

41. In the process of making oxygen gas from sulphuric acid, from whence is the oxygen in the first instance derived? Might not the same quantity of acid be made to yield an indefinite supply of gas?

42. It appears by experiment that the Sp. Gr. of H_2SO_4 vapor is 24.42. How does this agree with theory, and how do you explain the discrepancy?

43. It has been found by exact experiments that 100 parts of lead yield 146.45 parts of plumbic sulphate. What is the molecular weight of sulphuric acid? What assumption does your calculation involve (68)? Why do you regard this result as more trustworthy than that of the last problem?   Ans. 98.16.

44. How do the symbols of the hydrates of sulphuric acid compare with those of the crystalline salts of this acid?

45. Write the symbols of sulphuric acid and its two hydrates, representing them as compounds of SO_2 with hydroxyl. Point out the distinction between the ortho and meta acids, and show that a similar distinction may be made among the salts.

46. How many litres of sulphuric acid, $Sp. Gr. = 1.615$, can be made from 1,000 kilos. of pyrites, assuming that all the sulphur in the mineral is burnt?   Ans. 1444.4 litres.

47. How much sulphuric acid by weight, $Sp. Gr. = 1.501$, will be required, 1st. To neutralize 53 grammes of sodic carbonate? 2d. To dissolve 32.6 grammes of zinc? 3d. To precipitate completely 2.08 grammes of baric chloride?
        Ans. 81.666 grammes, 81.666 grammes, 1.633 grammes.

48. Represent the constitution of the various sulphates by graphic symbols.

49. In what does the symbol of dizincic sulphate differ from that of a sulphite?

50. If the specific gravity and molecular weight of a solid substance be given, how can you find the molecular volume of the substance in the solid condition?

51. How does the molecular volume of sulphur compare with that of selenium, 1st. In the solid condition? 2d. In the crystalline condition?

52. What is true of the molecular volumes of all substances in the state of gas?

53. Compare the molecular volumes of tellurium and bismuth.

54. What are the analogies, and what are the chief points of difference between sulphur, selenium, and tellurium?

55. Write the reaction of hydric selenide on a solution of plumbic acetate, also of potassic selenate on a solution of baric chloride?

56. Write the reaction when Molybdenite is roasted in the air.

57. Write the reaction of H_2S on a solution of molybdic acid in hydrochloric acid.

58. What is the relative proportion of tungstic anhydride in the two varieties of Wolfram?   Ans. 76.47 to 76.38 %.

59. Write the reaction of hydrochloric acid on Scheelite.

60. In what respects does tungsten resemble molybdenum?

61. What is the atomicity of tungsten and molybdenum, and what is the prevailing quantivalence in each case?

Division IV.

254. COPPER. $Cu = 63.5.$ — Dyad. One of the most abundant metals, and known from great antiquity. Of its ores, by far the most important is Copper Pyrites, $Fe=S_2=Cu$, which is found to a greater or less extent in almost all countries. This mineral resembles iron pyrites, but is distinguished from it by greater softness and a ruddier tint. The smelting of the ore is a complex process, and consists in an alternating series of roastings and meltings, during which the iron passes into the slags, while the copper accumulates in the successive "mattes," as they are called, until at last a nearly pure sub-sulphide is obtained. This is now heated in a current of air until the metal is partially oxidized, and then the mass is melted, when the following reaction results: —

$$2CuO + Cu_2S = 4Cu + SO_2. \qquad [295]$$

The crude metal thus obtained must, however, be subsequently refined. To this end it is first kept melted in the air for many hours, until all the impurities are oxidized; and then the oxides of copper, formed at the same time, are reduced by submitting the mass to the action of carbonaceous gases, which are generated by thrusting a stick of green wood under the molten metal.

255. *Metallic Copper. Cu.* — Found native crystallized in forms of the isometric system. Has a brilliant lustre, and a familiar reddish color. Has great hardness and tenacity. Is very ductile and malleable, and one of the best conductors of heat and electricity. Sp. Gr. 8.8. Fuses at about 780°. Volatilizes only at a very high temperature. Its vapor burns with a beautiful green flame, which shows in the spectroscope characteristic bands. Under ordinary conditions copper undergoes no change in the atmosphere, but if heated to redness in the air it is rapidly oxidized. In presence of acids or solutions of chlorides, like sea-water, copper absorbs oxygen from the air at the ordinary temperature, and is more or less rapidly corroded. A similar effect is also produced by aqua ammonia and solutions of ammonia salts. Out of contact with the air, dilute hydrochloric or sulphuric acids have but little action upon metallic

copper. If boiled with strong hydrochloric acid, it very slowly dissolves with the evolution of hydrogen gas. Under the same conditions sulphuric acid, if not too dilute, is decomposed by it, cupric sulphate is formed, sulphurous acid is evolved, and the reaction is similar to [265]. Nitric acid is the best solvent, but, singularly, the strongest acid has no action on the metal. When diluted with water, however, the action is very violent; cupric nitrate is formed, and a gas is evolved which is generally NO; but when the acid is very dilute this product is more or less mixed with N_2O.

256. *Cupric Oxides.* $[Cu_2]O$ and CuO. — Both of which act as basic anhydrides, although the salts of the second are by far the most stable and important compounds. $[Cu_2]O$ has a red color, and when melted into glass imparts to it a beautiful ruby or purple color. It is the Red Oxide of Copper of mineralogy, and is found massive and beautifully crystallized in various forms of the isometric system, also in splendid capillary tufts (Chalcotrichite). CuO is black, but imparts to glass a green color. It is found sparingly in nature, rarely crystallized (Black Oxide of Copper, or Melaconite). May be prepared by roasting copper or igniting the nitrate. Is very easily reduced by hydrogen [67] or carbonaceous materials, and is much used as an oxidizing agent in the process of organic analysis. The following reactions illustrate some of the relations of these oxides and their hydrates: —

When cold, $(Cu\text{-}O_2\text{=}SO_2 + 2K\text{-}O\text{-}H + Aq) =$
$$\mathbf{Cu\text{-}O_2\text{-}H_2} + (K_2\text{=}O_2\text{=}SO_2 + Aq). \quad [296]$$

By boiling, $(\underset{\text{Blue.}}{Cu\text{-}O_2\text{=}H_2} + Aq) = \underset{\text{Black.}}{\mathbf{CuO}} + (H_2O + Aq). \quad [297]$

By boiling with grape sugar,

$(2Cu\text{-}O_2\text{=}SO_2 + 4K\text{-}O\text{-}H - O + Aq) =$
$$\underset{\text{Red.}}{[\mathbf{Cu_2}]\mathbf{O}} + (2K_2\text{=}O_2\text{=}SO_2 + 2H_2O + Aq). \quad [298]$$

An orange-yellow hydrate, $4[Cu_2]O \cdot H_2O$, is precipitated on first warming the liquid, but this is rendered anhydrous by boiling.

257. *Cupric Sulphate* (*Blue Vitriol*). $Cu\text{=}O_2\text{=}SO_2 \cdot 5H_2O$. — The most important soluble salt of copper. Although when pure

it always crystallizes with five molecules of water, as above, yet it is capable of forming isomorphous mixtures with ferrous sulphate, $Fe\text{=}O_2\text{=}SO_2.7H_2O$. When in this mixture the copper is in excess, the crystals take $5H_2O$ and the form of cupric sulphate (Fig. 28). If, however, the iron is in excess, they take $7H_2O$ and the form of ferrous sulphate, similar to Fig. 26. The anhydrous salt is white, but becomes blue on uniting with water, for which it has a very strong affinity. Of the five molecules of water with which the crystalline salt is united, one is held much more firmly than the other four, and may be replaced by a molecule of an alkaline sulphate. This gives a reason for writing the symbol of the salt thus, $Ho_2, Cuo\text{≡}SO.4H_2O$. In like manner the symbols of several so-called basic salts may be written thus,

$$Ho,(CuO_2H)_3\text{≡}SO,$$
$$Ho_2,(CuO_2H)_4\text{≡}S \text{ (Brochantite)},$$
$$Ho,(CuO_2H)_5\text{≡}S.2H_2O,$$

in which the group CuO_2H acts as a monad radical. From solutions of cupric sulphate the copper is readily precipitated by Zn or Fe.

$$\mathbf{Zn} + (CuSO_4 + Aq) = \mathbf{Cu} + (ZnSO_4 + Aq). \quad [299]$$

258. *Carbonates.* — Malachite, $(CuO_2H)_2\text{=}CO$. Same compound may be obtained by mixing hot solutions of cupric sulphate and sodic carbonate. Azurite, $Cuo_3,Ho_2\text{viii}C_2$ or $Ho,Cuo\text{=}C\text{-}Cuo\text{-}C\text{=}Cuo,Ho$. Mysorin, $Cuo_2\text{≡}C$. The normal carbonate is not known.

259. *Nitrates.* — $Cuo\text{=}(NO_2)_2.6H_2O$ when crystallized below 60°, and $Cuo\text{=}(NO_2)_2.3H_2O$ when crystallized above 60°, a deliquescent blue salt. A green basic nitrate has the symbol $Ho_3,(CuO_2H)_3, Cuo\text{viii}N_2O$.

260. *Cupric Phosphate,* $Cuo_3\text{≡}(PO)_2$, is obtained on adding a solution of sodic phosphate to a solution of cupric sulphate.

261. *Cupric Silicate.* Dioptase, $Ho,(CuO_2H)\text{=}SiO$.

262. *Sulphides:* —

Copper Glance	$[Cu_2]S,$
Covelline (Indigo Copper)	$CuS,$
Copper Pyrites	$Fe\text{=}S_2\text{=}Cu,$
Erubescite	$Fe\text{=}S_2\text{=}([Cu_2]\text{-}S\text{-}[Cu_2]),$
Tetrahedrite	$[Cu_2]_3\text{≡}S_6\text{≡}Sb_2.ZnS.$

When H_2S is passed through the solution of a copper salt, a black precipitate falls having the composition $Cu_6S_5Ho_2$, which rapidly oxidizes in the air.

263. *Fluohydrate of Copper.* ($CuOH$)-Fl.

Chlorides. — Cuprous Chloride, [Cu_2] Cl_2. White compound, insoluble in water, crystallizes in tetrahedrons. Cupric Chloride, $CuCl_2 . 2H_2O$, crystallizes in green needles, very soluble in both water and alcohol. Cupric Oxichloride, (Cu_4O_3)=$Cl_2 . 4H_2O$, is much used as a paint (Brunswick green), and the mineral Atacamite is the same compound, with only one, or at most two, molecules of H_2O.

264. *Cupric Hydride.* CuH_2. — A brown powder, which gives, with hydrochloric acid, the following remarkable reaction : —

$$CuH_2 + (2HCl + Aq) = (CuCl_2 + Aq) + 2H\text{-}H. \quad [300]$$

265. *Ammoniated Compounds.* — When a solution of ammonia or of ammonia carbonate is added to a solution of a salt of copper, the light-green precipitate first produced readily dissolves in an excess of the reagent, producing a deep-blue solution; and this striking coloration is one of the most characteristic tests of the presence of copper. The effects are caused by the formation of certain remarkable compounds, in which a portion of the hydrogen of the ammonia appears to have been replaced by copper. The following are a few examples: —

$$(H_2,H_2,H_2 \equiv N_2 = [Cu_2]) = Cl_2, \qquad (H_2,H_2,(NH_4)_2 \equiv N_2 = [Cu_2]) = I_2,$$
$$(H_2,H_2,H_2 \equiv N_2 = Cu) = Cl_2, \qquad (H_2,H_2,(NH_4)_2 \equiv N_2 = Cu) = SO_4 . H_2O.$$

266. *Characteristic Reactions.* — The presence of copper in a solution may be readily detected, not only by ammonia as indicated above, but also by the action of polished iron (a needle, for example), which, in a feebly acid solution, soon becomes covered with a red metallic coating. Copper ores, when mixed with fluxes, are readily reduced on charcoal before the blowpipe, and this is one of the best means of recognizing such compounds.

267. *Uses.* — Besides the numerous uses of the metal itself, copper is employed in the arts still more extensively when alloyed with other metals. The varieties of brass and yellow metal are alloys of copper and zinc in different proportions,

while bronze, bell-metal, gun-metal, and speculum-metal are all essentially alloys of copper and tin.   Several of the compounds of copper are much used as paints.

268. MERCURY. $Hg = 200.$ — Dyad.   This element is not widely disseminated, but its ores are abundant in a few localities, of which the most noted are Idria in Austria, Almaden in Spain, New Almaden in California, and Huancavelica in Peru. The ores at all these localities consist chiefly of Cinnabar, HgS, but they frequently contain a small quantity of the metal in the native state.   They are easily smelted, the sulphur of the ore serving as fuel.   The assorted ores are arranged in layers in kilns of peculiar construction, and the mass kindled with brush-wood.   As the sulphur burns away, the mercury is volatilized, and the products thus formed are passed through earthen pipes ("aludels") or brick chambers, which condense the mercury vapor, while the SO_2 gas escapes into the atmosphere.

$$HgS + O=O = Hg + SO_2. \qquad [301]$$

In the Palatinate, mercury is obtained from cinnabar by mixing the ore with slaked lime and distilling in iron retorts.

$$4HgS + 4CaO = 3CaS + CaSO_4 + Hg. \qquad [302]$$

269. *Metallic Mercury. Hg.* — The only metal liquid at ordinary temperatures.   Freezes at —40°.   Boils at 350° and evaporates, but only with exceeding slowness at the ordinary temperature.   *Sp. Gr.* of liquid, 13.596.   Sp. Gr. of vapor by experiment, 100.7.   Has a brilliant metallic lustre, silver-white color.   In solid condition is malleable, crystallizes in octahedrons, *Sp. Gr.* 14.4.   In contact with the air pure mercury undergoes no change at the ordinary temperature, but if boiled in the atmosphere, it is slowly converted into HgO.   Hydrochloric acid is without action on the metal, and the same is true of dilute sulphuric acid.   Strong sulphuric acid, however, is decomposed by it [265].   The best solvent is nitric acid, which yields different products according to the proportions of metal, acid, and water used.   Chlorine, Bromine, Iodine, and Sulphur all enter into direct union with mercury.   By simple trituration the liquid metal admits of being mechanically mixed in a state of minute subdivision with chalk and with saccharine or oleaginous sub-

stances, and many important pharmaceutical preparations are made in this way, — blue-pills, mercurial ointments, etc.

270. *Oxides of Mercury.* — Mercurous Oxide, $[Hg_2]O$. Black powder, very unstable. Decomposed by exposure to light or to a very gentle heat. $[Hg_2]O = HgO + Hg$. Mercuric oxide, HgO. Red crystalline scales or yellow powder, according to mode of preparation. Stable compound, but decomposed at red heat into mercury and oxygen [228]. No corresponding hydrates are known, but both oxides form stable salts.

271. *Nitrates.* — Mercurous nitrate is obtained by dissolving metallic mercury in an excess of nitric acid diluted with four or five times its bulk of water. Mercuric nitrate is best obtained by dissolving mercuric oxide in an excess of nitric acid. These, like other salts of mercury, tend to form basic compounds.

Mercurous Nitrate $\quad [Hg_2]=O_2=N_2O_4 . 2H_2O,$

Dimercurous Nitrate $\quad ([Hg_2]\text{-}O\text{-}[Hg_2])=O_2=N_2O_4,$

Trimercurous Dinitrate

$\qquad ([Hg_2]\text{-}O\text{-}[Hg_2]\text{-}O\text{-}[Hg_2])=O_2=(N_2O_4\text{-}O\text{-}N_2O_4) . 3H_2O,$

Mercuric Nitrate $\quad Hg=O_2=N_2O_4 . 2H_2O,$

Dimercuric Nitrate $\quad (Hg\text{-}O\text{-}Hg)=O_2=N_2O_4 . 2H_2O,$

Trimercuric Nitrate $\quad (Hg\text{-}O\text{-}Hg\text{-}O\text{-}Hg)=O_2=N_2O_4 . H_2O.$

A solution of mercurous nitrate with caustic soda gives a black precipitate of mercurous oxide.

$$([Hg_2]=O_2=N_2O_4 + 2Na\text{-}O\text{-}H + Aq) =$$
$$[Hg_2]O + (2Na\text{-}O\text{-}NO_2 + H_2O + Aq). \quad [303]$$

A solution of mercuric nitrate with caustic soda gives a yellow precipitate of mercuric oxide.

$$(Hg=O_2=N_2O_4 + 2Na\text{-}O\text{-}H + Aq) =$$
$$HgO + (2Na\text{-}O\text{-}NO_2 + H_2O + Aq). \quad [304]$$

Mercurous nitrate, if heated, is converted into the red crystalline variety of mercuric oxide.

$$[Hg_2]=O_2=N_2O_4 = 2HgO + 2NO_2. \qquad [305]$$

272. *Sulphates.* — When mercury is gently heated with an excess of strong sulphuric acid, Mercurous Sulphate, $[Hg_2]=O_2=SO_2$

is formed; but if the heat be increased, and the evaporation carried to dryness, the first product is changed into Mercuric Sulphate, $Hg=O_2=SO_2$, which is a white crystalline powder, readily dissolving in a solution of common salt, but decomposed by pure water into a soluble acid and an insoluble basic salt. The last is known as turpeth-mineral. It has a yellow color, and its composition is expressed by the symbol,

$$(Hg\text{-}O\text{-}Hg\text{-}O\text{-}Hg)=O_2=SO_2.$$

Mercurous sulphate is also prepared for the manufacture of calomel by triturating together mercuric sulphate with a quantity of mercury equal to that which it already contains.

273. *Sulphides.* — Mercurous Sulphide, $[Hg_2]S$, obtained as a black precipitate on passing H_2S gas through the solution of a mercurous salt. Very unstable, like the corresponding oxide. Mercuric Sulphide (Vermilion, Cinnabar), HgS, is precipitated by the same reagent from the solution of a mercuric salt. This precipitate is also black, but when sublimed the substance acquires the peculiar vermilion tint. Vermilion is usually prepared by rubbing together mercury and sulphur, and subliming the black product. Crystals are frequently thus obtained identical in form with those of natural cinnabar (76).

274. *Chlorides.* — Mercurous Chloride, $[Hg_2]Cl_2$, may be obtained either as a white powder or in crystals (75), — 1st. By subliming a mixture of mercuric chloride and mercury,

$$HgCl_2 + Hg = [Hg_2]Cl_2. \qquad [306]$$

2d. By subliming a mixture of mercurous sulphate and common salt,

$$[Hg_2]SO_4 + 2NaCl = Na_2SO_4 + [Hg_2]Cl_2. \quad [307]$$

3d. By precipitation from a solution of mercurous nitrate,

$$([Hg_2]N_2O_6 + 2NaCl + Aq) =$$
$$[Hg_2]Cl_2 + (2NaNO_3 + Aq). \ [308]$$

Calomel is insoluble in water, alcohol, and ether. The Sp. Gr. of its vapor is only one half of that which the theory would require, — an anomaly which is explained as an effect of disassociation. Sublimes below a red heat without melting. When triturated with a solution of soda or potash, it is turned black, owing to the formation of (Hg_2) O, and when heated with alkaline chlorides it is converted into $Hg Cl_2$. In the presence of organic matter, acids, and air, this last change may take place, to some extent at least, at a temperature of 38° or 40°. Calomel is an invaluable medicine. It was first prepared by rubbing together in a mortar $Hg + Hg Cl_2$, but this product, although having all the medicinal properties of the white sublimate, had a brilliant black color, whence the name, from καλὸς μέλας.

275. *Mercuric Chloride* (*Corrosive Sublimate*). $Hg Cl_2$. — Crystalline (77) white solid, melting at 265°, boiling at 293°, and yielding a vapor whose Sp. Gr. (141.5) conforms very nearly to the theory. Soluble in water, alcohol, and ether. Forms salts with the alkaline chlorides as $2 Na Cl . Hg Cl_2$. May be prepared by subliming a mixture of mercuric sulphate and common salt, but adding a small amount of $Mn O_2$ to the mixture to prevent the formation of calomel. Also found when mercury is burnt in chlorine gas. Coagulates albumen, and forms with it, as well as with other albuminoid substances, stable compounds insoluble in water. Acts as a violent poison. Used for preserving from decay wood, dried plants, and other objects of natural history, and this effect appears to be due in part to its peculiar action on albuminoid compounds. It is also a valuable reagent, and is used to prepare other anhydrous chlorides.

Mercury forms, like copper, a large number of oxichlorides. It also combines with the other members of the chlorine group of elements. Among these compounds the most interesting is the iodide, $Hg I_2$, which affects two different crystalline forms distinguished also by striking differences of color. As obtained by precipitation

$$(Hg Cl_2 + 2 KI + Aq) = Hg I_2 + (2 KCl + Aq), \quad [309]$$

it appears as a crystalline red powder (75). This when heated changes its crystalline condition (77) and becomes yellow, but the yellow variety is changed back to the red by mere friction.

276. *Ammoniated Compounds.* — The compounds of mer-

cury, when acted on by ammonia or its salts, yield a large number of complex products. Among these the most remarkable
is a powerful base called Mercuramine, which is formed by the
action of aqua ammonia upon yellow precipitated oxide of mercury. There is a difference of opinion in regard to the arrangement of the atoms in this compound, but the most probable
symbol is $(\overset{\text{\tiny II}}{Hg},(HgO\overset{\text{\tiny I}}{H}),H{\equiv}N){\text -}O{\text -}H\,.\,H_2O$. The hydrate absorbs CO_2 from the air, and forms definite salts with all the
common acids. This compound is unstable, but when heated,
two molecules of the hydrate give up three molecules of water,
and there is left a dark brown product permanent in the air,
whose symbol may be represented after the type $[H_4N]_2O$.
The following are the symbols of a few only of the many mercurial compounds of this class: —

$H_2,H_2{\equiv}N_2{=}[Hg_2]$, formed by the action of ammonia gas on precipitated calomel.

$H_2[Hg_2]{\equiv}N_2{=}[Hg_2]$, black compound, formed from calomel by
action of aqua ammonia.

$(H_2,H_2,Hg{\equiv}N_2{=}Hg){=}Cl_2$, "White Precipitate," formed by adding
to aqua ammonia a solution of $HgCl_2$.

$(H_2,H_2,H_2{\equiv}N_2{=}Hg){=}Cl_2$, "Soluble White Precipitate."

277. *Characteristic Reactions and Uses.* — The salts of mercury, whether soluble or insoluble, are all reduced to the metallic state by a solution of stannous chloride. Any of the salts
heated in a closed tube with sodic carbonate give a sublimate of
minute globules of mercury. From solutions of its salts mercury is deposited as a gray film on metallic copper, and if short
lengths of copper wire thus coated and carefully dried be heated
in a closed tube, the sublimate is obtained as before.

The chief consumption of metallic mercury is in the treatment of gold ores. It is also used for silvering mirrors, for
making various philosophical instruments, and for other purposes in the arts. Large quantities are consumed in preparing its various compounds, and these are among the most important articles of the materia medica.

Questions and Problems.

1. Write the reaction of boiling sulphuric acid on copper.

2. Write the reaction of nitric acid on copper, — 1st, assuming that NO is the aeriform product; 2d, that it is N_2O.

3. Write the reaction which takes place when cupric nitrate is decomposed by heat.

4. Why does not concentrated nitric acid act on copper?

5. Represent the constitution of the hydrate $4[Cu_2]O \cdot H_2O$ in the typical form. How may it be regarded as related to the normal hydrate $[Cu_2]\!\!=\!\!Ho_2$?   Ans. It equals $4[Cu_2]\!\!=\!\!Ho_2 - 3H_2O$.

6. How may anhydrous cupric sulphate be used to detect the presence of moisture?

7. In what other way may the symbols of the different basic sulphates be written?
   Ans. The symbol of Brochantite may be written $(Cu\text{-}O\text{-}Cu\text{-}O\text{-}Cu\text{-}O\text{-}Cu)\!\!=\!\!O_2\!\!=\!\!SO_2 \cdot 3H_2O$, and the others in a similar way.

8. How may the symbols of the basic sulphates be derived from the hydrates?
   Ans. Disregarding the water of crystallization, we may regard Brochantite as formed from the condensed hydrate $4Cu\!\!=\!\!O_2\!\!=\!\!H_2$ by first eliminating $3H_2O$ and then replacing the remaining H_2 by SO_2.

9. If the symbol of Brochantite is written as in the text, to what order of sulphates does it belong?   Ans. Orthosulphates.

10. Show by graphic symbols that the radical CuO_2H must be a monad.

11. Represent by graphic symbols the composition of Malachite and Azurite.

12. Both Malachite and Azurite may be regarded as formed by the molecular union of cupric hydrate and cupric carbonate. Write the symbols on this theory.

13. Malachite is how related to cupric hydrate?
   Ans. It may be regarded as the hydrate doubly condensed with two of the hydrogen atoms replaced by CO thus, $Cu_2\!\!=\!\!O_4\!\!=\!\!CO, H_2$ or $Cu\!\!=\!\!O_2\!\!=\!\!CO \cdot Cu\!\!=\!\!O_2\!\!=\!\!H_2$. Symbol of Azurite in the same way becomes $Cu_3\!\!=\!\!O_6\!\!=\!\!(CO)_2, H_2$ or $2Cu\!\!=\!\!O_2\!\!=\!\!CO \cdot Cu\!\!=\!\!O_2\!\!=\!\!H_2$.

14. To what order of carbonates does Mysorin belong?

15   V

15. In what other ways may the symbol of the cupric nitrates be written?

Ans. $Cu_=O_2=(NO_2)_2$ and $Cu_2^=O_4^\equiv NO_2,H_3$, or $Cu_=O_2=(NO_2),H$. $Cu_=O_2=H_2$.

16. Write the symbol of dioptase in the same typical form.

Ans. $H_2,Cu\equiv O_4^\equiv Si$.

17. To what order of silicates may dioptase be referred?

Ans. Orthosilicates.

18. Write the reaction of solution of sodic phosphate on solution of cupric sulphate.

19. Represent the constitution of the various sulphides of copper by graphic symbols.

20. In what relation does the fluohydrate of copper stand to the hydrate and fluoride of the same metal?

Ans. It holds an intermediate position, as shown by the symbols $Cu_=Ho_2$, $Cu_=Ho,Fl$, $CuFl_2$.

21. Regarding the molecule of water in the common variety of Atacamite as water of constitution, how may the formula of this mineral be simplified?

Ans. It may be halved and written $(Cu\text{-}O\text{-}Cu)_=Ho, Cl$.

22. How is Atacamite related to cupric hydrate?

Ans. $2Cu_=Ho_2 = (Cu\text{-}O\text{-}Cu)_=Ho_2 + H_2O$, then replacing one atom of Ho in basic hydrate by Cl.

23. What do you find that is remarkable in the reaction of cupric hydride on hydrochloric acid? Compare it with reaction [236], and consider whether it indicates a difference of condition in hydrogen similar to that in oxygen.

24. Write the symbols of the ammonia compounds of copper in the vertical form.

25. What evidence can you find that a portion of the nitrogen atoms in two of the compounds stand in a different relation to the molecule from the others?

Ans. If the nitrogen atoms were all typical, we should expect the basic radicals to fix more than the equivalent of two univalent acid radicals.

26. Write the symbols of the hydrates which correspond to the different basic nitrates of mercury, and show how such basic hydrates may be derived from the assumed normal hydrates.

27. How is it possible that salts should exist corresponding to hydrates that cannot be isolated?

28. Show how turpeth-mineral may be derived from an assumed normal hydrate.

29. How would you seek to determine whether the black product obtained by grinding together $Hg + S$ is a mixture or a compound?

30. By experiment it appears that the specific gravity of calomel vapor is 118.5. What should it be theoretically? Into what is it probably decomposed when heated? Ans. 235.5; Hg and $HgCl_2$.

31. In administering calomel as medicine, what associations with other drugs should be avoided?

32. How may calomel be distinguished from corrosive sublimate?

33. What is the theoretical Sp. Gr. of $HgCl_2$, and why should you anticipate so great a difference between it and the experimental result?

Ans. 135.5. In such a dense vapor the deviation from Mariotte's law would probably be large.

34. Write the reaction which takes place when a mixture of mercuric sulphate and common salt are sublimed.

35. In cases of poisoning by corrosive sublimate, why should milk or the white of eggs be useful as temporary antidotes until the stomach can be emptied by an emetic or otherwise?

36. Write the symbols of the chloride, nitrate, sulphate, and carbonate of mercuramine.

37. Write the symbol of the oxide of mercuramine described above.

38. Represent the different ammoniated compounds of mercury by vertical symbols, and point out the type of each.

Division V.

278. CALCIUM. $Ca = 40.$ — Dyad. One of the most abundant and important constituents of the crust of the globe. The elementary substance is a soft, malleable metal, with a reddish tinge of color. Readily tarnishes in the air, and burns when heated, forming lime. Decomposes water at all temperatures, forming calcic hydrate.

$$2\mathbf{Ca} + \text{⊙-⊙} = 2\mathbf{CaO}.$$

$$Ca + 2H_2O = 2\,Ca\text{=}Ho_2 + \text{Ħ-Ħ}.$$

[310]

The metal is obtained with difficulty either by the electrolysis of the melted chloride or by decomposing the iodide with sodium.

279. *Calcic Carbonate.* $Ca\text{=}O_2\text{=}CO$ or $Cao\text{=}CO.$ — The chief lime mineral. Remarkable for the great variety of its crystalline forms. Dimorphous (Hexagonal and Orthorhombic). The hexagonal forms (Figs. 14, 16, 17, 40, 41, and 42) belong to the mineral species Calcite. The orthorhombic forms (74) to the species Aragonite. *Sp. Gr.* of Calcite 2.72, of Aragonite 2.94. The last is also distinguished from the first by superior hardness, and falling to powder when heated. The crystalline varieties of calcite are readily recognized by a very striking rhombohedral cleavage. Limestones, Oolite, Chalk, Marble, Travertine, Tufa, Calcareous Marl, are names of varieties of rocks, which consist chiefly or wholly of one or the other of these two minerals, generally of calcite. Many of these rocks make excellent building stones. All the varieties of calcic carbonate dissolve with effervescence in dilute nitric and other acids, and may thus be distinguished from the siliceous minerals which they sometimes outwardly resemble. Calcic carbonate, although nearly insoluble in pure water, is readily dissolved by water charged with CO_2. Thus it is held in solution by the water of lime districts, and to a greater or less extent by most spring water. Such water, when strongly charged, deposits calcic carbonate on exposure to the air, and thus are formed stalactites, tufa, and travertine. It also forms deposits in boilers, and decomposes the soap used in washing. (Hard water.) Calcic carbonate may be readily formed artificially by the reaction

$$(CaCl_2 + (NH_4)_2{=}CO_3 + Aq) =$$
$$Ca{=}CO_3 + (2(NH_4)Cl + Aq). \quad [311]$$

Singularly, however, if the products of the reaction are boiled together, the reverse change takes place; calcic chloride is formed, which dissolves, while ammonic carbonate is carried away with the steam.

280. *Calcic Oxide* (*Quick-lime*). *CaO.* — Obtained by burning limestone in kilns.

$$\mathbf{Ca{-}CO_3 = CaO + CO_2.} \quad [312]$$

Amorphous white solid. Very infusible, and emitting an intense white light when ignited (Drummond Light). Has strong affinity for water, and the chemical union is attended with the evolution of much heat (slaking). Exposed to the air, it gradually absorbs both water and carbonic anhydride (air slaking).

281. *Calcic Hydrate.* $Ca{=}Ho_2$. A light dry powder. Soluble in about 425 parts of cold water (lime-water). With a smaller quantity of water it forms a sort of emulsion called milk of lime, and with still less water it gives a somewhat plastic paste, which, mixed with sand, is ordinary mortar. Hydraulic cements, which harden under water, are made from limestones containing from fifteen to thirty-five per cent of finely divided silica or clay; also by intimately mixing with chalk a due proportion of clay under regulated conditions, and subsequently burning. Calcic hydrate acts on the skin like a caustic alkali, and is used by the tanners for removing hair from hides. It has a strong affinity for CO_2, and hence is used for rendering soda and potash caustic [97]. It is also employed for purifying coal-gas, and in many other processes of the arts. It is largely used as a manure. Whitewash is milk of lime mixed with a little glue.

282. *Chloride of Lime or Bleaching Powder,* $CaOCl_2$, is formed by passing chlorine gas into leaden chambers containing slaked lime, which absorbs the gas very rapidly.

$$CaO + Cl{-}Cl = (Ca{-}O){=}Cl_2. \quad [313]$$

Very much used in the arts for bleaching cotton goods. The cloth having been well washed and digested in a weak solution of chloride of lime, is passed into very dilute sulphuric acid, which liberates the chlorine in the fibre of the cloth. May also be used in the laboratory as a source of chlorine gas.

$$(CaOCl_2 + H_2SO_4 + Aq) =$$
$$(CaSO_4 + H_2O + Aq) + \text{Cl-Cl}. \quad [314]$$

283. *Calcic Peroxide.* $(Ca\text{-}O)\text{=}O.$ — Formed by adding H_2O_2 to lime-water, but is a very unstable compound.

284. *Calcic Sulphate.* $Ca\text{=}O_2\text{=}SO_2.$ — Second in importance of the lime minerals. It occurs in nature both in an anhydrous and hydrous form. The anhydrous mineral is called Anhydrite, the hydrous mineral is Gypsum. Anhydrite crystallizes in the orthorhombic system (77), and has *Sp. Gr.* $= 2.9$. Gypsum $(CaSO_4 . 2H_2O)$ crystallizes in the monoclinic system (Fig. 25), has *Sp. Gr.* $= 2.3$, and is softer than the first. Calcic sulphate is soluble in about 400 parts of water, and, like several of the lime salts, is much less soluble in hot water than in cold; and when water holding gypsum in solution is heated to a high tem-perature in steam-boilers, the whole is deposited in an insoluble condition $(CaSO_4 . \frac{1}{2}H_2O)$. It is a very common impurity of spring waters, and is another cause of their hardness, and of the crusts which they sometimes form on the inner surface of boilers. It is found in considerable quantity in the water of salt springs, and of the ocean. When these waters are evap-orated it is deposited before the common salt. Hence in nature we find that beds of rock-salt are usually associated with anhy-drite and gypsum. The last is by far the most abundant min-eral, forming in some places extensive rock deposits of great thickness. It is, moreover, found in beautifully transparent crystals (Selenite), which can be easily split into very thin plates, and it also forms the ornamental stone called alabaster. When heated, gypsum readily gives up its water of crystalliza-tion, and when not overburnt the dry product, if reduced to powder and made into a paste, again unites with water and sets into a hard mass. This reunion, however, will not take place if the gypsum has been heated above 300°; and anhydrite is then formed. The calcined gypsum, called Plaster of Paris, is used in immense quantities for making casts, and in various forms of stucco-work. Ground gypsum is also a valuable ma-nure, and finds other applications in the arts.

285. *Calcic Phosphate.* $Cao_3(PO)_2$. — The chief earthy constituent of the bones of animals. The animal obtains it from the plants, and the plant draws its supply from the soil. The grains of the cereals are especially rich in this bone-making material, and as the supply in the soil is usually limited, these plants, when cultivated year after year, soon exhaust it. Hence it is all important for the agriculturist to restore to his land the phosphates as fast as they are removed by the crops, and ground bones, guano, phosphorite, and other forms of calcic phosphate, are used for this purpose. The mineral Apatite is a crystalline variety (Fig. 14) of this same material, but contains also about eight per cent of calcic fluoride mixed with more or less calcic chloride. Its symbol may be written (Ca_5F) ix O_9 ix $(PO)_3$.

286. *Calcic Silicate* (*Tabular Spar*), $Cao=Si O$, is a not uncommon mineral. Formed on the surface of the grains of sand when mortar hardens; and the valuable qualities of hydraulic cements are probably due to a still more complete union of the same kind. An artificial stone of great strength may be made by first mixing together solutions of calcic chloride and sodic silicate, and then incorporating with the half-fluid mass a large proportion of sand.

287. *Calcic Fluoride* (*Fluor-Spar*). CaF_2. — An abundant mineral and the most important compound of fluorine. It is found both massive and crystallized in the forms of the isometric system, generally in cubes. Has octohedral cleavage. The pure material is colorless, but the native crystals are frequently beautifully colored, and are among the most splendid specimens of our mineral cabinets. Exposed to the light, they frequently exhibit a remarkable fluorescence, and many varieties of the mineral phosphoresce when heated. Although not very fusible by itself, fluor-spar forms a very fusible slag with gypsum and other earthy minerals frequently associated with lead ores. This property renders it a valuable *flux* in the process of smelting such ores, and hence the name fluor. In small quantities it is almost invariably associated with calcic phosphate, not only in the mineral kingdom, but also in the bones and teeth of animals.

288. *Calcic Chloride.* $Ca Cl_2$. — A deliquescent salt, readily obtained by dissolving calcic carbonate in hydrochloric acid. Also a secondary product in the preparation of ammonia [162].

$$CaCO_3 + (2HCl + Aq) =$$
$$(CaCl_2 + H_2O + Aq) + CO_2. \quad [315]$$

A useful reagent, and also employed, on account of its hygro-scopic qualities, for drying gases.

289. *Calcic Nitrate.* $Cao=(NO_2)_2$. — Also a very soluble deliquescent salt, which is formed in the soil, in cellars, in lime caverns, and wherever organic matter decays in contact with calcareous materials. Chiefly important as a source of saltpetre.

290. STRONTIUM, $Sr = 87.6$, and BARIUM, $Ba = 137$. — Dyads. The compounds of these elements are closely allied to the corresponding compounds of calcium, and the differences are only those which we should expect between members of the same chemical series. They are, however, far less abundantly distributed in nature. The most important native compounds are

Strontic Carbonate,	Strontianite,	$SrCO_3$,	Sp. Gr. 3.70.
Baric Carbonate,	Witherite,	$BaCO_3$,	Sp. Gr. 4.32.

These are isomorphous with Aragonite. No hexagonal forms corresponding to calcite are known. In like manner we have

Strontic Sulphate,	Celestine,	$SrSO_4$,	Sp. Gr. 3.95.
Baric Sulphate,	Heavy Spar,	$BaSO_4$,	Sp. Gr. 4.48.

These are isomorphous with anhydrite. No hydrous minerals corresponding to gypsum are known. Strontic sulphate is much less soluble in water than calcic sulphate, and baric sulphate is practically insoluble. Moreover, the solubility of these salts is not increased by the presence of weak acids. Hence a solution of calcic sulphate will give a precipitate in solutions containing either strontium or barium, and a solution of strontic sulphate only in the last. The sulphates are both easily prepared artifi-cially from solutions of corresponding chlorides by precipitation with sulphuric acid.

291. The *Strontic and Baric Nitrates* and the *Strontic and Baric Chlorides* are all soluble salts, but less soluble than the corresponding salts of calcium, the barium compounds being in each case the less soluble of the two. They are easily prepared by dissolving the native carbonates in dilute nitric or hydro-

chloric acids. Baric nitrate is precipitated from its aqueous
solution by strong nitric or hydrochloric acid in consequence of
its sparing solubility in these reagents. They may also be prepared from the native sulphates, as is illustrated by the following reactions : —

$$SrSO_4 + 4O = SrS + 4\textcircled{C}\textcircled{O}.$$

$$(SrS + 2HCl + Aq) = (SrCl_2 + Aq) + H_2S.$$ [316]

An intimate mixture of the powdered sulphate with some carbonaceous material is first intensely heated in a crucible. The
resulting product is then exhausted with water, and the solution
treated with hydrochloric or nitric acid as required.

292. *Strontic and Baric Hydrates* may also be prepared
from the solution of the sulphides, obtained as above, by the
reaction

$$CuO + (BaS + H_2O + Aq) =$$
$$CuS + (Ba=Ho_2 + Aq).$$ [317]

The relative solubility of the hydrates follows the inverse order
of that of the other salts, baric hydrate being much the most soluble and dissolving in twenty parts of water.

293. *Strontic and Baric Oxides* may be readily obtained by
igniting the nitrates. They slake when mixed with water, like
quick-lime.

294. *Strontic and Baric Peroxides* are prepared by heating
the oxides in an atmosphere of oxygen gas. They are more
stable than calcic peroxide, and baric peroxide is an important
reagent.

295. *Characteristic Reactions.* — Calcium, strontium, and
barium are all precipitated from their solutions by alkaline carbonates and by oxalic acid. They may be distinguished from
each other by the relative solubility of their sulphates,[1] and by
the colors of their flames, which show characteristic bands with
the spectroscope. The compounds of strontium impart to a
colorless flame a brilliant crimson color, and those of barium a

[1] Calcic sulphate gives an instantaneous precipitate in solutions of barium
salts, while in those of strontium the precipitate only forms after a perceptible
interval of time.

15 *

yellowish green.   Hence they are much used by makers of fire-works.   The soluble salts of barium are important reagents in the laboratory, and both the native and the artificial sulphate furnish an important white paint.

296. LEAD. $Pb = 207$.   Bivalent or quadrivalent.   One of the more abundant metallic elements, found chiefly in mineral veins.   Principal ore is Galena, PbS.   There is also a native Plumbic Carbonate called Cerusite ($PbCO_3$, $Sp.$ $Gr.$ 6.48), isomorphous with Aragonite, and a native Plumbic Sulphate called Anglesite ($PbSO_4$, $Sp.$ $Gr.$ 6.30), isomorphous with an-hydrite.

297. *Metallic Lead. Pb?* — $Sp.$ $Gr.$ 11.36.   Melting-point, 325°.   So soft that it can be moulded by pressure.   Obtained, 1st. By alternately roasting and melting the galena in a rever-beratory furnace.

Roasting stage,

$$3PbS + 3O \cdot O = PbS + 2PbO + 2SO_2, \text{ or}$$
$$2PbS + 2O \cdot O = PbS + PbSO_4; \qquad [318]$$

Melting stage, $PbS + 2PbO = 3Pb + SO_2,$ or
$$PbS + PbSO_4 = 2Pb + 2SO_2. \qquad [319]$$

2d.   By smelting the galena with scrap-iron in a blast-furnace,

$$PbS + Fe = FeS + Pb. \qquad [320]$$

Practically, however, both processes are far more complex than the reactions would indicate.   The ore is in all cases mixed with gangue, which can only be melted with the aid of some flux, and the slags thus formed contain a large amount of metal and must be smelted again.

Lead dissolves readily in *dilute* nitric acid, but is not acted on, or only very slightly, by either hydrochloric or sulphuric acids, unless concentrated and boiling.   Employed in number-less ways in the arts, both pure and alloyed, with other metals. Type-metal, britannia-metal, and solder are among the most im-portant of its alloys.

298. *Plumbic Oxide. PbO.* — Obtained by heating lead in a current of air, when, if the heat is not too great, a yellow pow-der is obtained called Massicot.   At a heat a little below red-

ness the oxide melts and crystallizes on cooling in yellowish red scales called Litharge. Largely used in the arts for making flint-glass, for glazing earthenware, and for preparing various paints and lead salts.

299. *Plumbic Peroxide.* PbO_2. — A dark-brown powder, very useful in the laboratory as an oxidizing agent. The bright red powder called Minium, obtained by still further roasting massicot at a low red heat, is a mixture of PbO_2 and PbO. There is also a suboxide, Pb_2O.

300. *Plumbic Hydrate.* — The normal hydrate, $Pb\text{=}Ho_2$, has never been obtained, but we can readily form

Diplumbic Hydrate　　　　　$(Pb\text{-}O\text{-}Pb)\text{=}Ho_2$,

Triplumbic Hydrate　　　　　$(Pb\text{-}O\text{-}Pb\text{-}O\text{-}Pb)\text{=}Ho_2$,

by the following reactions : —

$$2Pb\text{=}(NO_3)_2 + (4K\text{-}Ho + Aq) =$$
$$(Pb\text{-}O\text{-}Pb)\text{=}Ho_2 + (4K\text{-}NO_3 + H_2O + Aq). \quad [321]$$

$$((Pb_3O_2)\text{=}(C_2H_3O_2)_2 + 2(NH_4)\text{-}Ho + Aq) =$$
$$(Pb_3O_2)\text{=}Ho_2 + (2(NH_4)\text{-}(C_2H_3O_2) + Aq). \quad [322]$$

A plumbic hydrate is formed by the simultaneous action of air and water on lead, which is slightly soluble; and as all lead salts are poisonous, and even in minute quantities, if the dose is often repeated, may be injurious to health, it is not safe to use, for drinking, water which has been kept in cisterns lined with lead or drawn through lead pipes. The presence of nitrites, nitrates, or chlorides greatly increases the corrosive action of water on lead, while carbonates and sulphates exert a preservative influence.

301. *Plumbic Nitrate.* $Pb\text{=}(NO_3)_2$. — Obtained by dissolving litharge or lead in dilute nitric acid. Soluble in water, but insoluble in strong nitric acid.

$$PbO + (2H\text{-}NO_3 + Aq) = (Pb\text{=}(NO_3)_2 + H_2O + Aq). \quad [323]$$

$$3Pb + (8H\text{-}NO_3 + Aq) =$$
$$(3Pb\text{=}(NO_3)_2 + 4H_2O + Aq) + 2NO. \quad [324]$$

302. *Plumbic Acetate (Sugar of Lead).* $Pb\text{=}(C_2H_3O_2)_2$.

$3H_2O.$ — The most important soluble salt of lead, easily obtained by dissolving PbO in acetic acid. Lead has a great tendency to form basic salts (38). Hence a solution of the neutral acetate will dissolve a large additional quantity of litharge.

$$2\mathbf{PbO} + (Pb^=(C_2H_3O_2)_2 + Aq) =$$
$$((Pb\text{-}O\text{-}Pb\text{-}O\text{-}Pb)^=(C_2H_3O_2)_2 + Aq). \quad [325]$$

If CO_2 is now passed through this solution, the excess of PbO is precipitated as carbonate. Fresh portions of PbO may then be dissolved and the process repeated. The plumbic carbonate, which is obtained by this and other analogous methods, is very much used as a white paint under the name of white lead. The products of the different processes have not, however, the same composition, but are mixtures of the carbonate and hydrate in varying proportions.

303. *Plumbic Sulphate*, $PbSO_4$, is obtained as a white precipitate on adding sulphuric acid or a soluble sulphate to a solution of a salt of lead. It is practically insoluble in pure water and dilute sulphuric acid.

304. *Plumbic Phosphate* is found in nature in the mineral Pyromorphite, which is isomorphous with apatite and has an analogous constitution $(Pb_5Cl)^{ix}O_9^{ix}(PO)_3$. The mineral Mimetine is the corresponding isomorphous arseniate. A melted globule of plumbic phosphate assumes on cooling a peculiar radiated crystalline structure, which is very characteristic.

305. *Plumbic Chloride*, $PbCl_2$, may be obtained as a white crystalline powder by the reactions

$$PbO + (2HCl + Aq) = PbCl_2 + (H_2O + Aq). \quad [326]$$
$$(Pb(NO_3)_2 + 2HCl + Aq) =$$
$$PbCl_2 + (2HNO_3 + Aq). \quad [327]$$

It is only very slightly soluble in cold water, but in boiling water dissolves quite readily.

306. *Plumbates.* — Caustic alkalies dissolve PbO very freely, forming salts in which the lead plays the part of a negative radical. Hence the precipitate formed in reaction [321] dissolves in an excess of the reagent, and a solution of PbO in lime-water is used as a hair-dye.

307. *Characteristic Reactions.* — The lead compounds, in many of their reactions, are closely allied to the compounds of the first three elements of this group. For example, the soluble salts give precipitates with the alkaline carbonates and with oxalic acid. But in other reactions there are marked differences. Thus, 1. A strip of metallic zinc placed in a solution of plumbic acetate precipitates all the lead.

$$Zn + (Pb\text{=}(C_2H_3O_2)_2 + Aq) =$$
$$Pb + (Zn\text{=}(C_2H_3O_2)_2 + Aq). \quad [328]$$

2. Sulphuretted hydrogen gas passed through either an acid or an alkaline solution of a salt of lead gives a black precipitate of plumbic sulphide.

$$(Pb\text{=}Cl_2 + H_2S + Aq) = PbS + (2HCl + Aq). \quad [329]$$

When the solution is acidified with hydrochloric acid, the precipitate is first red, owing to the formation of $(Pb\text{-}S\text{-}Pb)\text{=}Cl_2$, but this is soon converted into the black sulphide. 3. Heated on charcoal before the blow-pipe, with reducing fluxes, the compounds of lead yield a soft, malleable bead of metal, and the charcoal immediately around the bead is at the same time coated with an incrustation of oxide which is orange-colored while hot, but becomes lemon-yellow when cold. By these reactions lead is easily distinguished from calcium, strontium, and barium. Indeed, the distinction is so marked, that, although the resemblances are very striking, it may be doubted whether lead belongs to the same chemical series.

Reactions and Problems.

1. Calcite and Aragonite are both not unfrequently found in acicular crystals. How may they be distinguished ?

2. Compare the molecular volumes of Calcite and Aragonite.

3. By igniting 100 parts of pure calcic carbonate, Dumas obtained exactly 56 parts of lime. What is the atomic weight of calcium ?

Ans. 40.

4. What assumptions are made in the last problem ? (19.)

5. How much CaO can be obtained from 100 kilogrammes of pure limestone?   How much $Ca=Ho_2$ will this amount yield?

Ans. 56 kilos. and 74 kilos.

6. How much limestone must be burnt to yield 560 kilos. of quick-lime?   How many cubic metres of CO_2 would be set free in the process?   Ans. 1,000 kilos. and 223.1 $\overline{m}^3$

7. In one cubic metre of limestone assumed to be pure calcic carbonate, $Sp.$ $Gr.$ 2.72, how many cubic metres of CO_2 are condensed?

Ans. 607.1 $\overline{m}^3$

8. What is the cause of the incrustation of boilers by calcic carbonate?

9. Lime-water is used to purify hard water.   Explain the reaction.

10. A bed of limestone, $Sp.$ $Gr.$ $=$ 2.75, and 100 metres thick, would make a bed of anthracite coal of what thickness?   Assume that the $Sp.$ $Gr.$ of anthracite is 1.8, and that it contains 90 per cent of carbon.   Ans. 20.37 metres.

11. In order to precipitate lime as completely as possible with ammonic carbonate, it is important to avoid an excess of ammonia salts, and to warm the liquid, but not to boil it.   Give the reasons for these precautions.   Also analyze reactions [311 and the reverse], and state the principle under which they may be brought.

12. One cubic decimetre of quick-lime, $Sp.$ $Gr.$ 3.18, will absorb how many cubic decimetres of water?   How many units of heat will be evolved by the change of state which the water undergoes?

Ans. 1.022 $\overline{d. m.}^3$

13. In burning quick-lime it is found that the process succeeds best in damp weather, and is facilitated by injecting steam into the kiln.   Why should you infer that this would be the case?   (58.)

14. Give an explanation of the hardening and adhesion of mortars and cements.

15. When milk of lime is spread over walls in the process of white-washing, what compound is formed on the surface?

16. How many cubic metres of CO_2 can be absorbed by a quantity of milk of lime, containing 112 kilos. of lime (CaO)?

17. When lime-water is shaken up with CO_2 it is rendered turbid. How do you explain the reaction, and to what application of lime-water in the laboratory does it point?

18. In order to render 100 kilos. of sal soda caustic how much quick-lime must be used?   [97.]   Ans. 52.83 kilos.

19. How many litres of chlorine gas would be absorbed by 100

kilos. of lime (CaO) first reduced to hydrate, and how much MnO_2 must be used to yield the requisite amount?

Ans. in part, 39.85 litres of chlorine.

20. Bleaching salts have been regarded as a mixture of calcic chloride with calcic hypochlorite. How would you write the symbol on this theory?

21. Represent by graphic symbols $CaCO_3$, CaO_2, $CaOCl_2$.

22. The percentage composition of gypsum is calcium, 23.26; sulphur, 18.61; oxygen, 37.21; water, 20.92. Calculate the symbol.

23. Is the incrustation of steam-boilers by insoluble calcic sulphate due to the same cause as the incrustation of salt-pans by gypsum? Explain the difference.

24. If the calcium contained in one cubic decimetre of anhydrite could be replaced by H_2, what would be the volume of the product formed?

25. If a concentrated solution of sodic sulphate is mixed with a concentrated solution of calcic chloride, the whole mass becomes solid. Write the reaction, and explain what becomes of the water of solution.

Ans. $(Na_2SO_4 + CaCl_2 + 2H_2O) = 2NaCl + CaSO_4 . 2H_2O.$

26. How could you detect the presence of sulphuric acid and lime in a solution of gypsum? Write the reactions

27. Represent the constitution of apatite by a graphic symbol.

28. How may you regard apatite as derived from calcic hydrate? What important part does fluorine play in the compound? Does not the presence of such a univalent element in this compound furnish an argument in favor of the diatomicity of calcium?

29. How much hydrochloric acid, $Sp. Gr.$ 1.1, will be required to dissolve 50 grammes of chalk, and how many litres of CO_2 could be thus obtained?

Ans. 179 grammes of acid and 11.16 litres of CO_2.

30. By what single reaction could you change a solution of calcic nitrate into a solution of nitre?

31. What evidence do you find in this section that calcium is bivalent?

32. Compare the molecular volumes of the native carbonates of strontium, barium, and lead with those of Aragonite and Calcite.

33. Write the reactions by which strontic and baric sulphates may be prepared from the corresponding nitrates or chlorides.

34. Analyze the reactions by which the chlorides and nitrates of

strontium and barium may be prepared from the corresponding sulphates, and show why such a circuitous method is necessary.

35. Compare the molecular volume of the sulphates of this group with that of the corresponding carbonates.

36. How may solutions of calcic and strontic sulphates be used to detect barium and strontium, even if mixed together in the same solution?

37. Knowing that sulphuric acid if in excess will completely precipitate barium and strontium, how can you detect the presence of lime in a solution containing all three?

38. On what does the use of the salts of barium as tests for sulphuric acid depend?

39. To how much SO_3 do 0.932 grammes of baric sulphate correspond? Ans. 0.320 grammes.

40. A quantity of Witherite weighing 0.591 grammes was dissolved in hydrochloric acid and precipitated with sulphuric acid. The precipitate when washed, dried, and ignited weighed 0.699 grammes. What per cent of barium does the mineral contain?
Ans. 69.37 per cent.

41. Baric and strontic carbonates are not, like calcic carbonates, easily decomposed when heated in the air, but readily give off CO_2 if heated in an atmosphere of hydrogen. How do you explain these facts? and do they confirm or otherwise your answer to question 13?

42. What is the percentage of lead in the three minerals Anglesite, Cerusite, and Galena? Ans. 68.32, 77.54, 86.62.

43. Analyze reactions [318 – 320] and state the general theory of the smelting process, including the removal of the gangue and the reduction of the ore.

44. Explain the peculiar action of lead with acid solvents. Why must the nitric acid be diluted, and to what extent?

45. How many kilos. of litharge can be obtained from 37.1 kilos. of lead, and what volume of oxygen gas would be absorbed in the process? Ans. 39.96 kilos. and 2 $\overline{m.}^3$

46. Represent the plumbic oxides and hydrates by graphic symbols, and show how the basic hydrates are related to the assumed normal hydrate.

47. The action of nitric acid on lead depends on the degree of concentration and on the temperature. Write the reaction assuming that N_2O is formed.

48. How many kilos. of crystallized sugar of lead can be made from 6.69 kilos. of litharge? Ans. 11.37 kilos.

49. How much litharge will a solution containing 11.37 kilos. of sugar of lead dissolve, assuming that triplumbic acetate is the product formed ?   Ans. 13.17 kilos. PbO.

50. Write the reaction of CO_2 on a solution of basic acetate of lead.

51. How may the basic acetates be regarded as derived from the normal hydrates ?

52. Write the reaction of dilute sulphuric acid on a solution of plumbic nitrate.

53. Represent the constitution of pyromorphite and mimetene by graphic symbols.

54. What is the derivation of the name pyromorphite ?

55. Will the whole of the lead be precipitated from its solution in acetic acid by an excess of $HCl + Aq$?

56. By what reagent may you precipitate the whole of the lead from a solution of one of its salts ?

57. Why should a solution of PbO in lime-water blacken the hair or any other organic material containing sulphur ?

58. How could you detect the presence of lead in water ?

59. From a solution containing all the members of this group, how could you separate the whole of the lead ?

60. The solubility of the compounds of the elements of this group diminishes, as a general rule, in proportion as the atomic weight of the metallic radical increases. Does this fact conform to the law which generally obtains in chemical series in regard to the chemical energy of the different members ?

W

Divisions VI. and VII.

308. MAGNESIUM. *Mg* = 24. — Dyad. One of the most widely distributed elements, although not so abundant as Calcium, with which it is usually associated. In some of its relations it is very closely allied to calcium, but also differs from it in many important respects.

309. *Metallic Magnesium*, *Mg*, is readily obtained by decomposing the anhydrous chloride with metallic sodium, also by electrolysis. It is a silver-white metal, melting at a red heat, and volatilizing at a high temperature in an atmosphere of hydrogen. It is malleable and ductile, is susceptible of a high polish, and does not tarnish in dry air. Heated in the air it takes fire and burns with great splendor [59], and it is now much used as a source of pure white light when great brilliancy is required. Boiling water acts upon the metal quite rapidly, but it decomposes cold water only very slowly.

310. *Magnesic Oxide* (*Calcined Magnesia*), *Mg O*, is obtained when the metal is burnt in air. It can also be obtained by calcining the carbonate or the nitrate. It is a bulky white powder, wholly infusible, and emitting a bright white light when heated before the blow-pipe. Intensely heated, it appears to volatilize unchanged. When mixed with water it slowly unites with it to form a hydrate. The oxide obtained by calcining the nitrate is much denser than that made from the carbonate, and possesses remarkable hydraulic qualities. When mixed with water, it soon sets forming a hard compact mass resembling marble. If the oxide is heated to a very high temperature, it loses its power of uniting with water, and dissolves only slowly even in the strongest acids. Crystallized *Mg O* (Figs. 5 to 7), Periclase, has been found in small grains imbedded in a limestone rock ejected from Vesuvius, but otherwise it does not occur uncombined in nature.

311. *Magnesic Hydrate*, $Mg\text{=}O_2\text{=}H_2$, is found native, crystallized in large hexagonal plates (76), Brucite. It can be readily formed artificially as above, also by adding caustic potassa, soda, or baryta to the solution of any of its salts. It is but very slightly soluble in water, yet sufficiently to give a distinct alkaline reaction (39). It absorbs CO_2 slowly from the air, but much more slowly than calcic hydrate.

312. *Magnesic Carbonate.* $Mg\text{=}O_2\text{=}CO.$ *Sp. Gr.* 3.056. — The mineral Magnesite, isomorphous with Calcite. Insoluble in pure water, but in carbonic acid water more soluble than calcic carbonate. This solution is much used as a medicine (liquid magnesia). If exposed to the air, the magnesic carbonate slowly separates in crystalline flakes, containing three atoms of water. Anhydrous magnesic carbonate is not readily obtained artificially. The precipitate obtained on adding to a boiling solution of a magnesia salt sodic carbonate is a mixture of magnesic carbonate and magnesic hydrate in variable proportions (Magnesia Alba). The product, however, appears to be rather a mixture of several definite compounds of these two salts; and a crystalline mineral is known called Hydromagnesite, which has the formula $H_4Mg_4O_{12}C_3 . 2H_2O$ or

$$Ho_4\text{≡}(\overset{IV}{C}\text{=}Mgo_2\text{=} C\text{=}Mgo_2\text{=} C) . 2H_2O.$$

Magnesic carbonate is found united with calcic carbonate in the mineral Dolomite (*Sp. Gr.* 2.9). This is by far the most abundant native compound of magnesium, and forms in many localities extensive beds of rocks. It occurs in large and well-defined crystals which are isomorphous with calcite and magnesite (Fig. 16). The mineral is somewhat variable in its composition, and may either be regarded as an isomorphous mixture of these two substances, or else as a definite compound mixed with an excess of one or the other of its constituents.

$$MgCO_3 + CaCO_3 \quad \text{or} \quad Mgo\text{=}(C\text{=}O_2\text{=}C)\text{=}Cao.$$

When calcined at not too high a temperature, the magnesic carbonate is alone decomposed, and a product obtained which forms an excellent hydraulic cement. From the calcined mass the magnesia can be dissolved out by carbonic acid water and freed from the lime. In this way pure magnesic carbonate is prepared.

313. *Magnesic Sulphate (Epsom Salt).* $MgSO_4 . 7H_2O.$ — The most important soluble salt of magnesia. Obtained from the bittern of sea-water, or by treating the native carbonates or Dolomite with sulphuric acid. It is a very common ingredient of mineral waters, like those of Epsom, and is formed when water saturated with gypsum filters through Dolomitic rocks.

The salt, with seven molecules of water, is dimorphous, crystallizing both in orthorhombic forms isomorphous with $ZnSO_4$. $7HO$, and in monoclinic forms isomorphous with $FeSO_4 . 7HO$. It may also be obtained crystallized with 1, 2, 3, ... 12 molecules of water under regulated conditions, chiefly of temperature. The compound $MgSO_4 . H_2O$ (Kieserite) is found in the Stassfurt salt-beds. Epsom salt is reduced to the same composition when heated to 150°, but the last molecule of water is retained even at 200°, and this leads us to believe that it forms a part of the molecule of the salt, whose formula would then be written, $Mgo{=}SO{=}Ho_2$. This opinion is confirmed by finding that this molecule of water may be replaced by the molecule of an alkaline sulphate, forming a double salt, which crystallizes with $6H_2O$ in the same form as magnesic sulphate with $7H_2O$. The symbol of the potash salt is

$$Mgo{=}(SO{=}O_2{=}OS){=}Ko_2 . 6H_2O.$$

Epsom salt dissolves in about three times its weight of cold water. It is a valuable medicine, but, like all the soluble salts of magnesium, it has a bitter, disgusting taste.

314. *Magnesic Silicates.* — The well-known minerals, Serpentine, Talc (Soap-Stone), and Chrysolite (Olivine), are essentially magnesic silicates; and in many other native silicates, including the Hornblendes, Augites, Chlorites, and some varieties of Mica, magnesium is one of the principal basic radicals.

315. *Magnesic Chloride.* $MgCl_2$. — Found dissolved in seawater, and the cause of its bitter taste. Obtained by dissolving magnesic carbonate in hydrochloric acid, and evaporating in an atmosphere of hydrochloric acid gas. If evaporated in the air, the salt is partially decomposed. Very fusible. Used for making magnesium. Forms double salts with alkaline chlorides (134).

316. *Characteristic Reactions.* — Magnesium, although closely related to calcium, is distinguished from the alkaline earths by the great solubility of its sulphate, also by its tendency to form soluble double salts with ammonium, in consequence of which no precipitate is formed in solutions of its salts either by ammonia or ammonic carbonate, when sufficient excess of some ammonia salt is present. The ammonic magnesian phosphate, however, $(NH_4)_2.Mg_2{\equiv}O_6{\equiv}P_2O_2 . 12H_2O$ is insoluble, and is formed whenever sodic phosphate is added to an ammoniacal solution of a magnesium salt. This reaction furnishes the most delicate test for magnesium salts.

317. ZINC. $Zn = 65.2$. — Dyad. One of the more abundant metallic elements. The principal ores are

Red oxide of Zinc[1]	ZnO	Hexagonal,
Blende	ZnS	Isometric,
Smithsonite	$Zno = CO$	Hexagonal,
Calamine	$Zno_2 \bar{=} Si . 2H_2O$	Trimetric.

The ores are reduced by first roasting or calcining until the metal is in the condition of an oxide, and then distilling with a mixture of coal in earthen retorts or muffles.

318. *Metallic Zinc. Zn.* — *Sp. Gr.* 6.8 to 7.2. Fuses at 500°. Boils at a red heat. The polished surface has a bright lustre, with a bluish tint, but soon tarnishes in moist air. Has a crystalline structure, but, although brittle both at a high and a low temperature, it may readily be rolled out into sheets at a temperature of about 140°. Sheet-zinc is nearly as cheap as sheet-iron; and since it does not rust, or at most only very superficially, it is preferable for many purposes. Iron, however, is a much stronger metal, and is frequently coated with zinc to protect it from rusting. It is then said to be galvanized. Zinc readily dissolves in dilute acids with the evolution of hydrogen, and is much used in the laboratory, together with dilute sulphuric acid, for making this gas. The metal is first granulated by pouring it, when melted, into water. When boiled with a solution of caustic soda or potash, it also dissolves with evolution of hydrogen.

$$\mathbf{Zn} + (2Ko\text{-}H + Aq) = (Ko_2\text{=}Zn + Aq) + \boxed{H}\text{-}\boxed{H}. \quad [330]$$

It is used as the electro-positive metal in the galvanic battery.

319. *Zincic Oxide, ZnO*, which is made in large quantities by burning zinc vapor at the mouth of the reduction furnaces, is a very light white powder, much used, when mixed with oil, as a white paint. A denser oxide is obtained by calcining zincic nitrate.

320. *Zincic Hydrate, $Zn\text{=}Ho_2$,* is formed by the reaction

$$(ZnSO_4 + 2K\text{-}Ho + Aq) = Zn\text{-}Ho_2 + (K_2SO_4 + Aq), \quad [331]$$

but is soluble in an excess of reagent.

---

[1] The color is due to the presence of a small amount of manganese.

321. *Zincic Carbonate, $ZnCO_3$,* is isomorphous with magnesite and calcite. When prepared by precipitation, a mixture of hydrate and carbonate is formed, as in (312).

322. *Zincic Sulphate (White Vitriol). $ZnSO_4 . 7H_2O.$* —Very soluble salt, isomorphous with Epsom salt, which it closely resembles in most of its chemical relations, forming similar double salts. Preparation as in [64]. Used in pharmacy.

323. *Zincic Chloride. $ZnCl_2.$* — A solution of zinc in hydrochloric acid can be concentrated by evaporation without decomposition. All the water is not driven off until the temperature reaches 250°. The result is a thick syrup, which forms, on cooling, a white, deliquescent solid, melting at 100°, called by the alchemists Butter of Zinc. It has an intense affinity for water, and by its aid the elements of water may frequently be removed from a chemical compound without producing any further change. Thus, alcohol may be converted by it into ether or ethelyne. According to the proportions used, we have

$$C_2H_6O - H_2O = C_2H_4 \quad \text{or} \quad 2C_2H_6O - H_2O = 2C_2H_5O. \ [332]$$
$$\text{Ethylene.} \hspace{9cm} \text{Ether.}$$

For the same reason it acts as a cautery on the skin. It is also used in solution as an antiseptic and disinfecting agent.

324. *Zinc and the Alcohol Radicals.* — Zinc Methide, $Zn = (CH_3)_2$; Zinc Ethide, $Zn = (C_2H_5)_2$; Zinc Amylide, $Zn = (C_5H_{11})_2.$ Observed Sp. Gr. of vapor, 3.29, 4.26, and 6.95 respectively. Obtained both by heating zinc with the iodides of methyl, ethyl, or amyl in sealed tubes, and by the action of zinc on the mercury compounds of the same radicals. They are all three colorless, transparent, strongly refracting, and mobile liquids. They are also volatile, boiling at the temperatures of 46°, 118°, and 220° respectively. They are, likewise, highly inflammable, and the first two take fire spontaneously in the air. As these compounds do not, as a whole, combine with any of the elements, their molecules are evidently saturated, and they are interesting as fixing beyond all doubt the atomic relations of zinc. Moreover, they are useful reagents in many processes of organic chemistry.

325. *Characteristic Reactions.* — Zinc, like magnesium, forms soluble double salts with ammonia, but it is easily distinguished by the fact that its sulphide is insoluble, not only in

solutions of the fixed alkalies, but also in those of ammonia and its salts. Hence it is precipitated from all alkaline solutions by sulphuretted hydrogen. The sulphide thus obtained is a white precipitate, soluble in dilute mineral acids, but insoluble in acetic acid.

326. INDIUM. $In = 72.$ $Sp.$ $Gr.$ 7.42. CADMIUM. $Cd = 112.$ $Sp.$ $Gr.$ 8.69. — Dyads. Two rare metallic elements associated with zinc. Indium only in exceedingly minute quantities, and at very few localities. Cadmium far more generally, and in much larger amounts. Indium is less volatile, and cadmium more volatile, than zinc, and hence in distilling zinc from its ores the cadmium is found in the "zinc dust" which is collected in the early stage of the process, while the indium comes over later with the great mass of the zinc, with which it remains alloyed. With sufficient differences to mark their individuality, these metals resemble zinc in almost every particular. They form similar oxides and hydrates, similar soluble salts with hydrochloric, nitric, and sulphuric acids, similar soluble compounds with ammonia salts, similar light-colored sulphides insoluble in alkaline solutions and acetic acid. Cadmium differs from the others in this respect, that its hydrate is insoluble in caustic soda or potash, its basic carbonate insoluble in excess of ammonic carbonate, and its yellow sulphide insoluble in dilute mineral acids. This sulphide is found in nature, and the mineral is called Greenockite. Zinc precipitates cadmium from solutions of its salts, and both zinc and cadmium precipitate indium. Indium and cadmium are more fusible than zinc, and form very fusible alloys. Indium melts at 176°, cadmium at 242°, and an alloy of cadmium with lead, tin, and bismuth has been made which melts at 60°. Cadmium boils at 860°, and the Sp. Gr. of its vapor has been found by observation to be 56.85. Indium and cadmium burn when heated before the blow-pipe, the first yielding a yellow, and the last a brown oxide, very unlike the white oxide of zinc. Although so closely allied to magnesium and zinc, these associated elements probably belong to a different although parallel series, and the relation between the atomic weights of the four elements is in harmony with this view. All these four metals show very characteristic bands with the spectroscope, and indium was first discovered by the well-marked indigo-blue band, from which it takes its name.

Questions and Problems.

1. Write the reaction of sodium on magnesic chloride.

2. When water is decomposed by magnesium, what are the products? Write the reaction. [43.]

3. How do you account for the intense brilliancy of the light emitted by burning magnesium? (95.)

4. Write the reaction of water on calcined magnesia. [45.]

5. Write the reaction of solution of caustic soda on solution of magnesic chloride.
Ans. $(MgCl_2 + 2NaHo + Aq) = MgHo_2 + (2NaCl + Aq.)$

6. Represent the composition of hydromagnesite by graphic symbols.

7. Represent, graphically, the compound radicals Mgo, Cao, Zno, and show their relations to hydroxyl.

8. Represent, graphically, the composition of Dolomite.

9. What do you understand by the term isomorphous mixture?

10. Explain the theory of the preparation of magnesic carbonate from Dolomite.

11. The symbol of magnesic sulphate may be written $MgSO_4$, or $Mg=O_2=SO_2$, or $Mgo=SO_2$. What different ideas do these forms suggest?

12. Write the reaction of sulphuric acid on the two constituents of dolomite, and show how pure Epsom salt may be thus prepared.

13. Write the reaction of a solution of gypsum on magnesic carbonate.

14. Represent by graphic symbols $MgSO_4 . H_2O$.

15. Represent by graphic symbols the composition of potassic magnesic sulphate, and explain the relations of the crystallized salt to Epsom salt.

16. Write the reaction of hydrochloric acid on magnesic carbonate.

17. Explain the decomposition which results when a solution of magnesic chloride is evaporated in the air, and why an atmosphere of HCl should prevent the change.

18. What is the difference between the relations of baric and magnesic carbonate to calcic carbonate?
Ans. The first is related to Aragonite, the second to Calcite.

19. What is the difference between the reactions of sodic carbon-

ate on solutions of calcic and magnesic salts, and on what does the difference depend? Write the reactions in the two cases.

20. What is the difference between the reaction of ammonic carbonate on the same solutions?

21. Write the reaction of sodic phosphate on a solution of magnesic and ammonic chloride.

Ans. $(MgCl_2 + NH_3 + H,Na_2{=}O_3{=}PO + Aq) =$
$$(NH_4),Mg{=}O_3{=}PO \ . \ 6H_2O + (2NaCl + Aq.)$$

22. Write the reactions when zinc blende and smithsonite are calcined.

Ans. $ZnCO_3 = ZnO + CO_2$, and $2ZnS + 3O{=}O =$
$$2ZnO + 2SO_2.$$

23. Write the reaction when zincic oxide is reduced.

Ans. $ZnO + C = Zn + OO.$

24. Write the reactions of dilute sulphuric, hydrochloric, and acetic acids on zinc.

25. What part does zinc play in reaction [330]?

26. In what different ways may the symbol of zincic hydrate be written? Ans. $Zn{=}O{=}_2H_2$, $Zn{=}Ho_2$, $Zno{=}H_2$.

27. When zincic hydrate dissolves in caustic soda, what is formed?

28. Write the reaction of sodic carbonate upon a solution of zincic sulphate, assuming that three molecules of zincic hydrate are formed to every two molecules of zincic carbonate.

Ans. $(5ZnSO_4 + 5Na_2CO_3 + 3H_2O + Aq) =$
$$2ZnCO_3 + 3ZnHo_2 + (5Na_2SO_4 + Aq) + 3OO_2.$$

29. In what different ways may the symbol of zincic sulphate be written, both the anhydrous salt and the salt with one molecule of water? Represent graphically.

30. Write the symbol of potassic zincic sulphate. What is the crystalline form of this double salt, and with how many molecules of water does it crystallize?

31. Write the reaction of ammonic sulphide on a solution of zincic sulphate.

Ans. $(ZnSO_4 + (NH_4)_2S + Aq) =$
$$ZnS + ((NH_4)_2SO_4 + Aq).$$

32. Write the reaction of sulphuretted hydrogen on a solution of zincic acetate.

33. Would zincic sulphide be precipitated from a solution of zincic chloride containing an excess of hydrochloric acid? What is the difference between this case and that of 32? (21.)

16

Cadmium.

34. Write the reaction of dilute sulphuric acid on cadmium.

35. Write the reaction of sodic hydrate on solution of cadmic sulphate.

36. Write the reaction of zinc on solution of indium chloride.

37. Write the reaction of sulphuretted hydrogen on solution of cadmic chloride.

38. By what reactions may cadmium be separated from zinc?
Ans. By metallic zinc, by ammonic carbonate, and by sulphuretted hydrogen.

39. What is the electrical order of magnesium, zinc, indium, and cadmium?

40. Assuming that the atomic weight of cadmium is 112, what inference may be drawn from the Sp. Gr. of its vapor in regard to the constitution of its molecule? Does the conclusion have any bearing on the other dyad elements?

Divisions VIII. and IX.

327. GLUCINUM. $Gl = 9.3.$ — Dyad. A metallic element, found only in the Beryl, $Glo_3^{\equiv}(Si_6O_6)^{\equiv}Al_2o$, the Chrysoberyl, $Glo = Al_2O_2$, and a few other rare minerals. The metal is very light, $Sp. Gr.$ 2.1, is malleable, has a bright white lustre, does not alter in the air even when heated, and does not decompose aqueous vapor at a red heat. It resembles aluminum, as do also its oxide, hydrate, and chloride the corresponding compounds of the same metal. The hydrate differs, however, from that of aluminum in several important respects. Although soluble in caustic alkalies, it is again precipitated on boiling the diluted solution. It dissolves in solutions of carbonate of ammonia, with which it forms a crystalline salt. It yields with sulphuric acid a well-crystallized sulphate, $GlSO_4 . 4H_2O$, which forms with potassic sulphate a double salt, $K_2, Gl^{\equiv}(SO_4)_2 . 2H_2O$, wholly different from alum. Lastly, it absorbs CO_2 from the air. The salts of this metal have an acid reaction and a sweet taste, whence the name from γλυκύς.

328. YTTRIUM, $Y = 61.7$, and ERBIUM, $E = 112.6$. — Dyads. Metallic elements associated together in Gadolinite, Yttrotantalite, and a few other very rare minerals. First recognized in the specimens from Ytterby, in Sweden, whence the names. In most of their relations they quite closely resemble glucinum. They differ, however, from it in forming insoluble oxalates, and hence are precipitated on adding an excess of oxalic acid to solutions of their salts. Their hydrates also are insoluble in caustic soda or potash, although they dissolve readily in solutions of ammonia and its carbonate. The oxide of yttrium is white, that of erbium slightly rose-colored. Oxide of erbium, when heated in a colorless flame, shines with a green light, although it does not volatilize; and with the spectroscope the unique phenomenon is seen of brilliant colored bands superimposed on a continuous spectrum. Moreover, solutions of erbium salts absorb the same colored rays which the ignited oxide emits; and when a luminous flame is viewed with a spectroscope through such a solution, dark bands are seen which have the same position as the luminous bands just mentioned. The salts of yttrium exhibit no phenomena of this kind.

329. CERIUM. $Ce = 92$. LANTHANUM. $La = 93.6$. DIDYMIUM. $D = 95$. — These three rare elements are found inseparably united in Cerite, Allanite, Lanthanite, Yttrocerite, Parisite, and several other very rare minerals. They are not unfrequently associated with the elements of the last section, which they resemble in many particulars, but they differ from them in forming with potassium insoluble double sulphates, and hence they are precipitated on adding an excess of potassic sulphate to solutions of their salts. They all yield oxides of the form RO, but cerium differs from the other two in forming a higher oxide, probably Ce_3O_4, which, when heated with hydrochloric acid, evolves chlorine. The oxides of cerium and lanthanum are more or less colored, and that of didymium is dark brown. The salts of didymium are pink or violet colored, and when in solution, even in small quantities, absorb powerfully certain rays of light; and the spectrum of a luminous flame viewed through such a solution shows a strong absorption band in the yellow and another in the green. As these bands differ wholly from those of erbium, they enable us to recognize with certainty the presence of didymium, as none of its associated elements produce any such effect. Moreover, since the characteristic absorption bands are seen with reflected as well as with transmitted light, we are enabled to extend this mode of investigation even to opaque solids.

In regard to the elementary substances but little is known. Cerium, which has been obtained by reducing its chloride with sodium, is a soft metal like lead. When polished, it exhibits a high metallic lustre, and its specific gravity is about 5.5.

Questions and Problems.

1. Some chemists regard glucina as a sesquioxide, like alumina, and hence write the symbol Gl_2O_3. What would then be the atomic weight of glucinum ?   Ans. 14.

2. By what two reagents may the elements of this section be divided into three groups ?   Ans. Oxalic acid and potassic sulphate.

3. When mixed with the other allied oxides, the amount of ceric oxide present may be determined by dissolving out of contact with the air a weighed amount of the mixed oxides in hydrochloric acid, to which some potassic iodide has been added, and then finding by [272] the quantity of iodine thus set free. Write the reactions illustrating the theory of the process.

Ans. in part. $Ce_3O_4 + 8HCl = 3CeCl_2 + 4H_2O + Cl\text{-}Cl$.

Division X.

330. NICKEL. $Ni = 58.8$. — Quantivalence usually two. One of the less abundant metallic elements. The chief native compounds are

Breithauptite	Hexagonal	$Ni_2^{\cdots}[Sb_2]$,
Kupfernickel	Hexagonal	$Ni_2^{\cdots}[As_2]$,
Chloanthite (Niccoliferous Smaltine)	Isometric	$Ni^{\cdots}[As_2]$,
Nickel Glance	Isometric	$Ni^{\cdots}[S_2,[As_2]]$,
Rammelsbergite	Orthorhombic	$Ni^{\cdots}[As_2]$,
Millerite	Hexagonal	$Ni = S$,
Bunsenite	Isometric	$Ni = O$,
Nickel Vitriol	Monoclinic	$Ni = O_2 = SO_2 . 7H_2O$,
Annabergite (Nickel green)	Monoclinic	$Ni_3^{\cdots}O_6^{\cdots}(As\,O)_2 . 8H_2O$,
Emerald Nickel (Zaratite)		$Ni_3^{\cdots}O_6^{\cdots}CO,H_4 . 4H_2O$,
Genthite		$[Ni,Mg]_4^{\text{viii}}O_8^{\text{viii}}Si_3O_2 . 6H_2O$.

The metal, however, is obtained chiefly from a niccoliferous iron pyrites (magnetic variety), which only contains the element as an accessory constituent. The native arsenides, and an impure regulus (called *speiss*) formed in the preparation of smalt, are the other sources of the nickel of commerce. The process of extracting the metal is complicated and tedious. It consists in roasting the ore, dissolving the resulting oxides in acid, and precipitating first the associated metals, and afterwards the nickel, by appropriate reagents. The chief difficulty is to separate from the nickel the more valuable cobalt, with which nickel is almost invariably associated, and to which it is very closely allied.

Metallic nickel, *Sp. Gr.* 8.82, has a silver-white color, a brilliant metallic lustre, and does not tarnish when exposed to the atmosphere. It has great tenacity and malleability, and, were it more abundant, would rival even iron in the number of its applications in the useful arts. Nickel resembles iron in many of its qualities. When pure, it is nearly as infusible as *wrought-*

iron, and may be forged in a similar way. When combined with a small amount of carbon, it may, like *cast-iron*, be fused in an ordinary wind furnace. Nickel is also, like iron, susceptible of magnetism, but the magnetic power is less marked, and, when heated, it loses this virtue at a much lower temperature. Moreover, like iron, nickel is soluble in dilute sulphuric or hydrochloric acids with evolution of hydrogen gas, but the action is less energetic, and the metal dissolves only slowly. The best solvents are nitric acid and aqua regia. Nickel forms with copper a brilliant white, hard, tenacious, malleable alloy, and a small amount of nickel will whiten a large body of copper. This alloy is much used for coinage, and as the basis of the better kinds of electrotype plate. German silver is an alloy of copper, zinc, and nickel in about the proportion of $5:3:2$. Nickel may also be alloyed with iron, and is a constant constituent of the metallic meteorites. Nickel readily combines with each of the members of the chlorine group of elements, but only in one proportion, and the compounds thus formed, NiF_2, $NiCl_2$, &c., are all soluble in water.

There are two oxides of nickel. The protoxide, NiO, is an olive-green powder, readily obtained by igniting either the nitrate or the carbonate of the metal. It is a basic anhydride, dissolving readily in the mineral acids, and forming the ordinary nickel salts, in all of which Ni *acts as a bivalent radical.* The sesquioxide, Ni_2O_3, is a black powder, also obtained by igniting the nitrate, but at a lower temperature. It is an unstable compound, and, when heated, is resolved into the lower oxide and oxygen gas. It is not a basic anhydride, and, when heated with the mineral acids, one third of the oxygen is given off as before, and a salt of the ordinary type is the result. In the sesquioxide, Ni is a quadrivalent, but the double atom (Ni_2) *acts as a sexivalent radical.* The tendency to form radicals of this last type, which is only foreshadowed in nickel, becomes a striking character in the elements which follow in our classification.

Of the crystallized soluble salts of nickel, the most common are

Niccolous Chloride	$NiCl_2 . 9H_2O,$
Niccolous Nitrate	$Ni=O_2^{=}(NO_2)_2 . 6H_2O,$
Niccolous Sulphate	$Ni,H_2^{\equiv}O_4^{\equiv}SO . 6H_2O,$
Dipotassic-niccolous Sulphate	$Ni,K_2^{\equiv}O_4^{\equiv}(SO_2)_2 . 6H_2O.$

The salts of nickel, both when crystallized and when in solution, have a characteristic green color; but, when rendered anhydrous by heat, this color changes to yellow. From their solutions the fixed alkalies precipitate a hydrate, and the alkaline carbonates a basic carbonate, of nickel, both forming pale-green precipitates. The first is probably the definite compound $Ni{=}O_2{=}H_2$; but the composition of the second varies with the temperature, strength, and proportions of the solutions employed, and the product is closely analogous to the precipitates, which are obtained under similar conditions from solutions of the salts of magnesium or zinc.

The salts of nickel readily combine both with ammonia and with the ammonium salts. A large number of products may thus be formed, which are easily soluble in water. The following crystalline compounds, which indirectly play an important part in some of the methods of qualitative analysis, will serve as types of the class: —

$$Ni\,Cl_2\,.\,6NH_3,\qquad\qquad NH_4Cl\,.\,Ni\,Cl_2\,.\,6H_2O.$$

From solutions of such ammoniacal compounds, and from other alkaline solutions containing nickel, the metal is precipitated as $[Ni_2]^{\underline{\underline{i}}}O_6^{\underline{i}}H_6$, both by chlorine gas and by the alkaline hypochlorites. The precipitate has an intense black color, and this reaction is one of the most delicate tests for nickel, but does not distinguish it from cobalt. Nickel is also precipitated from alkaline solutions by H_2S or by alkaline sulphides. The black precipitate thus obtained has the same composition as Millerite, NiS. It is insoluble in the dilute mineral acids, although in acid solutions of nickel salts H_2S gives no precipitate. Two other sulphides of the element, Ni_2S and NiS_2, have been described.

331. COBALT. $Co = 58.8$. — Quantivalence usually two. Associated with nickel in the same ores, but less abundantly distributed. Most of the minerals enumerated in the last section contain cobalt. When, however, this metal preponderates, they are in most cases classed as separate mineral species, and receive distinct names. No cobalt mineral corresponding to Kupfernickel or Breithauptite has been found, but we have

Smaltine	Isometric	$Co^{\equiv}[As_2]$,
Cobaltine	Isometric	$Co^{\equiv}[S_2,(As_2)]$,
Linnæite	Isometric	Co_3S_4,
Glaucodot	Orthorhombic	$Co^{\equiv}[S_2,(As_2)]$,
Syepoorite		$Co^=S$,
Cobalt Vitriol	Monoclinic	$Co^=O_2^=SO_2 . 7H_2O$,
Erythrite (Cobalt Bloom)	Monoclinic	$Co_3^{\equiv}O_6^{\equiv}(AsO)_2 . 8H_2O$.

To these must be added an impure oxide of cobalt (Earthy Cobalt), and a mineral called Remingtonite, which probably corresponds to Emerald Nickel. There is a variety of Linnæite, called Siegenite, which contains a large proportion of nickel; but no purely niccoliferous compound of this type is known.

In all their chemical relations, the two metals here associated resemble each other so closely that the description of nickel given above applies almost word for word to cobalt, and it is only necessary to indicate farther the points of difference.

Metallic cobalt rusts more readily than nickel, but less readily than iron. It is magnetic, and possesses valuable qualities, but is so costly that it has received no application in the arts.

Cobalt forms but one stable compound with either of the members of the chlorine group of elements, $CoCl_2$, &c.; but by dissolving Co_2O_3 in hydrochloric acid a red solution is obtained, which is supposed to contain Co_2Cl_6. The compound, however, is very unstable, for the solution evolves chlorine on the slightest elevation of temperature.

There are three well-marked oxides of cobalt. Cobaltous Oxide, CoO; Cobaltic Oxide, Co_2O_3; Cobaltous-cobaltic Oxide, Co_3O_4; but, besides these, several others have been distinguished, which are probably either mixtures or molecular aggregates of the first two. Not only is CoO a strong basic anhydride, like NiO, but also Co_2O_3 dissolves in acids, especially in acetic acid, forming salts. We have, therefore, to distinguish between cobaltous and cobaltic salts; but the last are very unstable and little known.

The ordinary cobaltous salts, when crystallized, are red, but are usually lilac-colored when anhydrous, and the pink solutions, which they yield with water, become blue when concentrated. On this change of color depends the virtue of certain sympathetic inks. From solutions of these salts, potassic or sodic hydrate precipitate $Co\text{-}O_2\text{=}H_2$, which has a delicate rose-color. The pale-blue precipitate, which generally falls first, is a basic salt of cobalt, but if warmed with an excess of the reagent, it soon acquires the composition and color of the normal hydrate. If exposed to the air this hydrate absorbs oxygen rapidly, and changes to a dingy-green color. The normal cobaltic hydrate is not known. The black precipitate obtained by the action of chlorine or the hypochlorites on alkaline solutions containing cobalt is the second anhydride of this hydrate, or $O_3\text{=}[\,Co_2\,]\text{=}O_2\text{-}H_2$. The same compound is formed when chlorine gas is passed through water or a solution of caustic potash holding cobaltous hydrate in suspension. When the alkali is used, the whole of the hydrate is converted into the cobaltic compound; but with pure water only two thirds as much are obtained. The compound of nickel formed under the same conditions is supposed to be the normal niccolic hydrate.

The tendency to form soluble compounds with ammonia and with the ammonium salts manifested by nickel, appears again and more prominently in the allied element cobalt. Moreover, there are cobaltic as well as cobaltous compounds of this class, and the last tend to pass into the first by absorbing oxygen when exposed to the air. The number of these compounds is very numerous. They have a very complex constitution, and in many cases at least are probably formed on the ammonia type. We may regard them as compounds of ammonio-cobalt bases, to several of which distinctive names have been given. The following scheme exhibits the relations of the more important compounds: —

Cobaltous Compounds.

$$Co\overset{\text{II}}{R} . 4NH_3, \qquad\qquad Co\overset{\text{II}}{R} . 6NH_3.$$

Cobaltic Compounds.

$[\,Co_2\,]\overset{\text{II}}{R_3} .\ \ 8NH_3$ Fusco-cobaltic salts.

$[\,Co_2\,]\overset{\text{II}}{R_3} . 10NH_3$ Roseo or Purpureo-cobaltic salts.

$[\,Co_2\,]\overset{\text{II}}{R_3} . 12NH_3$ Luteo-cobaltic salts.

In the above symbols $\overset{\text{II}}{R}$ stands for a bivalent acid radical, like (SO_4), (CO_3), (C_2O_4) or Cl_2, $(NO_3)_2$, &c. Substituting these in the general symbol, we obtain the specific symbols of the various salts of the assumed bases; but in most cases the crystallized salt contains in addition one or more molecules of water, which frequently play an important part in its constitution, and determine marked differences of qualities, as in the following typical compounds:—

Purpureo-cobaltic Chloride $[Co_2]Cl_6 \cdot 10NH_3$,
Roseo-cobaltic Chloride $[Co_2]Cl_6 \cdot 10NH_3 \cdot 2H_2O$,
Xantho-cobaltic Chloride $[Co_2]Cl_6 \cdot 10NH_3 \cdot N_2O_2 \cdot H_2O$.

Cobaltous oxide combines with many of the basic as well as with the acid anhydrides, yielding in several cases compounds distinguished by great brilliancy of coloring. The compound with $[Al_2]O_3$ is known as Thénard's blue, that with ZnO as Rinman's green. Such compounds are formed when the metallic oxides, moistened with a solution of cobaltous nitrate, are heated before the blow-pipe, and the production of the color is one of the most characteristic blow-pipe reactions.

Cobaltous oxide, when melted into glass or into the glaze of earthenware, imparts to the material an intense blue color, and the brilliancy and the depth of the color render the oxide one of the most valuable vitrifiable pigments, and this is its chief use in the arts. The blue pigment called smalt, used for coloring paper and dressing white calicoes, is a pulverized alkaline glass strongly colored with the oxide.

Cobalt is distinguished by the same reactions as nickel from all other metallic radicals. From nickel it is distinguished,— First, by the blue color which the oxide gives to borax glass. Secondly, by the fact that potassic nitrite precipitates[1] the cobalt from nitric or acetic acid solutions, while it does not precipitate nickel. Thirdly, by the circumstance that cyanide of cobalt forms, when boiled with a solution of potassic cyanide in contact with the air, a compound corresponding to potassic ferricyanide. The solution of potassic cobalti-cyanide is not decomposed by HgO or by alkaline hypochlorites, while from the solution of the cyanide of nickel and potassium, formed under

[1] Composition of precipitate according to S. P. Sadtler,

$$K_6, [Co_2]xii\,O_{12}\,xii\,(N_2O_2)_6 \cdot xH_2O.$$

the same circumstances, all the nickel is precipitated by the same reagents.

$$CoO + (2H\text{-}CN + Aq) = Co^=(CN)_2 + (H_2O + Aq.) \quad [333]$$

$$4Co^=(CN)_2 + (12K\text{-}CN + 4H\text{-}CN + Aq) + \odot \text{-} \odot = \\ (2K_6^{\underline{\underline{3}}}(C_{12}N_{12}Co_2) + 2H_2O + Aq). \quad [334]$$

$$NiO + (4K\text{-}CN + H_2O + Aq) = \\ (2K\text{-}CN . Ni^=(CN)_2 + 2K\text{-}O\text{-}H + Aq). \quad [335]$$

$$HgO + (2K\text{-}CN . Ni^=(CN)_2 + H_2O + Aq) = \\ Ni^=O_2H_2 + (2K\text{-}CN . Hg^=(CN)_2 + Aq). \quad [336]$$

Questions and Problems.

1. Represent by graphic symbols the constitution of Kupfernickel and Chloanthite.

2. In the symbol of Nickel Glance, in what relation does the sulphur stand to the arsenic? Could these elements replace each other by single atoms?

3. What is the distinction between Chloanthite and Rammelsbergite? Does the same distinction reappear in the corresponding compound of either of the allied elements?

4. Have any facts been stated which *prove* that nickel is sometimes quadrivalent?

5. Represent by a graphic symbol the constitution of niccolous sulphate.

6. Write the reaction of sulphuric acid, and also of hydrochloric acid, on Ni_2O_3.

7. Point out the analogies between nickel and zinc.

8. The precipitate first formed by ammonia or ammonic carbonate in solutions of the salts of nickel redissolves in an excess of the reagent, and does not form at all when a large amount of ammonic chloride is present. How do you explain these reactions?

9. In the native compounds of cobalt this element is more or less replaced by iron and nickel. Write the symbols of Smaltine and Cobaltine so as to indicate this fact.

10. Represent by graphic symbols the constitution of Linnæite, and also that of Co_2S_3 and CoS_2, the only other sulphides not mentioned in the text.

11. Represent by graphic symbols the constitution of the following oxides and oxysulphides, Co_3O_4, Co_6O_7, Co_2OS.

12. In what respects do the oxides and sulphides of cobalt differ from those of nickel?

13. Write the reaction of chlorine gas on cobaltous hydrate, first, when suspended in water, and, secondly, when suspended in solution of caustic potash. Write also the corresponding reactions which take place when hydrate of nickel is similarly treated.

14. Represent the composition of the ammonio-cobalt salts by typical symbols.

15. In potassic cobalti-cyanide what is the quantivalence of cobalt? Do the cobalt atoms change their atomicity in [334]?

16. Analyze reactions [333] to [336], and show that the differences in the relations of cobalt and nickel to the alkaline cyanides depend on differences in the atomic relations of the two elements. What part does the oxygen of the air play in [334]?

17. Potassic cobalti-cyanide is formed when cobaltous hydrate is boiled with a solution of potassic cyanide, there being free access of air. Write the reaction.

18. Write the reaction when a solution of potassic hypochlorite (K-O-Cl) is added to the product of reaction [335].

19. Point out the resemblances and the differences in the chemical relations of cobalt and nickel, and show how far they may be traced to the circumstance that the radical $[Co_2]$ is more stable than the radical $[Ni_2]$.

Division XI.

332. **MANGANESE.** $Mn = 55$. — Quantivalence two, four, six, and possibly eight. A tolerably abundant element, and widely diffused throughout the mineral kingdom, entering into the composition of a very large number of minerals. The following are the most characteristic or important: —

Pyrolusite	Orthorhombic	$Mn\,O_2$,
Braunite	Tetragonal	Mn_2O_3 or $(Mn\text{-}Si)^{\underline{\underline{}}}O_3$,
Hausmannite	Tetragonal	Mn_3O_4,
Psilomelane	Massive ⎫	Mixtures of different
Wad	Earthy ⎭	oxides,
Manganite	Orthorhombic	$O_2^{\underline{\underline{}}}[Mn_2] = O_2^{\underline{\underline{}}}H_2$,
Hauerite	Isometric	MnS_2,
Manganblende	Isometric	MnS,
Rhodonite	Triclinic	$Mn = O_2^{\underline{\underline{}}}Si\,O$,
Tephroite	Orthorhombic	$Mn_2^{\underline{\underline{}}}O_4^{\underline{\underline{}}}Si$,
Triplite	Orthorhombic	$([Fe,Mn]_2\text{-}F) = O_3^{\underline{\underline{}}}(PO)$?
Manganese Spar	Rhombohedral	$Mn = O_2^{\underline{\underline{}}}CO$,
Mangano-calcite	Orthorhombic	$[Ca,Mn] = O_2^{\underline{\underline{}}}CO$.

The elementary substance is a very hard and brittle metal, *Sp. Gr.* 8.013. It has a grayish-white color, is almost infusible, and very slightly magnetic. It oxidizes rapidly in moist air, and decomposes water even at the ordinary temperature. There appear to be two conditions of the metal corresponding to wrought and cast iron; but its properties have not been thoroughly studied. It is obtained with difficulty by reducing the oxide with carbon at a very high temperature, and as yet has found no applications in the arts. Corresponding to the three degrees of quantivalence of Manganese are three classes of compounds.

1. Manganous compounds, in which the quantivalence of the element is two. This class includes all the manganese minerals above enumerated, after manganblende, and all the common soluble salts of the metal. Among the last the most important are

Manganous Chloride $\qquad$ $Mn\,Cl_2$. (2 or $4H_2O$),

Manganous Sulphate $\qquad$ $Mn = O_2 = SO_2$. (4, 5, or $7H_2O$),

Dipotassic-manganous Sulphate $\quad K_2Mn\equiv O_4[SO_2]_2$. $6H_2O$.

There is also a Bromide, $MnBr_2$. $2H_2O$. The manganous compounds are distinguished by a delicate pink or red color. From solutions of the manganous salts, potassic or sodic hydrate precipitate a white hydrate, $Mn = O_2 = H_2$, which absorbs oxygen rapidly, and becomes brown when exposed to the air (Manganese Brown). In like manner sodic or potassic carbonate precipitate a white hydro-carbonate, which also becomes brown on drying. Ammonic carbonate also produces the same precipitate, and does not redissolve it when added in excess. Ammonic hydrate, on the other hand, gives no precipitate in solutions containing an excess of ammonic chloride, and redissolves the precipitate which first forms in simple aqueous solutions. Ammonio-manganous salts are thus formed, and two well-crystallized ammonio-manganous chlorides have been described, $MnCl_2$. $2NH_4Cl$. H_2O and $MnCl_2$. NH_4Cl . $2H_2O$.

In the solution of a manganous salt, sodic phosphate and ammonia produce, under regulated conditions, a highly crystalline precipitate having the composition $(NH_4)_2Mn_2\equiv O_6\equiv(PO)_2$. $2H_2O$. This precipitate yields on ignition a pyrophosphate of uniform composition, and on this reaction is based a valuable means of determining the amount of manganese in quantitative chemical analysis.

Manganous oxide, MnO, is easily obtained by reducing either of the higher oxides with hydrogen. It is an olive-green powder, which burns if heated in the air, thus forming the "*red oxide*" Mn_3O_4.

Manganous sulphide is precipitated on adding an alkaline sulphide to the solution of a manganous salt, as a flesh-colored hydrate, MnS . xH_2O; but this also in contact with the air rapidly oxidizes and turns brown. It readily dissolves in the dilute mineral acids, and also in acetic acid. The same tendency to form compounds, in which manganese presents a higher order of quantivalence, is exhibited by all the soluble manganous salts, and especially by the ammoniacal solutions just mentioned, which, when exposed to the air, rapidly absorb oxygen, become turbid, and deposit a brownish flocculent precipitate of manganic hydrate ($O_2^=[Mn_2]$=H_2=O_2?). So, also, when chlorine gas is passed through water holding manganous hydrate or carbonate in suspension, or through a solution of a manganous salt, to which an excess of sodic acetate has been added, the manganese is still further oxidized, and the brownish precipitate obtained is chiefly a hydrate of the dioxide $Mn O_2 . H_2O$. Bromine also produces a similar result.

2. *Manganic compounds, in which the quantivalence of the element is four.* Of these we must distinguish two divisions: *first*, those which have for their radical the single quadrivalent atom of manganese; *second*, those in which two such quadrivalent atoms act as a compound radical with a quantivalence of six. To the first division of the manganic compounds probably belong most of the native oxides. Pyrolusite, $Mn O_2$, has a crystalline form similar to that of Brookite, $Ti O_2$, which is an oxide of the well-marked tetrad element titanium; while Braunite, $Mn_2 O_3$, and Hausmannite, $Mn_3 O_4$, have a form which is nearly isomorphous with Rutile, an allotropic state of the same oxide (Fig. 37), but wholly unlike the forms of $Fe_2 O_3$ (Fig. 44) and $Fe_3 O_4$ (Fig. 33), two typical compounds, to which Braunite and Hausmannite, if containing the sexivalent radical $[Mn_2]$, must be closely allied. Manganite probably contains this radical, as it is isomorphous with the native ferric hydrate, Göthite.

Of the oxides of manganese, the red oxide, $Mn_3 O_4$, is the most stable. The higher oxides, when heated, are all resolved into $Mn_3 O_4$, and the native oxides thus become sources of oxygen gas [232]. When heated with sulphuric acid, they also give off oxygen and yield manganous sulphate [231]. When heated with hydrochloric acid, they liberate chlorine and yield manganous chloride [77]. Hence an important application of the native oxides in the arts. There are reasons for believing that the two atoms of oxygen in $Mn O_2$ stand in different relations to this molecular group (236), and the chloride of manganese, $Mn Cl_4$, recently isolated, affords still more conclusive evidence of the quadrivalent relations of this element. This manganic chloride is exceedingly unstable, and when gently heated breaks up into manganous chloride and chlorine gas.

To the second division of the manganic compounds belong manganic hydrate, $O_2^=[Mn_2]$=O_2=H_2, and several very unstable compounds, which have been formed by dissolving this hydrate in different acids. The sulphate, however, becomes stable when the hexad radical is associated in the salt with potassium. We thus obtain an interesting variety of alum,

$$K_2 [Mn_2]^{\text{viii}} O_8^{\text{viii}} [SO_2]_4 \cdot 24 H_2 O.$$

3. The most characteristic compounds of manganese are those in which the element is either sexivalent or octivalent, and the fact that a volatile fluoride of manganese is known, which contains at least six atoms of fluorine to every atom of manganese, indicates that the atomicity of the elements cannot be less than six. Indeed, the fluorides illustrate very strikingly the different degrees of quantivalence which manganese may assume, for we have MnF_2, MnF_4, $[Mn_2]F_6$, and MnF_6.

When an intimate mixture of $K\text{-}O\text{-}H$ and MnO_2 is roasted in a current of oxygen gas, the following reaction takes place:—

$$4\,\mathbf{K\text{-}O\text{-}H} + 2\,\mathbf{MnO_2} + \textcircled{O}\text{-}\textcircled{O} =$$
$$2\,\mathbf{K_2\text{-}O_2\text{-}MnO_2} + 2\,\mathbf{H_2O}. \quad [337]$$

On dissolving the resulting mass in water, and evaporating the *deep green* solution thus obtained (in vacuo), crystals are formed isomorphous with $K_2\text{-}O_2\text{-}SO_2$, in which the hexad atoms of manganese act as acid radicals, and we call the product potassic manganate. The acid corresponding to this compound has never been isolated, and only a few of its salts are known. They are all, like potassic manganate, exceedingly unstable.

On boiling a solution of potassic manganate, the following remarkable reaction results:—

$$(3K_2\text{-}O_2\text{-}MnO_2 + 3H_2O + Aq) =$$
$$\mathbf{MnO_2} \cdot \mathbf{H_2O} + (K_2\text{-}O_2[Mn_2]O_6 + 4K\text{-}O\text{-}H + Aq); \quad [338]$$

and a new compound called potassic permanganate is formed, in which the atoms of manganese appear to have a quantivalence of eight. The reaction takes place more readily if a stream of CO_2 is passed through the boiling solution to neutralize the $K\text{-}O\text{-}H$ as it forms, and when the solution is not too strong the carbonic anhydride of the atmosphere will in time determine the same change even at the ordinary temperature. The solution of $K_2\text{-}O_2\text{-}Mn_2O_6$ has a *deep violet* color, and the changing tints, during the reaction just described, present a very striking phenomenon. Hence the crude potassic manganate, obtained by melting together MnO_2 and $K\text{-}O\text{-}NO_2$, is commonly known as chameleon mineral; and the production of the characteristic green color, under similar conditions in a blow-pipe bead, is the best evidence of the presence of manganese.

Potassic permanganate, prepared as above, may be readily crystallized, and its crystals are isomorphous with those of potassic perchlorate; that is, $K_2\text{-}O_2[Mn_2]$xiiO_6 has the same form as $K\text{-}O\text{-}Cl{\equiv}O_3$. From potassic permanganate a number of other permanganates may be prepared, and also permanganic acid, a dark-colored volatile liquid. Permanganic acid is formed when the solution of a manganese salt is boiled with nitric acid and plumbic dioxide, and a violet color developed in the liquid under these conditions is a certain indication of the presence of manganese. The permanganates are more stable than the manganates, but still they readily part with a portion of their oxygen, and act as powerful oxidizing agents. A solution of potassic permanganate is much used for this purpose in the laboratory. For example, it changes ferrous into ferric salts.

$$(10Fe\text{-}O_2\text{-}SO_3 + K_2\text{-}O_2[Mn_2]O_6 + 8H_2\text{-}O_2\text{-}SO_3 + Aq) =$$
$$(5[Fe_2]{\equiv}O_6[SO_2]_3 + K_2\text{-}O_2\text{-}SO_3 + 2Mn\text{-}O_2\text{-}SO_3 + 8H_2O + Aq). \ [339]$$

The slightest excess of the permanganate is at once indicated by the color it imparts to the liquid, and the reaction is the basis of one of the most valuable methods of volumetric analysis. Both the manganates and the permanganates are at once decomposed by all organic tissues, which they rapidly oxidize, and a crude sodic permanganate is much used as a disinfecting agent.

333. IRON. $Fe = 56$. — Usually bivalent or quadrivalent, but rarely sexivalent. A universally diffused element, and the most abundant and important of the useful metals. As an accessory ingredient, it enters into the composition of almost every substance, and it is the chief metallic radical of a very large number of important minerals.

Oxides.

MAGNETITE	Isometric	$Fe,[Fe_2]^{viii}O_4,$
Magnesioferrite	Isometric	$Mg,[Fe_2]^{viii}O_4,$
FRANKLINITE	Isometric	$[Zn,Mn],[Fe_2]^{viii}O_4,$
HEMATITE		$[Fe_2]^{\equiv}O_3,$
SPECULAR IRON	Hexagonal,	
RED HEMATITE	Massive,	
CLAY IRON STONE	Massive,	
RED OCHRE	Massive,	
MENACCANITE		$(Ti\text{-}Fe)^{\equiv}O_3,$
Titanic Iron	Hexagonal.	

Hydrates.

Limnite	Massive	$[Fe_2]^{\equiv}O_6^{\equiv}H_6,$
Xanthosiderite	Massive	$O^{=}[Fe_2]^{\equiv}O_4^{\equiv}H_4,$
Göthite	Orthorhombic	$O_2^{\equiv}[Fe_2]^{=}O_2^{=}H_2,$
LIMONITE		$O_3^{\equiv}[Fe_2]_2^{\equiv}O_6^{\equiv}H_6,$
BROWN HEMATITE	Massive,	
BROWN CLAY IRON STONE	Massive,	
BOG ORE	Massive,	
YELLOW OCHRE	Massive.	

Carbonates.

SIDERITE		$Fe^{=}O_2^{=}CO,$
SPATHIC IRON	Rhombohedral,	
CLAY IRON STONE (of the coal-beds)	Massive,	
SPHÆROSIDERITE	Concretionary,	
Mesitite	Rhombohedral	$[Mg,Fe]^{=}O_2^{=}CO,$
Ankerite	Rhombohedral	$[Mg,Fe],Ca^{\equiv}O_4^{\equiv}(CO)_2,$

Sulphides.

Troilite	Massive	$FeS,$
Magnetic Pyrites	Hexagonal	Fe_7S_8 or $Fe_2S_2?$
Iron Pyrites	Isometric	$FeS_2,$
Marcasite	Orthorhombic	$FeS_2,$
Mispickel	Orthorhombic	$Fe^{=}[S_2,[As_2]].$

Sulphates.

Green Vitriol	Monoclinic	$H_2 Fe^{\equiv} O_4^{\equiv} SO . 6H_2O,$
Pisanite	Monoclinic	$H_2 [Fe,Cu]^{\equiv} O_4^{\equiv} SO . 6H_2O,$
Coquimbite	Hexagonal	$[Fe_2]^{\equiv}_3 O_6^{\equiv} [SO_2]_3 . 9H_2O,$
Jarosite	Rhombohedral	

$$4(O_2^{\equiv}[Fe_2]^{=}O_2^{=}SO_2) . ([K,Na]^{=}O_2^{=}SO_2) . 9H_2O,$$

Copiapite	Hexagonal?	$O^{=}[Fe_2]_2{}^{x}O_{10}{}^{x}[SO_2]_5 . 12H_2O,$
Raimondite	Hexagonal	$O_3^{\equiv}[Fe_2]_2^{\equiv}O_6^{\equiv}[SO_2]_3 . 7H_2O,$
Glockerite	Massive	$O_5{}^{x}[Fe_2]_2^{=}O_2^{=}SO_2 . 6H_2O,$
Fibroferrite	Fibrous	$O_4{}^{viii}[Fe_2]_3{}^{x}O_{10}{}^{x}[SO_2]_5 . 27H_2O,$
Botryogen	Monoclinic	

$$O_4{}^{viii}[Fe_2]_3{}^{x}O_{10}{}^{x}[SO_2]_5 . 3Fe^{=}O_2^{=}SO_2 . 36H_2O,$$

Voltaite	Isometric	$Fe, [Fe_2]^{viii}O_8{}^{viii}[SO_2]_4 . 24H_2O$

Phosphates and Arseniates.

Triphylite	Orthorhombic	$[Fe,Mn,Li_2]_3^{\equiv}O_6^{\equiv}(PO)_2,$
Vivianite	Monoclinic	$Fe_3^{\equiv}O_6^{\equiv}(PO)_2 . 8H_2O,$
Dufrenite	Orthorhombic	$O_3^{\equiv}[Fe_2]_2^{\equiv}O_6^{\equiv}(PO)_2 . 3H_2O,$
Cacoxenite	Radiated	$O_3^{\equiv}[Fe_2]_2^{\equiv}O_6^{\equiv}(PO)_2 . 12H_2O,$
Scorodite	Orthorhombic	$[Fe_2]^{\equiv}_3 O_6^{\equiv}(AsO)_2 . 4H_2O,$
Pharmacosiderite	Isometric	$O_{3}^{\equiv}[Fe_2]_4{}^{xviii}O_{18}{}^{xviii}(AsO)_6 . 15H_2O.$

Silicates.

Fayalite (iron olivine)		
	Orthorhombic?	$Fe_2^{\equiv}O_4^{\equiv}Si,$
Ilvaite (Yenite)	Orthorhombic	$R_3, [R_2]^{xii}O_{12}{}^{xii}Si_3?$
Schorlomite	Massive	$Ca_4 . [Fe_2]^{xiv}O_{14}{}^{xiv}[Ti,Si]_3^{\equiv}O_3.$

Compare also Columbite, Tantalite, and Wolfram (227) and (253).

334. *Metallurgy of Iron.* — Native iron of meteoric origin is not unfrequently found, but it is doubtful whether native iron of terrestrial origin exists, although instances of its occurrence have been reported. The commercial value of the metal is so small that only those ferriferous minerals which are at the same time rich, abundant, readily accessible, and easily smelted, can be utilized as ores. The useful ores, which are all either oxides, hydrates, or carbonates, are distinguished, in the list of iron minerals given above, by a difference of type; and the names

of the most important varieties of the different ores follow the names of the species to which they belong. These ores are found either in veins or in beds, associated with rocks of all ages and of very various characters, and the value of a given deposit frequently depends quite as much on its association with coal and lime, and on its proximity to a commercial centre, as on the richness of the ore. Hence the great wealth, which has been drawn from the deposits of clay iron-stone in the coal-beds of England, an ore which, intrinsically, is comparatively poor.

All the useful ores of iron, when not anhydrous oxides, are converted into this condition by roasting, and the oxides are easily reduced to the metallic state by simply heating the roasted ore with coal. The smelting process, however, also involves the fusion of the other mineral matter (gangue), with which the true ore is always mixed. This gangue will seldom fuse by itself, even at the high temperature of a blast furnace, and it is almost always necessary to mix the ore with some *flux* (usually limestone), which will unite with the gangue and form a fusible *slag*. The same end is sometimes attained, or at least an advantage is gained, by mixing different ores.

If the iron is reduced at a comparatively low temperature, as in a *bloomery forge*, the metal separates from the melted slag as a loosely coherent, spongy solid, the *bloom*, and is subsequently rendered compact by hammering and rolling while still at a welding heat. If the iron is reduced at a high temperature, as in a *blast furnace*, the metal unites with a small proportion of carbon and is thereby rendered fusible. Both the fused metal and the melted slag then drop together into the *crucible* of the furnace, and there the difference of density determines a perfect separation of the two molten liquids. The product of the first process is nearly a pure metal, and is called *wrought-iron*. The product of the second process contains a variable amount of carbon (from 2 to 5 per cent), and is known as *cast-iron*.

With the outward aspects of these two varieties of iron every one is familiar. Wrought-iron is so soft that it can be readily worked with files and other steel tools. It is very tough, and has great tenacity. It is exceedingly ductile and malleable. It readily fuses before a compound blow-pipe, and in small quantities may even be melted in a wind-furnace. It however requires, for its perfect fusion, a full white heat. But at a lower temperature it becomes soft and pliable, and in this condition can be *wrought* or welded on an anvil. It has a fibrous structure, but this is in a great measure due to the mechanical treatment it receives.

Cast-iron, on the other hand, has a granular or crystalline structure. It is much harder than wrought-iron, and proportionally more brittle. It is therefore neither malleable nor ductile, and cannot be wrought on the anvil like the former metal; but, as it melts at a much lower temperature, it is suitable for *castings*. Cast-iron differs greatly in quality, and the two extreme conditions are seen in the two commercial varieties known as *white iron* and *gray iron*. White iron has a brilliant white lustre and a lamellar crystalline fracture, is very brittle, and so hard that it cannot be worked with steel tools. It is, therefore, not suitable for casting, but may be used to advantage for making wrought-iron or steel. Gray iron has a darker lustre and a more granular fracture. It is much softer, and may be filed, drilled, or turned in a lathe. Although less fusible than white iron, it flows more freely when melted, and is better adapted for casting. It also contains, as a rule, less carbon, but the difference of qualities seems to depend more on the condition of the carbon than on the amount. In white iron *all* the carbon appears to be chemically combined with the metal, while in gray iron *the greater part* is disseminated in an uncombined form through the mass.[1] A form of white iron, called by the Germans *spiegeleisen* (mirror iron), which crystallizes in flat, brilliant tables, and contains about five per cent of carbon, has approximately the composition CFe_4, and another crystalline variety has been described, which nearly corresponds to CFe_8; but the existence of these compounds cannot be regarded as proved. Spiegeleisen, moreover, is not a pure ferro-carbide, but always contains manganese, the amount varying from 4 to 12 per cent. Indeed, manganese is a very common ingredient of cast-iron, as might be anticipated, seeing that manganesian minerals are so frequently associated with iron ores. Cast-iron also contains variable quantities of silicon, sulphur, and phos-

[1] When the fracture exhibits large, coarse grains, among which points of graphite are distinctly visible, the metal is said to be *mottled*. Mottled-iron is very tough, and is especially valued for casting ordnance. Of all three varieties of cast-iron, — the white, the mottled, and the gray, — the iron-masters distinguish several grades.

phorus, besides traces of other metals, such as aluminum, calcium, and potassium.

By melting cast-iron on the hearth of a reverberatory furnace, the carbon and the other impurities may be more or less thoroughly burnt out, and the metal converted into wrought-iron. At the same time a portion of the iron is oxidized, and a very fusible slag is formed by the union of the oxide with the silica always present.

The metal thickens as it becomes decarbonized, and the spongy *bloom* thus formed is easily separated from the melted slag, and hammered or rolled into bars, as before described. The greater part of the wrought-iron of commerce is made in this way, and the process is called "puddling," because the melted metal is stirred or puddled on the hearth of the furnace in order to expose the mass more effectually to the action of the air. The purest iron, thus prepared, still contains a small amount of carbon, which does not, however, impair its useful qualities. The other impurities of cast-iron, when not wholly removed, render the wrought-iron friable or brittle (*short*, in technical language), and are highly prejudicial. Sulphur makes the metal friable while hot (*red short*), while phosphorus and silicon make it brittle when cold (*cold short*).

That most valuable form of iron called steel holds an intermediate position between wrought and cast iron, and partakes, to a great extent, of the valuable qualities of both. At a white heat it may be worked on the anvil, like wrought-iron, and at a higher temperature, but still, within the range of a wind furnace, it may be melted and cast. If suddenly quenched in water, when red-hot, it becomes as hard and brittle as white cast-iron; and when subsequently heated to a regulated temperature, the *temper* may be reduced to any desired extent. It may thus be made soft and tough, or hard and elastic, at will, and on this remarkable quality its numerous and important applications to the useful arts depend. Good steel contains from 0.7 to 1.7 per cent of carbon, and it is made either by carbonizing wrought-iron, as in the ordinary *cementation* method, or, as in the Bessemer process, by decarbonizing cast-iron; but it is probable that the qualities of steel depend fully as much on some unknown causes as on the presence of carbon. It has even been doubted whether the presence of carbon is essential; and indeed, the whole subject is very obscure.

335. *Metallic Iron.* — The *Sp. Gr.* of the purest iron is 8.14, but cast-iron has sometimes a specific gravity as low as 7, and the density of the different varieties of the metal ranges between these extremes, the average for good bar-iron being 7.7. Iron is distinguished for its great susceptibility to magnetism, and in this respect it far surpasses both nickel and cobalt, the only other metals that exhibit this property in any marked degree. The susceptibility of iron to magnetic induction diminishes as its hardness increases, but at the same time its power of retaining the virtue is enhanced. Thus, iron can only be permanently magnetized when combined with carbon, as in steel, or with oxygen, as in the magnetic oxide or loadstone, Fe_3O_4, or with sulphur, as in magnetic pyrites, Fe_7S_8; but it is a fact worthy of notice, that spiegeleisen, specular iron, Fe_2O_3, and common pyrites, FeS_2, are almost indifferent to the action of a magnet, and the same is true of most other iron compounds.

At a high temperature iron burns readily, and under favorable conditions will sustain its own combustion (63). The product formed is Fe_3O_4. At a red heat it also decomposes water, yielding the same oxide as before, together with hydrogen gas. At the ordinary temperature, however, polished iron retains its lustre unimpaired, both in *dry* air and in *pure* water (free from air); but when exposed to both air and moisture, the surface soon becomes covered with rust. Moreover, this change is not merely superficial, but under favorable conditions proceeds until the whole mass of the metal is converted into a ferric hydrate, having the composition of Limonite. The change accelerates as it advances, and the rust first formed seems to act as a carrier of oxygen to the rest of the metal. The corrosion of wood and other organic fibre, when in contact with rusty nails, has been explained in a similar way. It is also a favorite theory that a coating of rust forms with the metal a voltaic combination, which actually decomposes the water present, and this is thought to account for the singular fact that iron-rust always contains ammonia.

Iron readily dissolves in dilute mineral acids, yielding a ferrous salt and hydrogen gas. It also dissolves in aqueous solution of carbonic acid if free from air. Concentrated sulphuric acid, even when boiled with iron, has but little action upon it. Nitric acid, on the other hand, rapidly dissolves the metal with

evolution of NO. It is a singular fact, however, that the most
concentrated nitric acid (*Sp. Gr.* 1.45) not only does not attack
iron, but so modifies its condition that it may subsequently be
kept for weeks in acid of the ordinary strength (*Sp. Gr.* not
less than 1.35) without the slightest alteration of the polish on
its surface. This same *passive condition* may also be induced
in other ways.

Iron enters into chemical combination with almost all the
non-metallic elements, and forms alloys with many of the metals. Corresponding to the three degrees of quantivalence are
three very distinct classes of compounds : first, the *ferrous* compounds, whose radical is a single bivalent atom of iron; secondly,
the *ferric* compounds, having a sexivalent radical consisting of
two quadrivalent atoms of iron ; and lastly, a few very unstable
salts called *ferrates*, analogous to the manganates, in which a
sexivalent atom of iron is the acid radical. The last class of
compounds, although practically unimportant, are interesting,
as they indicate the close relationship between iron and manganese ; but iron differs from all the associated elements in that
the two radicals $Fe^=$ and $[Fe_2]^{\underline{\underline{\equiv}}}$ form equally stable compounds,
and play an equally important part in the mineral kingdom ;
and this double aspect of the element is one of its most characteristic and important features.

336. *Ferrous Compounds.* — The crystallized ferrous compounds have, as a rule, a light green color, and ferrous oxide
imparts the same color to glass (152). The soluble ferrous
salts have a characteristic styptic taste. They are isomorphous
with the corresponding compounds of magnesium and zinc, and
quite as closely allied to them as to those of manganese, cobalt,
and nickel, — the elements with which iron is classed in the
scheme of this book. Thus, in nature, ferrous carbonate is as
intimately associated with the carbonates of magnesium and
zinc as with the carbonate of manganese, and the four bivalent
radicals replace each other in almost every proportion, not only
in the carbonates, but also in the silicates, and in a large number of other minerals. In like manner, ferrous sulphate (green
vitriol), like the sulphates of the same metals, and also those of
nickel and cobalt, crystallizes with seven molecules of water,
and forms double salts with the sulphates of the alkaline metals
(313), (322), (330). The sulphate is the most important of

the soluble ferrous salts, but all the following are also well known: —

Ferrous Chloride	$FeCl_2 . 4H_2O,$
Ferrous Nitrate	$Fe{=}O_2{=}(NO_2)_2 . 6H_2O,$
Ferrous Sulphate	$Fe{=}O_2{=}SO_2 . (7, 4, 3,$ or $2H_2O),$
Ferrous Oxalate	$Fe{=}O_2{=}C_2O_2 . 2H_2O,$
Ferrous Phosphate	$H_2,Fe_{2}{=}O_{6}{=}(PO)_2.$

In solutions of the ferrous salts, when protected from the air, the alkaline hydrates give a white precipitate of ferrous hydrate, $Fe{=}O_2{=}H_2,$ and the alkaline carbonates a similar white precipitate, which is a hydro-carbonate of variable composition. In the presence, however, of a large amount of NH_4Cl, neither ammonia nor ammonic carbonate give any precipitate, and the precipitation by the other alkaline reagents is in great measure prevented. The alkaline sulphides, nevertheless, precipitate the iron wholly as a hydrated ferrous sulphide, and so does also H_2S when the solution is alkaline, but not when the slightest excess of any mineral acid is present. Solutions of the ferrous salts, when exposed to the air, absorb oxygen, and the ferrous changes into a ferric compound. The same is true of the ferrous precipitates formed as just described, all of which are very rapidly oxidized as soon as they are exposed to the atmosphere. The products in any case are determined by various conditions, but the following are some of the most characteristic of the reactions: —

$$(4Fe{=}O_2{=}SO_2 + 2H_2{=}O_2{=}SO_2 + Aq) + O{=}O =$$
$$(2[Fe_2]{=}O_6{=}(SO_2)_3 + 2H_2O + Aq). \quad [340]$$

$$(20Fe{=}O_2{=}SO_2 + 6H_2O + Aq) + 5O{=}O = \qquad [341]$$
$$2(O_5{}^x[Fe_2]_2{=}O_2{=}SO_2 . 3H_2O) + (6[Fe_2]{=}O_6{=}(SO_2)_3 + Aq).$$

$$4Fe{=}O_2{=}H_2 + O{=}O = 2O{=}[Fe_2]{=}O_4{=}H_4. \quad [342]$$

337. *Ferric Compounds.* — Ferric oxide, when dissolved in melted borax, imparts to the glass a yellow or yellowish-red color, and most of the ferric compounds affect the same tints.

17   Y

They are isomorphous with the corresponding compounds of
aluminium, and closely allied to them in their chemical relations. The following are the most important of the soluble
normal salts: —

Ferric Chloride　　$[Fe_2]^{\scriptsize ii}_{\scriptsize ii}Cl_6 \cdot 6H_2O$, also with 5 or $12H_2O$,

Ferric Nitrate　　$[Fe_2]^{\scriptsize ii}_{\scriptsize ii}O_6^{\scriptsize iii}(NO_2)_6 \cdot 18H_2O$, also with $12H_2O$,

Ferric Acetate　　$[Fe_2]^{\scriptsize ii}_{\scriptsize ii}O_6^{\scriptsize iii}(C_2H_3O)_6 + Aq$,

Ferric Sulphate　　$[Fe_2]^{\scriptsize ii}_{\scriptsize ii}O_6^{\scriptsize iii}(SO_2)_3 \cdot 9H_2O$,

Diammonic-ferric Sulphate

$$(NH_4)_2 \cdot [Fe_2]^{\text{viii}}O_8^{\text{viii}}(SO_2)_4 \cdot 24H_2O,$$

Ferric Oxalate　　　　$[Fe_2]^{\scriptsize ii}_{\scriptsize ii}O_6^{\scriptsize iii}(C_2O_2)_3,$

Sodio-ferric Oxalate　$Na_6 \cdot [Fe_2]^{\text{xii}}O_{12}^{\text{xii}}(C_2O_2)_6 \cdot 6H_2O.$

Ferric acetate cannot be crystallized, and the ferric salts, as
a rule, crystallize with difficulty. All the well-marked radi-
cals of the type $[R_2]^{\scriptsize iii}_{\scriptsize ii}$ manifest a very strong tendency to form
basic compounds (38) [51], and the ferric salts furnish a strik-
ing illustration of the general principle. Most of the native
ferric salts are basic, and the symbols of a number of such compounds have already been given. Their mutual relations will
be best understood if they are studied in connection with the
various hydrates, from which they may be regarded as derived,
and a table of the possible ferric hydrates is easily made after
the principle of (151). Of the compounds which are thus theoretically possible, a large number are easily prepared, and a
still larger number are at times formed when the conditions
happen to be favorable; but as the compounds become more
basic, they soon lose every trace of crystalline structure, and
with this all evidence of definite chemical constitution disappears. The products are then amorphous or colloidal solids,
which present in their composition every possible gradation
between certain limits.[1]

---

[1] Solutions of various basic compounds are readily obtained either by dissolving freshly precipitated ferric hydrate in a solution of almost any ferric
salt, or by partially abstracting the acid of the salt by the cautious addition
of an alkali. A solution of ferric nitrate, for example, may thus be made to
take up seven additional atoms of $[Fe_2]$. On allowing such solutions to evaporate spontaneously, the basic compounds may frequently be obtained in the
solid state.

All the more basic salts are, as a rule, insoluble in water, but in several cases they affect both a soluble and an insoluble modification, and under certain conditions the first changes into the last on simply boiling the solution. The soluble condition appears in all cases to be a colloidal modification, and by dialysing (56) a solution of basic ferric chloride it is possible to remove almost all the acid radical, and obtain nearly a pure solution of ferric hydrate. This solution coagulates on standing, and the ferric hydrate thus passes through successive stages of dehydration. On boiling the water, the dehydration proceeds still further, until at last a hydrate corresponding to Göthite is formed. So also the voluminous hydrate, first precipitated by alkaline reagents from cold solutions of ferric salts, undergoes a similar change under the same conditions. These facts would lead us to infer that the "coagulation" of the solutions of the basic ferric salts is caused by the elimination of a certain quantity of water from the molecules of the compound.

The ferric compounds, although permanent in the air, are easily reduced to the ferrous condition by the feeblest reducing agents.

$$([Fe_2]Cl_6 + Aq) + Zn = (2FeCl_2 + ZnCl_2 + Aq). \quad [343]$$

$$([Fe]Cl_6 + H_2S + Aq) = S + (2FeCl_2 + 2HCl + Aq). \quad [344]$$

In solutions of ferric salts, the alkaline hydrates and carbonates all give a red precipitate of ferric hydrate, whose constitution varies with the conditions of the experiment, as indicated above. *This precipitate is insoluble in an excess of sodic or potassic hydrate.* In the same solutions potassic sulpho-cyanide strikes a deep red color, and potassic ferro-cyanide gives a deep blue precipitate. These reactions are very delicate, and enable us to detect the smallest amount of a ferric compound, even in the solution of a ferrous salt. The ferrous compound, under the same conditions, gives no color and a white precipitate.

338. *Chlorides.* $FeCl_2$ and $[Fe_2]Cl_6$. — By carefully heating crystallized ferrous chloride (336) out of contact with the air, the anhydrous compound can be obtained; but a solution of ferric chloride cannot be rendered anhydrous by evaporation, since the hydrous compound is decomposed by heat into hydrochloric acid and ferric oxide. Anhydrous ferrous chloride can

also be obtained by passing HCl over ignited metallic iron. Anhydrous ferric chloride can be prepared in a similar way, using Cl-Cl instead of HCl. The first yields a white, sublimate; the second, which is the most volatile, is deposited in brownish crystalline scales, and the Sp. Gr. of its vapor has been determined. There are fluorides, bromides, and iodides corresponding to the chlorides, but they have no special interest.

339. *Oxides.* — FeO, $[Fe_2]O_3$, $Fe,[Fe_2]^{viii}O_4$. — Ferrous oxide may be prepared by boiling in the surrounding water the voluminous white hydrate obtained when an alkali is added to the solution of a pure ferrous salt, every trace of air being carefully excluded. If exposed to the air, it rapidly absorbs oxygen, and $[Fe_2]O_3$ is the final result. A black pyrophoric powder, obtained by igniting ferrous oxalate in a close vessel, is a mixture of the same oxide with metallic iron. Ferric oxide is prepared for the arts by igniting green vitriol, or still better, ferric sulphate. It forms, even when most highly levigated, a very hard powder, much used for polishing glass and metallic surfaces (Colcothar, Crocus Martis, Rouge). It is also used as a red paint. Ferrous-ferric oxide is formed when either of the other oxides is intensely heated in the air, and must, therefore, be regarded as the most stable of this class of compounds. It is distinguished by its susceptibility to magnetism, and its crystalline form (74), which connects it with Spinel (352) and other allied isomorphous compounds. Besides the above, one or more intermediate oxides have been distinguished, but they are probably mixtures of the oxides already named. As has been already stated, both the anhydrous and the hydrous oxides are abundant native minerals, and important ores.

340. *Sulphides.* — The fusible product obtained by melting together iron and sulphur, and so much used in the laboratory for making H_2S, is essentially ferrous sulphide, FeS, although its composition is not absolutely constant. The same compound may be formed by mixing flowers of sulphur and iron-filings with water, and, since the resulting compound forms a coherent mass, this mixture is useful under certain conditions as a cement. Ferric disulphide, FeS_2 (Iron Pyrites), is by far the most abundant of the native metallic sulphides. It occurs in almost all mineral veins, and is known to the miners as *Mundic*. It is readily distinguished by its yellow color and great hard-

ness. The more compact varieties are very resisting minerals, but those of a looser texture rapidly crumble when exposed to the atmosphere, and this is especially true of the orthorhombic variety called *Marcasite*. The crumbling of many rocks is also caused by the oxidation of the pyrites which they contain. Although useless as an ore of iron, common pyrites is exceedingly valuable as a source of sulphur, and for the manufacture of sulphuric acid. The magnetic sulphide Fe_7S_8 has already been mentioned, and there is also a sulphide, Fe_3S_4, corresponding to the magnetic oxide, and another, Fe_2S_3, corresponding to ferric oxide. Moreover, sulphides of the composition Fe_8S and Fe_2S have been formed, but it is doubtful whether they are all definite compounds. The black precipitates, obtained when an alkaline sulphide is added to the solutions of ferrous and ferric salts, are either sulpho-hydrates (241) or molecular compounds of the sulphide and water. They are both very unstable products, and rapidly oxidize when exposed to the air.

341. *Ferrates.* — Potassic ferrate, $K_2O_2FeO_2$, may be prepared either by fusing ferric oxide with nitre or by passing chlorine gas through a very strong solution of potassic hydrate, in which ferric oxide is suspended. Both the fused mass of the first reaction, and the black powder deposited from the alkaline solution in the second, yield with water a beautiful violet-colored solution of potassic ferrate. This compound is very unstable, and has merely a theoretical interest. Ferrates of the alkaline earths are also known; but neither ferric acid nor any compounds corresponding to the permanganates have as yet been discovered.

Questions and Problems.

Manganese.

1. By what simple blow-pipe test may the presence of manganese in a mineral be recognized? How far is the color of the manganese minerals characteristic?

2. Compare the manganous with the niccolous and cobaltous salts, and show to what extent they resemble each other, as well as indicate the points of difference.

3. Compare the ammonio-salts of the same three elements, and

seek the cause of the difference of the effects which the atmospheric air produces when solutions of these salts are exposed to its influence.

4. Represent by graphic symbols the constitution both of manganous and manganic alum.

5. Write the reaction of potassic hydrate on a solution of manganous chloride, and the further reaction when the resulting precipitate is exposed to the atmospheric air. Assume that the final product is manganic hydrate.

6. Write the reaction of hydro-disodic phosphate and ammonic hydrate on a solution of manganous chloride, and also indicate the further change which takes place on igniting the resulting precipitate.

7. Make a list of the oxides of manganese, and show how far they correspond to the oxides of nickel and cobalt on the one side, and to those of iron on the other. Make also a similar comparison of the different hydrates. Compare also the different oxides and hydrates as regards their relative stability.

8. Of the metals thus far studied, which are precipitated from acid solutions, and which only from alkaline solutions, by H_2S?

9. By what solvents may the sulphides of manganese zinc and cobalt, when precipitated together, be separated?

10. In what other way may manganese, when in solution, be separated from nickel and cobalt?

11. To what relationship does the crystalline form of the native carbonates of manganese point?

12. By what means may manganese be separated from zinc when both are present in the same solution as acetates? If they are in the condition of chlorides, how may they be readily converted into acetates? How far may the same methods be used to separate manganese from the metallic radicals previously studied?

13. Write the reaction of the atmospheric oxygen on a solution of ammonio-manganous chloride.

14. Write the reaction of chlorine gas on manganous carbonate suspended in water.

15. Represent by graphic symbols the constitution of Pyrolusite, Braunite, and Hausmannite, and endeavor to harmonize the crystallographic relations stated above. Take also into consideration the relations of MnO_2 described in (236).

16. Represent by graphic symbols the constitution of Manganite and Göthite.

17. Write the reaction of sulphuric and also of hydrochloric acid on each of the three oxides, MnO_2, Mn_2O_3, and Mn_3O_4.

18. When a mixture of MnO_2 and oxalic acid is heated with dilute sulphuric acid, the products are manganous sulphate water and carbonic anhydride gas. Write the reaction, and calculate how much CO_2 would be formed for every gramme of MnO_2 taken.

19. Can you base on the reaction just written a method of determining the purity of the commercial "black oxide of manganese," which is frequently a mixture of the different native oxides, and is sometimes adulterated with sand.

20. Assuming that one gramme of a sample of the commercial oxide sets free, as above, 0.654 gramme of CO_2, how much bleaching salts could be manufactured with 1,000 kilos. of the oxide, assuming that the symbol of the bleaching salts is $(Ca\text{-}O)\text{=}Cl_2$?

21. Write the reaction of MnO_2 on $HCl + Aq$, assuming that $MnCl_4$ is first formed and subsequently decomposed by the heat employed.

22. Represent by a graphic symbol the constitution of manganic and manganous alum. (332) and (352).

23. State the distinction between the two classes of manganic compounds, and illustrate by representing the constitution of Mn_2O_3 first as a normal sesquioxide, and secondly as a molecular compound of manganous oxide and manganic dioxide.

24. Compare the manganic compounds with the corresponding compounds of nickel and cobalt. Consider in this connection the relative stability of the substances compared.

25. Represent the constitution of potassic manganate by a graphic symbol, and compare this with the graphic symbol of potassic sulphate.

26. How far does the isomorphism of the sulphates with the manganates indicate the quantivalence of the metallic radical in these compounds? What should you infer from the great difference in the stability of the two classes of salts in regard to the sexivalent condition of manganese?

27. Analyze reaction [337], and show that it turns on a change of quantivalence in the manganese atoms.

28. Is it necessary to assume a similar change of quantivalence in reaction [338]?

29. Represent the constitution of potassic permanganate by a graphic symbol, both on the assumption that the atoms are octivalent and also assuming that they are still sexivalent. Can you give any reasons why one symbol should be more probable than the other? Does not the fact that the permanganates are more stable than the manganates have a bearing on the question? How can you reconcile the isomorphism of the permanganates and the per-

chlorates, manganese being an artiad and chlorine a perissad element ?

30. Write the reaction when a solution of manganous chloride is boiled with free nitric acid and plumbic dioxide.

31. How could reaction [339] be used to determine the amount of iron in a given solution ?

32. What do you regard as the chief characteristic of manganese as compared with the allied metallic radicals ? and why does the study of its compounds have a peculiarly important bearing on chemical theories ?

33. Does not the study of the manganese compounds indicate a more rational use of the terminations *ous, ic, ite,* and *ate* in the nomenclature of chemistry ?

34. How may the principles of the nomenclature stated in Chapter X. be extended so as to express accurately the constitution of the more complex chemical compounds ? Give rules based on your own experience, and illustrate them by examples. Bear in mind, however, that, according to the best usage, the Greek numerals are employed, rather than the Latin, as prefixes.

Iron.

35. Compare the native compounds of manganese and iron, and point out the analogies as well as the differences which you observe.

36. Compare in the same way the native compounds of nickel and cobalt with those of iron, paying special attention to the sulphides and arsenides.

37. Compare the native compounds of magnesium and zinc with those of iron.

38. The mineral Pisanite indicates what relation between iron and copper ?

39. Why is not Pyrites included among the ores of iron ? State some of the circumstances on which the value of a bed of iron ore depends.

40. The *Sp. Gr.* of Pyrites is 5.2, that of Marcasite, 4.7, and that of Mispickel, 6.2. Compare the atomic volumes of these minerals.

41. Make a table giving the symbols of the minerals isomorphous with Iron Pyrites and Marcasite respectively.

42. Explain the theory of the " Blast Furnace,"[1] and show that the formation of slags of the right fusibility is essential to the success

---

[1] See Miller's Chemistry or Percy's Metallurgy

of the process, and that the proportion of flux must be differently adjusted according as cold or hot blast is used.

43. The slag formed both in the bloomery forge [1] and in the puddling process [1] is a *very* fusible *ferrous* silicate, having approximately the composition Fe_2O_4Si. Explain the theory of these processes, and show that the great fusibility of the slag is an essential condition of the production of wrought-iron. Could the loss of iron in the slag be avoided? How do you account for the low quantivalence of iron in this product? To what mineral does it correspond in composition?

44. Explain the theory of the Bessemer process [1] for refining cast-iron or making steel, and compare it with the puddling process. Consider especially the effects of the very high temperature attained in Bessemer's converter.

45. Compare together the qualities of iron in its three conditions of cast-iron, wrought-iron, and steel.

46. State the differences between the several varieties of cast-iron, gray, mottled, white, and spiegeleisen.

47. When white iron is dissolved in acid, all the carbon is converted into a volatile hydro-carbon oil, while under similar circumstances gray iron leaves a large residue of graphite. What conclusion do you draw from these facts?

48. Write the reaction when iron burns.

49. Write the reaction when steam is passed over red-hot iron.

50. Write the reaction when iron rusts, assuming, 1st. That the metal draws the oxygen wholly from the air; 2d. That water is decomposed and ammonia formed.

51. Write the reaction of an aqueous solution of carbonic acid on iron, assuming that no air is present. What is the nature of the solution thus obtained (279)?

52. Write the reaction of dilute sulphuric acid on iron, and inquire how much the acid should be diluted in order to obtain the best effect. In preparing ferrous sulphate, why is it best to use ferrous sulphide instead of metallic iron?

53. Write the rational symbol of dipotassic-ferrous sulphate, and compare its constitution with that of the isomorphous ferrous sulphate (336).

54. Compare the sulphates of magnesium, zinc, manganese, and iron, as regards the varying quantities of water of crystallization with which the several salts may combine.

[1] See Miller's Chemistry or Percy's Metallurgy.

17*

55. Pure ferrous nitrate may be obtained by dissolving ferrous sulphide in dilute nitric acid.   Write the reaction.

56. When metallic iron is dissolved in dilute nitric acid, the products are ferrous nitrate, ammonic nitrate, and water.   Write the reaction and compare it with the last.

57. Write the reaction of nitric acid (common strength) on iron, assuming that the products are ferric nitrate and nitric oxide.

58. Point out the ferrous and ferric compounds among the symbols on pages 378 and 379, and determine in each case the ratio which the quantivalence of the acid radical bears to that of the basic radicals, both $R=$ and $[R_2]\overline{\overline{\underline{\underline{\,}}}}$.

59. Ferrous phosphate is formed by precipitation on adding common sodic phosphate to the solution of a ferrous salt.   Write the reaction.

60. Ferrous oxalate is obtained on adding ammonic oxalate to a solution of ferrous sulphate.   Write the reaction.

61. Write the reaction which takes place when sodic hydrate is added to a cold solution of ferrous sulphate, the air being wholly excluded.   What further change takes place if the liquid is boiled in which the precipitate is suspended ?

62. Write the reaction of ammonic sulphide on a solution of ferrous sulphate, assuming that the precipitate fixes two molecules of water.

63. Write the reaction of sodic carbonate on a solution of ferric sulphate, assuming that the constitution of the product is analogous to that formed when the same reagent is added to a solution of magnesic sulphate.

64. Write the reaction of sodic carbonate on a solution of ferrous chloride, first, when the solution is cold, secondly, when it is boiling.

65. Ferric hydrate dissolves in a solution of acid potassic oxalate, forming potassio-ferric oxalate.   Write the reaction.   What practical application may be made of it ?

66. Normal ferric oxalate is precipitated when a slight excess of any ferric salt is mixed with a solution of ammonic oxalate.   Write the reaction.   The precipitated ferric oxalate readily dissolves in a solution of oxalic acid.   What compound is probably formed ?   When this solution is exposed to the sun, *ferrous* oxalate is precipitated, and CO_2 is evolved.   Write the reaction.

67. A solution of ferrous carbonate in $(CO_2 + Aq)$ deposits, when exposed to the air, a hydrate having the composition of Limonite. Write the reaction.   Under what circumstances might you expect

that a solution of ferrous carbonate would be formed in nature, remembering that the soil contains more or less ferric hydrate?· Under what circumstances would Siderite be deposited from such chalybeate waters (279)? Can you form any theory which accounts for the formation of beds of Siderite (clay iron-stone) in connection with the coal-measures?

68. Make a table of the possible ferric hydrates, and point out the relations of the native hydrates in your scheme.

69. By means of the table made as just directed, show in what relation the different native sulphates, phosphates, and arseniates stand to the hydrates.

70. Make a table illustrating how many nitrates, sulphates, or phosphates may be formed corresponding to any one of the possible hydrates.

71. Represent by graphic symbols the constitution of the basic sulphate $O_5[Fe_2]_2 = O_2 = SO_2$.

72. When to the solution of a ferric salt an alkali is added until it begins to occasion a permanent precipitate, and the solution is then raised to the boiling point, the whole or the greater part of the iron is precipitated as an insoluble basic salt. How do you explain the reaction?

73. Starting with a molecule of a ferric salt, show what products would result by the assimilation of successive molecules of ferric hydrate. Again, starting with one or more of the complex molecules thus obtained, and eliminating all the possible molecules of water, show what must be the constitution of the basic salts which would then be formed.

74. Have you observed that the solubility of salts in water has any connection with the number of atoms of typical hydrogen they contain? Cite examples in favor of this theory.

75. Cite different cases in which water is eliminated from a molecule on boiling the liquid in which the compound is dissolved or suspended.

76. When anhydrous ferrous sulphate is heated to redness, as in the process of making Nordhausen sulphuric acid (249), it is resolved into ferric oxide and into sulphurous and sulphuric anhydrides. Write the reaction.

77. The Nordhausen acid is now more frequently made by distilling anhydrous *ferric sulphate*. Write the reaction, and show how the sulphate may be regenerated and the same oxide used over and over again.

78. How could the reactions [343] and [339] be used to determine the relative amounts of the two iron radicals in a given mineral, assuming that it could be brought into solution without changing the atomic condition of the metal?

79. Baric carbonate precipitates all the iron from ferric, but not any of the metal from ferrous solutions. Moreover, ferrous hydrate precipitates ferric hydrate from the solutions of ferric salts. Write these reactions, and discuss the different relations of the two iron radicals to which they point.

80. By what characteristic reactions may the atomic condition of iron, when in solution, be easily determined?

81. Can one condition of iron be said to be more stable *absolutely* than the other?

82. What two wholly distinct relationships does iron manifest? Trace the lines of connection in each case. Point out also the specific characters by which iron is related to each member of the two groups of allied elements.

83. By what character are the elements classed with aluminum chiefly marked?

84. Compare the reaction of $(HCl + Aq)$ on Ni_2O_3, Co_2O_3, Mn_2O_3, Fe_2O_3, and show that the differences depend on the relative stability of the several hexad radicals.

85. In what way may magnesium, zinc, nickel, cobalt, and manganese be separated from aluminum, chromium, and iron?

86. Is there any reason for believing that in crystallized ferric chloride the water forms a part of the salt molecule? Write the reaction which takes place when the salt is heated.

87. Does the Sp. Gr. of anhydrous ferric chloride throw any light on the constitution of the ferric salts?

88. Write the reactions of $H\text{-}Cl$ and of $Cl\text{-}Cl$ on ignited metallic iron. Why should a ferrous compound be formed in the first case when a ferric compound is formed in the second?

89. When MnO_2 is melted into glass colored green by ferrous oxide, the color is either wholly removed, or, when originally very deep, is changed to yellow. How do you explain this reaction, and also the other familiar blow-pipe reactions of ferric oxide with a borax bead.

90. Ferric oxide, obtained by drying the hydrate at a temperature not exceeding 320°, dissolves easily in acids; but if heated to a low red heat, it suddenly glows, becomes denser, and after this dissolves in acids with difficulty. Are you acquainted with similar facts in

regard to any other metallic oxides? It is observed that the ignited oxide dissolves without difficulty in $(HCl + Aq)$ when the action is aided by ferrous chloride, zinc, stannous chloride, or some other reducing agent. How do you explain the reaction?

91. Write the reaction when FeS_2 is burnt in a current of air, assuming that the products are Fe_2O_3 and SO_2, and calculate how much sulphuric acid, *Sp. Gr.* 1.501, can be made from 1,000 kilos. of Pyrites.

92. In one process of purifying coal gas, the H_2S is absorbed by moist ferric oxide, and the sulphide thus formed is subsequently exposed to the air, when the oxide is "regenerated." Explain the reaction.

93. Pyrites appears to be formed in nature by the deoxidation of calcic sulphate, by means of organic matter in presence of chalybeate waters, and crystals have been formed artificially on twigs, in solutions of ferrous sulphate. Explain the reaction.

94. When SO_2 is passed through an alkaline solution of potassic ferrate, ferric oxide is precipitated, while potassic sulphate is formed in the solution. Write the reaction, and show that it may be used to determine the constitution of the ferrates.

95. The slag of a blast-furnace is essentially a double silicate of aluminum and calcium, in which the *atomic ratio*[1] of the two basic radicals, $Ca^=$ and $[Al_2]^{\equiv\equiv}$, is one to two. In the less fusible slags the total quantivalence of all the basic radicals is equal to that of the silicon, while in the most fusible slags it is only one half of that amount. Write the symbols of these silicates, assuming (as is usually the case) that the calcium is partially replaced by magnesium and iron.

[1] By the atomic ratio of a compound is meant the ratio between the total quantivalence of the several radicals which it contains.

Division XII.

342. CHROMIUM. $Cr = 52.2$. — Sometimes, although rarely, bivalent. Usually either quadrivalent or sexivalent. Many of the compounds of this element have a brilliant color, and are used as paints, and the name is derived from χρῶμα (color). The only important native compounds are

Chromite (Chrome Iron)　Isometric　$Fe,[Cr_2]^{viii}O_4$,
Crocoite　　　　　　　　Monoclinic　$Pb^=O_2^=CrO_2$.

The first is the ore from which all the chrome pigments used in the arts are indirectly prepared. It has an iron-black color, and has been found in abundance at a few localities, associated with serpentine. The second, although a very rare mineral, is well known on account of its brilliant red color, and in it the element chromium was first discovered (by Vauquelin in 1797).

343. *Metallic Chromium* may be prepared by reducing Cr_2O_3 with carbon at a very high temperature, and still more readily by reducing Cr_2Cl_6 with zinc, magnesium, or the alkaline metals. On account of its very great infusibility, it has never been obtained in compact masses, and its qualities are therefore imperfectly known. The whitish-gray porous mass, formed when the oxide is reduced by carbon, has a *Sp. Gr.* of 5.9. It is, like cast-iron, a combination of the metal with carbon, and consists of grains, which are as hard as corundum. The crystalline powder, obtained by reducing the chloride with zinc, has a *Sp. Gr.* of 6.81, and is undoubtedly a purer condition of the metal. When in fine powder, chromium takes fire below redness; but in its more compact forms it resists oxidizing agents as well as aluminum, and acts towards the different mineral acids in a similar way.

344. *Chromous Compounds.* — This class includes all those compounds of chromium in which the element is bivalent; but, since its atoms in this condition have still four strong affinities unsatisfied, the compounds of this order are all very unstable. The most important is $CrCl_2$, which is obtained by heating Cr_2Cl_6 to redness in a current of dry hydrogen. The white powder thus formed gives a blue solution with water, which, however, rapidly absorbs oxygen, and becomes green when ex-

posed to the air. Chromous hydrate, which falls as a dark brown precipitate on adding caustic potash to the blue solution, even decomposes water with evolution of hydrogen. The most stable of the chromous salts is $K_2, Cr^{\equiv}O_4^{\equiv}[SO_2]_2 \cdot 6H_2O$, which forms beautiful blue crystals isomorphous with the corresponding ferrous salt.

345. *Chromic Compounds.* — In these compounds the element is quadrivalent, but they all contain the sexivalent radical $[Cr_2]$. The commercial chromic oxide is a brilliant green powder, which is very much used in the arts, not only as a common paint (chrome green), but also as a vitrifiable pigment, since it imparts a beautiful green color to glass and to the glazing of porcelain ware. It may be prepared from the chromates in a great variety of ways, as is illustrated by the following reactions : —

$$4[\mathbf{Hg}_2]\text{-}\mathbf{O}_2\text{-}\mathbf{CrO}_2 = 2[\mathbf{Cr}_2]\mathbf{O}_3 + 8\mathbb{H}g + 5\mathbb{O}\text{-}\mathbb{O}. \quad [345]$$

$$(\mathbf{NH}_4)_2\text{-}\mathbf{O}_2\text{-}\mathbf{Cr}_2\mathbf{O}_5 = [\mathbf{Cr}_2]\mathbf{O}_3 + 4\mathbb{H}_2\mathbb{O} + \mathbb{N}\text{-}\mathbb{N}. \quad [346]$$

$$4\mathbb{C}r^{\equiv}\mathbb{O}_2,\mathbb{C}l_2 = 2[\mathbf{Cr}_2]\mathbf{O}_3 + 4\mathbb{C}l\text{-}\mathbb{C}l + \mathbb{O}\text{-}\mathbb{O}. \quad [347]$$

$$\mathbf{K}_2\text{-}\mathbf{O}_2\text{-}\mathbf{Cr}_2\mathbf{O}_5 + \mathbb{C}l\text{-}\mathbb{C}l =$$
$$[\mathbf{Cr}_2]\mathbf{O}_3 + 2\mathbf{KCl} + 2\mathbb{O}\text{-}\mathbb{O}. \quad [348]$$

The first two reactions are obtained by simply igniting the solid chromates. The third, by passing the vapor of chloro-chromic anhydride through a red-hot porcelain tube, and the last, by passing chlorine gas over ignited potassic dichromate. By the third reaction the oxide may be obtained in definite rhombohedral crystals (*Sp. Gr.* 5.21), which have the form and hardness of specular iron, and even the amorphous commercial oxide is so hard that, when finely levigated, it may be used like rouge for polishing glass. In this hard condition the oxide is almost insoluble in acids. There is, however, a less dense condition of the oxide (obtained by cautiously heating the hydrate), which dissolves freely in all the mineral acids. It has a darker color, and, like ferric oxide, changes suddenly with incandescence into the insoluble modification, if heated above a definite point. At the highest temperatures chromic oxide does not lose oxygen, and cannot be reduced by hydrogen. It may be melted by the heat of a forge fire, and the molten oxide forms, on cooling, a very hard dark-green crystalline solid.

There are a number of *chromic hydrates* corresponding to the ferric hydrates; but the different compounds cannot be isolated as readily, and their symbols have not been as accurately determined. When sodic or potassic hydrate is added to the solution of a chromic salt, the chromic hydrate first precipitated is dissolved by an excess of the reagent, but the precipitate reappears on boiling the liquid. These precipitates retain a portion of the alkali, which modifies the qualities of the hydrate, and this circumstance renders the investigation of these compounds very difficult. The only way to procure a pure hydrate is to precipitate with ammonia from boiling solutions. The light-blue precipitate thus obtained retains from one to seven molecules of water, according to the conditions under which it is dried.

The soluble chromic salts affect, as a rule at least, two modifications. In one state they have a violet color, and crystallize more or less readily, while in the other they have a green color, and are uncrystallizable. Thus we have, besides an anhydrous chromic sulphate, which is red and insoluble, the two following hydrous salts: —

Violet Sulphate (soluble and cryst.) $[Cr_2]^{\underline{\underline{ii}}} O_6^{\underline{\underline{ii}}} (SO_2)_3 . 15 H_2O,$

Green " (soluble but uncryst.) $[Cr_2]^{\underline{\underline{ii}}} O_6^{\underline{\underline{ii}}} (SO_2)_3 . 5 H_2O.$

The second is obtained by heating the crystals of the first to 100°. But the water thus driven off cannot be wholly water of crystallization, for on simply boiling a solution of the violet compound the same change of color and crystalline character takes place. There is evidently an essential alteration in the molecular structure of the compound, but further than this we have as yet no knowledge.

The best known of the chromic salts is *chrome alum*, which is easily prepared from commercial potassic bichromate by the reaction.

$$(K_2^{=}O_2^{=}Cr_2O_5 + H_2^{=}O_2^{=}SO_2 + 3SO_2 + Aq) =$$
$$(K_2[Cr_2]^{\text{viii}} O_8^{\text{viii}} (SO_2)_4 + H_2O + Aq). \quad [349]$$

This salt, like the other alums, crystallizes with $24 H_2O$ in octahedrons having a dark purple (nearly black) color, but which, when sufficiently thin, transmit a beautiful ruby red tint. Care must be taken in reducing the chromate that the temperature of the solution does not rise too high, for above $70°$ or $80°$ the change above described takes place, and the salt loses its power of crystallizing. By keeping, however, the green solution thus formed for several weeks, it gradually recovers its violet color, and then will yield the normal crystals.

346. *The Chromic Oxalates* form two interesting series of double salts. Those of the first class have a dark-blue, and those of the second class a ruby-red color. Thus we have

Blue Salt $K_6 [Cr_2]^{xii} O_{12}^{xii} (C_2 O_2)_6 . 6 H_2 O,$

Red Salt $K_2 [Cr_2]^{viii} O_8^{viii} (C_2 O_2)_4 . 8 H_2 O$ or $12 H_2 O.$

Ammonia gives no precipitate in solutions of these salts, neither does potassic hydrate, until they are boiled. Corresponding compounds are known containing $(NH_4)_2$, Na_2, Ba, Sr, Ca, or Mg in place of K_2, but with varying quantities of water of crystallization.

347. *Chromic Nitrate* may be obtained in dark purple crystals having the composition $[Cr_2]^{ii} O_6^{ii} (NO_2)_6 . 18 H_2 O$, by dissolving chromic hydrate in nitric acid, but the solution becomes green and uncrystallizable if heated beyond a limited degree.

348. *Chromic Chloride*, $[Cr_2]^{ii} Cl_6$, is prepared by passing chlorine gas through an intimate mixture of chromic oxide with carbon, heated to intense redness in a crucible [126], when the chloride sublimes and may be condensed in a second crucible covering the mouth of the first. It forms nacreous scales which have a beautiful peach-blossom color, and resist the action of the strongest acids. They are insoluble in cold water, and even in boiling water only dissolve, if at all, very slowly; but singularly, on the addition of the smallest quantity of chromous chloride, they dissolve immediately, generating much heat, and forming a *green* solution identical with that obtained by dissolving chromic hydrate in hydrochloric acid. A solution of the corresponding *violet* chloride may be formed by adding baric chloride to a solution of the violet sulphate; and it is worthy of notice that, while from this last solution argentic nitrate precipitates the whole of the chlorine, it only precipitates from a solution of the green compound one third of its chlorine, unless the liquid is boiled. Green crystals having the composition

z

$[Cr_2]Cl_6 . 12H_2O$ have been described, and compounds of chromic chloride with the alkaline chlorides are also known.

Besides the remarkable modifications of the chromic salts described above, most of them manifest a strong tendency to form basic compounds, but the principle which they illustrate has been already sufficiently discussed (337).

349. *Chlorhydrines.* — When hydrated chromic chloride is dried, it gives off, as the temperature increases, both water and hydrochloric acid, and compounds are formed which occupy an intermediate position between chromic chloride and chromic hydrate, and may be regarded as derived from the former by replacing one or more atoms of chlorine with hydroxyl. Thus we have

Chromic Chloride	$[Cr_2]\overset{\equiv}{}Cl_6,$
Chromic Penta-chlorhydrine	$[Cr_2]\overset{\equiv}{}Cl_5 , Ho . 4H_2O,$
Chromic Tetra-chlorhydrine	$[Cr_2]\overset{\equiv}{}Cl_4 , Ho_2.$
Chromic Dichlorhydrine	$[Cr_2]\overset{\equiv}{}Cl_2 , Ho_4,$
Chromic Hydrate	$[Cr_2]\overset{\equiv}{}Ho_6.$

The name *chlorhydrines* is now generally applied to bodies of this class, and it can easily be seen that they may be formed from water and the anhydrous chlorides by a simple metathesis. The compounds, whose symbols are given in (225) and (263), may be regarded as having a similar constitution, and the same is true of many other oxychlorides, oxyfluorides, &c.

350. *Chromates or Compounds in which Chromium is Sexivalent.* — These are the most characteristic and important of the compounds of this element, and the best known of all is *potassic dichromate*, which is manufactured on a large scale in the arts, and extensively used both in dyeing and in the preparation of various chrome pigments. It is made from native chrome iron, which is reduced to fine powder and roasted on the hearth of a reverberatory furnace with a mixture of chalk and potassic carbonate. The mixture is constantly stirred to hasten the oxidation, and the chalk facilitates the change by retaining the mass in a porous condition. From the product, water dissolves yellow potassic chromate, which is easily converted into the red dichromate by the addition of nitric acid, and the salt is then

separated and purified by repeated crystallizations. There are three potassic chromates, all of which yield anhydrous crystals easily soluble in water.

Potassic Chromate (Yellow)　　　　$K_2^= O_2^= Cr O_2$,

Potassic Dichromate (Orange Red)　$K_2^= O_2^= Cr_2 O_5$,

Potassic Trichromate (Dark Red)　　$K_2^= O_2^= Cr_3 O_8$.

The normal salt is isomorphous with potassic sulphate. It melts when heated, and is not decomposed by simple ignition; but when heated with reducing agents it yields chromic oxide mixed with some potassic salt. When in solution, it has an alkaline reaction, and is converted into the dichromate by the weakest acids. The dichromate also fuses without decomposition, but when heated to a high temperature it is converted into the normal salt and chromic oxide. In solution it has an acid reaction, and on the addition of potassic hydrate changes to the normal salt. Both salts possess great coloring power. The trichromate has merely a theoretical interest.

In another process of manufacturing the commercial chromates the chrome ore is simply roasted with lime. There is thus formed the normal *calcic chromate*, which, although itself only partially soluble in water, is converted by digestion with dilute sulphuric acid into a *dichromate*, which is very soluble, and from this solution the other chromate may be easily obtained by simple metathetical reactions. The chromates both of calcium and strontium dissolve readily in dilute acetic acid, while baric chromate is insoluble in this reagent; and on this fact is based an important method of qualitative analysis.

There are two plumbic chromates, which are not only important pigments and dyes, but are also interesting theoretically. Their symbols are usually written thus:—

Plumbic Chromate (Chrome Yellow)　　$Pb^= O_2^= Cr O_2$,

Diplumbic　"　(Chrome Orange)　$(Pb\text{-}O\text{-}Pb)^= O_2^= Cr O_2$.

The first falls as a brilliant yellow precipitate when a soluble chromate is added to a solution of plumbic acetate, and corresponds to the mineral Crocoite. It melts at a moderate heat, forming on cooling a red crystalline solid; but when strongly ignited it is decomposed, and a mixture of the second compound with chromic oxide is the result. The diplumbic chromate has a deep orange or red color, according to the mode of preparation. The finest vermilion-red is made by fusing the yellow chromate with nitre, and washing out the potassium salt with water, while an orange color is obtained in dyeing by passing the cloth through boiling lime-water, after chrome yellow has been fixed in its fibres by steeping it successively in solutions of plumbic acetate and potassic bichromate.

Several other metallic chromates, which are easily prepared by precipitation, are used in painting; but the coloring power of the chrome pigments is so great that they are frequently adulterated with chalk or some similar white material, and the tint is varied by mixing them with other paints. One variety of chrome green is a mixture of chrome yellow with Prussian blue.

The chromates are oxidizing agents, and fused plumbic chromate is sometimes used for this purpose in organic analysis. When heated with strong sulphuric acid they evolve oxygen gas [230]; with hydrochloric acid they evolve chlorine, and in both cases chromic salts are formed.

From the chromates we can easily prepare *chromic anhydride*, CrO_3, and the comparative stability of this compound illustrates most markedly the chief characteristic of the element chromium. The anhydride is most readily obtained by pouring one measure of a saturated solution of potassic dichromate into one and a half measures of concentrated sulphuric acid. As the liquid cools, chromic anhydride crystallizes from it in splendid crimson needles. This beautiful compound is permanent in the air, and melts at 190° without undergoing decomposition; but at a higher temperature it gives off oxygen gas, changing first into an intermediate brown oxide, Cr_3O_6, and afterwards into Cr_2O_3. It deliquesces in moist air, and dissolves in water in all proportions. This solution may be regarded as chromic acid, but the solution on evaporation yields crystals of the anhydride, and we have no evidence that a definite compound is formed. It is a very powerful oxidizing agent, and absolute alcohol inflames when brought in contact with the crystals.

Chlorochromic Anhydride, $Cr\overset{=}{}O_2, Cl_2$, a compound of the same type as the last, is distilled when a mixture of potassic dichromate, common salt, and sulphuric acid is heated in a glass retort. It is a blood-red volatile liquid, boiling at 118°, and yielding a vapor whose $\mathfrak{Sp. Gr.}$ (5.52) can be easily determined. It is at once decomposed by water into hydrochloric acid and chromic anhydride, and, like the last, is a powerful oxidizing agent; but it is chiefly interesting from its theoretical bearings. The existence also of $CrCl_6$ and $CrCl_4$ has been inferred from certain reactions, but they have never been isolated.

When potassic dichromate is dissolved in moderately strong hydrochloric acid at a gentle heat, there separate, on cooling, beautiful orange-colored needles, of a salt whose composition may be represented by the symbol $Cr^{\equiv}O_2,Cl,Ko$ or $K\text{-}O\text{-}(Cr^{\equiv}O_2,Cl)$, and another compound has been obtained whose symbol has been written $Cr^{\equiv}O_2,Cl,Ho \,.\, 2H_2Cl$. Their theoretical relations are obvious.

Another interesting compound belonging to the type of chromic anhydride is the fluoride, CrF_6. It distils when a mixture of fluor-spar, plumbic chromate, and sulphuric acid are heated in a leaden retort, and may be condensed (in a perfectly dry leaden receiver kept at a very low temperature) to a blood-red liquid; but the moment it comes in contact with moist air it is decomposed into hydrofluoric acid and chromic anhydride, and this reaction is one means of preparing the anhydride in a state of purity.

Lastly, there appears to be a perchromic acid corresponding to the permanganic acid. The compound in question is formed when to a solution containing peroxide of hydrogen and free hydrochloric or sulphuric acid is added a small quantity of some chromate. On shaking up the mixture with a few drops of ether, this solvent acquires a deep blue color, which is supposed to be due to perchromic acid, and the reaction serves as a very delicate test for chromium.

351. *Sulphides.* — The sulphides of chromium are unimportant. The black precipitate formed when ammonic sulphide is added to the solution of a chromous salt is probably CrS. A sesquisulphide, Cr_2S_3, may also be obtained as a black powder by passing H_2S over ignited Cr_2Cl_6. Like aluminic sulphide, it is decomposed by water, and cannot, therefore, be formed in an aqueous solution.

Questions and Problems.

1. In what order would you classify the elements allied to chromium, regarding only the stability of the compounds in which they act as bivalent radicals? Make a table illustrating this point.

2. In what order would you classify the same elements, regarding alone the stability of the several radicals $[R_2]^{\equiv}$? Compare the qualities of the several oxides and chlorides of these radicals.

3. What is the chief chemical characteristic of chromium? and how is this illustrated by reactions [345] to [348]?

4. Can you form any theory as to the cause of the difference between the blue and green modifications of the chromic salts? Compare (337).

5. Blue chromic oxalate is made by boiling a solution of 19 parts of potassic dichromate, 23 of potassic oxalate, and 55 of crystallized oxalic acid. The red salt is made in the same way with 19 parts of the dichromate, and 55 of oxalic acid only. Write the reactions.

6. What inference would you draw from the peculiar reactions of chromic chloride?

7. Explain the two methods of making potassic dichromate, and illustrate the process by reactions.

8. Represent by graphic symbols the constitution of the three potassic chromates.

9. The plumbic chromates may all be represented as containing the radical $(O\text{-}Pb_2)$, including the very rare mineral Phœnicochroite, which contains 23.1 CrO_3 and 76.9 PbO. Write the symbols of the three chromates on this assumption, and weigh their probability as compared with those given above. Compare the reactions of the plumbic with those of the potassic salts, and consider what bearing the general isomorphism of the chromates with the sulphates has on the question (296).

10. Illustrate by reactions the method of dyeing cloth with chrome orange.

11. Write the reaction of strong hydrochloric acid on potassic dichromate, assuming that the principal products are chromic chloride and chlorine gas.

12. When H_2S is passed through a solution of potassic dichromate supersaturated with sulphuric acid, sulphur is precipitated, and the color changes from red to green. Write the reaction.

13. A solution of potassic dichromate supersaturated with sulphuric acid is much used instead of nitric acid in the porous cup of

Grove's or Bunsen's voltaic cell (90). What is the theory of its action?

14. When a solution of potassic dichromate supersaturated with sulphuric acid is' boiled with oxalic acid, all the chromic acid is reduced to the condition of a chromic salt, and an equivalent amount of CO_2 is set free. Write the reaction, and show how it may be used to determine the quantity of CrO_3 in the dichromate.

15. The chromium in a soluble chromate may also be estimated as sesquioxide. By what reactions may this oxide be separated in a condition to be accurately weighed?

16. How may potassic chromate be used to separate barium from calcium and strontium?

17. It has been found by careful experiment that 10 grammes of chromic anhydride yield 7.6048 grammes of chromic oxide. We know also the Sp. Gr. of chlorochromic anhydride, and that this compound when brought in contact with water undergoes the change described above. Deduce the atomic weight of chromium, and state the steps in your reasoning.

18. Write the reaction by which chlorochromic anhydride is obtained in the reaction described in the text. It may also be made by distilling in a small retort a dry mixture of ferric chloride and chromic oxide. Write the reaction.

19. What is the relation of the compound $KCrO_3Cl$ to potassic chromate on the one side, and chlorochromic anhydride on the other?

20. Write the reaction by which CrF_6 is obtained in the reaction described above. It may also be prepared by distilling a mixture of potassic dichromate, ammonic fluoride, and sulphuric acid. Write the reaction.

21. Chromic fluoride is decomposed by glass, and for this reason we have not been able to analyze it, or to determine the density of its vapor satisfactorily. Its constitution is inferred from the products of its reaction with water. Is the conclusion trustworthy?

22. Write the reaction of ammonic sulphide on a solution of chrome alum.

Division XIII.

352. ALUMINUM. $Al = 27.4$. — Tetrad, but its compounds all contain the double atom $[Al_2] = 54.8$, which is a hexad radical. A very widely distributed element, and, after oxygen and silicon, the most abundant constituent of the rocky crust of the globe, of which it has been estimated that it forms about one twelfth. It occurs chiefly in combination with oxygen and silicon, and most of the siliceous minerals, and rocks, when not pure silica, contain aluminum as an essential ingredient. For a full enumeration of the aluminum minerals, the student must consult works on mineralogy. The following list comprises only such of the more characteristic native compounds as illustrate the chemical relations of the element.

Fluorides.

Cryolite	Orthorhombic	$[Al_2]F_6 \cdot 6NaF,$
Chiolite	Tetragonal	$[Al_2]F_8 \cdot 3NaF,$
Pachnolite	Monoclinic	$[Al_2]F_6 \cdot 3[Ca,Na_2]F_2 \cdot 2H_2O,$
Thomsenolite	Monoclinic	$[Al_2]F_6 \cdot 2[Ca,Na_2]F_2 \cdot 2H_2O.$

Oxides.

Spinel (Ruby)	Isometric	$Mg.[Al_2]^{\text{viii}}O_4,$
Gahnite	Isometric	$Zn.[Al_2]^{\text{viii}}O_4,$
Hercynite	Isometric	$Fe,[Al_2]^{\text{viii}}O_4.$

Corundum, *Sapphire*, Oriental Ruby, Oriental Topaz, Oriental
Amethyst, &c. Hexagonal $[Al_2]^{\text{iii}}O_3,$
Emery Massive $[Fe_2Al_2]^{\text{iii}}O_3.$

Hydrates.

Gibbsite	Hexagonal	$[Al_2]^{\text{iii}}O_{(\text{iii}}H_6,$
Beauxite	Massive	$O[Fe_2Al_2]^{\text{iii}}O_4^{\text{iii}}H_4,$
Diaspore	Orthorhombic	$O_2^{\text{iii}}[Al_2]^{\text{ii}}O_2^{\text{ii}}H_2,$
Chrysoberyl	Orthorhombic	$O_2^{\text{iii}}[Al_2]^{\text{ii}}O_2^{\text{ii}}G.$

Sulphates.

Alunogen   Monoclinic $[Al_2]^{\underline{\underline{\underline{iii}}}} O_6^{\underline{\underline{iii}}} (SO_2)_3 \cdot 18H_2O,$

Aluminite   Massive $O_2^{\underline{\underline{iii}}} [Al_2]^= O_2^= (SO_2) \cdot 9H_2O,$

Paraluminite   Massive $O_3 \times [Al_2]_2^x O_2^= (SO_2) \cdot 15H_2O,$

Alum-stone (Alunite)

       Rhombohedral $K_2, [Al_2]_3 \times\times O_{20} \times\times (SO_2)_3, H_{14},$ or

           $3(O_2^{\underline{\underline{iii}}} [Al_2]^= O_2^= SO_2) \cdot K_2^= O_2^= SO_2 \cdot 6H_2O.$

Octahedral Alums.

Potassium Alum   Isometric $K_2, [Al_2]^{viii} O_8^{viii} (SO_2)_4 \cdot 24H_2O,$

Ammonium Alum   " $(NH_4)_2, [Al_2]^{viii} O_8^{viii} (SO_2)_4 \cdot 24H_2O.$

Fibrous Alums.

Pickeringite   Fibrous $Mg, [Al_2]^{viii} O_8^{viii} (SO_2)_4 \cdot 22H_2O,$

Apjohnite   Fibrous $Mn, [Al_2]^{viii} O_8^{viii} (SO_2)_4 \cdot 22H_2O,$

Halotrichite   Fibrous $Fe, [Al_2]^{viii} O_8^{viii} (SO_2)_4 \cdot 22H_2O.$

Phosphates.

Lazulite   Monoclinic $H_2, Mg, [Al_2] \times O_{10} \times P_2,$

Turquois   Reniform $O_3^{\underline{\underline{iii}}} [Al_2]_2^{\underline{\underline{iii}}} O_6^{\underline{\underline{iii}}} (PO)_2,$

Wavellite   Orthorhombic $[Al_2]_3 \times viii O_{18} \times viii (PO)_4, H_6 \cdot 5H_2O.$

Silicates.

Andalusite   Orthorhombic $\Big\}$

Cyanite   Monoclinic $O^= [Al_2]^{\underline{\underline{iii}}} O_4^{\underline{\underline{iii}}} Si,$

Topaz   Orthorhombic $F_2^= [Al_2]^{\underline{\underline{iii}}} O_4^{\underline{\underline{iii}}} Si.$

Feldspars.

Anorthite   Triclinic $Ca, [Al_2]^{viii} O_8^{viii} Si_2,$

Labradorite   Triclinic $[Na_2, Ca], [Al_2]^{viii} O_8^{viii} Si_3 O_2,$

Leucite   Isometric $K_2, [Al_2]^{viii} O_8^{viii} Si_4 O_4,$

Oligoclase   Triclinic $[Ca, Na_2], [Al_2]^{viii} O_8^{viii} Si_5 O_6,$

Albite   Triclinic $Na_2, [Al_2]^{viii} O_8^{viii} Si_6 O_8,$

Orthoclase   Monoclinic $K_2, [Al_2]^{viii} O_8^{viii} Si_6 O_8.$

18

Clays.

Kaolinite	Orthorhombic	$H_2,[Al_2]^{\text{viii}}\,O_8^{\text{viii}}Si_2 \,.\, H_2O,$
Halloysite	Massive	$H_2,[Al_2]^{\text{viii}}\,O_8^{\text{viii}}Si_2 \,.\, 2H_2O,$
Pyrophyllite	Orthorhombic	$H_2,[Al_2]^{\text{viii}}\,O_8^{\text{viii}}Si_3 O_2,$
Agalmatolite	Massive	$H_2,[Al_2]^{\text{viii}}\,O_8^{\text{viii}}Si_4 O_4.$

Zeolites.

Thomsonite	Orthorhombic	$[Na_2, Ca],[Al_2]^{\text{viii}}\,O_8^{\text{viii}}Si_2 \,.\, 2\tfrac{1}{2}H_2O,$
Natrolite	Orthorhombic	$Na_2,[Al_2]^{\text{viii}}\,O_8^{\text{viii}}Si_3 O_2 \,.\, 2H_2O,$
Scolecite	Monoclinic	$Ca,[Al_2]^{\text{viii}}\,O_8^{\text{viii}}Si_3 O_2 \,.\, 3H_2O,$
Analcime	Isometric	$Na_2,[Al_2]^{\text{viii}}\,O_8^{\text{viii}}Si_4 O_4 \,.\, 2H_2O,$
Chabazite	Hexagonal	$Ca,[Al_2]^{\text{viii}}\,O_8^{\text{viii}}Si_4 O_4 \,.\, 6H_2O,$
Harmotome	Orthorhombic	$Ba,[Al_2]^{\text{viii}}\,O_8^{\text{viii}}Si_5 O_6 \,.\, 5H_2O,$
Heulandite	Monoclinic	$Ca,[Al_2]^{\text{viii}}\,O_8^{\text{viii}}Si_6 O_8 \,.\, 5H_2O,$
Stilbite	Orthorhombic	$Ca,[Al_2]^{\text{viii}}\,O_8^{\text{viii}}Si_6 O_8 \,.\, 6H_2O.$

To this list may be added the *Garnets*, the *Scapolites*, the *Epidotes*, the *Micas*, and the *Chlorites*, all large and important groups of minerals, which are chiefly silicates of aluminum, but which present differences of composition similar to those illustrated above. It is impossible, however, in the present state of the science, to deduce from the results of the analysis of many of these minerals any satisfactory or probable rational formula. The mineral Lapis Lazuli is a remarkable illustration of this fact. It has a definite crystalline form (Fig. 6), and has long been used as a paint under the name of ultramarine. It is a silicate of aluminum, calcium, and sodium, with a sulphide probably of iron and sodium; but numerous analyses have given no definite clew either to its rational formula or to the cause of its beautiful blue color. Nevertheless, the pigment is now made artificially in large quantities, by combining the ingredients in the proportions which the analyses have indicated, and this would seem to show that it is the theory and not the analysis which is at fault. This subject will be further discussed under silicon.

It will be noticed that among the native compounds of aluminum are included several of the precious stones, and also Emery, which yields an exceedingly hard powder very much used in polishing. From the clays the clay slates, and to a less extent from the rarer minerals Alum-stone and Beauxite, the alums and other soluble salts of aluminum are prepared. Cryolite, now imported from Greenland in large quantities, has become an important source of soda-ash. The feldspars, and more immediately the clays which result from their disintegration, are largely used in the manufacture of porcelain and the various kinds of earthenware. The coarser clays furnish the material for bricks. The slates, the porphyries, the granites, the trachytes, the green stones, the lavas, and other rocks, rich in aluminum, are used in building; but the other aluminous minerals, with few exceptions, find no important applications in the arts.

353. *Metallic Aluminum.* — Readily obtained by reducing either the chloride or the native fluoride (Cryolite) with metallic sodium. It has a brilliant white lustre, and possesses to a high degree all the qualities of a useful metal. It has a low specific gravity (2.56), but still a very great tenacity. It is singularly sonorous. It is very malleable and ductile. It is an excellent conductor of heat and electricity. It has a high melting point, although somewhat lower than that of silver. It does not tarnish in the air, and the molten metal does not oxidize, even when heated to a high temperature. Its present value, which depends solely on the cost of extraction, greatly limits the applications of aluminum in the arts; but, nevertheless, it is used to a limited extent for cheap jewelry, and in a few philosophical instruments, where it is important to combine lightness with strength. An alloy of copper with about ten per cent of pure aluminum, called aluminum bronze, has the color of gold, and an almost equal power of resisting atmospheric agents.

Neither sulphuric nor nitric acids, when cold and sufficiently diluted, attack aluminum, and nitric acid dissolves it only slowly when concentrated and boiling. Hot sulphuric acid, however, when not diluted with more than three or four parts of water, dissolves it rapidly with the evolution of hydrogen gas. The best *acid* solvent is hydrochloric acid, which acts on the metal at the ordinary temperature even when greatly diluted; but, singularly, the metal dissolves almost equally well in a solution of caustic soda or potash; and a comparison of the two following reactions will make evident one of the most important features in the chemical relations of this metal.

$$\mathbf{Al}\text{-}\mathbf{Al} + (6H\text{-}Cl + Aq) =$$
$$([Al\text{-}Al]\text{-}Cl_6 + Aq) + 3\mathrm{H}\text{-}\mathrm{H}. \quad [350]$$

$$\mathbf{Al}\text{-}\mathbf{Al} + (6Nao\text{-}H + Aq =$$
$$([Nao_6[Al\text{-}Al] + Aq) + 3\mathrm{H}\text{-}\mathrm{H}. \quad [351]$$

354. *Compounds in which* $[Al_2]$ *is the Basic Radical.* — The compounds of this class are isomorphous with, and resemble in almost every respect, excepting color, the corresponding ferric salt. Like the last, they have a great tendency to form basic salts, and they exhibit in general the same reactions which have been already described (337). The use of the soluble aluminic salts in the arts depends, — 1st. Upon their tendency to form insoluble basic compounds, and 2d. Upon the fact that these basic compounds, including the hydrates, eagerly absorb the soluble organic extracts used as dyes. When organic tissues, yarn or cloth, are dipped into a solution of a basic aluminic salt (compare note to page 386), or when in the process of calico-printing a similar preparation is transferred to the surface of the fabric in regular designs, the insoluble basic compounds, just referred to, are formed in the very fibre of the material, and become still more firmly incorporated when the tissue is exposed to the action of air, steam, or other agents in the process known as *ageing*. If now the yarn or cloth thus prepared is dipped in a dye-vat, the aluminic compound entangled in the fibre will seize and hold the coloring matter, and hence the name of mordants, from *mordeo (to take fast hold of)*, applied to these preparations of aluminum. The basic, ferric, chromic, and stannic salts act in a similar way, and are also used as mordants ; but while the colorless aluminic salts take the true color of the dye, the others modify the tint to a greater or less extent. Hence, in the process of calico-printing, various colors are obtained from the same bath, after the design has been printed on the cloth, with the appropriate mordants. When salts of aluminum are mixed in solution with dye-stuffs, and decomposed by an alkaline reagent, the insoluble hydrate or basic salt thus formed carries down a large amount of the coloring matter, and these colored precipitates, when dried, are used as pigments. (*Lakes.*)

Of the soluble salts of aluminum, which may be used as mordants, the most important are the alums, whose symbols have already been given (352). They alone crystallize readily, and can therefore be easily manufactured on a large scale in a condition which insures purity. The alkaline sulphate which they contain, although it determines the peculiar crystalline character of these double salts, is wholly worthless to the dyer, and it depends chiefly on the ruling price whether the ammonic or the potassic salt is employed in their manufacture. Sodic alum does not crystallize readily, and is therefore never used. The aluminic sulphate, which is the only useful part of the alums, is generally obtained by decomposing clay or shale, after it has been roasted at a low red heat with sulphuric acid. It is made in large quantities in England and Germany from a bituminous shale, found among the lowest beds of the coal measures, which contains a large quantity of iron pyrites disseminated through the mass. When this alum schist, or alum ore as it is called, is slowly burnt, one half of the sulphur of the pyrites is converted into sulphuric acid, which at once decomposes a portion of the aluminic silicate that the shale contains, thus yielding a certain amount of aluminic sulphate. At the same time ferrous sulphate is formed by the oxidation of the residue of the pyrites, and when the roasted mass is lixiviated with water both salts dissolve. Lastly, on adding to the solution, after concentration, potassic or ammonic sulphate, alum is formed, which is separated from the ferrous salt by crystallization.

A small amount of potassium alum is made in the Roman States from Alum-stone (352). This mineral, when roasted and exposed for several months to the action of air and moisture, crumbles into a sort of mud, which, when lixiviated, yields the well-known Roman alum.

Within the last few years the use of alum has been in a measure superseded by the introduction into commerce of pure aluminic sulphate, which is máde by the direct action of sulphuric acid on some of the purer varieties of clay, and freed from iron by means of sodic ferro-cyanide. This reagent is added to the solution so long as it occasions a blue precipitate, and after this settles the clear liquid is decanted and evaporated. The residue is known as *concentrated alum.* The salt may be crystallized in small scales, which have the composition given below.

A solution of basic aluminic acetate is also much used as a

mordant, especially for madder reds, under the name of red liquor. It is prepared by adding plumbic acetate to a solution of alum. The only important soluble salts of aluminum, which have not yet been mentioned, are the chloride and nitrate.

Aluminic Chloride	$[Al_2]'''Cl_6 . 12H_2O,$
Aluminic Nitrate	$[Al_2]'''O_6'''(NO_2)_6 . 18H_2O,$
Aluminic Sulphate	$[Al_2]'''O_6'''(SO_2)_3 . 18H_2O.$

The reactions of the aluminic salts, when in solution, differ from those of the corresponding ferric salts chiefly in the fact that the white aluminic hydrate, which is precipitated by the alkaline reagents, dissolves easily and perfectly in an excess of either potassic or sodic hydrate. A compound of aluminum may generally be recognized by the blue color, which is obtained when the solid, previously moistened with a solution of cobaltic nitrate, is intensely heated in the oxidizing flame of the blowpipe.

355. *Compounds in which* $[Al_2]$ *is the Acid Radical.* — Sodic aluminate, the same compound which is formed by [351], is now manufactured on a large scale from Beauxite. The pulverized mineral, mixed with sodic carbonate, is heated to bright redness, and the soluble aluminate thus formed separated from the insoluble residue by lixiviation and filtration. On evaporating the clear solution (in vacuo), a white amorphous solid is obtained, which has the composition already given. From solutions of this compound aluminic hydrate is precipitated on the addition of any soluble acid, or even on exposure to the carbonic acid of the atmosphere, and this new commercial product may be used with great advantage as a substitute for alum. A remarkable reaction occurs, when solutions of aluminic chloride and sodic aluminate are mixed together in atomic proportions, illustrating the singular twofold relations which the radical $[Al_2]$ may sustain.

$$([Al_2]'''Cl_6 + Na_6'''O_6'''[Al_2] + 6H_2O + Aq) =$$
$$2[Al_2]'''O_6'''H_6 + (6NaCl + Aq).\ [352]$$

Although other aluminates may be prepared, the salt just described is the only noteworthy example of this class of compounds. Spinel, however, and the allied minerals, may be regarded as meta-aluminates.

356. *Aluminic Chloride*, $[Al_2]^{\underline{\underline{\underline{\quad}}}}Cl_6$, is the only compound of aluminum with chlorine. It is made by passing chlorine gas into a mixture of aluminic oxide with carbon, heated intensely in an earthen retort, when the chloride distils over and condenses in the receiver in yellowish-white crystalline scales. It is a fusible solid, which volatilizes at a temperature only a few degrees above its melting-point, and the Sp. Gr. of its vapor confirms the theory of its constitution generally accepted. It eagerly unites with water, but, like ferric chloride, it cannot be recovered by evaporation when once dissolved. It forms double salts with the alkaline chlorides, and one of these, $[Al_2]^{\underline{\underline{\underline{\quad}}}}Cl_6 \cdot 2NaCl$, plays an important part in the preparation of aluminum.

357. *Aluminic Oxide*, Al_2O_3, forms, as we have seen, the mineral Corundum. It may be obtained artificially by igniting either ammonia, alum, or the hydrate obtained indirectly from Beauxite (352). It is a hygroscopic white powder, which adheres to the tongue, but does not become plastic when mixed with water. It affects, like ferric oxide, two conditions, and the change from one to the other is accompanied in like manner by a sudden incandescence. It may be fused by the compound blow-pipe, and the resulting transparent bead, like corundum, has a hardness only inferior to that of diamond. Moreover, colored crystals, resembling the ruby and the sapphire, have been obtained by art.

358. *Aluminic Sulphide*, $[Al_2]^{\underline{\underline{\underline{\quad}}}}S_3$, is formed when finely divided aluminum is burnt in the vapor of sulphur. It is a black powder, which is rapidly decomposed by water into H_2S and $[Al_2]^{\underline{\underline{\underline{\quad}}}}O_6^{\underline{\underline{\underline{\quad}}}}H_6$. Hence H_2S does not under any conditions precipitate aluminum from solutions of its salts, and the precipitate obtained with the alkaline sulphides is simply the normal hydrate.

Questions and Problems.

1. Why is not the atomic weight of aluminum doubled according to the principle of (19)?

2. Can the composition of the native fluorides of aluminum be expressed by unitary symbols (69)? Can you devise a process by which sodic carbonate may be made from Cryolite?

3. Compare together the minerals isomorphous with Spinel (352),

z

(333), (342), and show in what two ways their constitution may be expressed.

4. Compare the crystalline form and hardness of corundum with those of the allied sesquioxides.

5. Compare the native aluminic with the native ferric hydrates, and show how many of the possible hydrates are represented among the native aluminic salts. Use the table of ferric hydrates already made (Prob. 68, Div. XI.).

6. The symbol of Chrysoberyl may be written after the type of Spinel. What argument may be urged for the form given above?

7. Make a table of the known compounds of the two alum types.

8. On what principle are the aluminic silicates classified, and how do the several members of each group differ from each other?

9. Determine the atomic ratios between the various radicals in the several aluminic salts, sulphates, phosphates, and silicates. Consider, first, the *simple acid radicals*, and secondly, the *compound acid radicals* in these minerals.

10. What inference should you draw from a comparison of the symbols of the different aluminum compounds as regards the isomorphism of calcium with the alkaline radicals?

11. Some varieties of Pyrophyllite closely resemble Steatite. By what simple blow-pipe test can the two minerals be distinguished?

12. Write the reaction of sodium on sodio-aluminic chloride or fluoride, and calculate how much aluminum can be obtained theoretically for every kilogramme of sodium employed.

13. How does the *Sp. Gr.* of aluminum compare with that of the other useful metals?

14. Write the reaction of nitric acid and that of sulphuric acid on aluminum, assuming that nitric oxide is evolved in the first case, and hydrogen gas in the second.

15. Compare reactions [350] and [351], and point out the different relations of the radical $[Al_2]$ in the two cases.

16. Explain the peculiar relations of the aluminic salts on which their use as mordants depends.

17. Write the reaction which takes place when sodic-carbonate is added to a solution of alum, so long as the precipitate first formed is redissolved, assuming that in the basic aluminic sulphate, which remains in solution, the atomic ratio between the basic and acid radicals (SO_2) is as 3 : 1.

18. What are the relative intrinsic values of potassium-alum, am-

monium-alum, and crystallized aluminic sulphate, taking as the standard the quantity of normal aluminic hydrate which can be obtained from each? On what does the preference given to the alums as mordants chiefly rest?

19. Explain and illustrate by reactions the process of manufacturing alum from the alum shales, and also from pure clay.

20. Illustrate by reactions the change of Alum-stone into alum in the manufacture of Roman alum.

21. If a portion of the water obtained in the analyses of Aluminite and Paraluminite is water of constitution, how may the symbols be written?

22. Write the reaction of plumbic acetate on a solution of alum, assuming that in the basic acetate, which remains in solution, the atomic ratio is 3 : 1.

23. What are the two chief differences between the chemical relations of iron and aluminum? Illustrate the differences by reactions.

24. Explain and illustrate by reactions the method of manufacturing sodic aluminate. By what test could you determine when all the soda has been converted into sodic aluminate? Why evaporate solution *in vacuo?*

25. Write reaction of CO_2 on solution of sodic aluminate, and explain the use of this salt as a mordant.

26. Analyze reaction [352].

27. Show how Spinel could be derived from a tetrahydro-magnesic aluminate.

28. Write the reaction by which aluminic chloride is formed, and show that the Sp. Gr. of its vapor confirms the theory of its constitution generally accepted.

29. Write the reaction which takes place when a solution of aluminic chloride is evaporated to dryness. Consider whether the product formed by the union of the anhydrous chloride with water ought to be regarded as a chemical compound, and, if so, endeavor to represent its constitution by a rational symbol.

30. Compare the reactions of ammonic sulphide on an aluminic and on a ferric salt, and explain the cause of the difference.

31. In what order would you classify the several radicals $[R_2]^{\frac{i}{i}}$, regarding their electro-negative relations?

Divisions XIV. to XVI.

359. THE PLATINUM METALS. — The six metals which follow aluminum in our classification (Table II.) are always found in the native state, although more or less alloyed with each other. "Platinum Ore" is found in several countries, but at least nine tenths of the commercial supply comes from the Ural. It is everywhere obtained by washing alluvial material, generally in small rounded metallic grains, although masses of considerable size are occasionally found. The following analyses by Deville and Debray will give an idea of its composition : —

	Pt	Au	Fe	Ir	Rh	Pd	Cu	Ir-Os	Sand
Choco	86.20	1.00	7.80	0.85	1.40	0.50	0.60	0.95	0.95
California	85.50	0.80	6.75	1.05	1.00	0.60	1.40	1.10	2.95
Oregon	51.45	0.85	4.30	0.40	0.65	0.15	2.15	37.30	3.00
Australia	61.40	1.20	4.55	1.10	1.85	1.80	1.10	26.00	1.20
Russia	76.40	0.40	11.70	4.30	0.30	1.40	4.10	0.50	1.40

In this ore the grains of "Native Platinum," which have a steel-gray color, are always more or less mixed with those of a distinct mineral species called "Iridosmine,"[1] which have usually a lighter color, and consist chiefly of iridium and osmium, alloyed with small quantities of rhodium and ruthenium. Hence from the above analyses the amounts of iridosmine (Ir-Os) and sand must be subtracted in order to obtain the composition of native platinum proper.

In the old method of manufacturing platinum, the ore is treated with aqua-regia, which dissolves the platinum and the metals directly alloyed with it, but does not affect the iridosmine, the titaniferous iron, and other resisting minerals, which are frequently mixed with the "Native Platinum." To the solution thus obtained, when brought into suitable condition, ammonic chloride is added, which precipitates all the platinum [176] as ammonio-platinic chloride. This precipitate, when ignited, leaves the metal in a pulverulent condition (platinum

---

[1] Iridosmine is frequently associated with California gold, and is separated from it at the Assay Offices in considerable quantities. Being heavier than gold it sinks to the bottom of the crucible when the metal is fused.

sponge), which is welded into a compact mass by heat and pressure.

In the new method of Deville and Debray the platinum is first united to metallic lead, which, as it does not alloy with iri-dosmine, separates the platinum from the chief impurities in the ore. The lead is subsequently removed by cupellation, and the crude platinum purified by melting it in a crucible of lime with a powerful oxyhydrogen flame. Indeed, an alloy of platinum with a small amount of iridium and rhodium, well adapted for chemical vessels, may be obtained directly from the ore by fus-ing it with the same flame on a bed of lime, using a small amount of lime as a flux. The palladium and osmium present are thus volatilized, while the copper and iron form fusible com-pounds with the lime.

From the " platinum residues," as they are termed, the asso-ciated metals can only be separated by refined analytical meth-ods, and our knowledge of the chemical relations of these rare elements is still very imperfect. Necessarily, therefore, they must occupy a very subordinate place in an elementary treatise, and they are here, as elsewhere, classed together, more in con-sequence of their intimate association in nature and resemblances as metals, than from any well-defined chemical relationship.

360. RUTHENIUM ($Ru = 104.4$) is a white metal, very har and brittle, with difficulty fusible before the oxyhydrogen blow-pipe. $Sp.$ $Gr.$ when fused 11 to 11.4. It is scarcely at-tacked by nitro-muriatic acid, but it is easily oxidized when fused with potassic hydrate (especially if a little nitre be added), yielding potassic rutheniate, which forms with water an orange-colored solution. The pulverized metal heated in a current of air rapidly absorbs oxygen, and the oxides cannot be reduced by heat alone.

Five oxides are known, — First, RuO, which has a dark-gray color and metallic lustre. It is not acted on by acids, but is reduced by hydrogen at the ordinary temperature. Secondly, Ru_2O_3, which is the product when the metal is oxidized by the air. It has a deep-blue color, is also insoluble in acids, and is reduced by hydrogen, but only at a higher temperature. The corresponding hydrate, $[Ru_2]^{\dots}Ho_6$, which dissolves with yellow color in acids, but is insoluble in water or alkalies, is also known. Thirdly, RuO_2, which is a dark, greenish-blue powder, and the hydrate $Ru \equiv Ho_4$, which dissolves both in acids and alkalies. Fourthly, $Ru O_3$, which is the assumed anhydride of the yellow rutheniate, formed when the metal is ignited with a mixture of potassic hydrate with potassic nitrate or chlorate. This characteristic compound is decomposed, like potassic manganate, by acids and even by organic substances. Lastly, $Ru O_4$, which is a very volatile golden-yellow crystalline solid, melting at 58° and boiling at about 100°.

Ruthenium forms three chlorides: $Ru Cl_2$, which is known both as an insoluble black crystalline powder and as forming a fine blue solution; $[Ru_2] Cl_6$, which forms yellow solutions and soluble compounds with the alkaline chlorides, as $[Ru_2] Cl_6 . 4 KCl$; lastly, $Ru Cl_4$, known only in its double salts, $Ru Cl_4 . 2 KCl$ and $Ru Cl_4 . 2 (NH_4) Cl$, which, like the corresponding platinum salt, crystallizes in octahedrons (366), but appears to be dismorphous, as it forms under certain conditions hexagonal prisms.

When $H_2 S$ is passed through a solution of the yellow chloride, it partly precipitates the ruthenium as a sulphide, but at the same time it partially reduces $[Ru_2] Cl_6$ to $Ru Cl_2$, which gives to the supernatant liquid a fine azure-blue color. Zinc effects the same reduction, and this reaction is very delicate and characteristic.

361. OSMIUM ($Os = 199.2$). — In the most compact condition in which this metal has been obtained, it has $Sp. Gr. = 21.4$, and a bluish tinge of color resembling that of zinc. It has never been fused, but it slowly volatilizes at the temperature at which ruthenium and iridium melt. When finely divided, it is oxidized by nitric acid, but in its more compact state it resists even aqua-regia. When heated in a current of air, it oxidizes much more readily than ruthenium, passing at once to the highest degree of oxidation, $Os O_4$, and forming a volatile compound resembling $Ru O_4$. Indeed, when in powder, osmium is very combustible, and even when compact it takes fire at a temperature scarcely exceeding the melting-point of zinc, and its strong tendency to form this volatile oxide is the most striking character of the element. Its oxides and chlorides correspond almost precisely both in composition and chemical relations to those of ruthenium. The three lower oxides all form hydrates, but have no well-marked basic character. Osmic anhydride, $Os O_3$, is unknown, but potassic osmate, $K_2 \doteq O_2 \doteq Os O_2 . 2 H_2 O$,

can easily be obtained in large rose-colored octahedrons. The volatile oxide, OsO_4, just referred to, forms colorless acicular crystals, which are very fusible and freely soluble in water. It boils at about 100°, emitting an extremely irritating and deleterious vapor, whose pungent odor, resembling that of chlorine, is very characteristic. When pulverized osmium is heated in perfectly dry chlorine gas, there is first formed a blue-black sublimate of $OsCl_2$, and afterwards a red sublimate of $OsCl_4$. Osmious chloride gives a dark violet-blue solution, while osmic chloride gives a yellow solution; and when exposed to the air, the first rapidly changes to the last. By the action of reducing agents the change may be reversed. All the chlorides of osmium form double salts with the alkaline chlorides. The most interesting are the compounds corresponding to potassio-platinic chloride, $OsCl_4 \cdot 2KCl$, which forms beautiful red octahedral crystals, sparingly soluble in water, and $[Os_2]Cl_6 \cdot 6KCl \cdot 6H_2O$, which resembles a characteristic Rhodium compound mentioned below.

362. RHODIUM ($Rh = 104.4$) is a very hard grayish-white metal, barely fusible in an oxyhydrogen flame. *Sp. Gr.* after fusion 12.1. It is imperfectly malleable, but when alloyed with platinum may be easily worked. The pure metal is insoluble in acids, although when alloyed, in not too large quantity, with platinum, copper, bismuth, or lead, it dissolves with them in aqua-regia. Although unalterable in the air, rhodium combines both with oxygen and chlorine at a red heat. It is readily oxidized by fusion with nitre or peroxide of barium. Fused with potassic bisulphate, it is converted into soluble rhodio-potassic sulphate, and when heated with sodic or basic chlorides in a current of chlorine gas, it yields various double salts, which are likewise easily soluble.

Although several oxides of rhodium have been distinguished, the only one which as yet has been well defined is Rh_2O_3, Rhodic Oxide, and this compound evidently marks the prevailing quantivalence of the element. In this condition rhodium, unlike the elements with which it is associated, appears to be a well-marked basic radical, forming stable salts with several of the acids. Thus we have

Rhodic Hydrate　　　　　　$[Rh_2]\overset{\text{\tiny III}}{\,}O_6\overset{\text{\tiny II}}{\,}H_6,$

Rhodic Acetate　　　　　　$[Rh_2]\overset{\text{\tiny III}}{\,}O_6\overset{\text{\tiny II}}{\,}(C_2H_3O)_6 \cdot 5H_2O,$

Rhodic Nitrate	$[Rh_2]^{\underline{\underline{\underline{i}}}}O_6^{\underline{\underline{\underline{i}}}}(NO_2)_6 \cdot 4H_2O,$
Rhodic Sulphite	$[Rh_2]^{\underline{\underline{\underline{i}}}}O_6^{\underline{\underline{\underline{i}}}}(SO)_3 \cdot 6H_2O,$
Rhodic Sulphate	$\cdot \quad [Rh_2]^{\underline{\underline{\underline{i}}}}O_6^{\underline{\underline{\underline{i}}}}(SO_2)_3 \cdot 12H_2O,$
Potassio-rhodic Sulphate	$K_6[Rh_2]^{\text{xii}}O_{12}^{\text{xii}}(SO_2)_6.$

In like manner the only well-defined compound of rhodium
and chlorine is $[Rh_2]^{\underline{\underline{\underline{i}}}}Cl_6,$ a brownish-red, indifferent body, insoluble in all acids and alkalies. A solution of the chloride may
be obtained by dissolving R_2O_3 in hydrochloric acid, and from
this several well-crystallized soluble double chlorides may be
prepared, as

Potassio-rhodic Chloride	$[Rh_2]Cl_6 \cdot 6KCl \cdot 6H_2O,$
Sodio-rhodic Chloride	$[Rh_2]Cl_6 \cdot 6NaCl \cdot 24H_2O.$

They all have a ruby or rose color, whence the metal takes its
name, from ῥόδον, a rose.

363. IRIDIUM ($Ir = 196$) is a very hard, white, brittle
metal. Though even less fusible than rhodium, it has been
melted on lime with the oxyhydrogen flame and by the voltaic
arc. *Sp. Gr.* after fusion 21.15. The pure metal is not acted
on by any acid, but when alloyed with platinum it dissolves in
aqua-regia. It may also be rendered soluble by fusion with alkaline reagents, under the same conditions as rhodium. Unless
in very fine powder it does not oxidize when heated in the air.
It forms two principal oxides, Ir_2O_8 and $IrO_2,$ and the corresponding hydrates are readily obtained. The hydrates dissolve
in acids, but do not form definite oxygen salts unless associated
with other basic radicals. There are also chlorides corresponding
to the oxides, which form crystalline double salts with the alkaline chlorides, closely resembling the similar compounds already
described. Thus we have

Potassio-iridous Chloride	$[Ir_2]Cl_6 \cdot 6KCl \cdot 6H_2O,$
Sodio-iridous Chloride	$[Ir_2]Cl_6 \cdot 6NaCl \cdot 24H_2O,$

which contain the radical $[Ir_2]^{\underline{\underline{\underline{i}}}},$ and also

Potassio-iridic Chloride	$IrCl_4 \cdot 2KCl,$
Sodio-iridic Chloride	$IrCl_4 \cdot 2NaCl \cdot 6H_2O,$

which contain the radical $Ir^{\underline{\underline{\underline{i}}}},$ the last class being less soluble than the first. Most of the compounds of iridium have a strong coloring power, those containing the radical $[Ir_2]^{\equiv}$ giving in general green, and those containing the radical $Ir^=$ red solutions. The iridic compounds are the most stable, but under the action of reducing or oxidizing agents one condition of the element readily passes into the other, and the changes of color which then take place, giving under different conditions beautiful shades of purple, violet, and blue, are very striking and characteristic. Hence the name Iridium, from *iris, the rainbow*. Under certain circumstances this element appears to manifest still other degrees of quantivalence, and compounds containing both $Ir^=$ and $Ir^{\equiv}$ have been distinguished, the last acting as an acid radical in the product obtained by fusing iridium with nitre, which gives, with water, a deep blue solution, and is supposed to contain the compound $K_2^= O_2^= Ir\,O_2$; but our knowledge on this subject is still very imperfect.

364. PALLADIUM ($Pd = 106.6$). Sp. Gr. $= 11.4$.— This brilliant white metal resembles platinum more closely than either of its associates. Although best known as a subordinate constituent of platinum ore, it has also been found (in Brazil) native, in masses of considerable size. It is harder than platinum, has less tenacity, and is not so ductile; but, nevertheless, it can be wrought with facility. It cannot be fused in an ordinary wind-furnace, but before the compound blow-pipe it melts more readily than platinum, and if heated on lime is slowly volatilized, giving off a green vapor. Like the noble metals, its oxides and chlorides are reduced by heat alone. Yet when exposed to the air at a low red heat its surface becomes covered with an iridescent film of oxide, which is dispersed, however, at a higher temperature. Palladium is acted on by chemical agents more readily than platinum. Though only slightly attacked by pure hydrochloric or sulphuric acids, it dissolves readily in nitric acid, and also in aqua-regia, or in sulphuric acid when mixed with a small amount of nitric acid. It is also rendered soluble by fusion with alkaline reagents, under the same conditions as the preceding metals.

Palladium differs from the associated elements very markedly in that it affects most readily the condition of a bivalent positive radical. Thus we easily obtain, by dissolving the metal in the respective acids, the two following crystalline salts :—

Palladious Nitrate   (Brown) $Pd=O_2=(NO_2)_2,$
Palladious Sulphate   " $Pd=O_2=SO_2 . 2H_2O.$

The corresponding hydrate is precipitated by sodic carbonate from solutions of either of these salts as a dark brown powder. The oxide PdO, a black powder, is obtained by heating the nitrate to dull redness. The chloride $PdCl_2$ forms brown hydrous crystals, when a solution of the metal in aqua-regia is evaporated to dryness, and by uniting with other chlorides yields definite crystalline salts, as, for example, $PdCl_2 . 2KCl$, which is easily obtained in dull yellow prismatic crystals.

Palladium also forms another class of compounds in which its atoms are quadrivalent; but these are all very unstable. The chloride $PdCl_4$ has never been isolated, but the compound $PdCl_4 . 2KCl$, which has been obtained in red octahedral crystals, attests the relationship of this element to those with which it is classed.

But of all the characteristics of palladium the most noteworthy is the power which the metal possesses of absorbing hydrogen gas. It appears from the recent experiments of Professor Graham that, in the condition in which it is deposited by electrolysis, this metal will absorb or "occlude" nearly 1,000 times its volume of hydrogen, which amounts to about three fourths of one per cent of its weight, and in other conditions of the metal the power of absorption is very great, although not so large. The same phenomenon to a less degree has also been observed with platinum and iron, and considerable amounts of "occluded" hydrogen have been discovered in some of the meteors. The gas thus taken up by these metals is not simply mechanically condensed, as when absorbed by charcoal, but appears to be in a state of partial chemical combination like that of a solution or an alloy; for we find that, while the hydrogen is easily expelled by heat, it shows no tendency to escape into a vacuum. The gas, however, readily passes through a heated palladium or platinum plate by an action similar to dialysis (57), and these metals seem to partake more or less of a colloidal condition. By a similar action carbonic oxide passes through the iron walls of furnaces, and this class of phenomena, when further investigated, will undoubtedly be found to be quite general.

When a mass of palladium, charged as above described, is exposed to the air, it sometimes becomes suddenly heated from the oxidation of the hydrogen it contains, and the well-known power of platinum, especially when finely divided, as in the condition of *sponge* or the so-called *platinum black*, to determine the union of hydrogen and oxygen, and even to ignite a hydrogen jet, together with a large class of similar effects, may be explained on the same principle.

365. *Hydrogenium.* — The quantity of hydrogen " occluded" by palladium amounts to nearly one equivalent for each equivalent of the metal, and produces a marked change in its physical qualities. The volume of the metal is increased, its tenacity and conducting power for electricity diminished, and it acquires a slight susceptibility to magnetism, which the pure metal does not possess. From these facts Professor Graham infers that the metal charged with gas is an alloy of palladium and metallic hydrogen, which he prefers to call *hydrogenium,* and it would appear that in this remarkable product the anticipations of chemists in regard to the metallic condition of hydrogen have been realized. If this inference is correct, and if, as is generally the case, the volume of the alloy is equal to the sum of the volumes of the two metals, then the *Sp. Gr.* of hydrogenium (deduced from that of the alloy) must be about 2. The chemical qualities of this alloy are very remarkable. It precipitates mercury from a solution of its chloride, and in general acts as a strong reducing agent. Exposed to the action of chlorine, bromine, or iodine, the hydrogen leaves the palladium and enters into direct union with these elements. Moreover, from a palladium wire charged with the gas, and covered with calcined magnesia (to render the flame luminous), the hydrogen burns, when lighted by a lamp, like oil from a wick. So far, therefore, as its chemical activities are concerned, hydrogenium bears somewhat the same relation to hydrogen gas that ozone bears to ordinary oxygen. Palladium plate or wire is most readily charged with hydrogen by making it the negative pole of a galvanic battery in the process of electrolyzing water. (Fig. 84.)

366. PLATINUM. $Pt = 197.4.$ *Sp. Gr.* $= 21.5.$ — The extended use of this metal in practical chemistry has made its appearance familiar to every student of the science. Platinum utensils have been of inestimable value in chemical investiga-

tions, on account of the infusibility of the metal, and its wonderful power of resisting chemical agents. It not only does not
oxidize when heated in the air, but none of the acids singly act
upon it, and even aqua-regia dissolves it but slowly. The metal
is corroded when heated to redness in contact with the caustic
alkalies or alkaline earths, especially the hydrates of lithium or
barium, but the alkaline chlorides, carbonates, or sulphates may
be fused in platinum crucibles without injuring them. Dry chlorine has no action on the metal at any temperature, and both the
oxides and the chlorides are reduced by heat alone. Platinum,
however, readily alloys with several of the other metals, and care
must be taken to conduct no operations in platinum vessels by
which a fusible metal may be reduced. Phosphorus and sulphur
also act on platinum to a limited extent.

Platinum is very ductile and malleable, and two pieces of the
metal may be welded together at a white heat, although to melt
it the temperature of the oxyhydrogen flame is required.
Melted platinum absorbs oxygen from the air, and, like silver
(140), spits if suddenly cooled. The same phenomenon has
been observed with palladium and rhodium.

Platinum affects the condition both of a bivalent and a quadrivalent radical, but its affinities are at best very feeble. When
dissolved in aqua-regia the product first formed is probably
$PtCl_4 . 2HCl$, and from this solution a large number of other
compounds of the same type are easily obtained, and these are
the most important compounds of this element. We have, for
example,

Bario-platinic Chloride	$PtCl_4 . BaCl_2 . 4H_2O$,
Magnesio-platinic Chloride	$PtCl_4 . MgCl_2 . 6H_2O$,
Sodio-platinic Chloride	$PtCl_4 . 2NaCl . 6H_2O$,
Potassio-platinic Chloride	$PtCl_4 . 2KCl$,
Ammonio-platinic Chloride	$PtCl_4 . 2(NH_4)Cl$.

These salts have all a characteristic yellow color except in the
few cases where the second basic radical, having itself a strong
coloring power, modifies the result. The barium and sodium
salts crystallize in prisms. The magnesium salt, and the corresponding compounds of cadmium, zinc, copper, cobalt, and
manganese, which are isomorphous with it, crystallize in rhom-

bohedrons. The potassium and ammonium salts crystallize in regular octahedrons. The hydrous salts are all soluble in water, but the last two are nearly insoluble in water, and wholly insoluble in alcohol. They, therefore, can easily be obtained by precipitation, and on this fact are based several important methods of quantitative analysis. Moreover, compounds of the same general type may be formed with almost all the organic bases and vegetable alkaloids, and they furnish one of the simplest means of determining the molecular weight of such substances (68).

If the solution of platinum in aqua-regia is evaporated over a water-bath, the amorphous brownish-red residue (soluble both in water and alcohol) may be regarded as $PtCl_4$; but if the temperature is raised to 200° one half of the chlorine escapes, and the insoluble greenish-brown solid then obtained is $PtCl_2$. Platinous chloride is not acted on even by nitric or sulphuric acids, but, out of contact with the air, it dissolves unchanged in hydrochloric acid, although platinic chloride is formed if air has access to the solution. It also combines with other metallic chlorides, forming a large number of crystalline salts, as, for example,

Ammonio-platinous Chloride	$PtCl_2 . 2(NH_4)Cl,$
Potassio-platinous Chloride	$PtCl_2 . 2KCl,$
Argento-platinous Chloride	$PtCl_2 . 2AgCl,$
Zinco-platinous Chloride	$PtCl_2 . ZnCl_2,$
Bario-platinous Chloride	$PtCl_2 . BaCl_2 . 3H_2O.$

These salts are all readily prepared from the hydrochloric acid solution ($PtCl_2 . 2HCl + Aq$), and are generally distinguished by a red color.

367. *Platinous Hydrates*, $Pt=Ho_2$, which is obtained as a black powder by digesting platinous chloride with a solution of caustic potash, dissolves both in alkalies and acids, but the compounds thus formed are very unstable. Platinous nitrite and sulphite, however, form crystallizable double salts with several of the more basic radicals. Platinic Hydrate, $Pt\equiv Ho_4$, prepared indirectly from platinic chloride, is also soluble both in acids and alkalies. The compounds thus formed are all unstable, those in which the element acts as an acid radical being the more definite. Platinic sulphate and platinic nitrate, although they

have not been crystallized, are easily obtained in solution, the sulphate by evaporating a solution of the chloride with sulphuric acid, the nitrate by decomposing the sulphate with baric nitrate. Lastly, by cautiously heating the hydrates we can obtain the corresponding oxides, but if the temperature exceeds a limited degree they are at once completely reduced.

By acting on different platinum salts with ammonia, a remarkable class of compounds have been obtained, which are best regarded as salts of platinum bases, and as formed by the coalescing of two or more molecules of H_3N soldered together by atoms of $Pt^=$ or $P\mathrm{E}$, although they probably contain in some cases more complex platinum radicals. Similar compounds have also been formed with palladium and iridium; but, although highly interesting subjects of study on account of their manifold types and complex constitution, this new class of ammonia bases illustrate no principles not already fully discussed, and for a description of them we must refer to more extended works.

Questions and Problems.

1. Calculate the percentage composition of platinum ore, eliminating from the results given in (359) the quantity of iridosmine and sand with which the ore is mixed.

2. Explain the old method of working platinum ores, and illustrate the various steps in the process by reactions. To what extent are the associated metals precipitated by ammonic chloride?

3. Point out the relationship between the platinum metals and iron. Compare also these elements with each other, and consider especially the characteristics distinguishing the three groups into which they have been divided in Table II.

4. By what characters are the platinum metals as a class chiefly marked? Make a table which will bring into comparison the different double chlorides of these elements.

5. Explain, on the principle of dialysis, the transmission of hydrogen gas through the walls of a heated palladium or platinum tube.

6. Regarding the hydrogen condensed by platinum as chemically combined with the metal, cannot you find in this circumstance an explanation of the enhanced energy of the gas when in this condition. Consider the polarization of the negative platinum plate in a voltaic cell as an illustration of the same principle.

7. Show in what way the platinic salts may be used to determine the molecular weight of an organic base, and give an illustration of the principle.

8. Write the reactions by which platinic sulphate and nitrate may be prepared.

9. Write the reaction of a solution of platinic chloride on a solution of potassic nitrate. Platinic nitrate is one of the products.

10. Write the reaction of sodic carbonate on a solution of platinic sulphate, assuming that the chief product is platinic hydrate.

11. Write the reactions by which platinous hydrate may be prepared.

12. When platinous chloride dissolves in hydrochloric acid in contact with the air, what is the reaction?

13. Make a scheme illustrating the constitution or relations of the more important compounds of the platinum bases.

14. Explain a method of separating the platinum metals from each other.

Divisions XVII. to XIX.

368. TITANIUM. $Ti = 50.$ — Tetrad. No compounds corresponding to a lower degree of quantivalence are with certainty known. A comparatively rare element, but not unfrequently associated with iron. The most abundant native compound is Menaccanite or Titaniferous Iron, whose symbol has already been given among the iron ores. This mineral, however, is in most cases an isomorphous mixture of $(Ti\text{-}Fe)O_3$ and Fe_2O_3, sometimes containing also magnesium and manganese, and thus arise the numerous varieties which have been distinguished. The other important compounds are

Rutile, Brookite, and Octahedrite (2d or 4th System)		TiO_2,
Perofskite	(Rhombohedral)	$Ca = O_2 = TiO$,
Sphene	(Monoclinic)	$(Ca\text{-}O\text{-}Ti) = O_4 = Si.$

Titanium is also associated with columbium, tantalum, cerium, yttrium, and zirconium in a number of rare minerals.

369. *Metallic Titanium* has never been obtained as a massive metal, and its properties are very imperfectly known. As formed by decomposing the potassio-titanic fluoride with potassium it is a dark-green powder, showing under the microscope the color and lustre of iron. In this condition it is very combustible, readily dissolves in hydrochloric acid, and even decomposes water at the boiling-point.

370. *Titanic Chloride*, $TiCl_4$, is obtained by passing chlorine gas through an intimate mixture of titanic oxide and carbon intensely heated. It is a heavy, colorless liquid, boiling at 135°, and yielding a vapor whose Sp. Gr. $= 98.65$. Exposed to the air it absorbs moisture, and gradually solidifies, forming a crystalline hydrate which readily dissolves in water. From this solution, if sufficiently dilute, almost the whole of the titanium is precipitated as a hydrate on boiling, and the same is true of the solution formed by dissolving the native oxides (after fusion with an alkaline carbonate) in hydrochloric acid.

371. *Titanous Chloride*, Ti_2Cl_6, is formed by passing a mixture of $TiCl_4$ and $H\text{-}H$ through a red-hot porcelain tube. The compound is thus obtained in dark violet scales, which readily

dissolve in water forming a violet solution, but in contact with the air this solution gradually loses its color and deposits titanic hydrate. The same color is produced by boiling with tin a solution of titanic oxide in hydrochloric acid, and this reaction is the best test for titanium. The solution of titanous chloride is a very powerful reducing agent, which indicates that the radical $[Ti_2]^{\underline{\underline{i}}}$ is not a stable condition of the element.

372. *Titanic Bromide, and Iodide,* $TiBr_4$ and TiI_4, are fusible and volatile crystalline solids.

373. *Titanic Fluoride,* TiF_4, is a fuming, colorless liquid, obtained by distilling a mixture of fluor-spar and titanic oxide with sulphuric acid. This compound is resolved by water into soluble hydro-titanic fluoride and insoluble titanic oxyfluoride.

374. *Hydro-titanic Fluoride,* $TiF_4 . 2HF$, is the acid of a large class of salts which are easily made from the solution produced as just stated. The ammonium and potassium salts, which are the most important, both crystallize in white anhydrous scales.

375. *Titanic Hydrates.* — A large number of these hydrates have been distinguished, and they affect two very different modifications. Those obtained by precipitation with ammonia readily dissolve in acids, and when heated are converted into the anhydride with vivid incandescence. Those obtained by boiling dilute solutions of the chloride or sulphate are insoluble in all acids except strong sulphuric. They give off water more readily than the others, and the dehydration is not attended by the same incandescence. The composition of these hydrates depends on the temperature at which they are dried, and they may be regarded as derived from the normal hydrate by the method repeatedly illustrated and expressed by the general equation

$$n\,TiHo_4 - mH_2O = (O_m Ti_n)Ho_{4n-2m}. \qquad [353]$$

The two modifications have been obtained in the same degrees of hydration, and, so far as known, they are isomeric. Moreover, by dialysis a pure aqueous solution of titanic hydrate has been procured, which gelatinizes when concentrated, and evidently contains the compound in a colloidal condition.

376. *Titanic Oxide,* TiO_2, is chiefly interesting from the fact that it affects three different modifications, which are represented in nature by the minerals Rutile, Brookite, and Octa-

hedrite. These three isomeric bodies differ from each other in crystalline form, in density, and in hardness. Rutile, the most abundant, has the greatest hardness and density. Its crystals are tetragonal and isomorphous with those of SnO_2. Brookite, which stands next in hardness and density, affects forms of the orthorhombic system, which are approximately isomorphous with those of MnO_2. Lastly, Octahedrite is softer and less dense than either of the others, and its crystals, although tetragonal, differ essentially from those of Rutile. (Problem 2, page 144.) The same differences have been observed in crystals obtained artificially by decomposing TiF_4 or $TiCl_4$ with steam, and it is found that the nature of the product depends on the temperature at which the reaction takes place, the hardest and most dense crystals being formed at the highest temperature.

In its densest condition titanic oxide has a red color, and is insoluble in all acids; but the white anhydride, obtained by igniting titanic hydrate, is converted into a sulphate when heated with strong sulphuric acid, and may then be dissolved in water. The native oxides, also, may be rendered soluble by fusion with alkaline carbonates or bisulphates. It melts before the compound blow-pipe.

377. *Titanous Oxide*, Ti_2O_3, is obtained as a black powder when a stream of hydrogen is passed over ignited TiO_2. It dissolves in sulphuric acid, forming a violet solution, from which the alkalies precipitate a brown hydrate. A similar reduction takes place, and the same violet color is produced, when TiO_2 is dissolved in fused borax or microcosmic salt, and the bead heated before the blow-pipe on charcoal in contact with a small globule of tin.

378. *Titanic Sulphide*, TiS_2, is formed in large, brass-yellow, lustrous scales when a mixture of H_2S and $TiCl_4$ is passed through a glass tube heated to incipient redness. It is decomposed by water, and cannot, therefore, be obtained by precipitation.

379. *Nitrides.* — Titanium has a marked affinity for nitrogen, and combines with it in several proportions. When dry ammonia gas is passed over $TiCl_4$ it is rapidly absorbed with great elevation of temperature, and the resulting brown-red powder has the symbol $(H_{12}N_4Ti)^{\ddagger}Cl_4$. This compound, heated in a stream of ammonia gas, yields a copper-colored substance,

which is the nitride Ti_3N_4, and this, when further heated in a current of hydrogen, is converted into a second nitride (Ti_2N_2?) having a golden-yellow color and metallic lustre. A third violet-colored nitride has the symbol TiN_2. Lastly, the very hard copper-colored cubic crystals sometimes found adhering to the slags of iron-furnaces, and formerly mistaken for metallic titanium, have the composition expressed by the symbol Ti_5CN_4.

380. TIN. $Sn = 118.$ — *Bivalent and Quadrivalent.* The last is the most stable condition. The only valuable ore of tin is the oxide SnO_2, called in mineralogy Cassiterite or Tin Stone, and this is found at but few localities, chiefly in Cornwall, Malacca, Bolivia, Australia, Bohemia, and Saxony. This element is also an essential constituent of Tin Pyrites $[Zn,Fe]$, $[Cu_2]^{\equiv}S_4^{\equiv}Sn$, and is associated with columbium, titanium, zirconium, &c., in a few rare minerals, but its range in nature, so far as known, is very limited.

The metal is obtained by reducing the native oxide with coal; but, although in theory so simple, this process is in practice quite complicated. The ore requires, previous to smelting, a prolonged mechanical treatment, and in the furnace a large amount of metal passes into the slags, which therefore have to be worked over.

381. *Metallic Tin* has a familiar white color and bright lustre. It has a crystalline structure, and the breaking of the crystals against each other, when a bar of the metal is bent, produces the peculiar sound known as the *cry of tin.* By slowly cooling the fused metal distinct crystals can be obtained, which belong to the tetragonal system. The tenacity of tin is feeble, but it can readily be rolled and beaten into thin leaves, which are well known under the name of tin-foil. *Sp. Gr.* $= 7.3$. Melts at 222°. Boils at a white heat. Inferior conductor of heat or electricity.

Tin does not tarnish in a moist atmosphere which is free from sulphur, but when melted in the air it slowly oxidizes, and at a red heat decomposes steam. Hydrochloric acid dissolves the metal rapidly, the products being stannous chloride and hydrogen gas. It also dissolves slowly when boiled with dilute sulphuric acid, yielding stannous sulphate and liberating hydrogen as before. When the sulphuric acid is concentrated, SO_2 is evolved and stannous sulphate formed only so long as the tin

is in excess.   If the acid is in excess, sulphur separates and the
product is stannic sulphate.   Very strong nitric acid does not
act on the metal, but when somewhat diluted it converts the
tin into a white hydrate, insoluble in an excess of the acid.
Aqua-regia, if not too concentrated, dissolves tin as stannic
chloride, and the alkaline hydrates and nitrates also act upon it
at a high temperature.

Tin unites directly with most of the non-metallic elements,
and forms alloys with many of the metals.   The alloys with
copper have already been mentioned.   Pewter and plumber's
solder are alloys of tin and lead.   Britannia metal, an alloy of
brass, tin, lead, and bismuth, and the silvering of mirrors an
amalgam of tin and mercury.   On account of its beautiful lustre
and power of resisting atmospheric agents, tin is much used for
coating other metals.   The common tin ware is made of sheet-
iron thus protected.

382. *Stannous Chloride.* $SnCl_2$. — The anhydrous compound (butter of tin) obtained by heating mercuric chloride
with an excess of tin, or by heating the metal in hydrochloric
acid gas, is a fusible white solid with a fatty lustre, soluble in
water and alcohol.   The hydrous salt (tin salts), formed by
crystallizing the solution of tin in hydrochloric acid, has the
symbol $SnCl_2 . 2H_2O$.   The pure crystals dissolve perfectly in
a small amount of water, free from air, but a large amount of
water produces a partial decomposition.

$$(2SnCl_2 + 3H_2O + Aq) =$$
$$\mathbf{Sn_2OCl_2 . 2H_2O} + (2HCl + Aq). \quad [354]$$

So, also, when the solution is exposed to the air.

$$(6SnCl_2 + 4H_2O + Aq) + \text{⊙⊙} =$$
$$2(\mathbf{Sn_2OCl_2 . 2H_2O}) + (2SnCl_4 + Aq). \quad [355]$$

The oxychloride, which is milk white and insoluble (even in
dilute acids), renders the solution in both cases turbid.   Free
hydrochloric acid, tartaric acid, and sal ammoniac prevent the
decomposition.   Owing to the unsatisfied affinities of the tin
radical, stannous chloride is a powerful reducing agent (277),
and is much used for this purpose both in the laboratory and
the dye-house.   It also acts as a mordant.   Lastly, it forms
salts with several of the metallic chlorides.

Potassio-stannous Chloride　　$Sn\,Cl_2 \,.\, 2KCl \,.\, (1, 2, \text{or } 3H_2O)$,
Bario-stannous Chloride　　　$Sn\,Cl_2 \,.\, Ba\,Cl_2 \,.\, 4H_2O$.

383. *Stannic Chloride*, $Sn\,Cl_4$, may be made either by distilling a mixture of tin and mercuric chloride, the last being in
excess, or by heating tin in chlorine gas. It is a colorless, fuming liquid, boiling at 115°, and yielding a vapor whose Sp. Gr.
$= 132.7$. The liquid, exposed to the air, eagerly absorbs moisture, and changes into a crystalline solid. When mixed with
water intense heat is evolved, and a solution formed which yields
on evaporation rhombohedral crystals of $Sn\,Cl_4 \,.\, 5H_2O$. These
crystals, dried *in vacuo*, lose $3H_2O$, and there is reason to believe that the remaining $2H_2O$ are a part of the molecule of the
salt. If we regard the atoms of chlorine as trivalent, we can
easily see that such an atomic group would be possible, for we
might then have the univalent radical $(H\text{-}Cl\text{=}Cl) = Hcl$ replacing Ho, and the symbol of the dried salt would be written
$Sn \equiv Ho_2, Hcl_2$. The same principle may be applied in other
cases where the violence of the action indicates that a chemical
union has taken place between an anhydrous chloride and water.
Such bodies, however, may also be regarded as chlorhydrines
(349), to which molecules of HCl are united in place of water
of crystallization. Thus the symbol of the hydrous chloride we
have been discussing might be written $Sn \equiv Cl_2, Ho_2 \,.\, 2HCl$.

Although stannic chloride forms a clear solution with a small
amount of water, copious dilution determines the precipitation
of the greater part of the tin as an insoluble stannic hydrate.
Heat favors this decomposition, and, on the other hand, the presence of a large excess of hydrochloric acid prevents it. Stannic chloride unites with a considerable number of bodies both
organic and inorganic, and forms double salts with several of
the metallic chlorides. Ammonio-stannic chloride, $Sn\,Cl_4 \,.\,$
$2NH_4Cl$ (pink salts of the dyers) is isomorphous with the corresponding compound of platinum. An impure solution of
stannic chloride, made by dissolving tin in aqua-regia, is also
extensively used in dyeing for brightening and fixing certain
red colors.

There are two bromides and iodides of tin corresponding to
the chlorides. There is also a stannous fluoride, and although
stannic fluoride has not been isolated, a large number of double

stannic fluorides or fluostannates are known, which are isomorphous with the corresponding compounds of titanium and silicon.

384. *Stannous Hydrate.* — The precipitate which falls on adding an alkaline carbonate to a solution of stannous chloride is said to have the composition $Ho_2{=}(Sn_2{=}O)$. It is soluble in both alkalies and acids. Boiled with water or a weak solution of potash it is rendered anhydrous, but if boiled with a concentrated solution of this alkali it yields potassic stannate and metallic tin. The moist hydrate absorbs oxygen from the air, and acts, like the chloride, as a reducing agent. The only important oxygen salt corresponding to this hydrate is stannous sulphate.

385. *Stannic Hydrate*, like titanic hydrate, affects both a soluble and an insoluble modification. The hydrate precipitated when ammonia is added to a solution of stannic chloride dissolves readily both in acids and alkalies, while that obtained by boiling the same solution greatly diluted, or by acting on tin with nitric acid, is insoluble in acids, and dissolves less readily than the first in alkalies. The composition of these bodies varies with the temperature at which they are dried, and they are usually distinguished as stannic and meta-stannic hydrates. Like the corresponding compounds of titanium, they may be regarded as derived from a normal hydrate of either class by the elimination of successive molecules of water. The salts obtained by dissolving stannic hydrate in oxygen acids are unimportant. The sulphate is the most stable, but this is completely decomposed, and the tin precipitated as meta-stannic hydrate when the aqueous solution is diluted and boiled. The atoms $Sn{=}$ form much more stable compounds when they act as acid radicals. The alkaline stannates crystallize readily, and both potassic and sodic stannates, $(K$ or $Na)_2{=}O_2{=}SnO . 4H_2O$, are commercial products much used as mordants. Their efficacy depends on the fact that ammonic chloride and all acids, even the CO_2 of the atmosphere, decomposes these salts when in solution, and the stannic hydrate thus precipitated in the fibre of the cloth binds the coloring matter.

The compounds obtained by dissolving meta-stannic hydrate in alkaline solvents cannot be crystallized, but are precipitated on adding to the solution caustic potash. The potassium salt thus obtained, dried at 126°, has the composition $K_2{=}O_2{=}Sn_5O_9 . 4H_2O$.

It was formerly supposed that the peculiar qualities of the meta-stannic hydrates and the meta-stannates were due to the atomic grouping here represented, but this opinion has not been sustained by recent investigations. The water represented as water of crystallization cannot be removed without decomposing the salt, and is evidently water of constitution; so that we have good reason for writing the symbol $H_3,K_2 \times O_{10} \times (Sn_5 O_5)$ after the type of the normal stannates, and we may regard it as an example of the soluble colloidal hydrates, to which we have before referred (337). This view harmonizes with the facts that on boiling an aqueous solution of this compound meta-stannic hydrate is precipitated, and that by dialysis a solution both of meta-stannic and stannic hydrates in pure water may be obtained. The two classes of compounds are probably isomeric, but differ in the degree of molecular condensation.

386. *Oxides.* — Stannous Oxide, SnO, may be obtained in various ways, and its color differs according to the mode of preparation. It has a strong affinity for oxygen, and if set on fire when dry burns to stannic oxide.

Stannic oxide has been crystallized artificially, not only in the forms of Tin-stone isomorphous with Rutile, but also in forms isomorphous with Brookite. As obtained by igniting the hydrate, or by burning metallic tin, it is an amorphous white powder. It offers even greater resistance to the action of chemical agents than TiO_2. It is not attacked by acids even when concentrated. It is not dissolved by fusion with alkaline carbonates, but is rendered soluble by fusion with caustic alkalies. It is also taken up when fused with acid potassic sulphate, but separates completely when the fused mass is dissolved in water. Moreover, like titanic oxide it is very hard and infusible, but unlike that it is reduced to the metallic state when ignited in a stream of hydrogen gas.

Besides SnO and SnO_2 an intermediate oxide, Sn_2O_3, has been distinguished, but it does not form definite salts. Dissolved in hydrochloric acid it gives with auric chloride the beautiful purple precipitate known as Purple of Cassius (147).

387. *Sulphides.* — The dark-brown precipitate which falls when H_2S is passed through an acid solution of a stannous salt is SnS, and the dull yellow precipitate which forms under the same circumstances in a solution of a stannic salt is a hydrate

of SnS_2. The last of these dissolves readily in solutions of alkaline sulphides, and forms with them definite salts. It is also
soluble in the fixed alkaline hydrates, and in either case is precipitated unchanged when the alkali is neutralized with an acid.
Stannous sulphide, on the other hand, does not form salts with
the alkaline sulphides, and does not dissolve in solutions of these
compounds, unless, like the common yellow ammonic sulphide,
they contain an excess of sulphur, when it is converted into
SnS_2, and as such is precipitated on neutralizing the alkali.
It does, however, dissolve in the fixed alkaline hydrates, but
when an excess of acid is added to the solution a yellow precipitate of SnS_2 falls, containing only one half of the tin present.

The beautiful yellow flaky material known as mosaic gold,
and used in painting to imitate bronze, consists of anhydrous
stannic sulphide, and is obtained by subliming a mixture of tin,
sulphur, sal-ammoniac, and mercury. There is also a sesquisulphide, Sn_2S_3.

388. *Compounds with the Alcohol Radicals.* — These compounds are very numerous and highly important, theoretically,
because they establish beyond all doubt the atomic relations of
tin. Compounds have been obtained containing methyl, ethyl,
and amyl, either singly or associated together. Three compounds are known containing only tin and ethyl. Putting
$Et = (C_2H_5)$ we have

$$Sn\text{=}Et_2, \qquad (Sn\text{≡}Et_3)\text{-}(Sn\text{≡}Et_3), \qquad Sn\text{≡}Et_4.$$

All three are colorless oily liquids. The last is the most stable,
boiling at 181°, and yielding a vapor whose Sp. Gr. $=$ 116.
The others cannot be volatilized without decomposition, and
unite directly with oxygen, chlorine, bromine, and iodine. The
first, especially, like other stannous compounds, acts as a reducing agent, absorbing oxygen from the air, and precipitating silver from a solution of the nitrate. This is the only stannous
compound known among this class of bodies. In all the others
the tin atoms exert their maximum atom-fixing power, and they
may be regarded either as compounds of the radicals $(SnEt_3)\text{=}$
or $(SnEt_3)\text{-}$, or else as formed from stannic ethide by replacing
either one or more of the atoms of ethyl by other radicals.
The following are a few examples: —

Stanno-diethylic Bromide	$(SnEt_2)=Br_2,$
Stanno-diethylic Oxide	$(SnEt_2)=O,$
Stanno-diethylic Acetate	$(SnEt_2)=O_2=(C_2H_3O)_2,$
Stanno-diethylic Sulphate	$(SnEt_2)=O_2=SO_2,$
Stanno-triethylic Chloride	$(SnEt_3)-Cl,$
Stanno-triethylic Hydrate	$(SnEt_3)-O-H,$
Stanno-triethylic Oxide	$(SnEt_3)_2=O,$
Stanno-triethylic Carbonate	$(SnEt_3)_2=O_2=CO.$

The methyl and amyl compounds are formed after the same analogy, and also others which contain both methyl and ethyl. These compounds are either liquids or crystalline solids. The chlorides, bromides, and iodides are, as a rule, volatile and sparingly soluble in water. The oxides and oxygen salts, on the other hand, generally dissolve freely in water, and are more easily decomposed by heat. The vapor densities of several of these compounds are given in Table III., and this list might be greatly extended.

389. ZIRCONIUM. $Zr = 89.6.$ — Tetrad. Found only in Zircon, Eudialyte, and a few other very rare minerals. The elementary substance closely resembles silicon. It may be obtained by similar reactions in three corresponding states, amorphous, crystalline, and graphitoidal. Amorphous zirconium is a very combustible black powder. The crystals, *Sp. Gr.* 4.15, resemble antimony in color, lustre, and brittleness, and burn only at a very high temperature. The graphitoidal variety forms very light steel-gray scales. Zirconium is very infusible, is but slightly attacked by the ordinary acids, but hydrofluoric acid, and in some conditions aqua-regia, dissolve it rapidly.

390. *Zirconic Chloride, $ZrCl_4$,* is a white volatile solid (Sp. Gr. $= 117.6$), which dissolves easily and with evolution of heat in water. This solution, or the solution of the hydrate in hydrochloric acid, yields on evaporation a large mass of white silky needles, which, when heated, lose water and hydrochloric acid, leaving an oxychloride, $Zr_3O_4Cl_4$.

391. *Zirconic Fluoride, ZrF_4,* is likewise a volatile white solid, and forms a crystalline hydrate, $ZrF_4 . 3H_2O$, which is decomposed by heat, leaving pure ZrO_2. Zirconic fluoride unites with many other metallic fluorides, forming salts which are isomorphous with the corresponding compounds of silicon,

titanium, and tin. The following symbols illustrate the known types : —

Cadmio-zirconic Fluoride	$ZrF_4 . 2CdF_2 . 6H_2O,$
Tripotassio-zirconic Fluoride	$ZrF_4 . 3KF,$
Dipotassio-zirconic Fluoride	$ZrF_4 . 2KF,$
Potassio-zirconic Fluoride	$ZrF_4 . KF . H_2O,$
Sodio-zirconic Fluoride	$2ZrF_4 . 5NaF.$

392. *Zirconic Hydrate*, precipitated from the chloride by ammonia, and dried at 17°, has the symbol $Zr\equiv Ho_4$. Dried at a higher temperature, $(ZrO)\equiv Ho_2$. It is a yellowish, translucent, gummy mass, having a conchoidal fracture. The hydrate precipitated and washed cold dissolves easily in acids, and, very slightly, even in water; but when precipitated from hot solutions, or washed with hot water, it dissolves only in concentrated acids. Zirconic hydrate acts both as a base and an acid.

There are several zirconic sulphates. The normal salt can be crystallized, and the formation of a basic sulphate, which is precipitated when a neutral solution of zirconia in sulphuric acid is boiled with potassic sulphate, is one of the most characteristic reactions of zirconium. The salts of zirconium have an astringent taste, and the solutions redden turmeric paper.

The precipitated hydrate is insoluble in caustic alkalies, but when precipitated by a fixed alkaline carbonate, or, better, by a bicarbonate, it dissolves in an excess of the reagent. The alkaline zirconates can be obtained by fusion, and several definite crystalline zirconates of the more basic radicals have been studied.

393. *Zirconic Oxide* (*Zirconia*), ZrO_2, is obtained by heating the hydrate. Prepared at the lowest possible temperature it forms a white tasteless powder soluble in acids; but when heated to incipient redness it glows brightly, becomes denser and much harder, and is then insoluble in any acid excepting hydrofluoric and strong sulphuric. Zirconia has been crystallized artificially in the same form as Tin-stone and Rutile.

The mineral zircon is usually regarded as a silicate of zirconium, $Zr\equiv O_4\equiv Si$, but the symbol may also be written $[Zr,Si]\equiv O_2$, and this view harmonizes with the fact that the crystalline form is almost identical with that of ZrO_2, SnO_2 and TiO_2. Moreover, several isomorphous varieties of this mineral are known (Malacone, Oerstedite, &c.) in which the proportions of Zr and Si are quite variable. They are more or less hydrous, and for the most part comparatively soft, but, like pure ZrO_2, they become, when heated, exceedingly hard as well as more dense.

394. THORIUM. $Th = 115.7$. — The mineral Thorite, or Orangeite, is essentially a hydrous silicate of this exceedingly rare metallic element, which has also been found, but only as a subordinate constituent, in Euxenite, Pyrochlore, Monazite, Gadolinite, and Orthite. When Thorite is decomposed by hydrochloric acid a solution of thoric chloride, $ThCl_4$, is obtained, from which the caustic alkalies precipitate a hydrate insoluble in an excess of the reagent. A similar precipitate is obtained with the alkaline carbonates, but this readily dissolves when an excess is added to the solution. In the same solution a precipitate is obtained with oxalic acid, potassic sulphate, and potassic ferro-cyanide.

As the above reactions indicate, Thorium is allied in many of its properties to the metals of the glucinum and cerium groups, but in other respects it resembles more nearly zirconium, with which it is here associated. The anhydrous oxide ThO_2 is a white powder, which glows when heated, becomes more dense, and after ignition is insoluble in any acid except concentrated sulphuric. It has a high specific gravity, and by fusion with borax has been obtained in tetragonal crystals (Fig. 37) resembling those of Tin-stone, SnO_2, and Rutile, TiO_2. The anhydrous chloride is volatile, and the hydrated chloride forms a radiate crystalline mass like $ZrCl_4$. The chloride may be reduced by sodium, and the metal may be thus obtained as a gray lustrous powder which readily burns in the air.

Questions and Problems.

Titanium.

1. Compare by means of graphic symbols the composition of Perofskite and Menaccanite. Can they be regarded as similarly constituted?

2. Write the reaction by which titanic chloride is made.

3. According to the experiments of Isidore Pierre, 0.8215 gramme

of $TiCl_4$ yield 2.45176 grammes of $AgCl$. Calculate the atomic weight of titanium, and state clearly the course of reasoning by which the result is reached. Ans. 50.34.

4. Write the reaction which takes place when a dilute aqueous solution of $TiCl_4$ is boiled.

5. Write the reactions which take place when a solution of titaniferous iron in hydrochloric acid is boiled with tin, and explain the use of this reaction as a test for titanium.

6. Write the reaction by which TiF_4 is prepared, and also show how it is decomposed by water.

7. Represent the constitution of hydro-titanic fluoride by a graphic symbol, assuming that F is trivalent.

8. Represent in a tabular form the possible titanic hydrates.

9. Do the hydrates of any of the preceding elements present phenomena similar to those of titanic hydrate?

10. Write the reaction by which TiS_2 is prepared, and also the reactions by which crystals of TiO_2 may be obtained.

11. Compare the specific gravities and hardness of the native titanic oxides. What would these differences indicate in regard to the molecular constitution of these minerals?

12. Represent by graphic symbols the constitution of the nitrides of titanium.

13. Point out the analogies between titanium and the platinum metals. Is titanium in any way related to iron?

Tin.

14. Write the reactions of hydrochloric, nitric, and sulphuric acids on metallic tin.

15. Write the reaction of stannous chloride on solution of $HgCl_2$.

16. Write the reaction by which anhydrous $SnCl_2$ is prepared.

17. Analyze reactions [354] and [355], and explain the use of tin salts as a mordant.

18. Write the reactions by which anhydrous $SnCl_4$ is prepared.

19. Represent the constitution of hydrous stannic chloride by graphic symbols, and apply the same principle to the interpretation of other similar compounds.

20. Write the reaction when a dilute aqueous solution of stannic chloride is boiled, and explain the use of this solution as a mordant.

21. Write the reaction which takes place when stannous hydrate is boiled with a concentrated solution of potassic hydrate.

22. Make a table exhibiting the possible stannic hydrates, and explain the difference between the two classes of these compounds.

23. Write the reaction which takes place when a dilute aqueous solution of stannic sulphate is boiled.

24. Write the reaction which takes place when a solution of sodic stannate is boiled with ammonic chloride.

25. Represent the constitution of meta-stannic hydrate by graphic symbols, and explain the two opinions which have been entertained in regard to it, showing how far they are sustained by facts.

26. Write the reaction of H_2S on a solution of stannous or stannic chloride.

27. Write the reaction which takes place when SnS is dissolved in yellow ammonic sulphide, and that which follows on neutralizing the alkaline solvent with an acid. Write also the reactions when an alkaline hydrate is used as the solvent.

28. Point out the analogies and the differences between tin and titanium. By what simple reaction may the two elements be separated when in solution?

29. How is tin related to the platinum metals?

30. According to the experiments of Dumas, 100 parts of tin, when oxidized by nitric acid, yield 127.105 parts of SnO_2. What is the atomic weight of the element, assuming that the oxide has the constitution represented by the symbol?   Ans. 118.06.

31. On what facts do the conclusions in regard to the atomicity of tin and the constitution of its several compounds rest?

32. Show that the atomic weight of tin, deduced from the percentage composition and vapor densities of its compounds with the alcohol radicals, agrees with the value given above. Show, also, that these compounds fully illustrate the atomic relations of the elements.

33. State the reasons for classing zirconium and thorium with tin and titanium.

34. Point out the resemblances between zirconium and silicon, and give the reasons for classing zircon with tin-stone and rutile.

Division XX.

395. SILICON. $Si = 28$. — Tetrad. Most abundant of the elements after oxygen, forming, as is estimated, about one fourth of the rocky crust of the globe. Always found in nature united to oxygen either as quartz, SiO_2, or associated with more basic radicals in the various native silicates, many of whose symbols have already been given (333) (352). The elementary substance may be obtained in three different conditions, — amorphous, graphitoidal, and crystalline.

1. By decomposing $SiF_4 . 2KF$ with potassium or sodium, or by heating the same metals in a current of the vapor of $SiCl_4$, silicon is obtained as a dull-brown powder, which soils the fingers, and readily dissolves in hydrofluoric acid or a warm solution of caustic potash, although insoluble in water and the common acids. When ignited it burns brilliantly, but the grains soon become coated with a varnish of melted silicon, which protects them from the further action of the air.

2. The brown powder just described, when intensely heated in a closed crucible, becomes very much denser and darker in color, and afterwards is insoluble in hydrofluoric acid, and does not burn even in the oxyhydrogen flame. It does dissolve, however, in a mixture of hydrofluoric and nitric acids, or in fused potassic carbonate, and it deflagrates if intensely heated with nitre.

3. At the highest temperature of a wind-furnace silicon melts, and may be cast into bars which have a crystalline structure, a sub-metallic lustre, and a dark steel-gray color. Moreover, by reducing silicon in contact with melted aluminum or zinc the molten metal dissolves the silicon, and afterwards, on cooling, deposits it in definite crystals. These crystals have a reddish lustre and the form of diamond, which they almost rival in hardness.

396. *Silicic Anhydride or Silica.* SiO_2. — By far the most abundant of all mineral substances. The mineralogists distinguish two principal modifications, Quartz and Opal. Quartz crystallizes in the hexagonal system (Figs. 64 to 67), has a *Sp. Gr.* 2.5 to 2.8, is so hard that it cannot be cut with a file, and even in powder is but slightly acted on by hot solutions of caus-

tic alkalies. Opal is amorphous or colloidal, has a *Sp. Gr.* 1.9 to 2.3, is easily abraded with a file, and dissolves in alkaline solutions. Each of these mineral species exhibits numerous varieties, determined by differences of structure or admixtures of different bodies. Among those of quartz may be mentioned common quartz, milky quartz, smoky quartz, amethyst, chalcedony, carnelian, agate, onyx, flint, hornstone, jasper, sandstone, and sand. Among those of opal we have precious opal, common opal, jasper opal, wood opal, siliceous sinter, float-stone, and tripoli. These two conditions of SiO_2, however, are sometimes found alternating on the same specimen, and the chalcedonic varieties of quartz have frequently the appearance of opal, through which state they probably passed in the process of formation. The opals are more or less hydrous, but the water present is usually regarded as unessential.

Both in its crystalline and in its amorphous condition silica is insoluble in water and in all acids excepting hydrofluoric acid, which is its appropriate solvent. The heat of the oxyhydrogen flame is required for its fusion, but at this temperature it melts to a transparent glass, and may be drawn out into fine flexible elastic threads, the fused silica affecting the amorphous condition. When added in powder to melted sodic or potassic carbonate it causes violent effervescence, and if the silica is pure the product is a colorless glass. Unless the silica is in great excess the alkaline silicates thus obtained are soluble in water, and are generally known as *soluble* or *water glass.* They yield alkaline solutions, which are very much used in the arts, — 1. As a cement for hardening and preserving stone; 2. In preparing walls for fresco-painting; 3. For mixing with soap; and 4. In preparing mordanted calico for dyeing. The same solutions can be also made by digesting flints in strong solutions of the caustic alkalies at a high temperature under pressure.

397. *Silicic Hydrates.* — If to a solution of an alkaline silicate in water hydrochloric acid be added gradually, a gelatinous precipitate of silicic hydrate is formed, which, in its initial condition, probably has the composition $Ho_4 Si$; but in drying it passes through every degree of hydration, and the various hydrates which have been obtained in this and in other ways may be represented by the general formula

$$n Ho_4 Si - m H_2 O = Ho_{4n-2m}(O_m Si_n). \qquad [356]$$

They are all, however, very unstable bodies, some losing water at low temperatures, and others very hygroscopic, so that it is difficult to obtain definite compounds.

If, instead of making the experiment as just directed, a dilute solution of an alkaline silicate be poured into a considerable excess of hydrochloric acid, no precipitate is formed. The whole of the hydrate remains in solution mixed with the alkaline chlorides and free hydrochloric acid. These crystalloid substances, however, can readily be separated by dialysis from the colloid hydrate, and a pure solution of silicic hydrate may be thus obtained containing as much as five per cent of $Si\,O_2$. Moreover, by boiling in a flask the solution may be concentrated, until the quantity of silica reaches fourteen per cent. This solution is limpid, colorless, tasteless, and has a feebly acid reaction, which a very small quantity of K-Ho is sufficient to neutralize.

Evidently, then, silicic hydrate has both a soluble and an insoluble modification, but the last is by far the most stable condition. The concentrated solution, formed as above, in a few days completely gelatinizes. Moreover, even in a closed vessel this jelly gradually shrinks, spontaneously squeezing out the greater part of the water, until at last it becomes a hard mass resembling opal. When, however, the solution is quite dilute, it can be kept indefinitely without gelatinizing, and most spring and river waters hold an appreciable amount of silicic hydrate thus dissolved. The power of dissolving silica, which natural waters possess, is greatly enhanced by the presence of alkaline carbonates; and when the action of the alkaline liquid is aided by a high temperature, as in the case of hot springs, large quantities of silica are frequently dissolved, and such solutions have undoubtedly exerted an important agency in the geological history of the earth. Whenever a solution of silicic hydrate is evaporated to dryness, the whole of the silica is rendered insoluble and cannot afterwards be dissolved either in water or common acids.

398. *Silicates.* — Although it is impossible to isolate the numberless intermediate silicic hydrates comprehended in [356], yet we find in nature numerous mineral silicates formed after the same types, and which may be regarded as derived from the hydrates by replacing the hydrogen atoms with various basic radicals. These silicates, like silica itself, affect both the crystalline and the colloidal condition.

The crystalline silicates are represented by numerous well-defined mineral species, and by the rocks which are simply aggregates of such minerals. They have been formed in many ways; for example, — 1. By deposition from solution; 2. By the action of heated water or vapor on igneous and sedimentary rocks; 3. By the slow cooling of molten siliceous material.

The colloidal silicates are represented by the obsidians, the pitch-stones, and other volcanic rocks, which have probably always been formed by the sudden cooling of melted lavas. To the last class belong also the various artificial silicates we call glass, and the slags obtained in many metallurgical processes. Thus crown-glass is a silicate of sodium or potassium with calcium, flint-glass a silicate of either of these alkaline radicals with lead, and the slags silicates of calcium, magnesium, aluminum, and iron in various combinations. Since many of the basic hydrates and anhydrides may be melted with silica in almost every proportion, we do not find in the colloidal silicates the same definite composition as in the crystalline minerals, but they are probably in all cases mixtures of definite compounds.

Most of the silicates are fusible, and their fusibility is increased by mixture with each other. As a rule, those which contain the most fusible oxides melt the most readily, and the more readily in proportion as the base is in excess. Only the alkaline silicates above referred to are soluble in water. Most of the hydrous silicates, and many which are anhydrous but contain an excess of base, are decomposed by acids;[1] but the anhydrous, normal, or acid silicates are, as a rule, unaffected by any acid, except hydrofluoric, although they can be rendered soluble by fusion with an alkaline carbonate. When the fused mass is treated with $HCl + Aq$, evaporated to dryness, and again digested with the same acid, the silica remains as a gritty insoluble powder, and can at once be recognized. The presence of silica in a mineral can generally also be discovered by fusing a small fragment before the blow-pipe with microcosmic salt. This decomposes the mineral, but does not dissolve the silica, which is left floating in the clear bead.

[1] Soluble compounds of the basic radicals are thus formed, while the silica separates either as a gelatinous hydrate, or as a loose, anhydrous powder. Sometimes, however, the silica also dissolves, and generally it is taken up to a limited extent. In every case the silica becomes anhydrous, and completely insoluble if the solution is evaporated to dryness at the boiling-point of water.

399. *Constitution of Native Silicates.* — The symbols of many of the native silicates have already been given, and those of others will be discovered by solving the problems which follow this division. Moreover, the principles on which these symbols are written have been fully developed. There is still, however, an uncertainty in regard to the constitution of some of these minerals, and it is not always possible to deduce from the results of analysis a probable rational formula, even when these results are known to be essentially accurate. This uncertainty arises from several causes: — 1. We have no sure criterion of the purity of the mineral, since we are not able, as in the case of artificial products, to eliminate admixtures by repeated crystallizations; 2. The methods commonly used to determine the molecular weight of compounds (66) entirely fail in the case of these silicates, and this important element for fixing the symbol is therefore wanting[1] (23). Moreover, when the molecule is condensed (that is, contains several atoms of silicon) unavoidable inaccuracies in the processes may vitiate conclusions based on analysis alone; 3. The constant replacement of one radical by another (214) renders the composition of most silicates very complex, and we are frequently at a loss to determine the part which a given radical may play in the compound. This is especially true of hydrogen, for we have no certain means of deciding whether the atoms of this element in a hydrous silicate are a part of the molecule itself, or only connected with it in the water of crystallization.

400. *Symbols of Native Silicates.* — The composition of most native silicates may be so varied by replacements, without any essential change in external qualities, that such a mineral species cannot be distinguished as a compound of definite radicals, but merely as conforming to a certain general formula, and the only specific character is the *atomic ratio* between the several composite radicals of which the mineral may be supposed to consist (214). Thus the composition of common Garnet may in general be represented by the formula

$$\overset{\text{II}}{R}_{3}[\overset{\text{VI}}{R}_{2}]^{\text{xii}}O_{12}{}^{\text{xii}}\overset{\text{IV}}{Si}_{3},$$

---

[1] We have reason to hope that a more accurate knowledge of the laws which govern the molecular volume of compounds in the solid condition may hereafter supply this deficiency.

but $\overset{\text{II}}{R}$ may be either Ca, Mg, Fe, Mn, or Cr, and $\overset{\text{VI}}{[R_2]}$ either $[Al_2]$, $[Fe]_2$, or $[Cr_2]$, and garnets have been analyzed in which these several radicals are mixed together in every conceivable way consistent with the general formula, to which they all conform. *This formula, however, is merely the expression of a definite ratio between the atomicities of the several classes of radicals taken as a whole, and in the last analysis this ratio is itself the specific character.* Hence the great importance of the atomic ratio in mineralogy, and we have already seen how easily it can be calculated when the symbol of the mineral is given (Probs. 58 and 95, pages 394 and 397). On the other hand, from the ratio we can as easily construct the general formula of the mineral. Thus in the case of garnet the ratio between the dyad, hexad, and tetrad radicals is $6:6:12$, or $1:1:2$, which is evidently expressed in its simplest terms by the symbol above.

In works on mineralogy the atomic ratio is given for each of the native silicates, and in any case this ratio is easily deduced from the results of analysis by simply extending the method for finding the symbol of a body whose molecular weight is unknown (page 43). Having obtained the several quotients which represent the relative number of atoms on the supposition that the molecular weight is 100, we next multiply each of these quotients by the quantivalence of the respective radicals. Lastly, we add together these products for each class of replacing radicals, and compare the several sums thus obtained. For example, an actual analysis of the Bohemian Garnet (Pyrope) gave the following results : —

Si	19.30	or	SiO_2	41.35
$[Al_2]$	11.92	"	Al_2O_3	22.35
Fe	7.73	"	FeO	9.94
Mn	2.01	"	MnO	2.59
Mg	9.00	"	MgO	15.00
Ca	3.77	"	CaO	5.29
Cr	3.19	"	CrO	4.17
O	43.77			
	100.69			100.69

Dividing now each per cent by the atomic weight of the radical, and multiplying by its quantivalence, we obtain the following numbers : —

$$Si \quad (19.30 \div 28 \ ) \times 4 = 2.76 \qquad 2.76$$
$$[Al_2] \ (11.92 \div 54.8) \times 6 = 1.31 \qquad \overline{1.31}$$
$$Fe \quad (\ 7.73 \div 56 \ ) \times 2 = 0.27$$
$$Mn \quad (\ 2.01 \div 55 \ ) \times 2 = 0.07$$
$$Mg \quad (\ 9.00 \div 24 \ ) \times 2 = 0.75$$
$$Ca \quad (\ 3.77 \div 40 \ ) \times 2 = 0.19$$
$$Cr \quad (\ 3.19 \div 52.2) \times 2 = 0.12 \qquad \underline{1.40}$$

whence we deduce the ratio,

$$1.40 : 1.31 : 2.76 \quad \text{or} \quad 1 : 1 : 2 \text{ nearly.}$$

This ratio, although not exact, is as near the theory as we can expect, considering the material and methods used, and is as near as we usually obtain.

There is an uncertainty in the results of all calculations of this kind, which arises from the fact that we have no sure guide in selecting the radicals to be grouped together. Although it is true in general that replacements are limited to radicals of the same atomicity, yet most mineralogists admit that radicals of the form $[R_2]^{ii}$ may replace $3R^{ii}$, and some go so far as to reckon a part of the Si among the basic radicals. Hence our results are to a certain extent arbitrary, and in many cases give no satisfactory information as to the constitution of the mineral analyzed; but by deducing the atomic ratio according to the rule just given, we in all instances reduce the results, as it were, to the simplest terms, and bring them into a form in which they can be most conveniently compared with each other.

It is usual in works on mineralogy to present the results of analysis on the old dualistic plan, as if the mineral were formed by the union of various basic anhydrides with silicon. Starting with such data it is not, however, necessary to calculate the per cent of each radical in the assumed anhydrides before applying the above rule, because obviously by dividing the per cent of each anhydride by its molecular weight we shall obtain the same quotients as before. For example, in the analysis garnet cited above, where the data are given in both forms, we have

$$\overset{28}{Si} : \overset{60}{Si}O_2 = 19.30 : 41.35 \quad \text{or} \quad 19.30 \div 28 = 41.35 \div 60,$$

and so for each of the other values.

In the symbols of the silicates as formerly written on the dualistic theory, the atoms of oxygen were necessarily apportioned among the different radicals in proportion to their quantivalence, although this fundamental distinction between them was itself overlooked. Thus the general symbol of garnet would be written, dualistically,

$$3RO, R_2O_3, 3SiO_2,$$

and it is evident that the number of oxygen atoms is in each case a measure of the *relative* atomicities of the radicals with which they are associated. Hence the *atomic ratio* might also be found by comparing together the quantities of oxygen which the several assumed oxides contain, and this is the manner in which the calculation has generally been made hitherto. Hence, also, the *atomic ratio* has been called the *oxygen ratio*, and was long used in mineralogy before its true meaning was understood. But although the old method gives the same results as the new, it is not in harmony with our modern theories, and is practically less simple. Moreover, the principle is far more general than the old method would imply, and may be used with all classes of compounds as well as with those in which the radicals are cemented together by oxygen. Furthermore, it is sometimes useful to compare the atomic ratios of the complex radicals which may be assumed to exist in different minerals, and interesting relations may frequently be discovered in this way which the old method would entirely overlook. This has already appeared in solving the problems under aluminum, and requires no further illustration.

401. *Silicic Sulphide.* SiS_2. — When the vapor of CS_2 is passed over a mixture of silica and carbon intensely ignited, this compound is deposited in the colder part of the tube in "long, white, silky, flexible, asbestiform needles." It can be volatilized in a current of dry gas; but in contact with moist air, or when heated in aqueous vapor, it rapidly decomposes, the products being H_2S and amorphous silica, the latter of which retains the form of the sulphide. It undergoes a similar decomposition in contact with liquid water, but the silica formed dissolves completely, and the solution, when concentrated, yields the same singular vitreous hydrate, resembling opal, described above.

402. *Silicic Fluoride,* SiF_4, is a colorless gas (Sp. Gr. $= 52$)

which can only be reduced to the liquid state by great pressure and cold. It is easily prepared by the reaction

$$(SiO_2 + 2CaF_2 + 2H_2SO_4) = $$
$$2(CaSO_4 . H_2O) + SiF_4. \quad [357]$$

When brought in contact with the air it is at once decomposed by aqueous vapor and forms dense fumes. Passed into water it is absorbed in large quantities, and the products are silicic hydrate and hydro-silicic fluoride.

$$(3SiF_4 + 4H_2O + Aq) = $$
$$H_4O_4Si + 2(2HF . SiF_4 + Aq). \quad [358]$$

The same solution can also be obtained by dissolving silica in hydrofluoric acid. It forms, when saturated, a very sour, fuming liquid, which evaporates at 40° in a platinum vessel without leaving any residue. Hence a very simple way of testing the purity of silica.

The solution of hydro-silicic fluoride acts as a strong acid. It dissolves iron or zinc with the evolution of hydrogen, and decomposes many metallic oxides, hydrates, and carbonates, forming definite salts. It is therefore frequently called silico-fluoric acid ($H_2^=SiF_6$), and its salts are named silico-fluorides. The potassium salt, $K_2^=SiF_6$, and the barium salt, $Ba^=SiF_6$, are both sparingly soluble in water, and may, therefore, be readily obtained by precipitation. Moreover, since the corresponding sodium and strontium salts are much more soluble, this reagent may be used to distinguish potassium from sodium, but more especially barium from strontium. Several of the silico-fluorides may be readily crystallized.

Ammonic silico-fluoride	$(NH_4)_2^=SiF_6 . xH_2O,$
Cupric silico-fluoride	$Cu^=SiF_6 . 7H_2O,$
Manganous silico-fluoride	$Mn^=SiF_6 . 7H_2O.$

403. *Silicic Chloride, SiCl_4,* is formed by passing a current of chlorine gas through an intimate mixture of silica and carbon heated intensely in a porcelain tube.

$$SiO_2 + C_2 + 2Cl\text{-}Cl = 2CO + SiCl_4. \quad [359]$$

It is a colorless, volatile liquid (*Sp. Gr.* 1.52), boiling at 50°, and is decomposed by water into hydrochloric acid and silicic hydrate. **Sp. Gr.** of vapor 5.94. It is also slowly decomposed by H_2S.

$$Si\,Cl_4 + H_2S = Si\,Cl_3,Hs + HCl. \qquad [360]$$

The new product is a colorless liquid, boiling at 96°, and yielding a vapor whose **Sp. Gr.** = 5.78.

When the vapor of $Si\,Cl_4$ is passed through a white-hot porcelain tube it undergoes a partial oxidation, and is in part converted into an oxychloride,

$$2Si\,Cl_4 + O = Si_2\,O\,Cl_6 + Cl\text{-}Cl, \qquad [361]$$

the oxygen required coming from the glazing of the tube. This compound is also a colorless fuming liquid, resembling the chloride. It boils at 138°, and has **Sp. Gr.** = 10.05.

404. *Silicic Bromide, $SiBr_4$,* may be formed in a similar way, and closely resembles the chloride, but is less volatile, boiling at 153°, and crystallizing at from 12° to 15°. **Sp. Gr.** of vapor 12.05. The compound $Si\,Cl_3,I$, **Sp. Gr.** = 7.25, is also known.

405. *Silicic Iodide, SiI_4,* is a colorless crystalline solid, melting at 120°.5, and boiling at about 290°. **Sp. Gr.** of vapor 19.12. It crystallizes in regular octahedrons, and is obtained by passing iodine vapor in a stream of CO_2 over ignited silicon.

406. *Silicic Hydride. SiH_4.*—One of the silicic ethers (409), when heated with sodium, furnishes this remarkable compound in a pure condition.

$$4((C_2H_5)_3\text{-}O_3\text{-}SiH) = 3((C_2H_5)_4\text{-}O_4\text{-}Si) + SiH_4. \quad [362]$$

The sodium induces the chemical change by its mere presence. The composition of silicic hydride has been determined by the following reaction : —

$$SiH_4 + (2K\text{-}O\text{-}H + H_2O + Aq) =$$
$$(K_2\text{-}O_2\text{-}SiO + Aq) + 4H\text{-}H. \quad [363]$$

It is a colorless gas, which inflames at a very low temperature (under some conditions spontaneously), and yields when burnt silicic anhydride and water.

407. *Silicic Hydrochloride*, $SiHCl_3$, is a colorless inflammable liquid, obtained by passing HCl over ignited silicon. It has **Sp. Gr.** = 4.64, and may be regarded as the chloride of the radical $(SiH)^{\equiv}Cl_3$, corresponding to chloroform $(CH)^{\equiv}Cl_3$, among the compounds of carbon. The corresponding bromine and iodine compounds are also known. When mixed with water these substances are decomposed, and a voluminous white powder is formed which has been called leukon.

$$2SiHCl_3 + 3H_2O = (SiOH)_2^= O + 6HCl. \quad [364]$$

Leukon dissolves in the alkaline hydrates or carbonates, yielding an alkaline silicate and evolving hydrogen. It also decomposes water, and acts in general as a reducing agent.

408. *Silicic Ethide*, $Si(C_2H_5)_4$, and *Silicic Methide*, $Si(CH_3)_4$, are two colorless volatile liquids, prepared by heating $SiCl_4$ with zinc ethide and zinc methide in sealed tubes. They boil respectively at 30° and 153°, and their vapors have a **Sp. Gr.** of 3.08 and 5.13. Also another compound has been described whose symbol may be written $O^=Si_2^{\equiv}(C_2H_5)_6$.

409. *Silicates of the Organic Radicals or Silicic Ethers.* — A large number of these compounds have been prepared, containing the radicals methyl, ethyl, and amyl, either singly or associated in different combinations. They are all colorless volatile liquids, highly combustible, and having for the most part an ethereal odor. We give in the following table the symbols, the boiling-points, and the vapor-densities of several of the most interesting ethers, and of the chlorhydrines (349) derived from them.

	Sp. Gr. of Liquid.	Boiling-point.	Vapor-density.	
			Obs.	Calc.
$(CH_3)_4^= O_4^{\equiv} Si$	1.059	121° – 122°	5.38	5.26
$(CH_3)_3^= O_3^= Si\text{-}Cl$	1.195	114°.5 – 115°	5.58	5.42
$(CH_3)_2^= O_2^= Si^= Cl_2$	1.259	98° – 103°	5.66	5.57
$(CH_3)\text{-}O\text{-}Si^{\equiv}Cl_3$		82° – 86°	5.66	5.73
$(CH_3)_6^{\equiv} O_6^{\equiv} Si_2 O$	1.144	201° – 202°.5	9.19	8.93
$(C_2H_5)_4^= O_4^{\equiv} Si$	0.968	165° – 166°	7.32	7.27

	Sp. Gr. of Liquid.	Boiling-point.	Vapor-density.	
			Obs.	Calc.
$(C_2H_5)_3{\equiv}O_3{\equiv}Si\text{-}H$		134°		5.68
$(C_2H_5)_3{\equiv}O_3{\equiv}Si\text{-}Cl$	1.048	157°	7.05	6.81
$(C_2H_5)_2{\equiv}O_2{\equiv}Si{=}Cl_2$	1.44	137°	6.76	6.54
$(C_2H_5)\text{-}O\text{-}Si{\equiv}Cl_3$	1.291	104°	6.38	6.22
$(C_2H_5)_6{\equiv}O_6{\equiv}Si_2O$	1.020		12.02	11.86
$(C_2H_5)_3,(C_2H_3O){\equiv}O_4{\equiv}Si$		190°		7.69
$(CH_3)_2,(C_2H_5)_2{\equiv}O_4{\equiv}Si$	1.004	143° – 146°	6.18	6.23
$(CH_3),(C_2H_5)_3{\equiv}O_4{\equiv}Si$	0.981	155° – 157°		6.72
$(C_2H_5)_2,(C_5H_{11})_2{\equiv}O_4{\equiv}Si$	0.915	245° – 250°		10.12
$(C_2H_5),(C_5H_{11})_3{\equiv}O_4{\equiv}Si$	0.913	280° – 285°		11.57

The following equations illustrate some of the reactions by which these compounds have been prepared : —

$$4\,C_2H_5\text{-}O\text{-}H + SiCl_4 = (C_2H_5)_4{\equiv}O_4{\equiv}Si + 4HCl. \quad [365]$$

$$3((C_2H_5)_4{\equiv}O_4{\equiv}Si) + SiCl_4 = 4(C_2H_5)_3{\equiv}O_3{\equiv}SiCl. \quad [366]$$

$$(C_2H_5)_4{\equiv}O_4{\equiv}Si + SiCl_4 = 2(C_2H_5)_2{\equiv}O_2{\equiv}SiCl_2. \quad [367]$$

$$(C_2H_5)_3{\equiv}O_3{\equiv}SiCl + C_5H_{11}\text{-}O\text{-}H =$$
$$(C_2H_5)_3, (C_5H_{11}){\equiv}O_4{\equiv}Si + HCl. \quad [368]$$

$$3(C_2H_5)\text{-}O\text{-}H + SiHCl_3 = (C_2H_5)_3{\equiv}O_3{\equiv}SiH + 3HCl. \quad [369]$$

$$6(C_2H_5)\text{-}O\text{-}H + Si_2OCl_6 = (C_2H_5)_6{\equiv}O_6{\equiv}Si_2O + 6\,HCl. \quad [370]$$

In general, these reactions may be obtained by simply heating together the several factors, enclosed if necessary in sealed tubes. The process is usually complicated by accessory changes, and a mixed product results, which must be purified by repeated fractional distillation.

Questions and Problems.

1. Compare the properties of silicon in its different conditions with those of boron.

2. Make a table illustrating the relations of the possible hydrates of silicon.

3. Required the general formula of the following mineral species whose atomic ratios are given in the table: —

	$\overset{I}{R}$	$\overset{II}{R}$	$\overset{VI}{[R_2]}$	Si	H	Formula required.
Anorthite		1	3	4		$\overset{II}{R},[R_2]^{viii}O_8{}^{viii}Si_2$
Sarcolite		1	1	2		$\overset{II}{R_3}[R_2]^{xii}O_{12}{}^{xii}Si_3$
Epidote		1	2	3		$\overset{II}{R_6},[R_2]_4{}^{xxxvi}O_{36}{}^{xxxvi}Si_9$
Vesuvianite		3	2	5		$\overset{II}{R_{18}},[R_2]_4{}^{lx}O_{60}{}^{lx}Si_{15}$
Leucite	1		3	8		$\overset{I}{R_2},[R_2]^{viii}O_8{}^{viii}Si_4 O_4$
Beryl		1	1	4		$\overset{II}{R_3},[R_2]^{xii}O_{12}{}^{xii}Si_3 O_6$
Iolite		1	3	5		$\overset{II}{R_2},[R_2]_2{}^{xvi}O_{16}{}^{xvi}Si_5 O_2$
Oligoclase	1		3	10		$\overset{I}{R_2},[R_2]^{viii}O_8{}^{viii}Si_5 O_6$
Natrolite	1		3	6	2	$\overset{I}{R_2},[R_2]^{viii}O_8{}^{viii}Si_3 O_2 \cdot 2H_2O$
Analcime	1		3	8	2	$\overset{I}{R_2},[R_2]^{viii}O_8{}^{viii}Si_4 O_4 \cdot 2H_2O$
Harmotome		1	3	10	5	$\overset{II}{R},[R_2]^{viii}O_8{}^{viii}Si_5 O_6 \cdot 5H_2O$
Stilbite		1	3	12	6	$\overset{II}{R},[R_2]^{viii}O_8{}^{viii}Si_6 O_8 \cdot 6H_2O$

The number of atoms of oxygen, which form the vinculum in each of the above formulæ, is always necessarily equal to the total atomicity of all the basic radicals, and as many atoms of oxygen are associated with the acid radical as are required to complete the molecule. The last evidently serve to bind together the atoms of silicon when they are in excess over the number required to neutralize the base (151). The precise form we give to the symbols is in great measure arbitrary, and must be determined from many circumstances, which do not influence the results of analysis; and the great advantage of expressing these results in the form of an atomic ratio is found in the fact that they are thus reduced to the simplest terms, and exhibited independently of all hypothesis, leaving each student to construct the formulæ according to his own theoretical conceptions.

4. Represent the constitution of Anorthite, Sarcolite, and Beryl by graphic symbols.

5. In the following table the percentage composition of a number of native silicates is given on the usual plan, as if they were composed of basic anhydrides and silica. It is required in each case to deduce the atomic ratio and construct the formula.

	Na_2O	K_2O	Li_2O	FeO	CaO	MgO	Al_2O_3	Fe_2O_3	SiO_2	H_2O	Ratio.
Wollastonite					48.3				51.7		1 : 2
Pyroxene				8.0	24.9	13.4			53.7		1 : 2
Spodumene			6.4				29.4		64.2		1 : 2
Petalite	1.2		3.3				17.8		77.7		1 : 4
Forsterite						57.14			42.86		1 : 1
Iron-Garnet					17.3	12.4		33.1	37.2		1 : 1 : 2
Zoisite					37.3		22.8		39.9		1 : 2 : 3
Ilvaite				31.5	12.3			23.4	32.8		3 : 2 : 5
Sarcolite	4.1				33.4		22.8		39.7		1 : 1 : 2
Andesine	6.53	1.08			5.77	1.08	24.28	1.58	59.60		1 : 3 : 8
Analcime	14.1						23.3		54.4	8.2	1 : 3 : 8 : 2
Heulandite					9.2		16.9		59.1	14.8	1 : 3 : 12 : 5

6. It was formerly supposed that the symbol of silica was Si_2O_3, corresponding to that of boric acid, B_2O_3, when $Si = 21$ and $O = 16$. What facts can you adduce in support of the symbol adopted in this book?

7. Deduce the atomic weight of silicon from the data of (409) according to the principle of (19). It is assumed that the percentage composition of the various compounds has been accurately determined by analysis.

8. Point out the analogies between the properties of silicic fluoride and chloride, and those of the corresponding compounds of boron.

9. Compare the chemical qualities of silicon with those of the elements immediately preceding it in our classification. To which element is it more closely allied?

10. Compare the chemical qualities of silicon with those of carbon, and illustrate by examples the analogies between those elements.

11. Point out the examples of chlorhydrines in the table of (409).

12. Describe and illustrate by reactions the methods by which the silicic ethers and chlorhydrines are prepared.

Division XXI.

410. CARBON. $C = 12.$ — Tetrad.   One of the most
widely diffused, and one of the most important elements in the
scheme of terrestrial nature.   United to the three aeriform elements, oxygen, hydrogen, and nitrogen, it forms the chief solid
substratum of all organized structures.   Combined with oxygen
it forms the carbonic anhydride of the atmosphere, which is the
food of the whole vegetable world.   In a nearly pure condition,
or combined with hydrogen, it is found in the strata, forming
those deposits of coal and petroleum which are such great stores
of light, heat, and motive power (64).   Lastly, it is an essential
constituent of the limestones and Dolomites, which constitute
an important part of the rocky crust of the globe (279) (312).
The elementary substance is found in nature in three very different conditions, namely, coal, graphite, and diamond.

411. *Coal.* — All organized tissues, and many other carbonaceous materials, when heated without free access of air, are
charred; that is, the volatile ingredients are driven off, and more
or less of the carbon is left behind in an uncombined condition.
Common charcoal, animal charcoal, lamp-black, ivory-black, &c.
are all artificial products of this kind, and mineral coal is the
charred remains of the rank vegetation of an early geological
epoch.   Since carbon is, under all circumstances, infusible and
non-volatile, coal frequently retains the structure of the organic
tissue from which it was derived, and this element may therefore
be regarded as the skeleton of all organic forms, which in the
process of growth gather around this solid nucleus the elements
of air and water.   The great porosity of many kinds of coal,
which results from its organic structure, renders it a powerful
absorbent both of aeriform and liquid materials, and hence the
use of wood-charcoal as a disinfecting, and of bone-black as a
decolorizing, agent.   The ready combustibility of coal is, however, the most characteristic and important, as it is the most
familiar, quality of this variety of carbon, which is peculiarly
adapted for its all-important uses as fuel, not only on account of
its high calorific power, but also because it retains its solid condition at the highest furnace heat, and because the product of
its combustion is an invisible innocuous gas, the appropriate

food of the plant.   In its more porous conditions coal is a non-conductor of heat and electricity, has a low specific gravity and a high specific heat, both varying, however, in different varieties between quite wide limits.

412. *Graphite* has usually a foliated structure, and is found occasionally in small six-sided tables belonging to the third system, but it is also met with in compact amorphous masses. From its frequent association with crystalline minerals, evidently the products of aqueous action, we naturally infer that it must have been formed in a similar way; but the nature of the process is not understood.   Graphite is very soft, leaving a black shining streak on paper, and has a *Sp. Gr.* $= 1.209$.   It is practically incombustible, although it burns slowly in an oxyhydrogen flame. It has a metallic lustre, and, since it also conducts electricity nearly as well as the metals, it has been called metallic carbon.

The carbon which separates from some varieties of cast-iron when the molten metal slowly cools is in the condition of graphite, and the cavities in iron slags are sometimes lined with crystalline plates of the same material.   Moreover, when coal is intensely heated in a close vessel, it acquires the characteristic lustre and conducting power of the same mineral, and a similar product is formed in the iron retorts in which illuminating gas is manufactured.   Ordinary coke also sometimes approaches the same condition, but all these materials are very hard, and thus differ from true graphite.

Graphite may be obtained in a state of minute sub-division by heating with strong sulphuric acid the coarsely pulverized mineral, previously mixed with one fourteenth of its weight of potassic chlorate, and, after washing with water and drying, igniting the residue.   If this process is many times repeated the graphite is converted into a yellow crystalline product which has been called graphitic acid, and which has been regarded as a peculiar compound of the graphitoidal condition of carbon. Analysis gives the symbol $C_{11}H_4O_5$.

413. *Diamond.* — This well-known gem is also a crystalline condition of carbon.   It affects the forms of the monometric system, and may be cleaved in directions which are parallel to the faces of the regular octahedron.   Its peculiar brilliancy is due to a very high refractive and dispersive power united to a strong lustre called adamantine.   The effect is greatly increased

by the lapidary, who cuts numerous facets on the gem, which reflect and disperse the light in various directions. Diamond is the hardest substance known, and can therefore only be cut with its own powder. Opaque stones called "black diamonds," which are otherwise valueless, are pounded up and used for this purpose. On account of its great hardness the diamond is also used for cutting glass, and the convex faces of the crystals enable them to bear the necessary pressure without breaking. The diamond burns at a high temperature much more readily than graphite, and in an atmosphere of pure oxygen sustains its own combustion, yielding CO_2 like all other forms of carbon. It is a poor conductor of electricity, but when intensely heated in the voltaic arc it suddenly acquires this power, becomes specifically lighter, and is converted into a kind of coke. The diamond has never been made artificially, and we have no knowledge as to its origin. It is found in alluvial soil at only a few localities, chiefly in India, Borneo, and Brazil.

It will thus be seen that carbon presents the most remarkable example of allotropism which has been observed in nature, and the essential differences between the three states appear chiefly in the form, density, and capacity for heat, which we sum up in the table below : —

	Crystalline Form.	Sp. Gr.	Sp. Heat.
Wood Charcoal	Amorphous	0.300	0.2415
Graphite	Hexagonal	2.300	0.2027
Diamond	Isometric	3.500	0.1469

In all these forms carbon is chemically the same, and yields the same product (CO_2) when burnt. It is not only non-volatile and infusible, but does not even soften in the hottest fire; although in the experiments of Despretz, with a voltaic battery of intense energy, it appears to have undergone incipient fusion, and to have been partially volatilized. Lastly, although combustible at a high temperature, yet under ordinary conditions carbon effectually resists, and for an indefinite period, the action of all atmospheric agents, and its uses for fuel on the one hand, and for printing-ink on the other, are remarkable illustrations of the singular twofold aspects of this element in the economy of nature.

CARBON AND OXYGEN, OR SULPHUR.

414. *Carbonic Anhydride.* CO_2. — With this aeriform product of ordinary combustion the student must have already become familiar. Although a gas under ordinary conditions, it can be condensed by pressure and cold to a colorless limpid liquid, which freezes by its own evaporation to a light flocculent solid, outwardly resembling snow, a condition in which it is used to produce a great degree of cold. As a gas it is distinguished by the absence of all those qualities which affect the senses, and hence, although playing such an important part in nature, it escaped notice until the year 1757, when it was first discovered by Dr. Black. It is not only a product of the combustion of all carbonaceous materials, and of the slow oxidation of organic tissues called decay, but it is also one of the chief products of respiration, and of the other processes of animal life. Carbonic anhydride is likewise formed during fermentation, and is the cause of the effervescence in all fermented liquids. It is a product of volcanic action, and is copiously evolved from the earth in many localities, especially in volcanic districts. As it is much heavier than the air, 𝔖𝔭. 𝔊𝔯. $= 1.529$, it not unfrequently collects in wells, mines, and caverns, and it is the choke-damp which has occasioned so many serious accidents; for, although not, properly speaking, poisonous, the free secretion of carbonic anhydride from the body is an essential condition of life, and this is arrested as soon as the amount in the atmosphere exceeds a few per cent. Hence also the necessity of ventilating crowded apartments.

Although an immense flood of carbonic anhydride is being constantly poured into the atmosphere from the various sources just enumerated, yet in the beautiful balance of creation the plant restores the equilibrium which these causes tend to disturb. This product of animal life, of decay, and of combustion is the food of the vegetable world, and, as has been stated (64), the sun's rays acting on the leaves of the plant undo the work of destruction, and while the plant fixes the carbon in its tissues, the oxygen is restored to the atmosphere. While the plant is an apparatus of reduction, the animal is an apparatus of combustion, in which the carbon it receives with its food is burnt in each act of life, and every breath carries back carbonic anhydride to the atmosphere, ready to be reabsorbed by the plant, and repass through the phases of organic life.

Water dissolves very nearly its own volume of carbonic anhydride gas (53), and this important agent is as universally diffused through the waters of the globe as it is through the atmosphere, and sustains the same intimate relations to the plants and animals which inhabit the water as it does to those which live in the air. Moreover, in this condition of solution carbonic anhydride is a very active and important agent in the mineral kingdom, exerting a powerful solvent action on many minerals which would be otherwise unaffected by water, and thus causing extensive geological changes. (279), (312), and Prob. 67, page 394.

Although the solution of CO_2 in water acts in all respects like a simple solution (54), yet there are reasons for regarding it as a solution of carbonic acid, and writing its symbol thus, $(H_2\text{-}O_2\text{-}CO + Aq)$. It has an acid reaction (39), and dissolves iron with the evolution of hydrogen gas (335). Moreover, it neutralizes many basic hydrates, and such reactions are most simply regarded as examples of direct metathesis, thus: —

$$(Ca\text{-}O_2\text{-}H_2 + H_2\text{-}O_2\text{-}CO + Aq) =$$
$$Ca\text{-}O_2\text{-}CO + (2H_2O + Aq). \quad [371]$$

Carbonic acid is a weak dibasic acid, and forms two distinct classes of salts, the most important of which have already been described (123), (124), &c., and, as may be inferred from what has been said, carbon is next to silicon the most abundant acid radical in the mineral kingdom.

The quantity of CO_2 formed by the burning of a known weight of carbon can be collected and weighed with the greatest accuracy, and it was thus that the atomic weight of carbon was determined. Dumas found in a series of very accurate experiments that 100 parts of pure carbon yield exactly 366.66 + parts of CO_2.

415. *Carbonic Oxide*, CO, is, like CO_2, a colorless gas, but contains in the same volume only one half as much oxygen, and its molecules not being saturated, act as powerful dyad radicals (69). The gas is devoid of odor or taste, is very poisonous, is but slightly soluble in water, and has never been condensed to the liquid state. When ignited it burns with a blue flame, and

when in contact with heated metallic oxides it acts as a powerful reducing agent, in each case eagerly absorbing more oxygen without changing its volume. It is formed abundantly in all furnaces and grates whenever the first product of combustion, always CO_2, subsequently passes through a mass of ignited carbonaceous combustible, and it plays an important part in many metallurgical processes, not unfrequently occasioning a great loss of heat by escaping combustion. It is also formed when steam is passed over ignited coal, and it is a chief ingredient in the so-called water gas.

Carbonic oxide may be obtained in a pure condition by a number of chemical reactions, of which the following is the most available : —

$$K_4^=(Fe\,C_6N_6) + 6H_2^=O_2^=SO_2 + 6H_2O =$$
Potassic Ferrocyanide.
$$Fe^=O_2^=SO_2 + 2K_2^=O_2^=SO_2 + 3(NH_4)_2^=O_2^=SO_2 + 6\,CO. \quad [372]$$

So, also, when oxalic acid is dehydrated, — best by heating the crystals with concentrated sulphuric acid, — it breaks up into CO_2 and CO, which are evolved in equal volumes, and the CO may be isolated by passing the gas through a solution of caustic alkali which absorbs the CO_2.

$$H_2^=O_2^=C_2O_2 - H_2O = CO_2 + CO. \quad [373]$$

In theoretical chemistry CO is chiefly interesting as an important acid radical, and when acting in this capacity it is usually known as carbonyl. It is the acid radical not only in the normal carbonates, but also in almost all of the organic acids. The following beautiful synthetical reaction, obtained by simply heating carbonic oxide gas with potassic hydrate, illustrates the relations of this radical to an important class of organic acids.

$$K\text{-}O\text{-}H + CO = K\text{-}O\text{-}(CO\text{-}H). \quad [374]$$
Potassic Formate.

Under the influence of direct sunlight, carbonic oxide combines directly with chlorine, forming $CO^=Cl_2$, called phosgene gas. This compound is at once decomposed both by water and ammonia (NH_3), and in each of the resulting reactions the radical CO evidently retains its integrity.

$$CO^=Cl_2 + H_2O = 2HCl + CO_2, \quad [375]$$

$$CO^=Cl_2 + 4H_3N = H_2,H_2^=N_2^=CO + 2NH_4Cl. \quad [376]$$
Urea.

416. *Oxalic Acid.* $H_2{=}O_2{=}C_2O_2 . 2H_2O.$ — The anhydride of this acid, C_2O_3, has never been obtained, and the acid itself forms the first term of an important series of compounds, all of which contain hydrogen. Strictly, therefore, it cannot be classed with the simple compounds of carbon and oxygen, but nevertheless it is best studied in this connection.

The calcic and potassic salts of oxalic acid are found in the juices of many plants, and when organic bodies are oxidized by nitric acid or similar agents, this acid is one of the most common products. It is made in the arts by the action of nitric acid on sugar or starch, and also by heating sawdust with caustic potash.

Oxalic acid easily crystallizes in prisms which have the composition indicated above. These crystals lose their water of crystallization at 100°, and at 160° the body itself is broken up, the products being carbonic anhydride and formic acid; but the greater part of the last is still further decomposed into water and carbonic oxide, and a portion of the oxalic acid always sublimes unchanged.

$$C_2H_2O_4 = CH_2O_2 + CO_2 \text{ and } CH_2O_2 = H_2O + CO. \quad [377]$$

When, however, the acid is heated with glycerine, the reaction is arrested at the first stage, and yields the equivalent quantity of formic acid.

Oxalic acid is both diatomic and dibasic. Thus we have

Normal Potassic Oxalate $\qquad\qquad K_2{=}O_2{=}C_2O_2 . H_2O,$
Acid Potassic Oxalate (Salt of Sorrel). $H,K{=}O_2{=}C_2O_2 . H_2O,$
Super-acid Potassic Oxalate $H,K{=}O_2{=}C_2O_2 . H_2{=}O_2{=}C_2O_2 . 2H_2O.$

The last is usually regarded as a molecular compound. With the exception of the alkaline salts, the oxalates are, as a rule, insoluble or difficultly soluble in water, and on the great insolubility of calcic oxalate several important analytical processes depend.

Calcic oxalate, when heated, is converted into calcic carbonate.

$$Ca{=}O_2{=}C_2O_2 = Ca{=}O_2{=}CO + CO. \quad [378]$$

When, however, the acid itself is heated with an excess of lime, we obtain a somewhat different result.

$$H_2{=}O_2{=}C_2O_2 + 2CaO = 2Ca{=}O_2{=}CO + H{-}H. \quad [379]$$

Oxidizing agents convert oxalic acid into CO_2 (Prob. 18, page 391) by removing the typical hydrogen.

$$H_2{=}O_2{=}C_2O_2 + O = H_2O + 2CO_2. \qquad [380]$$

Substances having a strong attraction for water transform the acid into CO_2 and CO [373].

Argentic oxalate, when heated, is resolved with explosion into metallic silver and CO_2.

$$Ag_2{=}O_2{=}C_2O_2 = Ag{-}Ag + 2CO_2. \qquad [381]$$

On the other hand, when an amalgam of potassium is heated in an atmosphere of CO_2, the gas is absorbed and potassic oxalate results.

$$K{-}K + 2CO_2 = K_2{=}O_2{=}C_2O_2. \qquad [382]$$

These reactions all justify the rational symbol assigned to oxalic acid, and by writing the symbol as in the margin the relation of the atoms is made more evident. We thus see that dry oxalic acid may be regarded as formed by the union of two atoms of the compound radical $(Ho{-}CO){-}$, held together by one affinity of each of the carbon radicals, which, when not thus satisfied, may join the radical to any other group of atoms that is in the condition to hold it. This radical is called oxatyl, and dry oxalic acid is evidently the corresponding radical substance. Oxatyl, as is evident, is not only univalent, but also monobasic, and therefore must transform any group of atoms to which it is united into an acid. Moreover, the basicity of such an acid will be measured by the number of atoms of oxatyl which it contains. Now nearly all the so-called organic acids may be regarded as compounds of oxatyl with the different hydrocarbon radicals. Those containing one atom of oxatyl are monobasic, those containing two atoms are dibasic, those containing three are tribasic. Oxatyl, however, must itself be regarded as a compound of carbonyl with hydroxl, and thus we arrive at this important general principle. *The basicity of an organic acid is determined by the number of atoms of Ho which it contains associated with carbonyl.*[1] Moreover, it now appears why the basicity may be

$$H{-}O{-}C{=}O$$
$$\mid$$
$$H{-}O{-}C{=}O$$

[1] This theory of the constitution of organic acid, which has been recently advanced and abundantly illustrated by Professor Frankland, of London, is one

less than the atomicity; for the last is measured by the *total* number of *Ho* atoms present, however united to the nucleus of the compound (43). But while the hydrogen of all the *Ho* atoms in a compound may be displaced by very positive metals, or compound radicals of either class, we can only displace *by double decomposition with bases* the hydrogen of those atoms which are associated with carbonyl.

The explanation of this important principle seems to be that, while a strong positive metal, such as sodium, will, like a powerful magnetic pole, increase the attraction of the point of affinity to which it is opposed, and thus give to it an energy it would not otherwise possess, yet in the ordinary metathetical reactions the atoms of hydrogen cannot be displaced unless they are in a polar condition, such as is determined by their association with carbonyl.

417. *Carbonic Sulphide.* CS_2. — Charcoal burns in an atmosphere of sulphur vapor with almost as much energy as in oxygen, forming a colorless gas, which at the ordinary temperature of the air condenses to a very volatile liquid, distinguished for its very great refractive and dispersive power, and much used in the arts as a solvent of phosphorus, sulphur, and caoutchouc. The compound CS has never been obtained in a free state, but the following reactions indicate that it exists as an acid radical in certain sulphur salts (38).

$$K_2S + CS_2 = K_2^=S_2^=CS. \qquad [383]$$

$$(Pb^=O_2^=(NO_2)_2 + K_2^=S_2^=CS + Aq) =$$
$$Pb^=S_2^=CS + (2K\text{-}O\text{-}NO_2 + Aq). \ [384]$$

$$Pb^=S_2^=CS + (H_2S + Aq) = PbS + (H_2^=S_2^=CS + Aq). \ [385]$$

CARBON AND NITROGEN.

418. *Cyanogen. CN.* — Although carbon will not combine directly with nitrogen, yet when heated in an atmosphere of this gas, and in the presence of a strong alkaline base, the two elements unite with the alkaline metals, and the resulting pro-

of the most important contributions recently made to Chemistry, and the author would here acknowledge his great indebtedness to the papers of this eminent chemist in the preparation of the present division of this work.

duct contains the compound radical CN, with which the student is already familiar, under the name of cyanogen.

$$K_2=O_2=CO + 4C + N\equiv N = 2K\text{-}CN + 3CO. \quad [386]$$

Like carbonyl, cyanogen is a very strong negative or acid radical, and, if we accept the theory of Frankland, we need admit no other acid radical than these two "in investigating the whole range of organic compounds."[1]   In many of its chemical relations cyanogen closely resembles the elements of the chlorine group, forming many compounds which are analogous to the corresponding chlorides, bromides, and iodides, but in other respects it differs widely from these elements, both on account of its compound nature, and the singularly complex relations of the two elements of which it consists.   Its univalent condition is an obvious result of the atomicities of its two constituents.

419. *Cyanogen Gas*, $CN\text{-}CN$ or $Cy\text{-}Cy$, bears the same relation to the radical CN that chlorine gas bears to the element chlorine (69), (113).   It is easily made by heating mercuric cyanide.

$$\mathbf{HgCy_2} = Hg + Cy\text{-}Cy. \quad [387]$$

At the same time a brown non-volatile product is formed which is called paracyanogen.   This body is isomeric with the gas, but probably represents a more condensed molecular condition, and is converted wholly into cyanogen when heated in an inert atmosphere.

Cyanogen has been condensed to a liquid, boiling at $-20°.7$, and freezing below $-34°$, which is its melting-point.   The gas is colorless, has a suffocating odor, and is poisonous.   It burns with a beautiful flame, which recalls the color of peach-blossoms, and the products of its combustion are CO_2 and $N\equiv N$.   It dissolves in water, but not so freely as in alcohol.   The aqueous solution, moreover, is not permanent, for the cyanogen slowly unites with the elements of water, changing into ammonic oxalate.

$$CN\text{-}CN + 4H_2O = (NH_4)_2=O_2=C_2O_2. \quad [388]$$

---

[1] There is, however, a class of somewhat obscure acids, formed by the action of $H_2=O_2=SO_2$ on various organic substances, in which the radical $(Ho\text{-}SO_2)$ appears to play the same part as the radical oxatyl in the compounds just noticed.   Such bodies were formerly said to be copulated or conjugated, and these terms, though latterly discarded, were not wholly inappropriate.

On the other hand, when ammonic oxalate is heated the action
is reversed, and these facts show how easily carbonyl and cyanogen are convertible. Cyanogen unites directly with potassium,
forming $K\text{-}CN$.

420. *Hydrocyanic Acid.* $H\text{-}CN$. — The anhydrous acid (a
combustible and very volatile liquid) is most readily obtained
by passing H_2S over $Hg\,Cy_2$, but a solution of the acid in water
(the prussic acid of pharmacy) may be made by distilling potassic cyanide or ferro-cyanide with dilute sulphuric acid.

Hydrocyanic acid has the peculiar odor of bitter almonds,
and is intensely poisonous. It is a very unstable body, and
both the hydrous and the anhydrous acid undergo spontaneous
decomposition, which is greatly accelerated by the action of the
light. When diluted with water, and mixed with a mineral
acid, it is more permanent, but it is so volatile that even the
very dilute acid used in pharmacy rapidly loses strength when
exposed to the air.

By absorption of the elements of water both ammonic oxalate
and ammonic formate are slowly formed in the aqueous acid.
The first by a reaction similar to [388], and the second thus,

$$H\text{-}CN + 2H_2O = NH_4\text{-}O\text{-}(CO\text{-}H). \qquad [389]$$
Ammonic Formate.

When the vapor of ammonic formate is passed through a red-
hot tube, the last reaction is reversed. In like manner, when
hydrocyanic acid is mixed with hydrochloric acid (both concentrated), we have

$$H\text{-}CN + HCl + 2H_2O = H\text{-}O\text{-}(CO\text{-}H) + NH_4\text{-}Cl. \quad [390]$$
Formic Acid.

421. *Cyanides.* — Hydrocyanic acid reddens litmus feebly,
and potassic cyanide has an alkaline reaction (39). It however
freely dissolves $Hg\,O$, forming $Hg\,Cy_2$, and in a similar way (or
more readily by metathesis from potassic cyanide) a large number of metallic cyanides may be obtained. The alkaline cyanides are very soluble in water, and several of the cyanides of
the heavier metals, like $Hg\,Cy_2$, dissolve to a limited extent.
Most of them, however, are insoluble in pure water, but with
few exceptions they all dissolve freely in solutions of the alkaline cyanides, with which they form double salts, and solutions
of $Ag\,Cy$ and $Au\,Cy$ in $(K\,Cy + Aq)$ are very much used in

the process of electroplating. The double cyanides are a still more definite and numerous class of salts than the simple cyanides. Among them we may cite as examples

$$Ag\,Cy \,.\, KCy \quad \text{and} \quad Zn\,Cy_2 \,.\, 2KCy.$$

All these cyanides contain cyanogen as such, and, with few exceptions, when heated with dilute hydrochloric acid, they yield HCy, and, if soluble, are violent poisons. There is, however, another class of compounds formed by combining with the alkaline cyanides the cyanides of iron, cobalt, chromium, platinum, and a few of the rarer metals, which do not evolve HCy under the influence of hydrochloric acid, and have not the same deadly character. Moreover, the metals which they contain cannot be displaced by the usual metathetical methods. Hence we have come to the conclusion that these bodies are not simple cyanides of the metals, but contain far more complex radicals, of which the metals just mentioned form a part. The most important of these compounds are described in the next two sections.

422. *Ferrocyanides.* $R_4^{\equiv}(Fe\,C_6N_6)$ or $R_4^{\equiv}Cfy$. — Potassic ferrocyanide (yellow prussiate of potash), $K_4^{\equiv}Cfy$, is an important commercial product, manufactured on a large scale by fusing nitrogenized animal matter with potassic carbonate and iron-filings, lixiviating the resulting mass with water, and crystallizing. The salt forms large yellow, square, tabular crystals, is very much used in dyeing, and is the primary source of all the cyanogen compounds. It may also be made from KCy or HCy by the following reactions : —

$$FeS + 6K\text{-}CN = K_4^{\equiv}(Fe\,C_6N_6) + K_2S. \qquad [391]$$

1. $2Fe_2O_3 + 3FeO + 18H\text{-}CN =$
$$[Fe_2]_2\text{xii}(Fe\,C_6N_6)_3 + 9H_2O. \; [392]$$
Prussian Blue.

2. $[Fe_2]_2\text{xii}Cfy_3 + (12K\text{-}Ho + Aq) =$
$$2[Fe_2]^{\equiv}Ho_6 + (3K_4^{\equiv}Cfy + Aq). \; [393]$$

When fused, the ferrocyanide is partially decomposed, yielding potassic cyanide, which is made in great quantities in this

$$K_4^{\equiv}(Fe\,C_6N_6) = 4K\text{-}CN + Fe\,C_2 + N\text{-}N. \qquad [394]$$

way. By previously mixing the ferrocyanide with potassic carbonate a larger product is obtained, but less pure, as potassic cyanate is formed at the same time.

$$K_4^{\overline{\equiv}}(Fe\,C_6N_6) + K_2^{\cdot}O_2^{\cdot}CO =$$
$$5K\text{-}CN + K\text{-}O\text{-}CN + Fe + CO_2. \quad [395]$$

From the solution of the potassium salt various ferrocyanides are easily prepared by simple metathesis, and several of them have striking and characteristic colors. Thus, when the solution is mixed with hydrochloric acid and ether, hydro-ferrocyanic acid is precipitated.

$$K_4^{\overline{\equiv}}Cfy + 4HCl = H_4^{\overline{\equiv}}Cfy + 4KCl. \quad [396]$$

With a ferric salt we obtain Prussian blue (ferric ferrocyanide).

$$(2[Fe_2]^{\overline{\equiv}}Cl_6 + 3K_4^{\overline{\equiv}}Cfy + Aq) =$$
$$[Fe_2]_2^{\text{xii}}Cfy_3 + (12KCl + Aq). \quad [397]$$

Hence the origin of the name cyanogen (κύανος γεννάω).

With a ferrous salt the precipitate is white or nearly so, but becomes blue in contact with the air.

$$(Fe^{\cdot}Cl_2 + K_4^{\overline{\equiv}}Cfy + Aq) = \underset{\text{White.}}{K_2,Fe^{\overline{\equiv}}Cfy} + (2KCl + Aq).$$
$$[398]$$
$$12K_2,Fe^{\overline{\equiv}}Cfy + 3\,O^{\cdot}O = \underset{\text{Blue.}}{2[Fe_2]_2^{\text{xii}}Cfy_3} + 6K_4^{\overline{\equiv}}Cfy + 2Fe_2O_3.$$

With cupric salts we have a red precipitate.

$$(2Cu^{\cdot}O_2^{\cdot}SO_2 + K_4^{\overline{\equiv}}Cfy + Aq) =$$
$$Cu_2^{\overline{\equiv}}Cfy + (2K_2^{\cdot}O_2^{\cdot}SO_2 + Aq). \quad [399]$$

The soluble ferrocyanides, as a rule, crystallize readily, and the crystals usually contain several molecules of water, thus:—

$(NH_4)_4^{\overline{\equiv}}Cfy \cdot 3H_2O$, $(NH_4),K_3^{\overline{\equiv}}Cfy$, $(NH_4)_2,K_2^{\overline{\equiv}}Cfy$,
$Na_4Cfy \cdot 12H_2O$, $Na,K_3^{\overline{\equiv}}Cfy \cdot 6H_2O$, $Ba_2^{\overline{\equiv}}Cfy \cdot 6H_2O$,
$K_2,Ba^{\overline{\equiv}}Cfy \cdot 3H_2O$, $Zn_2^{\overline{\equiv}}Cfy \cdot 3H_2O$, $(C_2H_5)_4^{\overline{\equiv}}Cfy \cdot 6H_2O$.

423. *Ferricyanides.* — By passing $Cl\text{-}Cl$ through a solution of $K_4^{\overline{\equiv}}Cfy$ a compound is formed, $K_6^{\overline{\equiv}}[Cfy_2]$, containing the hexad radical $(Cfy\text{-}Cfy)^{\overline{\equiv}}$, which sustains the same relation to

Cfy that $Ti^{\underline{z}}$ bears to $[Ti_2]^{\underline{z}}$. On evaporating the solution we obtain the salt in deep-red crystals, which are an article of commerce under the name of red prussiate of potash.

$$(2K_4{^\equiv}Cfy + Cl\text{-}Cl + Aq) =$$
$$(K_6^{\equiv}[\,Cfy_2] + 2KCl + Aq).\;[400]$$

Other ferricyanides may be obtained from the potassium salts by metathesis.

$$H_6^{\equiv}[\,Cfy_2],\; Na_6^{\equiv}[Cfy_2]\,.\,H_2O,\; Na_2,K_3^{\equiv}[Cfy_2],\; K_2,Ba_2^{\equiv}[Cfy_2]\,.\,3H_2O.$$

With a solution of potassic ferricyanide ferrous salts give a deep-blue precipitate called Turnbull's blue.

$$(3Fe\text{=}Cl_2 + K_6^{\equiv}[\,Cfy_2] + Aq) =$$
$$Fe_3^{\equiv}[\,Cfy_2] + (6KCl + Aq).\;[401]$$

Ferric salts, on the other hand, give no precipitate, and it will be noticed that, while these salts give a blue precipitate with the ferrocyanides, the ferrous salts give a blue precipitate only with the ferricyanides. Hence, a simple means of distinguishing the two classes of salt.

424. *Other Compounds of Cyanogen.* — Chlorine forms with cyanogen three polymeric compounds.

$Cy\text{-}Cl$ (Sp. Gr. 30.7), $(Cy_2)\text{=}Cl_2$ (Sp. Gr. 61.5),
    Gas.   Liquid.
                    $(Cy_3)\text{=}Cl_3$ (Sp. Gr. 92.1).
                            Solid.

In like manner there are three polymeric oxygen acids.

$H\text{-}O\text{-}Cy$, $H_2\text{=}O_2\text{=}(Cy_2)$, $H_3\text{=}O_3\text{=}(Cy_3)$.
Cyanic Acid.   Dicyanic Acid.   Cyanuric Acid.

The tendency to polymerism (70), here manifested, is a remarkable feature of the cyanogen compounds, and gives rise to products of great complexity, most of which, however, have been but little studied. Their condensed molecules are evidently held together by complex radicals formed by the coalescing of several atoms of cyanogen, and it is evident that the atomicity of such radicals must be equal to the number of elementary atoms of any one kind, nitrogen or carbon, of which they consist. On the same principle the constitution of the ferro- and ferri-cyanides, as well as that of paracyanogen, may be explained.

425. *Cyanates.* — Cyanic acid, referred to above, forms an important class of salts which have a great theoretical interest on account of the remarkable transformations of which many of them are susceptible. Potassic cyanate is readily prepared by dropping litharge into the fused cyanide, or ferrocyanide, so long as the oxide is reduced.

$$KCy + PbO = K\text{-}O\text{-}Cy + Pb. \qquad [402]$$

In order to crystallize the salt the fused mass should be exhausted with alcohol of 80%, since on evaporating an aqueous solution the salt is slowly decomposed. The same change takes place rapidly when the salt is heated with potassic hydrate.

$$K\text{-}O\text{-}CN + K\text{-}O\text{-}H + H_2O = K_2\text{=}O_2\text{=}CO + NH_3. \quad [403]$$

When potassic cyanate is mixed in solution with ammonic sulphate a metathesis takes place, but the resulting ammonic cyanate is at once transformed into a remarkable compound-ammonia or amine (167) called urea,

$$NH_4\text{-}O\text{-}CN = H_2,H_2^{\equiv}N_2\text{=}CO, \qquad [404]$$

and by this reaction the synthesis of this complex organic product was first obtained.

The most interesting of the cyanates are the compounds called cyanic ethers, in which methyl, ethyl, &c. are the basic radicals. They are easily obtained,

$$K\text{-}O\text{-}Cy + K,C_2H_5\text{=}O_2\text{=}SO_2 = K_2\text{=}O_2\text{=}SO_2 + C_2H_5\text{-}O\text{-}Cy, \quad [405]$$

$$\underset{\text{Distilled together.}}{}$$

and the investigation of the many wonderful transformations of which they are susceptible was one of the most important steps in the progress of organic chemistry.

As cyanic acid when heated with an excess of potash yields ammonia, so these cyanic ethers yield various amines.

$$H\text{-}O\text{-}CN + 2K\text{-}O\text{-}H = K_2\text{=}O_2\text{=}CO + H,H,H^{\equiv}N.$$

$$C_2H_5\text{-}O\text{-}CN + 2K\text{-}O\text{-}H = K_2\text{=}O_2\text{=}CO + H,H,C_2H_5^{\equiv}N. \qquad [406]$$

$$\underset{\text{Ethylamine.}}{}$$

The following reactions are equally instructive : —

$$C_2H_5\text{-}O\text{-}CN + 2K\text{-}O\text{-}C_2H_5 = K_2\text{=}O_2\text{=}CO + (C_2H_5)_3\text{=}N. \quad [407]$$

$$\underset{\text{Triethylamine.}}{}$$

$$C_2H_5\text{-}O\text{-}CN + H\text{-}O\text{-}C_2H_3O =$$
$$\underset{\text{Acetic Acid.}}{}\quad \underset{\text{Ethylacetamide.}}{H, C_2H_5, C_2H_3O \doteq N} + CO_2. \quad [408]$$

$$2\,C_2H_5\text{-}O\text{-}CN + H_2O = \underset{\text{Diethylcarbamide.}}{H_2(C_2H_5)_2 N_2 \doteq CO} + CO_2. \quad [409]$$

The above reactions will appear more simple if the symbols of the cyanic ethers are written after the ammonia type thus, $C_2H_5, CO \doteq N$, and that this is their true constitution is rendered probable by the fact that a body has recently been discovered called cyanetholine, which appears to be a true cyanic ether. It is made by the reaction

$$Na\text{-}O\text{-}C_2H_5 + CyCl = NaCl + C_2H_5\text{-}O\text{-}Cy; \quad [410]$$

and when acted upon by potash it yields, not ethylamine, but common alcohol. (Prob. 3, page 77.)

426. *Sulpho-cyanates.* — By fusing potassic cyanide with sulphur we obtain the sulphur salt corresponding to potassic cyanate, or $K\text{-}S\text{-}Cy$, and from this, as from the cyanate, a large number of compounds may be derived. Potassic sulpho-cyanate, although without action on the ferrous compounds, strikes a deep-red color in a solution which contains the least trace of a ferric salt, and for this reason is a very useful reagent.

CARBON AND HYDROGEN.

427. "*Organic Chemistry.*" — It has already been stated that organized beings consist of materials composed chiefly of carbon, hydrogen, oxygen, and nitrogen; but few as are the chemical elements concerned in the processes of organic life, nevertheless the number of compounds which have been discovered in the tissues of animals and plants, or formed by their chemical metamorphosis, is exceedingly great. Such compounds are called *Organic Compounds*, and in works on chemistry they are usually studied together under the separate head of *Organic Chemistry.*

While the molecules of mineral compounds consist for the most part of only a few atoms, those of organic compounds frequently contain a very large number, and the diversity in organic chemistry is obtained, not by multiplying the number of elements, but by varying the molecular grouping. It was formerly supposed that the great complexity thus produced was sustained by what was called the vital principle; but although the cause which determines the growth of organized beings is still a perfect mystery, we now know that the materials of which they consist are subject to the same laws as mineral matter, and the complexity may be traced to a peculiar quality of carbon already described.[1] The atoms of carbon are prone to combine among themselves, and the same tendency which appears in several of the elements to a limited extent is developed in the case of carbon to a very high degree. Carbon is the skeleton of an organic compound in a peculiar sense. Its atoms, locked together like so many vertebræ, form the framework to which the other elements are fastened, and thus a complex molecular structure is rendered in a wonderful measure compact and stable.

Organic chemistry is simply the chemistry of the compounds of carbon, and has no distinctive character except that which the peculiar qualities of this singular element give. Moreover, although in a compendium of the science it may be convenient, or even necessary, to distinguish between mineral and organic chemistry on account of the great preponderance and importance of the compounds of carbon; yet in a work on Chemical Philosophy, where the object is not to enumerate facts, there seems to be no good reason for departing, in the case of this single element, from the general scheme, or treating it more fully than is required to illustrate the new and important principles which it presents to our notice. Indeed, in an elementary work no other course is possible, since a mere list of the known compounds of carbon would fill a large volume.

428. *Hydrocarbons.* — If we conceive that the carbon atoms of the successive molecules are held together by the smallest possible number of bonds, then, as shown in (34), the symbols of the possible hydrocarbon compounds of this class would be expressed by the general symbol $C_n H_{2n+2}$, and each number of the series would differ from the preceding by CH_2. Again, if we conceive that the skeleton of carbon atoms, instead of presenting at either end an open affinity as in Fig. *a*, forms a closed chain as in Fig. *b*, the hydrocarbon atoms of this second class would be expressed by $C_n H_{2n}$, and form another series with a constant difference as before of CH_2. Lastly, if we start with

---

[1] The student should very carefully review (34) in this connection.

a nucleus of carbon atoms grouped together as in Fig. c, form-

Fig. a.   Fig. b.   Fig. c.

ing the hydrocarbon C_6H_6, and add to this successive incre-
ments of CH_2, we obtain still a third series of hydrocarbons
expressed by the symbol C_nH_{2n-6}.

Each of the above symbols represents a series of actual compounds, of which many members are known, as shown in the
table on page 477. Moreover, the hydrocarbons of any one
series all sustain the same general relations to chemical reagents,
undergo similar changes when exposed to the same influences,
and present a regular gradation in their physical properties corresponding to the change in their composition. Compounds so
related are said to be *homologues*, and such a series is called an
homologous series.

Obviously, however, the three series, whose relations have
been just described, do not include all the possible hydrocarbons,
for, starting with any one of the more complex molecules of the
first class, in which the carbon atoms are united by the smallest
possible number of bonds, we may assume that the open bonds
are successively closed two by two by the more intimate union of
the carbon atoms among themselves, and we shall thus obtain a
derived series, whose successive members differ by the quantity
H_2. The general symbol of such a series would be $C_nH_{2(n-m)+2}$,
the first term being C_nH_{2n+2}, m standing for the number of
the required term counting from the first. Compounds thus
related are termed *isologues*, and it is obvious that those hydrocarbons in the three series of homologues exhibited above,
which contain the same number of carbon atoms, are members
of the same series of isologues; but it is also obvious that besides these three an indefinite number of parallel homologous
series are theoretically possible. The student will best understand the relations of this scheme by tabulating the possible
compounds, arranging the homologues in parallel columns with
the isologues on the same horizontal line. He will thus see

that there is no limit to the number of hydrocarbons, except that fixed by the instability of the resulting molecules.

A table, prepared as just directed, would not, however, exhibit all the possibilities in this scheme of the hydrocarbons, since we may conceive of the atoms of each of the more complex compounds as arranged in different ways, and thus giving rise to one or more isomeric modifications. For example, we may construct the symbol of the hydrocarbon C_4H_{10} as indicated by either of the rational formulæ $(C\text{-}C\text{-}C\text{-}C)$x H_{10} or $C\equiv(CH_3)_3,H$, and with a little ingenuity the student will readily discover in any case the number of such commutations possible, only he must carefully distinguish between a mere arbitrary change in the relative position of the atoms and a fundamental difference of arrangement. The last alone implies a difference of qualities in the substance which the formulæ represent, and indicates the possibility of isomeric modifications. Review in this connection (70).

It must not be supposed that all the hydrocarbons which our theory prefigures are actually possible, that is, represent compounds which either have been or may be isolated; for as yet the theory has taken into account but one condition, namely, the atom-fixing power of carbon, and many causes may intervene to render unstable the compounds which are, from this one point of view, theoretically possible. As the number of carbon atoms increases, a condition is soon reached, when, if we may so express it, the molecule cannot sustain its own weight, and in all cases the atoms must be so grouped as to preserve certain polar relations between its several parts. As yet, however, we do not understand the laws which determine molecular stability, and cannot, therefore, foresee the result in a given case, so that we are unable to control our algebraic method. Still, with all this uncertainty the theory has its value, and not only serves for the time to classify our facts, but gives us one of those glimpses of the order of creation which are the greatest privilege that the student of nature enjoys.

But with all the limitations which the conditions of stability impose, the number of possible hydrocarbons must be very large, and the compounds actually known can form but a very small portion of those which may hereafter be isolated. The series of homologues given on page 477 include the greater part as well as the most important of the known compounds of this class. Of other series a few members here and there have been recognized, but in regard to most of these our knowledge is imperfect and uncertain. Many hydrocarbons are found in a free state in nature, but mixed together in the petroleums, and in those combustible gases like the fire-damps of coal-mines which are evolved from the earth in many localities. Others are found among the products of the dry distillation of coal, wood, or other organic tissues, and in either case the individual compounds are isolated by various processes of fractional distillation. Others, again, have been obtained by various chemical reactions, and of these a few of the more characteristic are given below:—

Marsh Gas Series.
$$C_nH_{2n+2}.$$

		B. P.
Methylic Hydride	CH_4	
Ethylic Hydride	C_2H_6	
Propylic Hydride	C_3H_8	
Butylic Hydride	C_4H_{10}	0°.0
Amylic Hydride	C_5H_{12}	30°.2
Hexylic Hydride	C_6H_{14}	61°.3
Heptylic Hydride	C_7H_{16}	90°.4
Octylic Hydride	C_8H_{18}	119°.5
Nonylic Hydride	C_9H_{20}	150°.8

Acetylene Series.
$$C_nH_{2n-2}$$

Acetylene	C_2H_2
Allylene	C_3H_4
Crotonylene	C_4H_6
Valerylene	C_5H_8
Allyl?	C_6H_{10}

Olefiant Gas Series.
$$C_nH_{2n}$$

		B. P.
Ethylene	C_2H_4	
Propylene	C_3H_6	—17°.8
Butylene	C_4H_8	+35°.0
Amylene	C_5H_{10}	55°.0
Hexylene	C_6H_{12}	39°.0
Heptylene	C_7H_{14}	65°.0
Octylene	C_8H_{16}	95°.0
Nonylene	C_9H_{18}	125°.0
Decatylene	$C_{10}H_{20}$	174°.9
Endecatylene	$C_{11}H_{22}$	195°.8
Dodecatylene	$C_{12}H_{24}$	216°.2
Tridecatylene	$C_{13}H_{26}$	235°
Cetene	$C_{16}H_{32}$	
Cerotene (paraffine)	$C_{27}H_{54}$	270°
Melene	$C_{30}H_{60}$	375°

Essential Oils.
$$C_nH_{2n-4}$$

Oil of Turpentine	$C_{10}H_{16}$

Phenyl Series.
$$C_nH_{2n-6}$$

		B. P.
Benzol	C_6H_6	82°
Toluol	C_7H_8	111°
Xylol	C_8H_{10}	129°
Cumol	C_9H_{12}	148°
Cymol	$C_{10}H_{14}$	175°

Several of the terms in the above series are represented by at least two isomeric compounds. Thus we find in the Pennsylvania petroleums, mixed with the last six members of the marsh gas series, five other hydrocarbons, C_4H_{10} to C_8H_{18}, identical in composition, but having boiling-points uniformly eight degrees higher. The common difference between these boiling-points (which have been determined with great accuracy) is very nearly 30°, and it is probable that a similar constancy would appear in all series of truly homologous compounds, and the discrepancies noticeable in several members of the series as above exhibited are probably to be referred to the fact that bodies are here included which do not belong to the same type.

429. *Marsh Gas Series.* $C_n H_{2n+2}$. — Molecules having this composition must necessarily be closed and saturated. Hence the hydrocarbons of this class are indifferent bodies, but they readily yield substitution compounds containing chlorine and bromine. Thus, when we act on marsh gas (CH_4) with chlorine, hydrochloric acid is formed, and we obtain either CH_3Cl, $CHCl_3$, CCl_4, or C, the products of the reaction varying with the conditions of the experiment and the proportions of the factors. Marsh gas may be obtained perfectly pure from zinc methide (324), which is decomposed by water, as shown by the following reaction : —

$$Zn\text{=}(CH_3)_2 + 2H_2O = Zn\text{=}O_2\text{=}H_2 + 2CH_4. \quad [411]$$

By a similar reaction ethylic and amylic hydrides can be obtained from zinc ethide and zinc amylide.

The first member of the series has long been known as a product of the decomposition of vegetable tissue under water, and hence the trivial name Marsh Gas. It is the chief constituent of the fire-damp of coal-mines, and of common illuminating gas obtained by the dry distillation of coal. It is most conveniently prepared by heating potassic acetate with a large excess of potassic hydrate mixed with quicklime.

$$K\text{-}O\text{-}C_2H_3O + K\text{-}O\text{-}H = K_2\text{=}O_2\text{=}CO + CH_4. \quad [412]$$

It can also be obtained by either of the following reactions, but they have only a theoretical interest.

$$CCl_4 + 4H\text{-}H = 4HCl + CH_4. \qquad [413]$$

$$CHCl_3 + 3H\text{-}H = 3HCl + CH_4. \qquad [414]$$

$$CS_2 + 2H_2S + 4Cu = 4CuS + CH_4. \quad [415]$$

The first two reactions are obtained by reducing carbonic chloride or chloroform with nascent hydrogen, the last by passing H_2S gas mixed with CS_2 vapor over ignited copper.

Marsh gas has no sensible qualities, and has never been liquefied. Like the other members of the series it is highly combustible, and burns with a luminous flame.

Marsh gas and its homologues may be regarded as hydrides of radicals having the general form C_nH_{2n+1}, and we are already acquainted with many compounds in which these atomic groups manifest a marked individuality. Ethylic iodide is easily prepared, and by acting on this compound with zinc we obtain a hydrocarbon which may be regarded as the corresponding radical substance.

$$2\,C_2H_5\text{-}I + Zn = ZnI_2 + C_2H_5\text{-}C_2H_5. \qquad [416]$$

In like manner similar products may be obtained with several of the homologous compounds, and by using iodides of two radicals simultaneously the so-called double or mixed radicals may be produced.

$$CH_3\text{-}I + C_2H_5\text{-}I + Zn = ZnI_2 + CH_3\text{-}C_2H_5. \qquad [417]$$

These hydrocarbons, however, are all isomeric, if not identical, with the normal terms of the marsh gas series.

430. *Olefiant Gas Series.* C_nH_{2n}. — Molecules of this type are not necessarily closed, but are capable of fixing two additional monad atoms, and of acting as dyad radicals. The first member of the series was discovered by an association of Dutch chemists in 1795, who, noticing its characteristic property of combining directly with chlorine, called it Olefiant (oil making) Gas, because the product of this union is a thick flowing liquid. This product, long known as the Oil of the Dutch chemists, is ethylene chloride, $C_2H_4Cl_2$. Ethylene bromide and ethylene iodide may be formed in a similar way, and the tendency to form compounds of this type distinguishes this class of hydrocarbons, which are called, for this reason, *olefines.* Moreover, the hydrogen atoms of the bivalent radical may all be replaced by chlorine or bromine, and the resulting compound still retain the same typical character. This is shown by the following reactions : —

$$C_2H_4 + Br\text{-}Br = (C_2H_4)\text{=}Br_2, \qquad [418]$$

$$(C_2H_4)^{\cdot}Br_2 + K\text{-}O\text{-}H = C_2H_3Br + KBr + H_2O, \quad [419]$$

$$C_2H_3Br + Br\text{-}Br = (C_2H_3Br)^{\cdot}Br_2, \quad [420]$$

$$(C_2H_3Br)^{\cdot}Br_2 + K\text{-}O\text{-}H = C_2H_2Br_2 + KBr + H_2O, \quad [421]$$

which may be repeated with the successive products, until at last we obtain C_2Br_4 and $(C_2Br_4)^{\cdot}Br_2$ as the final results.

Olefiant gas is most readily obtained by heating alcohol with several times its volume of strong sulphuric acid. The reaction is somewhat complicated, but the result is a dehydration of the alcohol, and the same effect may be produced with zincic chloride (323).

$$C_2H_6O - H_2O = C_2H_4. \quad [422]$$

Like marsh gas this aeriform hydrocarbon has no sensible qualities save a slight odor, due probably to a trace of ether. It has, however, been liquefied, and is slightly soluble in water. Containing twice as much carbon in the same volume, it burns with a more luminous flame than the lighter gas, and the illuminating power of coal-gas is due in no inconsiderable measure to its presence. Olefiant gas combines directly, not only with chlorine, bromine, &c., but also with the hydrogen acids.

$$C_2H_4 + HI = C_2H_5I. \quad [423]$$

Moreover, it unites with hypochlorous acid, forming a chlor-hydrine.

$$C_2H_4 + H\text{-}O\text{-}Cl = (C_2H_4)^{\cdot}Ho,Cl. \quad [424]$$

These reactions of olefiant gas illustrate in general the chemical relations of this series of hydrocarbons; but it is probable that several of those included in the list on page 477, although isomeric with terms of the series, are really formed after a different type. A large number of them are only known as constituents of petroleum or products of dry distillation, and have not been prepared by any intelligible process.

431. *Acetylene Series.* C_nH_{2n-2}. *Acetylene.* — This gas is formed by the direct union of its elements, when the current from a powerful voltaic battery passes between carbon poles in an atmosphere of hydrogen. It may also be obtained by the action of water on potassic carbide.

$$K_2C_2 + 2H_2O = 2K\text{-}O\text{-}H + C_2H_2. \quad [425]$$

It is not unfrequently a product of the incomplete combustion of bodies containing carbon and hydrogen, and it may also be prepared in other ways. Acetylene acts as a dyad or tetrad radical, combining with nascent hydrogen to form C_2H_4 (ethylene), with bromine to form $C_2H_2Br_2$ or $C_2H_2Br_4$, and with hydrobromic acid to form C_2H_3Br or $C_2H_4Br_2$. It is not yet determined whether these bodies are identical with the isomeric compounds of the olefiant gas series. When the gas is passed through a solution of cuprous chloride in ammonia, a highly explosive compound is formed as a red precipitate, which has the composition $(C_2H[Cu_2])_2O$, and acts as a basic anhydride. The other hydrocarbons of the series have similar chemical relations, but have not been thoroughly studied.

432. *Allyl.* — When allylic iodide is digested with sodium and distilled, we obtain a hydrocarbon which has the composition C_6H_{10}.

$$Na\text{-}Na + 2(C_3H_5)\text{-}I = 2Na\text{-}I + C_3H_5\text{-}C_3H_5. \quad [426]$$

This product, moreover, unites directly with one or two molecules either of $Br\text{-}Br$ or $H\text{-}I$, and in general its chemical relations are those of a homologue of acetylene. But, as the above reaction indicates, it may also be regarded as the radical substance (22) corresponding to allyl, and this view is sustained by the fact that there is an isomeric hydrocarbon having similar chemical relations, but different physical qualities, which is more probably the fifth member of the acetylene series.

433. *Essential Oils.* C_nH_{2n-4}. — Oil of Turpentine and many other essential oils have a composition represented by the symbol $C_{10}H_{16}$, and there are a few others which, although also isomeric, must be represented by a multiple of this symbol; but no other members of the series are known. Oil of turpentine combines both with the hydrogen acids and with water, forming compounds in which ($C_{10}H_{16}$) acts either as a dyad or a tetrad radical, and others in which the double molecule acts as a hexad radical. Thus we have

$$(C_{10}H_{16})\text{''}H,Cl, \quad (C_{10}H_{16})\text{≡}H_2,Cl_2, \quad (C_{20}H_{32})\text{''}H,Cl, \quad (C_{20}H_{32})\text{≡}H_3,Cl_3.$$

Exposed to the air oil of turpentine absorbs oxygen, yielding a resinous product, and the same is true to a greater or less degree of the other essential oils. They all appear to have simi-

EE

lar chemical relations, and are singularly susceptible of allotropic conditions; but on what the differences between these isomeric bodies depend we are as yet ignorant.

434. *Phenyl Series.* C_nH_{2n-6}. — The hydrocarbons of this class are found in coal-tar and Rangoon petroleum, and are isolated by fractional distillation. Benzol, or benzine, is very much used in the arts, but the commercial product is more or less mixed with the associated hydrocarbons. When pure, benzol becomes solid at a low temperature, melting only at $5°.5$. Benzol may be obtained artificially by heating benzoic or phthalic acid with an excess of lime.

$$C_7H_6O_2 + CaO = CaCO_3 + C_6H_6.$$
Benzoic Acid.   Benzol.

$$C_8H_6O_4 + 2CaO = 2CaCO_3 + C_6H_6.$$
Phthalic Acid.   Benzol.

[427]

Benzol, when treated with chlorine or bromine, yields a number of substitution products. By the action of nitric acid we obtain (31)

Nitro-benzol $C_6H_5(NO_2)$,

Dinitro-benzol $C_6H_4(NO_2)_2$,

and when acted on by reducing agents (as zinc and hydrochloric acid, sulphuretted hydrogen, &c.), nitro-benzol is converted into aniline (167), and thus becomes the source of the aniline dyes.

$$C_6H_5(NO_2) + 3H_2S = C_6H_5(NH_2) + 2H_2O + S_3. \quad [428]$$

The other hydrocarbons of this series may be regarded as containing the same group of carbon atoms as benzol, and as derived from it by replacing one or more of its hydrogen atoms with the radicals methyl, ethyl, or amyl. It is evident that by replacing several atoms of hydrogen with methyl we should obtain a body of the same composition as by replacing a single atom with a radical richer in carbon, and we have abundant evidence that compounds thus obtained, though isomeric, are not identical.

The radical C_6H_5, called *Phenyl*, appears to be the nucleus of all the hydrocarbons of this series. By acting on boiling benzol with bromine, we obtain the bromide of this radical,

$$C_6H_6 + Br\text{-}Br = C_6H_5\text{-}Br + H\text{-}Br, \qquad [429]$$

and when this product is treated with sodium a hydrocarbon is formed which is regarded as the corresponding radical substance.

$$2\,C_6H_5\text{-}Br + Na\text{-}Na = C_6H_5\text{-}C_6H_5 + 2NaBr. \quad [430]$$

Benzol is then phenylic hydride, and its homologues are hydrides of more complex radicals, which may be designated as methyl-phenyl, dimethyl-phenyl, &c. Besides the hydrocarbons included in the five series just described we know also a few others. Of these the best studied are phenylene, C_6H_4, and cinnamene, C_8H_8, corresponding to the symbol C_nH_{2n-8}, and napthaline, $C_{10}H_8$, corresponding to C_nH_{2n-12}. They all combine with chlorine and bromine, and have in general the chemical relations of artiad radicals. The last of these especially yields with these elements, besides the direct compounds, a very large number of substitution products, and the careful investigation of these bodies by Laurent was an important step in the progress of chemistry (31).

435. *Hydrocarbon Radicals.* — It is evident from the principles developed in (22) and (28), and still further illustrated in (34), that, by eliminating successive atoms of hydrogen, each of the possible hydrocarbons of the scheme exhibited above may yield a series of compound radicals, and that the atomicity of such radicals is equal in any case to the number of hydrogen atoms thus lost.

Such of these radicals as contain an even number of hydrogen atoms are necessarily artiads, and isomeric with either actual or possible hydrocarbons. Moreover, it follows from (428) that we may have several artiad radicals isomeric with each of the more complex compounds. Thus we may have two radicals $(C_2H_2)^=$ and $(C_2H_2)^{\equiv}$ isomeric with acetylene, and the same is true of each of the homologues of this hydrocarbon. Indeed, parallel to each series of hydrocarbons, except the first, we may have one or more series of artiad radicals isomeric, term by term, with the normal compounds, and the number of possible isomers in any case is the same as the number of the series in the order of isologues (428). It is, however, an open question whether such hydrocarbons as ethylene or acetylene are essentially different from the radicals of the same composition (69), and we do not distinguish the radicals by separate names.

The hydrocarbon radicals which contain an odd number of hydrogen atoms are necessarily perissads, and cannot, without

reduplication, exist in a free state [416], [417], and [426].
Nevertheless, the radicals homologous with methyl and phenyl
play such an important part in numberless chemical reactions,
and preserve their integrity through so many changes, that, although only known in combination, their individuality is as well
marked as that of the elements themselves.   Hence it is with
reason that they have received distinctive names.   With most
of these the student is already familiar, but to those previously
noticed we may here add Vinyl, $C_2H_3\text{-}$, Glyceryl, $C_3H_5^{\equiv}$ (the
trivalent condition of allyl), and the radical of chloroform, $CH^{\equiv}$,
which are all important perissads.

436   *Oxygenated Radicals.* — Unless associated with some
very powerful basic radical, like the alkaline metals, the simple
hydrocarbons always form basic or positive radicals (40).   To
every such radical, however, corresponds an acid or negative
radical having the same atomicity, which is generated by replacing a portion of the hydrogen with oxygen (34).   Thus : —.

Methyl	CH_3	yields	Formyl	CHO	or	$CO\text{-}H,$
Ethyl	C_2H_5	"	Acetyl	C_2H_3O	"	$CO\text{-}CH_3,$
Propyl	C_3H_7	"	Propionyl	C_3H_5O	"	$CO\text{-}C_2H_5,$
Butyl	C_4H_9	"	Butyryl	C_4H_7O	"	$CO\text{-}C_3H_7,$
Amyl	C_5H_{11}	"	Valeryl	C_5H_9O	"	$CO\text{-}C_4H_9,$
Allyl	C_3H_5	"	Acryl	C_3H_3O	"	$CO\text{-}C_2H_3,$

Ethylene C_2H_4 yields Glycolyl $CO\text{-}CH_2$ and Carbonyl $(CO)_2$
Propylene C_3H_6 " Lactyl $CO\text{-}C_2H_4$ " Malonyl $(CO)_2\text{=}CH_2,$
Acetylene C_4H_8 " Acetonyl $CO\text{-}C_3H_6$ " Succinyl $(CO)_2\text{=}C_2H_4.$

If the theory of (416) is correct, it is evident that the virtue
of these oxygenated radicals depends entirely on the number of
atoms of carbonyl which are generated in the hydrocarbon
radical, and we find that only those atoms of hydrogen can be
replaced which are so related to the molecule that the atoms of
carbonyl thus formed may have an open bond, and by the
addition of Ho be converted into oxatyl.   Hence the number
of oxygen atoms which can thus be introduced into the radical
can never exceed its atomicity, and the basicity of the acids,
formed by the union of the resulting negative radicals with $Ho,$
is equal to the number of oxygen atoms which any such negative radical contains.

ALCOHOLS AND THEIR DERIVATIVES.

437. *Definition.* — The name of alcohol is applied to a class of bodies which resemble common vinic alcohol chiefly in that under like conditions they are susceptible of similar reactions. They are produced in a variety of processes, especially by fermentation ; but the reactions cannot usually be traced. They may be regarded as hydrates of the hydrocarbon radicals (40), or as formed from the hydrocarbons themselves by replacing one or more atoms of hydrogen with hydroxyl, and their atomicity (43) depends on the number of atoms of Ho thus introduced into the molecule. Hence we have monatomic, diatomic, triatomic alcohols, &c., and these are still further subdivided according to the class of hydrocarbons from which they are derived. Moreover, each alcohol is one of a group of compounds which may be derived from each other by simple reactions, not affecting the arrangement of the atoms in the carbon skeleton that may be regarded as the nucleus of the group. The compounds thus related have frequently little in common, and in more extended works would be classed under their appropriate heads. Our only object is to exhibit a few of the general principles and wonderful relations which the study of organic chemistry has revealed, and this will best be gained by associating with each class of alcohols those of their derivatives which have the same atomicity.

MONATOMIC COMPOUNDS.

1. MARSH GAS SERIES.

438. *Alcohols.* — This very important class of compounds may be regarded as derived from the normal hydrocarbons of the marsh gas series by replacing a single atom of hydrogen with Ho, and consequently they are hydrates of the radicals of the methyl series (40). Of these bodies the following are known : —

		Boiling-point.
Methylic Alcohol	$CH_3\text{-}O\text{-}H$	66°.5
Ethylic Alcohol	$C_2H_5\text{-}O\text{-}H$	78°.4
Propylic Alcohol	$C_3H_7\text{-}O\text{-}H$	96°
Butylic Alcohol	$C_4H_9\text{-}O\text{-}H$	109°

		Melting-point.	Boiling-point.
Amylic Alcohol	$C_5H_{11}\text{-}O\text{-}H$	—20°	132°
Hexylic Alcohol	$C_6H_{13}\text{-}O\text{-}h$		
Heptylic Alcohol	$C_7H_{15}\text{-}O\text{-}H$		
Octylic Alcohol	$C_8H_{17}\text{-}O\text{-}H$		178°
Cetylic Alcohol	$C_{16}H_{33}\text{-}O\text{-}H$	50°	
Cerotic Alcohol	$C_{27}H_{55}\text{-}O\text{-}H$	79°	
Melissic Alcohol	$C_{30}H_{61}\text{-}O\text{-}H$	85°	

The lower members of the series are liquids, the higher solids, and the boiling-point increases about 19° for every addition of CH_2. The following reactions illustrate the production of methylic alcohol from marsh gas : —

$$CH_4 + Cl\text{-}Cl = HCl + CH_3\text{-}Cl, \qquad [431]$$

$$CH_3\text{-}Cl + Ag\text{-}O\text{-}C_2H_3O = Ag\,Cl + CH_3\text{-}O\text{-}C_2H_3O, \quad [432]$$

$$CH_3\text{-}O\text{-}C_2H_3O + K\text{-}O\text{-}H = K\text{-}O\text{-}C_2H_3O + CH_3\text{-}O\text{-}H; \; [433]$$

and the same method applied to the homologues of marsh gas yields other members of the alcohol series.

We may also start with olefiant gas, and having combined this with HCl we may convert the C_2H_5Cl thus formed into common alcohol by the same series of reactions as before, or we may reach the same result by combining olefiant gas with sulphuric acid and distilling the product with water.

$$H_2\text{=}O_2\text{=}SO_2 + C_2H_4 = H,C_2H_5\text{=}O_2\text{=}SO_2. \qquad [434]$$

$$H,C_2H_5\text{=}O_2\text{=}SO_2 + H\text{-}O\text{-}H = H_2\text{=}O_2\text{=}SO_2 + C_2H_5\text{-}O\text{-}H. \; [435]$$

Propylic alcohol may be obtained from C_3H_6 by similar reactions, but these processes applied to the other members of the olefiant series either give no results or yield compounds which, although resembling the true alcohols, and isomeric with them, manifest in their reactions an essential difference of molecular structure. These bodies have been called pseudo-alcohols.

By means of the following reactions we may ascend from one member of the alcohol series to the next higher : —

$$C_2H_5\text{-}O\text{-}H + H_2\text{=}O_2\text{=}SO_2 = H,C_2H_5\text{=}O_2\text{=}SO_2 + H_2O. \; [436]$$

$$K,C_2H_5\text{=}O_2\text{=}SO_2 + K\text{-}CN = K_2\text{=}O_2\text{=}SO_2 + C_2H_5\text{-}CN. \quad [437]$$

$$C_2H_5\text{-}CN + 2H\text{-}H = H,H,C_3H_7\text{=}N. \qquad [438]$$

$$2(H,H,C_3H_7\text{=}N) + N_2O_3 =$$
$$2\,C_3H_7\text{-}O\text{-}H + H_2O + 2N\text{-}N. \quad [439]$$

Common alcohol is always obtained in the arts by the fermentation of grape sugar (480), and other compounds of the series are not unfrequently formed in small amounts during the same process.

The typical hydrogen of the alcohols may be replaced by sodium or potassium.

$$2H\text{-}O\text{-}C_2H_5 + K\text{-}K = 2K\text{-}O\text{-}C_2H_5 + H\text{-}H. \quad [440]$$

An alcohol in which the oxygen has been replaced by sulphur may be obtained by the following reaction : —

$$K,C_2H_5\text{=}O_2\text{=}SO_2 + K\text{-}S\text{-}H = K_2\text{=}O_2\text{=}SO_2 + C_2H_5\text{-}S\text{-}H. \quad [441]$$

This sulphur alcohol is called *mercaptan*, and a corresponding selenium alcohol is also known.

By the action of oxidizing agents the alcohols are converted first into aldehydes and then into acids,

$$\underset{\text{Alcohol.}}{C_2H_5\text{-}Ho} + O = \underset{\text{Aldehyde.}}{C_2H_3O\text{-}H} + H_2O,$$

$$\underset{\text{Aldehyde.}}{C_2H_3O\text{-}H} + O = \underset{\text{Acetic Acid.}}{C_2H_3O\text{-}Ho} ; \qquad [442]$$

but only in a few cases can the process be arrested at the first stage.

439. *Fat Acids.* — The acids formed by the oxidation of the monatomic alcohols belong to a remarkable series of organic compounds, of which more members are now known than of any other. These acids may be regarded as hydrates of the oxygenated radicals of the methyl series (40), (436), or as formed from the hydrocarbons homologous with marsh gas by replacing one atom of hydrogen with oxatyl (416). The following are known : —

			Melting-point.	Boiling-point.
Formic Acid	$H\text{-}O\text{-}CHO$	or $Ho\text{-}(CO\text{-}H)$ [1]	$+1°$	$100°$
Acetic Acid	$H\text{-}O\text{-}C_2H_3O$	" $Ho\text{-}(CO\text{-}CH_3)$	$+17°$	$117°$
Propionic Acid	$H\text{-}O\text{-}C_3H_5O$	" $Ho\text{-}(CO\text{-}C_2H_5)$		$141°$
Butyric Acid	$H\text{-}O\text{-}C_4H_7O$	" $Ho\text{-}(CO\text{-}C_3H_7)$	$-20°$	$161°$
Valeric Acid	$H\text{-}O\text{-}C_5H_9O$	" $Ho\text{-}(CO\text{-}C_4H_9)$		$175°$
Caproic Acid	$H\text{-}O\text{-}C_6H_{11}O$	" $Ho\text{-}(CO\text{-}C_5H_{11})$	$+5°$	$198°$
Œnanthylic Acid	$H\text{-}O\text{-}C_7H_{13}O$	" $Ho\text{-}(CO\text{-}C_6H_{13})$		$212°$
Caprylic Acid	$H\text{-}O\text{-}C_8H_{15}O$	" $Ho\text{-}(CO\text{-}C_7H_{15})$	$14°$	$236°$
Pelargonic Acid	$H\text{-}O\text{-}C_9H_{17}O$	" $Ho\text{-}(CO\text{-}C_8H_{17})$	$18°$	$260°$
Capric Acid	$H\text{-}O\text{-}C_{10}H_{19}O$	" $Ho\text{-}(CO\text{-}C_9H_{19})$	$27°$	
Lauric Acid	$H\text{-}O\text{-}C_{12}H_{23}O$	" $Ho\text{-}(CO\text{-}C_{11}H_{23})$	$44°$	
Myristic Acid	$H\text{-}O\text{-}C_{14}H_{27}O$	" $Ho\text{-}(CO\text{-}C_{13}H_{27})$	$54°$	
Palmitic Acid	$H\text{-}O\text{-}C_{16}H_{31}O$	" $Ho\text{-}(CO\text{-}C_{15}H_{31})$	$62°$	
Margaric Acid	$H\text{-}O\text{-}C_{17}H_{33}O$	" $Ho\text{-}(CO\text{-}C_{16}H_{33})$	$60°$	
Stearic Acid	$H\text{-}O\text{-}C_{18}H_{35}O$	" $Ho\text{-}(CO\text{-}C_{17}H_{35})$	$69°$	
Arachidic Acid	$H\text{-}O\text{-}C_{20}H_{39}O$	" $Ho\text{-}(CO\text{-}C_{19}H_{39})$	$•75°$	
Behenic Acid	$H\text{-}O\text{-}C_{22}H_{43}O$	" $Ho\text{-}(CO\text{-}C_{21}H_{43})$	$76°$	
Cerotic Acid	$H\text{-}O\text{-}C_{27}H_{53}O$	" $Ho\text{-}(CO\text{-}C_{26}H_{53})$	$78°$	
Melissic Acid	$H\text{-}O\text{-}C_{30}H_{59}O$	" $Ho\text{-}(CO\text{-}C_{29}H_{59})$	$88°$	

Formic acid is found in nettles, and is secreted by ants. Valeric acid is found in the valerian root, pelargonic acid in the essential oil of the Pelargonium roseum, and cerotic acid in beeswax. Chinese wax is cerylic cerotate, spermaceti cetylic palmitate, and the natural fats are mixtures of salts of various acids of the group, in which glyceryl, C_3H_5, is the basic radical. Several of these acids may be procured by the oxidation of albuminous compounds. Propionic and butyric acids are produced in some kinds of fermentation, and acetic acid is made in the arts in large quantities from the products of the dry distillation of wood and other similar substances.

The formation of the fat acids by the oxidation of the corresponding alcohol is illustrated by the reactions already given [442]. They may also be formed from the cyanides of the alcohol radicals, and the method is interesting as indicating their molecular constitution.

1 The student will not fail to notice that all dashes used in connection with the hydrocarbon radicals must refer exclusively to the carbon atoms, since the hydrogen atoms, being united to the carbon skeleton by their only bond, can present no open affinity.

$$H\text{-}CN + HCl + 2H_2O = NH_4Cl + (H\text{-}CO)\text{-}Ho.$$
$$C_2H_5\text{-}CN + HCl + 2H_2O = NH_4\text{-}Cl + (C_2H_5\text{-}CO)\text{-}Ho.$$
[443]

So also

$$C_2H_5\text{-}CN + K\text{-}Ho + H_2O = (C_2H_5\text{-}CO)\text{-}Ko + NH_3. \quad [444]$$

On the other hand, when the ammonic salts of these acids are heated with P_2O_5 they are converted back into the cyanides of the radicals of the methyl series,

$$(CH_3\text{-}CO)\text{-}(NH_4)o + 2P_2O_5 = CH_3\text{-}CN + 4H\text{-}O\text{-}PO_2, \quad [445]$$

and from the cyanide thus obtained the corresponding alcohol may be produced by [438], and in this way [442] is reversed.

The acid may also be converted into the alcohol by another remarkable series of reactions, of which the following series is an example : —

$$(CH_3\text{-}CO)\text{-}Ko + (H\text{-}CO)\text{-}Ko =$$
Potassic Acetate. Potassic Formate.
$$(CH_3\text{-}CO)\text{-}H + Ko_2\text{-}CO. \quad [446]$$
Acetic Aldehyde. Potassic Carbonate.

$$(CH_3\text{-}CO)\text{-}H + H\text{-}H = C_2H_5\text{-}O\text{-}H. \quad [447]$$

The potassic salt of the acid is first distilled with potassic formate, and the aldehyde thus obtained transformed into alcohol by nascent hydrogen. Starting now with ethylic alcohol, we can convert it into ethylic cyanide by [436] and [437], and then by [438] or [444] we can produce propionic acid. Thus we are able to pass from one fat acid to the next as from one alcohol to the next, and since formic acid can be made directly from its elements [374] the synthesis of this whole class of organic compounds is, theoretically at least, possible.

All these reactions seem to indicate that the fat acids contain the radicals of the methyl series united to oxatyl, and this view, is rendered more probable by the fact that sodic acetate may be formed by the direct combination of CO_2 with sodic methide.

$$(CH_3)\text{-}Na + CO_2 = (CH_3\text{-}CO)\text{-}Nao. \quad [448]$$

Again, it appears that, when the acids of this series are acted upon by nascent oxygen in the process of electrolysis, CO_2 is

formed, and the radical assumed to have been previously united
to the oxatyl is thus set free.

$$2(CH_3\text{-}CO)\text{-}Ho + O = CH_3\text{-}CH_3 + H_2O + 2CO_2. \quad [449]$$

If this theory of the constitution of the fat acids is correct, it
is obvious that if we could replace the radical hydrogen of formic acid with the radicals methyl, ethyl, &c., we should obtain
the successive members of the series. The direct substitution
has not been accomplished, but with acetic ether an analogous
series of reactions has been obtained.

$$2C_2H_5\text{-}O\text{-}(CO\text{-}CH_3) + Na\text{-}Na =$$
$$2C_2H_5\text{-}O\text{-}(CO\text{-}CH_2Na) + H\text{-}H. \quad [450]$$

$$C_2H_5\text{-}O\text{-}(CO\text{-}CH_2Na) + CH_3I =$$
$$C_2H_5\text{-}O\text{-}(CO\text{-}C_2H_5) + NaI. \quad [451]$$

$$C_2H_5\text{-}O\text{-}(CO\text{-}CH_2Na) + C_2H_5I =$$
$$C_2H_5\text{-}O\text{-}(CO\text{-}C_3H_7) + NaI. \quad [452]$$

440. *Formic Acid*, on account of its peculiar constitution as
the first member of the series, presents some special reactions
which are highly instructive. Thus, when heated with strong
sulphuric acid,

$$(H\text{-}CO)\text{-}Ho = H_2O + CO. \quad [453]$$

So also when acted on by chlorine gas,

$$(H\text{-}CO)\text{-}Ho + Cl\text{-}Cl = 2HCl + CO_2. \quad [454]$$

It even acts as a reducing agent,

$$(H\text{-}CO)\text{-}Ho + HgO = Hg + H_2O + CO_2. \quad [455]$$

441. *Acetic Acid*, the acidifying principle of vinegar, is the
best known of all the lower members of this series of compounds, and the student has already become familiar with it in
many reactions. The remarkable substitution products which
it yields with chlorine have already been described (31), and
the manner in which it breaks up when acted on by PCl_5 has
also been illustrated (29). By this last reaction a chloride of
the assumed oxygenated radical (acetyl) is obtained.

442. *Isomers of the Fat Acids.* — It is obvious that with the higher members of the acetic acid series one or more isomeric modifications are possible, depending upon the different ways in which the atoms of the hydrocarbon radical may be grouped (428). Such differences of structure have been actually realized by means of reactions similar to [450 *et seq.*], using, however, as the starting-point, the products obtained by replacing two or all three of the hydrogen atoms of the acid radical in ethylic acetate with sodium.

$$C_2H_5\text{-}O\text{-}(CO\text{-}CHNa_2) + 2CH_3I =$$
$$2NaI + C_2H_5\text{-}O\text{-}(CO\text{-}CH\text{=}(CH_3)_2). \quad [456]$$

$$C_2H_5\text{-}O\text{-}(CO\text{-}CNa_3) + 3CH_3I =$$
$$3NaI + C_2H_5\text{-}O\text{-}(CO\text{-}C\text{≡}(CH_3)_3). \quad [457]$$

By acting on these ethylic salts with *K-Ho*, the corresponding potassic salts are readily obtained, from which the acids themselves may be easily set free.

Now the first of these products is isomeric, but not identical, with butyric acid (boiling at 152° instead of 161°), and the second sustains a similar relation to valeric acid. By exhibiting the symbols graphically, the difference of structure will be made evident, and it will appear that, although reactions like [451] yield the normal acids of the series, reactions similar to the last must necessarily give the so-called iso-acids. It can also be discovered how many isomers are possible in any case.

443. *Ethers.* — These compounds are the anhydrous oxides of the alcohol radicals (40), and our common ether, $(C_2H_5)_2\text{=}O$, may be taken as the type of the class. It is prepared by the action of sulphuric acid on alcohol, and the process may be divided into two stages: —

$$C_2H_5\text{-}O\text{-}H + H_2\text{=}O_2\text{=}SO_2 = H,C_2H_5\text{=}O_2\text{=}SO_2 + H_2O.$$
$$[458]$$
$$H,C_2H_5\text{=}O_2\text{=}SO_2 + C_2H_5\text{-}O\text{-}H = H_2\text{=}O_2\text{=}SO_2 + (C_2H_5)_2\text{=}O.$$

The alcohol and sulphuric acid, mixed in equivalent proportions, are heated in a retort, when the water and ether distil over together, and if the loss is supplied by fresh alcohol (flowing slowly into the retort through a tube adapted to the tubulature) the same quantity of sulphuric acid will convert an unlimited quantity of alcohol into ether.

Ether may be reconverted into alcohol by reversing the above reaction, thus : —

$$(C_2H_5)_2\text{-}O + 2H_2\text{=}O_2\text{=}SO_2 = 2H,C_2H_5\text{=}O_2\text{=}SO_2 + H_2O. \qquad [459]$$

$$H,C_2H_5\text{=}O_2\text{=}SO_2 + H\text{-}O\text{-}H = H_2\text{=}O_2\text{=}SO_2 + C_2H_5\text{-}O\text{-}H.$$

By using in the second stage of "*etherification*" an alcohol containing a different radical, mixed ethers as they are termed may in some cases be obtained.

$$H,C_5H_{11}\text{=}O_2\text{=}SO_2 + C_2H_5\text{-}O\text{-}H =$$
$$H_2\text{=}O_2\text{=}SO_2 + C_2H_5,C_5H_{11}\text{=}O. \quad [460]$$

Other bodies of this class have been formed, thus : —

$$2 CH_3\text{-}O\text{-}H + Na\text{-}Na = 2 CH_3\text{-}O\text{-}Na + H\text{-}H.$$
$$\qquad [461]$$
$$CH_3\text{-}O\text{-}Na + C_2H_5I = NaI + CH_3\text{-}O\text{-}C_2H_5.$$

444. *Compound Ethers.* — We include under this head the numberless salts of the hydrocarbon radicals usually distinguished as different kinds of ether. These bodies are, for the most part, volatile, and have an agreeable odor which resembles that of fresh fruit, and several of them are used by the confectioners as essences. They are produced by reactions similar to those employed in the preparation of metallic salts.

$$C_2H_5\text{-}Cl + \underset{\text{Argentic Acetate.}}{Ag\text{-}O\text{-}C_2H_3O} = AgCl + \underset{\text{Acetic Ether.}}{C_2H_5\text{-}O\text{-}C_2H_3O}. \quad [462]$$

$$C_2H_5\text{-}O\text{-}Na + \underset{\text{Butyrylic Chloride.}}{C_4H_7O\text{-}Cl} = NaCl + \underset{\text{Butyric Ether.}}{C_2H_5\text{-}O\text{-}C_4H_7O}. \quad [463]$$

$$H,C_5H_{11}\text{=}O_2\text{=}SO_2 + \underset{\text{Potassic Acetate.}}{K\text{-}O\text{-}C_2H_3O} =$$
$$H,K\text{=}O_2\text{=}SO_2 + \underset{\text{Amylic Acetate.}}{C_5H_{11}\text{-}O\text{-}C_2H_3O}. \quad [464]$$

$$C_2H_5\text{-}O\text{-}H + H\text{-}O\text{-}C_2H_3O = C_2H_5\text{-}O\text{-}C_2H_3O + H_2O. \quad [465]$$

In reactions like the last, when a weak acid is unable by itself to produce the decomposition of the alcohol, the presence of a strong mineral acid will sometimes determine the formation of the ether. The reaction is then best expressed as if in two stages.

$$C_2H_5\text{-}O\text{-}H + H_2\text{=}O_2\text{=}SO_2 = H,C_2H_5\text{=}O_2\text{=}SO_2 + H_2O.$$

$$H,C_2H_5\text{=}O_2\text{=}SO_2 + H\text{-}O\text{-}C_7H_5O = \tag{466}$$

$$\underset{\text{Benzoic Acid.}}{}$$

$$H_2\text{=}O_2\text{=}SO_2 + C_2H_5\text{-}O\text{-}C_7H_5O.$$

$$\underset{\text{Benzoic Ether.}}{}$$

$$C_4H_9\text{-}O\text{-}H + HCl = C_4H_9\text{-}Cl + H_2O.$$

$$\tag{467}$$

$$C_4H_9\text{-}Cl + H\text{-}O\text{-}CHO = HCl + C_4H_9\text{-}O\text{-}CHO.$$

When acted on by strong alkaline bases the compound ethers yield a metallic salt and an alcohol.

$$C_2H_5\text{-}O\text{-}C_2H_3O + K\text{-}O\text{-}H = K\text{-}O\text{-}C_2H_3O + C_2H_5\text{-}O\text{-}H. \tag{468}$$

Since the ethers are quite insoluble in water, such reactions are best obtained in alcoholic solutions, and this kind of decomposition is frequently called *saponification*. At a high temperature the ethers may be *saponified* by water alone.

445. *Anhydrides.* — The simple and mixed ethers are anhydrides, but the name is usually confined to the oxides of the acid radicals. Acetic anhydride may be obtained by the following reaction,

$$K\text{-}O\text{-}C_2H_3O + C_2H_3O\text{-}Cl = KCl + (C_2H_3O)_2\text{=}O, \tag{469}$$

and propionic, butyric, and valerianic anhydrides may all be prepared in a similar way. Formic anhydride, however, has not as yet been formed. In contact with water these anhydrides dissolve only slowly, in measure, as they are converted into the corresponding acids.

446. *Haloid Ethers.* — The term *haloid* means resembling common salt, and is applied to those compounds which, like *salt*, are formed after the simple type of HCl, and includes the cyanides, chlorides, bromides, &c., of the hydrocarbon radicals. These ether-like bodies are formed in a great variety of reactions.

$$C_2H_5\text{-}O\text{-}H + HCl = C_2H_5\text{-}Cl + H_2O. \tag{470}$$

$$3\,C_5H_{11}\text{-}O\text{-}H + PCl_3 = H_2\text{=}O_2\text{=}POH + 3\,C_5H_{11}\text{-}Cl. \tag{471}$$

$$5\,C_2H_5\text{-}O\text{-}H + I_5 + P = H_3\text{=}O_3\text{=}PO + 5\,C_2H_5\text{-}I + H_2O. \tag{472}$$

$$CH_4 + Cl\text{-}Cl = CH_3\text{-}Cl + H\text{-}Cl. \tag{473}$$

When acted on by an alcoholic solution of potash, all the haloid ethers, except the cyanides, are converted into alcohols.

$$C_5H_{11}\text{-}Cl + K\text{-}O\text{-}H = KCl + C_5H_{11}\text{-}O\text{-}H. \quad [474]$$

The reaction of the cyanides has already been given [444].

The haloid ethers are allied to the hydrogen acids, and like these combine with ammonia, and by the action of potash on the salts thus formed various amines may be obtained.

$$NH_3 + C_2H_5\text{-}I = (N\equiv C_2H_5,H_3)\text{-}I.$$

$$(N\equiv C_2H_5,H_3)\text{-}I + K\text{-}O\text{-}H = KI + H_2O + H_2,C_2H_5\equiv N. \quad [475]$$
Ethylamine.

Ethylic iodide, heated in a sealed tube with water, is converted into common ether.

$$2C_2H_5\text{-}I + H_2O = (C_2H_5)_2\text{-}O + 2HI. \quad [476]$$

Methylic chloride, when acted on by chlorine, yields the following substitution products, and it will be noticed that the boiling-point increases in proportion as the atoms of hydrogen are replaced.

	B. P.		B. P.		B. P.		B. P.
$CH_3\text{-}Cl$	$-21°$,	CH_2Cl_2	$31°$,	$CHCl_3$	$60°.8$,	CCl_4	$78°$.

The compound $CHCl_3$ is called chloroform, and is an anæsthetic agent made in large quantities by heating alcohol or wood spirit (methylic alcohol) with a solution of chloride of lime (282). When boiled with an alcoholic solution of potash, chloroform is converted into potassic formiate, and chlorine gas, under the influence of sunlight, changes it into carbonic chloride.

$$CHCl_3 + 4K\text{-}O\text{-}H = 3KCl + K\text{-}O\text{-}(CO\text{-}H) + 2H_2O. \quad [477]$$

Bromoform, $CHBr_3$, and Iodoform, CHI_3, are also known.

447. *Aldehydes.* — These bodies, already mentioned as the products of the imperfect oxidation of the alcohols [442], may also be obtained by distilling a mixture of potassic formate with the potassic salt of the acid corresponding to the aldehyde required.

$$K\text{-}O\text{-}(CO\text{-}H) + K\text{-}O\text{-}(CO\text{-}CH_3) =$$
$$K_2\text{-}O_2\text{-}CO + H\text{-}(CO\text{-}CH_3). \quad [478]$$
Acetic Aldehyde.

The aldehydes are distinguished by a strong affinity for oxygen. They not only absorb oxygen gas from the air, but they reduce argentic oxide, and when heated with alkaline hydrates they evolve hydrogen, passing in each case into the corresponding acid.

$$H\text{-}(CO\text{-}CH_3) + O = H\text{-}O\text{-}(CO\text{-}CH_3). \qquad [479]$$
$$\text{Aldehyde.} \qquad\qquad\qquad \text{Acetic Acid.}$$

$$H\text{-}(CO\text{-}CH_3) + Ag_2O = H\text{-}O\text{-}(CO\text{-}CH_3) + Ag\text{-}Ag. \quad [480]$$

$$H\text{-}(CO\text{-}CH_3) + K\text{-}O\text{-}H = K\text{-}O\text{-}(CO\text{-}CH_3) + H\text{-}H. \quad [481]$$

By nascent hydrogen (water and sodium amalgam) the aldehydes are converted back into alcohol.

$$H\text{-}(CO\text{-}CH_3) + H\text{-}H = C_2H_5\text{-}O\text{-}H. \qquad [482]$$

Most of them yield crystalline compounds with ammonia.

$$H\text{-}(CO\text{-}CH_3) + NH_3 = NH_4\text{-}(CO\text{-}CH_3). \qquad [483]$$

So also by dissolving potassium in aldehyde we obtain the reaction

$$2H\text{-}(CO\text{-}CH_3) + K\text{-}K = 2K\text{-}(CO\text{-}CH_3) + H\text{-}H. \quad [484]$$

The aldehydes are named after the corresponding acids. The first is formic aldehyde $H\text{-}(CO\text{-}H)$, and the seven succeeding terms of the same series have been obtained. Of acetic aldehydes there are three polymeric modifications. The normal compound is a very volatile liquid, boiling at 21° and having a strong suffocating odor.

448. *Ketones.* — This name is applied to a class of compounds outwardly resembling the alcohols and having a pleasant ethereal odor. They are isomeric with the aldehydes, but differ from them widely in their chemical relations, for they are comparatively inactive bodies, and show no tendency to unite with oxygen. They are most readily obtained by distilling the potassic or calcic salts of the monatomic acids.

$$Ca\text{=}O_2\text{=}(CO\text{-}CH_3)_2 = Ca\text{=}O_2\text{=}CO + (CH_3)_2\text{=}CO. \quad [485]$$
$$\text{Calcic Acetate.} \qquad\qquad\qquad\qquad \text{Acetone.}$$

$$Ca\text{=}O_2\text{=}(CO\text{-}C_2H_5)_2 = Ca\text{=}O_2\text{=}CO + (C_2H_5)_2\text{=}CO. \quad [486]$$
$$\text{Calcic Propionate.} \qquad\qquad\qquad\qquad \text{Propione.}$$

It will be noticed that the two ketones thus obtained differ by $2\,CH_2$, although the initial acids only differ by CH_2; but by distilling an intimate mixture of the two salts we can obtain the intermediate term of the series, namely, $CH_3, C_2H_5=CO$.

Ketones can also be obtained by acting on acetyl chloride or its homologues with zinc methide or ethide.

$$2\,(CH_3\text{-}CO)\text{-}Cl + Zn=(CH_3)_2 = Zn\,Cl_2 + 2\,(CH_3)_2=CO. \quad [487]$$

Moreover, they have been formed by the action of carbonic oxide on sodic ethide and the homologous compounds.

$$2\,Na\text{-}C_2H_5 + CO = Na\text{-}Na + (C_2H_5)_2=CO. \quad [488]$$

449. Pseudo-Alcohols. — By the action of nascent hydrogen the ketones are converted into compounds isomeric, but not identical with the alcohols.

$$(CH_3)_2=CO + H\text{-}H = (CH_3)_2=CH\text{-}Ho. \quad [489]$$

The bodies of this class are also called *secondary alcohols*, and are distinguished by the prefix iso. Their relations to the normal alcohols are illustrated by the following symbols : —

$(CH_3\text{-}CH_2)\text{-}Ho,$
Ethylic Alcohol.

$(CH_3\text{-}CO)\text{-}H,$
Aldehyde.

$(CH_3\text{-}CO)\text{-}Ho,$
Acetic Acid.

$(C_2H_5\text{-}CH_2)\text{-}Ho,$
Propylic Alcohol.

$(C_2H_5\text{-}CO)\text{-}H,$
Aldehyde.

$(C_2H_5\text{-}CO)\text{-}Ho,$
Propionic Acid.

$(CH_3)_2=CH\text{-}Ho,$
Isopropylic Alcohol.

$(CH_3)_2=CO.$
Acetone.

As common alcohol passes by oxidation first into aldehyde and then into acetic acid so normal propylic alcohol, when oxidized, yields similar products. But under the same conditions the isopropylic alcohol gives acetone, which, although isomeric with propionic aldehyde, cannot be converted by further oxidation into propionic acid, and it is evident that such a change would not be possible without a complete remodelling of the molecule. The difference between these isomeric alcohols, indicated by their reactions, is still further manifested in their boiling-points, since while the normal alcohol boils at 96°, the pseudo-alcohol boils at 87°. Besides the isopropylic two other pseudo-alcohols have been obtained which probably belong to the same class.

Isoamylic Alcohol	$(CH_3, C_3H_7{=}CH)\text{-}Ho,$
Isohexylic Alcohol	$(CH_3, C_4H_9{=}CH)\text{-}Ho.$

Lastly a pseudo-alcohol has been discovered, isomeric with butylic alcohol, which appears to be constituted after still a third type, and to be the first of a class of *tertiary alcohols*.

Pseudo-butylic Alcohol $(CH_3)_3{=}C\text{-}Ho.$

If we represent by $\mathfrak{R}$ any univalent hydrocarbon-radical, the general symbols of the three classes of alcohols we have distinguished would be as follows : —

$\mathfrak{R}\text{-}CH_2\text{-}Ho,$	$\mathfrak{R}_2{=}CH\text{-}Ho,$	$\mathfrak{R}_3{=}C\text{-}Ho.$
Primary Alcohol.	Secondary Alcohol.	Tertiary Alcohol.

2. VINYL SERIES.

450. *Vinylic Alcohol.* — Acetylene like ethylene dissolves in sulphuric acid, and when the product is distilled with water we obtain the hydrate of the radical vinyl or vinylic alcohol.

$$H_2{=}O_2{=}SO_2 + C_2H_2 = H,C_2H_3{=}O_2{=}SO_2.$$

$$H,C_2H_3{=}O_2{=}SO_2 + H\text{-}O\text{-}H = H_2{=}O_2{=}SO_2 + C_2H_3\text{-}O\text{-}H. \quad [490]$$

This alcohol is isomeric both with acetic aldehyde and the oxide of ethylene.

$C_2H_3\text{-}O\text{-}H,$	$(CH_3{=}CO)\text{-}H,$	$C_2H_4{=}O.$
Vinylic Alcohol.	Acetic Aldehyde.	Ethylenic Oxide.

No acid has been obtained from it by the action of oxidizing agents.

451. *Allylic Alcohol.* — The second term of the vinyl series may be formed from glycerine by the following reactions.

$$2C_3H_5{=}O_3{=}H_3 + [P_2]{=}I_4 =$$
Glycerine.
$$2C_3H_5\text{-}I + 2H_2{=}O_2{=}POH + I\text{-}I. \quad [491]$$
Allylic Iodide.

$$2C_3H_5\text{-}I + Ag_2{=}O_2{=}C_2O_2 = 2AgI + (C_3H_5)_2{=}O_2{=}C_2O_2. \quad [492]$$
Argentic Oxalate.   Allylic Oxalate.

$$(C_3H_5)_2{=}O_2{=}C_2O_2 + 2H_3N =$$
$$(H_2N)_2{=}C_2O_2 + 2C_3H_5\text{-}O\text{-}H. \quad [493]$$
Oxamide.   Allylic Alcohol.

R F

When dehydrated by phosphoric anhydride (184) this alcohol gives allylene the second member of the acetylene series.

$$(C_3H_5)\text{-}O\text{-}H \longrightarrow H_2O = C_3H_4. \qquad [494]$$

Oil of garlic is the sulphide of allyl $(C_3H_5)_2\text{=}S$ and oil of mustard the sulphocyanate $C_3H_5\text{-}S\text{-}CN$.

When acted on by oxidizing agents, allylic alcohol yields both an aldehyde and an acid, and the following symbols indicate the relations and probable constitution of the three bodies.

$$(CH_2\text{=}CH\text{-}CH_2)\text{-}Ho, \quad (CH_2\text{=}CH\text{-}CO)\text{-}H, \quad (CH_2\text{=}CH\text{-}CO)\text{-}Ho.$$
Allylic Alcohol.   Acrolein (Aldehyde).   Acrylic Acid.

452. *Acrolein* is formed abundantly during the dry distillation of fats or similar glycerides (474). and the pungent odor of its vapor, so intensely irritating to the eyes, is familiar to every one. It may be best procured by the action of dehydrating agents, such as phosphoric anhydride or sulphuric acid, on glycerine, from which it differs by $2H_2O$.

$$(CH_2\text{-}CH\text{-}CH_2)\text{=}Ho_3 \longrightarrow 2H_2O = (CH_2\text{=}CH\text{-}CO)\text{-}H. \quad [495]$$
Glycerine.   Acrolein.

453. *Acrylic or Oleic Series of Acids.* — Acrylic acid is the first member of a large and important series of acids, which are associated with the acids of the acetic series in the natural fats and oils. Only those members of the series are included in the following list which we have reason to believe are constituted like acrylic acid. Of the constitution of the other fat acids of this class we have as yet no knowledge.

Acrylic Acid	$C_3H_4O_2$	or	$Ho\text{-}(CO\ CH\text{=}CH_2)$,
Crotonic Acid	$C_4H_6O_2$	"	$Ho\text{-}(CO\text{-}CH\text{=}C_2H_4)$,
Angelic Acid	$C_5H_8O_2$	"	$Ho\text{-}(CO\text{-}CH\text{=}C_3H_6)$,
Pyroterbic Acid	$C_6H_{10}O_2$	"	$Ho\text{-}(CO\text{-}CH\text{=}C_4H_8)$,
Oleic Acid	$C_{18}H_{34}O_2$	"	$Ho\text{-}(CO\text{-}CH\text{=}C_{16}H_{32})$.

These acids are closely allied to those of the acetic series. Acrylic acid under the influence of nascent hydrogen changes into propionic acid, and when acted on by bromine it yields a simple derivative of the same compound.

$$Ho\text{-}(CO\text{-}CH\text{=}CH_2) + H\text{-}H = Ho\text{-}(CO\text{-}C_2H_5).$$

$$Ho\text{-}(CO\text{-}CH\text{=}CH_2) + Br\text{-}Br = Ho\text{-}(CO\text{-}C_2H_3Br_2). \quad [496]$$

Moreover, when heated with caustic potash *all* the acids of the above list break up into two acids of the acetic series, one of which is always acetic acid itself.

$$Ho\text{-}(CO\text{-}CH\text{=}CH_2) + 2K\text{-}O\text{-}H =$$
$$Ko\text{-}(CO\text{-}CH_3) + Ko\text{-}(CO\text{-}H) + H\text{-}H. \quad [497]$$

$$Ho\text{-}(CO\text{-}CH\text{=}C_2H_4) + 2K\text{-}O\text{-}H =$$
$$Ko\text{-}(CO\text{-}CH_3) + Ko\text{-}(CO\text{-}CH_3) + H\text{-}H. \quad [498]$$

$$Ho\text{-}(CO\text{-}CH\text{=}C_3H_6) + 2K\text{-}O\text{-}H =$$
$$Ko\text{-}(CO\text{-}CH_3) + Ko\text{-}(CO\text{-}C_2H_5) + H\text{-}H. \quad [499]$$

$$Ho\text{-}(CO\text{-}CH\text{=}C_4H_8) + 2K\text{-}O\text{-}H =$$
$$Ko\text{-}(CO\text{-}CH_3) + Ko\text{-}(CO\text{-}C_3H_7) + H\text{-}H. \quad [500]$$

$$Ho\text{-}(CO\text{-}CH\text{=}C_{16}H_{32}) + 2K\text{-}O\text{-}H =$$
$$Ko\text{-}(CO\text{-}CH_3) + \underset{\text{Salt of Palmitic Acid.}}{Ko\text{-}(CO\text{-}C_{15}H_{31})} + H\text{-}H. \quad [501]$$

The alkali appears to act on the olefines (430), assumed to exist in the radicals of these compounds, and replaces them with H_2, thus forming acetic acid in every case, while at the same time it converts the olefine itself into another acid of the acetic series.

454. *Secondary Acids.* — Acids isomeric with those of the acrylic series have been obtained by means of reactions which indicate the structure of the resulting molecules, and a comparison of the reactions of these artificial products with those of the normal acids shows that the rational symbols we have assigned to the latter must be essentially correct. The symbol of oxalic ether may be written $Et\text{-}O\text{-}(CO\text{-}CO)\text{-}O\text{-}Et$, and there are good reasons for writing the symbols of the zinc compounds of the monad radicals (324) thus, $(Zn\mathfrak{R})\text{-}\mathfrak{R}$, indicating, as is undoubtedly the case, that the group $(Zn\mathfrak{R})\text{-}$ acts as a monad radical. When now a body of this class acts on oxalic ether, the following reaction takes place : —

$$Et\text{-}O\text{-}(CO\text{-}CO)\text{-}O\text{-}Et + 2(Zn\mathfrak{R})\text{-}\mathfrak{R} =$$
$$Et\text{-}O\text{-}(CO\text{-}C\mathfrak{R}_2)\text{-}O\text{-}(Zn\mathfrak{R}) + Et\text{-}O\text{-}(Zn\mathfrak{R}). \quad [502]$$

If next water is added, the product of the last reaction undergoes a still further change,

$$Et\text{-}O\text{-}(CO\text{-}C\mathfrak{R}_2)\text{-}O\text{-}(Zn\mathfrak{R}) + 2H_2O =$$
$$Zn\text{=}O_2\text{=}H_2 + H\mathfrak{R} + Et\text{-}O\text{-}(CO\text{-}C\mathfrak{R}_2)\text{-}O\text{-}H, \quad [503]$$

and the whole effect, as will be seen, is to replace one atom of oxygen in the radical of oxalic acid with two atoms of a radical of the methyl series. Lastly, if we subject one of these acids, thus synthetically obtained, to a dehydrating agent (PCl_3 or P_2O_5), the result is an isomer of the acrylic series.

$$Et\text{-}O\text{-}(CO\text{-}C\mathfrak{R}_2)\text{-}O\text{-}H - H_2O = Et\text{-}O\text{-}(CO\text{-}C\mathfrak{R}\text{=}\mathfrak{R}). \quad [504]$$

Here $\mathfrak{R}$ stands for a dyad radical of the olefiant series, and the symbols of the compounds which have been obtained in this way are given below. By comparing these with the symbols of the normal isomers, the difference of structure will be evident.

	Secondary Acids.	Normal Acids.
Methyl-acrylic Acid	$H\text{-}O\text{-}(CO\text{-}C(CH_3)\text{=}CH_2)$	$H\text{-}O\text{-}(CO\text{-}CH\text{=}C_2H_4)$
Methyl-crotonic "	$H\text{-}O\text{-}(CO\text{-}C(CH_3)\text{=}C_2H_4)$	$H\text{-}O\text{-}(CO\text{-}CH\text{=}C_3H_6)$
Ethyl-crotonic "	$H\text{-}O\text{-}(CO\text{-}C(C_2H_5)\text{=}C_2H_4)$	$H\text{-}O\text{-}(CO\text{-}CH\text{=}C_4H_8)$

When treated with potash, the secondary acids break up like the normal compounds, but *they* only give *acetic acid* when the dyad radical is *ethylene*, and after writing these reactions, according to the models given above, it will be seen not only that these facts confirm the opinion already expressed in regard to the nature of the change, but also that the close coincidence between theory and observation gives strong grounds for believing that we have gained positive knowledge in regard to the structure of the bodies we have been studying.

455. *Tertiary Acids.* — By means of the following reaction a second isomer of crotonic acid has been obtained, which must have a structure differing from either of the other two conditions of this compound. Compare [444].

$$\underset{\text{Allylic Cyanide.}}{(CH_2\text{=}CH\text{-}CH_2)\text{-}CN} + K\text{-}O\text{-}H + H_2O =$$
$$\underset{\text{Potassic } \beta \text{ Crotonate.}}{(CH_2\text{=}CH\text{-}CH_2\text{-}CO)\text{-}O\text{-}K} + NH_3. \quad [505]$$

3. PHENYL SERIES.

456. *Benzoic Alcohol.* — If the peculiar grouping of the carbon atoms represented in Fig. *c* (428) is an essential character in the structure of the radical phenyl and its homologues, it is obvious that the lowest normal alcohol of this series, formed after the type of common alcohol, must have the composition represented by the symbol $(C_6H_5\text{-}CH_2)\text{-}O\text{-}H$. This body is Benzoic Alcohol, and the corresponding aldehyde and acid are the well-known compounds Oil of Bitter Almonds and Benzoic Acid.

$$(C_6H_5\text{-}CH_2)\text{-}O\text{-}H, \qquad (C_6H_5\text{-}CO)\text{-}H, \qquad (C_6H_5\text{-}CO)\text{-}O\text{-}H.$$
Benzoic Alcohol.   Oil of Bitter Almonds.   Benzoic Acid.

Benzoic alcohol may be prepared by treating oil of bitter almonds with an alcoholic solution of potassic hydrate.

$$2(C_6H_5\text{-}CO)\text{-}H + K\text{-}O\text{-}H =$$
$$(C_6H_5\text{-}CO)\text{-}O\text{-}K + (C_6H_5\text{-}CH_2)\text{-}O\text{-}H.$$

It may also be made from toluol (methyl-phenylic hydride) (434).

$$C_6H_5\text{-}CH_3 + Cl\text{-}Cl = (C_6H_5\text{-}CH_2)\text{-}Cl + HCl.$$
Toluol.   Toluic Chloride.

$$(C_6H_5\text{-}CH_2)\text{-}Cl + K\text{-}O\text{-}H = KCl + (C_6H_5\text{-}CH_2)\text{-}O\text{-}H.$$

Moreover, benzoic acid, when acted on by nascent hydrogen, is reduced in part, first to benzoic aldehyde (oil of bitter almonds), and then to benzoic alcohol.

The essential oil of cumin is a mixture of cymol, $C_{10}H_{14}$, and cuminic aldehyde, from which may be derived on the one side cumylic alcohol homologous with benzoic alcohol and on the other cuminic acid homologous with benzoic acid.

$$(C_9H_{11}\text{-}CH_2)\text{-}O\text{-}H, \qquad (C_9H_{11}\text{-}CO)\text{-}H, \qquad (C_9H_{11}\text{-}CO)\text{-}O\text{-}H.$$
Cumylic Alcohol.   Cuminic Aldehyde.   Cuminic Acid.

Sycocerylic alcohol $(C_{17}H_{27}\text{-}CH_2)\text{-}O\text{-}H$, obtained from a resin brought from New South Wales, is supposed to be another member of this series.

457. *Phenols.* — By comparing the symbols of the normal alcohols, of either class, as given above, or still better when

exhibited by one of the graphic methods, the student will see
that the peculiarity in their structure consists mainly in the circumstance that two atoms of hydrogen are attached to the
same carbon atom, to which the atom of hydroxyl is also united,
so that when these atoms of hydrogen are replaced by an atom
of oxygen, the radical oxatyl $H\text{-}O\text{-}CO\text{-}$ is formed in the molecule, and this, as has been shown, appears to be the acidifying
principle of all the organic acids.   Hence by a very simple replacement, which does not alter the molecular structure, the
alcohol changes into an acid.

Such now is the structure of benzoic alcohol, but such would
not be the condition if the Ho were united directly to one of
the carbon atoms, which form the nucleus of the radical
phenyl, and it can easily be seen that the resulting product,
$C_6H_5\text{-}O\text{-}H$, could not change into an acid, at least of the oxatyl
type, without disturbing the peculiar atomic grouping shown in
Fig. c (428).   Compounds thus constituted are called *Phenols*.

The compound $C_6H_5\text{-}O\text{-}H$ is a well-known commercial product, called carbolic acid.   The more appropriate name is
phenylic alcohol, since it is a secondary or pseudo-alcohol of the
phenyl series, differing from the true alcohols in that it does not
yield by oxidation a homologue of benzoic acid.   As we might
expect, however, the different hydrogen atoms of the radical
may be replaced by Cl, Br, or NO_2, and a great number of
substitution products may be thus obtained, of which the best
known is the so-called Picric Acid ($C_6H_2(NO_2)_3)\text{-}O\text{-}H$.

Phenylic alcohol is one of the products of the dry distillation
of coal, and it is procured for the arts, from the coal-tar of the
gas-works.   It may also be formed by distilling salicylic acid
with baryta or lime, or by the action of nitrous acid on aniline
(167).

$$H\text{-}O\text{-}(CO\text{-}C_6H_4)\text{-}O\text{-}H + CaO = C_6H_5\text{-}O\text{-}H + Ca\text{=}O_2\text{=}CO.$$
Salicylic Acid.   Phenylic Alcohol.

[506]

$$H_2C_6H_5\text{=}N + H\text{-}O\text{-}NO = C_6H_5\text{-}O\text{-}H + H_2O + N\text{-}N.$$
Aniline.   Nitrous Acid.

Phenylic alcohol smells like wood-tar creosote, and is an
equally powerful antiseptic agent.   Indeed, it constitutes the
greater part of the so-called coal-tar creosote.   There is sometimes associated with it a small quantity of an homologous com-

pound, which has been named cresylic alcohol, and this is the only other phenol which has as yet been obtained. It closely resembles the first, has the symbol $C_7H_7\text{-}O\text{-}H$, and is therefore isomeric with benzoic alcohol. The student should seek to exhibit by graphic symbols the difference in the structure of these two isomeric compounds, on which the wide differences in their properties and chemical relations depend, and thus show also why a normal alcohol isomeric with phenylic alcohol cannot be produced.

458. *Acids of the Phenyl Series.* — Benzoic acid, formerly exclusively obtained by sublimation from gum benzoin, is now more frequently procured from hippuric acid (168), which is found abundantly in the urine of herbivorous animals. When hippuric acid is boiled with hydrochloric acid, the radical benzoyl (C_7H_5O) in this amide changes place with H of $H\text{-}O\text{-}H$, and the products are glycocol and benzoic acid. Only two other acids of this series are known. The normal series probably includes

Benzoic Acid	$H\text{-}O\text{-}(CO\text{-}C_6H_5)$,
Tolnylic Acid	$H\text{-}O\text{-}(CO\text{-}C_7H_7)$ or $H\text{-}O\text{-}(CO\text{-}C_6H_4\text{-}CH_3)$,
Cuminic Acid	$H\text{-}O\text{-}(CO\text{-}C_9H_{11})$ or $H\text{-}O\text{-}(CO\text{-}C_6H_4\text{-}C_3H_7)$.

This class of compounds has been comparatively little studied, and future investigation will probably bring to light not only other members of the series, but also other series of related acids, differing from the normal compounds by peculiarities of structure or slight variations in composition. One such compound is already known, and this bears the same relation to benzoic acid that crotonic acid bears to acetic acid,

$$H\text{-}O\text{-}(CO\text{-}CH_3),$$
Acetic Acid.

$$H\text{-}O\text{-}(CO\text{-}CH\text{=}C_2H_4),$$
Crotonic Acid.

$$H\text{-}O\text{-}(CO\text{-}C_6H_5),$$
Benzoic Acid.

$$H\text{-}O\text{-}(CO\text{-}C_6H_3\text{=}C_2H_4) ;$$
Cinnamic Acid.

and when heated with potassic hydrate cinnamic acid breaks up into benzoic and acetic acids, thus : —

$$H\text{-}O\text{-}(CO\text{-}C_6H_3\text{=}C_2H_4) + 2K\text{-}O\text{-}H =$$
$$K\text{-}O\text{-}(CO\text{-}C_6H_5) + K\text{-}O\text{-}(CO\text{-}CH_3) + H\text{-}H. \text{ [507]}$$

Salicylic acid is another compound belonging to the phenyl group, and its relation to benzoic acid is indicated below. The volatile oil of meadow-sweet (*Spiræa ulmaria*) is supposed to be the aldehyde of this acid, and the oil of wintergreen, called also chequer-berry (*Gaultheria procumbens*), is methyl salicylic acid.

$$H\text{-}O\text{-}(CO\text{-}C_6H_5),$$
Benzoic Acid.

$$H\text{-}O\text{-}(CO\text{-}C_6H_4)\text{-}O\text{-}H,$$
Salicylic Acid.

$$H\text{-}(CO\text{-}C_6H_4)\text{-}O\text{-}H,$$
Oil of Meadow-sweet.

$$H\text{-}O\text{-}(CO\text{-}C_6H_4)\text{-}O\text{-}CH_3.$$
Oil of Wintergreen.

These compounds, however, being diatomic, more properly belong under the next head.

DIATOMIC COMPOUNDS.

459. *Glycols.* — The dyad radicals of the ethylene series may combine with two atoms of hydroxyl, and the diatomic hydrates thus formed constitute an interesting class of alcohols which are usually called glycols, and whose relations to the water-type have been already explained (41). The following reactions illustrate three of the methods by which these bodies may be produced : —

1. $$C_2H_4 + Br\text{-}Br = C_2H_4\text{=}Br_2.$$ [508]

2. $$C_2H_4\text{=}Br_2 + 2Ag\text{-}O\text{-}C_2H_3O =$$
$$2AgBr + C_2H_4\text{=}O_2\text{=}(C_2H_3O)_2.$$ [509]

3. $$C_2H_4\text{=}O_2\text{=}(C_2H_3O)_2 + 2K\text{-}O\text{-}H =$$
Diacetic Glycol.
$$2K\text{-}O\text{-}(C_2H_3O) + C_2H_4\text{=}O_2\text{=}H_2.$$ [510]
Ethyl Glycol.

1. $$C_2H_4 + H\text{-}O\text{-}Cl = C_2H_4\text{=}Ho,Cl.$$ [511]
Monochlorhydrine of Glycol.

2. $$C_2H_4\text{=}Ho,Cl + Ag\text{-}O\text{-}C_2H_3O =$$
$$AgCl + C_2H_4\text{=}O_2\text{=}(C_2H_3O),H.$$ [512]

3. $$C_2H_4\text{=}O_2\text{=}(C_2H_3O),H + K\text{-}O\text{-}H =$$
Mono-acetic Glycol.
$$K\text{-}O\text{-}C_2H_3O + C_2H_4\text{=}O_2\text{=}H_2.$$ [513]
Ethyl Glycol.

$$C_3H_5\text{=}Ho_2,Cl + H\text{-}H = HCl + C_3H_6\text{=}O_2\text{=}H_2.$$ [514]
Monochlorhydrine of Glycerine.   Propyl Glycol.

The normal glycols, like all normal alcohols, are easily oxi-

dized, and on account of their diatomic nature a reaction similar to [442] may be once repeated with each of these bodies.
Every such glycol thus yields two acids, whose relations may
be best indicated by writing the symbols as below : —

$H\text{-}O\text{-}(CH_2\text{-}CH_2)\text{-}O\text{-}H$,
Ethylic Glycol.

$H\text{-}O\text{-}(CO\text{-}CH_2)\text{-}O\text{-}H$,
Glycollic Acid.

$H\text{-}O\text{-}(CO\text{-}CO)\text{-}O\text{-}H$,
Oxalic Acid.

$H\text{-}O\text{-}(CH_2\text{-}CH_2\text{-}CH_2)\text{-}O\text{-}H$,
Propylic Glycol.

$H\text{-}O\text{-}(CO\text{-}CH_2\text{-}CH_2)\text{-}O\text{-}H$,
Paralactic Acid.

$H\text{-}O\text{-}(CO\text{-}CH_2\text{-}CO)\text{-}O\text{-}H$,
Malonic Acid.

$H\text{-}O\text{-}(CH_2\text{-}C_2H_4\text{-}CH_2)\text{-}O\text{-}H$,
Butylic Glycol.

$H\text{-}O\text{-}(CO\text{-}C_2H_4\text{-}CH_2)\text{-}O\text{-}H$,

$H\text{-}O\text{-}(CO\text{-}C_2H_4\text{-}CO)\text{-}O\text{-}H$.
Succinic Acid.

In these symbols those hydrogen atoms which are associated
with CO are strongly basic, and those which are associated
with CH_2, although also typical and replaceable under certain
conditions, cannot be displaced by the usual metathetical methods (21). In this we find the explanation of the fact stated
in (41), that the acids homologous with glycollic acid are only
monobasic, although diatomic and the acids homologous with
oxalic acid, both dibasic and diatomic. Of the glycols included
in the list given in the section just referred to only the first is
supposed to have the constitution exhibited above. It is probable that in the others the atoms are differently arranged.

The following-derivatives of ethylic glycol will further illustrate the chemical relations of this class of compounds : —

Cyanhydrine	$C_2H_4\text{=}Ho,CN$,
Bromhydrine	$C_2H_4\text{=}Ho,Br$,
Dibromhydrine (ethylene dibromide)	$C_2H_4\text{=}Br_2$,
Bromo-ethylic Glycol	$C_2H_4\text{=}(C_2H_5)\,O,Br$,
Sulphur Glycol	$C_2H_4\text{=}S_2\text{=}H_2$.

Compare also the products of [509], [511], and [512].

460. *Ethylenic Oxide or Ether*, which has already been
mentioned as isomeric with both vinylic alcohol and acetic

22

aldehyde, is another of the derivatives of ethylic glycol. It may be produced thus: —

$$C_2H_4\text{-}O_2\text{=}H_2 + HCl = C_2H_4\text{=}Ho,Cl + H_2O.$$

$$C_2H_4\text{=}Ho,Cl + K\text{-}O\text{-}H = \underset{\text{Ethylenic Oxide.}}{C_2H_4\text{=}O} + H_2O + KCl. \qquad [515]$$

The following reactions illustrate the remarkable relations of this compound: —

$$C_2H_4\text{=}O + H\text{-}H = C_2H_5\text{-}O\text{-}H. \qquad [516]$$

$$C_2H_4\text{=}O + O\text{=}O = H\text{-}O\text{-}(CO\text{-}CH_2)\text{-}O\text{-}H. \qquad [517]$$

$$C_2H_4\text{=}O + H\text{-}Cl = C_2H_4\text{=}Ho,Cl. \qquad [518]$$

$$C_2H_4\text{=}O + H_2O = C_2H_4\text{=}O_2\text{=}H_2. \qquad [519]$$

It precipitates many oxides from solutions of their salts.

$$MgCl_2 + 2C_2H_4\text{=}O + 2H_2O =$$
$$2C_2H_4\text{=}Ho,Cl + Mg\text{=}O_2\text{=}H_2. \quad [520]$$

By expressing these reactions in a graphic form the student will see that they are all possible without a disruption of the original molecule, and this accounts for the great difference between the behavior of ethylenic oxide and that of ethylic ether, which in other respects is similarly constituted.

461. *Condensed Glycols.* — The peculiar constitution of ethylenic oxide, just referred to, gives rise to a class of glycols in which the basic radical consists of two or more atoms of ethylene soldered together by atoms of oxygen (38). Thus, representing ethylene by $Et = C_2H_4$, we have,

Glycol $\qquad\qquad Et\text{=}O_2\text{=}H_2,$
Diethylenic Glycol $\quad(Et\text{-}O\text{-}Et)\text{=}O_2\text{=}H_2,$
Triethylenic Glycol $\quad(Et\text{-}O\text{-}Et\text{-}O\text{-}Et)\text{=}O_2\text{=}H_2,$
Tetrethylenic Glycol $(Et\text{-}O\text{-}Et\text{-}O\text{-}Et\text{-}O\text{-}Et)\text{=}O_2\text{=}H_2,$
Pentethylenic Glycol $(Et\text{-}O\text{-}Et\text{-}O\text{-}Et\text{-}O\text{-}Et\text{-}O\text{-}Et)\text{=}O_2\text{=}H_2,$
Hexethylenic Glycol $(Et\text{-}O\text{-}Et\text{-}O\text{-}Et\text{-}O\text{-}Et\text{-}O\text{-}Et\text{-}O\text{-}Et)\text{=}O_2\text{=}H_2.$

These bodies are formed by direct synthesis when glycol and ethylenic oxide are heated together for many days in sealed tubes, but they are more readily produced by the following reactions: —

$$C_2H_4\text{=}Br_2 + C_2H_4\text{=}Ho_2 = 2C_2H_4\text{=}Ho,Br, \qquad [521]$$

$$C_2H_4^=Ho,Br + C_2H_4^=Ho_2 = (C_2H_4\text{-}O\text{-}C_2H_4)^=Ho_2 + H\text{-}Br, \quad [522]$$

$$C_2H_4^=Ho,Br + (C_2H_4\text{-}O\text{-}C_2H_4)^=Ho_2 =$$
$$(C_2H_4\text{-}O\text{-}C_2H_4\text{-}O\text{-}C_2H_4)^=Ho_2 + HBr, \quad [523]$$

and so on.

The last reactions are also obtained by heating together the original factors in closed tubes. The several changes succeed each other, and thus more and more complex molecules are gradually built up. However great the condensation, these condensed molecules contain but two typical atoms of hydrogen, and when oxidized only four of the H atoms in the radical can be replaced with oxygen as in the normal glycol. At least this is true of diethylenic and triethylenic glycol, and with these alone the reactions have been studied. The symbols of the acids resulting from the oxidation in the two cases may be written,

$$(C_2H_4\text{-}O\text{-}C_2O_2)^=O_2^=H_2, \quad \text{and} \quad (C_2H_4\text{-}O\text{-}C_2H_4\text{-}O\text{-}C_2O_2)^=O_2^=H_2.$$

The compound $(C_2H_4\text{-}O\text{-}C_2H_4)^=O_2$ is also known, and these remarkable bodies derive a special interest from the fact that the study of the phenomena which they present has furnished the key to the explanation of the more complex phenomena of the same kind with which we are already familiar in the mineral kingdom.

462. *Monobasic Acids.* 1. *Lactic Family.* — This family of acids, which represents the first stage in the oxidation of the glycols, is at the present time especially interesting, because the phenomena of isomerism have been here studied with more success than in any other class of compounds of equal complexity. According to our view, the normal glycol is one which admits of two degrees of oxidation, as represented in (459). Such a glycol may be represented by the general symbol $Ho\text{-}(CH_2\text{-}(CH_2)_n\text{-}CH_2)\text{-}Ho$, where $(CH_2)_n$ stands for any olefine, and common glycol is the first term of the series, for which $n = o$. The glycols actually known, however, with the exception of the first, belong to a different type, represented by the symbol $Ho\text{-}(CH_2\text{-}CHR)\text{-}Ho$, in which R stands for a radical of the methyl series, and which is capable of variation, not only by changing this radical, but also, as in the normal series, by the addition of $(CH_2)_n$ between the two carbon atoms

of the original type. Moreover, it is evident that we might have still a third class of glycols corresponding to the general symbol $Ho\text{-}(CH_2\text{-}(CH_2)_n\text{-}C\mathfrak{R}_2)\text{-}Ho$.

From these three classes of glycols we should evidently obtain, at the first stage of oxidation, three classes of acids, thus :—

Normal.   Secondary.   Tertiary.

$$Ho\text{-}(CO\text{-}CH_2)\text{-}Ho, \quad Ho\text{-}(CO\text{-}CH\mathfrak{R})\text{-}Ho, \quad Ho\text{-}(CO\text{-}C\mathfrak{R}_2)\text{-}Ho \ ;$$

Normal Olefine.

$$Ho\text{-}(CO\text{-}(CH_2)_n\text{-}CH_2)\text{-}Ho,$$

Secondary Olefine.

$$Ho\text{-}(CO\text{-}(CH_2)_n\text{-}CH\mathfrak{R})\text{-}Ho,$$

Tertiary Olefine.

$$Ho\text{-}(CO\text{-}(CH_2)_n\text{-}C\mathfrak{R}_2)\text{-}Ho \ ;$$

and the term olefine may be appropriately used to distinguish the succeeding members of each series from the first. Moreover, it is equally evident that by replacing with univalent radicals the hydrogen of the non-basic hydroxyl we may obtain a whole group of acids corresponding·to each of the members of the above scheme. These last acids we shall call etheric, and we will next endeavor to show that the symbols which have been assigned to the known members of the lactic family of acids are legitimately deduced from observed facts.

463. *Normal Acids.* — Only three members of this series are known.

Glycollic Acid	$Ho\text{-}(CO\text{-}CH_2)\text{-}Ho,$
Paralactic Acid	$Ho\text{-}(CO\text{-}CH_2\text{-}CH_2)\text{-}Ho,$
Paraleucic Acid	$Ho\text{-}(CO\text{-}(CH_2)_4\text{-}CH_2)\text{-}Ho.$

The symbol of glycollic acid may be inferred from that of glycol, since the acid is a product of the direct oxidation of this diatomic alcohol. The symbol of paralactic acid may be referred back to that of ethylene, which we assume to be $(CH_2\text{-}CH_2)$, by means of the following reactions :—

1. $(CH_2\text{-}CH_2) + COCl_2 = Cl\text{-}(CO\text{-}CH_2\text{-}CH_2)\text{-}Cl.$

2. $Cl\text{-}(CO\text{-}CH_2\text{-}CH_2)\text{-}Cl + 3KHo =$ [524]

β Chloropropionylic Chloride.

$$Ko\text{-}(CO\text{-}CH_2\text{-}CH_2)\text{-}Ho + 2KCl + H_2O.$$

Potassic Paralactate.

So also

$$CN\text{-}(CH_2\text{-}CH_2)\text{-}Ho + KHo + H_2O =$$
$$\text{Cyanhydrine.}$$
$$Ko\text{-}(CO\text{-}CH_2\text{-}CH_2)\text{-}Ho + NH_3. \quad [525]$$
$$\text{Potassic Paralactate.}$$

The body called paraleucic acid was formed by reactions similar to [524], using amylene instead of ethylene, but it has not yet been completely investigated.

464. *Secondary Acids.* — This series includes the most important acids of the lactic family, and corresponds to the series of known glycols. For this reason its members are regarded by Frankland as the normal compounds. The following are here classed :—

Glycollic Acid	$Ho\text{-}(CO\text{-}CHH)\text{-}Ho,$
Lactic Acid	$Ho\text{-}(CO\text{-}CHMe)^1\text{-}Ho.$
Oxybutyric Acid	$Ho\text{-}(CO\text{-}CHEt)^1\text{-}Ho,$
Valerolactic Acid	$Ho\text{-}(CO\text{-}CHPr)^1\text{-}Ho,$
Leucic Acid	$Ho\text{-}(CO\text{-}CHBu)^1\text{-}Ho.$

Glycollic acid may be regarded as belonging to both the normal and secondary series. Under certain conditions it is formed in the oxidation of common alcohol.

$$2Ho\text{-}(CH_2\text{-}CH_2\text{-}H) + 3O\text{=}O =$$
$$\text{Alcohol.}$$
$$2Ho\text{-}(CO\text{-}CH_2)\text{-}Ho + 2H_2O. \quad [526]$$
$$\text{Glycollic Acid.}$$

The constitution of lactic acid is made evident by the following considerations. It has already been shown that the symbol of aldehyde must be $H\text{-}(CO\text{-}CH_3)$. When this is acted on by PCl_5 we obtain a compound isomeric with ethylene chloride by the reaction

$$H\text{-}(CO\text{-}CH_3) + PCl_5 = Cl_2\text{=}(CH\text{-}CH_3) + POCl_3. \quad [527]$$
$$\text{Aldehyde.} \qquad\qquad \text{Ethylidene Chloride.}$$

This product, however, differs from ethylene chloride both in its physical and chemical properties, and it must therefore be the chloride of a distinct radical, to which has been given the name of ethylidene. Moreover, the mode of its production (190) leaves no doubt in regard to its constitution, and then by

---

^{1} $Me = (CH_3)\text{-},$ $\quad Et = (C_2H_5)\text{-},$ $\quad Pr = (C_3H_7)\text{-},$ $\quad Bu = (C_4H_9)\text{-}.$

exclusion we fix the symbol of ethylene as well; for, as is evident, the atoms C_2H_4, to form a dyad radical, must be grouped in one or two ways, either

$$-(CH_2\text{-}CH_2)\text{-}, \qquad \text{or} \qquad =(CH\text{-}CH_3).$$
Ethylene.   Ethylidene.

Now, as the cyanhydrine of ethylene yields paralactic acid, so the cyanhydrine of ethylidene yields common lactic acid.

$$Ho, CN=(CH\text{-}Me) + K\text{-}Ho + H_2O =$$
Cyanhydrine of Ethylidene.
$$Ko\text{-}(CO\text{-}CHMe)\text{-}Ho + NH_3. \quad [528]$$
Salt of Lactic Acid.

We can now interpret the following reaction by which lactic acid is obtained from propionic acid : —

1. $Ho\text{-}(CO\text{-}CH_2\text{-}CH_3) + Cl\text{-}Cl =$
Propionic Acid.
$$Ho\text{-}(CO\text{-}CHCl\text{-}CH_3) + HCl.$$
Chloropropionic Acid.
[529]

2. $Ho\text{-}(CO\text{-}CHCl\text{-}Me) + 2 KHo =$
$$Ko\text{-}(CO\text{-}CHMe)\text{-}Ho + KCl + H_2O.$$

We are thus able to show to what part of the radical of propionic acid the hydrogen atom replaced by chlorine belonged. Moreover, it is evident that the acid which would be obtained by the action of water on β chloropropionylic chloride (463) must differ from that formed as above, and we can understand the reason why. Lastly, since lactic acid has also been formed by the oxidation of propylic glycol, we conclude that the constitution of this body must be $Ho\text{-}(CH_2\text{-}CHMe)\text{-}Ho$, as intimated in (462).

For the methods by which the constitution of the other members of this series has been established we must refer the student to more extended works. The examples given are sufficient to illustrate the general course of the reasoning.

465. *Etheric Secondary Acids.* — No secondary olefine acids are known, but by simple metathetical methods we can easily replace the hydrogen of the non-basic hydroxyl in the compounds of this series with various radicals, and the following bodies will serve as examples of the products thus obtained : —

Methyl-glycollic Acid	$Ho\text{-}(CO\text{-}CH_2)\text{-}Meo,$
Ethyl-lactic Acid	$Ho\text{-}(CO\text{-}CHMe)\text{-}Eto,$
Aceto-lactic Acid	$Ho\text{-}(CO\text{-}CHMe)\text{-}Aco.$[1]

[1] $Ac = \text{-}(CO\text{-}CH_3).$

466. *Tertiary Acids.* — The following are known : —

Dimethoxalic Acid　　　　Ho-$(CO$-$CMe_2)$-Ho,
Ethomethoxalic Acid　　　Ho-$(CO$-$CMeEt)$-Ho,
Diethoxalic Acid　　　　　Ho-$(CO$-$CEt_2)$-Ho.

Our knowledge of the constitution of these acids is based on the beautiful synthetical method (454) by which they were produced by Professor Frankland, who has also obtained etheric acids belonging to this division, but no corresponding olefines have been discovered.

467. *Isomerism in the Lactic Family.* — The number of possible isomeric combinations in this family of acids is evidently infinite. The following are two of the known examples : —

Ho-$(CO$-CH_2-$CH_2)$-Ho,
　Paralactic Acid.

Ho-$(CO$-$CHEt)$-Ho,
　Oxybutyric Acid.

Ho-$(CO$-$CHMe)$-Ho,
　Lactic Acid.

Ho-$(CO$-$CMe_2)$-Ho,
　Dimethoxalic Acid.

Ho-$(CO$-$CH_2)$-Meo,
　Methyl-glycollic Acid.

Ho-$(CO$-$CH_2)$-Eto.
　Ethyl-glycollic Acid.

468. *Lactic Acid* is by far the most important member of the family to which it gives name, and one of the most common of the organic acids. It is the acid of sour milk and sauerkraut, and is a general product of putrefactive fermentation. The acid contained in the gastric juice and many other animal fluids is said to be paralactic acid. The salts of lactic acid are very numerous, and those of the bivalent metals bind two atoms of the acid radicals. By the action of HI lactic acid may be converted into propionic acid.

Ho-$(CO$-CH-$Me)$-Ho + $2HI$ =
　Lactic Acid.　　　Ho-$(CO$-CH_2-$Me)$ + H_2O + I-I. [530]
　　　　　　　　　Propionic Acid.

469. *Monobasic Acids.* 2. *Pyruvic Series.* — Two members only are well known : —

Glyoxalic Acid　　　　Ho-$(CO$-$CO)$-H,
Pyruvic Acid　　　　　Ho-$(CO$-$CO)$-Me.

The first may be regarded as the semi-aldehyde of oxalic acid, a compound called glyoxal being the full aldehyde, thus : —

Ho-$(CO$-$CO)$-Ho,　　　Ho-$(CO$-$CO)$-H,　　　H-$(CO$-$CO)$-H.
　Oxalic Acid.　　　　　　Glyoxalic Acid.　　　　　Glyoxal.

Both glyoxalic acid and glyoxal are formed when common alcohol is oxidized by nitric acid.

$$Ho\text{-}(CH_2\text{-}CH_3) + O_3 = H\text{-}(CO\text{-}CO)\text{-}H + 2H_2O.$$
$$\phantom{Ho\text{-}(}\underset{\text{Alcohol.}}{\phantom{CH_2\text{-}CH_3}}\underset{\text{Glyoxal.}}{\phantom{H\text{-}(CO\text{-}CO)\text{-}H}}$$

$$H\text{-}(CO\text{-}CO)\text{-}H + O = Ho\text{-}(CO\text{-}CO)\text{-}H.$$
$$\underset{\text{Glyoxal.}}{\phantom{H\text{-}(CO\text{-}CO)\text{-}H}}\underset{\text{Glyoxalic Acid.}}{\phantom{Ho\text{-}(CO\text{-}CO)\text{-}H}}$$

[531]

Glyoxalic acid reduces argentic oxide like an aldehyde, and passes into oxalic acid.

$$Ho\text{-}(CO\text{-}CO)\text{-}H + O = Ho\text{-}(CO\text{-}CO)\text{-}Ho. \quad [532]$$
$$\underset{\text{Glyoxalic Acid.}}{\phantom{Ho\text{-}(CO\text{-}CO)\text{-}H}}\underset{\text{Oxalic Acid.}}{\phantom{Ho\text{-}(CO\text{-}CO)\text{-}Ho.}}$$

Compare (479).

The relations of these compounds to the acids of the lactic family are equally close.

$$Ho\text{-}(CO\text{-}CO)\text{-}H + H\text{-}H = Ho\text{-}(CO\text{-}CH_2)\text{-}Ho.$$
$$\underset{\text{Glyoxalic Acid.}}{\phantom{Ho\text{-}(CO\text{-}CO)\text{-}H}}\phantom{ + H\text{-}H = }\underset{\text{Glycollic Acid.}}{\phantom{Ho\text{-}(CO\text{-}CH_2)\text{-}Ho.}}$$

[533]

$$Ho\text{-}(CO\text{-}CO)\text{-}Me + H\text{-}H = Ho\text{-}(CO\text{-}CHMe)\text{-}Ho.$$
$$\underset{\text{Pyruvic Acid.}}{\phantom{Ho\text{-}(CO\text{-}CO)\text{-}Me}}\phantom{ + H\text{-}H = }\underset{\text{Lactic Acid.}}{\phantom{Ho\text{-}(CO\text{-}CHMe)\text{-}Ho.}}$$

470. *Dibasic Acids.* 1. *Succinic Series.* — Of this important series of acids, which represents the second stage in the oxidation of the normal glycols, the following members are known : —

Oxalic Acid	$Ho\text{-}(CO\text{-}CO)\text{-}Ho,$
Malonic Acid	$Ho\text{-}(CO\text{-}CH_2\text{-}CO)\text{-}Ho,$
Succinic Acid	$Ho\text{-}(CO\text{-}(CH_2)_2\text{-}CO)\text{-}Ho,$
Pyrotartaric Acid	$Ho\text{-}(CO\text{-}(CH_2)_3\text{-}CO)\text{-}Ho,$
Adipic Acid	$Ho\text{-}(CO\text{-}(CH_2)_4\text{-}CO)\text{-}Ho,$
Pimelic Acid	$Ho\text{-}(CO\text{-}(CH_2)_5\text{-}CO)\text{-}Ho,$
Suberic Acid	$Ho\text{-}(CO\text{-}(CH_2)_6\text{-}CO)\text{-}Ho,$
Anchoic Acid	$Ho\text{-}(CO\text{-}(CH_2)_7\text{-}CO)\text{-}Ho,$
Sebacic Acid	$Ho\text{-}(CO\text{-}(CH_2)_8\text{-}CO)\text{-}Ho,$
Roccellic Acid	$Ho\text{-}(CO\text{-}(CH_2)_{15}\text{-}CO)\text{-}Ho.$

With the exception of the first, each compound in the series admits of one or more modifications, the possible isomeric forms rapidly increasing with the number of carbon atoms in the olefine radical ; but the exact constitution of these bodies has been definitely fixed in only a few cases. The relation of the normal acids to the olefine radicals, which they are assumed to contain, is indicated by the following general synthetical method, by which they may be produced: —

$$CN\text{-}(CH_2)_n\text{-}CN + 2K\text{-}Ho + 2H_2O =$$

Cyanide of Radical.

$$Ko\text{-}(CO\text{-}(CH_2)_n\text{-}CO)\text{-}Ko + 2NH_3. \quad [534]$$

Potassic Salt of Dibasic Acid.

When, on the other hand, these acids are acted on by agents, which determine the elimination of CO_2 from their molecules, they are converted first into monobasic acids of the acetic series, and then into hydrides of the olefine radicals. In some cases the action of heat alone is sufficient to produce the result, but in most cases the body must be heated with some caustic alkali or earth. It will readily be seen that by eliminating first one and then a second molecule of CO_2 from the dibasic acid, the two compounds on the same line would be successively formed. The name is omitted when it is not known that the product has been obtained by the reaction just indicated.

$Ho\text{-}(CO\text{-}CO)\text{-}Ho,$ Oxalic Acid.	$Ho\text{-}(CO\text{-}H),$ Formic Acid.	$H\text{-}H,$ Hydrogen Gas.
$Ho\text{-}(CO\text{-}CH_2\text{-}CO)\text{-}Ho,$ Malonic Acid.	$Ho\text{-}(CO\text{-}CH_3),$ Acetic Acid.	$CH_4,$ Marsh Gas.
$Ho\text{-}(CO\text{-}C_2H_4\text{-}CO)\text{-}Ho,$ Succinic Acid.	$Ho\text{-}(CO\text{-}C_2H_5),$ Propionic Acid.	$C_2H_6,$
$Ho\text{-}(CO\text{-}C_6H_{12}\text{-}CO)\text{-}Ho,$ Suberic Acid.	$Ho\text{-}(CO\text{-}C_6H_{13}),$	C_8H_{14} Hexylene Hydride.
$Ho\text{-}(CO\text{-}C_8H_{16}\text{-}CO)\text{-}Ho,$ Sebacic Acid.	$Ho\text{-}(CO\text{-}C_8H_{17}),$	C_8H_{18} Octylene Hydride.

It will thus be seen how closely the acids of the succinic series are related to those of the acetic series, and the same point is still further illustrated by the following beautiful series of reactions by which acetic acid has been converted into malonic acid and the order of the changes described above reversed.

$$Ho\text{-}(CO\text{-}CH_3) + Cl\text{-}Cl = Ho\text{-}(CO\text{-}CH_2Cl) + HCl.$$

$$Ho\text{-}(CO\text{-}CH_2Cl) + KCy = KCl + Ho\text{-}(CO\text{-}CH_2Cy). \quad [535]$$

$$Ho\text{-}(CO\text{-}CH_2CN) + 2KHo = Ko\text{-}(CO\text{-}CH_2\text{-}CO)\text{-}Ko + NH_3.$$

In the same way succinic acid has been obtained from propionic acid, and formic acid may be changed into oxalic acid still more readily.

$$2Ho\text{-}(CO\text{-}H) + 2K\text{-}O\text{-}H =$$
$$Ko\text{-}(CO\text{-}CO)\text{-}Ko + 2H_2O + H\text{-}H.$$

471. *Succinic Acid* was originally prepared by distilling amber, and takes its name from the Latin name (*succinium*) of this fossil resin; but it is now generally obtained by the fermentation of crude calcic malate. It occurs ready formed in amber, in certain lignites, in some varieties of turpentine, and in several plants. This acid is a frequent product of the oxidation of organic substances, and is always formed together with other products when the fat acids are oxidized by nitric acid. Succinic acid itself singularly resists the action even of powerful oxidizing agents. It forms, like oxalic acid, three classes of salts, neutral acid, and super acid. When distilled it breaks up into water and an anhydride.

$$Ho\text{-}(CO\text{-}C_2H_4\text{-}CO)\text{-}Ho = O\text{=}((CO)_2\text{=}C_2H_4) + H_2O. \quad [536]$$

Under the influence of nascent oxygen produced by electrolysis it yields ethylene carbonic anhydride and water.

$$Ho\text{-}(CO\text{-}C_2H_4\text{-}CO)\text{-}Ho + O = C_2H_4 + 2CO_2 + H_2O. \quad [537]$$

472. *Dibasic Acids.* 2. *Fumaric Series.* — Two sets of isomeric compounds are known corresponding to two terms of a series of acids, which stand in the same relation to the succinic series that the acrylic bears to the acetic. Thus we have

Fumaric Maleic or Isomaleic Acids $Ho\text{-}(CO\text{-}C_2H_2\text{-}CO)\text{-}Ho$,
Itaconic Citraconic or Mesaconic Acids $Ho\text{-}(CO\text{-}C_3H_4\text{-}CO)\text{-}Ho$.

The first term admits of only four modifications, and the choice of symbols for fumaric and maleic acids is limited by the fact that when acted on by nascent hydrogen they both give succinic acid. Furthermore, both acids combine directly with two atoms of bromine, and though the immediate products of this union are different, yet both bromo and isobromo-succinic acids, as they are called, produce the same succinic acid when the bromine is replaced by hydrogen.

The second term may be varied in no less than eleven different ways, and the three formulæ belonging to the three known acids cannot at present be recognized.

These bodies, however, are related to pyrotartaric acid, just as the first set are to succinic acid. All three yield this product when acted on by nascent hydrogen, and all three combine with bromine, forming brominated acids which hydrogen converts into the same pyrotartaric acid as before.

Fumaric and Maleic acids are both formed during the distillation of malic acid, from which they differ only by one molecule of water.

$$Ho\text{-}(CO\text{-}CH_2\text{-}CHHo\text{-}CO)\text{-}Ho =$$
Malic Acid.

$$Ho\text{-}(CO\text{-}C_2H_2\text{-}CO)\text{-}Ho + H_2O. \quad [538]$$
Fumaric or Maleic Acid.

Malic acid is the acid principle of apples, and of many other fruits. Fumaric acid is also found in certain plants, but maleic acid has not been met with ready formed in nature. Itaconic and citraconic acids are products of the distillation of citric acid. The third terms of both groups are products of special processes which cannot be traced.

TRIATOMIC COMPOUNDS.

473. *Triatomic Alcohols, or Glycerines.* — Common glycerine is the hydrate of the triad radical (C_3H_5)≡ and has all the characteristics of a triatomic alcohol. The natural fats are mixtures of various salts of the same radicals associated with acids of the acetic or oleic groups. When boiled with alkalies these salts are decomposed, a hydrate of the radical (glycerine) is formed, and alkaline salts of the fat acids result. The last are familiarly known as soaps, and such reactions are termed *saponification.* We can also saponify the fats with plumbic oxide, and then the lead soap (or " plaster ") being insoluble in water, while the glycerine is soluble, the products are easily separated. The fats may even be saponified by water alone, if acting at a high temperature, and glycerine is produced in the arts in large quantities by distilling the fats in a current of superheated steam. The products of the decomposition pass over together ; but, in consequence of their insolubility and low specific gravity, the fat acids separate from the glycerine in the

condenser. The reaction in one case is represented by the following equation : —

$$(C_3H_5)^{\equiv}O_3^{\equiv}(C_{18}H_{35}O)_3 + 3H_2O =$$

Stearine.

$$(C_3H_5)^{\equiv}O_3^{\equiv}H_3 + H_3^{\equiv}O_3^{\equiv}(C_{18}H_{35}O)_3. \quad [538]$$

Glycerine.   Stearic Acid.

Glycerine, like all the true alcohols, readily exchanges H_2 of its radical for O under the influence of oxidizing agents, and the acid product is called glyceric acid. Theory would lead us to expect two stages in this process, and two corresponding acids, thus : —

$$(CH\text{-}CH_2\text{-}CH_2)^{\equiv}O_3^{\equiv}H_3,$$

Glycerine.

$$(CH\text{-}CH_2\text{-}CO)^{\equiv}O_3^{\equiv}\bar{H}_2,\overset{+}{H},$$

Glyceric Acid.

$$(CO\text{-}CH\text{-}CO)^{\equiv}O_3^{\equiv}\bar{H},\overset{+}{H}_2,$$

Tartronic Acid.

the first being triatomic and monobasic and the second triatomic and dibasic. The second acid has not as yet been produced by the direct oxidation of glycerine, but there can be little doubt that tartronic acid, which is formed by the spontaneous decomposition of nitro-tartaric acid, is the acid in question.

When acted on by HI, glycerine is converted into isopropylic iodide.

$$(CH_2\text{-}CH_2\text{-}CH)^{\equiv}Ho_3 + 5HI =$$

$$(CH_3)_2^{\equiv}(CH)\text{-}I + 3H_2O + 2I\text{-}I. \quad [539]$$

The relations of glycerine to allylic alcohol and propylic glycol are illustrated by [491 *et seq.*] and [514].

Under the action of HCl glycerine exchanges Ho for Cl in two successive stages, and by means of PCl_5 all three atoms of Ho may be thus replaced.

$$(C_3H_5)^{\equiv}Ho_3, \quad (C_3H_5)^{\equiv}Ho_2, Cl, \quad (C_3H_5)^{\equiv}Ho, Cl_2, \quad (C_3H_5)^{\equiv}Cl_3.$$

Glycerine.   Monochlorhydrine.   Dichlorhydrine.   Trichlorhydrine.

The compound $(C_3H_5)^{\equiv}Br_3$ may be formed by a similar reaction, and by acting on this first with argentic acetate and then saponifying the "acetine" thus produced, glycerine may be regenerated. When acted on by a mixture of nitric and sulphuric acid glycerine yields a highly explosive compound, nitroglycerine, which may be regarded as a nitrate of glyceryl, or $(C_3H_5)^{\equiv}O_3^{\equiv}(NO_2)_3$ (31).

Theory would lead us to expect anhydrides of glycerine. The first anhydride (called *Glycide*) would have the symbol $(C_3H_5)^{\equiv} O,Ho$, and although this body itself is not known, several of what may be regarded as its derivatives have been obtained.

$$(C_3H_5)^{\equiv} O,Ho, \quad (C_3H_5)^{\equiv} O,Cl, \quad (C_3H_5)^{\equiv} O,I, \quad (C_3H_5)^{\equiv} Ho,Cl,Br.$$

By reactions similar to [521 *et seq.*], condensed glycerines have been formed. Thus we have

$$(C_3H_5\text{-}O\text{-}C_3H_5)^{\equiv} O_4^{\equiv} H_4, \qquad (C_3H_5\text{-}O\text{-}C_3H_5\text{-}O\text{-}C_3H_5)^{\equiv} O_5^{\equiv} H_5,$$
$$\text{Diglyceric Alcohol.} \qquad\qquad \text{Triglyceric Alcohol.}$$

which are evidently alcohols of higher atomicity than glycerine. Like similar polybasic compounds, they may be regarded as derived from a group of two or three molecules of glycerine by the elimination of a sufficient number of atoms of water to furnish the oxygen required to bind together the basic radicals (151). Continuing this elimination still further we should obtain a series of anhydrides, one of which is known, viz. $(C_3H_5^{\equiv} O_2^{\equiv} C_3H_5)^{\equiv} O_2^{\equiv} H_2$, and also a corresponding chlorhydrine $(C_3H_5^{\equiv} O_2^{\equiv} C_3H_5)^{\equiv} Ho,I$.

The following reactions illustrate the formation of some of the above compounds : —

$$(C_3H_5)^{\equiv} Ho,Cl_2 + K\text{-}O\text{-}H = C_3H_5^{\equiv} O,Cl + H_2O + KCl.$$
$$(C_3H_5)^{\equiv} O,Cl + HBr = (C_3H_5)^{\equiv} Ho,Br,Cl. \qquad [541]$$
$$(C_3H_5)^{\equiv} O,Cl + KI = (C_3H_5)^{\equiv} O,I + KCl.$$

474. *Ethers of Glycerine.* — By the action of $Na\text{-}O\text{-}C_2H_5$ upon mono-, di-, and tri-chlorhydrine, we can replace either one, two, or all three of the atoms of typical hydrogen in glycerine with ethyl. The products have been called ethylines.

$$(C_3H_5)^{\equiv} O_3^{\equiv} (C_2H_5),H_2, \quad (C_3H_5)^{\equiv} O_3^{\equiv} (C_2H_5)_2,H, \quad (C_3H_5)^{\equiv} O_3^{\equiv} (C_2H_5)_3$$
$$\text{Ethyline.} \qquad\qquad \text{Diethyline.} \qquad\qquad \text{Triethyline.}$$

By heating glycerine with acetic acid the typical atoms of hydrogen may be replaced by the radical acetyl in the same three proportions : —

$$(C_3H_5)^{\equiv} O_3^{\equiv} (C_2H_3O),H_2,$$
$$\text{Mono-acetine.}$$
$$(C_3H_5)^{\equiv} O_3^{\equiv} (C_2H_3O)_2,H,$$
$$\text{Diacetine.}$$
$$(C_3H_5)^{\equiv} O_3^{\equiv} (C_2H_3O)_3.$$
$$\text{Triacetine.}$$

Using in a similar way acids higher in the series, bodies similar to the fats may be produced. The natural oils and fats are mixtures of such salts, chiefly those of palmitic stearic and oleic acids. The solid fats consist chiefly of stearines and palmitines, and the liquid fats of oleines. The so-called drying oils, which when exposed to the air absorb oxygen and change to a dry resinous mass, are for the most part "glycerides" of acids not belonging to the acetic series, although closely related to it. All glycerides, when heated in the air, are decomposed and yield among other products acrolein whose penetrating odor is highly characteristic. This volatile body is formed abundantly when glycerine is heated with substances having a strong attraction for water, such as phosphoric anhydride, sulphuric acid, or still better acid potassic sulphate.

$$(C_3H_5)^{\equiv}O_3^{\equiv}H_3 = 2H_2O + (C_2H_3 \text{-} CO)\text{-}H. \qquad [542]$$

Propylic alcohol, propylic glycol, and glycerine are all closely related compounds, and may be regarded as derived from the same hydrocarbon,

$$C_3H_7\text{-}Ho = C_3H_8O, \quad C_3H_6^{\equiv}Ho_2 = C_3H_8O_2, \quad C_3H_5^{\equiv}Ho_3 = C_3H_8O_3,$$

and hence common glycerine is distinguished as propylic glycerine. Amylic glycerine, the only other compound of the series which has been produced, has not been thoroughly investigated.

475. *Tribasic Acid.* — A triatomic acid of this class has been obtained from glycerine by the following reaction : —

$$C_3H_5^{\equiv}Br_3 + 3KCy = 3KBr + C_3H_5^{\equiv}Cy_3.$$

$$[543]$$

$$\underset{\text{Glyceryl Cyanide.}}{C_3H_5^{\equiv}(CN)_3} + 3KHo + 3H_2O = \underset{\text{Potassic Tricarballylate.}}{C_3H_5^{\equiv}(CO\text{-}Ko)_3} + 3NH_3.$$

The tricarballylic acid may be regarded as the third stage of oxidation from an unknown hexyl glycerine, and aconitic acid, found in the roots and leaves of monkshood, is the corresponding acryloid compound.

Acetoid.	Acryloid.
$Ho\text{-}CO\text{-}C_3H_7,$	$Ho\text{-}CO\text{-}C_3H_5,$
Butyric Acid.	Crotonic Acid.
$(Ho\text{-}CO)_3^{\equiv}C_3H_5,$	$(Ho\text{-}CO)_3^{\equiv}C_3H_3.$
Tricarballylic Acid.	Aconitic Acid.

Aconitic acid may be obtained by cautiously heating citric acid, but at the temperature of 160° it loses CO_2 and is converted into itaconic acid, already mentioned among the diatomic compounds.

$$(Ho\text{-}CO)_3\text{=}C_3H_3 - CO_2 = (Ho\text{-}CO)_2\text{=}C_3H_4. \quad [544]$$
$$\text{\small Aconitic Acid.} \qquad\qquad \text{\small Itaconic Acid.}$$

Citric acid, the well-known acid principle of the lemon, but which is also found in many other fruits, although only tribasic, is tetratomic and therefore belongs to the next division. It differs from aconitic acid by only a single molecule of water,

$$(Ho\text{-}CO)_3\text{=}C_3H_4\text{-}Ho - H_2O = (Ho\text{-}CO)_3\text{=}C_3H_3, \quad [545]$$
$$\text{\small Citric Acid.} \qquad\qquad\qquad \text{\small Aconitic Acid.}$$

and hence the transformations which it undergoes when heated (472).

TETRATOMIC COMPOUNDS.

476. *Tetratomic Alcohol.* — Erythrite, a white crystalline material extracted from various lichens, is regarded as an alcohol of this class. It combines with the fat acids, forming ethers, and it contains, as the symbol given below indicates, four atoms of typical hydrogen. The following reaction exhibits its constitution, and the symbols which follow show its relations to butylic alcohol.

$$C_4H_6\text{≡}Ho_4 + 7HI = C_4H_8\text{=}H.I + 4H_2O + 3I\text{-}I. \quad [546]$$
$$\text{\small Erythrite.} \qquad\qquad \text{\small Butylene Iodo-hydride.}$$

$$C_4H_{10}, \qquad C_4H_{10}O, \qquad C_4H_{10}O_2, \qquad C_4H_{10}O_3, \qquad C_4H_{10}O_4.$$
$$\text{\small Butylic Hydride.} \;\; \text{\small Butylic Alcohol.} \;\; \text{\small Butylic Glycol.} \;\; \text{\small Unknown Glycerine.} \;\; \text{\small Erythrite.}$$

Theory would lead us to expect three acids from the oxidation of erythrite, but of these only one is known. The second derivative is tartaric acid, whose tetratomic and dibasic character, already illustrated (209), is thus explained: —

$$C_4H_6\text{≡}O_4\text{≡}\overline{H}_4, \quad C_4H_4O\text{≡}O_4\text{≡}\overline{H}_3,\overset{+}{H}, \quad C_4H_2O_2\text{≡}O_4\text{≡}\overline{H}_2,\overset{+}{H}_2, \quad C_4O_3\text{≡}O_4\text{≡}\overline{H},\overset{+}{H}_3.$$
$$\text{\small Erythrite.} \qquad\quad \text{\small Unknown.} \qquad\qquad \text{\small Tartaric Acid.} \qquad\qquad \text{\small Unknown.}$$

Citric acid, $C_6H_4O_3\text{≡}O_4\text{≡}\overline{H},\overset{+}{H}_3$, is a homologue of the unknown third derivative, and may be regarded as derived in the same way from an unknown alcohol of this series.

Tartaric acid is closely allied both to malic and succiuic acids. Malic acid is a homologue of tartaronic acid, and both have already been mentioned. As the following symbols show, they differ, each from the next in order, by a single atom of oxygen.

$$C_4H_6O_4, \qquad\qquad C_4H_6O_5, \qquad\qquad C_4H_6O_6,$$
$$\text{or} \qquad\qquad \text{or} \qquad\qquad \text{or}$$
$$C_4H_4O_2\text{=}O_2\text{=}\overset{+}{H}_2, \qquad C_4H_3O_2\text{=}O_3\text{=}\overset{-}{H},\overset{+}{H}_2, \qquad C_4H_2O_2\text{=}O_4\text{=}\overset{-}{H}_2,\overset{+}{H}_2.$$
$$\text{Succinic Acid.} \qquad\qquad \text{Malic Acid.} \qquad\qquad \text{Tartaric Acid.}$$

When tartaric acid is heated with HI it is reduced first to malic acid, and then to succinic acid, and on the other hand by treating bromo- and dibromo- succinic acids with water and argentic oxide the reverse change may be effected. The remarkable isomeric modifications of tartaric acids have already been noticed (70), (85).

HEXATOMIC COMPOUNDS.

477. *Mannite.* — No well-defined pentatomic compounds are known, but several hexatomic compounds have been distinguished, and it is probable that many of saccharine bodies belong to this class. By extracting common manna (the exudation from several species of ash) with boiling alcohol we easily obtain a highly crystalline white solid, slightly sweet to the taste, which is called *mannite*. This substance is a hexatomic alcohol, and its composition is represented by the symbol $C_6H_8\text{≡}O_6\text{≡}H_6$. Its constitution is indicated by the following circumstances: 1. When treated with a mixture of nitric and sulphuric acids it yields a product similar to nitro-glycerine $C_6H_8\text{≡}O_6\text{≡}(NO_2)_6$. 2. It forms numerous compounds with the fat acids, in which, as before, six atoms of hydrogen are replaced by the acid radical; for example, the symbol of the compound with stearic acid is $C_6H_8\text{≡}O_6\text{≡}(C_{18}H_{35}O)_6$. 3. It is acted on by HI in a similar manner to erythrite and glycerine.

$$C_6H_8\text{≡}Ho_6 + 11HI = C_6H_{12}\text{=}HI^1 + 6H_2O + 5I\text{-}I. \quad [547]$$

4. By means of oxidizing agents mannite may be converted into two acids, — mannitic acid, $H_6\text{≡}O_6\text{≡}C_6H_6O$, and saccharic acid, $H_6\text{≡}O_6\text{≡}C_6H_4O_2$, — which bear the same relation to this hexatomic alcohol that glyceric and tartaronic acids bear to glycerine.

---

1 The products obtained in [539], [546], and [547], although isomeric with

478. *Saccharine and Amylaceous Bodies.* — Woody fibre, or cellulose, starch, gum, and sugar, together with water, constitute the great mass of all vegetable organism, and are the materials on which the animal chiefly subsists. But although these bodies play such an important part both in vegetable and animal physiology, we have but little knowledge of their chemical constitution beyond their empirical formulæ. They have been divided into three classes, — 1st. The Amyloses, including woody fibre, starch, and gum, all of which are materials incapable of crystallization, and for the most part organized. 2d. Sucroses, including cane sugar, sugar of milk, and the sugars from different varieties of manna, which have a crystalline structure, but are not susceptible of direct fermentation. 3d. Glucoses, including grape sugar and fruit sugar, which, under the influence of yeast, break up into alcohol and carbonic anhydride.

These bodies contain hydrogen and oxygen in the proportions to form water, and therefore have been called the hydrates of carbon ; but there is no reason for believing that the atoms are grouped as this name would indicate. The composition of the bodies of each class is essentially the same, and may be represented by the following symbols : —

Amyloses, $C_6H_{10}O_5$; Sucroses, $C_{12}H_{22}O_{11}$; Glucoses, $C_6H_{12}O_6$.

It is probable, however, that some of them ought to be represented by multiples of these formulæ, and several of them contain in addition one or more molecules of water of crystallization.

The glucoses have evidently the simplest molecular structure of this class of bodies. They consist for the most part of two isomeric substances which are most readily distinguished by the action which they exert when in solution on the plane of polarization of a ray of light. One turns the plane to the right and the other to the left (85), and hence they have been called

---

the iodides of the alcohol radicals, are not identical with them. If treated with Ag_2O and H_2O, they are converted into pseudo-alcohols similar to iso-propylic alcohol, and their symbols may be written on either of the two types represented in the reactions just referred to. Thus we may write

$$C_6H_{12}=HI, \quad \text{or} \quad (C_2H_5),(C_3H_7)=(CH)\text{-}I.$$

Hexylene Iodo-hydride.   Iso-hexylic Iodide.

Dextrose and Levulose. They are found mixed together in honey, in the juices of acid fruits, and in the uncrystallizable sirups, called molasses, formed in the extraction of sugar, and they may readily be produced artificially by the action of dilute acids and certain ferments on the different varieties of starch and sugar. When common starch is heated with dilute sulphuric acid, it changes into dextrose ; but a variety of starch extracted from the dahlia-root changes under the same conditions into levulose. Cane-sugar under similar influence forms a mixture of dextrose and levulose.

$$C_{12}H_{22}O_{11} + H_2O = C_6H_{12}O_6 + C_6H_{12}O_6. \quad [548]$$

Sucrose.   Dextrose.   Levulose.

The acid acts merely by its presence, and remains unchanged during the process. Nitric acid oxidizes glucose to saccharic or oxalic acids ; and under the influence of nascent hydrogen levulose changes to mannite. We may, therefore, regard it as the aldehyde of this hexatomic alcohol.

$C_6H_{14}O_6$, $C_6H_{12}O_6$, $C_6H_{12}O_7$, $C_6H_{10}O_8$.

Mannite.   Levulose.   Mannitic Acid.   Saccharic Acid.

By the action of nitric acid on milk, sugar, or gum-arabic, an acid isomeric with saccharic acid called mucic acid is formed, and by the gentle action of nitric acid on saccharic acid tartaric acid may be produced.

All the amylaceous and saccharine bodies form more or less stable compounds with strong bases, and most of them when treated with a mixture of nitric and sulphuric acids yield products similar to nitro-glycerine, of which gun-cotton (31) is the best known.

479. *Glucosides.* — Under the prolonged influence of heat, glucose has been united with acetic, butyric, stearic, and benzoic acids, and a class of compounds obtained similar to the fats. The compound formed with acetic acid is represented by the symbol ($C_6H_4O_5$)$\equiv$(C_2H_3O)$_6$. These glucosides are interesting because they are probably allied to a class of substances found in many plants, which under the influence of ferments yield glucose, together with other bodies. The most important are : —

1. Amygdaline, found in bitter almonds, together with an

albuminous substance called synaptase, which when the almond meats are bruised determines the following reaction : —

$$C_{20}H_{27}NO_{11} + 2H_2O = C_7H_6O + HCN + 2C_6H_{12}O_6. \quad [549]$$

Amygdaline.   Oil of Bitter   Glucose.
              Almonds.

2. Salicine, contained in the pith of the willow and poplar, which in presence of certain ferments is decomposed as follows : —

$$C_{13}H_{18}O_7 + H_2O = C_7H_8O_2 + C_6H_{12}O_6. \quad [550]$$

Salicine.   Saligenine.   Glucose.

3. Tannine or Tannic Acid, widely diffused in the bark of plants, and well known for forming an insoluble compound with gelatine (as in tanning leather), and for producing a black color (ink) with ferric salts. This body when exposed in a moist state to the air, or treated with dilute acid, forms glucose and gallic acid.

$$C_{27}H_{22}O_{17} + 4H_2O = 3C_7H_6O_5 + C_6H_{12}O_6. \quad [551]$$

Tannine.   Gallic Acid.   Glucose.

480. *Fermentation.* — This term is applied to a number of remarkable chemical processes, which depend upon the life and growth of a very low order of organized beings, belonging chiefly to the vegetable kingdom. These organisms are the efficient part of what is called the ferment or yeast. The fermenting material is their appropriate food, and the products of fermentation are in some unknown way determined by the vital process, different ferments, that is different organisms, producing different results. Moreover, we can frequently distinguish between the growth and propagation of these organisms, and the normal vital process, by which the products of fermentation are evolved ; the first requiring the presence of certain materials, chiefly albuminous, which otherwise take no part in the chemical change. The germs of these living beings are widely diffused, floating even in the atmosphere, and begin at once to grow as soon as a fermentable liquid and the right temperature supply the conditions of active life. Fermentation, therefore, may set in without the apparent addition of any ferment, and on the other hand the change may be prevented by sealing up the material in air-tight cans previously heated to such a temperature as will insure the destruction of all living germs.

The principal modes of fermentation are : —

1. Alcoholic fermentation caused by a fungus, the Torvula cerevisiæ, commonly called yeast, which converts glucose into alcohol and carbonic anhydride, forming, however, at the same time a small amount of succinic acid and glycerine.

$$C_6H_{12}O_6 = 2\,C_2H_6O + 2\,CO_2. \qquad [552]$$

2. Acetous fermentation, induced by the Mycoderma vini, by which alcohol is changed into vinegar.

3. Lactic fermentation, in which the Penicillium glaucum converts saccharine materials into lactic acid.

$$\underset{\text{Glucose.}}{C_6H_{12}O_6} = \underset{\text{Lactic Acid.}}{2\,C_3H_6O_3.} \qquad [553]$$

4. Butyric fermentation, supposed to be caused by an animal, in which lactic acid, formed as above, is changed into butyric acid.

$$2\,C_3H_6O_3 = C_4H_8O_2 + 2\,CO_2 + 2H\text{-}H. \qquad [554]$$

5. Mucous fermentation, which sugar undergoes under the influence of the " mucous ferment," giving rise to the escape of carbonic anhydride and hydrogen, and the formation of mannite, together with a peculiar gum and a mucilaginous substance.

481. *Conclusion.* — The different forms of fermentation are but lower modes of the manifestation of that obscure power by which animals and plants not only prepare the materials of their tissues, but also secrete from their organisms the various products of their vital processes. As has been shown, we have been able, to a limited extent, to achieve in our laboratories the same results, and we can see no limit to our synthetical methods. Nevertheless, we have not been able as yet to produce any of the materials which make up the great mass of the tissues of all organized beings, and this, which is true of the gum, starch, and woody fibre of plants, is true to a still greater degree of such materials as albumen, caseine, gelatine, fibrine, &c., which are the main constituents of the animal body. In regard to the composition of these nitrogenized compounds we have no knowledge except that which may be obtained by ultimate

analysis; and although we have every reason to believe that future investigation will reveal their molecular constitution, so far as they are simple chemical compounds, yet in most cases the *substance* of these bodies cannot be isolated from the organic structure which determines in a great measure their distinctive qualities; and not only has man never been able to make the simplest organic cell, but the whole process of its growth and development is utterly beyond the range of his conceptions. Moreover, even in regard to those simpler products of organic life which we have been able to reach by synthesis, we have no knowledge of the processes by which they are formed in organic nature.

The vegetable kingdom is a great laboratory, in which the sun's rays manufacture from the gases of the atmosphere, and from a few earthy salts of the soil, the different materials which the organic builders employ. The animal, unlike the plant, has not the power of forming the substance of its tissues from inorganic compounds, but it receives from the vegetable laboratory the materials required ready formed. It transmutes these products into a thousand shapes in order to adapt them to its wants; but its peculiar province is to assimilate and consume, not to produce. The nitrogenized compounds just referred to are the portion of its food which supplies the constant waste attending all the vital processes. The non-nitrogenized starch and sugar, although they form the greater part of our food, are never incorporated into the tissues of the body, but are merely the fuel by which its temperature is maintained. Here, however, chemistry stops, and the science of physiology begins.

In closing this summary of facts, we must remind the student that, as we stated in the introduction, we have made no attempt at completeness. Although the chief characteristics of all the chemical elements have been illustrated, yet important classes of compounds have been necessarily left unnoticed, and this is especially true in the last division of the book. Organic chemistry presents such a vast array of facts that the attempt to comprehend the whole field would simply lead to confusion, and serve no useful end. We have, therefore, limited our scope to those classes of compounds whose molecular structure is well understood, and our great object has been to illustrate the methods by which a knowledge of this structure has been reached. It is by these methods that the new philosophy of chemistry is chiefly distinguished from the old, and to them we shall especially direct the student's attention in the questions which follow. He should not content himself, however, with simply answering these questions, but, by an exhaustive study of all the reactions which have been given, and by a constant use of graphic symbols, endeavor to become imbued with the spirit of the philosophy which it has been the object of this book to illustrate.

Questions and Problems.

Carbon and Oxygen.

1. Deduce the atomic weight of carbon, and state the facts and principles on which the conclusion is based.

2. When the product of the combustion of coal is CO, what proportion of the calorific power of the fuel is lost ? (61).

3. Is the combination of CO_2 with additional carbon in passing through a mass of incandescent coal attended with an evolution or an absorption of heat ? Estimate the amount of the effect produced.

4. Illustrate by examples and seek to establish by reactions or other facts the oxatyl theory of the constitution of organic acids.

Carbon and Nitrogen.

5. On what facts is the symbol of cyanogen gas based ?

6. In what respects does HCy resemble, and how does it differ, from the hydrogen acids of the chlorine group ?

7. What is the distinction between the two classes of double metallic cyanides ?

8. Represent by graphic symbols the constitution of several of the polymeric compounds of cyanogen, including the ferro and ferricyanides of potassium.

9. What proof is furnished by the reactions of (425) that the amine and amide compounds, there mentioned, have the constitution represented by the symbols assigned to them ?

10. Repeat the reactions given in (425), writing the symbol of cyanic ether after the ammonia type.

11. Represent by graphic symbols the constitution of cyanic

ether and cyanetholine respectively, and give the reactions from which the symbols are deduced.

12. Urea, when in solution in water, changes into ammonic carbonate. Write the reaction.

Carbon and Hydrogen.

13. How many essentially different modes of grouping are possible with a carbon skeleton of four atoms, assuming that no atom is united to any one of its neighbors by more than one of its affinities? How many with a skeleton of five atoms, &c.?

14. Make a table of the possible hydrocarbons in series of homologues and isologues.

15. How many essentially different modes of grouping are possible with the compounds C_6H_{14}, C_6H_{12}, and C_6H_6?

16. Is the number of H atoms in the molecule of a hydrocarbon necessarily an even number?

17. Is any evidence given of the synthesis of marsh gas?

18. Why may the three expressions C_2H_5-C_2H_5, C_2H_7-CH_3 and C_4H_{10} represent identical compounds?

19. Explain the manner in which the successive hydrogen atoms of C_2H_4 may be replaced by bromine.

20. Write the symbols of the different hydrocarbons of the phenyl series on the assumption that they all contain the radical C_6H_5 united to the radicals of the methyl series, and show how many isomeric modifications are possible in each case.

21. Describe the method of preparing aniline from benzol.

22. Show by graphic symbols the relations of the radicals allyl and glyceryl.

23. Illustrate by graphic symbols the relations of the oxygenated to the simple hydrocarbon radicals, and explain the principle stated in (436).

Monatomic Alcohols, &c. Marsh Gas Series.

24. Represent graphically the constitution of the alcohols of the marsh gas series, and show that the reactions of (438) sustain your theory.

25. Write a series of reactions by which the synthesis of propylic alcohol can be effected, starting with mineral substances.

26. Analyze reactions [438] and [439], and trace the action of nascent hydrogen and N_2O_3 in these cases as illustrating their use as reagents in organic chemistry.

27. What general method of preparing the amines (167) is indicated by [438]?

28. Show that the constitution of acetic acid may be deduced from [374], [443], [448], and [449].

29. Write a series of reactions by which acetic acid may be converted into propionic acid.

30. What is the use of P_2O_5 as a reagent in organic chemistry [445]?

31. Analyze reaction [444] and show what an important effect can be produced by the action of potassic hydrate on the cyanide of a hydrocarbon radical. Compare [389].

32. What conclusions would you deduce from reactions [450] to [452] in regard to the constitution of the fat acids? Illustrate by developing in full the rational formula of butyric acid.

33. What are the several sources of palmitic acid?

34. Compare the constitution of iso-butyric and iso-valeric acids obtained by [456] and [457] with the normal compounds. Are other isomers possible?

35. Write the reactions by which methylic ether is prepared.

36. Explain the process of etherification as illustrated by [458] and [459]. What is the essential difference of conditions in the two reactions?

37. Write the reactions by which common ether may be obtained after [461].

38. Make a table of the different ethers.

39. All the hydrogen atoms of methylic ether may be replaced by chlorine in successive pairs. Write the symbols of the compounds thus formed.

40. Analyze reactions [461] as illustrating the use of sodium as a reagent in organic chemistry.

41. Describe the methods of preparing the compound ethers, and compare them with the reactions by which mineral salts are obtained.

42. Show in what way the presence of a strong acid assists the reactions expressed by [466] and [467].

43. To what does saponification correspond in mineral chemistry?

44. Write the reaction of water on acetic ether.

45. Write the reaction by which butyric anhydride may be prepared.

46. Write the reaction of water on acetic anhydride.

47. Compare the effects of PCl_3 and PCl_5 when used as reagents in organic chemistry, so far as illustrated by [471] and [34].

48. In what manner may the haloid ethers be converted into amines ?

49. Chloroform may be regarded as the chloride of the trivalent radical CH. Do you know of any reaction which illustrates this point ?

50. Analyze the reactions by which the aldehydes are formed, and show how far they indicate the constitution of these bodies.

51. Write the reaction which takes place when the aldehydes are heated with potassic hydrate.

52. Represent by graphic symbols the constitution of the aldehydes and ketones, and show that the chemical relations of the two classes of isomeric compounds are the result of a difference of atomic grouping. Show also that your theory of the constitution of these bodies is a legitimate inference from the reactions, of which they are susceptible.

53. Illustrate by graphic symbols the difference between the pseudo-alcohols and the normal compounds and the relations in which they stand to the ketones and aldehydes respectively. Show that the symbols assigned to the normal and secondary alcohols are legitimately deduced.

54. Compare by the graphic method the constitution of the three classes of alcohols. Take heptyl alcohol with its isomers as an example, and point out the differences in the carbon skeletons of these isomeric compounds. In what does a normal alcohol consist ?

55. Make a table exhibiting the relations of the different compounds of the marsh gas series including hydrocarbons, alcohols, acids, aldehydes, acetones, and ethers.

Vinyl Series.

56. The differences between the vinylic and ethylic alcohols may be referred to what differences in the structure of the carbon skeleton of these two classes of compounds ? What proof have you that such a difference exists ?

57. Compare by the graphic method the difference between vinylic alcohol, acetic aldehyde, and ethylenic oxide, and give the reasons for your mode of grouping the atoms.

58. Why should you not expect to obtain an acid from vinylic

alcohol by the action of oxidizing agents, when allylic alcohol yields both an aldehyde and an acid ?

59. Write the reaction by which allylic alcohol is converted into acrolein and acrylic acid.

60. How far is the change from glycerine into acrolein attended with a change of type ?

61. In what does the difference between the structure of the acids of the acrylic and acetic series consist ?

62. Carefully analyze the reactions by which different types of structure in the acrylic series have been obtained, and show that the conclusions reached are legitimate.

63. How and under what conditions does PCl_3 act as a dehydrating agent ?

64. In what way does [444] and [505] indicate the structure of β crotonic acid ?

65. Give the general symbols of the three classes of acryloid acids.

Phenyl Series.

66. Represent the constitution of benzoic alcohol by graphic symbols, and show how far its structure resembles that of the alcohol of the ethylic series containing the same number of carbon atoms. Compare the carbon skeletons of the two compounds.

67. Why is it that carbolic acid, although homologous with benzoic alcohol, differs from it so greatly in its chemical relations ?

68. How is toluol related to benzol, and by what series of reactions may the first be changed into the last ?

69. How is cressylic alcohol related to carbolic acid ? Represent with graphic symbols the structure of the two bodies.

70. Write the reaction by which benzoic acid is produced from hippuric acid (168).

71. Represent graphically the relations of cinnamic to benzoic acid, and point out the difference of structure in the carbon skeleton of the two compounds. What similar relations have previously been noticed ?

72. Represent graphically the relations of salicylic acid to benzoic acids. What acid stands in a similar relation to acetic acid ?

73. Make a table exhibiting the relations of the different compounds of the radical phenyl, with their possible homologues, and show how far the reactions, which have been given, indicate their molecular structure.

Diatomic Alcohols, &c.

74. Describe the several processes by which the glycols may be produced.

75. Illustrate by graphic symbols the constitution and relations of the different derivatives of ethylic glycol, especially of the chlorhydrines, bromhydrines, &c.

76. Point out the differences between the chemical relations of ethylic oxide (common ether) and ethylenic oxide, and show how far they may be explained by differences of structure.

77. Describe the reactions, by which condensed glycols may be produced, and cite examples of similar compounds from the mineral kingdom. What proof is there that these compounds have the structure assigned to them, and why can greater certainty be reached in regard to the structure of these bodies than in regard to that of the mineral products they are said to explain?

78. Illustrate by graphic symbols the structure of the three chief classes of acids of the lactic family, and show in each case how the conclusion has been reached.

79. Construct the graphic symbols of ethylene and ethylidene, and give the reasons for the forms adopted.

80. Show that the constitution of the known glycols can be inferred from that of the acids of the lactic family.

81. What is meant by an olefine acid? In what way must the carbon atoms in the olefines be arranged? Show that the conclusion is trustworthy.

82. Compare the reaction of potassic hydrate on cyanhydrine of ethylene and on cyanhydrine of ethylidene. Can you draw any legitimate inference in these cases as to the structure of the resulting compounds?

83. Explain the term etheric acids. Has any example of such compounds been previously given?

84. Represent by graphic symbols the constitution of the isomeric compounds cited in (467), and inquire whether further variations are possible.

85. Write the reactions, 1. of lactic acid on sodic carbonate, 2. of sodium on sodic lactate, 3. of ethylic iodide on disodic lactate.

86. What is the general action of *HI* as a reagent in organic chemistry? [530.]

87. Write the reaction of potassic hydrate on cyanide of ethylene, and show how far this establishes the constitution of succinic acid.

88. Write the reaction which takes place when one molecule of CO_2 is eliminated from malonic acid by the action of heat, or when succinic acid is decomposed in a similar way if heated with lime.

89. Write the reaction when suberic acid is heated with excess of baryta.

90. What is the general action of lime or baryta when heated with an organic acid ?

91. Show by graphic symbols how the acids of the succinic series are related to those of the acetic series, and describe the methods by which one class of compounds may be converted into the other.

92. Show that reactions [536] and [537] confirm the conclusion already reached in regard to the constitution of succinic acid.

93. In what isomeric form may the symbol of succinic acid be written, and what radical would it then contain, in place of ethylene ? What proof have you that it does contain ethylene ?

94. Succinic acid is formed when butyric acid is oxidized (by nitric acid). Write the reaction.

95. Write the general symbols of the three classes of the succinates both of univalent and bivalent radicals.

96. What is the characteristic of an acryloid acid ? Show that fumaric acid conforms to this type.

97. Show by graphic symbols the possible forms of the first term of the fumaric series.

98. Show how far the fact that both fumaric and maleic acids yield succinic acid, under the influence of nascent hydrogen, fixes their symbols. Show also that the brominated compounds may be different; while the further products obtained by the action of nascent hydrogen on the last may be identical.

99. Represent graphically some of the possible forms of the second term of the fumaric series, and trace the relations of these compounds to pyrotartaric acid.

100. Compare the graphic symbols of succinic, fumaric, and malic acids.

Triatomic Compounds.

101. Write the reaction on stearine, 1. of solution of potassic hydrate, 2. of plumbic oxide and water, 3. of superheated steam.

102. Compare the graphic symbols of glycerine, glyceric acid, and tartaronic acid, and explain their atomic and basic relations.

103. How far do the reactions [514] and [539] indicate the construction of the basic radical of glycerine ?

104. Write the reaction by which the several chlorhydrines of glycerine are obtained, and point out their relations to the triatomic character of the compound.

105. Compare the anhydrides of glycerine with the polybasic mineral compounds.

106. Give the symbols of the three stearines and the three oleines corresponding to the three acetines.

107. Exhibit by graphic symbols the relations of glycerine to acrolein.

108. Compare graphically the relations of propylic alcohol, propylic glycol, and glycerine.

109. A normal alcohol may be converted into an acid either by oxidation or by a reaction similar to [543]; compare the results obtained, and show the bearing of the facts on the oxatyl theory of organic acids.

110. Write the symbols of the different acids which might theoretically be formed by the oxidation of the assumed hexyl glycerine.

111 Compare the graphic symbols of tricarballylic and aconitic acids.

112. Compare the graphic symbols of citric, aconitic, and itaconic acids, and explain the change of the first into the last through the second.

Tetratomic Alcohols, &c.

113. Make a table exhibiting the relations of tartaric and citric acids to the tetratomic alcobols.

114. When tartaric acid is reduced by Hl, it changes first into malic and then into succinic acid. Write the reactions and inquire how far they aid in establishing the constitution of the bodies involved.

115. Compare the carbon skeletons of one or more of each of the classes of acids which have been studied, and show that the variations are limited to a few principal types. Then, by attaching atoms of H, Ho, NH_2, $COHo$ or O to these skeletons, illustrate the relations of the various classes of compounds which may be formed around a common nucleus.

CHAPTER XX.

Complex Amines.

482. *Aniline Colors.* — These beautiful products of modern chemistry, which are so highly valued on account of their brilliant hues and wonderful tinctorial power, belong to the class of compounds called amines, whose chemical relations have been already described (167). They are, so far as known, highly complex bodies of the ammonia type, and will serve to extend our knowledge of this class of compounds, connecting them with the compounds of the hydro-carbon radicals, with which we have become more recently acquainted. The processes by which the aniline dyes are prepared in the arts consist chiefly in the oxidation of a mixture of aniline and toluidine, but the precise reactions involved can seldom be traced. Nevertheless we have been able to reach a general knowledge of their constitution, although it must be held subject to revision by the results of the ever-widening investigations, which the great interest of these beautiful bodies invites.

The process by which aniline is obtained from benzol has been already described, and toluidine is prepared in precisely the same way from toluol (434). By the action of oxidizing agents on these *monamines* we can obtain four distinct *triamine* bases, whose salts are all deeply colored. Each molecule of the monamine loses by oxidation two atoms of hydrogen, and then three of these dehydrated molecules coalesce to form one molecule of the complex triamine, thus :—

$$3\ C_6H_5\text{-}N\text{=}H_2 - 6H = C_{18}H_{12}{}^{vi}N_3\text{=}H_3.$$
Aniline.   Violaniline.

$$2\ C_6H_5\text{-}N\text{=}H_2 + C_7H_7\text{-}N\text{=}H_2 - 6H = C_{19}H_{14}{}^{vi}N_3\text{=}H_3.$$
Aniline.   Toluidine.   Mauvaniline.

$$C_6H_5\text{-}N\text{=}H_2 + 2\ C_7H_7\text{-}N\text{=}H_2 - 6H = C_{20}H_{16}{}^{vi}N_3\text{=}H_3.$$
Aniline.   Toluidine.   Rosaniline

$$3\ C_7H_7\text{-}N\text{=}H_2 - 6H = C_{21}H_{18}{}^{vi}N_3\text{=}H_3.$$
Toluidine.   Chrysotoluidine.

The simplest conception we can form of the constitution of these products is indicated below : —

$$C_6H_4$$
$$NH \quad NH$$
$$C_6H_4\text{-}NH\text{-}C_6H_4$$
Violaniline.

$$C_7H_6$$
$$NH \quad NH$$
$$C_6H_4\text{-}NH\text{-}C_6H_4$$
Mauvaniline.

$$C_7H_6$$
$$NH \quad NH$$
$$C_7H_6\text{-}NH\text{-}C_6H_4$$
Rosaniline.

$$C_7H_6$$
$$NH \quad NH$$
$$C_7H_6\text{-}NH\text{-}C_7H_6$$
Chrysotoluidine.

and it can easily be seen that such a grouping might readily result, if we assume that of the two atoms of hydrogen which each molecule of the monamine loses, one is torn from the nitrogen atom and the other from the benzol nucleus. All we know, however, with any certainty, is that there remain three atoms of typical hydrogen, which may be further replaced by various hydro-carbon radicals, and this is expressed by the first set of symbols.

Of these bases rosaniline is practically the most important. The usual process by which its compounds are manufactured in the arts consists of three stages : first, the conversion of benzol and toluol (obtained from coal-tar naphtha by fractional distillation) into nitro-benzol and nitro-toluol (434) ; second, the reduction of these nitro-compounds (usually by mixing them with acetic acid and iron-turnings) to aniline and toluidine [428] ; third, the oxidation of a mixture of these bases, in about the proportions of one of aniline to two of toluidine, by means of arsenic acid. To this end the mixture is treated with a concentrated sirupy solution of the reagent, and the whole mass is heated to about 150°, and kept at this temperature under constant stirring for several hours. The crude product, a resinous solid with a bronze-like lustre, is dissolved in boiling water, and a large excess of sodic chloride added, which precipitates chloride of rosaniline in crystals, that reflect beautiful changing green hues like beetles' wings, but are red by transmitted light, and yield with alcohol or acetic acid deep red solutions. From the chloride the other salts of the same base may be readily prepared, including the hydrate, $C_{20}H_{19}N_3 \cdot 2H_2O$, which falls as a

brownish-yellow precipitate on adding caustic soda or ammonia
to a solution of any of the aniline reds of commerce, but when
purified it is colorless, becoming, however, rose-red on exposure
to any acid, even the carbonic acid of the atmosphere. It is
a singular fact in regard to all the bases mentioned above, that,
while all their salts are such powerful pigments, they are themselves colorless. The hydrate of rosaniline is insoluble in ether
or coal-tar, nearly so in water, only slightly soluble in aqua
ammonia, but dissolves with readiness in alcohol, with which it
forms deep red solutions. With acids it forms three classes of
salts, neutral, acid, and di-acid, which crystallize readily. It is
the last of these which are so remarkable for their beetle-like
lustre and give such beautiful rose-red solutions, and they are
the true coloring compounds. A great variety of these, including besides the arseniate the chloride, nitrate, sulphate, chromate, acetate, oxalate, and tannate, are used in the arts and
known under fanciful names, such as magenta, azaliene, fuch-
sine, roseine, &c. They are most of them freely soluble in
water and alcohol, but the tannate is so insoluble that it is used
for fixing the color upon calico and recovering the dye from
nearly spent solutions.

It was discovered by Hofmann that the three atoms of typical
hydrogen remaining in rosaniline may be replaced by the hydro-carbon radicals, and these replacements give rise to beautiful *violet* and *blue* pigments. The so-called Hofmann's violets
and blues are salts of mono, di, or tri phenylic, ethylic, or methylic rosaniline; and the further the substitution is carried, the
more do the blue tints preponderate in the resulting dye. The
phenylic compounds are obtained by heating the salts of rosaniline with aniline under pressure, and the ethylic or methylic
compounds may be prepared by treating the rosaniline salts
with the iodides or bromides of ethyl or methyl.

Besides the definite compounds, whose chemical relations
have been described above, there are prepared in the arts a
very great variety of other aniline dyes, including greens, yel-
lows, blacks, and indeed almost every color. They are all
probably compounds of one of the four bases described above,
or of analogous bases derived from them, but they are frequently mixtures, and from the empirical processes by which
they are prepared we can draw no definite conclusion as to
their precise constitution.

Complex Amides.

483. *Urea* N_2H_4CO. — This compound has already been mentioned as an example of a diamide (168), and its synthesis by the transformation of ammonic cyanate has been explained [404]. It is a substance of very great physiological interest. It has been found in several of the fluids of the animal body, and forms a large constituent of the vitreous humor of the eye. With all the higher animals it is the final product of the oxidation of their tissues, and the chief form in which they are eliminated from the body after having discharged the functions of life. It takes its name from the secretion of the kidneys, of whose solid constituents it forms by far the largest part, and after being voided by the body it is soon converted into carbonic dioxide and ammonia, the two substances which, together with water, are the principal food of the vegetable world (481) (64). This change is apparently induced by certain highly unstable bodies, with which urea is associated in the urine, and consists simply in the assimilation of one molecule of water to each molecule of urea, thus: —

$$N_2H_4CO + H_2O = 2NH_3 + CO_2. \qquad [555]$$

The same change may be produced by strong sulphuric acid and by various alkaline reagents, also by heating with water alone in sealed tubes to temperatures above the boiling point.

Urea acts as a feeble base, forming salts with the stronger acids, and of these the nitrate, $(N_2H_4CO)HNO_3$, and the oxalate, $(N_2H_4CO)_2H_2C_2O_4$, are the most readily crystallized. It also forms definite compounds with several metallic oxides and with many salts. In all these cases there is no replacement of the hydrogen atoms of the urea; but its molecules combine directly with those of the acid, oxide, or salt, as in the above examples. Such a reaction as this, however, is a characteristic of an amine (167), and not what we should anticipate of the neutral amide of carbonic acid, whose acid amide forms the well-known ammonic carbamate (168) and (174). But, unlike a true diamine, one molecule of urea does not neutralize two molecules of a monobasic acid, but only one, as in the above examples. Hence some chemists do not regard urea as the true carbamide, but only a compound isomeric with it, and the following formulæ represent possible views of its constitution : —

$$NH_4\text{-}O\text{-}CN \qquad (NH_2)_2\text{=}CO \qquad NH,NH_2\text{=}C\text{-}Ho \qquad NH_4\text{-}N\text{=}CO.$$
$$\text{Ammonic Cyanate.} \qquad \text{Carbamide.} \qquad \text{Urea ?} \qquad \text{Urea ?}$$

Against each of these, however, we might urge plausible objections, and the simple carbamide formula, which is here adopted as a provisional mode of explaining the relations of the compound, is not less probable than either of the others.

In whatever way we may write the symbol of the urea molecule, its single carbon atom must be directly united to one or both of the two nitrogen atoms with which it is associated. Hence arises an intimate relationship between urea and the compounds of cyanogen, from which it is so readily derived. Urea, when heated under regulated conditions, yields besides other products both cyanic and cyanuric acids, thus : —

$$N_2H_4CO + AgNO_3 = Ag\text{-}O\text{-}CN + NH_4NO_3. \qquad [556]$$
$$\text{Solution of urea evaporated with argentic nitrate.}$$

$$6N_2H_4CO + 6HCl = 2H_3\text{=}O_3\text{=}C_{3\pm 3} + 6NH_4Cl. \qquad [557]$$
$$\text{Compound of urea and hydrochloric acid heated to 145°.}$$

$$3N_2H_4CO = 3NH_3 + H_3\text{=}O_3\text{=}C_3N_3. \qquad [558]$$
$$\text{Urea heated alone to 150° - 170°.}$$

The last reaction is accompanied by another, in which a considerable portion of the urea is converted into a compound similar to itself called Biuret.

$$2N_2H_4CO = NH_3 + N_3H_5C_2O_2,$$
$$\text{Biuret.}$$

or possibly $NH_2\text{-}CO\text{-}NH\text{-}CO\text{-}NH_2.$
$$\text{Biuret ?}$$

484. *Compound Ureas.* — The atoms of hydrogen in urea may be replaced by various hydrocarbon positive radicals. Thus compounds are known in which either one, two, or three of the four hydrogen atoms in the urea molecules are replaced by ethyl or methyl, but the substitution of the fourth hydrogen atom by these radicals has not been effected. Ethyl-urea, diethyl-urea, and triethyl-urea may be prepared by the action of ethylic cyanate on ammonia, ethylamine, or diethylamine respectively[1] (compare also [409]). Of these bodies diethyl-urea is especially noteworthy, because it admits of two isomeric

[1] Ethylic cyanate is without action on triethylamine, and an analysis of the reactions above described will show that there is a difference of condition in this case, which probably explains why the fourth atom of hydrogen in urea cannot be replaced by this method, which succeeds so well for the first three.

modifications (according as it is obtained by the reaction of ethylic cyanate on ethylamine or of potassic cyanate on diethyl-ammonic sulphate), which may be represented thus : —

$$(H, C_2H_5=N)-CO-(N=C_2H_5,H) \qquad (H,H=N)-CO-(N=C_2H_5,C_2H_5)$$

The first of these when treated with alkalies yields besides CO_2 simply ethylamine, the second a mixture of diethylamine with ammonia.

By means of the dyad radical ethylene we can bind together two molecules of urea into a still more complex group. Thus, by the action of cyanic acid on ethylene diamine (167), we obtain

$$H_2N-CO-NH-C_2H_4-HN-CO-NH_2,$$
Ethyelene-diurea.

and by the action of the same reagent on diethyl-ethylene-di-amine, or that of ethylic cynate on ethylene-diamine, we ob-tain compounds differing from the last only in that two of the hydrogen atoms are replaced by ethyl. These compounds furnish another example of isomerism, similar to that described above, but of a more complex type. When decomposed by alkalies, the first yields besides CO_2 a mixture of diethyl-ethyl-ene-diamine with ammonia, the second a mixture of ethylene-diamine with ethylamine. A graphic representation of these reactions will further show that two other isomeric modifica-tions of the same compound are also possible ; the one giving, under the conditions above mentioned, a mixture of ethylene-diamine with diethylamine, and the other a mixture of ethyl-ethylene-diamine, ethylamine and ammonia.

The properties and reactions of these compound ureas are analogous to those of urea itself. They act like feeble amine bases, but as a rule they unite less readily with acids than normal urea.

485. *Monureides.* — The atoms of hydrogen in urea may be replaced by acid as well as by positive radicals, and there thus results a most remarkable class of compounds, which have all the characters of true amides. Those which are formed after the type of the single urea molecule are called *monureides*, to distinguish them from the more complex though similar pro-ducts having the type of a doubly condensed urea molecule, the *diureides*. These highly complex bodies, like the simpler amides, are acid when the replacing radical contains one or

more atoms of **oxatyl**. Otherwise, they are neutral or feebly basic. The monureides may be regarded as formed by the union of one molecule of an acid with one molecule of urea, accompanied by the elimination of one or two molecules of water, a reaction, through which one or two of the hydrogen atoms in the urea molecule become replaced by the acid radical, thus : —

$$Ho_2\text{=}\,C_2H_2O + \left.\begin{array}{c} CO \\ H_2 \\ H_2 \end{array}\right\} N_2 - H_2O = Ho\text{-}\,C_2H_2O \left.\begin{array}{c} CO \\ H_3 \end{array}\right\} N_2$$

Glycollic Acid.　　　Urea.　　　　　　　　Glycoluric Acid.

$$Ho_2\text{=}\,C_2H_2O + \left.\begin{array}{c} CO \\ H_2 \\ H_2 \end{array}\right\} N_2 - 2H_2O = C_2H_2O \left.\begin{array}{c} CO \\ H_2 \end{array}\right\} N_2$$

Glycolyl Urea (Hydantoin).

In like manner we may derive, at least theoretically, the several monureides included in the second and third columns of the following table from the corresponding acids included in the first column. Monobasic acids can of course yield only one derivative, and that must be neutral. Dibasic acids, on the other hand, yield two, one acid and one neutral.

Acids.	Monureides. — H_2O	Monureides. — $2H_2O$
$Ho_2\text{=}\,CO$ Carbonic Acid.	$Ho\text{-}CO \left.\begin{array}{c} CO \\ H_3 \end{array}\right\} N_2$ Allophanic Acid.	
$Ho_2\text{=}\,C_2O_2$ Oxalic Acid.	$Ho\text{-}C_2O_2 \left.\begin{array}{c} CO \\ H_3 \end{array}\right\} N_2$ Oxaluric Acid.	$C_2O_2 \left.\begin{array}{c} CO \\ H_2 \end{array}\right\} N_2$ Paraban.
$Ho_2\text{=}\,C_3O_3$ Mesoxalic Acid.	$Ho\text{-}C_3O_3 \left.\begin{array}{c} CO \\ H_3 \end{array}\right\} N_2$ Alloxanic Acid.	$C_3O_3 \left.\begin{array}{c} CO \\ H_2 \end{array}\right\} N_2$ Alloxan.
$Ho\text{-}C_2H_3O$ Acetic Acid.	$C_2H_3O \left.\begin{array}{c} CO \\ H_3 \end{array}\right\} N_2$ Acetyl Urea.	
$Ho_2\text{=}\,C_2H_2O$ Glycollic Acid.	$Ho\text{-}C_2H_2O \left.\begin{array}{c} CO \\ H_3 \end{array}\right\} N_2$ Glycoluric Acid.	$C_2H_2O \left.\begin{array}{c} CO \\ H_2 \end{array}\right\} N_2$ Hydantoin.

Acids.	*Monureïdes.*	*Monureïdes.*

$$Ho_2 = C_3H_2O_2$$
Malonic Acid.

$$\left.\begin{array}{l}CO \\ C_3H_2O_2 \\ H_2\end{array}\right\} N_2$$
Barbituric Acid.

$$\bar{Ho}, \overset{+}{Ho_2} = C_3HO_2$$
Tartronic Acid.

$$\left.\begin{array}{l}CO \\ \bar{Ho}\text{-} C_3HO_2 \\ H_2\end{array}\right\} N_2$$
Dialuric Acid.

$$H\text{-}(CO\text{-}CO)\text{-}Ho$$
Glyoxalic Acid.

$$\left.\begin{array}{l}CO \\ H\text{-}(CO\text{-}CO) \\ H_3\end{array}\right\} N_2$$
Allanturic Acid.

486. *Diureïdes.* — These may be regarded as formed by the union of a monureïde with an additional molecule of urea, the combination involving as before the elimination of one or two molecules of water. The following are a few examples : —

$$\left.\begin{array}{l}CO \\ Ho\text{-} C_2H_2O \\ H_3\end{array}\right\} N_2 + \left.\begin{array}{l}CO \\ H_2 \\ H_2\end{array}\right\} N_2 - 2H_2O = \left.\begin{array}{l}C \\ CO \\ C_2H_2O \\ H_4\end{array}\right\} N_4$$

Glycoluric Acid.   Urea.   Glycoluril.

$$\left.\begin{array}{l}CO \\ H\text{-}C_2O_2 \\ H_3\end{array}\right\} N_2 + \left.\begin{array}{l}CO \\ H_2 \\ H_2\end{array}\right\} N_2 - H_2O = \left.\begin{array}{l}C \\ CO \\ H\text{-}C_2O_2 \\ H_5\end{array}\right\} N_4$$

Allanturic Acid.   Urea.   Allantoin.

$$\left.\begin{array}{l}CO \\ Ho\text{-} C_3HO_2 \\ H_2\end{array}\right\} N_2 + \left.\begin{array}{l}CO \\ H_2 \\ H_2\end{array}\right\} N_2 - 2H_2O = \left.\begin{array}{l}C \\ C \\ \bar{Ho}\text{-} C_3HO_2 \\ H_2\end{array}\right\} N_4$$

Dialuric Acid.   Urea.   Uric Acid.

$$\left.\begin{array}{l}CO \\ C_3H_2O_2 \\ H_2\end{array}\right\} N_2 + \left.\begin{array}{l}CO \\ H_2 \\ H_2\end{array}\right\} N_2 - 2H_2O = \left.\begin{array}{l}C \\ C \\ C_3H_2O_2 \\ H_2\end{array}\right\} N_4$$

Barbituric Acid.   Urea.   Xanthine.

$$\left.\begin{array}{l}C \\ C \\ C_3H_2O \\ H_2\end{array}\right\} N_4$$

Hypoxanthine.

It must not be inferred that the equations either of this or of
the last section represent actual processes by which the various
urides have been prepared. They merely indicate the most
probable theory in regard to the constitution and chemical relations of these bodies which we have been able to form. The
substances themselves are either products of the animal organism,
or else have been prepared from such products by different chemical processes, and our only knowledge in regard to their molecular structure has been derived from a study of their properties, and of the chemical changes in which they are formed
or broken up. For the evidence on which the rational symbols here given are based we refer the student to the memoirs
of Baeyer, in the *Annalen der Chemie und Pharmacie,* containing the results of his very extended investigations of this class
of compounds.[1]

487. *Uric Acid* is not only the most important of the ureides,
but it is the source from which almost all the rest have been
derived. It is a constant product of the animal organism, resulting from the imperfect oxidation of the nitrogenized tissues.
With the reptiles, birds, and insects it forms (in combination
with ammonia) the chief part, and in some cases nearly the
whole, of their solid excrements ; but in mammalia the oxidation
proceeds further in the body and the product voided is princi-
pally urea. Nevertheless, uric acid is always present in human
urine, and in certain abnormal states of the system the amount
becomes increased to an injurious extent, giving rise to sedi-
ment, gravel, or calculi. In some forms of gout all the fluids
of the body become saturated with it, and in combination with
soda it is deposited in the joints, forming what are familiarly
known as chalk stones.

Uric acid, when pure, forms a white crystalline powder,
which under the microscope exhibits definite and characteristic crystalline forms ; but the crude acid is more or less tinted
by the coloring matter of the urinary secretion, from which it
is prepared. When heated, it decomposes without melting,
yielding a sublimate of cyanuric acid, ammonic cyanate (or
urea), and ammonic carbonate, leaving a carbonaceous residue

[1] See, also, an article in Silliman's Journal, vol. 96, page 289, by Dr. W.
Gibbs, in which rational symbols for these bodies are theoretically deduced
from either the known or assumed polymeric forms of cyanic acid.

behind.   It is almost insoluble in water and the dilute mineral
acids; but it dissolves readily in alkaline solutions, since it
forms with the alkaline radicals more or less soluble salts.   It
also forms salts with several of the more basic metallic radicals, which may either replace one or two of its typical hydrogen atoms.   We have, therefore, in several cases both an acid
and a basic salt of the same radical.   But while we can only
replace two of the hydrogen atoms with metallic radicals we
can replace three with ethyl.

The rational formula of uric acid has already been given.
It is based chiefly on the following considerations.   When the
acid is treated with a mixture of hydrochloric acid and potassic chlorate (a strong oxidizing acid), it is converted wholly
into a mixture of alloxan and urea,

$$\underset{\text{Uric Acid.}}{N_4 H_4 C_5 O_3} + O + H_2 O = \underset{\text{Alloxan.}}{N_2 H_2 C_4 O_4} + \underset{\text{Urea.}}{N_2 H_4 CO}. \quad [559]$$

Now the first effect of the oxidation would be naturally to remove the hydrogen atoms from the hydrocarbon radical we
have assumed to exist in uric acid, changing it into the hypothetical compound $N_4 H_2 C_5 O_3$, and then this, by absorbing two
molecules of water, gives at once alloxan and urea.

$$\underset{\text{Uric Acid.}}{Ho\text{-}C_2 H O_2 \left. \begin{matrix} C \\ C \\ H_2 \end{matrix} \right\} N_4} \quad \underset{\text{Hypothetical Intermediate.}}{\left. \begin{matrix} C \\ C \\ C_3 O_3 \\ H_2 \end{matrix} \right\} N_4} + 2H_2 O = \underset{\text{Alloxan.}}{C_3 O_3 \left. \begin{matrix} CO \\ H_2 \end{matrix} \right\} N_2} + \underset{\text{Urea.}}{H_2 \left. \begin{matrix} CO \\ H_2 \end{matrix} \right\} N_2}. \quad [560]$$

Further, when alloxan is boiled with an alkaline solution it
yields urea and the mesoxalate of the alkaline radical.   Lastly,
mesoxalic acid is a crystalline solid resembling oxalic acid, and
like it is dibasic.   As its composition is well determined there
can be no question that it contains the radical $C_3 O_3$, and is the
third term of a series of which carbonic acid and oxalic acid
are the other three.

$$\underset{\text{Carbonic Acid.}}{Ho_2 = CO} \qquad \underset{\text{Oxalic Acid.}}{Ho_2 = C_2 O_2} \qquad \underset{\text{Mesoxalic Acid.}}{Ho_2 = C_3 O_3.}$$

This completes the chain of evidence, but the student will not
fail to see that it has a weak point.

The view of the constitution of uric acid here adopted is
further supported by a reaction observed by Strecker, who
found that, when treated with hydriodic acid, one molecule of
uric acid breaks up into one molecule of glycocoll ($Ho, NH_2 =$

C_2H_2O), three molecules of ammonia and three of carbonic dioxide. Now if uric acid contains, as we have assumed, the tartronyl radical, it must have the graphic symbol given below, leaving the parts in brackets undeveloped (473), and by comparing this with the symbols of tartronic acid and glycocoll on either side, it can readily be seen that the products are precisely such as might be expected from the action of the reagent used, assuming of course that our theory is correct.

$$\overset{O\ \ H\ \ O}{Ho\text{-}\overset{\shortmid}{\underset{\underset{Ho}{\shortmid}}{C}}\text{-}\overset{\shortmid}{C}\text{-}\overset{\shortmid}{C}\text{-}Ho} \qquad \overset{O\ \ H\ \ O}{(NH_2)\text{-}\overset{\shortmid}{\underset{\underset{Ho}{\shortmid}}{C}}\text{-}\overset{\shortmid}{C}\text{-}\overset{\shortmid}{C}\text{-}(N_3C_2)} \qquad \overset{O\ \ H}{(NH_2)\text{-}\overset{\shortmid}{\underset{\underset{Ho}{\shortmid}}{C}}\text{-}\overset{\shortmid}{C}\text{-}H.}$$

| Tartronic Acid. | Uric Acid. | Glycocoll. |

Uric acid is remarkable for the facility with which it is altered by oxidizing agents, and for the great number of definite and crystallizable compounds obtained, either in this manner or by treating the immediate products of oxidation with various reagents. The following list includes all the more important derivations: —

Derivatives of Uric Acid, $N_4H_4C_5O_3$.

Allantoin,	$N_4H_6C_4O_3$	Hydantoin,	$N_2H_4C_3O_2$
Allanturic Acid,	$N_2H_4C_3O_3$	Hydurilic Acid,	$N_4H_5C_4O_6$
Allituric Acid,	$N_4H_6C_6O_4$	Leucoturic Acid,	$N_4H_4C_6O_5$
Alloxan,	$N_2H_2C_4O_4$	Mesoxalic Acid,	$H_2C_3O_5$
Alloxanic Acid,	$N_2H_4C_4O_5$	Murexide,	$N_6H_8C_8O_6$
Alloxantin,	$N_4H_4C_8O_7 \cdot 3H_2O$	Mycomelic Acid,	$N_4H_4C_4O_2$
Barbituric Acid,	$N_2H_4C_4O_3$	Oxaluric Acid,	$N_2H_4C_3O_4$
Bromo-barbituric ⎰	Br	Paraban,	$N_2H_2C_3O_3$
Acid, ⎱	$N_2H_3C_4O_3$	Pseudo-uric Acid,	$N_4H_6C_5O_4$
Dibromo-barbituric ⎰	Br_2	Stryphnic Acid,	$N_5H_8C_4O_4$
Acid, ⎱	$N_2H_2C_4O_3$	Thionuric Acid,	$N_2H_5C_4O_6S$
Dibarbituric Acid,	$N_4H_6C_8O_5$	Uramil,	$N_3H_5C_4O_3$
Dialuric Acid,	$N_2H_4C_4O_4$	Urinilic Acid,	$N_7H_7C_8O_6$
Diliuric Acid,	$N_3H_3C_4O_5$	Uroxanic Acid,	$N_4H_{10}C_5O_8$
Glycoluric Acid,	$N_2H_6C_3O_3$	Violantin,	$N_6H_6C_4O_9$
Glycoluril,	$N_4H_6C_4O_2$	Violuric Acid,	$N_3H_3C_4O_4$
Hydantoic Acid,	$N_2H_4C_3O_3$	Xanthine,	$N_4H_4C_5O_2$

It must not be supposed that the term *acid*, used in connection with so many of these compounds, implies that they all have the constitution of true organic acids, that is, contain one or more atoms of oxatyl. That there are among them true acid amides (168) has already been shown, but in most cases the apparent acid reaction arises from the power, which many amides possess, of exchanging one or more of their atoms of typical hydrogen for the basic radicals of metallic hydrates, and this relation undoubtedly shows that the molecules of these bodies are in a polar condition not unlike, although less marked, than that of the true acid molecules of the water type.

For the various processes by which the uric acid derivatives have been prepared we must refer the student to Watt's Dictionary of Chemistry, from which, with some alterations, the above table has been taken. But in spite of the apparent complexity of the results, the chemical changes involved in the production of these bodies may be referred to a few types. We may have : —

First. The breaking up of a diureide into a monureide and urea.

$$\left.\begin{matrix} C \\ CO \\ C_2H_2O \\ H_4 \end{matrix}\right\}N_4 + H_2O = \left.\begin{matrix} CO \\ C_2H_2O \\ H_4 \end{matrix}\right\}N_2 + \left.\begin{matrix} CO \\ H_2 \end{matrix}\right\}N_2 \qquad [561]$$

Glycoluril.   Hydantoin.   Urea.

By boiling a solution of glycoluril with acids, and the reaction [560] given above is an example of a similar change.

Secondly. The formation of a biureide from a ureide.

$$2N_2H_2C_4O_4 - O = N_4H_4C_8O_7. \qquad [562]$$

Alloxan.   Alloxantin.

By the action of hydric sulphide or nascent hydrogen on a solution of alloxan.

Thirdly. A modification of the more complex radical of the ureide, without altering its relations to the compound.

$$\left.\begin{matrix} CO \\ C_3O_3 \\ H_2 \end{matrix}\right\}N_2 + O = \left.\begin{matrix} CO \\ C_2O_2 \\ H_2 \end{matrix}\right\}N_2 + CO_2 \qquad [563]$$

Alloxan.   Paraban.

By gently warming alloxan with nitric acid.

$$N_4H_4C_5O_3 + O + H_2O = N_4H_6C_4O_3 + CO_2.$$

Uric Acid.   Allantoin.

By boiling uric acid with water and plumbic dioxide.

$$N_4H_6C_4O_3 + H_2 = N_4H_6C_4O_2 + H_2O. \qquad [564]$$

Allantoin.   Glycoluril.

By the action of sodium amalgam on a solution of allantoin.

$$\left.\begin{matrix} CO \\ C_2H_2BrO \\ H_3 \end{matrix}\right\}N_2 = HBr + \left.\begin{matrix} CO \\ C_2H_2O \\ H_2 \end{matrix}\right\}N_2 \qquad [565]$$

Bromacetyl Urea.   Hydantoin.

By the action of ammonia.

$$\left.\begin{array}{c}CO\\C_3H_2O_2\\H_2\end{array}\right\}N_2 - H + NO_2 = \left.\begin{array}{c}CO\\C_3H(NO_2)O_2\\H_2\end{array}\right\}N_2 \quad [566]$$

Barbituric Acid.   Nitrobarbituric or
Diluturic Acid.

By the action of nitric acid.

$$\left.\begin{array}{c}CO\\C_3O_3\\H_2\end{array}\right\}N_2 + H_2O = Ho\text{-}\left.\begin{array}{c}CO\\C_3O_3\\H_3\end{array}\right\}N_2 \quad [567]$$

Alloxan.   Alloxanic Acid.

Fourthly. A breaking up of the ureide into ammonia and the hydrate of its principal radical.

$$\left.\begin{array}{c}CO\\C_3O_3\\H_2\end{array}\right\}N_2 + 3H_2O = CO_2 + Ho_2\text{=}C_3O_3 + 2NH_3 \quad [568]$$

Alloxan.   Mesoxalic Acid.

$$\left.\begin{array}{c}CO\\C_3H_2O_2\\H_2\end{array}\right\}N_2 + 3H_2O = CO_2 + Ho_2\text{=}C_3H_2O_2 + 2NH_3 \quad [569]$$

Barbituric Acid.   Malonic Acid.

By heating with solutions of caustic alkalies.

It will, of course, be understood that in the actual processes two or more of such reactions as have been here illustrated may concur or may succeed each other. Indeed, it has been found very difficult to isolate them.

488. *Allantoin and Murexide* are the only bodies among the uric acid derivatives which have any other interest than that which is connected with their chemical composition, and the only special interest attaching to allantoin arises from the isolated fact that it appears to be an essential constituent of the allantoic liquid. Murexide, however, is a most brilliant purple pigment, and before it was superseded by the aniline colors was manufactured on a large scale. It can be readily prepared by adding ammonia to the solution of alloxan and alloxantin, which is obtained by dissolving uric acid in dilute nitric acid under regulated conditions, and the production of a purple color under such circumstances is a delicate test for uric acid. Murexide crystallizes in brilliant garnet-colored prisms, which appear gold-green by reflected light. It gives with water a rich purple solution, but is insoluble in alcohol or ether. It appears to be the ammonium salt of a very complex amide, which has been called purpuric acid; but although the ammonium radical may be readily replaced by various metals the

amide itself has not been isolated, and our knowledge in regard to these beautiful compounds is as yet too limited to enable us to assign to them any probable rational symbols. Similar products are obtained by the action of potassic cyanides on picric acid (457), and these isopurpurates, as they are called, are isomeric with the corresponding uric acid derivatives.

489. *Guanine and Guanidine.* — The first of these compounds resembles uric acid, and is found associated with it in some kinds of guano, but it forms an amorphous instead of a crystalline powder, and has basic rather than acid relations. Ultimate analysis gives the empirical symbol $H_5N_5C_5O$, and it may be regarded as derived from xanthine by replacing the radical HO by H_2N, — a view of its constitution which is sustained by the fact that when treated with nitrous acid it yields that well-known diureide,

$$2H_5N_5C_5O + O{=}O = 2C_5H_4N_4O_2 + H_2O + N{\equiv}N. \quad [570]$$
$$\underset{\text{Guanine.}}{} \qquad \underset{\text{Xanthine.}}{}$$

An equally interesting reaction is obtained by digesting guanine with a mixture of hydrochloric acid and potassic chlorate, when it breaks up into paraban and a remarkable amine called guanidine.

$$H_5N_5C_5O + H_2O + O_3 =$$
$$\underset{\text{Guanine.}}{} \qquad H_5N_3C + H_2N_2C_3O_3 + CO_2. \quad [571]$$
$$\underset{\text{Guanidine.}}{} \quad \underset{\text{Paraban.}}{}$$

There are also formed at the same time, although in smaller quantities, xanthine, oxaluric acid, and urea.

Guanidine is a crystalline solid having a strong basic reaction, absorbing CO_2 from the air, and forming with acids crystalline salts, which, like $H_5N_3C \cdot HCl$, contain for every molecule of a monobasic acid one molecule of the amine. It can be formed synthetically by heating iodide of cyanogen with an alcoholic solution of ammonia in a closed tube, and this reaction leaves no doubt in regard to its molecular structure.

$$N{\equiv}C{-}I + 2H_3N = HN{=}C{=}(NH_2)_2 \cdot HI. \quad [572]$$

Guanidine has also been obtained by heating with the same solution, and under similar conditions, chlorpicrin, a product of the action of chlorine on picric acid.

$$CCl_3(NO_2) + 3NH_3 =$$
$$\underset{\text{Chlorpicrin.}}{} \qquad H_5N_3C \cdot HCl + 2HCl + HNO_3. \quad [573]$$

The interpretation of this reaction is aided by the fact that when the same chlorpicrin is distilled with alcohol and sodium it yields an ether which is a true ortho-carbonate, thus : —

$$C \equiv Cl_3(NO_2) + 4Na\text{-}O\text{-}C_2H_5 =$$
$$(C_2H_5)_4 \equiv O_4 \equiv C + 3NaCl + NaNO_2. \quad [574]$$

The same ether, heated with aqua ammonia in a closed tube, gives guanidine.

$$Et_4 \equiv O_4 \equiv C + 3NH_3 = 4Et\text{-}O\text{-}H + HN \equiv C \equiv (NH_2)_2. \quad [575]$$

There are also known a number of well-marked amine bases, which may be regarded as derived from guanidine by replacing one, two, or three atoms of its typical hydrogen by hydrocarbon radicals.

490. *Glycocyamin and Glycocyamidine, Creatine and Creatinine.* — By passing chloride of cyanogen and ammonia gas simultaneously into anhydrous ether, the ammonic chloride which is formed separates out, while there remains in solution one of the simplest and at the same time most remarkable compounds of the amide group.

$$CN\text{-}Cl + 2NH_3 = \underset{\text{Cyanamide.}}{NH_2\text{-}CN} + NH_4Cl. \quad [576]$$

Now we can directly unite the cyanamide thus formed with glycocoll, and the product is called glycocyamine, which when acted upon by dry *HCl* yields an allied base called glycocyamidine. The constitution of these bodies can be inferred with great certainty from the simple synthetical process by which the first is formed, interpreted by reactions [572] and [576]. It will be noticed that the factors in these two reactions are nearly the same, and the difference in the products depends on slight variations of conditions. Indeed, guanidine may be obtained by the action of NH_3 on the chloride as well as on the iodide of cyanogen, only it is not then the chief product, for the reaction tends to take the form of [576] rather than of [572]. An analysis of these reactions will show that the difference in the results depends on the circumstance that, while in [576] the two atoms in the cyanogen radical remain united by the three original bonds, in [572] one of these bonds is let loose, forming points of attachment to which the two radicals H and NH_2 join themselves. Now the union of glycocoll with cyanamide probably depends on a similar change, so that in the resulting glycocyamine the two atoms in the original cyanogen radical remain joined by two bonds, while the two parts of the glycocoll molecule, NH_2 and $HO\text{-}C_2H_2O$, unite to the points of attachment which the breaking of the third bond furnishes. The subsequent production of glycocyamide is simply an example of the change from a monad to a dyad radical by the elimination of HO with which we are so familiar (485).

The interest attaching to the above compounds arises from the fact that there is found in muscular juice a crystalline base called *creatine* (supposed to have important physiological relations), which is the first homologue of glycocyamine, and which yields, when treated with acids, a second base, *creatinine*, that is the first homologue of glycocyamide. Thus we have the following triamides : —

$$\left.\begin{array}{c}C\\H_5\end{array}\right\}N_3 \qquad \left.\begin{array}{c}C\\Ho\text{-}C_2H_2O\\H_4\end{array}\right\}N_3 \qquad \left.\begin{array}{c}C\\C_2H_2O\\H_3\end{array}\right\}N_3$$

Guanidine.   Glycocyamine.   Glycocyamidine.

$$\left.\begin{array}{c}C\\Ho\text{-}C_2H_2O\\CH_3\\H_3\end{array}\right\}N_3 \qquad \left.\begin{array}{c}C\\C_2H_2O\\CH_3\\H_2\end{array}\right\}N_3$$

Creatine.   Creatinine.

Both creatine and creatinine have been found not only in muscular flesh, but also in the urine, in the blood, and in other animal fluids ; but it is difficult to determine to what relative extent they exist in the living body, since, while strong acids convert creatine into creatinine, alkaline reagents change creatine back to creatinine, and these changes may take place in the processes of extraction. These bases unite directly with acids, forming well-crystallized salts, and one molecule of base neutralizes in each case one molecule of a monobasic acid.

Creatine has been formed synthetically by a process which plainly indicates its molecular constitution ; for as glycocyamine results from the union of cyanamide with glycocoll, so creatine is the product of the union of cyanamide with methylglycocoll, a compound usually called sarcosine, and the reactions below, which show that sarcosine is really methyl-glycocoll, complete the evidence.

1st. Synthesis of glycocoll.

$$Ho\text{-}(C_2H_2O)\text{-}C' + N^\equiv H_3 = Ho\text{-}(C_2H_2O)\text{-}N^\equiv H_2 + HCl. \quad [577]$$

Chloracetic Acid.   Glycocoll.

2d. Synthesis of sarcosine.

$$Ho\text{-}(C_2H_2O)\text{-}Cl + \underset{\text{Methylamine.}}{N^=(CH_3),H_2} =$$

$$\underset{\text{Sarcosine.}}{Ho\text{-}(C_2H_2O)\text{-}N^=(CH_3),H} + HCl. \quad [578]$$

491. *Caffeine and Theobromine.* — These well-known organic bases which are regarded as the active agents in tea and coffee on the one hand, and in the cacao-bean on the other, are closely allied to the class of compounds we have been studying. They are probably the methyl substitution products of a simpler amide not yet discovered. That caffeine is methyl-theobromine there is no doubt, for theobromine can be converted into caffeine by a simple process of substitution. It is also probable that theobromine itself contains methyl, for when caffeine is oxidized by chlorine and water it yields well-known dimethyl products. Moreover, these products are the methylated forms of two well-known uric acid derivatives, viz. alloxanthine and paraban, indicating that caffeine and theobromine are allied to the diureides. Now it appears from their empirical symbols that theobromine differs from xanthine by just $(CH_2)_2$, thus : —

$$\underset{\text{Xanthine.}}{C_5H_4N_4O_2} \qquad \underset{\text{Theobromine.}}{C_7H_8N_4O_2} \qquad \underset{\text{Caffeine.}}{C_8H_{10}N_4O_2.}$$

But theobromine can not be simply dimethyl-xanthine, for this last compound has been made, and although isomeric with theobromine is not the same substance. When caffeine is treated with baric hydrate there is formed during the first stage of the process a new base called caffeidine, but this is subsequently decomposed, and the ultimate products of the reaction are, besides carbonic dioxide and ammonia, formic acid, methylamine, and sarcosine. Creatine similarly treated yields, besides carbonic dioxide and ammonia, only sarcosine, and these reactions indicate that the unknown amide, of which caffeine is a methylated substitution product, is allied to creatine, probably containing like this the glycol radical.

492. *Vegetable Alkaloids.* — The active principles of many medicinal or poisonous plants are crystallizable bodies, which closely resemble in their general properties and chemical relations the complex amines or basic amides we have been studying. Several of them, like quinine and morphine, are well-known articles of the materia medica, and are perhaps the

most valuable medicinal agents which we possess. As a general rule they are soluble in water, have a strong, bitter taste, and form well-marked crystalline salts with acids. Hence the name of vegetable alkaloids. The number of these bodies now known is exceedingly large. The dried juice of the poppy, which we call opium, alone contains not less than eight distinct bases. Two of the alkaloids, conine and nicotine, from the hemlock and tobacco plant respectively, are volatile oily liquids, and they do not contain oxygen. The great body, however, of the alkaloids are oxygenated compounds, and cannot be distilled without decomposition. These two classes of alkaloids correspond to the volatile amines on the one hand, and the non-volatile ammonium bases on the other; but no safe conclusion in regard to their constitution can be drawn from this seeming analogy, for not only are the facts we have been studying sufficient to show that the class of amines or alkaline amides includes many non-volatile oxygenated bases, but all the natural alkaloids combine directly with acids in forming salts. Moreover, in several cases we are able to substitute hydrocarbon radicals for one or more of the hydrogen atoms of the alkaloid, and obtain bodies which, like the ammonium bases, eliminate water when they combine with acids.

Among the most important of the vegetable alkaloids may be mentioned morphine, narcotine, and codeine from opium; quinine and cinchonine from cinchona bark; strychnine and brucine from nux-vomica and other strychnos plants; aconitine from the monkshood; atropine from belladonna and stramonium; veratrine from the white hellebore. All these substances have been carefully studied, and their general properties and chemical relations are accurately known. Their empirical formulæ show that with few exceptions they must be very complex bodies, but beyond this very little has been made out in regard to their chemical constitution. In several cases the number of replaceable atoms of hydrogen have been determined, and in others the natural alkaloid has been proved to be a methylated substitution product of a simpler base, but in no case has the molecular structure been fully developed. The great difficulty encountered in investigating the constitution of these bodies arises from the fact that we know of no reagent by which we can replace nitrogen by monad radicals, and thus

break up the alkaloid into the several atomic groups of which
it consists, without decomposing the radicals also. The student
should study in this connection the important investigation of
Matthiessen [1] on morphine and codeine, and that of Schiff [2] on
conine, the first alkaloid which has been produced synthetically.

493. *Amine-Amides, or Alkamides.* — It must have been
noticed that with the complex compounds we have been recently studying, the clear distinction between amines and
amides previously drawn (167, 168) is almost wholly obscured.
The effect of introducing several radicals, both acid and basic,
into the same ammonia group, cannot be traced to any general
principle. The resulting molecule has sometimes basic and
sometimes acid relations. Hence it is that we have been
obliged to class with the amides so many substances having
well-marked alkaline properties, and for this reason many
chemists distinguish a third class of compounds under the ammonia type, to which they give the name of amine-amides or
alkamides (alkaline amides). An alkamide is frequently defined as a compound of the ammonia type, in which the hydrogen atoms are in part replaced by basic and in part by acid
radicals; but we prefer to give to the term the simple meaning
which the derivation indicates, for urea, which contains only an
acid radical, is one of the best-defined bodies of the class, at
least if we accept the view of its constitution usually taken.
The distinction has not been before made in this book, because
the study of the alkamides cannot well be separated from that
of the true amides to which they are so closely related; and
since several of the more important of these compounds have
already been described, further examples are unnecessary.

[1] Proceedings of the Royal Society of London, XVII. 455; also, Ann.
Chem. und Pharm., VII. Supplementband, 170.

[2] Berichte der Deutschen chem., Gesellschaft, Jahrgang, III. 946.

Alcohols and their Derivatives.

494. *Chlorals.* — The white solid which is the ultimate result of the action of chlorine gas on absolute alcohol is a compound of alcohol with one of its chlorinated derivates called chloral. When the crude product of this reaction is treated with strong sulphuric acid the chloral separates out, and may be decanted and purified by repeated distillation over lime. It is a thin colorless oil, having a pungent odor and astringent taste, boiling at 98°6, with *Sp. Gr.* = 1.49 and Sp. Gr. = 74.04. It readily dissolves in water, yielding a neutral solution which does not precipitate nitrate of silver, but in so dissolving it enters into combination, and if the amount of water is small the union is attended with a marked elevation of temperature. If the amount taken is about one eighth of the weight of the chloral the whole mass solidifies, and the white translucent solid thus formed is the familiar preparation which is now so highly valued as an anesthetic agent. *Chloral Hydrate* has a strong, pungent, ethereal odor, volatilizes gradually in the air, and distils without decomposition when heated. It melts at 50° to 51°, boils at 97° to 99°, has *Sp. Gr.* = 1.61 and Sp. Gr. = 39.84, showing that chloral and water are disassociated at 100°. This substance was discovered by Liebig in 1832, but it is only recently that its valuable medicinal qualities have been appreciated or its chemical relations fully understood.

Chloral is a chlor-aldehyde, and has the same structure as acetic aldehyde, but contains Cl_3 in place of the H_3 in the methyl radical.

$$CH_3\text{-}CO\text{-}H \qquad\qquad CCl_3\text{-}CO\text{-}H.$$
Acetic Aldehyde.   Acetic Chloral.

Its constitution is shown by the following reactions: 1st. Acetic aldehyde when acted on by chlorine gas, under regulated conditions, is converted into chloral. 2d. Chloral when acted on by nascent hydrogen changes back to aldehyde. 3d. Chloral combines with NH_3, forming a compound corresponding to aldehyde ammonia. 4th. Oxidizing agents convert chloral into chloracetic acid (31) and [479].

ith a solution of
· with a formiate

of the alkaline metal, and the value of the hydrate as an anesthetic agent seems to depend on the fact that a similar reaction takes place in the blood.

$$(CCl_3)\text{-}CO\text{-}H + (K\text{-}O)\text{-}H = K\text{-}O\text{-}(CO\text{-}H) + CCl_3\text{-}H. \quad [579]$$

Chloral. Potassic Formate. Chloroform.

When chloral is heated with nitric acid there is formed, besides chloracetic acid, which is the direct product of the oxidation due to this reagent, also a small amount of a substance called chlorpicrin. The last is the product of a metathesis between the radicals of the acid and the chloral, thus : —

$$(CCl_3)\text{-}CO\text{-}H + (H\text{-}O)\text{-}NO_2 =$$
Chloral.
$$H\text{-}O\text{-}(CO\text{-}H) + CCl_3\text{-}(NO_2). \quad [580]$$
Formic Acid. Chlorpicrin.

It will be noticed that while in this reaction the radical CCl_3 changes place with HO, in the previous reaction it changed place with KO, and this fact is a most striking illustration of the theory of chemical polarity. Chlorpicrin is an oily liquid, usually obtained by the action of chlorine on picric acid, and may be regarded as chloroform in which the remaining hydrogen atom has been replaced by NO_2.

Chloral combines not only with water and with ethylic alcohol, but also with other alcohols of the same family, with urea, and with several amides. These products are generally regarded as molecular compounds, but it is more probable that they have the constitution represented in the scheme below : —

$(CH_3\text{-}CH)\text{=}O$	$(CCl_3\text{-}CH)\text{=}O.$
Acetic Aldehyde.	Chloral.
	$(CCl_3\text{-}CH)\text{=}Ho_2.$
	Chloral Hydrate.
	$(CCl_3\text{-}CH)\text{=}Eto,Ho.$
	Chloral Hydro-ethylate.
$(CH_3\text{-}CH)\text{=}Eto_2$	$(CCl_3\text{-}CH)\text{=}Eto_2.$
Acetal.	Chloral Diethylate.

As here represented, the compounds, with water and alcohol, are intermediate terms between chloral and another substitution product, which bears the same relation to acetal [1] that chloral

---

[1] Acetal is a well-known product of the oxidation of ethylic alcohol. It contains the radical ethylidene, and differs both in $Sp. Gr.$ and boiling-point from an isomeric compound containing ethylene, which has also been isolated.

bears to acetic aldehyde. These formulæ are supported by the fact that, while aldehyde chloral and chloral hydrate are all converted by PCl_5 into ethylidene chloride (31) (464), the compound of chloral with alcohol yields, under the same conditions, a substance represented by the symbol (CCl_3-CH)-Eto, Cl, and not the normal products of the action of PCl_5 on chloral and alcohol separately, as we should expect if they were present as such in the compound in question.

It has been stated above that acetic chloral may be formed from acetic aldehyde by the direct action of chlorine gas under regulated conditions. It is simply necessary that there should be present with the aldehyde lumps of marble to absorb the HCl, which is formed by the reaction; for HCl converts acetic aldehyde into crotonic aldehyde, and this product is then the only point of attack for the chlorine gas. Thus it is that when chlorine acts on acetic aldehyde without any check, the final product is not acetic chloral, but a new chloral derived from crotonic aldehyde (453).

$$(CH_3\text{-}CH\text{=}CH\text{-}CO)\text{-}H \qquad (CCl_3\text{-}CH\text{=}CH\text{-}CO)\text{-}H.$$

Crotonic Aldehyde.   Crotonic Chloral.

Crotonic chloral resembles outwardly acetic chloral, and forms a similar compound with water. It is the only other chloral which has thus far been isolated; but an insoluble isomeric modification of common chloral is known whose relations are not yet understood.

495. *Mellitic Acid.* — This compound has long been known as a constituent of the mineral mellite or honeystone, which is mellitate of aluminum, $[Al_2]C_6O_6 . 9H_2O$, and is found in reddish-yellow octahedral crystals in the brown coal at several localities; but it is only recently that its remarkable chemical relations have been discovered. It has been shown by Bayer that this acid is hexabasic and belongs to the phenyl group. It may be regarded as derived from benzol, C_6H_6, by replacing all the six atoms of hydrogen with oxatyl. Benzoic acid, it will be remembered, is benzol with one of the hydrogen atoms replaced by oxatyl, and Bayer has not only been able to identify three of the four intermediate acids which are theoretically possible, but he has also shown that each of the three is capable of two isomeric modifications. Thus we have : —

Normal Series.	Isomeric Series.	2d Isomeric Series.	
Benzol.			$C_6H_6.$
Benzoic Acid.			$C_6H_5\text{-}(CO\text{-}Ho).$
Terephthalic Acid.	Isophthalic Acid.	Phthalic Acid.	$C_6H_4\text{=}(CO\text{-}Ho)_2.$
Trimellitic Acid.	Trimesic Acid.	Hemimellitic Acid.	$C_6H_3\text{≡}(CO\text{-}Ho)_3.$
Pyromellitic Acid.	Prehnitic Acid.	Mellophanic Acid.	$C_6H_2\text{≡}(CO\text{-}Ho)_4.$
			$C_6H \text{≣}(CO\text{-}Ho)_5.$
Mellitic Acid.			$C_6 \text{ vi } (CO\text{-}Ho)_6.$

The isomeric modifications probably result from a variation of the order in which the hydrogen and oxatyl atoms are attached to the carbon atoms of the primary nucleus (428, Fig. c.) and (456).

One of the compounds included in the above scheme has certain other remarkable chemical relations which point with great certainty to its molecular constitution. Phthalic acid is not only a derivation of benzol, but also of naphthaline; for this well-known hydrocarbon (434), when heated with strong oxidizing agents, yields a mixture of phthalic and oxalic acids. Assuming it proved that phthalic acid has the benzol nucleus, the best theory we can form in regard to this reaction gives to the molecule of naphthaline the singular constitution represented below; and it can be seen by comparing the three graphic symbols placed side by side that the reaction is thus fully explained.

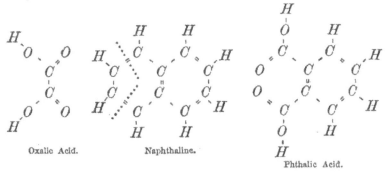

Oxalic Acid.   Naphthaline.   Phthalic Acid.

If this theory is correct, it follows that in phthalic acid the two oxatyl groups are united to adjacent carbon atoms of the nucleus, and that its constitution is so far determined. Again, it will be noticed that these adjacent carbon atoms are united by a double bond, and that in the closed chain, of which they are a part, the links are joined by double and single bonds alternating. Now it is evident that if either of these double bonds could be exchanged for a single one, the nucleus would

be able to attach to itself two additional hydrogen atoms, six
in all, and that if, besides, we could break the chain between
the two adjacent atoms above referred to, the nucleus could
hold yet two more, and we should then have suberic acid (470).
Now all these transformations appear to be possible, for we
have been able to prepare the following series of bodies :—

Phthalic Acid,　　　　　　　　$C_6H_4 = (CO\text{-}Ho)_2$.
Hydro-phthalic Acid,　　　　　$C_6H_6 = (CO\text{-}Ho)_2$.
Tetrahydro-phthalic Acid,　　　$C_6H_8 = (CO\text{-}Ho)_2$.
Hexahydro-phthalic Acid,　　　$C_6H_{10} = (CO\text{-}Ho)_2$.
Suberic Acid,　　　　　　　　$C_6H_{12} = (CO\text{-}Ho)_2$.

We are also acquainted with still another derivative of benzol
called tartro-phthalic acid, which differs from hexahydro-phthalic acid only in that there is associated with each oxatyl group,
and attached to the same carbon atom, HO in place of H.
Tartro, hexahydro, and tetrahydro-phthalic acids are related
by a peculiar kind of homology to tartaric succinic and maleic
acids respectively, which will be evident on bringing together
their graphic symbols. The theory that in all these acids except suberic the two oxatyl groups are joined to adjacent carbon atoms is sustained by other considerations than the one we
have given here, but for these we must refer the student to the
original memoirs.

The graphic symbol of naphthaline being so symmetrical, it
would seem impossible to determine on which side the division
of the nucleus takes place in the reaction represented above;
but there are conditions in which even this can be traced. We
have written below the symbol of naphthaline so as to indicate
in a measure its bilateral structure, and on the same line we
have given the symbols of two of its well-marked substitution
products, which are very numerous : —

$C_4H_4 = C_2 = C_4H_4$　　　　$C_4H_4 = C_2 = C_4Cl_2O_2$　　　　$C_4H_3Cl = C_2 = C_4Cl_4$.
Naphthaline.　　　　　　　Dichlordioxynaphthaline.　　　　Pentachlornaphthaline.

Now the first of these derivatives when oxidized gives phthalic
acid like naphthaline itself, while under the same conditions the
second gives tetrachlorphthalic acid. Evidently, then, in the
first case the substitution is confined to one side of the naphthaline molecule, and the division which accompanies the oxidation takes place on the same side ; while in the second case not

only all the hydrogen atoms on one side are replaced, but also one on the other, and the division takes place on the side of the single chlorine atom; for were the nucleus divided on the other side we should have not tetrachlorphthalic but monochlorphthalic acid.   These reactions, moreover, furnish very strong evidence in favor of the theory of the structure of the naphthaline molecule stated above.   Since, as we obtain a body having the structure of phthalic acid on whichever side we divide the molecule, it is evident that the two sides must have the same structure, so that if we are not mistaken in regard to the structure of phthalic acid there can remain but little doubt in regard to that of naphthaline.   Now phthalic acid, when heated with an excess of lime, yields benzol, and benzol, when oxidized under certain conditions, yields benzoic and phthalic acid, reactions which may be almost said to prove that this acid contains the benzol or phenyl nucleus.   The simple relations of phthalic to benzoic acid are evident.

If, with Kekulé, we number the carbon atoms of the phenyl nucleus from 1 to 6, and assume that in phthalic acid the two oxatyl radicals are united to the first and second atoms of the nucleus, then it is evident that, without altering the general structure, two modifications of it may be obtained by changing the position of the oxatyl radical, which can also be attached either to the first and third or to the first and fourth atoms of the closed chain.   Now there is good reason for believing that such is the position of the radicals in isophthalic and terephthalic acids respectively, but for the evidence we must refer to the original papers.[1]

[1] Ann. Chem. und Pharm., VII. Supplementband, 1; also CXLIX. 27; also Jour. Chem. Soc. of London, Vol. IX. 872.

Quinone Group.

496. *Quinone.* — The artificial production of alizarine, the coloring principle of madder, is not only one of the most remarkable achievements of modern chemistry, but is also a direct corroboration of the validity of the mode of reasoning which the new philosophy of the science has introduced. Alizarine was actually *constructed* by following out the indications of a theory of its *molecular structure,* to which a study of its reactions and those of allied compounds had led. In order to make clear the course of the investigation we must go back to the discovery of quinone in 1838. This body was obtained by the oxidation of quinic acid, a vegetable acid found in cinchona bark, where it is combined with cinchonine and quinine. Quinone is a volatile solid, crystallizing by sublimation in shining yellow needles, which have the composition indicated by the empirical symbol $C_6H_4O_2$. When heated with a mixture of hydrochloric acid and potassic chlorate it is rapidly converted into tetrachlorquinone, $C_6Cl_4O_2$, a compound which is identical with chloranil, a product of the action of the same agents on carbolic acid, aniline, and other well-known bodies of the phenyl group. But although these reactions indicated a close relationship with the class of compounds formed around the carbon nucleus, represented in Fig. c., page 457, the first satisfactory theory in regard to the molecular structure of quinone was that advanced by Graebe in 1868.[1] He concluded, as the result of a very extended investigation of the whole class of allied compounds, first, that the molecule of quinone contains the phenyl nucleus; secondly, that the two atoms of oxygen in this molecule are united together by a common bond, thus forming a dyad radical which aids in binding together two adjacent carbon atoms of the phenyl nucleus, thus: so that, according to his view, quinone may be regarded as derived from benzol by replacing two neighboring hydrogen atoms in its molecules by the radical $=[O_2]$.

$$
\begin{array}{ccc}
 & H & \\
 & | & \\
 & C & \\
 & \diagup \quad \diagdown & \\
H\text{-}C & & C\text{-}O \\
 & & \| \\
H\text{-}C & & C\text{-}O \\
 & \diagdown \quad \diagup & \\
 & C & \\
 & | & \\
 & H &
\end{array}
$$

[1] Untersuchungen über die Chinongruppe, Ann. der Chem. und Pharm., CXLVI.

The above conclusions are based chiefly on the following facts. In support of the first we have a large number of reactions besides those mentioned above, whose concurrent testimony leaves no doubt that the benzol and the quinone group of compounds are formed around the same carbon nucleus, so that if we accept Kekulé's [1] theory in regard to the first, we must extend it also to the last. In support of the second, we have the fact that when by reactions, which are well understood, the oxygen of the quinone molecule is replaced by hydroxyl or chlorine, the two atoms are exchanged for only two atoms of these monad radicals, and not for four, as would be the case if the oxygen atoms were united to the carbon nucleus by all four of their bonds. Thus, when quinone is acted on by hydriodic acid it yields hydroquinone, whose symbol is $C_6H_4{=}Ho_2$, and oxidizing agents change this body back to quinone. Again, when tetrachlorquinone, $C_6Cl_4O_2$, is acted on by phosphoric chloride the products are C_6Cl_6 and free chlorine gas. It is impossible, however, in a few words, to do justice to the arguments which Graebe advances in support of his theory, which will be found clearly stated in the paper already referred to.

In studying the derivatives of quinone Graebe recognized certain general characteristics, which he attributed to their supposed molecular structure. Of these, the most striking, after the two just illustrated, is the fact that two of the monad atoms, H or Cl, associated with the oxygen radical, ${=}[O_2]$, in the molecular group may be readily replaced by Ho, H_2N, or HSO_3, the product being an acid, an amide, or a sulpho-acid. This well-marked character of the quinone group of compounds Graebe attributes to the influence of the atomic group $[C_2O_2]$ on the rest of the molecule, which, as he supposes, throws the neighboring atoms into a polar condition, similar to that produced by CO in the organic acids and aldehydes. The three characteristics of the quinone group we have signalized are better illustrated by the chlorine derivatives of quinone than by quinone itself. Take, for example, tetrachlorquinone or

---

[1] Kekulé originated the theory in regard to the molecular structure of the radical phenyl which has been presented in this book. For the evidence on which it is based we must refer to Kekulé's well-known work on Organic Chemistry, as it is too extended to be given here ; also, Ann. Chem. und Pharm., CXXXVII. 129.

chloranil, mentioned above, which has the following chemical relations : —

1. Reducing agents readily convert chloranil into tetrachlor-hydroquinone, $C_6Cl_4=Ho_2$, a compound which oxidizing agents as readily change back to chloranil, and whose atoms of hydrogen may be replaced by metals or organic radicals, giving such bodies as $C_6Cl_4=Ko_2$, $C_6Cl_4=Eto_2$, $C_6Cl_4=Aco_2$.

2. When acted on by phosphoric chloride, chloranil yields C_6Cl_6 and free chlorine, as stated above.

3. If chloranil is dissolved in a solution of potassic hydrate, a metathesis takes place between Cl_2 in the first and Ko_2 in the last, in conformity with the third characteristic we have described, and if the proportions are rightly regulated there crystallize out from the solution red needles of potassic chloranilate, $Ko_2=C_6Cl_2=[O_2]$. From a solution of this salt hydrochloric or sulphuric acids precipitate chloranilic acid, $Ho_2=C_6Cl_2=[O_2]$, in similarly colored crystals.

Trichlorquinone, $C_6Cl_3HO_2$, yields also similar derivatives, which for the most part contain C_6Cl_3H in place of C_6Cl_4, but when treated with potassic hydrate it yields chloranilic acid, the same product which is obtained from tetrachlorquinone, showing that the single remaining hydrogen atom is one of the two replaced in the reaction.

497. *Naphtho-quinone.* — Graebe's next step, in the course of investigation we are following, was to recognize in the compound we have called dichlordioxynaphthaline (495) a body having the same general structure as quinone. In a paper published in 1869,[1] he showed that this body, which he calls dichlornaphtho-quinone,[2] has the same general characteristics as tetra- or tri-chlorquinone. Thus it appears,

1st. That dichlornaphtho-quinone, when acted on by reducing agents, yields dichlorhydronaphtho-quinone,

$$C_{10}H_4Cl_2=[O_2] + H\text{-}H = C_{10}H_4Cl_2=Ho_2.$$

Moreover, in this compound, as in tetrachlorhydro-quinone, Ho_2 may be replaced by Aco_2.

2d. That dichlornaphtho-quinone yields with phosphoric chloride the compound $C_{10}H_3Cl_5$, by which it is evident that, as in

[1] Ann. der Chem. und Pharm., CXLIX.

[2] The German name for quinone is chinon, and the names of the different quinone derivatives are formed from this root.

the case of tetrachlorquinone, the group $[O_2]$ is replaced by Cl_2, although at the same time a further replacement of the hydrogen atoms of the original naphthaline molecule is effected so that no free chlorine is evolved.

3d. That when dichlornaphtho-quinone is dissolved in a solution of potassic hydrate there are formed cherry-red needles of the potassic salt, of an acid corresponding to chloranilic acid, and from this salt, by the action of hydrochloric acid, the acid itself is readily obtained, as a yellow precipitate having the composition expressed by the symbol $Ho\text{-}C_{10}H_4Cl\text{-}[O_2]$. It will be noticed that in the reactions by which the so-called chloroxynaphthalic acid is formed only one atom of chlorine is replaced by hydroxyl, and not two, as in the case of chloranilic acid. The acid is a coloring matter, dyeing wool a scarlet or orange color, but has no affinity for alumina mordants.

The above facts certainly justified the theory of Graebe in regard to the constitution of these derivatives of naphthaline, and since his paper was published naphthoquinone itself, $C_{10}H_6[O_2]$, has been obtained. Thus the word "quinone" has become the name of a class of compounds, and indicates the peculiar molecular structure we have described.

Dichlornaphtho-quinone and chloroxynaphthalic acid were discovered by Laurent, 1836–40, and the great similarity, as indicated by ultimate analysis, between the last and alizarine was noticed soon after. Indeed, chloroxynaphthalic acid was for some time regarded as chlorinated alizarine, and this opinion was apparently confirmed by the fact that both these substances yield phthalic acid by decomposition with nitric acid. But about six years since Martius and Griess succeeded in replacing the single atom of chlorine in chloroxynaphthalic acid with hydrogen, and a coloring matter was obtained having the formula $C_{10}H_6O_3$, which is identical with that assigned to alizarine by Strecker. This body, however, did not prove to be alizarine, although it was supposed at the time to be isomeric with it.

498. *Anthraquinone and Alizarine.* — Graebe, now associated with Liebermann, beginning the investigation of alizarine at the point we left it in the last section, naturally inferred, from the resemblance to chloroxynaphthalic acid, that the coloring matter of madder might be a similar acid, though derived

from a different quinone, and, in order to obtain some clew to the hydrocarbon to which it is related, these chemists sought as a first step to reduce natural alizarine by heating it with powdered zinc, adopting a method first suggested by Bayer for reducing similar compounds. The result was a solid body, which was soon recognized as identical with anthracene, a hydrocarbon ($C_{14}H_{10}$) associated with naphthaline in coal-tar, and it was of course at once inferred that alizarine was the quinone acid of this well-known hydrocarbon, thus : —

$$C_{14}H_{10} \qquad\qquad C_{14}H_8O_2 \qquad\qquad Ho_2{=}C_{14}H_6{=}[O_2].$$

Anthracene.   Anthraquinone.   Anthraquinonic Acid or Alizarine.

The formula of alizarine thus deduced, although differing from that of Strecker, agreed with that of Schunk, who had made a most extended investigation of the constituents of madder. Before, however, this theory of the constitution of alizarine could be established, it was essential to reverse the process of reduction and produce alizarine from anthracene, and the first step was to obtain the anthraquinone. Here again Graebe was aided by the previous investigations of Laurent, who long before had obtained an oxygenated derivative of anthracene, which he called, in accordance with a peculiar nomenclature of his own, anthracenuse. The substance had been re-examined by Anderson, who gave it the symbol $C_{14}H_8O_2$, and in it Graebe and Liebermann at once recognized the required quinone. It only now remained to replace two atoms of the hydrogen in this body by hydroxyl, in order to settle the question whether alizarine is the quinone acid of anthracene or not. The method was obvious. Anthraquinone was heated with bromine, which, replacing two of its hydrogen atoms, yielded the compound $C_{14}H_6Br_2[O_2]$, and this heated to 180° with a solution of potassic hydrate gave an intense blue solution, from which hydrochloric acid precipitated a yellow crystalline powder identical in every respect with the alizarine obtained from madder.

This was the first instance of the artificial production of a vegetable coloring matter, and we have dwelt at more length than usual on the history of this beautiful discovery, because it affords an admirable illustration of the methods of modern chemistry.[1] Before the discovery could be applied in the arts

[1] In preparing this section we have been aided by an interesting paper of W. H. Perkins (Journal of Chem. Soc. of London, for 1870, page 133), in which specimens of prints made with artificial alizarine are given.

it was of course essential that the synthetical process should be modified so as to adapt it to a manufacturing scale, and this has been in a great measure accomplished by substituting for bromine sulphuric acid, which when heated with anthraquinone converts it into a sulpho acid, $(HSO_3)_2 = C_{14}H_6 = [O_2]$, and this, like the corresponding bromine compound, yields alizarine when heated with potassic hydrate.

499. *Purpurine.* — There is associated with alizarine in madder a second coloring material called purpurine, but as it is not absorbed by mordanted calicoes it has little commercial value. Like alizarine, it is reduced to anthracene by zinc powder, and the result of its ultimate analysis agrees very well with the symbol $Ho_3 = C_{14}H_5 = [O_2]$, but we have no further proof of its correctness. A third coloring principle has also been distinguished, called pseudopurpurine, whose analysis gave results corresponding to the symbol $Ho_4 = C_{14}H_4 = [O_2]$. It is probable that all three of these coloring materials occur in the madder-root as glucosides.

500. *Constitution of Anthracene.* — We have now distinguished three quinones, viz. benzoquinone, naphthoquinone, and anthraquinone. Graebe and Liebermann have shown in their recent paper [1] that the last has the chief characteristics we have distinguished in the other two, and that it gives similar derivatives. It only remains to add a few works in regard to its molecular constitution. In the paper just referred to Graebe and Liebermann advance the theory that the anthracene molecule has a structure which may be represented thus : —

Anthracene.

and hence that anthracene bears the same relation to naphthaline that naphthaline bears to benzol (428) and (495). This theory is not only rendered probable by the similar chemical relations of those three hydrocarbons which we have been

[1] Ann. der Chem. und Pharm., VII. Supplementband, 1870, 312.

studying, but it also furnishes a satisfactory explanation of two synthetical processes by which anthracene has been produced.

1. When benzylchloride, C_6H_5-CH_2-Cl, is heated with water in a closed tube to 180°, anthracene is one of the chief products. If we suppose that the production of the hydrocarbon results from the coalescing of two molecules of the chloride, the reaction may be indicated thus : —

and it can readily be seen that if each molecule of the chloride gives up a molecule of HCl and an atom of H, we shall have the two halves of a molecule of anthracene as represented above.

2. Anthracene may be also formed by passing a mixture of benzol and styrol (cinamene) vapors through a red-hot tube, and the same graphic symbol gives a very simple account of its production.

This synthesis was observed by Berthelot, who also obtained anthracene under similar conditions from toluol and also from a mixture of benzol and ethylene. Both processes admit of a similar simple explanation based on the above formula. In the last case the chief product is styrol, which probably precedes the formation of anthracene.

The three hydrocarbons, benzol, naphthaline, and anthracene, form a well-defined series, whose successive members differ from each other, not, as in the alcohol family, by CH_2, but by C_4H_2, and to this corresponds a difference of about 140° in the boiling-points.

	C_6H_6	Diff.	$C_{10}H_8$	Diff.	$C_{14}H_{10}$.
B. P.	80°	136°	216°	144°	360°

Apart from similar differences which the gradations in the series necessarily determine, these bodies strikingly resemble each other both in their physical and chemical qualities. The last point has been illustrated in this chapter so far as regards the formation of the quinone derivatives, and the impression produced by the facts here presented would be strengthened by a further study of the subject. All this of course indicates a similarity in the molecular structure of these bodies, and the cumulative evidence in favor of the theory here adopted is therefore much greater than that which can be obtained in regard to either of the substances separately.

501. *Chrysene and Pyrene.* — Since the identification of anthraquinone it has been discovered that two other hydrocarbons associated with naphthaline and anthracene, among the least volatile of the products of the distillation of coal-tar, were capable of yielding derivatives belonging to the class of quinones. The names chrysene and pyrene were given by Laurent to impure products, and it is only very recently that these bodies have been isolated and their composition accurately determined.[1] Chrysene, $C_{18}H_{12}$, makes evidently the fourth term of the naphthaline series, differing from anthracene by C_4H_2, and its molecule may be regarded as formed from that of anthracene by the addition of another phenyl nucleus, thus: Pyrene, $C_{16}H_{10}$, although not belonging to the same series, appears to be similarly constituted, and may be regarded as phenylene-naphthaline $(C_{10}H_6)''(C_6H_4)$. Chryso-quinone, $C_{18}H_{10}[O_2]$, has the chief characteristics of a true quinone, but in pyrene-quinone, $C_{16}H_8[O_2]$, the characters are less strongly marked.

---

[1] Graebe und Liebermann, Ann. Chem. und Pharm., CLVIII., 285 and 299. June, 1871.

Electrical Measurements.

502. *Fundamental Laws.* — The following formulæ express the most important properties of electrical currents : —

(1.) $C = F\dfrac{K^2}{Lm}$.   (2.) $C = \dfrac{E}{R}$.   (3.) $Q = Ct$.   (4.) $W = C^2Rt$.   (5.) $W = QE$.

The first defines strength of current as a magnitude proportional to the force which it exerts on a magnetic pole under constant conditions. These conditions are the strength of pole, m, the length of the conductor, L, — assumed, as in the common form of galvanometer, to be bent in a circle around the pole, — and the radius of this circle, K. The unit of force is that force which imparts to one gramme of matter the velocity of one metre in one second, and the unit pole that pole which at a distance of one metre repels a similar and equal pole with the unit force.

The second is Ohm's formula (88), and expresses the principle, which can be readily demonstrated experimentally, that the strength of current, as defined by (1), is directly proportional to the electromotive force of the given circuit, and inversely proportional to the resistance of the circuit. It also involves the still further truth that in *different parts* of the *same circuit*, where the strength of current is necessarily the same (88), the difference of tension or potential [1] between any two points is always proportional to the resistance between these points.

The third expresses a truth first verified experimentally by

---

[1] The influence of the electromotive force extends throughout the circuit, causing at every cross section of the conductor what we may call an *electrical pressure*, which regulates the flow of the electrical current. This pressure is greatest at the surface of the active plate where the power originates, and diminishes as we proceed round the circuit in either direction. At some intermediate section where the opposite currents neutralize each other the pressure is zero, and as we move back from this neutral point against the negative current we encounter an ever-increasing "negative" pressure, while in the opposite direction we meet an ever-increasing "positive" pressure. What we here call electrical pressure is called above tension or potential, and without attempting to give a theoretical conception of its nature, it is sufficient to say that it is a force measured at any point of the circuit by the tendency of the current to leave the conductor. Ohm's formula holds not only for the whole circuit, but also for any part of it; but in such cases E stands, not for the whole electromotive force, but for the difference of tension between the two ends of the portion under consideration.

Faraday, that the quantity of electricity which passes any point of a circuit, as measured by the amount of electrolysis, is proportional to the strength of the current and the time during which it flows.

The fourth expresses an important law, first demonstrated experimentally by Joule, that the work done by a current (e. g. the quantity of heat generated) is proportional to the square of the current, to the time during which it acts, and to the resistance which it encounters. It should be remembered in this connection that the unit of force acting through one metre does the unit of work; that the force of gravity acting on one gramme of matter through one metre does 9.8 units of work, equal to one metre-gramme, and that the unit of heat (12) is equivalent to 4157.25 units of work or 423.8 metre-grammes.

The fifth is involved in the previous three, from which it is readily deduced, and expresses the fact that the work done in any portion of the circuit is proportional to the quantity of electricity which passes over it and to the difference of tension between the two ends.

503. *Kirchhoff's Laws.* — The following propositions may be deduced from the general theory of electrical currents : —

1. *The sum of the currents which approach any point is always equal to those which recede from it.*

Or, if we distinguish the first by a plus and the second by a negative sign, we may say more generally : —

The sum of all the currents which meet at a point is equal to zero.

2. *On any continuous line of conductors the sum of the products of the resistances of the several parts by the strength of the current in each part is equal to the sum of the electromotive forces included in the same closed circuit.*

The last proposition holds true of every circuit which may be traced in any system of conductors and batteries, however complicated the maze; only currents flowing in opposite directions, with reference to the given circuit, must be distinguished by opposite signs. Moreover, the sum is equal to zero when there is no electromotive force on the line of conductors under consideration.

504. *Electrical Units.* — In the following problems the val-

ues C, R, or r and E of Ohm's formula are assumed to be measured in terms of the following units: First, the *unit of current* is that which would produce, by the electrolysis of water, 1 $\overline{c.\ m.}^3$ of hydrogen and oxygen gas (measured under standard conditions) in one minute. Secondly, the *unit of resistance* is that offered by a pure silver or copper wire 1 m. long, and 1 m. m. in diameter at 0°. Lastly, the unit of *electromotive force* is that which transmits a *unit current* against a *unit resistance* in a *unit of time*.

By means of the magnetic and thermal relations given by (1) and (4) above, it is possible to express the values of the three elements of an electrical current in terms of the fundamental units of space, weight and time, the metre, the gramme, and the second. The following formulæ in which $L =$ length, $M =$ mass or weight, and $T =$ time, are easily deduced, involving only simple mechanical principles : —

Velocity $= V = \dfrac{L}{T}$.

Force $= F = \dfrac{MV}{T} = \dfrac{ML}{T^2}$.

Work $= W = FL = \dfrac{ML^2}{T^2}$.

Work in metre-grammes $= \dfrac{ML^2}{T^2} \cdot \dfrac{1}{9 \cdot 8}$.

Strength of pole [1] $= m = \dfrac{L^{\frac{3}{2}} M^{\frac{1}{2}}}{T}$.

Strength of current [2] $= C = \dfrac{L^{\frac{1}{2}} M^{\frac{1}{2}}}{T}$.

Quantity of electricity $= Q = CT = L^{\frac{1}{2}} M^{\frac{1}{2}}$.

Electro-motive force $= E = \dfrac{W}{Q} = \dfrac{M^{\frac{1}{2}} L^{\frac{3}{2}}}{T^2}$.

Resistance $= R = \dfrac{E}{C} = \dfrac{L}{T} = V$.

The values of C, R, and E, when the several factors in the formulæ expressing their values are each taken equal to unity, are called the electromagnetic units. Thus the unit of resist-

---

[1] This value is readily obtained by considering that the force exerted between the two poles must be $F = \dfrac{mm'}{D^2}$ or $= \dfrac{m^2}{D^2}$ when the two poles are equal. Hence, $m = D \sqrt{F}$.

[2] Readily derived from value of C, (1).

ance is a velocity of one metre a second.[1] These absolute units, however, are of an order of magnitude which is unsuitable for ordinary measurements, but the following very small multiples or submultiples may be used to advantage : —

For R the Ohm	equal to 10^7 absolute units of resistance.			
" " " Megohm	" " 10^{13}	"	" " "
" " " Microhm	" " 10	"	" " "
" E " Volt	" " 10^5	"	" " electromotive force.
" " " Megavolt	" " 10^{11}	"	" " " "
" " " Microvolt	" " 10^{-1}	"	" " " "
" C " Farad	" " 10^{-8}	"	" " quantity per second.
" " " Megafarad	" " 10^{-2}	"	" " " " "
" " " Microfarad	" " 10^{-14}	"	" " " " "

The unit current is a current of one Farad a second.

A pure copper or silver wire 1 m. m. in diameter and 48.61 metres long has a resistance of one Ohm at 65° F., and the Committee of the British Association on Electrical Standards have carefully constructed a standard Ohm of which copies are readily accessible. Further, we have a closely approximate standard of electromotive force in the Daniell's cell, which, according to Sir W. Thompson, is equal to 1.079 Volts, or 1 Volt = 0.9268 of force of Daniell's cell. One Volt equals about 500.6 of the old units, and a current of one Megafarad per second will yield during one minute by the electrolysis of water 10.3 $\overline{\text{c. m.}}^3$ of gas very nearly.

The admirable instruments now constructed for the purpose enable us to use the B. A. units, as they are called, with great facility, but in solving the following problems the older system will be found more convenient. The student, however, should familiarize himself with both ; but he should bear in mind that values in Ohm's Volts and Farads must be reduced to absolute units before they can be substituted for C, R, or E in Ohm's formula.

Questions and Problems.

1. What resistance does the current suffer in an iron wire 50 metres long and 5 m. m. diameter? Sp. R. of iron 7.

Ans. 14 units.

2. Assuming that the Sp. R. of copper is 1.3 and that of iron 7, what must be the diameter of an iron wire which will oppose no greater resistance to the current than a copper wire of 2 m. m. diameter?

Ans. 4.64 m. m.

---

[1] For the interpretation of this remarkable analytical result see pamphlet by the author on Absolute System of Electrical Measurements.

3. It is found by experiment that a wire of German silver, 7.201 m. long and 1.5 m. m. diameter, opposes the same resistance to the current as a wire of pure silver 10 m. long and $\frac{1}{2}$ m. m. diameter. What is the Sp. R. of German silver.   Ans. 12.5.

4. It is required to make with 132.8 grammes of pure silver, a wire which will offer a resistance of 81 units. What must be its length and diameter ?   *Sp. Gr.* of silver = 10.57.

Solution. Representing by x the length in *metres*, and by y the diameter in *millimetres*, we deduce by [1] $y^2 x \frac{\pi}{4} 10.57 = 132.8$ and by the laws of conduction $\frac{x}{y^2} = 81$.   Whence $x = 36$ m. and $y = \frac{2}{3}$ m. m.

5. What is the length and diameter of an iron wire weighing 97.38 grammes, which offers a resistance of 9,072 units ? It is known that the *Sp. Gr.* of the iron = 7.75 and its Sp. R. = 7.
Ans. Length, 144 m.   Diameter, $\frac{1}{3}$ m. m.

6. From a given wire there are four branches, of which the resistance is respectively 10, 20, 30, and 40. Required the total resistance when the current passes simultaneously through the four branches.

Solution. The resistance in the first branch may be represented by a normal silver wire 10 m. long and 1 m. m. diameter. If we call the area of a transverse section of this wire s, then the resistance in the other three branches will be represented by normal wires of the same length, but having on the cross sections the areas $\frac{1}{2}s$, $\frac{1}{3}s$ and $\frac{1}{4}s$ respectively. If next we conceive of these wires as merged in one, having the common length 10 m. and an area on the section equal to $(1 + \frac{1}{2} + \frac{1}{3} + \frac{1}{4})s$, it is evident that such a wire will represent the resistance required. Hence we easily deduce,
Ans. 4.8.

7. A closed circuit has two branches through which the current passes simultaneously. In one branch $r = 100$. What length of copper wire 5 m. m. diameter must be used for the other that the total $r = 50$?   : Ans. 2,500 metres.

8. A conductor has two branches, one having $r = 756$, the other so adjusted that when the current passes at the same time through both, the *total* resistance equals 540. Required the length of a German silver wire $\frac{1}{2}$ m. m. diameter and Sp. R. = 12.5, which, when inserted in the adjusted branch, will increase the *total* resistance to 630.

Solution. By principle of last problem we easily find that the resistance in the adjusted branch before insertion equals 1,890, and after insertion, 3,780. The difference between these values, 1,890, is the resistance due to the inserted wire. Hence its length must be 37.8 metres.

9. We have a battery of six Daniells cells, in each of which $E = 475$, $R = 15$, and the external resistance against which the battery is to work, $r = 10$. The cells may be arranged, 1st, as six single elements; 2d, as three double elements;[1] 3d, as two three-fold elements; 4th, as one six-fold element. Required the current strength in each case.   Ans. 28.5, 43.8, 47.5 and 38.0 respectively.

10. We have a battery of twelve Grove cells, in each of which $E = 830$, and $R = 18$, to work against an external resistance of $r = 24$. Required the strength of current when the cells are arranged, 1st, as twelve single; 2d, as six two-fold; 3d, as four three-fold; 4th, as three four-fold; 5th, as two six-fold, and 6th, as one twelve-fold element.

Ans. 41.5, 63.8, 69.2, 66.4, 55.3, and 32.5 respectively.

11. With a single cell, where E and R have a constant value, what is the maximum strength of current, and under what conditions would it be obtained?

Ans. $\dfrac{E}{R}$, when the external resistance is nothing.

12. With n cells in each of which E and R have the same value, what is the maximum strength of current, and under what conditions would it be obtained?

Ans. $n \dfrac{E}{R}$, when the cells are arranged as one n-fold element, and work against no external resistance.

13. With n cells as above, working against a given external resistance r, how should they be arranged so as to obtain the maximum value of C?

Ans. So as to make the internal resistance equal to that of the external circuit.

Solution. If x represents the number of compound elements formed with the n cells when C in Ohm's formula is a maximum, we should evidently have under this condition x compound elements, each formed of $\dfrac{n}{x}$ cells. The electromotive force of such an arrangement would be $x E$. The internal resistance would be $x R \div \dfrac{n}{x} = \dfrac{x^2}{n} R$ (compare problems 8 and 9), and the strength of the maximum current required,

$$C = \frac{x E}{\dfrac{x^2}{n} R + r}$$

---

[1] By double elements is meant a group of two cells coupled for quantity (§ 89) and equivalent to a large cell having plates of twice the size. Six double elements are six such groups arranged for intensity, and the other terms have a similar meaning.

The first differential coefficient of this function of x when C is a maximum must be equal to zero. Hence,

$$\frac{\left(\frac{x^2}{n}R+r\right)E - 2\frac{x^2}{n}RE}{\left(\frac{x^2}{n}R+r\right)^2} = 0$$

or
$$r = \frac{x^2}{n}R.$$

That is, the strength of the current is at its maximum when the internal equals the external resistance, as stated above. Those who are not familiar with the elementary principles of the differential calculus may satisfy themselves of the truth of this result by comparing the answers obtained to problems 8 and 9.

14. We have, in the first place, for a single cell of a given combination working against a feeble resistance, the value $C = \frac{E}{R+r}$; in the second place, for n cells of the same combination working against n times the resistance, the identical value $C = \frac{nE}{nR+nr}$. In "strength" the two currents are equal, but are they identical?

15. In a given cell $E = 475$; $R = 15$. The current passes through 30 metres pure copper wire 2 m. m. diameter. It is required to arrange 8 cells so that C may be the greatest possible.

    Ans. They should be arranged as two four-fold elements.

16. We have a battery of four Bunsen cells ($E = 800, R = 4$ each), coupled as four single elements. The circuit is closed through 500 grammes of pure copper wire. Required the greatest strength of current, and the dimensions of the wire that this maximum may be obtained.

17. A simple Voltaic cell, whose electromotive force E is known, working against an unknown total resistance R' (both external and internal), produces a given effect upon a galvanometer. Another cell differently constructed, working against a total resistance R'', also unknown, produces the same effect upon the galvanometer. It is also observed that a measured length l of normal copper wire, inserted in the first circuit, produces on the galvanometer the same difference of effect as a length l' inserted in the second circuit. Required the electromotive force E' of the second cell.

Solution. We easily deduce from Ohm's formula the two equations $\frac{E}{R'} = \frac{E'}{R''}$ and $\frac{E}{R'+l} = \frac{E'}{R''+l'}$, whence we obtain,—

    Ans. $E' = E\frac{l'}{l}$.

18. In order to determine the electromotive force of a Bunsen's cell, it was compared, as in last problem, with a Daniell's cell whose electromotive force was known to be 470. After adjusting the external resistances so that both produced the same effect upon the galvanometer, it was found that the insertion of 5.6 m. of copper wire into the first circuit caused the same change in the instrument as the insertion of 3.29 metres of the same wire in the circuit of the Daniells cell. What was the electromotive force sought?

Ans. 800.

19. A battery of 40 Bunsen's cells remains closed for an hour, and during that time furnishes a current whose strength $C = 30$. How much zinc will be consumed in this time, assuming that there is no local action?

Solution. Such a current would produce, by the electrolysis of water, $30 \overline{\text{c. m.}}^8$ of gas in one minute, or 1.8 litres in one hour. Of this gas 1.2 litres or 1.2 criths would be hydrogen. The chemical equivalent of zinc being 32.6, the amount of zinc dissolved in each cell must be $1.2 \times 32.6 = 39.12$ criths, and in the forty cells 1564.8 criths, equal to 140 grammes, the answer required.

20. In an electrotype apparatus, Fig. 85, 16.36 grammes of copper were deposited on the negative mould in 24 hours. What was the strength of current?   Ans. 6 units.

21. In an electrotype apparatus the electromotive force of the single cell employed is 420, and the internal resistance 5. The external resistance, including decomposing· cell, is 0.25. How much copper will be deposited on the negative mould in one hour, and how much zinc will be dissolved in the battery during the same time?   Ans. 9.088 grammes copper and 9.346 grammes of zinc.

22. Thirty-two Grove cells ($E = 830$, $R = 20$ each) are connected as 4 eight-fold compound elements and the current employed to work an electro-silvering apparatus, in which the total resistance external to the battery was equivalent to 10. Required the number of grammes of silver deposited each hour, and the number of grammes of zinc dissolved during the same time in the battery.

Ans. 64.24 grammes of silver and 77.56 grammes of zinc.

23. Assuming that the external resistance cannot be changed, could the same number of cells of the battery described in last problem be so arranged as to deposit more silver in the same time?

Ans. They could not.

Could they be so arranged as to deposit the same amount of silver with less expense of zinc? What would be the most economical arrangement, and under these conditions how much silver would be deposited in one hour and how much zinc dissolved?

Answer to last question, 30.25 grammes silver, and 9.13 grammes of zinc.

24. What is the current through 25 Ohm with a tension of 5 Volts?

Ans. $C = \dfrac{E}{R} = \dfrac{5 \times 10^2}{25 \times 10^7} = 0.5 \times 10^{-2}$ or 0.5 Megafarad.

25. What is the work done by a current of 5 Megafarads per second through a resistance of 10 Ohms?

Ans. $W = C_2 Rt = (5 \times 10^{-2})^2 \times 10 \times 10^7 = 250,000$ units per second.

26. What is the work done by one thousand Farads in falling in tension one Volt?

Ans. $W = QE = 1000 \times 10^{-8} \times 10^5 = 1000 \times 10^{-3} = 1$ unit of work. Hence, 9,800 Voltfarads equal one metregramme.

27. What would be the answers to Problem 10 in B. A. units? Assuming that nine tenths of the external resistance is in a coil of platinum wire surrounded by a kilogramme of water, how high would the temperature of the water be raised in ten minutes?

28. Assuming that in the system of conductors represented in Fig. 3, E represents the electromotive force of the voltaic element, R the total resistance of the main conductor $a E$ b, R_1 and R_2 the resistances of the two conductors into which the main stream divides, find the values of the

three corresponding currents C, C_1, and C_2 in terms of E, R, R_1, and R_2. Prove also that $C_1 : C_2 = R_2 : R_1$, and further, that $C_1 = C\dfrac{R_2}{R_1 + R_2}$ or $C_2 = C\dfrac{R_1}{R_1 + R_2}$. Lastly, show that the equivalent resistance of any number of branches may be found by adding together the reciprocals of each branch and taking the reciprocal of this sum. A conductor like R_2, which diverts a portion of the main current from R_1, is called a shunt, and if R_1 is the coil of a galvanometer the galvanometer would be said to be shunted by R_2, and by adjusting the value of R_2 to R_1 we can cause a known fraction of the whole current to pass through the instrument.

29. In the system of conductors represented in Fig. 4, called Wheatstone's bridge, no current passes over the bridge between c and d when $R_1 : R_2 = R_3 : R_4$. Prove the truth of this proposition,

and show how it may be applied for measuring resistances when we have a set of standard resistance coils.

30. In the system of conductors, represented in Fig. 5, prove that no current passes in the portion $a\,E^1\,b$ when $\dfrac{E^1}{E} = \dfrac{R_0}{R + R_0}$, and consider how the system may be used for comparing the electromotive force of different cells.

TABLE I.

FRENCH MEASURES.

Measures of Length.

1 Kilometre	=	1000	Metres.	1 Metre	=	1.000	Metre.
1 Hectometre	=	100	"	1 Decimetre	=	0.100	"
1 Decametre	=	10	"	1 Centimetre	=	0.010	"
1 Metre	=	1	"	1 Millimetre	=	0.001	"

			Logarithms.	Ar. Co. Log.
1 Kilometre	=	0.6214 Mile.	9.7933 712	0.2066 188
1 Metre	=	3.2809 Feet.	0.5159 930	9.4840 070
1 Centimetre	=	0.3937 Inch.	9.5951 742	0.4048 258

The metre is one ten-millionth of a quadrant of the globe.

Measures of Volume.

1 Cubic Metre	$\overline{m.}^3$	=	1000.000	Litres.
1 Cubic Decimetre	$d.\overline{m.}^3$	=	1.000	"
1 Cubic Centimetre	$\overline{c.\,m.}^3$	=	0.001	"

			Logarithms.	Ar. Co. Log.
1 Cubic Metre	=	35.31660 Cubic Feet.	1.5479 790	8.4520 210
1 Cubic Decimetre	=	61.02709 Cubic Inches.	1.7855 226	8.2144 774
1 Cubic Centimetre	=	0.06103 " "	8.7855 226	1.2144 774
1 Litre	=	0.22017 Gallon.	9.3427 581	0.6572 419
1 Litre	=	0.88066 Quart.	9.9448 083	0.0551 917
1 Litre	=	1.76133 Pints.	0.2458 407	9.7541 593

FRENCH WEIGHTS.

1 Kilogramme	=	1000	Grammes.	1 Gramme	=	1.000	Gramme.
1 Hectogramme	=	100	"	1 Decigramme	=	0.100	"
1 Decagramme	=	10	"	1 Centigramme	=	0.010	"
1 Gramme	=	1	"	1 Milligramme	=	0.001	"

			Logarithms.	Ar. Co. Log.
1 Kilogramme	=	2.20462 Pounds Avoirdupois.	0.3433 337	9.6566 663
1 "	=	2.67922 " Troy.	0.4280 083	9.5719 917
1 Gramme	=	15.43235 Grains.	1.1884 321	8.8115 679
1 Crith	=	0.089578 Grammes.	8.9522 014	1.0477 986

TABLE II.

ELEMENTARY ATOMS.

Perissad Elements	Atomic Weights	Symbols of Molecules	Quantivalence	Artiad Elements	Atomic Weights	Symbols of Molecules	Quantivalence
Hydrogen	1.0	$H\text{-}H$	I	Copper	63.4	$Cu?$	II
Fluorine	19.0	$F\text{-}F$	"	Mercury	200.0	Hg	"
Chlorine	35.5	$Cl\text{-}Cl$	"	Calcium	40.0	$Ca?$	"
Bromine	80.0	$Br\text{-}Br$	"	Strontium	87.6	$Sr?$	"
Iodine	127.0	$I\text{-}I$	"	Barium	137.0	$Ba?$	"
Lithium	7.0	$Li\text{-}Li$	"	Lead	207.0	$Pb?$	"
Sodium	23.0	$Na\text{-}Na$	"	Magnesium	24.0	$Mg?$	"
Potassium	39.1	$K\text{-}K$	"	Zinc	65.2	$Zn?$	"
Rubidium	85.4	$Rb\text{-}Rb$	"	Indium	72.0	$In?$	"
Cæsium	133.0	$Cs\text{-}Cs$	"	Cadmium	112.0	Cd	"
Silver	108.0	$Ag\text{-}Ag?$	"	Glucinum	9.3	$G?$	"
Thallium	204.0	$Tl\text{-}Tl?$	I or III	Yttrium	61.7	$Y?$	"
Gold	197.0	$Au{\equiv}Au?$	III	Erbium	112.6	$E?$	"
Boron	11.0	$B{\equiv}B?$	"	Cerium	92.0	$Ce?$	"
Nitrogen	14.0	$N{\equiv}N$	III or V	Lanthanum	93.6	$La?$	"
Phosphorus	31.0	$P{\equiv}P_2$		Didymium	95.0	$D?$	"
Arsenic	75.0	$As{\equiv}As_2$	"	Nickel	58.8	$Ni?$	"
Antimony	122.0	$Sb{\equiv}Sb_2?$	"	Cobalt	58.8	$Co?$	"
Bismuth	210.0	$Bi{\equiv}Bi_2?$	"	Manganese	55.0	$Mn?$	II or IV
Vanadium	51.37	$V{\equiv}V?$	"	Iron	56.0	$Fe?$	"
Uranium	120.0	$U{\equiv}U?$	"	Chromium	52.2	$Cr?$	"
Columbium	94.0	$Cb{\equiv}Cb?$	V	Aluminum	27.4	$Al?$	"
Tantalum	182.0	$Ta{\equiv}Ta?$	"	Ruthenium	104.4	$Ru?$	"
				Osmium	199.2	$Os?$	"
				Rhodium	104.4	Rh	"
				Iridium	196.0	$Ir?$	"
Artiad Elements.				Palladium	106.6	$Pd?$	"
				Platinum	197.4	$Pt?$	"
Oxygen	16.0	$O{=}O$	II	Titanium	50.0	$Ti?$	"
				Tin	118.0	$Sn?$	"
Sulphur	32.0	$S{=}S$	II or VI	Zirconium	89.6	$Zr?$	IV
Selenium	79.4	$Se{=}Se$	"				
Tellurium	128.0	$Te{=}Te$	"	Thorium	231.4	$Th?$	"
Molybdenum	96.0	$Mo?$	VI	Silicon	28.0	$Si?$	"
Tungsten	184.0	$W?$	"	Carbon	12.0	$C?$	"

TABLE III.

Specific Gravity of Gases and Vapors.

Names.	Symbols.	Sp. Gr. Air = 1.	Sp. Gr. H-H=1.	Half Molecular Weight.	Logarithms.
Air		1.000	14.43		1.1593
Hydrogen	H-H	0.0693	1.00	1.00	0.0000
Acetylic Hydride (Aldehyde)	C_2H_3O-H	1.532	22.10	22.00	1.3424
Acetylic Chloride	C_2H_3O-Cl	2.87	41.42	39.25	1.5938
Acetic Anhydride	$(C_2H_3O)_2$=O	3.47	50.07	51.00	1.7076
Acetic Acid	H-O-C_2H_3O	2.083	30.07	30.00	1.4771
Aluminic Chloride	$[Al_2]\equiv Cl_6$	9.34	134.80	133.90	2.1268
Aluminic Bromide	$[Al_2]\equiv Br_6$	18.62	268.79	267.40	2.4272
Aluminic Iodide	$[Al_2]\equiv I_6$	27.	389.60	408.40	2.6111
Antimonious Chloride	$Sb\equiv Cl_3$	7.8	112.70	114.20	2.0577
Triethylstibine	$(C_2H_5)_3\equiv Sb$	7.23	104.40	104.50	2.0191
Arsenic	$As_2\equiv As_2$	10.6	153.00	150.00	2.1761
Arseniuretted Hydrogen	$H_3\equiv As$	2.695	38.90	39.00	1.5911
Triethylarsine	$(C_2H_5)_3\equiv As$	5.29	76.35	81.00	1.9085
Kakodyl	$(CH_3)_2As$-$(CH_3)_2As$	7.10	102.50	105.00	2.0212
Arsenious Chloride	$As\equiv Cl_3$	6.3	90.90	90.75	1.9578
Arsenious Iodide	$As\equiv I_3$	16.1	232.40	228.00	2.3579
Bismuthous Chloride	$Bi\equiv Cl_3$	11.35	163.90	158.25	2.1994
Boric Methide	$(CH_3)_3\equiv B$	1.931	27.90	28.00	1.4472
Boric Ethide	$(C_2H_5)_3\equiv B$	3.401	49.10	49.00	1.6902
Boric Fluoride	$B\equiv F_3$	2.37	34.20	34.00	1.5315
Boric Chloride	$B\equiv Cl_3$	3.942	56.85	58.75	1.7690
Boric Bromide	$B\equiv Br_3$	8.78	126.80	125.50	2.0986
Methylic Borate	$(CH_3)_3\equiv O_3\equiv B$	3.59	51.80	52.00	1.7160
Ethylic Borate	$(C_2H_5)_3\equiv O_3\equiv B$	5.14	74.20	73.00	1.8633
Bromine	Br-Br	5.54	79.50	80.00	1.9031
Hydrobromic Acid	H-Br	2.71	39.10	40.50	1.6075
Carbonic Tetrachloride	$C\equiv Cl_4$	5.415	78.14	77.00	1.8865
Marsh Gas	CH_4	0.5576	8.05	8.00	0.9031
Phosgene Gas	$C\equiv O, Cl_2$	3.399	49.00	49.50	1.6946
Dicarbonic Hexachloride	$[C$-$C]\equiv Cl_6$	8.157	117.70	118.50	2.0737
Dicarbonic Tetrachloride	$[C$=$C]\equiv Cl_4$	5.82	84.00	83.00	1.9191
Dicarbonic Dichloride	$[C\equiv C]$=Cl_2			47.50	1.6767
Carbonic Oxide	C=O	0.967	13.95	14.00	1.1461
Carbonic Anhydride	$C\equiv O_2$	1.529	22.06	22.00	1.3424
Carbonic Sulphide	$C\equiv S_2$	2.645	38.17	38.00	1.5798
Chlorine	Cl-Cl	2.44	35.22	35.50	1.5502
Hydrochloric Acid	H-Cl	1.27	18.32	18.25	1.2613
Chromic Oxychloride	$Cr\equiv O_2, Cl_2$	5.5	79.40	77.6	1.8935
Columbic Chloride	$Cb\equiv Cl_5$	9.6	138.60	135.70	2.1326
Columbic Oxychloride	$Cb\equiv O, Cl_3$	7.9	114.00	108.20	2.0342
Cyanogen	CN-CN	1.806	26.06	26.00	1.4150
Hydrocyanic Acid	H-CN	0.947	13.67	13.50	1.1303
Ethyl	C_2H_5-C_2H_5	2.0	28.86	29.00	1.4624
Ethylic Chloride	(C_2H_5)-Cl	2.219	32.02	32.25	1.5065
Ethylic Oxide (Ether)	$(C_2H_5)_2$=O	2.586	37.32	37.00	1.5682
Ethylic Hydrate (Alcohol)	C_2H_5-O-H	1.613	23.28	23.00	1.3617

TABLE III. (Continued.)

Names.	Symbols.	Sp.Gr. Air =1.	Sp.Gr. H-H=1.	Half Molecular Weight.	Loga- rithms.
Ethylene (Olefiant Gas)	C_2H_4	0.978	14.11	14.00	1.1461
" Chloride (Dutch Liq.)	$(C_2H_4)=Cl_2$	3.443	49.69	49.50	1.6946
Ethylene Oxide	$(C_2H_4)=O$	1.422	20.52	22.00	1.3424
Ethylene Hydrate (Glycol)	$(C_2H_4)=O_2=H_2$			31.00	1.4914
Ferric Chloride	$[Fe_2]\equiv Cl_6$	11.39	164.40	162.50	2.2108
Iodine	$I-I$	8.716	125.90	127.00	2.1038
Hydriodic Acid	$H-I$	4.443	64.12	64.00	1.8062
Mercury	Hg	6.976	100.70	100.00	2.0000
Mercuric Ethide	$(C_2H_5)_2=Hg$	9.97	143.90	129.00	2.1106
Mercuric Methide	$(CH_3)_2=Hg$	8.29	119.60	115.00	2.0607
Mercuric Chloride	$Hg=Cl_2$	9.8	141.50	135.50	2.1319
Mercuric Bromide	$Hg=Br_2$	12.16	175.60	180.00	2.2553
Mercuric Iodide	$Hg=I_2$	15.9	229.60	227.00	2.3560
Mercurous Chloride	$[Hg_2]=Cl_2$	8.21	118.50	235.50	2.3720
Nitrogen	$N\equiv N$	0.971	14.00	14.00	1.1461
Ammonia	$H_3\equiv N$	0.591	8.535	8.51	0.9294
Methylamine	$H_2,(CH_3)\equiv N$	1.08	15.59	15.50	1.1903
Aniline	$H_2,(C_6H_5)\equiv N$	3.21	46.33	46.50	1.6675
Nitrous Oxide	N_2O	1.527	22.04	22.00	1.3424
Nitric Oxide	NO	1.038	14.97	15.00	1.1761
Nitric Peroxide	NO_2	1.72	24.82	23.00	1.3617
Osmic Tetroxide	$Os\,O_4$	8.89	128.30	131.60	2.1193
Oxygen	$O=O$	1.1056	15.95	16.00	1.2041
Aqueous Vapor	$H_2=O$	0.6235	8.998	9.00	0.9542
Phosphorus	$P_2\equiv P_2$	4.42	63.78	62.00	1.7924
Phosphuretted Hydrogen	$H_3\equiv P$	1.184	17.09	17.00	1.2304
Phosphorous Chloride	$P\equiv Cl_3$	4.742	68.44	68.75	1.8373
Phosphoric Oxychloride	$P\equiv O, Cl_3$	5.3	76.49	76.75	1.8851
Oxide of Triethylphosphine	$((C_2H_5)_3\equiv P)=O$	4.6	66.39	67.00	1.8261
Selenium, at 771°	$Se=Se$	5.68	81.96	79.40	1.8998
Seleniuretted Hydrogen	$H_2=Se$	2.795	40.33	40.70	1.6096
Silicic Methide	$(CH_3)_4\equiv Si$	3.083	44.49	44.00	1.6435
Silicic Ethide	$(C_2H_5)_4\equiv Si$	5.13	74.03	72.00	1.8573
Silicic Fluoride	$Si\equiv F_4$	3.600	51.95	52.00	1.7160
Silicic Chloride	$Si\equiv Cl_4$	5.989	85.72	85.00	1.9294
Ethylic Silicate	$(C_2H_5)_4\equiv O_4\equiv Si$	7.82	105.60	104.00	1.0170
Stannic Ethide	$(C_2H_5)_4\equiv Sn$	8.021	115.80	117.00	2.0682
Stannic Dimethylo-diethide	$(CH_3)_2,(C_2H_5)_2\equiv Sn$	6.838	98.68	103.00	2.0128
Stannic Chloro-triethide	$Cl,(C_2H_5)_3\equiv Sn$	8.430	121.70	120.20	2.0799
Stannic Dichloro-diethide	$Cl_2,(C_2H_5)_2\equiv Sn$	8.710	125.70	123.50	2.0917
Stannic Chloride	$Sn\equiv Cl_4$	9.199	132.70	130.00	2.1139
Sulphur above 860°	$S=S$	2.23	32.18	32.00	1.5051
Sulphur at 450°	S_6	6.617	95.50	96.00	1.9823
Sulphuretted Hydrogen	$H_2=S$	1.191	17.19	17.00	1.2304
Sulphurous Anhydride	$S\equiv O_2$	2.234	32.24	32.00	1.5051
Sulphuric Anhydride	$S\equiv O_3$	2.763	39.87	40.00	1.6021
Tantalic Chloride	$Ta\,Cl_5$	12.8	184.70	179.70	2.2546
Titanic Chloride	$Ti\,Cl_4$	6.836	98.65	96.00	1.9823
Zinc Ethide	$(C_2H_5)_2=Zn$	4.259	61.46	61.60	1.7896
Zirconic Chloride	$Zr\equiv Cl_4$	8.15	117.60	115.80	2.0637

LOGARITHMS AND ANTILOGARITHMS.

LOGARITHMS OF NUMBERS.

Natural Numbers.	0	1	2	3	4	5	6	7	8	9	Proportional Parts.								
											1	2	3	4	5	6	7	8	9
10	0000	0043	0086	0128	0170	0212	0253	0294	0334	0374	4	8	12	17	21	25	29	33	37
11	0414	0453	0492	0531	0569	0607	0645	0682	0719	0755	4	8	11	15	19	23	26	30	34
12	0792	0828	0864	0899	0934	0969	1004	1038	1072	1106	3	7	10	14	17	21	24	28	31
13	1139	1173	1206	1239	1271	1303	1335	1367	1399	1430	3	6	10	13	16	19	23	26	29
14	1461	1492	1523	1553	1584	1614	1644	1673	1703	1732	3	6	9	12	15	18	21	24	27
15	1761	1790	1818	1847	1875	1903	1931	1959	1987	2014	3	6	8	11	14	17	20	22	25
16	2041	2068	2095	2122	2148	2175	2201	2227	2253	2279	3	5	8	11	13	16	18	21	24
17	2304	2330	2355	2380	2405	2430	2455	2480	2504	2529	2	5	7	10	12	15	17	20	22
18	2553	2577	2601	2625	2648	2672	2695	2718	2742	2765	2	5	7	9	12	14	16	19	21
19	2788	2810	2833	2856	2878	2900	2923	2945	2967	2989	2	4	7	9	11	13	16	18	20
20	3010	3032	3054	3075	3096	3118	3139	3160	3181	3201	2	4	6	8	11	13	15	17	19
21	3222	3243	3263	3284	3304	3324	3345	3365	3385	3404	2	4	6	8	10	12	14	16	18
22	3424	3444	3464	3483	3502	3522	3541	3560	3579	3598	2	4	6	8	10	12	14	15	17
23	3617	3636	3655	3674	3692	3711	3729	3747	3766	3784	2	4	6	7	9	11	13	15	17
24	3802	3820	3838	3856	3874	3892	3909	3927	3945	3962	2	4	5	7	9	11	12	14	16
25	3979	3997	4014	4031	4048	4065	4082	4099	4116	4133	2	3	5	7	9	10	12	14	15
26	4150	4166	4183	4200	4216	4232	4249	4265	4281	4298	2	3	5	7	8	10	11	13	15
27	4314	4330	4346	4362	4378	4393	4409	4425	4440	4456	2	3	5	6	8	9	11	13	14
28	4472	4487	4502	4518	4533	4548	4564	4579	4594	4609	2	3	5	6	8	9	11	12	14
29	4624	4639	4654	4669	4683	4698	4713	4728	4742	4757	1	3	4	6	7	9	10	12	13
30	4771	4786	4800	4814	4829	4843	4857	4871	4886	4900	1	3	4	6	7	9	10	11	13
31	4914	4928	4942	4955	4969	4983	4997	5011	5024	5038	1	3	4	6	7	8	10	11	12
32	5051	5065	5079	5092	5105	5119	5132	5145	5159	5172	1	3	4	5	7	8	9	11	12
33	5185	5198	5211	5224	5237	5250	5263	5276	5289	5302	1	3	4	5	6	8	9	10	12
34	5315	5328	5340	5353	5366	5378	5391	5403	5416	5428	1	3	4	5	6	8	9	10	11
35	5441	5453	5465	5478	5490	5502	5514	5527	5539	5551	1	2	4	5	6	7	9	10	11
36	5563	5575	5587	5599	5611	5623	5635	5647	5658	5670	1	2	4	5	6	7	8	10	11
37	5682	5694	5705	5717	5729	5740	5752	5763	5775	5786	1	2	3	5	6	7	8	9	10
38	5798	5809	5821	5832	5843	5855	5866	5877	5888	5899	1	2	3	5	6	7	8	9	10
39	5911	5922	5933	5944	5955	5966	5977	5988	5999	6010	1	2	3	4	5	7	8	9	10
40	6021	6031	6042	6053	6064	6075	6085	6096	6107	6117	1	2	3	4	5	6	8	9	10
41	6128	6138	6149	6160	6170	6180	6191	6201	6212	6222	1	2	3	4	5	6	7	8	9
42	6232	6243	6253	6263	6274	6284	6294	6304	6314	6325	1	2	3	4	5	6	7	8	9
43	6335	6345	6355	6365	6375	6385	6395	6405	6415	6425	1	2	3	4	5	6	7	8	9
44	6435	6444	6454	6464	6474	6484	6493	6503	6513	6522	1	2	3	4	5	6	7	8	9
45	6532	6542	6551	6561	6571	6580	6590	6599	6609	6618	1	2	3	4	5	6	7	8	9
46	6628	6637	6646	6656	6665	6675	6684	6693	6702	6712	1	2	3	4	5	6	7	7	8
47	6721	6730	6739	6749	6758	6767	6776	6785	6794	6803	1	2	3	4	5	5	6	7	8
48	6812	6821	6830	6839	6848	6857	6866	6875	6884	6893	1	2	3	4	4	5	6	7	8
49	6902	6911	6920	6928	6937	6946	6955	6964	6972	6981	1	2	3	4	4	5	6	7	8
50	6990	6998	7007	7016	7024	7033	7042	7050	7059	7067	1	2	3	3	4	5	6	7	8
51	7076	7084	7093	7101	7110	7118	7126	7135	7143	7152	1	2	3	3	4	5	6	7	8
52	7160	7168	7177	7185	7193	7202	7210	7218	7226	7235	1	2	2	3	4	5	6	7	7
53	7243	7251	7259	7267	7275	7284	7292	7300	7308	7316	1	2	2	3	4	5	6	6	7
54	7324	7332	7340	7348	7356	7364	7372	7380	7388	7396	1	2	2	3	4	5	6	6	7

Natural Numbers	0	1	2	3	4	5	6	7	8	9	Proportional Parts.								
											1	2	3	4	5	6	7	8	9
55	7404	7412	7419	7427	7435	7443	7451	7459	7466	7474	1	2	2	3	4	5	5	6	7
56	7482	7490	7497	7505	7513	7520	7528	7536	7543	7551	1	2	2	3	4	5	5	6	7
57	7559	7566	7574	7582	7589	7597	7604	7612	7619	7627	1	2	2	3	4	5	5	6	7
58	7634	7642	7649	7657	7664	7672	7679	7686	7694	7701	1	1	2	3	4	4	5	6	7
59	7709	7716	7723	7731	7738	7745	7752	7760	7767	7774	1	1	2	3	4	4	5	6	7
60	7782	7789	7796	7803	7810	7818	7825	7832	7839	7846	1	1	2	3	4	4	5	6	6
61	7853	7860	7868	7875	7882	7889	7896	7903	7910	7917	1	1	2	3	4	4	5	6	6
62	7924	7931	7938	7945	7952	7959	7966	7973	7980	7987	1	1	2	3	3	4	5	6	6
63	7993	8000	8007	8014	8021	8028	8035	8041	8048	8055	1	1	2	3	3	4	5	5	6
64	8062	8069	8075	8082	8089	8096	8102	8109	8116	8122	1	1	2	3	3	4	5	5	6
65	8129	8136	8142	8149	8156	8162	8169	8176	8182	8189	1	1	2	3	3	4	5	5	6
66	8195	8202	8209	8215	8222	8228	8235	8241	8248	8254	1	1	2	3	3	4	5	5	6
67	8261	8267	8274	8280	8287	8293	8299	8306	8312	8319	1	1	2	3	3	4	5	5	6
68	8325	8331	8338	8344	8351	8357	8363	8370	8376	8382	1	1	2	3	3	4	4	5	6
69	8388	8395	8401	8407	8414	8420	8426	8432	8439	8445	1	1	2	2	3	4	4	5	6
70	8451	8457	8463	8470	8476	8482	8488	8494	8500	8506	1	1	2	2	3	4	4	5	6
71	8513	8519	8525	8531	8537	8543	8549	8555	8561	8567	1	1	2	2	3	4	4	5	5
72	8573	8579	8585	8591	8597	8603	8609	8615	8621	8627	1	1	2	2	3	4	4	5	5
73	8633	8639	8645	8651	8657	8663	8669	8675	8681	8686	1	1	2	2	3	4	4	5	5
74	8692	8698	8704	8710	8716	8722	8727	8733	8739	8745	1	1	2	2	3	4	4	5	5
75	8751	8756	8762	8768	8774	8779	8785	8791	8797	8802	1	1	2	2	3	3	4	5	5
76	8808	8814	8820	8825	8831	8837	8842	8848	8854	8859	1	1	2	2	3	3	4	5	5
77	8865	8871	8876	8882	8887	8893	8899	8904	8910	8915	1	1	2	2	3	3	4	4	5
78	8921	8927	8932	8938	8943	8949	8954	8960	8965	8971	1	1	2	2	3	3	4	4	5
79	8976	8982	8987	8993	8998	9004	9009	9015	9020	9025	1	1	2	2	3	3	4	4	5
80	9031	9036	9042	9047	9053	9058	9063	9069	9074	9079	1	1	2	2	3	3	4	4	5
81	9085	9090	9096	9101	9106	9112	9117	9122	9128	9133	1	1	2	2	3	3	4	4	5
82	9138	9143	9149	9154	9159	9165	9170	9175	9180	9186	1	1	2	2	3	3	4	4	5
83	9191	9196	9201	9206	9212	9217	9222	9227	9232	9238	1	1	2	2	3	3	4	4	5
84	9243	9248	9253	9258	9263	9269	9274	9279	9284	9289	1	1	2	2	3	3	4	4	5
85	9294	9299	9304	9309	9315	9320	9325	9330	9335	9340	1	1	2	2	3	3	4	4	5
86	9345	9350	9355	9360	9365	9370	9375	9380	9385	9390	1	1	2	2	3	3	4	4	5
87	9395	9400	9405	9410	9415	9420	9425	9430	9435	9440	0	1	1	2	2	3	3	4	4
88	9445	9450	9455	9460	9465	9469	9474	9479	9484	9489	0	1	1	2	2	3	3	4	4
89	9494	9499	9504	9509	9513	9518	9523	9528	9533	9538	0	1	1	2	2	3	3	4	4
90	9542	9547	9552	9557	9562	9566	9571	9576	9581	9586	0	1	1	2	2	3	3	4	4
91	9590	9595	9600	9605	9609	9614	9619	9624	9628	9633	0	1	1	2	2	3	3	4	4
92	9638	9643	9647	9652	9657	9661	9666	9671	9675	9680	0	1	1	2	2	3	3	4	4
93	9685	9689	9694	9699	9703	9708	9713	9717	9722	9727	0	1	1	2	2	3	3	4	4
94	9731	9736	9741	9745	9750	9754	9759	9763	9768	9773	0	1	1	2	2	3	3	4	4
95	9777	9782	9786	9791	9795	9800	9805	9809	9814	9818	0	1	1	2	2	3	3	4	4
96	9823	9827	9832	9836	9841	9845	9850	9854	9859	9863	0	1	1	2	2	3	3	4	4
97	9868	9872	9877	9881	9886	9890	9894	9899	9903	9908	0	1	1	2	2	3	3	4	4
98	9912	9917	9921	9926	9930	9934	9939	9943	9948	9952	0	1	1	2	2	3	3	4	4
99	9956	9961	9965	9969	9974	9978	9983	9987	9991	9996	0	1	1	2	2	3	3	3	4

ANTILOGARITHMS.

Loga-rithms.	0	1	2	3	4	5	6	7	8	9	Proportional Parts.								
											1	2	3	4	5	6	7	8	9
.00	1000	1002	1005	1007	1009	1012	1014	1016	1019	1021	0	0	1	1	1	1	2	2	2
.01	1023	1026	1028	1030	1033	1035	1038	1040	1042	1045	0	0	1	1	1	1	2	2	2
.02	1047	1050	1052	1054	1057	1059	1062	1064	1067	1069	0	0	1	1	1	2	2	2	2
.03	1072	1074	1076	1079	1081	1084	1086	1089	1091	1094	0	0	1	1	1	1	2	2	2
.04	1096	1099	1102	1104	1107	1109	1112	1114	1117	1119	0	1	1	1	1	2	2	2	2
.05	1122	1125	1127	1130	1132	1135	1138	1140	1143	1146	0	1	1	1	1	2	2	2	2
.06	1148	1151	1153	1156	1159	1161	1164	1167	1169	1172	0	1	1	1	1	2	2	2	2
.07	1175	1178	1180	1183	1186	1189	1191	1194	1197	1199	0	1	1	1	1	2	2	2	2
.08	1202	1205	1208	1211	1213	1216	1219	1222	1225	1227	0	1	1	1	1	2	2	2	3
.09	1230	1233	1236	1239	1242	1245	1247	1250	1253	1256	0	1	1	1	1	2	2	2	3
.10	1259	1262	1265	1268	1271	1274	1276	1279	1282	1285	0	1	1	1	1	2	2	2	3
.11	1288	1291	1294	1297	1300	1303	1306	1309	1312	1315	0	1	1	1	2	2	2	2	3
.12	1318	1321	1324	1327	1330	1334	1337	1340	1343	1346	0	1	1	1	2	2	2	2	3
.13	1349	1352	1355	1358	1361	1365	1368	1371	1374	1377	0	1	1	1	2	2	2	3	3
.14	1380	1384	1387	1390	1393	1396	1400	1403	1406	1409	0	1	1	1	2	2	2	3	3
.15	1413	1416	1419	1422	1426	1429	1432	1435	1439	1442	0	1	1	1	2	2	2	3	3
.16	1445	1449	1452	1455	1459	1462	1466	1469	1472	1476	0	1	1	1	2	2	2	3	3
.17	1479	1483	1486	1489	1493	1496	1500	1503	1507	1510	0	1	1	1	2	2	2	3	3
.18	1514	1517	1521	1524	1528	1531	1535	1538	1542	1545	0	1	1	1	2	2	2	3	3
.19	1549	1552	1556	1560	1563	1567	1570	1574	1578	1581	0	1	1	1	2	2	3	3	3
.20	1585	1589	1592	1596	1600	1603	1607	1611	1614	1618	0	1	1	1	2	2	3	3	3
.21	1622	1626	1629	1633	1637	1641	1644	1648	1652	1656	0	1	1	2	2	2	3	3	3
.22	1660	1663	1667	1671	1675	1679	1683	1687	1690	1694	0	1	1	2	2	2	3	3	3
.23	1698	1702	1706	1710	1714	1718	1722	1726	1730	1734	0	1	1	2	2	2	3	3	4
.24	1738	1742	1746	1750	1754	1758	1762	1766	1770	1774	0	1	1	2	2	2	3	3	4
.25	1778	1782	1786	1791	1795	1799	1803	1807	1811	1816	0	1	1	2	2	2	3	3	4
.26	1820	1824	1828	1832	1837	1841	1845	1849	1854	1858	0	1	1	2	2	3	3	3	4
.27	1862	1866	1871	1875	1879	1884	1886	1892	1897	1901	0	1	1	2	2	3	3	3	4
.28	1905	1910	1914	1919	1923	1928	1932	1936	1941	1945	0	1	1	2	2	3	3	4	4
.29	1950	1954	1959	1963	1968	1972	1977	1982	1986	1991	0	1	1	2	2	3	3	4	4
.30	1995	2000	2004	2009	2014	2018	2023	2028	2032	2037	0	1	1	2	2	3	3	4	4
.31	2042	2046	2051	2056	2061	2065	2070	2075	2080	2084	0	1	1	2	2	3	3	4	4
.32	2089	2094	2099	2104	2109	2113	2118	2123	2128	2133	0	1	1	2	2	3	3	4	4
.33	2138	2143	2148	2153	2158	2163	2168	2173	2178	2183	0	1	1	2	2	3	3	4	4
.34	2188	2193	2198	2203	2208	2213	2218	2223	2228	2234	1	1	2	2	3	3	4	4	5
.35	2239	2244	2249	2254	2259	2265	2270	2275	2280	2286	1	1	2	2	3	3	4	4	5
.36	2291	2296	2301	2307	2312	2317	2323	2328	2333	2339	1	1	2	2	3	3	4	4	5
.37	2344	2350	2355	2360	2366	2371	2377	2382	2388	2393	1	1	2	2	3	3	4	4	5
.38	2399	2404	2410	2415	2421	2427	2432	2438	2443	2449	1	1	2	2	3	3	4	4	5
.39	2455	2460	2466	2472	2477	2483	2489	2495	2500	2506	1	1	2	2	3	3	4	5	5
.40	2512	2518	2523	2529	2535	2541	2547	2553	2559	2564	1	1	2	2	3	4	4	5	5
.41	2570	2576	2582	2588	2594	2600	2606	2612	2618	2624	1	1	2	2	3	4	4	5	5
.42	2630	2636	2642	2649	2655	2661	2667	2673	2679	2685	1	1	2	2	3	4	4	5	6
.43	2692	2698	2704	2710	2716	2723	2729	2735	2742	2748	1	1	2	3	3	4	4	5	6
.44	2754	2761	2767	2773	2780	2786	2793	2799	2805	2812	1	1	2	3	3	4	4	5	6
.45	2818	2825	2831	2838	2844	2851	2858	2864	2871	2877	1	1	2	3	3	4	5	5	6
.46	2884	2891	2897	2904	2911	2917	2924	2931	2938	2944	1	1	2	3	3	4	5	5	6
.47	2951	2958	2965	2972	2979	2985	2992	2999	3006	3013	1	1	2	3	3	4	5	5	6
.48	3020	3027	3034	3041	3048	3055	3062	3069	3076	3083	1	1	2	3	4	4	5	6	6
.49	3090	3097	3105	3112	3119	3126	3133	3141	3148	3155	1	1	2	3	4	4	5	6	6

ANTILOGARITHMS.

Loga-rithms.	0	1	2	3	4	5	6	7	8	9	Proportional Parts.								
											1	2	3	4	5	6	7	8	9
.50	3162	3170	3177	3184	3192	3199	3206	3214	3221	3228	1	1	2	3	4	4	5	6	7
.51	3236	3243	3251	3258	3266	3273	3281	3289	3296	3304	1	2	2	3	4	5	5	6	7
.52	3311	3319	3327	3334	3342	3350	3357	3365	3373	3381	1	2	2	3	4	5	5	6	7
.53	3388	3396	3404	3412	3420	3428	3436	3443	3451	3459	1	2	2	3	4	5	6	6	7
.54	3467	3475	3483	3491	3499	3508	3516	3524	3532	3540	1	2	2	3	4	5	6	6	7
.55	3548	3556	3565	3573	3581	3589	3597	3606	3614	3622	1	2	2	3	4	5	6	7	7
.56	3631	3639	3648	3656	3664	3673	3681	3690	3698	3707	1	2	3	3	4	5	6	7	8
.57	3715	3724	3733	3741	3750	3758	3767	3776	3784	3793	1	2	3	3	4	5	6	7	8
.58	3802	3811	3819	3828	3837	3846	3855	3864	3873	3882	1	2	3	4	4	5	6	7	8
.59	3890	3899	3908	3917	3926	3936	3945	3954	3963	3972	1	2	3	4	5	5	6	7	8
.60	3981	3990	3999	4009	4018	4027	4036	4046	4055	4064	1	2	3	4	5	6	6	7	8
.61	4074	4083	4093	4102	4111	4121	4130	4140	4150	4159	1	2	3	4	5	6	7	8	9
.62	4169	4178	4188	4198	4207	4217	4227	4236	4246	4256	1	2	3	4	5	6	7	8	9
.63	4266	4276	4285	4295	4305	4315	4325	4335	4345	4355	1	2	3	4	5	6	7	8	9
.64	4365	4375	4385	4395	4406	4416	4426	4436	4446	4457	1	2	3	4	5	6	7	8	9
.65	4467	4477	4487	4498	4508	4519	4529	4539	4550	4560	1	2	3	4	5	6	7	8	9
.66	4571	4581	4592	4603	4613	4624	4634	4645	4656	4667	1	2	3	4	5	6	7	9	10
.67	4677	4688	4699	4710	4721	4732	4742	4753	4764	4775	1	2	3	4	5	7	8	9	10
.68	4786	4797	4808	4819	4831	4842	4853	4864	4875	4887	1	2	3	4	6	7	8	9	10
.69	4898	4909	4920	4932	4943	4955	4966	4977	4989	5000	1	2	3	5	6	7	8	9	10
.70	5012	5023	5035	5047	5058	5070	5082	5093	5105	5117	1	2	4	5	6	7	8	9	11
.71	5129	5140	5152	5164	5176	5188	5200	5212	5224	5236	1	2	4	5	6	7	8	10	11
.72	5248	5260	5272	5284	5297	5309	5321	5333	5346	5358	1	2	4	5	6	7	9	10	11
.73	5370	5383	5395	5408	5420	5433	5445	5458	5470	5483	1	3	4	5	6	8	9	10	11
.74	5495	5508	5521	5534	5546	5559	5572	5585	5598	5610	1	3	4	5	6	8	9	10	12
.75	5623	5636	5649	5662	5675	5689	5702	5715	5728	5741	1	3	4	5	7	8	9	10	12
.76	5754	5768	5781	5794	5808	5821	5834	5848	5861	5875	1	3	4	5	7	8	9	11	12
.77	5888	5902	5916	5929	5943	5957	5970	5984	5998	6012	1	3	4	5	7	8	10	11	12
.78	6026	6039	6053	6067	6081	6095	6109	6124	6138	6152	1	3	4	6	7	8	10	11	13
.79	6166	6180	6194	6209	6223	6237	6252	6266	6281	6295	1	3	4	6	7	9	10	11	13
.80	6310	6324	6339	6353	6368	6383	6397	6412	6427	6442	1	3	4	6	7	9	10	12	13
.81	6457	6471	6486	6501	6516	6531	6546	6561	6577	6592	2	3	5	6	8	9	11	12	14
.82	6607	6622	6637	6653	6668	6683	6699	6714	6730	6745	2	3	5	6	8	9	11	12	14
.83	6761	6776	6792	6808	6823	6839	6855	6871	6887	6902	2	3	5	6	8	9	11	13	14
.84	6918	6934	6950	6966	6982	6998	7015	7031	7047	7063	2	3	5	6	8	10	11	13	15
.85	7079	7096	7112	7129	7145	7161	7178	7194	7211	7228	2	3	5	7	8	10	12	13	15
.86	7244	7261	7278	7295	7311	7328	7345	7362	7379	7396	2	3	5	7	8	10	12	13	15
.87	7413	7430	7447	7464	7482	7499	7516	7534	7551	7568	2	3	5	7	9	10	12	14	16
.88	7586	7603	7621	7638	7656	7674	7691	7709	7727	7745	2	4	5	7	9	11	12	14	16
.89	7762	7780	7798	7816	7834	7852	7870	7889	7907	7925	2	4	5	7	9	11	13	14	16
.90	7943	7962	7980	7998	8017	8035	8054	8072	8091	8110	2	4	6	7	9	11	13	15	17
.91	8128	8147	8166	8185	8204	8222	8241	8260	8279	8299	2	4	6	8	9	11	13	15	17
.92	8318	8337	8356	8375	8395	8414	8433	8453	8472	8492	2	4	6	8	10	12	14	15	17
.93	8511	8531	8551	8570	8590	8610	8630	8650	8670	8690	2	4	6	8	10	12	14	16	18
.94	8710	8730	8750	8770	8790	8810	8831	8851	8872	8892	2	4	6	8	10	12	14	16	18
.95	8913	8933	8954	8974	8995	9016	9036	9057	9078	9099	2	4	6	8	10	12	15	17	19
.96	9120	9141	9162	9183	9204	9226	9247	9268	9290	9311	2	4	6	8	11	13	15	17	19
.97	9333	9354	9376	9397	9419	9441	9462	9484	9506	9528	2	4	7	9	11	13	15	17	20
.98	9550	9572	9594	9616	9638	9661	9683	9705	9727	9750	2	4	7	9	11	13	16	18	20
.99	9772	9795	9817	9840	9863	9886	9908	9931	9954	9977	2	5	7	9	11	14	16	18	20

CONSTANT LOGARITHMS.

	Logarithms.	Ar. Co. Log.
Circumf. of circle when $R = 1$, $(\frac{\pi}{2} = 1.5708)$	0.1961	9.8039
" " " " $D = 1$, $(\pi = 3.1416)$	0.4971	9.5028
Area of circle when $R^2 = 1$, $(\pi = 3.1416)$	0.4971	9.5028
" " " " $D^2 = 1$, $(\frac{\pi}{4} = 0.7854)$	9.8951	0.1049
" " " " $C^2 = 1$, $(\frac{1}{4\pi} = 0.0796)$	8.9008	1.0992
Surface of sphere when $R^2 = 1$, $(4\pi = 12.5664)$	1.0992	8.9008
" " " " $D^2 = 1$, $(\pi = 3.1416)$	0.4971	9.5028
" " " " $C^2 = 1$, $(\frac{1}{\pi} = 0.3183)$	9.5028	0.4971
Solidity of sphere when $R^3 = 1$, $(\frac{4}{3}\pi = 4.1888)$	0.6221	9.3779
" " " " $D^3 = 1$, $(\frac{\pi}{6} = 0.5236)$	9.7190	0.2810
" " " " $C^3 = 1$, $(\frac{1}{6\pi^2} = 0.0169)$	8.2275	1.7724
Weight of one litre of Hydrogen (0.0896 grammes)	8.9522	1.0478
" " " " " Air (1.293 ")	0.1116	9.8884
" " " " " " (14.43 criths)	1.1594	8.8406
Per cent of Oxygen in air by weight (0.2318)	9.3651	0.6349
" " " Nitrogen " " " " (0.7682)	9.8855	0.1145
Mean height of Barometer (76 c. m.)	1.8808	8.1192
Coefficient of expansion of Air (0.00366)	7.5635	2.4365
Latent Heat of Water (79)	1.8976	8.1024
" " " Free Steam (537)	2.7300	7.2700
To reduce 𝔖𝔭.𝔊𝔯. to Sp. Gr., or reverse, add to log.	1.1594 or 8.8406
" " Sp. Gr. to Sp. Gr., " " " " "	5.9522 or 4.0478
" " 𝔖𝔭.𝔊𝔯. to Sp. Gr., " " " " "	7.1116 or 2.8884
" " grammes to criths, " " " " "	1.0478 or 8.9522

INDEX.

The numbers of this Index refer to pages; those following dashes are references to reactions, into which the given substance enters as an important factor. To use the index with copies of the first edition, add ten to the number of all pages above the two hundredth.

A TREATISE ON LOGIC;

Or, The Laws of Pure Thought. Comprising both the Aristotelic and
Hamiltonian Analyses of Logical Forms, and some Chapters on
Applied Logic. By FRANCIS BOWEN, Alford Professor of Moral
Philosophy in Harvard College. *Sixth Thousand.* 12mo. Cloth.
450 pp. $2.00.

Extract from the Preface.

" Among English authors, after Sir William Hamilton, I have been chiefly
indebted to Prof. Mansel; and have also derived much help from Thompson's
excellent ' Outlines of the Laws of Thought '; but the work would not have been
carried on in the same spirit in which my predecessors began it, if I had not ven-
tured respectfully to dissent from some of their doctrines, and even to present some
opinions which will very likely be found to have no other merit than that of origi-
nality. . . . . Throughout the work I have kept constantly in view the wants
of learners, much of it having been first suggested while attempting to expound
the science in my own class-room."

From James Walker, D. D., LL.D., late President of Harvard University.

" It is, so far as I am able to judge, singularly complete, and yet is brought
within reasonable limits. As an English text-book in this department of philosophy I have seen nothing to be compared with it."

From E. O. Haven, LL. D., late President of University of Michigan.

" I have examined the ' Treatise on Logic ' by Prof. Francis Bowen with great
care, having, indeed, used it as a text-book, and have found it the most thorough
and systematic text-book on the subject with which I am acquainted. I think it
fully supplies the purpose for which it was written, and in the hands of a good
teacher, it furnishes all the aid that he or his class will need."

From Prof. W. D. Wilson, Hobart College, Geneva, N. Y.

" It is, in my opinion, an admirable compend of what is now taught as Logic ;
presenting with great clearness and skill the rival systems of Aristotle and Hamilton, with a very full and fair exhibit of the thoughts and opinions of all others
whose writings are of note on the subject."

2

THE METAPHYSICS OF SIR WILLIAM HAMILTON.

Collected, Arranged, and Abridged for the Use of Colleges and Private Students. By FRANCIS BOWEN, A. M., Alford Professor of Moral Philosophy in Harvard College. Ninth Thousand. 12mo. Cloth. Price, $2.00.

The publisher takes pleasure in stating that this work has met with great favor, and has already been introduced as a text-book in all the principal colleges and institutions of learning in the country.

Extract from the Editor's Preface.

"As any course of instruction in the Philosophy of Mind at the present day must be very imperfect which does not comprise a tolerably full view of Hamilton's Metaphysics, I have endeavored, in the present volume, to prepare a text-book which should contain, in his own language, the substance of all that he has written upon the subject. For this purpose, the 'Lectures on Metaphysics' have been taken as the basis of the work ; and I have freely abridged them by striking out the repetitions and redundancies in which they abound, and omitting also, in great part, the load of citations and references that they contain, as these are of inferior interest except to a student of the history of philosophy, or as marks of the stupendous erudition of the author."

The Rev. Dr. Walker, late President of Harvard University, in a note to the editor, says of the book : "Having examined it with some care, I cannot refrain from congratulating you on the success of the undertaking. You have given the Metaphysics of Sir William Hamilton in his own words, and yet in a form admirably adapted to the recitation-room, and also to private students."

Prof. J. Torrey, University of Vermont.

"The editor has left scarcely anything to be desired. The work presents in short compass the Philosophy of Sir W. Hamilton, in his own language, more completely and satisfactorily than many students would find it done by the author himself in the whole series of his voluminous and scattered productions."

From the North American Review.

"Mr. Bowen's eminence as a scholar, thinker, and writer in this department, his large experience as a teacher, and his experimental use of the 'Lectures' as a textbook, might have given the assurance, which he has fully verified, that so delicate an editorial task would be thoroughly, faithfully, and successfully performed. We cannot doubt that if Sir William were still living, the volume would have his cordial *imprimatur ;* and the students of our colleges are to be congratulated that the labors of the great master of Metaphysical Science are now rendered much more availing for their benefit, than they were made, perhaps than they could have been made, by his own hand."

Milton Keynes UK
Ingram Content Group UK Ltd.
UKHW042313190124
436367UK00003B/140